The Many Deaths of
The Black Company

The MANY DEATHS of The BLACK COMPANY

GLEN COOK

TOR®

A TOM DOHERTY ASSOCIATES BOOK / NEW YORK

THE MANY DEATHS OF THE BLACK COMPANY

Omnibus copyright © 2009 by Glen Cook
Water Sleeps copyright © 1999 by Glen Cook
Soldiers Live copyright © 2000 by Glen Cook

A Tor Book
Published by Tom Doherty Associates, LLC
175 Fifth Avenue
New York, NY 10010

www.tor-forge.com

Tor® is a registered trademark of Tom Doherty Associates, LLC.

ISBN 978-0-7653-2401-6

First Tor Trade Paperback Edition: January 2010

Printed in the United States of America

0 9 8 7 6

Contents

WATER SLEEPS

BOOK THREE
of
GLITTERING STONE

For John Ferraro
and all the wonderful
Ducklings, all in a row.
It was a great
little party.

I

In those days the Black Company did not exist. This I know because there were laws and decrees that told me so. But I did not feel entirely insubstantial.

The Company standard, its Captain and Lieutenant, its Standardbearer and all the men who had made the Company so terrible, had passed on, having been buried alive at the heart of a vast desert of stone. "Glittering stone," they whispered in the streets and alleys of Taglios, and "Gone to Khatovar," they proclaimed from on high, the mighty making what they had been so determined to prevent for so long over into a great triumph once the Radisha or Protector or somebody decided that people ought to believe that the Company had fulfilled its destiny.

Anyone old enough to remember the Company knew better. Only fifty people had ventured out onto that plain of glittering stone. Half of those people had not been Company. Only two of those fifty had returned to lie about what had happened. And a third who had come back to retail the truth had been killed in the Kiaulune wars, far away from the capital. But the deceits of Soulcatcher and Willow Swan fooled no one, then or now. People simply pretended to believe them because that was safer.

They might have asked why Mogaba needed five years to conquer a Company that had passed on, squandering thousands of young lives to bring the Kiaulune domains under the Radisha's rule and into the realm of the Protector's twisted truths. They might have mentioned that people claiming to be Black Company had held out in the fortress Overlook for years after that, until the Protector, Soulcatcher, finally became so impatient with their intransigence that she invested her own best sorceries in a two-year project that reduced that huge fortress to white powder, white rubble and white bones. They might have raised these points. But they remained silent instead. They were afraid. With cause, they were afraid.

The Taglian empire under the Protectorate is an empire of fear.

During the years of defiance, one unknown hero won Soulcatcher's eternal hatred by sabotaging the Shadowgate, the sole gateway to the glittering plain. Soulcatcher was the most powerful sorcerer alive. She might have become a Shadowmaster to eclipse those monsters the Company had pulled down during its earlier wars on Taglios' behalf. But with the Shadowgate sealed she could not conjure killer shadows more powerful than the few score she had controlled when she worked her treachery on the Company.

Oh, she *could* open the Shadowgate. One time. She did not know how to close it again, though. Meaning everything inside would be free to wriggle out and begin tormenting the world.

Meaning that for Soulcatcher, party to so few of the secrets, the choice must be all or very little. The end of the world or making do.

For the moment she is making do. And pursuing continuous researches. She is the Protector. Fear of her steeps the empire. There are no challenges to her terror. But even she knows this age of dark concord cannot endure.

Water sleeps.

In their homes, in the shadowed alleyways, in the city's ten thousand temples, nervous whispers never cease. *The Year of the Skulls. The Year of the Skulls.* It is an age when no gods die and those that sleep keep stirring restlessly.

In their homes, in the shadowed alleyways or fields of grain or in the sodden paddies, in the pastures and forests and tributary cities, should a comet be seen in the sky or should an unseasonable storm strew devastation or, particularly, if the earth should shake, they murmur, "Water sleeps." And they are afraid.

They call me Sleepy. I was withdrawn as a child, hiding from the horrors of my childhood inside the comfort and emotional safety of daydreams and nightmares. Any time I did not have to work, I went away in there to hide. The evil could not touch me there. I knew no safer place till the Black Company came to Jaicur.

My brothers accused me of sleeping all the time. They resented my ability to get away. They did not understand. They died without ever understanding. I slept on. I did not waken fully till I had been with the Company for several years.

I keep these Annals today. Somebody must and no one else can, though the Annalist title never devolved upon me formally.

There is precedent.

The books must be written. The truth must be recorded even if fate decrees that no man ever reads a word I write. The Annals are the soul of the Black Company. They recall that this is who we are. That this is who we were. That we persevere. And that treachery, as it ever has, failed to suck the last drop of our blood.

We no longer exist. The Protector tells us so. The Radisha swears it. Mogaba, that mighty general with his thousand dark honors, sneers at our memory and spits on our name. People in the streets declare us no more than an evil, haunting memory. But only Soulcatcher does not watch over both shoulders to see what might be gaining ground.

We are stubborn ghosts. We will not lie down. We will not cease to haunt them. We have done nothing for a long time but they remain afraid. Their guilt cannot stop whispering our name.

They *should* be afraid.

Somewhere in Taglios, every day, a message appears upon a wall, written in chalk or paint or even animal blood. Just a gentle reminder: *Water Sleeps.*

Everyone knows what that means. They whisper it, aware that there is an enemy out there more restless than running water. An enemy who will, somehow, someday, lurch forth from the mouth of his grave and come for those who played at betrayal. They know no power that can prevent it. They were warned ten thousand times before they gave in to temptation. No evil can preserve them.

Mogaba is afraid.

Radisha is afraid.

Willow Swan is so afraid he barely functions, like the wizard Smoke before him, whom he indicted and tormented for his cowardice. Swan knew the Company of old, in the north, before anyone here recognized it as more than a dark memory of ancient terror. The years have seen no calluses form on Swan's fear.

Purohita Drupada is afraid.

Inspector-General Gokhale is afraid.

Only the Protector is not afraid. Soulcatcher fears nothing. Soulcatcher does not care. She mocks and defies the demon. She is mad. She will laugh and be entertained while being consumed by fire.

Her lack of fear leaves her henchmen that much more troubled. They know she will drive them before her, into the grinding jaws of destiny.

Occasionally a wall will carry another message, a more personal note: *All Their Days Are Numbered.*

I am in the streets every day, either going to work, going to spy, listening, capturing rumors or launching new ones within the anonymity of *Chor Bagan*, the Thieves' Garden even the Greys have not yet been able to extirpate. I used to disguise myself as a prostitute but that proved to be too dangerous. There are people out there who make the Protector seem a paragon of sanity. It is the world's great good fortune that fate denies them the power to exercise the fullest depth and sweep of their psychoses.

Mostly I go around as a young man, the way I always did. Rootless young men are everywhere since the end of the wars.

The more bizarre the new rumor, the faster it explodes out of Chor Bagan and the more strongly it gnaws the nerves of our enemies. Always, always, Taglios must enjoy a sense of grim premonition. We must provide them their ration of omens, signs and portents.

The Protector hunts us in her more lucid moments but she never remains interested long. She cannot keep her attention fixed on anything. And why should she be concerned? We are dead. We no longer exist. She herself has declared that to be the reality. As Protector, she is the great arbiter of reality for the entire Taglian empire.

But: *Water Sleeps.*

3

In those days the spine of the Company was a woman who never formally joined, the witch Ky Sahra, wife of my predecessor as Annalist, Murgen, the Standardbearer. Ky Sahra was a clever woman with a will like sharp steel. Even Goblin and One-Eye deferred to her. She would not be intimidated, not even by her wicked old Uncle Doj. She feared the Protector, the Radisha and the Greys no more than she feared a cabbage. The malice of evils as great as the deadly cult of Deceivers, their messiah the Daughter of Night and their goddess Kina, intimidated Sahra not at all. She had looked into the heart of darkness. Its secrets inspired in her no dread. Only one thing made Sahra tremble.

Her mother, Ky Gota, was the incarnation of dissatisfaction and complaint. Her lamentations and reproaches were of such amazing potency that it seemed she must be an avatar of some cranky old deity as yet undiscovered by man.

Nobody loves Ky Gota except One-Eye. And even he calls her the Troll behind her back.

Sahra shuddered as her mother limped slowly through a room gone suddenly silent. We were not in power now. We had to use the same few rooms for everything. Only a short while ago this one had been filled with loafers, some Company, most of them employees of Banh Do Trang. We all stared at the old woman, willing her to hurry. Willing her to overlook this opportunity to socialize.

Old Do Trang, who was so feeble he was confined to a wheelchair, rolled over to Ky Gota, evidently hoping a show of concern would keep her moving.

Everyone always wanted Gota to go somewhere else.

This time his sacrifice worked. She had to be in a lot of discomfort, though, not to take time to harangue all who were younger than she.

Silence persisted till the old merchant returned. He owned the place and let us use it as our operational headquarters. He owed us nothing, but nevertheless, shared our danger out of love for Sahra. In all matters his thoughts had to be heard and his wishes had to be honored.

Do Trang was not gone long. He came back rolling wearily. The man behind the liver spots seemed so fragile it had to be a miracle that he could move his chair himself.

Ancient he was, but there was an irrepressible twinkle in his eyes. He nodded. He seldom had anything to say unless someone else said something incredibly stupid. He was a good man.

Sahra told us, "Everything is in place. Every phase and facet has been double-checked. Goblin and One-Eye are sober. It's time the Company speaks up." She glanced around, inviting comments.

I did not think it was time. But I had said my piece when I was planning this. And had been outvoted. I treated myself to a shrug of despair.

There being no new objections, Sahra said, "Start the first phase." She waved at her son. Tobo nodded and slipped out.

He was a skinny, scruffy, furtive youngster. He was Nyueng Bao, which meant he had to be a sneak and a thief. His every move had to be watched. In consequence he was so generally observed that no individual examined in detail what he actually did so long as his hands did not stray toward a dangling purse or some treasure in a vendor's stall. People did not look for what they did not expect to see.

The boy's hands stayed behind his back. While they were there, he was not considered a threat. He could not steal. No one noticed the small, discolored blobs he left on any wall he leaned against.

Gunni children stared. The boy looked so strange in his black pajama clothing.

Gunni raise their children polite. Gunni are peaceable folk, in the main. Shadar children, though, are wrought of sterner stuff. They are more bold. Their religion has a warrior philosophy at its root. Some Shadar youths set out to harass the thief.

Of course he was a thief! He was Nyueng Bao. Everyone knew all Nyueng Bao were thieves.

Older Shadar called the youngsters off. The thief would be dealt with by those whose responsibility that was.

The Shadar religion has its streak of bureaucratic rectitude, too.

Even such a small commotion attracted official attention. Three tall, grey-clad, bearded Shadar peacekeepers wearing white turbans advanced through the press. They looked around constantly, intently, oblivious to the fact that they traveled in an island of open space. The streets of Taglios are packed, day and night, yet the masses always find room to shrink away from the Greys. The Greys are all men with hard eyes, seemingly chosen for their lack of patience and compassion.

Tobo drifted away, sliding through the mob like a black snake through swamp reeds. When the Greys inquired about the commotion, no one could describe him as anything but what prejudice led them to presume. A Nyueng Bao thief. And there was a plague of those in Taglios. These days the capital-city boasted plenty of every kind of outlander imaginable. Every layabout and lackwit and sharpster from the length and breadth of the empire was migrating to the city. The population had tripled in a generation. But for the cruel efficiencies of the Greys, Taglios would have become a chaotic, murderous sink, a hellfire fueled by poverty and despair.

Poverty and despair existed in plentitude but the Palace did not let any disorder take root. The Palace was good at ferreting out secrets. Criminal careers tended to be short. As did the lives of most who sought to conspire against the Radisha or the Protector. Particularly against the Protector, who did not concern herself deeply with the sanctity of anyone else's skin.

In times past, intrigue and conspiracy had been a miasmatic plague afflicting every life in Taglios. There was little of that anymore. The Protector did not approve. Most Taglians were eager to win the Protector's approval. Even the priesthoods avoided attracting Soulcatcher's evil eye.

At some point the boy's black clothing came off, leaving him in the Gunni-style loincloth he had worn underneath. Now he looked like any other youngster, though with a slightly jaundiced cast of skin. He was safe. He had grown up in Taglios. He had no accent to give him away.

4

It was the waiting time, the stillness, the doing nothing that there is so much of before any serious action. I was out of practice. I could not lean back and play tonk or just watch while One-Eye and Goblin tried to cheat each other. And I had writer's cramp, so could not work on my Annals.

"Tobo!" I called. "You want to go see it happen?"

Tobo was fourteen. He was the youngest of us. He grew up in the Black Company. He had a full measure of youth's exuberance and impatience and overconfidence in his own immortality and divine exemption from retribution. He enjoyed his assignments on behalf of the Company. He was not quite sure he believed in his father. He never knew the man. We tried hard to keep him from becoming anyone's spoiled baby. But Goblin insisted on treating him like a favorite son. He was trying to tutor the boy.

Goblin's command of written Taglian was more limited than he would admit. There are a hundred characters in the everyday vulgate and forty more reserved to the priests, who write in the High Mode, which is almost a second unspoken, formal language. I use a mixture recording these Annals.

Once Tobo could read, "Uncle" Goblin made him do all his reading for him, aloud.

"Could I do some more buttons, Sleepy? Mom thinks more would get more attention in the Palace."

I was surprised he talked to her that long. Boys his age are surly at best. He was rude to his mother all the time. He would have been ruder and more defiant still if he had not been blessed with so many "uncles" who would not tolerate that stuff. Naturally, Tobo saw all that as a grand conspiracy of adults. Publicly. In private, he was amenable to reason. Occasionally. When approached delicately by someone who was not his mother.

"Maybe a few. But it's going to get dark soon. And then the show will start."

"What'll we go as? I don't like it when you're a whore."

"We'll be street orphans." Though that had its risks, too. We could get caught by a press gang and forced into Mogaba's army. His soldiers, these days, are little better than slaves, subject to a savage discipline. Many are petty criminals given an option of rough justice or enlistment. The rest are children of poverty with nowhere else to go. Which was the standard of professional armies men like Murgen saw in the far north, long before my time.

"Why do you worry so much about disguises?"

"If we never show the same face twice, our enemies can't possibly know who they're looking for. Don't ever underestimate them. Especially not the Protector. She's outwitted death itself more than once."

Tobo was not prepared to believe that or much else of our exotic history. Though not as bad as most, he was going through that stage where he knew everything worth knowing and nothing his elders said—particularly if it bore any vaguely educational hue—was worth hearing. He could not help that. It went with the age.

And I was my age and could not help saying things I knew would do no good. "It's in the Annals. Your father and the Captain didn't make up stories."

He did not want to believe that, either. I did not pursue it. Each of us must learn to respect the Annals in our own way, in our own time. The Company's diminished circumstance makes it difficult for anyone to grasp tradition. Only two Old Crew brothers both survived Soulcatcher's trap on the stone plain and the Kiaulune wars afterward. Goblin and One-Eye are haplessly inept at transmitting the Company mystique. One-Eye is too lazy and Goblin too inarticulate. And I was still practically an apprentice when the Old Crew ventured onto the plain in the Captain's quest for Khatovar. Which he did not find. Not the Khatovar he was looking for, anyway.

I am amazed. Before long I will be a twenty-year veteran. I was barely fourteen when Bucket took me under his wing. . . . But I was never like Tobo. At fourteen I was already ancient in pain. For years after Bucket rescued me, I grew younger. . . .

"What?"

"I asked why you look so angry all of a sudden."

"I was remembering when I was fourteen."

"Girls have it so easy—" He shut up. His face drained. His northern ancestry became apparent. He was an arrogant and spoiled little puke but he did have brains enough to recognize it when he stepped into a nest of poisonous snakes.

I told him what he knew, not what he did not. "When I was fourteen, the Company and Nyueng Bao were trapped in Jaicur. Dejagore, they call it here." The rest does not matter anymore. The rest is safely in the past. "I almost never have nightmares now."

Tobo had heard more than he ever wanted to about Jaicur already. His mother and grandmother and Uncle Doj had been there, too.

Goblin says we'll be impressed by these buttons," Tobo whispered. "They won't just make spooky lights, they'll prick somebody's conscience."

"That'll be unusual." Conscience was a rare commodity on either side of our dispute.

"You really knew my dad?" Tobo had heard stories all his life but lately wanted to know more. Murgen had begun to matter in a more than lip-service fashion.

I told him what I had told him before. "He was my boss. He taught me to read and write. He was a good man." I laughed weakly. "As good a man as belonging to the Black Company let him be."

Tobo stopped. He took a deep breath. He stared at a point in the dusk some-where above my left shoulder. "Were you lovers?"

"No, Tobo. No. Friends. Almost. But definitely not that. He didn't know I was a woman till just before he left for the glittering plain. And I didn't know he knew till I read his Annals. Nobody knew. They thought I was a cute runt who just never got any bigger. I let them think that. I felt safer as one of the guys."

"Oh."

His tone was so neutral I had to wonder. "Why did you even ask?" Surely he had no reason to believe I had behaved differently before he knew me.

He shrugged. "I just wondered."

Something must have set him off. Possibly an "I wonder if . . ." from Goblin or One-Eye, say, while they were sampling some of their homemade elephant poison.

"I didn't ask. Did you put the buttons behind the shadow show?"

"That's what I was told to do."

A shadow show uses cutout puppets mounted on sticks. Some of their limbs are manipulated mechanically. A candle behind the puppets casts their shadows on a screen of white cloth. The puppeteer uses a variety of voices to tell his story as he maneuvers his puppets. If he is sufficiently entertaining, his audience will toss him a few coins.

This particular puppeteer had performed in the same place for more than a generation. He slept inside his stage setup. In so doing, he lived better than most of Taglios' floating population.

He was an informer. He was not beloved of the Black Company.

The story he told, as most were, was drawn from the myths. It sprang from the Khadi cycle. It involved a goddess with too many arms who kept devouring demons.

Of course it was the same demon puppet over and over. Kind of like real life, where the same demon comes back again and again.

Just a hint of color hung above the western rooftops.

There was an earsplitting squeal. People stopped to stare at a bright orange light. Glowing orange smoke wobbled up from behind the puppeteer's stand. Its strands wove the well-known emblem of the Black Company, a fanged skull with no lower jaw, exhaling flames. The scarlet fire in its left eye socket seemed to be a pupil that stared right down inside you, searching for the thing that you feared the most.

The smoke thing persisted only a few seconds. It rose about ten feet before it dispersed. It left a frightened silence. The air itself seemed to whisper, "Water sleeps."

Whine and flash. A second skull arose. This one was silver with a slightly bluish tint. It lasted longer and rose a dozen feet higher before it perished. It whispered, "My brother unforgiven."

"Here come the Greys!" exclaimed someone tall enough to see over the crowd. Being short makes it easy for me to disappear in groups but also makes it tough for me to see what is happening outside them.

The Greys are never far away. But they are helpless against this sort of thing. It can happen anywhere, any time, and has to happen before they can react. Our supposed ironclad rule is that perpetrators should never be nearby when the buttons speak. The Greys understand that. They just go through the motions. The Protector must be appeased. The little Shadar have to be fed.

"Now!" Tobo murmured as four Greys arrived. A shriek erupted from behind the puppeteer's stage. The puppeteer himself ran out, spun and leaned toward his stage, mouth wide open. There was a flash less bright but more persistent than its predecessors. The subsequent smoke image was more complex and lasted longer. It appeared to be a monster. The monster focused on the Shadar. One of the Greys mouthed the name "Niassi."

Niassi would be a major demon from Shadar mythology. A similar demon under another form of the name exists in Gunni belief.

Niassi was a chieftain of the inner circle of the most powerful demons. Shadar beliefs, being heretical Vehdna, include a posthumous, punitive Hell but also definitely include the possibility of a Gunni-like Hell on earth, in life, managed by demons in Niassi's employ, laid on for the particularly wicked. Despite understanding that they were being taunted, the Greys were rocked. This was something new. This was an attack from an unanticipated and sensitive direction. And it came on top of ever more potent rumors associating the Greys with vile rites supposedly practiced by the Protector.

Children disappear. Reason suggests this is inevitable and unavoidable in a city so vast and overcrowded, even if there is not one evil man out there. Babies vanish by wandering off and getting lost. And horrible things do happen to good people. A clever, sick rumor can reassign the numb evil of chance to the premeditated malice of people no one ever trusted anyway.

Memory becomes selective.

We do not mind a bit lying about our enemies.

Tobo yelled something insulting. I started to pull him away, dragging him toward our den. Others began to curse and mock the Greys. Tobo threw a stone that hit a Grey's turban.

It was too dark for them to make out faces. They began to unlimber bamboo wands. The mood of the crowd turned ugly. I could not help but suspect that there was more to the devil display than had met the eye. I knew our tame wizards. And I knew that Taglians do not lose control easily. It takes a great deal of patience and self-control for so many people to live in such unnaturally tight proximity.

I looked around for crows, fluttering bats, or anything else that might be spies for the Protector. After nightfall all our risks soar. We cannot see what might be watching. I held onto Tobo's arm. "You shouldn't have done that. It's dark enough for shadows to be out."

He was not impressed. "Goblin will be happy. He spent a long time on that. And it worked perfectly."

The Greys blew whistles, summoning reinforcements.

A fourth button released its smoke ghost. We missed the show. I dragged Tobo through all the shadowtraps between the excitement and our headquarters. He would be explaining to some uncles soon. Those for whom paranoia remains a way of life will be those who will be around to savor the Company's many revenges. Tobo needed more instruction. His behavior could have been exploited by a clever adversary.

Sahra summoned me as soon as we arrived, not to chastise me for letting Tobo take stupid risks but to observe as she launched her next move. It might be time Tobo walked into something that would scare some sense into him. Life underground is unforgiving. It seldom gives you more than one chance. Tobo had to understand that in his heart.

After Sahra grilled me about events outside, she made sure Goblin and One-Eye were acquainted with her displeasure, too. Tobo was not there to defend himself.

Goblin and One-Eye were not cowed. No forty-something slip of a lass could overawe those two antiques. Besides, they put Tobo up to half his mischief.

Sahra said, "I'll raise Murgen now." She seemed unsure about that. She had not consulted Murgen much recently. We all wondered why. She and Murgen were a genuine romantic love match straight out of legend, with all the appurtenances seen in the timeless stories, including gods defied, parents disappointed, desperate separations and reunions, intrigues by enemies and so forth. It remained only for one of them to go down into the realm of the dead to rescue the other. And Murgen was tucked away in a nice cold underground hell right now, courtesy of the mad sorceress Soulcatcher. He and all the Captured lived on, in stasis, beneath the plain of glittering stone, in a place and situation known to us only because Sahra could conjure Murgen's spirit.

Could the problem be the stasis? Sahra got a day older every day. Murgen did not. Had she begun to fear she would be older than his mother before we freed the Captured?

Sadly, after years of study, I realize that most history may really pivot on personal considerations like that, not on the pursuit of ideals dark or shining.

Long ago Murgen learned to leave his flesh while he slept. He retained some of that ability but, sadly, it was diminished by the supernatural constraints of his captivity. He could do nothing outside the cavern of the ancients without being summoned forth by Sahra—or, conceivably, chillingly, by any other necromancer who knew how to reach him.

Murgen's ghost was the ultimate spy. Outside our circle none but Soulcatcher could detect his presence. Murgen informed us of our enemies' every plot—those that we suspected strongly enough to ask Sahra to investigate. The process was cumbersome and limited but still, Murgen constituted our most potent weapon. We could not survive without him.

And Sahra was ever more reluctant to call him up.

God knows, it is hard to keep believing. Many of our brothers have lost their faith and have drifted away, vanishing into the chaos of the empire. Some may be rejuvenated once we have had a flashy success or two.

The years have been painful for Sahra. They cost her three children, an agony no loving parent should have to bear. She lost their father as well but suffered little by that deprivation. No one who remembered the man spoke well of him. She suffered with the rest of us during the siege of Jaicur.

Maybe Sahra—and the entire Nyueng Bao people—had angered Ghanghesha. Or maybe the god with the several elephant heads just enjoyed a cruel prank at the expense of his worshipers. Certainly Kina got a chuckle out of pulling lethal practical jokes on her devotees.

Goblin and One-Eye were not usually present when Sahra raised Murgen. She did not need their help. Her powers were narrow but strong, and those two could be a distraction even when they tried to behave.

Those antiques being there told me something unusual was afoot. And old they are, almost beyond reckoning. Their skills sustain them. One-Eye, if the Annals do not lie, is on the downhill side of two hundred. His youthful sidekick lags less than a century behind.

Neither is a big man. Which is being generous. Both are shorter than me. And never were taller, even long before they became dried-up old relics. Which was probably when they were about fifteen. I cannot imagine One-Eye ever having been anything but old. He must have been born old. And wearing the ugliest, filthiest black hat that ever existed.

Maybe One-Eye goes on forever because of the curse of that hat. Maybe the hat uses him as its steed and depends on him for its survival.

That crusty, stinking glob of felt rag will hit the nearest fire before One-Eye's corpse finishes bouncing. Everyone hates it.

Goblin, in particular, loathes that hat. He mentions it whenever he and One-Eye get into a squabble, which is about as often as they see one another.

One-Eye is small and black and wrinkled. Goblin is small and white and wrinkled. He has a face like a dried toad's.

One-Eye mentions that whenever they get into a squabble, which is about as often as there is an audience but nobody to get between them.

They strain to be on their best behavior around Sahra, though. The woman has a gift. She brings out the best in people. Except her mother. Though the Troll is much worse away from her daughter.

Lucky us, we do not see Ky Gota much. Her joints hurt her too bad. Tobo helps care for her, our cynical exploitation of his special immunity from her vitriol. She dotes on the boy—even if his father was foreign slime.

Sahra told me, "These two claim they've found a more effective way to materialize Murgen. So you can communicate directly." Usually Sahra had to talk for Murgen after she raised him up. I do not have a psychic ear.

I said, "If you bring him across strong enough so the rest of us can see and hear him, then Tobo ought to be here, too. He's suddenly got a lot of questions about his father."

Sahra peered at me oddly. I was saying something but she did not get what I meant.

"Boy ought to know his old man," One-Eye rasped. He stared at Goblin, waiting to be contradicted by a man who did not know his. That was their custom. Pick a fight and never mind trivia like facts or common sense. The debate about whether or not they were worth the trouble they caused went back for generations.

This time Goblin abstained. He would make his rebuttal when Sahra was not around to embarrass him with an appeal to reason.

Sahra nodded to One-Eye. "But first we have to see if your scheme really works."

One-Eye began to puff up. Somebody dared suggest that *his* sorcery needed field-testing? Come on! Forget the record! *This* time—

I told him, "Don't start."

Time had caught up with One-Eye. His memory was no longer reliable. And lately he tended to nod off in the middle of things. Or to forget what had gotten him exercised when he roared off on a rant. Sometimes he ended up contradicting himself.

He was a shadow of the dried-up old relic he was when first I met him, though he got around under his own power still. But halfway through any journey, he was likely to forget where he was bound. Occasionally that was good, him being One-Eye, but mostly it was a pain. Tobo usually got the job of keeping him headed in the right direction when it mattered. One-Eye doted on the kid, too.

The little wizard's increasing fragility did make it easier to keep him inside, away from the temptations of the city. One moment of indiscretion could kill us all. And One-Eye never quite caught on to what it meant to be discreet.

Goblin chuckled as One-Eye subsided. I suggested, "Could you two concentrate on what you're supposed to be doing?" I was haunted by the dread that one day One-Eye would doze off in the midst of a deadly spell and leave us all up to our ears in demons or bloodsucking insects distraught about having been plucked from some swamp a thousand miles away. "This is important."

"It's always important," Goblin grumbled. "Even when it's just 'Goblin, give me a hand here, I'm too lazy to polish the silver myself,' they make it sound like the world's about to end. Always important? Hmmph!"

"I see you're in a good mood tonight."

"Gralk!"

One-Eye heaved himself out of his chair. Leaning on his cane, muttering unflattering remarks about me, he shuffled over to Sahra. He had forgotten I was female. He was less unpleasant when he remembered, though I expect no special treatment because of that unhappy chance of birth.

One-Eye became dangerous in a whole new way the day he adopted that cane. He used it to swat people. Or to trip them. He was always falling asleep between here and there but you never knew for sure if his nap was the real thing. That cane might dart out to tangle your legs if he was pretending.

The dread we all shared was that One-Eye would not last much longer. Without him, our chances to continue avoiding detection would plummet. Goblin would try hard but he was just one small-time wizard. Our situation offered work for more than two in their prime.

"Start, woman," One-Eye rasped. "Goblin, you worthless sack of beetle snot, would you get that stuff over here? I don't want to hang around here all night."

Sahra had had a table set up for them. She used no props herself. At a fixed time she would concentrate on Murgen. She usually made contact quickly. At her time of the month, when her sensitivity went down, she would sing in Nyueng Bao. Unlike some of my Company brothers, I have a poor ear for languages. Nyueng Bao mostly eludes me. Her songs seem to be lullabies. Unless the words have double meanings. Which is entirely possible. Uncle Doj talks in riddles all the time but insists he makes perfect sense if we would just listen.

Uncle Doj is not around much. Thank God. He has his own agenda—though even he does not seem clear on what that is anymore. The world keeps changing on him, not in ways he likes.

Goblin brought a sack of objects without challenging One-Eye's foul manners. He deferred to One-Eye more lately, if only for efficiency's sake. He wasted no time making his opinions known if work was not involved, though.

Even though they were cooperating, laying out their tools, they began bickering about the placement of every instrument. I wanted to paddle them like they were four-year-olds.

Sahra began singing. She had a beautiful voice. It should not have been buried this way. Strictly speaking, she was not employing necromancy. She was not laying an absolute compulsion on Murgen, nor was she conjuring his shade—Murgen was still alive out there. But his spirit could escape his tomb when summoned.

I wished the other Captured could be called up, too. Especially the Captain. We needed inspiration.

A cloud of dust formed slowly between Goblin and One-Eye, who stood on opposite sides of the table. No, it was not dust. Nor was it smoke. I stuck a finger in, tasted. That was a fine, cool, water mist. Goblin told Sahra, "We're ready."

She changed tone. She began to sound almost wheedling. I could pick out even fewer words.

Murgen's head materialized between the wizards, wavering like a reflection on a rippling pond. I was startled, not by the sorcery but by Murgen's appearance. He looked just like I remembered him, without one new line in his face. None of the rest of us looked the same.

Sahra had begun to look something like her mother had back in Jaicur. Not as heavy. Not with the strange, rolling waddle caused by problems of the joints. But her beauty was going fast. In her, that had been a wonder, stretching on way past the usual early, swift-fading characteristic of Nyueng Bao women. She did not talk about it but it preyed upon her. She had her vanity. And she deserved it.

Time *is* the most wicked of all villains.

Murgen was not happy about being called up. I feared he suffered the malaise afflicting Sahra. He spoke. And I had no trouble hearing him, though his words were an ethereal whisper.

"I was dreaming. There is a place . . ." His irritation faded. Pale horror replaced it. And I knew he had been dreaming in the place of bones he described in his own Annals. "A white crow . . ." We had a problem indeed if he preferred a drift through Kina's dreamscapes to a glimpse of life.

Sahra told him, "We're ready to strike. The Radisha ordered the Privy Council convened just a little while ago. See what they're doing. Make sure Swan is there." Murgen faded from the mist. Sahra looked sad. Goblin and One-Eye began excoriating the Standardbearer for running away.

"I saw him," I told them. "Perfectly. I heard him, too. Exactly like I always imagined a ghost would talk."

Grinning, Goblin told me, "That's because you hear what you expect to hear. You weren't really listening with your ears, you know."

One-Eye sneered. He never explained anything to anybody. Unless maybe to Gota if she caught him sneaking back in in the middle of the night. Then he would have a story as convoluted as the history of the Company itself.

Sounding like a woman pretending not to be bitter, Sahra said, "You can bring Tobo in. We know there won't be any explosions or fires, and you melted only two holes through the tabletop."

"A base canard!" One-Eye proclaimed. "That happened only because Frogface here—"

Sahra ignored him. "Tobo can record what Murgen has to say. So Sleepy can use it later. It's time for us to turn into other people. Send a messenger if Murgen finds out anything dangerous."

That was the plan. I was even less enthusiastic about it now. I wanted to stay and talk to my old friend. But this thing was bigger than a bull session. Bigger than finding out if Bucket was keeping well.

6

Murgen drifted through the Palace like a ghost. He found that thought vaguely amusing, though nothing made him laugh anymore. A decade and a half in the grave destroyed a man's sense of humor.

The rambling stone pile of the Palace never changed. Well, it got dustier. And it needed repairs ever more desperately. Credit that to Soulcatcher, who did not like having hordes of people underfoot. Most of the original vast professional staff had been dismissed and replaced by occasional casual labor.

The Palace crowned a sizable hill. Each ruler of Taglios, generation after generation, tagged on an addition, not because the room was needed but because that was a memorial tradition. Taglians joked that in another thousand years there would be no city, just endless square miles of Palace. Mostly in ruin.

The Radisha Drah, having accepted that her brother, the Prahbrindrah Drah, had been lost during the Shadowmaster wars, and galvanized by the threat of the Protector's displeasure, had proclaimed herself head of state. Traditionalists in the ecclesiastical community did not want a woman in the role, but the world knew this particular woman had been doing the job practically forever anyway. Her weaknesses existed mainly in the ambitions of her critics. Depending who did the pontificating, she had made one of two great mistakes. Or possibly both. One would be betraying the Black Company when it was a well-known fact that nobody ever profited from such treachery. And the other error, of particular popularity with the senior priests, would be that she had erred in employing the Black Company in the first place. The terror of the Shadowmasters being expunged in the interim, by agency of the Company, did not present a counterargument of any current merit.

Unhappy people shared the meeting chamber with the Radisha. The eye automatically went to the Protector first. Soulcatcher looked exactly as she always had, slimly androgynous, yet sensual, in black leather, a black mask, a black helmet and black leather gloves. She occupied a seat slightly to the left of and behind the Radisha, within a curtain of shadow. She did not put herself forward but there was no doubt who made the ultimate decisions. Every hour of every day the Radisha found another reason to regret having let this particular camel shove her nose into the tent. The cost of having tried to get around fulfilling an unhappy promise to the Black Company was insupportable already. Surely, keeping her promises could not have been so painful. What possibly could have happened that would be worse than what she suffered now had she and her brother helped the Captain find the way to Khatovar?

At desks to either hand, facing one another from fifteen feet, stood scribes who struggled valiantly to record anything said. One group served the Radisha. The other was in Soulcatcher's employ. Once upon a time there had been disagreements after the fact about decisions made during a Privy Council meeting.

A table twelve feet long and four wide faced the two women. Four men sat behind its inadequate bulwark. Willow Swan was situated at the left end. His once-marvelous golden hair had gone grey and stringy. At higher elevations, it had grown extremely sparse. Swan was a foreigner. Swan was a bundle of nerves. Swan had a job he did not want but could not give up. Swan was riding the tiger.

Willow Swan headed up the Greys. In the public eye. In reality, he was barely a figurehead. If his mouth opened, the words that came out were pure Soulcatcher. Popular hatred deservedly belonging to the Protector settled upon Willow Swan instead.

Seated with Swan were three running-dog senior priests who owed their standing to the Protector's favor. They were small men in large jobs. Their presence at Council meetings was a matter of form. They would not take part in any actual debate, though they might receive instructions. Their function was to agree with and support Soulcatcher if she happened to speak. Significantly, all three represented Gunni cults. Though the Protector used the Greys to enforce her will, the Shadar had no voice in the Council. Neither did the Vehdna. That minority simmered continuously because Soulcatcher arrogated to herself much that properly applied only to God, the Vehdna being hopelessly monotheistic and stubborn about keeping it that way.

Swan was a good man inside his fear. He spoke for the Shadar when he could.

There were two other men, of more significance, present. They were positioned behind tall desks located back of the table. They perched atop tall stools and peered down at everyone like a pair of lean old vultures. Both antedated the coming of the Protector, who had not yet found a suitable excuse for getting rid of either, though they irritated her frequently.

The right-hand desk belonged to the Inspector-General of the Records, Chandra Gokhale. His was a deceptive title. He was no glorified clerk. He controlled finances and most public works. He was ancient, hairless, lean as a snake and twice as mean. He owed his appointment to the Radisha's father. Until the latter days of the Shadowmaster wars, his office had been a minor one. The wars caused that office's influence and power to expand. And Chandra Gokhale was never shy about snatching at any strand of bureaucratic power that came within reach. He was a staunch supporter of the Radisha and a steadfast enemy of the Black Company. He was also the sort of weasel who would change all that in an instant if he saw sufficient advantage in so doing.

The man behind the desk on the left was more sinister. Arjana Drupada was a priest of Rhavi-Lemna's cult but there was not one ounce of brotherly love in the man. His official title was Purohita, which meant, more or less, that he was the Royal Chaplain. In actuality, he was the true voice of the priesthoods at court. They had forced him upon the Radisha at a time she was making desperate concessions in order to gain support. Like Gokhale, Drupada was more interested in control than he was in doing what was best for Taglios. But he was not an entirely cynical manipulator. His frequent moral bulls got up the Protector's nose more often even than the constant, quibbling financial caveats of the Inspector-General. Physically, Drupada was known for his shock of wild white hair. That clung to his head like a mad haystack, the good offices of a comb being completely unfamiliar.

Only Gokhale and Drupada seemed unaware that their days had to be numbered. The Protector of All the Taglias was not enamored of them at all.

The final member of the Council was absent. Which was not unusual. The Great General, Mogaba, preferred to be in the field, harrying those designated as his enemies. He viewed the infighting in the Palace with revulsion.

None of which mattered at the moment. There had been Incidents. There were Witnesses to be Brought Forward. The Protector was not pleased.

Willow Swan rose. He beckoned a Grey sergeant out of the gloom behind the two old men. "Ghopal Singh." Nobody remarked on the unusual name. Possibly he was a convert. Stranger things were happening. "Singh's patrol watches an area immediately outside the Palace, on the north side. This afternoon one of his patrolmen discovered a prayer wheel mounted on one of the memorial posts in front of the north entrance. Twelve copies of this sutra were attached to the arms of the wheel."

Swan made a show of turning a small paper card so the light would fall upon the writing there. The lettering appeared to be in the ecclesiastical style. Swan failed to appreciate his own ignorance of Taglian letters, though. He was holding the card inverted. He did not, however, make any mistakes when he reported what the prayer card had to say.

"*Rajadharma.* The Duty of Kings. Know you: Kingship is a trust. The King is the most exalted and conscientious servant of the people."

Swan did not recognize the verse. It was so ancient that some scholars attributed it to one or another of the Lords of Light in the time when the gods still handed down laws to the fathers of men. But the Radisha Drah knew it. The Purohita knew it. Someone outside the Palace had leveled a chiding finger.

Soulcatcher understood it, too. Its object, she said, "Only a Bhodi monk would presume to chastise this house. And they are very few." That pacifistic, moralistic cult was young and still very small. And it had suffered during the war years almost as terribly as had the followers of Kina. The Bhodi refused to defend themselves. "I want the man who did this." The voice she used was that of a quarrelsome old man.

"Uh . . ." Swan said. It was not wise to argue with the Protector but that was an assignment beyond the capacities of the Greys.

Among Soulcatcher's more frightening characteristics was her seeming ability to read minds. She could not, really, but never insisted that she could not. In this instance she found it convenient to let people believe what they wanted. She told Swan, "Being Bhodi, he will surrender himself. No search will be necessary."

"Hunh?"

"There is a tree, sometimes called the Bhodi Tree, in the village of Semchi. It is a very old and highly honored tree. The Bhodi Enlightened One made his reputation loafing in the shade of this tree. The Bhodi consider it their most holy shrine. Tell them I will make kindling wood out of the Bhodi Tree unless the man who rigged that prayer wheel reports to me. Soon." Soulcatcher employed the voice of a petty, vindictive old woman.

Murgen made a mental note to send Sahra a suggestion that the guilty man be prevented from reaching the Protector. Destruction of a major holy place would create thousands of new enemies for Soulcatcher.

Willow Swan started to speak but Soulcatcher interrupted.

"I do not care if they hate me, Swan. I care that they do what I tell them to do when I tell them to do it. The Bhodi will not raise a fist against me, anyway. That would put a stain on their kharma."

A cynical woman, the Protector.

"Get on with it, Swan."

Swan sighed. "Several more of those smoke shows appeared tonight. One was much bigger than any seen before. Once again the Black Company sigil was part of all of them." He brought forward another Shadar witness, who told of being stoned by the mob but did not mention the demon Niassi.

The news was no surprise. It was one of the reasons the Council had been convened. With no real passion, the Radisha demanded, "How could that happen? Why can't you stop it? You have men on every street corner. Chandra?" She appealed to the man who knew just how much it cost to put all those Greys out there.

Gokhale inclined his head imperially.

As long as the Radisha did the questioning, Swan's nerve stood up. She could not hurt him in ways he had not been hurt before. Not the way the Protector could. He asked, "Have you been out there? You should disguise yourself and go. Like Saragoz in the fairy tale. Every street is clogged with people. Thousands sleep where others have to walk over them. Breezeways and alleyways are choked with human waste. Sometimes the press is so thick you could murder somebody ten feet from one of my men and never be noticed. The people playing these games aren't stupid. If they're really Company survivors, they're especially not stupid. They've already survived everything ever thrown at them. They're using the crowds for cover exactly the way they'd use the rocks and trees and bushes out in the countryside. They don't wear uniforms. They don't stand out. They're not outlanders anymore. If you really want to nail them, put out a proclamation saying they all have to wear funny red hats." Swan's nerve had peaked high. That was not directed at the Radisha. Soulcatcher, speaking through her, had issued several proclamations memorable for their absurdity. "Being steeped in Company doctrine, they wouldn't be anywhere around when the smoke emblems actually formed. So far, we haven't even figured out where they come from."

Soulcatcher unleashed a deep-throated grunt. It said she doubted that Swan could figure out much of anything. His nerve guttered like a dying lamp. He began to sweat. He knew he walked a tightrope with the madwoman. He was tolerated like a naughty pet for reasons clear only to the sorceress, who sometimes did things for no better reason than a momentary whim. Which could reverse itself an instant later.

He could be replaced. Others had been. Soulcatcher did not care about facts, insurmountable obstacles or mere difficulties. She cared about results.

Swan offered, "On the plus side there's no evidence, even from our most eager informants, that suggests this activity is anything but a low-grade nuisance. Even if Black Company survivors are behind it—and even with tonight's escalation."

Soulcatcher said, "They'll *never* be anything but a nuisance." Her voice was that of a plucky teenage girl. "They're going through the motions. They lost heart when I buried all their leaders." That was all spoken in a powerful male voice, by someone accustomed to unquestioning obedience. But those words amounted to an oblique admission that Company members might, after all, still be alive, and the final few words included in a rising inflection betraying potential uncertainty. There were questions about what had happened on the plain of glittering stone that Soulcatcher herself could not answer. "I'll worry when they call them back from the dead."

She did not know.

In truth, little had gone according to anyone's plan out there. Her escape, with Swan, had been pure luck. But Soulcatcher was the sort who believed Fortune's bright countenance was her born due.

"Probably true. And only marginally significant if I understood your summons."

"There are Other Forces Afoot," Soulcatcher said. This voice was a sybil's, rife with portent.

"The Deceivers have been heard from," the Radisha announced, causing a general startled reaction that included the disembodied spy. "Lately we've had reports from Dejagore, Meldermhai, Ghoja and Danjil about men having been slain in classic Strangler fashion."

Swan had recovered. "In classic Strangler work, only the killers know that it happened. They aren't assassins. The bodies would go through their religious rites and be buried in some holy place."

The Radisha ignored his remarks. "Today there was a strangling here. In Taglios. Perhule Khoji was the victim. He died in a joy house, an institution specializing in young girls. Such places aren't supposed to exist anymore, yet they persist." That was an accusation. The Greys were charged with crushing that sort of exploitation. But the Greys worked for the Protector and the Protector did not care. "I gather that anything you can imagine can still be found for sale."

Some people blamed a national moral collapse on the Black Company. Others blamed the ruling family. A few even blamed the Protector. Fault did not matter, nor did the fact that most of the nastier evils had existed almost since the first mud hut went up alongside the river. Taglios *had* changed. And desperate people will do what they must to survive. Only a fool would expect the results to be pretty.

Swan asked, "Who was this Perhule Khoji?" He glared over his shoulder. He had a scribe of his own recording the meeting back there in the darkness. Plainly, he wondered why the Radisha was familiar with this particular murder when he was not. "Sounds like the guy got something he had coming. You sure it wasn't just his adventure with the little girls gone bad?"

"Quite possibly Khoji did deserve what happened," the Radisha said with bitter sarcasm. "He was Vehdna, so he'll be talking it over with his god about now, I would imagine. His morals don't interest us, Swan. His position does. He was one of the Inspector-General's leading assistants. He collected taxes in the Checca and east waterfront areas. His death will cause problems for months. His areas were some of our best revenue producers."

"Maybe somebody who owed—"

"His child companion survived. And he did call for help. The sort of men who handle troublemakers in those places arrived while it was happening. Stranglers did it. It was an initiation killing. The Strangler candidate was inept. Nevertheless, with the help of his arm-holders, he managed to break Khoji's neck."

"So they were captured."

"No. The one they call Daughter of Night was there. Overseeing the initiation."

So the strong-arm guys would have been scared witless once they recognized her. No Gunni or Shadar wanted to believe the Daughter of Night was just a nasty young woman, not a mythic figure. Few Taglians of those religions would find the courage to interfere with her.

"All right," Swan conceded. "That would mean real Stranglers. But how did they recognize the Daughter of Night?"

Exasperated, Soulcatcher snapped, "She told them who she was, you ninny! 'I am the Daughter of Night. I am the Child of Darkness Forthcoming. Come to my mother or become prey for the beasts of devastation in the Year of the Skulls.' Typically portentous stuff." Soulcatcher's voice had become the mid-range monotone of an educated skeptic. "Not to mention that she was vampire-white and a prettier duplicate of my sister as a child."

The Daughter of Night feared no one and nothing. She knew that her spiritual parent, Kina the Destroyer, the Dark Mother, would shelter her—even though that goddess had stirred not at all for more than a decade. Rumors about the Daughter of Night had run through the underside of society for years. A lot of people believed she was what she claimed. Which only added to her power over the popular imagination.

Another rumor, losing currency with time, credited the Black Company with having forestalled Kina's Year of the Skulls back about the time the Taglian state chose to betray its hired protectors.

The Deceivers and Company alike had a psychological strength vastly exceeding their numbers. Being social ghosts made both groups more frightening.

What signified most was that the Daughter of Night had come to Taglios itself. And that she had shown herself publicly. And where the Daughter of Night went, the chieftain of all Deceivers, the living legend, the living saint of the Stranglers, Narayan Singh, surely followed like a faithful jackal and worked his evils, too.

Murgen considered aborting his mission to warn Sahra to call everything off till this news could be assessed. But it would be too late to stop everything now, whatever else was happening.

Narayan Singh was the most hated enemy of the Black Company still standing upright. Not Mogaba, nor even Soulcatcher, who was an old, old adversary, were as eagerly hunted as was Narayan Singh. Nor did Singh harbor any love for the Company. He had gotten himself caught once. And had spent a long time being made uncomfortable by people overburdened with malice. He had debts he would love to collect, should it please his goddess to permit that.

The Privy Council, as was customary, degenerated into nagging and finger-pointing soon afterward, with the Purohita and Inspector-General both maneuvering to get a rung up on one another, and maybe on Swan. The Purohita could count on the backing of the three tame priests—unless Soulcatcher had other ideas. The Inspector-General usually enjoyed the support of the Radisha.

These squabbles were generally prolonged but trivial, more symbol than substance. The Protector would let nothing she disapproved of come out of them.

As Murgen started to leave, his presence never having been detected, two Royal Guards rushed into the chamber. They headed for Willow Swan, though he was not their captain. Perhaps their news was something they did not care to share with the unpredictable Protector, their official commander. Swan listened for a moment, then slammed a fist onto the tabletop. "Damn it! I knew it had to be more than a nuisance." He bulled past the Purohita, giving the man a look of contempt. There was no love lost there.

It has started already, Murgen thought. Back to Do Trang's warehouse, then. He could prevent nothing already in motion, but he could get word to those still at headquarters so they could get after Narayan and the Daughter of Night as soon as possible.

7

Sahra changed faces as easily as an actor swaps masks. Sometimes she was the cruel, cunning, coldly calculating necromancer who conspired with the Captured. Sometimes she was just the near-widow of the Standardbearer and official Annalist of the Company. Sometimes she was just Tobo's doting mother. And whenever she went out into the city, she was Minh Subredil, another being entirely.

Minh Subredil was an outcast, the half-breed by-blow of a priest of Khusa and a Nyueng Bao whore. Minh Subredil knew more about her antecedents than did half the people on the streets of Taglios. She talked to herself about them all the time. She would tell anyone she could trap into listening.

Minh Subredil was a woman so pathetic, so shunned by fortune, that she was an old, bent thing decades before her time. Her signature, which made her recognizable to people who never had encountered her, was the small statue of Ghanghesha she carried everywhere. Ghanghesha, who was the god in charge of good luck in Gunni and some Nyueng Bao belief. Minh Subredil talked to Ghanghesha when there was nobody else who would listen.

Widowed, Minh Subredil supported her one child by doing scut-work day labor at the Palace. Each morning well before dawn she joined the assembly of unfortunates who gathered at the northern servants' postern in hopes of gaining work. Sometimes she was joined by her dead husband's retarded sister Sawa. Sometimes she brought her daughter, though seldom anymore. The girl was getting old enough to be noticed.

Subassistant housekeeper Jaul Barundandi would come out and announce the number of positions available for the day, then would select the people to fill them. Barundandi always chose Minh Subredil because, though she was too ugly to demand sexual favors of, she could be counted upon to kick back a generous percentage of her salary. Minh Subredil was a desperate creature.

Barundandi was amused by Subredil's omnipresent statue. A devout Gunni of the cult of Khusa, he often included in his prayers a petition that he be spared Subredil's sort of luck. He would never admit it to his henchmen but he did favor Subredil some because of her poor choice of a father. Like most villains, he was wicked only most of the time and mainly in small-minded ways.

Subredil, as Ky Sahra, never prayed. Ky Sahra had no use for gods. Unaware of his tiny soft spot, she did have in mind a destiny for Jaul Barundandi. When the time came. The subassistant would have ample opportunity to regret his predations.

There would be many, many regrets, spanning the length and breadth of the Taglian empire. When the time came.

We went out through the maze of confusion and distraction spells Goblin and One-Eye have spent so many years weaving throughout the neighborhood, a thousand layers of gossamer deception so subtle only the Protector herself might notice them. If she was looking. But Soulcatcher does not roam the streets looking for enemy hideouts. She has the Greys and her shadows and bats and crows to do that work. And those are too dim to notice that they are being guided away from or subtly ushered through the area in a manner that left it seeming no more remarkable than any other. The two little wizards spent most of their time maintaining and expanding their maze of confusion. People not trusted no longer got within two hundred yards of our headquarters. Not without being led.

We had no trouble. We wore strands of yarn tied around our left wrists. These enchanted loops softened the confusion spells. They let us see the truth.

Thus we often knew what the Palace intended before plans went into motion. Minh Subredil, or sometimes Sawa, listened in while the plans were being made.

I muttered, "Isn't it awfully early for us to be out?"

"Yes. But there will be others already there when we take our place." There are a lot of desperate people in Taglios. Some will camp as near the Palace as the Greys will allow.

We did reach the Palace area hours earlier than ever before. But there were rounds of the darkness to make, brothers of the Company to visit in their hiding places. In each instance the voice of the witch came out of the wreckage that was Minh Subredil. Sawa tagged along behind and drooled out of the corner of her twisted mouth.

Most of the men did not recognize us. They did not expect to do so. They expected to receive a code word from those in charge that would expose us as messengers. They got that word. Chances were good they were in some disguise themselves. Every Company brother was supposed to create several characters he could assume in public. Some did better than others. The worst were called upon to risk the least.

Subredil glanced at the fragment of moon sneaking a peek through a crack in the clouds. "Minutes to go."

I grunted, nervous. It had been a while since I had been involved in anything directly dangerous. Other than wandering around the Palace or going to the library, of course. But nobody was likely to stick me with sharp objects there.

"Those clouds look like the kind that come right before the rainy season." If they were, that season would be early. Which was not a pleasant thought. During the rainy season that is what it does, in torrents, every day. The weather can be truly ferocious, with dramatic temperature shifts and hailstorms, and thunder like all the gods of the Gunni pantheon are drunk and brawling. But mainly I do not like the heat.

Taglians divide their year into six seasons. Only during the one they call winter is there any sustained relief from the heat.

Subredil asked, "Would Sawa even notice the clouds?" She was a stickler for staying in character. In a city ruled by darkness you never knew what eyes watched from the shadows, what unseen ears were pricked to overhear.

"Uhm." That was about as intelligent a thing as Sawa ever said.

"Come." Subredil took my arm, guiding me, which was what she always did when we went to work at the Palace. We approached the main north entrance, which was only two-score yards from the service postern. A single torch burned there. It was supposed to show the Guards who might be outside. But it was situated so poorly it only helped them see the honest people. As we drew closer, someone who had sneaked in along the foot of the wall jumped up and enveloped the torch in a sack of wet rawhide.

The crude, startled remark of one of the guards carried clearly. Now, would he be incautious enough to come see what had happened?

There was no reason to believe he would not. The Royal Guards had had no trouble for almost a generation.

The sliver of moon vanished behind a cloud. As it went, something moved at the Palace entrance.

Now came the tricky part, making it look like we screwed up a sure thing by going in right at a shift change.

A sound of scuffling. A startled cry. Somebody else demanding what was going on. A rattle and clatter as people rushed the gate. Clang of metal. A scream or two. Whistles. Then within fifteen seconds, answering whistles from several directions. Exactly according to plan. In moments the whistles from the Palace entrance became shrilly desperate.

When first the idea was broached, there had been serious debate about whether or not the attack should be the real thing. It seemed likely taking the entrance would be easy. A strong faction, made up of men tired of waiting, just wanted to bust in and kill everybody. While that might have offered a certain amount of satisfaction, there was little chance Soulcatcher could be destroyed, and such wholesale murder would do nothing to liberate the Captured, which was supposed to be our primary mission.

I had convinced everyone that we needed to launch an old-fashioned, Annals-based game of misdirection. Make the enemy think we were up to one thing when actually we wanted to accomplish something else entirely. Get them running hard to head us off in one direction when we were following a completely different course.

With Goblin and One-Eye now so old, our deceits have to be increasingly intellectual. Those two do not have the strength or stamina to create and maintain massive battlefield illusions. And, though willing to share their secrets, they had not been able to arm Sahra for the struggle. Her talent did not extend in that direction.

The first Greys charged out of the darkness, into the ambushes waiting to receive them. For a while it was a vicious slaughter. But, somehow, a few managed to get through to support the Guards barely hanging on at the Palace entrance.

Subredil and I moved into position against the foot of the wall, between the big entrance and the servants' postern. Subredil hugged her Ghanghesha and whimpered. Sawa clung to Subredil and drooled and made strange little frightened noises.

Though the attackers piled up heaps of Greys, they never quite managed to break through the defense of the entryway. Then help arrived from inside. Willow Swan and a platoon of Royal Guards burst through the gateway. The attackers scattered instantly. So fast, in fact, that Swan screeched, "Hold up! There's something wrong!"

The night lit up. The air filled with hurtling fireballs. Their like had not been seen since the heavy fighting at the end of the Shadowmaster wars. Lady had created those weapons in vast numbers and a few had been husbanded carefully since then. The men employing them had not been involved in the attack on the entrance. They clung to the fire plan, which counted on everyone being able to pick Swan out from amongst the Guards and Greys.

His life depended on it.

Fire fell to the side of the group away from Subredil and me. Willow was afraid. When fire swiftly shifted to fall on the entry and cut him off, he was supposed to retreat toward the service entrance. Past us.

Good old Swan. He must have read my script. As his men were being torn apart by fireballs just yards away, he skittered along, hand against the wall, staying just steps ahead of destruction. Molten stone and chunks of burning flesh flew over his head and ours and I realized that I had underestimated the fury of my weapons, perhaps fatally. It was definitely a mistake to have committed so many.

Swan stumbled over Minh Subredil's ankle. Somehow, when he hit the cobblestones, he found himself face-to-face with a drooling idiot. Who had a dagger's point neatly positioned under his chin. "Don't even breathe," she whispered.

Fireballs hitting the Palace wall melted their way right in. The wooden gateway was on fire. There was plenty of light by which our brothers could see us signal that we had gotten our man. Fire became more accurate. The resistance to the Greys coming to help became less porous. A second apparent attack came forward. A couple of those brothers collected Swan. They kicked and cursed us. And took our weapons with them when they went away, part of a general retreat as the attack wave fled from no evident resistance.

As they disappeared into the darkness, the thing that we had feared most occurred.

Soulcatcher came out on the battlements above to see what was happening. Subredil and I knew because all fighting ceased within seconds once somebody spotted her. Then a storm of fireballs flashed her way.

We were lucky. She was sufficiently unprepared that she could do nothing but duck. Our brothers then did what they were supposed to do. They got the heck out of there. They got downhill and lost amongst the population before the Protector could release her bats and crows.

It was my belief that the activity would have all the nearby part of the city in an uproar within minutes. The men were supposed to help that along by launching absurd rumors. If they remained calm enough.

Subredil and Sawa moved two dozen yards closer to the servants' postern. We had just settled down to drool and be held and whimper while we watched the corpses burn when a frightened voice demanded, "Minh Subredil. What are you doing here?"

Jaul Barundandi. Our boss. I did not look up. And Subredil did not respond until Barundandi stirred her with a toe and asked again, not unkindly. She told him, "We were going to be here early. Sawa needs to work bad." She looked around. "Where are the others?"

There had been others. Four or five even more eager to be first in line. They had fled. That might mean trouble. No telling what they might have seen before they ran. An early stray fireball was supposed to have panicked and scattered them before Swan got to us but I could not recall that having happened.

Subredil turned more toward Barundandi. I held on to her tighter and whimpered. She patted my shoulder and murmured something indistinct. Barundandi seemed to buy it, particularly when Subredil discovered that one of her Ghanghesha's trunks had broken off, and she began to cry and search our surroundings.

Several of Barundandi's associates were out as well, looking around, asking one another what happened. The same thing was going on at the main entrance, where stunned Guards and sleep-fuddled functionaries asked one another what had happened and what they should do and, holy shit! some of those fires burned all the way through the wall and it was six or eight feet thick! Shadar from as far as a mile away were arriving, gathering dead and wounded Greys and also trying to figure out what had happened.

Jaul Barundandi's voice gentled further. He beckoned his assistants. "Help these two inside. Be gentle. The high and the mighty may want to talk to them."

I hoped my start did not give us away. I had counted on getting inside early but it had not occurred to me that anyone might be interested in what two near-untouchables might have seen.

8

I need not have worried. We were interviewed by a seriously distracted Guard sergeant who seemed to be going through the motions mainly as a sop to Jaul Barundandi. The subassistant had evidently suffered an overinspiration of ambition in thinking he could win favor by providing eyewitnesses to the tragedy.

His solicitude began to fade once he had little to gain. A few hours after we were taken inside, while excitement still gripped the Palace and a thousand outrageous rumors circulated, while leading Guardsmen and Greys kept bringing in more and more trusted armed men and sending out more and more spies to watch the regular soldiers in their barracks, just in case they were in on the attack somehow, Minh Subredil and her idiot sister-in-law were already hard at work. Barundandi had them cleaning the chamber where the Privy Council met. A huge mess had been left there. Somebody had lost her temper and had worked out her anger by tearing the place up.

Barundandi told us, "Expect to work very hard today, Minh Subredil. Few workers showed up this morning." He sounded bitter. He would not garner much kickback because of the raid. It did not occur to him to be thankful he was still alive. "Is she all right?" He meant me. Sawa. I was still doing a credible job of shaking.

"She will manage as long as I stay close. It would not be good to put her anyplace where she cannot see me today."

Barundandi grunted. "So be it. There's work enough here. Just don't get in anybody's way."

Minh Subredil bowed slightly. She was good at being unobtrusive. She seated me at a wide table about a dozen feet long, piled up lamps and candlesticks and whatnot that had gotten thrown around. I invoked Sawa's narrow focus and went to work cleaning them. Subredil began cleaning floors and furniture.

People came and went, many of them important. None of them noticed us except the Inspector-General of the Records, Chandra Gokhale, who kicked Subredil irritably because she was scrubbing the floor where he wanted to walk.

Subredil got back onto her knees, bowing and begging pardon. Gokhale ignored her. She began cleaning up spilled water, showing no emotion whatsoever. Minh Subredil took that sort of thing. But I suspect Ky Sahra had just formed a definite opinion about which of our enemies should follow Willow Swan into captivity.

The Radisha appeared. The Protector was with her. They settled into their places. Jaul Barundandi appeared soon afterward, meaning to get us out of there. Sawa seemed to notice nothing. Her focus on a candlestick was too narrow.

A tall Shadar captain bustled in. He announced, "Your Highness, the preliminary tally shows ninety-eight dead and one hundred twenty-six injured. Some of those will die from their wounds. Minister Swan hasn't been found but many of the bodies are burned too badly to identify. Many that were hit by fireballs caught fire and burned like greasy torches." The captain had trouble remaining calm. He was young. Chances were good he had not seen the consequences of battle before.

I kept working hard to shove myself way down deep into character. I had not been this close to Soulcatcher since she held me prisoner outside Kiaulune fifteen years ago. Those were not happy memories. I prayed she did not remember me.

I went all the way down into my safe place. I had not been there since my captivity. The hinges on the door were rusty. But I got inside and got comfortable while remaining Sawa. I had just enough attention left to catch most of what was happening around me.

The Protector suddenly asked, "Who are these women?"

Barundandi fawned. "Pardon, Great Ones. Pardon. My fault. I did not know the chamber was to be used."

"Answer the question, Housekeeper," the Radisha ordered.

"Certainly, Great One." Barundandi kowtowed halfway to the floor. "The woman scrubbing is Minh Subredil, a widow. The other is her idiot sister-in-law, Sawa. They are outside staff employed as part of the Protector's charity program."

Soulcatcher said, "I feel I have seen one or both of them before."

Barundandi bowed deeply again. The attention frightened him. "Minh Subredil has worked here for many years, Protector. Sawa accompanies her when her mind is clear enough for her to accomplish repetitive tasks."

I felt him trying to decide whether or not to volunteer the news that we had witnessed the morning's attack from up close. I clung to my safe place so hard that I did not catch what happened during the next few minutes.

Barundandi chose not to volunteer us for questioning. Perhaps he reasoned that too intensive an attention paid to us might expose the fact that he was charging us half our feeble salaries for the right to work our hands into raw, aching crabs.

The Radisha finally told him, "Go away, Housekeeper. Let them work. The fate of the empire will not be decided here today."

And Soulcatcher waved a gloved hand, shooing Barundandi out, but then halted him to demand, "What is that the woman has on the floor beside her?" Meaning Subredil, of course, since I was seated at the table.

"Uh? Oh. A Ghanghesha, Great One. The woman never goes anywhere without it. It's an obsession with her. It—"

"Go away now."

So it was that Sahra, at least, sat in on almost two hours of the innermost powers' responses to our assault.

After a while I came forward again, enough to follow most of it. Couriers came and went. A picture of generally upright behavior by the army and people took shape. Which was to be expected. Neither had any real reason to rise up right now. Which was nothing but good news to the Radisha.

Positive intelligence just made the Protector more suspicious, though. The old cynic.

"No prisoners taken," she said. "No corpses left behind. Quite possibly no serious casualties suffered. Nor any great risks endured, if you examine it closely. They fled as soon as there was a chance someone would hit back. What were they up to? What was their real purpose?"

Reasonably, Chandra Gokhale pointed out, "The attack appears to have been sustained with exceptional ferocity till you yourself appeared on the battlements. Only then did they run."

The Shadar captain volunteered, "Several survivors and witnesses report that the bandits argued amongst themselves about your presence, Protector. It seems they expected you to be away from the Palace. Evidently the attack would not have been undertaken had they known you were here."

One of my touches of misdirection. I hoped it did some good.

"That makes no sense. Where would they get that idea?" She did not expect an answer and did not wait for one. "Have you identified any of the burned bodies?"

"Only three, Protector. Most are barely recognizable as human."

The Radisha asked, "Chandra, how bad was the physical damage? Do you have an assessment yet?"

"Yes, Radisha. It was bad. Extremely bad. The wall appears to have suffered some structural damage. The full extent is being determined right now. It's certain to be a weak point for a while. You might consider putting up a wooden curtain-wall in front of what is going to become a construction area. And think hard about bringing in troops."

"Troops?" the Protector demanded. "Why troops?" Her voice, long neutral, became suspicious. When you have no friends at all, paranoia is an even more natural outlook than it is for brothers of the Black Company.

"Because the Palace is too big to defend with the people you have here now. Even if you arm the household staff. An enemy doesn't need to use any of the regular entrances. He could climb the outside wall where no one is watching and attack from inside."

The Radisha said, "If he tried that, he'd need maps to get around. I've never seen anyone but Smoke, who was our court wizard a long time ago, who could get around this place without one. You have to have an instinct."

The Inspector-General observed, "If the attack *was* undertaken by elements descended from the old Black Company—and the employment of fireball weapons would suggest *some* connection, even though we *know* that the Company was exterminated by the Protector—then they *may* have access to hallway maps created when the Liberator and his staff were quartered here."

The Radisha insisted, "You can't chart this place. I know. I've tried."

Thank Goblin and One-Eye for that, Princess. Long, long ago the Captain had those two old men scatter confusion spells liberally, everywhere. There were things he had not wanted the Radisha to find. Things that remained hidden still, among them those ancient volumes of the Annals that supposedly explain the Company's secret beginnings but which have been a complete disappointment so far. Minh Subredil knows how to get to them. Whenever she gets the chance, Minh Subredil tears out a few pages and smuggles them out to me. Then I sneak them into the library and when no one is watching, I translate them a few words at a time, looking for that one phrase that will show us how to open the way for the Captured.

Sawa cleaned brass and silver. Minh Subredil cleaned floor and furniture. The Privy Council and their associates came and went. The level of panic declined as no new attacks developed. Too bad we did not have the numbers to stir them up again every few hours.

Soulcatcher remained uncharacteristically quiet. She had known the Company longer than anyone but the Captain, Goblin and One-Eye, though from the outside. She would accept nothing at face value. Not yet.

I hoped she broke a mental sprocket trying to figure it out, though I feared she had already done so, because she kept wondering about the burned bodies and Willow Swan. Could I have planned so obviously that she was confused only because she kept looking for something beyond the kidnapping?

I finished the last candlestick. I did not look around, did not say anything, just sat there. It was difficult to focus my thinking away from the danger seated across the room when my fingers were not busy. I gave praise to God, silently, as I had learned was proper for a woman when I was little. Equal praise was due Sahra's insistence on staying in character.

Both served me well.

At some point Jaul Barundandi came back. Under the eyes of the Great Ones, he was not an unkind boss. He told Subredil it was time to leave. Subredil bestirred Sawa. As I got to my feet, I made some sounds of distress.

"What is that?" Barundandi asked.

"She's hungry. We haven't eaten all day." Usually the management did provide a few scraps. That was one of the perks. Subredil and Sawa sometimes husbanded some of their share and took it home. That established and sustained the women's habit of carrying things out of the Palace.

The Protector leaned forward. She stared intently. What had we done to tickle her suspicion? Was she just so ancient in her paranoia that she needed no clue stronger than intuition? Or was it possible that she really *could* read minds, just a touch?

Barundandi said, "We'll go to the kitchen, then. The cooks overprepared badly today."

We shuffled out behind him, each step like leaping another league out of winter toward spring, out of darkness into light. Four or five paces outside the meeting chamber, Barundandi startled us by running a hand through his hair and gasping. He told Subredil, "Oh, it feels good to get out of there. That woman gives me the green willies."

She gave me the green willies, too. And only the fact that I had gone deep into character to deal with them saved me giving myself away. Who would suspect that much humanity in Jaul Barundandi? I got a grip on Subredil's arm and shook.

Subredil responded to Barundandi softly, submissively agreeing that the Protector might be a great horror.

The kitchens, normally off limits to casual labor, was a dragon's hoard of edible treasures. With the dragon evicted. Subredil and Sawa ate till they could barely waddle. They loaded themselves with all the plunder they thought they would be allowed to carry off. They collected their few coppers and headed for the servants' postern before anyone could think of something else for them to do, before any of Barundandi's cronies realized that the customary kickbacks had been overlooked.

There were armed guards outside the postern. That was new. They were Greys rather than soldiers. They did not seem particularly interested in people going out. They did not bother with the usual cursory search casuals had to endure so nobody carried off the royal cutlery.

I wish our characters had more curiosity in them. I could have used a closer look at the damage we had done. They were putting up scaffolding and erecting a wooden curtain-wall already. The glimpses I did catch awed me. I had only read about what the later versions of those fireball throwers could do. The face of the Palace looked like a model of dark wax that someone had stuck repeatedly with a white-hot iron rod. Not only had stone melted and run, some had been vaporized.

We had been released much earlier than usual. It was only mid-afternoon. I tried to walk too fast, eager to get away. Subredil refused to be rushed. Ahead of us stood quiet crowds who had come to stare at the Palace. Subredil murmured something about ". . . ten thousand eyes."

9

I erred. That mass of people had not come just to examine our night's work and marvel that the Protector's dead men could be so frisky. They were interested in four Bhodi disciples at the memorial posts that stood a dozen yards in front of the battered entrance, outside the growing curtain-wall. One disciple was mounting a prayer wheel onto one of the posts. Another two were spreading an elaborately embroidered dark red-orange cloth on the cobblestones. The fourth, shaved balder and shinier than a polished apple, stood before a Grey who was sixteen at the oldest. The Bhodi disciple had his arms folded. He looked through the youngster, who seemed to be having trouble getting across the message that these men had to stop doing what they were doing. The Protector forbade it.

This was something that would interest even Minh Subredil. She stopped walking. Sawa clung to her arm with one hand and cocked her head so she could watch, too.

I felt terribly exposed standing out there, a dozen yards from the silent gawkers.

Reinforcements for the young Grey arrived in the person of a grisled Shadar sergeant who seemed to think the Bhodi's problem was deafness. "Clear off!" he shouted. "Or you'll be cleared."

The Bhodi with folded arms said, "The Protector sent for me."

Not having gotten Murgen's report yet, Sahra and I had no idea what this was about.

"Huh?"

The disciple preparing the prayer wheel announced its readiness. The Sergeant growled, swatted it off the post with the back of his hand. The responsible disciple bent, picked it up, began remounting it. They were not violent people, the Bhodi disciples, nor did they resist anything, but they were stubborn.

The two spreading the prayer rug were satisfied with their work. They spoke to the man with folded arms. He bowed his head slightly, then raised his eyes to meet those of the elder Shadar. In a voice loud but so calm it was disturbing, he proclaimed, "*Rajadharma*. The Duty of Kings. Know you: Kingship is a trust. The King is the most exalted and conscientious servant of the people."

Not one witness had any trouble hearing and understanding those words.

The speaker settled himself on the prayer rug. His robes were an almost identical shade. He seemed to fade into a greater whole.

One of the secondary disciples passed him a large jar. He raised that as though in offering to the sky, then dumped its contents over himself. The Shadar sergeant looked as rattled as the youngster. He peered around for help.

The prayer wheel was back in place. The disciple responsible set it spinning, then backed off with the two who had spread the prayer rug.

The disciple on the rug struck flint to steel and vanished in a blast of flame just as I recognized the odor of naphtha. Heat hit me like a blow. I was in character strongly enough to whimper and grab Subredil with both hands. She resumed moving, eyes wide, stunned.

The man inside the flames never cried out, never moved till all life was gone and the charred husk left behind toppled over.

Crows circled above, cursing in their own tongue. So Soulcatcher knew. Or soon would.

We continued moving, into the now-animated crowd and through, heading home. The Bhodi disciples who had helped prepare the ritual suicide had disappeared already, while all eyes were fixed on the burning man.

I can't believe he did that!" I said, still climbing out of Sawa's smelly rags and crippled personality. Word had beaten us home. The suicide was all anyone wanted to discuss. Our own nighttime effort had become secondary. That was over and they had survived.

Tobo definitely did not believe it. He mentioned that in passing and insisted on telling us everything his father had seen inside the Palace last night. He referred to notes he had made with Goblin's help. He was thoroughly proud of the job he had done and wanted to rub our noses in it. "But I couldn't really get him to *talk* to me, Mom. Anything I asked seemed to be just an irritation. It was like he just wanted to get it over with so he could go away."

"I know, dear," Sahra said. "I know. He's that way with me, too. Here's some nice bread they let us bring home. Eat something. Goblin. What did they do with Swan? Is he healthy?"

One-Eye cackled. He said, "Healthy as a man with cracked ribs can be. Scared shitless, though." He cackled again.

"Cracked ribs? Explain."

Goblin told her, "Somebody with a grudge against the Greys got overexcited. But don't worry about it. The guy is going to have plenty of opportunity to be sorry he let his feelings get the best of him."

"I'm exhausted," Sahra said. "We spent the whole day in the same room as Soulcatcher. I thought I would burst."

"*You* did? It was all I could do not to run out of there screaming. I concentrated so hard on being Sawa that I missed half of what they said."

"What didn't get said might be more important. Soulcatcher was really suspicious about the attack."

"I told you, go for the throat!" One-Eye barked. "While they still didn't believe in us. Kill them all and you wouldn't have to sneak around trying to figure out how to get the Old Man out. You could make those guys at the library do your research for you."

"We'd've just gotten killed," Sahra said. "Soulcatcher was already looking for trouble. The news about the Daughter of Night did that. Speaking of whom, I want you two looking for her, and Narayan, too."

"Too?" Goblin asked.

"Soulcatcher will hunt them with a great deal of enthusiasm, I expect."

I observed, "Kina must be stirring again. Narayan and the girl wouldn't come to Taglios unless they were confident of her protection. Which means the girl will start copying the Books of the Dead again, too. Sahra, tell Murgen to keep an eye on them." Those terrible, ancient volumes were buried in the same cavern as the Captured. "I had a thought while we were up there—after I ran out of candlesticks and didn't have anything else to do. It's been a long time since I read Murgen's Annals. It didn't seem like they had much bearing on what we're trying to do. Being so modern. But when I was sitting there, just a few feet from Soulcatcher, I got a really creepy feeling that I had missed something. And it's been so long since I studied those things, I can't guess what."

"You should have time. We'll need to lie pretty low for a few days."

"You'll be going to work, won't you?"

"It would be suspicious if I didn't."

"I'm going to the library. I located some histories that go back to the earliest days of Taglios."

"Yeah?" One-Eye croaked, jerked himself out of a half-sleep. "Then find out for me why the hell the ruling gang are only princes. The territories they rule are bigger than most kingdoms around here."

"A question that never would have occurred to me," I said politely. "Or to any native of this end of the world, probably. I'll ask." If I remembered.

Nervous laughter came from the shadows in the back of the warehouse. Willow Swan. Goblin said, "He's playing tonk with some guys he knew in the old days."

Sahra said, "We should get him out of the city. Where can we keep him?"

"I need him here," I said. "I need to ask him about the plain. That's why we grabbed him first. And I'm not going off to some place in the country when I've finally started getting somewhere at the library."

"Soulcatcher might have him marked somehow."

"We've got two half-ass wizards of our own. Have them check him over. They add up to one competent—"

"You watch your mouth, Little Girl."

"I forget myself, One-Eye. You two together add up to half as much as either one alone."

"Sleepy has a point. If Soulcatcher marked him, you two ought to be able to find out."

One-Eye snapped, "Use your head! If she'd marked him, she'd already be here. She wouldn't be up there asking her lackeys if they'd found his bones yet." The little man climbed out of his chair, creaking and groaning. He headed for the shadows at the rear of the warehouse but not toward Swan's voice.

I said, "He's right." I headed to the back myself. I had not seen Swan up close for fifteen years. Behind me, Tobo started grilling his mother about Murgen. He was upset because his father had been indifferent.

Seemed to me there was a good chance Murgen did not understand who Tobo was. He had trouble with time. He had had that problem since the siege of Jaicur. He might think it was still fifteen years ago and he was stumbling away into a possible future.

S wan stared at me for a few seconds after I stepped into the light of the lamp illuminating the table where he was playing cards with the Gupta brothers and a corporal we called Slink. "Sleepy, right? You haven't changed. Goblin or One-Eye put some kind of hex on you?"

"God is good to the pure of heart. How are your ribs?"

Swan ran fingers through the remnants of his hair. "So that's the story." He touched his side. "I'll live."

"You're taking it well."

"I needed a vacation. Nothing's in my hands now. I can relax until she finds me again."

"Can she do that?"

"You the Captain now?"

"The Captain is the Captain. I design ambushes. Can she find you?"

"Well, son, this looks like the fabled collision between the unstoppable whatsis and the immovable thingee. I don't know where to lay my bets. Over here we got the Black Company with four hundred years of bad and tricky. Over there you got Soulcatcher with four centuries of mean and crazy. It's a toss-up, I guess."

"She doesn't have you marked somehow?"

"Only with scars."

The way he said that made me feel I knew exactly what he meant. "You want to come over to our side?"

"You're kidding. You pulled all that stuff this morning just to ask me to join the Black Company?"

"We pulled all that stuff this morning to show the world that we're still here and that we could do what we want, whenever we want, Protector or no Protector. And to take you so I can question you about the plain of glittering stone."

He looked at me for several seconds, then checked his cards. "There's a subject that hasn't come up in a while."

"You going to be stubborn about it?"

"You kidding? I'll talk your ear off. But I'll bet you don't learn a damned thing you didn't already know." He discarded a black knave.

Slink jumped on the card, laid down a nine-queen spread, discarded a red queen and grinned. He needed to see One-Eye about those teeth.

"Shit!" Swan grumbled. "I missed this game. How did you people learn? It's the simplest damn game in the world but I never met a Taglian who could figure it out."

I observed, "You learn fast when you play with One-Eye. Scoot over, Sin. Let me play while I pick this guy's brain." I pulled up a stool, studying Swan every second. The man knew how to get into a character. This was not the Willow Swan that Murgen wrote about or the Swan that Sahra saw when she visited the Palace. I picked up my five cards from the next deal. "This ain't a hand, it's a foot. How come you're so relaxed, Swan?"

"No stress. You can't have a worse hand than mine. I don't got no two cards of the same suit."

"No stress?"

"As of today I got nothing to do but lean back and take it easy. Just play tonk till my honey comes and takes me home."

"You're not afraid? Reports I've had said you're shakier than Smoke used to be."

His features hardened. That was not a comparison he liked. "The worst has happened, hasn't it? I'm in the hands of my enemies. But I'm still healthy."

"There's no guarantee you'll stay that way. Unless you cooperate. Darn! I'm going to have to rob a poor box if this keeps on." Play had not gotten all the way back to me before the hand ended. I did not win.

"I'll sing like a trained crow," Swan said. "Like a chorus. But I can't do you much good. I was never as close to the center as you may think."

"Possibly." I watched his hands closely as he dealt. It seemed like a moment when a skilled manipulator's ego might compel him to show himself how good he was at pulling fast moves. If he had any moves, he would not get them by me. I learned the game from One-Eye, too. "Prove it. Tell me how Soulcatcher kept you two alive long enough to get off the plain."

"That's an easy one." He completed a straight deal. "We ran away faster than the ghosts chasing us could run. We were riding those black horses the Company brought down from the north."

I had ridden those enchanted beasts a few times myself. That could be the answer. They could outdistance any normal horse and could run almost forever without tiring. "Maybe. Maybe. She didn't have any special talisman?"

"Not that she mentioned to me."

I looked down at another terrible hand. Grilling Swan could get expensive. I am not one of the better tonk players in the gang. "What happened to the horses?"

"Far as I know, they're all dead. Time or magic or wounds got them. And the queen bitch wasn't happy about that, either. She don't like walking and she ain't fond of flying."

"Flying?" Startled, I discarded a card I should have kept. That allowed one of the Guptas to go down and take me for another couple of coppers.

Swan said, "I think I'm going to like playing with you. Yeah. Flying. She's got a couple of them carpets that was made by the Howler. And she just ain't real good with them. I can tell you that from personal experience. Your deal. Ain't nothing like falling off of one of them suckers while it's hauling ass, even if you're only five feet high."

One-Eye materialized. He looked about as bright and alert as he ever did these days. "Room for one more?" His breath smelled of alcohol.

Swan grumbled, "I know that voice. No. I figured you out twenty-five years ago. I thought we got your ass at Khadighat. Or maybe it was Bhoroda or Nalanda."

"I'm quick on my feet."

Slink said, "You're in only if you show some money up front and you agree not to deal."

"And you keep your hands on top of the table all the time," I added.

"You smite me to the heart, Little Girl. People might get the idea you don't trust me not to cheat."

"Good. That'll save them a lot of time and pain."

"Little girl?" Swan asked. There was a whole different look in his eye suddenly.

"One-Eye's got diarrhea of the mouth. Sit down, old man. Swan was just telling us about Soulcatcher's magic carpets and how she doesn't like flying. And I'm wondering if we couldn't find some way to take advantage of that."

Swan looked from one of us to the other. I watched One-Eye's hands as he picked up his first bunch of cards. Just in case he might have done something to this deck sometime in the past. "Little girl?"

"Is there an echo in here?" Slink asked.

"Is that suddenly a problem?" I asked.

"No! No." Swan showed me the palm of his free hand. "I'm just getting a lot of surprises here. Soulcatcher thought she was pretty solid on the Company survivors. But I've already run into four people who are known to be dead, including the world's ugliest wizard and that Nyueng Bao woman who acts like she's in charge."

One-Eye growled, "Don't you go talking about Goblin that way. He's my pal. I'll have to stand up for him. Someday." He snickered.

Swan ignored him. "And you. That we had down as a man."

I shrugged. "Not many knew. And it's not important. The dope with the eye patch and smelly hat should've had sense enough not to mention it in front of an outsider." I glared.

One-Eye grinned, drew a card from the pile, discarded. "She's feisty, Swan. Smart, too. Designed the plan that pulled you in. You started on another one, Little Girl?"

"Several. I think Sahra will want the Inspector-General next, though."

"Gokhale? He can't tell us anything."

"Say it's personal. Swan. You know anything about Gokhale? He dabble in little girls like Perhule Khoji used to?"

One-Eye gave me an evil look. Swan stared. My mess-up this time. I had given something away.

Too late to fuss about it. "Well?"

"Actually, yes." Swan was pale. He focused on his cards, having trouble keeping his hands steady. "Those two and several others in that office. Common interests brought them together. The Radisha doesn't know. She doesn't want to know." He discarded out of turn. He had lost his zest for the game.

I realized what the problem was. He thought my speaking freely meant I expected to elevate him to a higher plane before long. "You're all right, Swan. Long as you behave. Long as you answer questions when you're asked. Hell, I got to save you. There's a bunch of guys buried under the glittering plain that want to talk to you about that when they get back." Might be interesting to watch him talk it over with Murgen.

"They're still *alive*?" The idea seemed to stun him.

"Very alive. Just frozen in time. And getting angrier by the minute."

"I thought . . . Great God . . . shit."

"Do not speak so on the name of God!" Slink growled.

Slink was Jaicuri Vehdna, too. And much less lapsed than I. He managed prayers at least once a day and temple several times a month. The local Vehdna thought he was a Dejagoran refugee employed by Banh Do Trang because he had done the Nyueng Bao favors during the siege there. Most of our brothers endured genuine employment and worked hard to resemble pillars of the local community.

Swan swallowed, said, "You people ever eat? I ain't had nothing since yesterday."

"We eat," I said. "But not like you're used to. It's true what they say about Nyueng Bao. They don't eat anything but fish heads and rice. Eight days a week."

"Fish will do right now. I'll save the bitching till my belly's full."

"Slink," I said. "We need to send a kill team down to Semchi to watch the Bhodi Tree. The Protector's probably going to try to smash it. We could make some friends if we save it." I explained about the Bhodi disciple who burned himself and Soulcatcher's threat to turn the Bhodi Tree into kindling. "I'd like to go myself, just to see if the Bhodi nonviolent ethic is strong enough to make them stand around while somebody destroys their most holy shrine. But I have too much work to do here." I tossed my cards in. "In fact, I have work to do now."

I was tired but figured I could study Murgen's Annals for a few hours before I passed out.

As I walked away, Swan whispered, "How the hell does she know all that? And is she really a she?"

"Never checked personally," Slink said. "I have a wife. But she's definitely got some female habits on her."

What the devil did that mean? I am just one of the guys.

These were exciting times. I found myself eager to be up and outside, where things were happening. The impact of our boldness would have reached every cranny of the city by now. I gobbled cold rice and listened to Tobo complain, again, that his father had paid him no attention.

"Is there something I can do about that, Tobo?"

"Huh?"

"Unless you think I can go back there and tell him to shape up and talk to his kid, you're wasting your time and mine bitching about it. Where's your mother?"

"She left for work. A long time ago. She said they'd be suspicious if she didn't show up today."

"Probably would be. They'll be real edgy about everything for a while. How about instead of fussing about what's happened already, you spend some time thinking about what you'll do next time you see your father? And in the meantime, you can stay out of trouble by keeping notes for me whenever anybody questions the prisoner."

His glower told me he was no more excited about being offered work than any boy his age would be. "You're going out, too?"

"I have to go to work." It would be a good day to get to the library early. The scholars were supposed to be gone most of the day. There was supposed to be a big meeting of the bhadrhalok, which was a loosely associated group of educated men who did not like the Protector and who found the institution of the Protectorate objectionable. Jokingly, they referred to themselves as a band of intellectual terrorists. Bhadrhalok means, more or less, "the respectable people" and that was exactly what they thought they were. They were all educated, high-caste Gunni, which meant, right away, that a vast majority of the Taglian population regarded them with no sympathy at all. Their biggest problem with the Protector was that she held their self-confident, arrogant assumption of superiority in complete contempt. As revolutionaries and terrorists, they were less incandescent than any of the low-caste social clubs that existed on every residential block in the city. I doubt that Soulcatcher wasted two spies watching them. But they had great fun, fulminating and crying on one another's shoulders about the world going to hell in a goat cart driven by the demon in black. And every week or so it got most of the library crew out of my way.

I did what I could to encourage their seditious fervor.

I got off to a slow start. Not thirty yards from the warehouse exit I ran into two of our brothers doing donkey work for Do Trang while standing lookout. One made gestures indicating that they had something to report. Sighing, I strolled over. "What's the story, River?" The men called him Riverwalker. I did not know him by any other name.

"We got shadowtraps that's been sprung. We got ourselves some new pets."

"Oh, no. Darn." I shook my head.

"That's not good?"

"Not good. Run, report it to Goblin. I'll stick with Ran till you get back. Don't dawdle. I'm late for work." Not true, but Taglians have little sense of urgency, and the concept of punctuality is alien to most.

Shadows in the shadowtraps. Not a good eventuation, for sure. Near as we could determine, Soulcatcher had no more than two dozen manageable shadows left under control. As many more had gone feral in the remote south and were developing reputations as rakshasas, which were demons or devils but not quite like those my northern forebrethren knew. Northern demons seemed to be solitary beings of considerable power. Rakshasas are communal and pretty weak individually. But deadly. Very deadly.

In ancient myth, of course, they are much more powerful. They swat each other over the head with mountaintops, grow two heads for every one chopped off by a hero, and collect the beautiful wives of kings who are really gods incarnate but do not remember that fact. Things must have been much more exciting in olden times—even if they did not make a lot of sense from day to day.

Catcher would keep a close eye on her shadows. They were her most valuable resource. Which meant that if they had been sent out to spy, she should know exactly where each was supposed to have gone. At least that is the way I would have done it if I were committing irreplaceable resources. I did that for every single man we committed to Willow Swan's capture. I knew how they were going to get to their places and how they were going to get home and everything they were supposed to do in between. And just like I figured Soulcatcher might, I would have gone looking for them personally if they had failed to return home.

Goblin came hobbling into the early morning light, cursing all the way. He wore the all-covering brown wool of a veyedeen dervish. He hated the outfit, however necessary it was to disguise himself when he was outside. I did not blame him. The wool was hot. It was supposed to remind the holy men of the hell they were escaping by devoting themselves to chastity, asceticism and good works. "What the hell is this shit?" he growled. "It's hot enough to boil eggs out here already."

"The boys say we've caught something in our shadowtraps. I thought you might want to do something about that before Mama comes looking for her babies."

"Shit. More work—"

"Old man, you just had something in your mouth I wouldn't even want in my hand."

"Vehdna priss. Get the flock out of here before I give you a real language lesson. And bring home something decent to eat when you come back. Like maybe a cow."

More than once he and One-Eye had conspired to kidnap one of the sacred cattle that wander the city. To date, their efforts have come to naught because none of the men will go along. The majority have Gunni backgounds.

It took no time at all to learn that our shadow captives were not the only shadows that had run wild just before dawn. Rumor was rife. The stories of the murders the shadows committed banished news of the attack on the Palace and the self-immolation of the Bhodi disciple. The killings were closer to home and closer in time. And they were grotesque. The corpse of a man whose life has been devoured by a shadow is a twisted husk of the creature that was.

I insinuated myself into the crowd surrounding the doorway of a family where there had been multiple deaths. You can do that when you are little and limber and know how to use your elbows. I arrived just in time to watch them bring the bodies out. I was hoping they would be exposed to the public eye. Not that I wanted to see them myself. I saw plenty of those kinds of bodies during the Shadowmaster wars. I just thought the people ought to see what Soulcatcher could do. She needed all the enemies she could get.

The bodies were enshrouded already. But there was talk.

I traveled on, learning that most of the dead had been people who lived on the streets. And there had been a lot of those, taken in no obvious pattern whatsoever. It looked like Soulcatcher had sent the shadows out just to demonstrate that she had the power and the will to kill.

The deaths had evoked no great fear. People thought it was over. Most of them did not know any of the dead so were not angry, either. Curiosity and revulsion were the common emotions.

I considered turning back to tell Goblin to fix the captured shadows so they would go out killing again tonight and every night thereafter, till Soulcatcher tracked them down. She would not look for trappers if she thought her pets had gone rogue. And the shadows would create a lot more enemies for her before their terror ended.

At first it seemed the Greys had faded from the streets. They were less in evidence than usual. But as I skirted Chor Bagan, it became evident why. They had the place under siege, apparently on the assumption that any Black Company survivors, having been branded bandits by the Protector, would hide themselves amongst Taglios' homegrown thieves and villains. Amusing.

Sahra and I insist that we have as little to do with the criminal element as possible—over One-Eye's objections. And ignoring Banh Do Trang's occasional lapses. That element included folk of dubious morals and discipline who might serve us up for enough blood money to buy one more jar of illegal wine. I hoped they and the Greys had fun. I hoped somebody forgot the rules and their day turned bloody. That would make life easier for me and mine.

Any trip across town exposes you to the cruel truth about Taglios. Beggary exists there like nowhere else in the world. Were someone to sweep the city clean and organize the beggars into regiments, they would number more than the biggest army the Captain put together in the days of the Shadowmaster wars. If you look the least bit foreign or prosperous, they come at you in waves. Every attempt is made to exploit your pity. Not far from Do Trang's warehouse there is a boy with neither hands nor lower legs. Somehow, blocks of wood have been affixed in their place. He crawls around with a bowl in his mouth. Every cripple over the age of fifteen claims to be a wounded hero of the wars. The children are the worst. Often they have been maimed deliberately, their limbs deformed evilly. They are sold to men who then feel they own them because they feed them a handful of toasted grain every few days.

A new mystery of the city is that men of that stripe seem to run the risk of cruel tortures and their own careers as deformed beggars. If they do not watch their backs very, very carefully.

My route took me near one such. He had one arm he could use to drag himself around. The rest of his limbs were twisted ruins. His bones had been crushed to gravel but he had been kept alive by a dedicated effort. His face and exposed skin were covered with burn scars. I paused to place one small copper in his bowl.

He whimpered and tried to crawl away. He could still see out of one eye.

Everywhere you looked, life proceeded in the unique Taglian fashion. Every vehicle in motion had people hanging off it, sponging a ride. Unless it was the ricksha of a rich man, perhaps a banker from Kowlhri Street, who could afford outrunners armed with bamboo canes to keep people off. Shopkeepers often sat on top of their tiny counters because there was no other space. Workmen jogged hither and yon with backbreaking loads, violently cursing everyone in their way. The people argued, laughed, waved their arms wildly, simply stepped to the side of the street where no one was lying to defecate when the need came upon them. They bathed in the water in the gutters, indifferent to the fact that a neighbor was urinating in the same stream fifteen feet away.

Taglios is an all-out, relentless assault upon all the senses but engages none so much as it does the sense of smell. I hate the rainy season but without its protracted sluicings-out, Taglios would become untenable even for rats. Without the rains, the endemic cholera and smallpox would be far worse than they are—though the rainy times bring outbreaks of malaria and yellow fever. Disease of every sort is common and accepted stoically.

And then there are the lepers, whose plight gives new depth of meaning to horror and despair. Never do I find my faith in God so tested as when I consider the lepers. I am as terrified by them as anyone but I do know enough about some individuals to realize that very few are being visited by a scourge they deserve. Unless the Gunni are right and they are paying for evils done in previous lives.

Up above it all are the kites and crows, the buzzards and vultures. For the eaters of carrion, life is good. Till the dead wagons come to collect the fallen.

The people come from everywhere, from five hundred miles, to find their fortunes. But Fortune is an ugly, two-faced goddess.

When you have lived with her handiwork for half a generation, you hardly notice anymore. You forget that this is not the way life has to be. You cease to marvel at just how much evil man can conjure simply by existing.

12

The library, created by and bequeathed to the city by an earlier mercantile prince who was much impressed by learning, strikes me as a symbol of knowledge rearing up to shed its light into the surrounding darkness of ignorance. Some of the city's worst slums wash right up against the wall enclosing its ground. The beggars are bad around its outer gates. Why is a puzzlement. I have never seen anyone toss them a coin.

There is a gateman but he is not a guard. He lacks even a bamboo cane. But a cane is unnecessary. The sanctity of the place of knowledge is observed by everyone. Everyone but me, you might say.

"Good morning, Adoo," I said as the gateman swung the wrought iron open for me. Though I was a glorified sweeper and fetch-it man, I had status. I appeared to enjoy the favor of some of the bhadrhalok.

Status and caste grew more important as Taglios became more crowded and resources grew less plentiful. Caste has become much more rigidly defined and observed in just the last ten years. People are desperate to cling to the little that they have already. Likewise, the trade guilds have grown increasingly powerful. Several have raised small, private armed forces that they use to make sure immigrants and other outsiders do not trample on their preserves, or that they sometimes hire out to temples or others in need of justice. Some of our brothers have done some work in that vein. It generates revenue and creates contacts and allows us glimpses inside otherwise closed societies.

Outside, the library resembles the more ornate Gunni temples. Its pillars and walls are covered with reliefs recalling stories both mythical and historical. It is not a huge place, being just thirty yards on its long side and sixty feet the other way. Its main floor is elevated ten feet above the surrounding gardens and monuments, which themselves cap a small knoll. The building proper is tall enough that inside there is a full-size hanging gallery all the way around at the level where a second floor should be, then an attic of sorts above that, plus a well-drained basement below the main floor. I find that interior much too open for comfort. Unless I am way down low or way up high, everyone can watch what I am doing.

The main floor is an expanse of marble, brought from somewhere far away.

Upon it, in neat rows, stand the desks and tables where the scholars work, either studying or copying decaying manuscripts. The climate is not conducive to the longevity of books. There is a certain sadness to the library, a developing air of neglect. Scholars grow fewer each year. The Protector does not care about the library because it cannot brag that it contains old books full of deadly spells. There is not one grimoire in the place. Though there is a lot of very interesting stuff—if she bothered to look. But that sort of curiosity is not part of her character.

There are more glass windows in the library than anywhere else I have ever seen. The copyists need a lot of light. Most of them, these days, are old and their sight is failing. Master Santaraksita often goes on about the library having no future. No one wants to visit it anymore. He believes that has something to do with the hysterical fear of the past that began to build soon after the rise of the Shadowmasters, when he was still a young man. Back when fear of the Black Company gained circulation, before the Company ever appeared.

I stepped into the library and surveyed it. I loved the place. In another time I would gladly have become one of Master Santaraksita's acolytes. If I could have survived the close scrutiny endured by would-be students.

I was not Gunni. I was not high caste. The former I could fake well enough to get by. I had been surrounded by Gunni all my life. But I did not know caste from within. Only the priestly caste and some selected commercial-caste folks were permitted to be literate. Though familiar with the vulgate and the High Mode both, I could never pretend to have grown up in a priestly household fallen on hard times. I had not grown up in much of any kind of household.

I had the place entirely to myself. And there was no obvious cleaning that needed doing right away.

It ever amazed me that no one actually lived in the library. That it was more holy or more frightening than a temple. The kangali—the parentless and homeless and fearless boys of the street, who run in troops of six to eight—see temples as just another potential resource. But they would not trouble the library.

To the unlettered, the knowledge contained in books was almost as terrible as the knowledge bound up in the flesh of a creature as wicked as Soulcatcher.

I had one of the best jobs in Taglios. I was the main caretaker at the biggest depository and replicatory of books within the Taglian empire. It had taken three and a half years of scheming and several carefully targeted murders to put me into a position I enjoyed way too much. Always before me was the temptation to forget the Company. The temptation might have gotten me had I had the social qualifications to be anything but a janitor who sneaked peeks into books when nobody was looking.

In quick order I conjured the tools of my purported trade, then hurried to one of the more remote copying desks. It was out of the way, yet offered a good line of vision and good acoustics so I would not be surprised doing something both forbidden and impossible.

I had gotten caught twice already, luckily both times with *Tantric* books illuminated with illustrations. They thought I was sneaking peeks at dirty pictures. Master Santaraksita himself suggested I go study temple walls if that sort of thing appealed to me. But I could not help feeling that he began to harbor a deep suspicion after the second incident.

They never threatened me with dismissal or even punishment, but they made it clear I was out of line, that the gods punish those who exceed caste and station. They were, of course, unaware of my origins or associations, or of my disinclination to accept the Gunni religion with all its idolatry and tolerance for wickedness.

I dug out the book that purported to be a history of Taglios' earliest days. I would not have been aware of it had I not noticed it being copied from a manuscript so old that much of it had appeared to be in a style of calligraphy resembling that of the old Annals I was having so much trouble deciphering. Old Baladitya, the copyist, had had no difficulty rendering the text in modern Taglian. I have salvaged the moldy, crumbling original. I had it hidden. I had a notion that by comparing versions I could get a handle on the dialect of those old Annals.

If not, Girish could be offered a chance to translate for the Black Company, an opportunity he ought to pounce on considering the alternative available at that point.

I already knew that the books I wanted to translate were copies of even earlier versions, at least two of which had been transcribed originally in another language entirely—presumably that spoken by our first brothers when they came down off the plain of glittering stone.

I started at the beginning.

It was an interesting story.

Taglios began as a collection of mud huts beside the river. Some of the villagers fished and dodged crocodiles, while others raised a variety of crops. The city grew for no obvious reason beyond its being the last viable landing before the river lost itself in the pestilential delta swamps, in those days not yet inhabited by the Nyueng Bao. Trade from upriver continued overland to "all the great kingdoms of the south." Not a one of those was mentioned by name.

Taglios began as a tributary of Baladiltyla, a city great in oral histories and no longer in existence. It is sometimes associated with some really ancient ruins outside the village of Videha, which itself is associated with the intellectual achievements of a "Kuras empire" and is the center of ruins of another sort entirely. Baladiltyla was the birthplace of Rhaydreynak, the warrior king who nearly exterminated the Deceivers in antiquity and who harried the handful of survivors into burying their sacred texts, the Books of the Dead, in that same cavern where Murgen now lay entombed with all the old men in their cobwebs of ice.

Not all this was information from the book I was reading. As I went, I made connections with things I had read or heard elsewhere. This was very exciting stuff. For me.

Here was an answer for Goblin. The princes of Taglios could not be kings because they honored as their sovereigns the kings of Nhanda, who raised them up. Of course Nhanda was no more and Goblin would want to know why, in that case, the Taglian princes could not just crown themselves. There were plenty of precedents. From the looks of the history of the centuries before the coming of the Black Company, that had been the favorite pastime of anybody who could get three or four men to follow him around.

I overcame a powerful urge to rush ahead and look for the era when the Free Companies of Khatovar exploded upon the world. What had happened before that would help explain what had happened when they did.

A sudden, startled thrill ran through me. I was not alone anymore. A long time had passed. The sun had swung several hours across the sky. The quality of the light within the library had changed. It had become a much paler version of its morning self. Presumably the clouds had passed away.

I did not jump or, I hope, show any immediate outward reaction. But I did have to respond visibly to my awareness of the presence of whoever was standing behind me. Perhaps it was his breath that alerted me. The curry and garlic were strong. Certainly I never heard a sound.

I brought my heartbeat under control, smoothed my features, turned.

The Master of the Library, my boss, Surendranath Santaraksita, met my gaze. "Dorabee. I believe you were reading." At the library they know me as Dorabee Dey Banerjae. An honorable name. A man of that name died beside me in a skirmish near the Daka Woods a long time ago. He did not need it anymore and I would do it no harm.

I did not speak. The truth would be hard to deny if the Master had been there long. I was halfway through the book, which was of the bound sort and contained no illustrations whatsoever, not even one *Tantric* passage.

"I have been watching you for some time, Dorabee. Your interest and skill are both evident. It's clear that you read better than most of my copyists. Yet it's equally obvious that you aren't of the priestly caste."

My face was still as old cheese. I was wondering if I should kill him and how I could dispose of the corpse if I did. Perhaps the Stranglers could be framed. . . . No. Master Santaraksita was old but still hale enough to throw me around if I tried to throttle him. Being small has definite disadvantages at times. He had eight inches on me but at the moment that seemed like several feet. And someone else was moving around at the other end of the library. I heard voices.

I did not drop my eyes the way a menial should. Master Santaraksita already knew I was more than a curious sweeper, though a good one. I kept the place spotless. That was a Company rule. Our public characters had to be morally straight and excellent workers. Which did not make some of the men at all happy.

I waited. Master Santaraksita would decide his own fate. He would decide the fate of the library that he loved.

"So. Our Dorabee is a man of more talents than we suspected. What else do you do that we don't know about, Dorabee? Can you write, as well?" I did not answer, of course. "Where did you learn? It has long been the contention of many of the bhadrhalok that those not of the priestly caste do not have the mental facility to learn the High Mode."

Still I did not speak. Eventually he would commit to movement in some direction. I would respond accordingly. I hoped I could avoid destroying him and his brethren and stripping the library of whatever might be useful. That was the course One-Eye wanted to follow years ago. Never mind being subtle. Never mind not alerting Soulcatcher to what was happening right under her nose.

"You have nothing to say? No defense?"

"A pursuit of knowledge needs no defense. Sri Sondhel Ghosh the Janaka declared that in the Garden of Wisdom there is no caste." Albeit in an age when caste had much less meaning.

"Sondhel Ghosh spoke of the university at Vikramas, where all the students had to pass an exhaustive examination before they were allowed to enter the grounds."

"Do we suppose many students of any caste were admitted who were unable to read the *Panas* and *Pashids*? Sondhel Ghosh was not called the Janaka for nothing. Vikramas was the seat of Janai religious study."

"A janitor who knows about a religion long dead. We are indeed entering the Age of Khadi, where all is turned upon its head." Khadi is the favored Taglian name for Kina, in one of her less vicious aspects. The name Kina is seldom spoken, lest the Dark Mother hear and respond. Only the Deceivers want her to come around. "Where did you acquire this skill? Who taught you?"

"A friend started me out a long time ago. After we buried him, I continued to teach myself." My gaze never left his face. For a goofy old boffin, whose stuffiness was grist for the mockery of the younger copyists, he seemed remarkably flexible mentally. But then, he might be brighter than he seemed. He might realize that he could buy himself a float downriver to the swamps if the wrong words passed his lips.

No. Master Surendranath Santaraksita did not yet live in a world where one who read and cherished sacred texts also cut throats and trafficked with sorcerers, the dead and rakshasas. Master Surendranath Santaraksita did not think of himself that way, but he was a sort of holy hermit, self-consecrated to preserve all that was good in knowledge and culture. This much I had discovered already, through continuous observation. I had figured out, also, that we might not often agree on what was good.

"You just wish to learn, then."

"I lust after knowledge the way some men lust after pleasures of the flesh. I've always been that way. I can't help it. It's an obsession."

Santaraksita leaned a little closer, studying me with myopic eyes. "You are older than you seem."

I confessed. "People think I'm younger than I am because I'm small."

"Tell me about yourself, Dorabee Dey Banerjae. Who was your father? Of what family was your mother?"

"You will not have heard of them." I considered refusing to elaborate. But Dorabee Dey Banerjae did have a story. I had been rehearsing it for seven years. If I just stayed in character, it would all be true.

Stay in character. Be Dorabee caught reading. Let Sleepy worry about what to do when it was time for Sleepy to come back onstage.

"You denigrate yourself overmuch," Santaraksita said at one point. "I may have known your father . . . if he was the same Dollal Dey Banerjae who could not resist the Liberator's call for recruits when he raised the original legion that triumphed at Ghoja Ford."

I had named dead Dorabee's father already. I could not take that back now. How could he know Dollal, anyway? Banerjae was one of the oldest and most common of traditional Taglian surnames. Banerjaes were mentioned in the text I had been reading till moments ago. "That may have been him. I never knew him well. I do recall him boasting that he was one of the first to enroll. He marched off with the Liberator to defeat the Shadowmasters. He never came back from Ghoja Ford." I did not know much more about Dorabee's family. Not even his mother's name. In all Taglios how could it be possible I would encounter anyone who remembered the father? Fortune is indeed a goddess filled with caprice. "Did you know him well?" If that was so, the librarian might have to go—just that would make my exposure inevitable.

"No. Not well. Not well at all." Now Master Santaraksita seemed disinclined to say more. He seemed worrisomely thoughtful. After a moment he told me, "Come with me, Dorabee."

"Sri?"

"You brought up the university at Vikramas. I have a list of the questions the gate guards put to those who wanted to enroll. Curiosity impels me to subject you to the same examination."

"I know little about Janai, Master." If the truth were told, I was a bit shaky on the tenets of my own religion, always having been afraid to examine it too closely. Other religions do not stand up to the rigorous application of reason, for all we have things like Kina stalking the earth, and I really did not want to find myself stumbling over any boulders of absurdity protruding from the bedrock of my own faith.

"The examination was not religious in nature, Dorabee. It tested the prospective student's morals, ethics and ability to think. Janaka monks did not wish to educate potential leaders who would come to their calling with the stain of darkness upon their souls."

That being the case, I had to get into character very deeply indeed. Sleepy, the Vehdna soldier girl from Jaicur, had stains on her soul blacker than a shadow of all night falling.

Then what did you do?" Tobo asked.

Around a mouthful of spicy Taglian-style rice, I told him, "Then I went out and made sure the library was clean." And Surendranath Santaraksita remained where he was, stunned into immobility by the answers he had received from a lowly sweeper. I could have told him that anyone who paid attention to the storytellers in the street, the sermons of mendicant priests, and the readily available gratuitous advice of hermits and yogis, could have satisfied most of the Vikramas questions. Darn it, a Vehdna woman from Jaicur could do it.

"We got to kill him," One-Eye said. "How you want to do it?"

"That's always your solution these days, isn't it?" I asked.

"The more we get rid of now, the fewer there'll be around to aggravate me in my old age."

I could not tell if he was joking. "When you start getting old, we'll worry about it."

"Guy like that will be easy, Little Girl. He won't be looking for it. Bam! He's gone. And nobody'll care. Strangle his ass. Leave a rumel on him. Blame it on our old buddy Narayan. He's in town, we need to put all kinds of shit off on him."

"Language, old man." One-Eye babbled on, putting a name to animal waste in a hundred tongues. I turned my back. "Sahra? You've been very quiet."

"I've been trying to digest what I picked up today. By the way, Jaul Barundandi was distraught because you stayed home. Tried to take your kickback out of my wages. He finally found Minh Subredil's limit. I threatened to scream. He would've called my bluff if his wife hadn't been around somewhere. Are you sure it's safe to let this librarian live? If it looked natural, no one would suspect—"

"It may not be safe but it could pay dividends. Master Santaraksita wants to make some kind of experiment out of me. To see if a low-caste dog really can be taught to roll over and play dead. What about Soulcatcher? What about the shadows? Did you learn anything?"

"She loosed everything she had. Just an impulse. No master plan except to remind the city of her power. She expected the victims to be immigrants who live in the streets. No one much cares about them. Only a handful of shadows got back before dawn. Our captives won't be missed until tomorrow."

"We could go catch a few more—"

"Bats," Goblin said, inviting himself to take a seat. One-Eye appeared to have dozed off. He still had hold of his cane, though. "Bats. There's bats out there tonight."

Sahra offered a confirming nod.

Goblin said, "Back before we marched against the Shadowmasters, we killed all the bats. Had bounties on them big enough for bat hunters to make a living. Because the Shadowmasters used them to spy."

I recalled a time when crows were murdered relentlessly because they might be acting as Soulcatcher's far-flying eyes. "You're saying we should stay in tonight?"

"Mind like a stone ax, this old gal."

I asked Sahra, "What did Soulcatcher think about our attack?"

"It didn't come up where I could hear." She pushed some sheets from the old Annals across. "The Bhodi suicide bothered her more. She's afraid it might start a trend."

"A trend? There could be more than one monk goofy enough to set himself on fire?"

"She thinks so."

Tobo asked, "Mom, are we going to call up Dad tonight?"

"I don't know right now, dear."

"I want to talk to him some more."

"You will. I'm sure he's interested in talking to you, too." She sounded like she was trying to convince herself.

I asked Goblin, "Would it be possible for you to keep that mist thing going all the time so we could keep Murgen connected and any time we wanted, we could just send him where we needed to know about something?"

"We're working on it." He took off on a technical rant. I did not understand a word but I let him roll. He deserved to feel good about something.

One-Eye began to snore. The smart would stay out of reach of his cane anyway.

I said, "Tobo could keep notes all the time. . . ." I had had this sudden vision of the son of the Annalist taking over for the father, the way it goes in Taglian guilds, where trades and tools pass down generation after generation.

"In fact," One-Eye said, as though no time had passed since the last remark, and as though he had not been faking sleep a moment ago, "right now's the time you could play you a really great big ol' hairy-assed, old-time Company dirty trick, Little Girl. Send somebody down to the silk merchants' exchange. Have them get you some silk, different colors. Big enough to make up copies of them scarves the Stranglers use. Them rumels. Then we start picking off the guys we don't like anyway. Once in a while we leave one of them scarves behind. Like with that librarian."

I said, "I like that. Except the part about Master Santaraksita. That's a closed subject, old man."

One-Eye cackled. "Man's got to stand by what he believes."

"It *would* get a lot of fingers pointing," Goblin said.

One-Eye cackled again. "It would point them in some other direction, too, Little Girl. And I'm thinking we don't want much more attention coming our way right now. I'm thinking maybe we're closer to figuring things out than any of us realizes."

"Water sleeps. We have to be taken seriously."

"That's what I'm saying. We use them scarves to take out informants and guys who know too much. Librarians, for instance."

"Would I be correct in my suspicion that you've been thinking about this for a while and by chance you just happen to have a little list all ready to go?" Very likely any such list would include all the people responsible for his several failed attempts to establish himself in the Taglian black markets.

He cackled. He took a swipe at Goblin with his cane. "And you said she's got a mind like a flint hatchet."

"Bring me the list. I'll discuss it with Murgen next time I see him."

"With a ghost? They got no sense of perspective, you know."

"You mean maybe he's seen everything and knows what you're really up to? Sounds like a perspective to me. Makes me wonder how far the Company might've gone if our forebrethren had had a ghost to keep an eye on you."

One-Eye grumbled something about how unfair and unreasonable the world was. He had been singing that song the whole time I had known him. He would keep it up after he became a ghost himself.

I mused, "You think we could get Murgen to winkle out the source of the stink that keeps coming from the back, there, where Do Trang hides his crocodile skins? I know it's not them. Croc hides have a flavor all their own."

One-Eye scowled. He was ready to change the subject now. The odor in question came from his beer- and liquor-manufacturing project, hidden in a cellar he and Do Trang thought nobody knew about. Banh Do Trang, once our benefactor for Sahra's sake, now was practically one of the gang because he had a powerful taste for One-Eye's product, a huge hunger for illegal and shadowy income, and he liked having tough guys on the payroll who would work hard for very little money. He thought his vice was a secret he shared only with One-Eye and Gota. The three of them got drunk together twice a week.

Alcohol is a definite Nyueng Bao weakness.

"I'm sure it's not worth the trouble, Little Girl. It's probably dead rats. Bad rat problem in this town. Do Trang puts rat poison out all the time. By the pound. No need to waste Murgen's time chasing rodents. You've both got better things to do."

I would be talking over a lot of things with Murgen if I could deal with him directly. If we could catch and keep his attention. I would like to know firsthand everything that ordinarily came to me through other people. I imply no malice, particularly from Sahra, but people do reshape information according to their own prejudices. Including even me, possibly, though until now, my objectivity has been peerless. All my predecessors, though . . . their reports must be read with a jaundiced eye.

Of course, most of them made the same observation in regard to their own predecessors. So we are all in agreement. Everyone is a liar but us. Only Lady was unabashedly self-congratulating. She missed few opportunities to remind those who came later how brilliant and determined and successful she was, turning the tide of the Shadowmaster wars when she had nothing to begin building upon but herself. Murgen was, putting it charitably, less than sane much of the time. Because I lived through many of the times and events he recollected, I have to say he did pretty good. Most of what he recorded *could* be true. I cannot contradict him. But a lot he set down does seem fanciful.

Fanciful? Last night I had a long chat with his ghost. Or spirit. Or ka. Whatever that was. If that was really Murgen and not some trick played on us by Kina or Soulcatcher.

We can never be one-hundred-percent certain that anything is exactly what it appears to be. Kina is the Mother of Deceit. And Soulcatcher, to quote a man far wiser and more foul of mouth than I, is a mudsucking lunatic.

15

"This is excellent," I enthused again as Sahra summoned Murgen once more. She herself betrayed no enthusiasm for the task. Tobo's hovering did nothing to improve her temper. "Before he does anything else, I want to have him check on Surendranath Santaraksita."

"So you don't trust the librarian after all," One-Eye said. He chuckled.

"I think he's all right but why hand him a chance to break my heart if I can avoid it by keeping an eye on him?"

"How come it's got to be my eye?"

"There's not a sharper one available, is there? And you already turned down a chance to work on the Annals. I've got to do some heavy studying in those tonight. I might be on the track of something."

The little wizard grunted.

"I think I found something at the library today. If Santaraksita doesn't trip me up, I may have an outside view of the first coming of the Company by the end of the week." An independent historical source has been a goal almost as long as has been our desire for a look at uncontaminated editions of the earliest three volumes of the Annals.

Sahra had something else on her mind. "Barundandi wants me to bring Sawa to work, Sleepy."

"No. Sawa is on hiatus. She's sick. She has cholera, if that's what it takes. I'm finally starting to make some real headway. I'm not going to let that slide now."

"He's also been asking about Shiki." Back when Tobo had accompanied his mother to the Palace occasionally, she had called him Shikhandini, which was a joke Jaul Barundandi never got because he was not the sort to pay attention to historical mythology. One of the kings of legendary Hastinapur had had a senior wife who seemed to be barren. A good Gunni, he prayed and made sacrifice faithfully, and eventually one of the gods stepped down from heaven to tell him he could have what he wanted, which was a son, but he was going to get it the hard way, for the son would be born a daughter. And, as they say, it came to pass that the wife brought forth a daughter whom the king then named Shikhandin, a name that also existed in the female form Shikhandini. It is a long and not that interesting story, but the girl grew up to become a mighty warrior.

The trouble started when it came time for the prince to take a bride.

Many of our public characters have obscure allusions or jokes built into them. That helped make things more interesting for the brothers playing the roles.

I asked, "Do we have any reason to snatch Barundandi? Other than his general sliminess?" I thought he was most useful right where he was. Any replacement was sure to be as venal and unlikely to be as kind to Minh Subredil. "And could we even get him out where we could touch him?"

Nobody suggested a strategic reason for grabbing the man. Sahra wanted to know, "Why do you ask?"

"Because I do think we could lure him. If we dress Tobo up pretty, then refuse to cooperate unless Barundandi meets him outside . . ."

Sahra was not offended. The ruse is a legitimate weapon of war. She looked thoughtful. "Maybe Gokhale instead?"

"Perhaps. Though he might want someone younger. We can ask Swan. I was thinking of catching Gokhale in that place where the Deceivers killed that other one." The enemy's leading personalities seldom left the Palace. Which was why we had chosen to go get Willow Swan.

Sahra began to sing. Murgen was reluctant again tonight. I said, "Murgen should look at that joy house, too. He'd be the best way for us to check it out." Though, no doubt, we could find several brothers willing to risk themselves in an extended recon.

Sahra nodded, did not break the rhythm of her lullaby.

"We might even . . ." No. We could not just burn the place once Gokhale had been inside long enough to become seriously engaged. Nobody would understand why I wanted to waste a perfectly good whorehouse—though a few might find a deadly fire highly amusing.

One-Eye looked like he was sleeping again but was not. Without opening his eyes, he asked, "You know where you're going, Little Girl? You got some kind of overall plan?"

"Yes." I was surprised to find that I really believed that. Intuitively, somewhere inside, though I had not known it consciously, I had engineered a master plan for the liberation of the Captured and the resurrection of the Company. And it was starting to come together. After all these years.

Murgen showed up muttering about a white crow. He was distracted. I asked the wizards, "You figured out how to anchor him here yet?"

"Always some damned thing," One-Eye grumbled. "Whatever you do, it's never enough."

"It can be done," Goblin admitted. "But I still don't see why we would want to."

"He hasn't been very cooperative. He doesn't want to be here. He's losing his connection to the real world. He'd rather sleep and wander those caverns." I took a stab in the dark. "And put on his white wings. Be Khadi's messenger."

"White wings?"

They did not read the Annals. "The albino crow that turns up sometimes. Sometimes Murgen is inside it. Because Kina puts him there. Or used to put him there and now he keeps stumbling back in, the way he kept stumbling around in time once Soulcatcher got him started."

"How do you know that?"

"I read sometimes. And once in a while I even read the Annals and try to figure out what Murgen didn't tell us. What he might not actually have known himself. Right now he may be enamored of being the white crow because that way he gets into actual flesh that ranges outside the caverns. Or he may just be falling under the influence of Kina as she wakes up again. But none of that ought to matter much right now. Right now we have a bunch of spying we need him to do. I want to be able to twist his arm if I have to."

The mission comes first. Murgen himself taught me that.

Sahra said, "Sleepy's right. Anchor him. Then I'll grab him by the nose and kick his behind until I've got his undivided attention." She seemed suddenly optimistic, as though taking a direct approach with her husband was some totally new concept fraught with unexpected hope.

She went straight to outright confrontation, drawing Tobo in to support her.

Maybe she *could* rebuild Murgen's ties with the outside world.

I turned to the others. "I found another Kina myth this morning. In this one her father didn't trick her into going to sleep. She died. Then her husband got so upset that—"

"Husband?" Goblin squeaked. "What husband?"

"I don't know, Goblin. The book didn't name names. It was written for people who grew up in the Gunni religion. It assumes you know who they're talking about. When Kina died, her husband was so grief-stricken he grabbed up her corpse and started doing that stomping dance Murgen talks about her doing in his visions. He got so violent that the other gods were afraid he would destroy the world. So her father threw an enchanted knife that cut her up into about fifty pieces and every place one of the chunks fell became a holy place for Kina's worshippers. Just reading between the lines and guessing, I'd say Khatovar is where her head hit the ground."

"I got a notion One-Eye was on the right track back when he was going to desert and retire."

One-Eye gawked. Goblin saying something positive about anything he ever did? "The hell I was. I just had an attack of juvenile angst. I got over it and got responsible again."

"There's a new concept," I observed. "One-Eye responsible."

"For catastrophes and afflictions, maybe," Goblin said.

One-Eye said, "I don't get the Kina story. If she died back at the beginning of the world, how could she be giving us trouble for the last twenty or thirty years?"

"It's religion, dimwit," Goblin barked. "It don't got to make sense."

"Kina is a goddess," I said. "I guess gods can't ever be completely dead. I don't know, One-Eye. I didn't make it up, I just reported it. Look, the Gunni don't believe anybody dies really. Their soul goes on."

"Heh-heh-heh," Goblin chuckled. "If these Gunni got it right, you're in deep shit, runt boy. You got to keep going 'round on the Wheel of Life till you get it right. You got a lot of karma to work off."

"Stop. Now," I snapped. "We're supposed to be working."

Work. Not the favorite swear word of either man.

I told them, "You get Murgen nailed down. Or chained down. Whatever it takes to keep him under control. Then you help Sahra try to get through to him. I have a suspicion things are going to get exciting before long and we'll need him wide awake and cooperative."

One-Eye grumbled, "Sounds to me like you don't plan to be here looking over our shoulders."

I was up already. "Clever man. I have some reading and some translating to do. You can manage without me. If you concentrate."

One-Eye told Goblin, "We got to get that little bit into the sack with some guy'll pork her brains out." His cure for all ills, even at his age.

I paused to say, "When he's given everything else the once-over, have him search for Narayan and the Daughter of Night." I did not need to explain how badly we needed to keep those two from achieving their ends.

I've got it!" I shouted, running back to the corner where Murgen's friends and family were trying to torment him into taking a broader interest in the world of the living. "I found it! I've got it!"

"I hope you ain't gonna give it to me," One-Eye grumbled.

My excitement was so loud and intense even Murgen, who was caught in the mist and being a real pain about his situation, paused to study me.

"I had a feeling, an intuition the other day, that the answer was in the Annals. In Murgen's Annals. And I'd just overlooked it. Maybe because it had been so long since I read them and I wouldn't have thought to look for it back then."

"And, behold!" One-Eye sneered. "There it was. In ink of gold on myrex-tinted paper, with little scarlet arrows saying, 'Here it is, Little Girl. The secret of the—' "

"Stuff it, dustbag," Goblin snapped. "I want to hear what Sleepy found." Though it would have been him doing the sarcasm if One-Eye had not beat him to it.

"It's the whole thing with the Nyueng Bao. Well, maybe not all of it," I said as Sahra scowled at me. "But the part with Uncle Doj and Mother Gota and why they came out of the swamp when they didn't have a debt of honor like your brother, Sahra." Sahra's brother Thai Dei was under the glittering plain with Murgen, serving as his bodyguard because of what Murgen and the Company had done to help the Nyueng Bao during the siege of Jaicur. "Sahra, you must know some of this."

"That may be true, Sleepy. But you'll have to tell us what you're talking about first."

"I'm talking about whatever it was that The Thousand Voices stole from the Temple of Ghanghesha sometime between the end of the siege and when Uncle Doj and your mother invited themselves to come stay with you here in Taglios. Murgen touches on it over and over, lightly, but I don't think he ever really caught on completely. Whatever it was that The Thousand Voices stole, Uncle Doj called it 'the Key.' From other internal evidence, I think it had to be another key to the Shadowgate, like the Lance of Passion." The Thousand Voices was what the Nyueng Bao called Soulcatcher. "I think if we had that key, we could open the way for the Captured."

If I was guessing right here, I had created a whole new line of inquiry: Why the Nyueng Bao?

Sahra began shaking her head slowly.

"Am I wrong? What is the Key, then?"

"I'm not saying you're wrong, Sleepy. I'm saying I don't want you to be right. There are things I wouldn't want to be true."

"What? Why?"

"Myths and legends, Sleepy. Ugly myths and legends. Some of them I'm not supposed to know. And I know I don't know them all. Probably none of the worst. Doj was their curator and keeper. As you are for the Black Company. But Doj never shared his secrets. Tobo, find your grandmother. Bring her here. Get Do Trang, too, if he's here."

Bewildered, the boy shuffled away.

A spectral whisper came out of the device where Murgen waited. "Sleepy may be right. I recall suspecting something like that and wondering if I could find a good history of the Nyueng Bao so I could figure it out. You'll need to question Willow Swan, too."

I said, "I'll do that later. Separately. Swan doesn't need to know what's happening. Are you paying attention now, Standardbearer? Do you have any idea where we're at and what we're doing?"

"I do." His tone was resigned, though. Like mine when I know I have to get up in the morning, want to or not.

"Tell me about the Temple of Ghanghesha, then. Both of you. Why would this Key have been kept there?"

Sahra did not want to talk about it. Her whole body said she was caught up in a ferocious internal struggle.

"Why is this so hard?" I asked.

"There is old evil in my people's past. I'm only vaguely familiar with it. Doj knows the whole truth. The rest of us just understand that our ancestors were guilty of a great sin and until we expiate it, our whole race is condemned to live in bitter destitution in the swamp. The temple was a holy place long before some Nyueng Bao began to adopt Gunni beliefs. It protected something. Possibly the Key you mentioned. The thing Uncle Doj has been looking for."

"Where did the Nyueng Bao come from, Sahra?" That question had intrigued me since childhood. Each few years hundreds of those strange people would pass through Jaicur on pilgrimage. They were quiet and orderly and stayed to themselves. And a year after they arrived from the north, they would pass through again, going back that way. Even at the height of the power of the Shadowmasters, that cycle had continued. Nobody knew where they went. Nobody ever cared.

"Out of the south somewhere, a long time ago."

"From beyond the Dandha Presh?" I could not imagine subjecting little children and old folks to the rigors of a journey of that magnitude. The pilgrimage had to be very important indeed.

"Yes."

"But there are no pilgrimages anymore." The one that had ended up with hundreds of Nyueng Bao dying in Jaicur was the last of which I was aware.

"The Shadowmaster and the Kiaulune wars made the next few times impossible. There's supposed to be a pilgrimage every four years. Each Nyueng Bao De Duang has to make the pilgrimage at least once as an adult. For a while the lack was no problem. But now the Protector will not permit the people to meet their obligations," Banh Do Trang rasped from his wheelchair, having arrived in time to catch the drift of my interrogation. "There are things we do not discuss with those who aren't Nyueng Bao."

I got the feeling he was saying the same thing twice at one time, one way for my benefit and another for Sahra's. This could be ticklish. We dared not offend Banh Do Trang, whose friendship we needed. If we lost him, we also risked losing Sahra, whose value to the Company could not be calculated.

Nothing is ever simple and straightforward.

I told the old man the way I had it figured. Ky Gota waddled in just as I started. My eyes widened as One-Eye gallantly offered her his seat. It is a world just chock-full of wonders. The little wizard went and got another seat, which he set next to Gota's. The two of them sat there leaning on their canes like a couple of temple gargoyles. A ghost of ancient beauty peeked out of the wide, permanent scowl that Gota used for a face.

I explained the situation. "But here's the mystery. Where is the Key today?"

Nobody volunteered that information.

"I'd think that if The Thousand Voices still had it, she'd be running down to Ki-aulune every month to round up a new gaggle of killer shadows. It if *could* open the Shadowgate safely. And if Uncle Doj had it, he wouldn't be roaming around looking for it. He'd be back in the swamp blithely letting the rest of us go to *al-Sheil* in a handcart. Am I wrong? Mother Gota? You know the man. You must be able to offer something."

Able, perhaps. Willing, of course not. The big thing that stands out, to my ear, about the Company's sojourn in the south, is the stubborn silence of so many people. About everything. Like if we even discovered our own birthdays, that would be something we could use against them. The fact that the Company now consists almost entirely of native soldiers has not helped at all. Our life does not attract the knowledgeable, educated portion of the population. If a priest offered to sign on, we would send him downriver, knowing for certain that he was a spy.

"You got the damned gimmick?" One-Eye asked.

"Who?"

"You, Little Girl. The villainess, you. I didn't forget that you were Soulcatcher's guest for a while, when she caught you on the road coming back from running that message for Murgen. I haven't forgotten that when our sweet old Uncle Doj rescued you it was incidental. He was looking for his missing trinket, the Key. Not so?"

"That's all true. But I didn't bring anything away from that. Except a few new scars and the rags on my back."

"What we need to know then is has Soulcatcher been looking for the Key?"

"We don't know for sure. But she does fly down south occasionally and patrols the old ground like she's looking for something." We knew that, courtesy of Murgen. Though till now, her behavior had made no sense.

"So who else could've snatched this prize?" One-Eye did not press Gota for any information. The way to get around Gota was to ignore her. In time, she would insist that she be noticed.

I remembered a pale, ragged little girl who, though just four years old, had seemed ageless, silent and patient, confidently unfrightened by her captivity. The Daughter of Night. She never spoke to me once. She acknowledged my existence only when she had to, because if she irritated me too much, I might take all of what little food Soulcatcher allowed us. I should have strangled her then. But at that time I did not know who she was.

At that time I was having trouble remembering who *I* was. Soulcatcher had drugged me and gone down inside me and found half what made me me, then had tried *being* me in order to infiltrate the Company. I still wonder how well she really knows me. Certainly I do not want her to find out that I survived the Kiaulune wars. She might have the emotional weapons to crush me.

"Narayan came to get the Daughter of Night," I mused aloud. "But I caught only glimpses of him. An extremely skinny little man in a filthy loincloth who didn't look anything like the terrible monster he was supposed to be. It didn't occur to me it was him till I realized I wasn't going to be released, too. Since I couldn't see what they were doing, I don't know if they took anything with them. Murgen, you saw them then. I have it written down that you did. Did they take anything away that might have been this key?"

"I don't know. Believe it or not, you really do miss some things out here." He seemed piqued.

I realized I had not bothered to hear what he had to report. I asked.

"Not much useful," Sahra told me, cutting Murgen off before he could retell everything from the beginning.

"Can you find them now?" I foresaw trouble. There was an unwilling connection to Kina. If the dark goddess was stirring again, he would have to be careful not to attract divine attention. "We have these priorities regarding the Daughter of Night: Kill her. Failing that: Kill her sidekick. Failing that: Make sure she can't copy the Books of the Dead, which I'm sure she'll start doing again as soon as she develops a reliable connection with Kina. Finally: Recapture anything she and Singh might have carried off when Narayan rescued her."

One-Eye stopped nodding off long enough to clap his hands lazily. "Tear 'em up, Little Girl. Tear 'em up."

"Sarky old reprobate."

One-Eye snickered.

Goblin said, "You want another angle, find out from your library pals who makes bound blank books. Go to them and find out who's ordered some recently. Or bribe them to let you know when anybody does."

"Gosh," I said. "Somebody who actually uses his brain to think. The delight of the world is that its wonders never cease. Where the devil did Murgen go?"

Sahra said, "You just told him to find Narayan Singh and the Daughter of Night."

"I didn't mean right this second. I wanted to know if he found out anything about Chandra Gokhale we can use."

"Pressure getting to you, Little Girl?" One-Eye's tone was so sweet I wanted to pop him. "Relax. Now's the time when you don't want to force anything."

A couple of men from the duty crew, Runmust Singh and a Shadowlander dubbed Kendo Cutter by his squad mates, invited themselves into the staff meeting. Kendo reported, "There's all kinds of screaming going on out there tonight. I sent out word everybody should hole up someplace where there's plenty of light."

Sahra said, "The shadows are hunting."

I said, "We'll be all right here. But just to be safe, Goblin, why don't you make the rounds with Kendo and Runmust? We don't want any surprise. Sahra, will Soulcatcher let the shadows run completely wild?"

"To make her point? You're the Annalist. What do the books say about her?"

"They say she's capable of anything. She has no connection with the humanity of anyone else. It must be very lonely to be her."

"What?"

"We agree our next target should be Chandra Gokhale?"

Sahra eyed me oddly. That had been decided already. Unless some better opportunity fell into our laps, we would eliminate the Inspector-General, without whom the tax system and the bureaucratic side of government would stumble and stagger. He also seemed the most vulnerable of our enemies. And his removal would leave the Radisha more isolated than ever, cut off by the Protector on one hand, the priests on the other, and unable to turn anywhere because she was the Radisha, the Princess unapproachable, in some respects a demi-goddess.

It had to be lonely to be her, too.

Subtlety and finesse.

I asked, "What did we do today to frighten the world?" Then I realized that I knew the answer. It had been part of the plan for capturing Swan. All the brotherhood would have avoided any risks. Tonight there would be shows from buttons previously planted. There would be more again tomorrow night. Smoke-and-light shows proclaiming "Water sleeps," or "My brother unforgiven," or "All their days are numbered." There would be more, somewhere, every evening from now on.

Sahra mused, "Someone who wasn't one of us brought in another prayer wheel and mounted it on a memorial post outside the north entrance. It hadn't been noticed yet when I left."

"Same message?"

"I presume."

"That's scary. That could be a potent one. *Rajadharma.*"

"It has the Radisha thinking already. That monk burning himself definitely got her attention."

Story of my life. Here I spend months working out every tiny detail of a marvelous plan and I get upstaged by a lunatic with a fire fetish.

"So those Bhodi nuts found a good message. You think we could steal some of their thunder?"

One-Eye chuckled evilly.

"What?" I demanded.

"Sometimes I amaze myself."

Goblin, about to leave with Runmust and Kendo, observed, "You been amazed at yourself for two hundred years. Mainly 'cause nobody else bothers to get interested in insects."

"You better not go to sleep any time soon, Frogface—"

"Gentlemen?" Sahra said. Gently. Yet she grabbed the attention of both wizards. "Can we stick to business? I need some sleep."

"Absolutely!" Goblin said. "Absolutely! If the old fart has an idea, let's get it out here before it dies of loneliness."

"You may continue your assignment."

Goblin stuck out his tongue but left.

"Amaze the rest of us, One-Eye," I suggested. I did not want him dozing off before he shared his wisdom.

"Next time one of those Bhodi loons lights himself up, we have the smoke and flames carry our message. 'Water Sleeps.' And a new one I thunk up, 'Nor Even Death Destroy.' You got to admit, that's got a nice religious ring to it."

"Indeed," I agreed. "What the heck does it mean?"

"Little Girl, don't you start in on me—"

The ghost of evils past whispered, "I found them."

Murgen was back.

I did not ask who. "Where?"

"The Thieves' Garden."

"Chor Bagan? The Greys have it under siege."

And they were still serious about getting the place cleaned out, Murgen said.

17

Sahra wakened me well before dawn, which is not my best time of day. When I opted for a military career, we were besieged in my hometown. I just knew that once we got out of there, we would sleep till noon, we would eat fresh food all the time and there would be plenty of it and never, ever, would we have to go out in the rain again. In the meantime, I took the best I could get, which was the Black Company during the siege, with the water fifty feet deep. The only thing resembling fresh food was the long pig Mogaba and his Nar friends were enjoying. Unless you counted the occasional lame rat or slow-witted crow.

"What?" I grumbled. Personally, I am convinced that even the priests of happy-go-lucky old Ghanghesha are not required to be pleasant before an hour much closer to noon than this was.

"I have to go to the Palace. You have to appear at the library. If we want to snatch Narayan and the girl right in front of the Greys, we need to start planning right now."

She was right. But that did not mean I had to accept it gracefully.

Every Company member inside Do Trang's complex, and Banh himself, gathered over a crude breakfast. Only Tobo and Mother Gota were absent. But they would have no part in any of this. I thought.

Nobody from outside could be included now, because shadows were on the prowl.

"We got a plan all worked out," One-Eye announced proudly.

"I'm sure it's one stroke of genius after another," I replied as I made a groggy effort to collect a bowl of cold rice, a mango and a bowl of tea.

"First thing, Goblin goes up there in his dervish outfit. Then Tobo comes strutting along. . . ."

Good morning, Adoo," I murmured distractedly as the gateman admitted me to the library grounds. I was worried about leaving Goblin and One-Eye to operate on their own. My mother instinct at work, they said, both showing nasty teeth as they reminded me that every hen has to trust her chicks on their own sometime. A point well made. Though few hens have to worry about their chicks getting drunk, forgetting what they are doing and wandering off in search of adventure in a city where there is not even one other skinny little black man or ugly little white character.

Adoo nodded his greeting. He never had anything to say.

Inside the library I went to work immediately, though only a couple of copyists had arrived before me. Sometimes Dorabee focused as intently as Sawa did. That helped turn off the worries.

Dorabee? Dorabee Dey Banerjae!"

I started awake, amazed that I had fallen asleep. I had squatted down on my heels in a corner, in a fashion common amongst Gunni and Nyueng Bao but not common among Vehdna, Shadar or many of the ethnic minorities. We Vehdna favor sitting on the floor or on a cushion, cross-legged. Shadar like low chairs or stools. Not owning at least a crude stool is the truest mark of poverty amongst the Shadar.

I was in character even in my sleep.

"Master Santaraksita?"

"Are you ill?" He sounded concerned.

"Tired. I didn't sleep well. The *skildirsha* were hunting last night." I used the Shadowlander name for the shadows. That did not trouble Santaraksita. It had become part of the language under the Protectorate. "The screams kept waking me up."

"I understand. I did not enjoy a sound sleep myself, though not for that reason. I was unaware of the horror till I saw its marks this morning."

"The *skildirsha* show a proper respect for the priestly class, then."

The faintest twitch of his lip told me he had not missed the joke. "I am properly appalled, Dorabee. This is evil unlike any we have ever known. The blind misfortune of flood or plague or disaster we must endure stoically. And against the darkness even the gods themselves sometimes contend in vain. But to send out a pack of these shadows to do murder randomly and often, and for no reason even an insane man can comprehend, that is evil of the sort the northerners used to preach."

Dorabee managed a credible job of looking slack-jawed.

"I'm sorry. I'm exercised. You probably never saw any of the outsiders." He placed the same stress on "outsiders" that many Taglians used when they meant the Black Company specifically.

"I did. I saw the Liberator himself once when I was little. And I saw the one they called the Lieutenant after she came back from Dejagore. I was pretty far away but I remember it because that was the same day she killed all the priests. And the Protector. I saw her a couple of times." I was making it up as I went but that was the sort of thing most adult Taglians could claim. The Company had been in and out of the city for years before the final campaign against Longshadow and the fortress Overlook. I rose. "I'll get back to work now."

"You do your job well, Dorabee."

"Thank you, Master Santaraksita. I try."

"Indeed." He seemed to be having trouble getting something out. "I have decided that you will be allowed access to any books not in the restricted section." Restricted books were those not available in multiple copies. Only the most favored scholars were allowed near those. So far, I had been able to determine only a handful of the titles of the books so set aside. "When you have no other obligations." Part of my day, every day, I spent just waiting to be told about something I needed to do.

"Thank you, Master Santaraksita!"

"I'll expect you to be able to discuss them."

"Yes, Master Santaraksita."

"We have set our feet upon an unknown road, Dorabee. An exciting and frightening journey lies ahead." His prejudices were such that he actually meant what he said. Me reading had twisted his universe all out of shape and now he was going to conspire in this perverted vermiculation.

I took my broom in hand. Exciting and frightening things would be happening elsewhere in my universe. And I hated every second that I was not there to control them.

The little dervish in brown wool seemed completely lost inside himself. He was busy talking to himself, paying no attention to the surrounding world. Most likely he was quoting to himself from the sacred texts of the Vehdna, as understood by his peculiar splinter sect. Though tired and irritable, the Greys did not challenge him immediately. They had been taught to honor all holy men, not just those already secure within the Shadar truths. Any devoted stalker after wisdom would find his path leading him to enlightenment eventually.

Tolerance of such seekers was common to all Taglians. The welfare of the soul and the spirit were of grave concern to most. The Gunni, indeed, considered the seeking of enlightenment to be one of the four key stages of an ideally lived life. Once a man successfully raised up and provided for his children, he should put all things material, all ambition and pleasure, aside. He should go into a forest to live as a hermit or become a mendicant seeker or in some other way should live out his final years looking for the truth and purifying his soul. Many of the greatest names in Taglian and southern history are those of kings and rich men who chose just such a path.

But human nature being human nature . . .

The Greys did not, however, let the dervish follow his quest into Chor Bagan. A sergeant intercepted him. His associates surrounded the holy man. The sergeant said, "Father, you cannot go in that direction. This street has been closed to traffic by order of Minister Swan." Even dead, Swan had to take the blame for Soulcatcher's policies.

The dervish apparently failed to notice the Greys till he actually collided with the sergeant. "Huh?"

The younger Greys laughed. Men enjoy seeing their prejudices confirmed. The sergeant repeated his message. He added, "You must turn right or left. We're rooting out the evils infesting what lies straight ahead." He possessed a touch of wit.

The dervish looked first right, then left. He shivered, then announced, "All evil is the result of metaphysical error," in a raspy little voice and started along the street to the right. It was a very strange street. It was almost empty of humanity. In Taglios that was something seldom seen.

A moment later the Shadar sergeant squealed in surprise and pain. He began slapping his side.

"What's the matter?" another Grey asked.

"Something bit me . . ." He squealed again, which indicated that he was in a great deal of agony, for Shadar were proud of their ability to endure pain without outcry or even flinching.

Two of the sergeant's men tried to lift his shirt while a third clung to his arm in an effort to keep him immobile. He shrieked again.

Smoke began to boil out of his side.

The Greys were so startled they backed away. The sergeant went down. He went into convulsions. Smoke continued to boil up. It assumed a form none of the Greys wanted to see.

"Niassi!"

The demon Niassi began to whisper secrets no Shadar wanted to hear.

Grinning to himself, Goblin slipped into Chor Bagan. He disappeared long before anyone wondered if there might not be a connection between the sergeant's discomfort and the veyedeen dervish.

Greys arrived from all directions. Officers barked and cursed and drove them back to their stations before the denizens of Chor Bagan seized the opportunity to escape. Obviously this was a distraction meant to give their prey the chance to run.

A crowd had begun to gather, too. Among them was a Nyueng Bao boy who picked his moment, cut a purse and fled past the Greys, one of whom recalled him from the evening when one of their own got stoned. Discipline began to collapse.

The Grey officers tried. And managed rather well, considering. Only a few people escaped Chor Bagan. And a half-dozen slipped inside, among them a skinny little old man in the all-enveloping yellow of a leper.

One-Eye was not pleased. He was sure strategy had had nothing to do with it being him who had to assume the yellow. Goblin was up to something wicked.

The six raiders approached the target tenement from front and rear, in loose teams of three. One-Eye was around front. People cleared off fast when they saw the yellow. Lepers were held in absolute terror.

None of the men wanted to carry out a raid in broad daylight. It was not the Company way. But darkness was denied us till Soulcatcher pulled her shadows back off the streets. And the consensus of the Annalists and wizards was that it was less likely that the Daughter of Night could summon Kina's help during daylight. Daytime also offered a better chance of taking her by surprise.

Each team paused to make sure every man still wore his yarn bracelet before they stormed into the tenement. Each wizard set loose an array of previously prepared low-grade confusion spells that buzzed through the ramshackle structure like a swarm of drunken mosquitoes. The attackers passed inside, stepping over and around frightened, shivering families who, till now, had considered themselves wildly fortunate to have a roof over their heads, even if that meant renting floor space in a hallway. Both teams posted a man who would make sure no one went outside. Another two men met at the foot of the rickety stair. They would prevent movement up or down. Goblin and One-Eye met at the cellar entrance and shared a few complaints about being desperately undermanned, then a few exaggerated courtesies as each offered the other the opportunity to go down into the enemy's den first.

Goblin finally accepted on the basis of superior youth, quickness and alleged intelligence. He launched a couple of luminary floating stars into the pit, where the darkness was blacker than Kina's heart.

"Here!" Goblin said. "Ha! We've got—"

Something like a flaming tiger burst out of nowhere. It leaped at Goblin. A shadow drifted in from the side. It flicked something long and thin that looped around the little wizard's neck.

One-Eye's cane came down on Narayan's wrist hard enough to crack bone. The living saint of the Strangler lost his rumel, which flew across the cellar.

One-Eye's off hand tossed something over Goblin's head, toward the source of the tiger. A ghostly light floated up like a wisp of luminescent swamp gas. It moved suddenly, enveloping a young woman. She began to slap at herself, trying to wipe it off.

Goblin did something quick, while she was distracted. She collapsed. "Goddamn! Goddamn! It worked. I'm a genius. Admit it. I'm a fucking genius."

"Who's a genius? Who came up with the plan?"

"Plan? What plan? Success is in the details, runt. Who came up with the details? Any damned fool could've said let's go catch them two."

Both men tied limbs as they nattered.

One-Eye said, "Plan the details on this. We got to get out of here with these people. Through all the Greys in the world."

"Already covered. They've got so much trouble they won't have time to worry
about any damned lepers." He started trying to get a yellow outfit over the head of
the Daughter of Night. "Remind me to warn them back at the shop that this one
can put together an illusion or two."

"I know that's the way its *supposed* to go." One-Eye began dragging Narayan
Singh into another yellow outfit. In a moment Goblin would trade his brown for
yellow, too. Upstairs, the four Company brothers, all of Shadar origin, were turning
themselves into Greys. "I'm saying it ain't got a prayer of working."

"That because I planned it?"

"Absolutely. You're beginning to catch on. Welcome to reality."

"It goes to shit in our hands, you can blame it on Sleepy, not me. It was her idea."

"We got to do something about that girl. She thinks too damned much. Will
you quit farting around? Them goddamn Greys out there are going to have time to
go home for lunch."

"Don't hit him so hard. You want him to walk out of here under his own power."

"You talking to me? What the hell you doing with . . . get your hand out of
there, you old pervert."

"I'm putting a control amulet over her heart, you dried-up old turd. So she
won't embarrass us before we get her home."

"Oh, yeah. Sure you are. But why don't I look on the bright side? At least you're
interested in girls again. She built as nice as her mother?"

"Better."

"Watch your mouth. The place might be haunted. And I got a suspicion maybe
some of those ghosts can talk to each other, no matter what Murgen claims." One-
Eye began to bully the groggy Narayan Singh up the steps.

I do believe this is going to work," One-Eye crowed. The combination of Greys and
lepers seemed the perfect device for exiting the Thieves' Garden—particularly now
that the real Greys were running around distracted.

"I don't want to break your heart, old-timer," Goblin said. "But I think we done
been fished." He was looking over his shoulder.

One-Eye looked back. "Shit!"

A small flying carpet dropped toward them, accompanied by crows making no
sounds at all. Soulcatcher. And her very stance suggested mischievous glee.

She threw something.

"Spread out!" Goblin barked. "Don't let those two get away." He faced the
descending carpet, heart in this throat. If it came to a direct face-off, he was going to get splattered like a stomped egg. He extended a gloved hand, caught the

falling black globule, whipped his arm in a circle and launched the missile back into the sky.

Soulcatcher shrieked, outraged. The people of Taglios did not have that kind of nerve. She drove the carpet to one side, avoiding the black globe. And well she moved when she did.

Her luck had served her yet again. A screaming fireball ripped right through the space she had vacated, the same kind of fireball that had eaten all those holes in the Palace wall and had set the bodies of so many men burning like bad fat candles. She continued to dive. Two more fireballs barely missed her. She put a tenement between herself and the sharpshooters. She was extremely angry but did not let rage cloud her thinking.

Above her, her crows began bursting like soundless fireworks. Blood, flesh and feathers rained down.

In seconds she figured it out, conversing with herself in a committee of voices.

They had not been hiding inside Chor Bagan after all. She could not have caught anyone trying to slip away like this if they had not come in to retrieve something they did not want found. "They're here in the city. But we haven't found them. We haven't seen a trace or heard a rumor that they didn't want to reach our ears. Until now. That takes wizardry. That bold little one. That was the toad man. Goblin. Though the Great General of the Armies Mogaba assures us that he saw the body himself. Who else is alive? Could the Great General himself be less trustworthy than he would like us to believe?"

That was not possible. Mogaba had no other friends. He was committed in perpetuity.

Soulcatcher brought her carpet to earth, stepped off, folded its light bamboo frame, rolled the carpet around that, surveyed the street. They had come down this way. From up there. What could they have wanted desperately enough to have exposed themselves so thoroughly? Anything they thought that important would be something she was bound to find very interesting herself.

I t took just one whispered word of power to illuminate the cellar. The squalor was appalling. Soulcatcher turned slowly. A man and his daughter, apparently. An old man and a young woman, anyway. One lamp. Discarded clothing. A few handfuls of rice. Some fish meal. Why the writing instruments and ink? What was this? A book. Somebody had just begun writing in it in an unfamiliar alphabet. She caught a spot of black movement in the corner of her eye. She whirled, crouching, fearing an attack by a rogue shadow. The *skildirsha* maintained an especially potent hatred for those who dared command them.

A rat fled, dropping the object of its curiosity. Soulcatcher knelt, picked up a long strip of black silk with an antique silver coin sewn into one corner. "Oh. I see."

She began to laugh like a young girl catching on late to the meaning of an off-color joke. She collected the book, surveyed the scene once more before leaving. "Dedication sure doesn't pay."

Once in the street again, she reassembled her carpet, unconcerned about snipers. Those people would be long gone and far away. They knew their business. But crows should be tracking them.

She froze, staring upward but not really seeing the white crow on the peak of the tenement roof. "How did they find out where those two were?"

What happened?" Sahra demanded as soon as she came in, before she began shedding Minh Subredil's rags.

I was still Dorabee Dey Banerjae myself. "We lost Murgen somehow. Goblin thought they had him anchored, but he went away while we were all out and I don't know how to get him back."

"I meant what happened in the Thieves' Garden. Soulcatcher was out there. Whatever she tried to pull didn't work out but she came back a different person. I didn't get to hear everything she told the Radisha but I do know she found something or figured out something that changed her whole attitude. Like everything suddenly stopped being fun."

I said, "Oh. I don't know. Maybe Murgen can tell us. If we can get him back here."

Goblin joined us. He was pushing a sleeping One-Eye in Banh Do Trang's spare wheelchair. He announced, "They're resting peacefully. Drugged. Narayan was distraught. The girl took it pretty calmly. We need to worry about her."

"What's wrong with him?" I asked, indicating One-Eye.

"He's worn out. He's an old man. I want to see you have half the energy he does when you get to be half his age."

Sahra asked, "Why do we need to worry about the girl?"

"Because she's her mother's daughter. She doesn't have much skill with it yet because she hasn't had anybody to teach her, but she's got the natural ability to become a substantial sorceress. Maybe even as powerful as her mother but without Lady's rudimentary sense of ethics. It reeks off her—"

"'Tain't the only thing she reeks of, neither," One-Eye chirped. "First thing you do with that little honey, you throw her in a vat of hot water. Then throw in a couple, four lumps of lye soap and let her soak for a week."

Sahra and I exchanged glances. If she was bad enough to offend One-Eye, she had to be ripe indeed.

Goblin grinned from ear to ear but eschewed temptation.

I said, "I hear you ran into the Protector."

"She was on a roof or somewhere waiting for something to happen. She didn't get what she expected. A couple of fireballs and she ducked and stayed ducked."

"You made it home without being followed?" I knew the answer because I knew they knew the stakes. They would not have come anywhere near here had they had the slightest doubt that that was safe.

I had to ask, even knowing that if they had failed, the warehouse would be buried in Greys already.

"We were ready to deal with the crows."

"All but one," One-Eye grumbled.

"What?"

"I saw a white one up there. It didn't try to follow us, though."

Once again Sahra and I exchanged glances. Sahra said, "I'm going to change and relax and get something to eat. Let's meet in an hour. If you could find it in your heart, Goblin, you might try to get Murgen back here."

"You're the necromancer."

"You're the one who claimed he anchored him. One hour."

Goblin began grumbling to himself. One-Eye chuckled and made no offer to help. He asked me, "You ready to kill your librarian yet?"

I did not tell him so but I was slightly more open to the suggestion tonight. Surendranath Santaraksita seemed to suspect that Dorabee Dey Banerjae was something more than he pretended. Or maybe I was just paranoid enough to hear things Santaraksita never intended to say. "You don't worry about Master Santaraksita. He's being very good to me. Today he told me I can look at any book I want. Unless it's in the restricted stacks."

"Woo!" One-Eye breathed. "Somebody finally found the way to her heart. Who'd'a thunk a book would do it? Name the first one after me, Little Girl."

I waved a fist under his nose. "I'd knock out your last tooth and call you Mushy but I was brought up to respect my elders—even if they're rambling, demented and senile." For all its One True God focus, my religion contains a strong taint of ancestor worship. Every Vehdna believes his forefathers can hear his prayers and can in-

tercede with God and his saints. If he feels he has been properly treated. "I'm going
to follow Sahra's example."

"You holler if you want to get in practice for your new boyfriend." His cackle
ended abruptly as Gota limped around me. When I glanced back, One-Eye appeared
to be sound asleep again. Must have been some other old fool running his mouth.

During the siege of Jaicur, I announced that never again would I be picky about
what I ate. That I would respond to anything offered me with a smile of gratitude and a spoken "Thank you." But time has a way of wearing away at such vows.
I was nearly as sick of rice and smoked fish as Goblin and One-Eye were. Breaking
the tedium with the occasional supper of rice and fish meal did not seem to help. I
am confident that it is their diet that makes the Nyueng Bao such a humorless
people.

I ran into Sahra, who had bathed and let her hair down and relaxed, looking a
decade younger, so that it was easy to see how, a decade earlier still, she could have
been every young man's fantasy. "I still have a little money I took off somebody who
picked the wrong side down south," I told her, waving a tiny piece of fish caught between two bamboo chopsticks. Nyueng Bao refuse to adopt innovative utensils that
have been in common use amongst everyone else in this part of the world for centuries. Those who did the cooking in Do Trang's complex were all Nyueng Bao.

"What?" Sahra was completely baffled.

"I'll give it up. If we can buy a pig with it." Vehdna are not supposed to eat pork.
But I made the mistake of being born female, so I probably do not have a seat reserved in Paradise anyway. "Or anything else that doesn't go through the water like
this." I made a wiggly motion with one hand.

Sahra did not understand. Food was a matter of indifference to her—so long as
she got some. Fish and rice forever were perfectly fine. And she was probably right.
There are plenty of people out there who have to eat chhatu because they cannot afford rice. And others cannot afford any food at all. Though Soulcatcher seemed to
be thinning those out now.

Sahra started to tell me something about a rumor that another Bhodi disciple
was going to present himself at the entrance to the Palace and demand an audience
with the Radisha. But we were approaching the lighted area where we worked our
wickednesses of evenings and she saw something there that made her stop.

I started to say, "Then we need to get somebody next to him—"

Sahra growled, "What the hell is *he* doing here?"

I saw it now. Uncle Doj was back, probably determined to invite himself into
our lives again. His timing seemed interesting and suspect.

I also found it interesting that Sahra spoke Taglian when she was stressed. She
had some definite points of contention with her own people, though around the

warehouse nobody used Nyueng Bao except Mother Gota, who did so only to remain a pain.

Uncle Doj was a wide little man who, though on the brink of seventy, was
mostly muscle and gristle, and in recent years, bad temper. He carried a long,
slightly curved sword he called Ash Wand. Ash Wand was his soul. He had told me
so. He was some sort of priest but would not bother to explain. His religion involved martial arts and holy swords, though. He was nobody's uncle in reality.
Uncle was a title of respect among Nyueng Bao, and they all seemed to consider
Doj a man worthy of the greatest respect.

Uncle Doj has meandered in and out of our lives since the siege of Jaicur, always
more distraction than contribution. He could be underfoot for years at a stretch,
then would disappear for weeks or months or years. This latest time he had been
out of the way for more than a year. When he did turn up, he never bothered reporting what he had been doing or where he had been, but judging from Murgen's
observations and my own, he was still searching for his Key diligently.

Curious, him materializing so suddenly after my epiphany. I asked Sahra, "Did
your mother happen to leave the warehouse today?"

"That question occurred to me, too. It might be worth pursuit."

Very little warmth existed between mother and daughter. Murgen was not the
cause but absolutely had become the symbol.

Uncle Doj was supposed to be a minor wizard. I never saw any evidence to support that, other than his uncanny skill with Ash Wand. He was old and his joints
were getting stiff. His reflexes were fading. But I could not think of anyone who
would remotely be his match. Nor have I ever heard of anyone else dedicating his
life to a piece of steel the way he has.

Maybe I did have evidence of his being a wizard, I reflected. He never had any
trouble getting through the mazes Goblin and One-Eye had created to save us the
embarrassment of unexpected walk-ins. Those two ought to tie him down till he explained how he did that.

I asked Sahra, "How do you want to handle this?"

Her voice was edged with flint. "Far as I'm concerned, we can lump him right
in there with Singh and the Daughter of Night."

"The enemy of my enemy is my enemy, huh?"

"I never liked Doj much. By Nyueng Bao standards he's a great and honorable
man, a hero due great respect. And he's the embodiment of everything I find distasteful about my people."

"Secretive, huh?"

She betrayed a hint of a smile. In that she was as guilty as any other Nyueng
Bao. "That's in the blood."

Tobo noticed us watching and talking. He darted over. He was excited enough
to forget he was a surly young man. "Mom. Uncle Doj is here."

"So I see. He say what he wants this time?"

I touched her arm gently, cautioning her. No need to start butting heads.

Doj, of course, was aware of our presence. I never saw a man so intensely aware of his environment. He might have heard every word we whispered, too. I put no store in the chance that time had weathered his sense of hearing. He gobbled rice and paid us no heed.

I told Sahra, "Go say hello. I need a second to put my face on."

"I ought to send for the Greys. Have them raid the place. I'm too tired for this." She did not bother to keep her voice down.

"Mom?"

I held Doj's eye. My face was cold. My voice held no emotion whatsoever as I asked, "What is the Key?" Bound, gagged, Narayan Singh and Daughter of Night watched and waited their turn.

The faintest flicker of surprise stirred in Doj's eyes. I was not the sort he expected to be a questioner.

I was in character again, a borrowed one based on a gang enforcer who had offended us a few years ago, Vajra the Naga. The gang was out of business and Vajra the Naga had gone on to a better world but his legacy occasionally proved useful.

Doj enjoyed the reasonable expectation that he would not be tortured. I had no intention of taking it that far. With him. The Company's fortunes and those of the Nyueng Bao had become so intermingled that I could not brutalize Doj without alienating our most useful allies.

Doj volunteered nothing. Nor did I expect him to be any more vocal than a stone. I told him, "We need to open the way onto the glittering plain. We know you don't have the Key. We do know where to start looking for it. We'll be pleased to return it to you once we release our brothers." I paused, giving him time to surprise me by replying. He did not.

"You are, perhaps, philosophically opposed to opening the way. We're going to disappoint you on that. The way will open. Somehow. You have only the option of participating or not participating."

Doj's eyes shifted, just for an instant. He wanted to read Sahra's stance.

Hers was plain. She had a husband trapped under the glittering plain. The wishes of the lone priest of some obscure, never-explained cult carried no weight with her.

Not even Banh Do Trang or Ky Gota offered demonstrative support, though both would favor him mainly out of decades of inertia.

"If you don't cooperate, then we won't return the Key when we're done with it. And *we* will determine what constitutes cooperation. The first step is to put an end to all of the normal Nyueng Bao equivocation and evasion and selective deafness."

Vajra the Naga was not a character I liked to adopt too often. A naga was a mythical serpent being that lived beneath the earth and had no sympathy whatever for anything human. The trouble with the character was that I could slip into it like it had been tailored for me. It would take only a small emotional distortion to turn me into Vajra the Naga.

"You have something we want. A book." I was betting a lot on my having reasoned out or intuited the course of various hidden events based upon what I had gotten from Murgen and his Annals. "It's about so-by-so and this thick, bound in tan vellum. The writing inside is in an untrained hand in a language no one has spoken for seven centuries. Specifically, it is a nearly complete copy of the first volume of the Books of the Dead, the lost sacred texts of the Children of Kina. Chances are you didn't know that."

Narayan and even the Daughter of Night reacted to that.

I continued, "The book was stolen from the fortress Overlook by the sorcerer called the Howler. He concealed it because he didn't want Soulcatcher to get it, nor did he want the child to have it. You either saw him hide it or stumbled onto it soon after he did. You concealed it somewhere you feel is safe. Ignoring the fact that nothing can remain hidden forever. Some eyes will discover anything eventually."

Once again I allowed Doj time for remarks. He chose to pass on the opportunity.

"You have a choice in all this. I remind you, though, that you're getting old, that your chosen successor is buried under the plain with my brothers, and that you have no allies more favorable than Gota, whose enthusiasm has to be suspect at this late date. You may choose to say nothing, ever, in which case truth will follow you into the darkness. But the Key will remain here. In other hands. Have you had enough to eat? Has Do Trang been a good host? Will somebody help our guest find something to drink? We shouldn't be scorned for our failures of hospitality."

"You didn't get a word out of him," One-Eye complained as soon as Doj was out of earshot.

"I didn't expect to. I just wanted him to have something to think about. Let's talk to these two. Scoot Singh over here, take the gag off and turn him so he can't get cues from the girl." She was spooky. Even bound and gagged, she radiated a disturbingly potent presence. Put her in the company of people already prepared to believe that she was touched by the dark divine and it was easy to understand why the Deceiver cult was making a comeback. Interesting, though, that that was a recent phenomenon. That for a decade she and Narayan had been fugitives painstakingly taking control of the few surviving Deceivers and evading the Protector's agents, and now, just as *we* feel we are up to tugging a few beards, *they* began making their survival known, too.

I had no trouble seeing where the Gunni imagination would find connections and portents and wild harbingers of the Year of the Skulls.

"Narayan Singh," I said in my Vajra the Naga voice. "You're a stubborn old man. You should have been dead long ago. Perhaps Kina does favor you. Which would suggest that here in my hands is where the goddess wants you to be." We Vehdna are good at blaming everything on God. Nothing can happen that is not the will of God. Therefore, He has already measured the depth of the brown stuff and has decided to toss you in. "And these are bloody hands, make no mistake."

Singh looked at me. He did not fear much. He did not recognize me. If our paths had crossed before, I had been too minor an annoyance for him to recall.

The Daughter of Night remembered me, though. She was thinking that I was a mistake she would not be making again. I was thinking maybe she was a mistake *we* ought not to make, however useful a tool she might become. She almost scared Vajra the Naga, who had been too dense to comprehend fear in personal terms.

"You're troubled by events but aren't afraid. You rely upon your goddess. Good. Let me provide assurances. We won't harm you. Assuming you cooperate. However much we owe you."

He did not believe a word of that and I did not blame him. That was the usual sort of "hold out a feather of hope" a torturer used to leverage cooperation from the doomed. "In this case, the pain will all be directed elsewhere."

He tried to turn to look at the girl.

"Not just there, Narayan Singh. Not only there. Though that's where we'll start. Narayan, you have something we want. We have several things we believe to be of value to you. I'm prepared to make an exchange, sworn in the names of all our gods."

Narayan had nothing to say. Yet. But I began to sense that his ears might be open to the right words.

The Daughter of Night sensed that, too. She squirmed. She tried to make some kind of noise. She was going to be as stubborn and crazy as her mother and aunt. Must be the blood.

"Narayan Singh. In another life you were a vegetable seller in the town called Gondowar. Every other summer you would go off to lead your company of *tooga*." Singh looked uncomfortable and puzzled. This was nothing he expected. "You had a wife, Yashodara, whom you called Lily in private. You had a daughter, Khaditya, which was maybe just a little too clever a naming. You had three sons: Valmiki, Sugriva and

Aridatha. Aridatha you've never seen because he wasn't born until after the Shadow-masters carried the able men of Gondowar off into captivity."

Narayan looked more uncomfortable and troubled than ever. His life before the coming of the Shadowmasters was a lost episode. Since his unexpected salvation, he had dedicated himself solely to his goddess and her Daughter.

"Those times were so unsettled that you have since proceeded on the reasonable assumption that nothing of your former life survived the coming of the Shadowmasters. But that assumption is a false one, Narayan Singh. Yashodara bore you that third son, Aridatha, and lived to see him become a grown man. Though she endured great poverty and despair, your Lily survived until just two years ago." In fact, until just after we located her. I still did not know for certain if some of my brothers had not grown overly zealous in their eagerness to locate Narayan. "Of your sons, Aridatha and Sugriva still live, as does your daughter Khaditya, though she has used the name Amba since she learned, to her horror, that her very father was the Narayan Singh of such widespread infamy."

By stealing Lady's baby, Narayan had ensured that his name would live on amongst those of the great villains. Everyone over a certain age knew the name and a score of evil stories burdening it—the majority of them fabrications or accretions of stories formerly attached to some other human demon whose ignominy had been nibbled up by time.

I had his attention despite his determination to remain indifferent. Family is critically important to all but a handful of us.

"Sugriva continues in the produce business, although his desire to escape your reputation led him first to move to Ayodahk, then to Jaicur when the Protector decided she wanted the city repopulated. He felt everyone would be strangers there and he could create a more favorable past for himself."

Both captives noted my unfortunate use of "Jaicur." Which did not give them anything they could use but which did tell them I was not Taglian. No Taglian would call that city anything but Dejagore.

I continued, "Aridatha grew into a fine young man, well-formed and beautiful. He's a soldier now, a senior noncommissioned officer in one of the City Battalions. His rise has been rapid. He has been noticed. There's a good chance he'll be chosen to become one of the career commissioned officers the Great General had been imposing on the army."

I fell silent. No one else spoke. Some were hearing this for the first time, though Sahra and I had started looking for those people a long time ago.

I got up and went out, got myself a large cup of tea. I cannot abide the Nyueng Bao tea-making ceremonies. I am, of course, a barbarian in their eyes. I do not like the tiny little cups they use, either. When I have some tea, I want to get serious about it. Make it strong and bitter and toss in a glob of honey.

I seated myself in front of Narayan again. No one had spoken in my absence. "So, living saint of the Stranglers, have you truly put aside all the chains of the earth? Would you like to see your Khaditya again? She was little when you left. Would you like to see your grandchildren? There are five of them. I can say the word and inside a week we can have one of them here." I sipped tea, looked Singh in the eye and let his imagination toy with the possibilities. "But *you* are going to be all right, Narayan. I'm going to see to that personally." I showed him my Vajra the Naga smile. "Will somebody show these two to their guest rooms?"

"That all you're going to do?" Goblin asked once they were gone.

"I'm going to let Singh think about the life he never lived. I'll let him think about losing what's left of that. *And* about losing his messiah. When he can avoid all those tragedies just by telling us where to find the souvenir he carried away from Soulcatcher's hideout down by Kiaulune."

"He won't take a deep breath without getting permission from the girl."

"We'll see how he handles having to make his own decisions. If he stalls too long and we get pressed, you can put a glamour on me that'll make him think I'm her."

"What about her?" One-Eye asked. "You going to personally work on her, too?"

"Yes. Starting right now. Put some of those choke spells on her. One on each wrist and ankle. And double them up around her neck." We had done some herding, amongst other things, over the years and One-Eye and Goblin, being incredibly lazy, had developed choke spells that constricted tighter and tighter as an animal moved farther away from a selected marker point. "She's a resourceful woman with a goddess on her side. I'd prefer to kill her and be done with it but we won't get any help from Singh if we do. If she does manage to escape, I want complete success to be fatal. I want near success to render her unconscious from lack of air. I don't want her having regular contact with any of our people. Remember what her aunt, Soulcatcher, did to Willow Swan. Tobo. Has Swan said anything that might interest us?"

"He just plays cards, Sleepy. He does talk all the time but he never says anything. Kind of like Uncle One-Eye."

Whisper. "You put him up to that, didn't you, Frogface?"

"Sounds like Swan to me," I said. I shut my eyes, began massaging my brow between thumb and forefinger, trying to make Vajra the Naga go away. His reptilian lack of connection was seductive. "I'm so tired—"

"Then why the hell don't we all just retire?" One-Eye croaked. "For a whole goddamned generation it was the Captain and his next year in Khatovar shit that beat us into the ground. Now it's you two women and your holy crusade to resurrect the Captured. Find yourself a guy, Little Girl. Spend a year screwing his brains out. We're not going to get those people out of there. Accept that. Start believing that they're dead."

He sounded exactly like the traitor in my soul that whispered in my mind every night before I fell asleep. The part about accepting that the Captured were never going to be coming back, anyway. I asked Sahra, "Can we call up our favorite dead man? One-Eye, ask him what he thinks of our plan."

"Bah! Frogface, you deal with this. I need a little medicinal pick-me-up."

Almost smiling despite her aching joints, Gota waddled out behind One-Eye. We would not see those two for a while. If we were lucky, One-Eye would get drunk fast and pass out. If we were not, he would come staggering out looking to feud with Goblin and we would have to restrain him. That could turn into an adventure.

"Well. Here's our prodigal." Sahra finally had Murgen back in the mist box.

I told him, "Tell me about the white crow."

Puzzled, "I go there sometimes. It's not voluntary."

"We took Narayan Singh and the Daughter of Night out of Chor Bagan today. There was a white crow there. You weren't here."

"I wasn't there." More puzzled. Even troubled. "I don't remember being there."

"I think Soulcatcher noticed it. And she knows her crows."

Murgen continued, "I wasn't there but I remember things that happened. This can't be happening to me again."

"Just calm down. Tell us what you know."

Murgen proceeded to report everything Soulcatcher said and did after she ducked our snipers. He would not tell us how he knew. I do not think he could.

Sahra said, "She does know that we have Singh and the girl."

"But did she guess why? The Company has an old grudge with those two."

"She'll need to see bodies to be convinced there was nothing more to it than that. She's still not completely satisfied that Swan is dead. A very suspicious woman, the Protector."

"A Narayan corpse would be easy—if we could make it credible. There're a million skinny, filthy little old men with green teeth out there. But we'd sure come up short on beautiful twenty-year-old women with blue eyes and skin paler than ivory."

"The Greys will definitely become more active now," Sahra said. "Whatever she suspects or doesn't, the Protector wants no one going about any tricky business in her city."

"A point the Radisha might argue. Which reminds me of something that's been knocking around the back of my head. Listen to this and tell me what you think."

21

As the Bhodi disciples made their way through the crowds, more than one on-looker reached out to slap their backs. The disciples took that with poor grace. It told them that many of the witnesses were there to be entertained.

The rite proceeded as before, but more quickly as it was evident that the Greys anticipated trouble and had instructions to head it off.

The kneeling priest in orange burst into flames just as the Greys began man-handling his assistants out of the way.

A gout of smoke leaped upward. A Black Company skull formed inside it, an evil eye seeming to stare deep into the souls of all the witnesses. A voice filled the morning. "All their days are numbered."

And the wooden curtain-wall shielding the reconstruction came to life. Glowing lime characters as tall as a man proclaimed "Water Sleeps," and "My Brother Unforgiven." They crawled slowly back and forth.

Soulcatcher herself materialized on the ramparts overhead. Her rage was palpable.

A second and larger cloud of smoke burst off the burning disciple. A face—the best representation of the Captain's that One-Eye and Goblin could manage—told the awed and silent thousands, "*Rajadharma!* The Duty of Kings. Know you: King-ship is a Trust. The King is the most exalted and conscientious servant of the people."

I began to slide away from there. This was sure to sting the Protector into some impulsive and self-defeating response.

Or maybe not. She did nothing obvious, though a sudden breeze came along. It blew the smoke away. But it fanned the flames consuming the Bhodi disciple. The smell of burning flesh spread out downwind.

22

When Master Santaraksita wanted to know why I was late, I told the truth. "Another Bhodi disciple set himself on fire in front of the Palace. I went to watch. I couldn't help myself. There was sorcery involved." I described what I had seen. As so many of the actual eyewitnesses also had, Santaraksita seemed both repelled and intrigued.

"Why do you suppose those disciples are doing that, Dorabee?"

I knew why they were doing it. It took no genius to fathom their motives. Only their determination remained a puzzle. "They're trying to tell the Radisha that she's not fulfilling her obligations to the Taglian people. They consider the situation so desperate that they've chosen to send their message by a means that can't be ignored."

"I, too, believe that to be the case. The question remains: What can the Radisha *do*? The Protector won't go away just because some people believe she's bad for Taglios."

"I have a great deal to do today, Sri, and I'm starting late."

"Go. Go. I must assemble the bhadrhalok. It's possible we can present the Radisha with some means of shaking the Protector's grip."

"Good luck, Sri." He would need it. Only the most outrageous good luck since the beginning of time was going to give him and his cronies the tools to undo Soulcatcher. Chances were good the bhadrhalok had no idea how dangerous an opponent they had chosen.

I dusted and mopped and checked the rodent traps and after a while noticed that most everyone had gone away. I asked old Baladitya the copyist where everyone was. He told me that the other copyists had ducked out as soon as the senior librarians had gone off to their bhadrhalok meeting. They knew that the bhadrhalok would do nothing but it would take them hours of grumbling and talking and arguing to get it done, so they made themselves a holiday.

It was not an opportunity to be refused. I began examining books, even going so far as to penetrate the restricted stacks. Baladitya knew nothing. He could not see three feet in front of his face.

23

Jaul Barundandi partnered Minh Subredil with a young woman named Rahini and sent them to work in the Radisha's own quarters, under the direction of a woman named Narita, a fat, ugly creature possessed by an inflated conception of her own importance. Narita complained to Barundandi, "I need six more women. I'm supposed to clean the council chamber again after I complete the royal suite."

"Then I suggest you pick up a broom yourself. I'll be back in a few hours. I expect to see progress. I've given you the best workers available." Barundandi went elsewhere to be unpleasant to someone else.

The fat woman took it out on Subredil and Rahini. Subredil did not know who Narita was. The woman had not worked in the royal chambers before. As Subredil steered a mop around, she whispered, "Who is this woman who is so bitter?" She stroked her Ghanghesha.

Rahini glanced right and left but did not raise her eyes. "You must understand her. She is Barundandi's wife."

"You two! You aren't being paid to gossip."

"Pardon, ma'am," Sahra said. "I didn't understand what to do and didn't want to trouble you."

The fat woman scowled for a moment but then turned her displeasure in another direction. Rahini smiled softly, whispered, "She's in a good mood today."

As the hours passed and her knees and hands and muscles began to ache, Sahra realized that she and Rahini had been delivered to Barundandi's wife more for who they were than for the work they could do. They were not bright and they were not among the more attractive workers. Barundandi wanted Narita to believe that these were the kind of women he always employed. Elsewhere, no doubt, he and his chief assistants would take full advantage of their bit of power over the unfortunate and the desperate.

It was not a good day for exploring. There was more work than three women could possibly complete. Sahra got no chance to collect additional pages from the hidden Annals. Then, not many hours after the day started, conditions within the Palace became much less relaxed. The high and the mighty began to show themselves, moving rapidly here and there. Rumor came, apparently passing right through stone walls.

Another Bhodi disciple had burned himself to death outside and the Radisha was completely distraught. Narita herself confided, "She's very frightened. Many things are happening over which she has no control. She has gone to the Anger Chamber. She does so almost every day now."

"The Anger Chamber?" Sahra murmured. She had not heard of this before, but till recently she never worked this close to the heart of the Palace. "What is that, ma'am?"

"A room set aside where she can tear her hair and clothing and rage and weep without having her emotions poison surroundings used for other purposes. She won't come out until she can face the world in complete calm."

Subredil understood: It was a Gunni thing. Only Gunni would come up with an idea like that. Gunni religion personified everything. It had a god or goddess or demon, a deva or rakshasa or yaksha or whatever for everything, usually with several aspects and avatars and differing names, none of whom were seen much nowadays but who had been very busy way back when.

Only an extremely wealthy Gunni would come up with a conceit like an Anger Chamber—a Gunni cursed with a thousand rooms she did not know how to use.

Later in the day Subredil contrived to be allowed to service the freshly evacuated Anger Chamber. It was small and contained nothing but a mat on a polished wooden floor and a small shrine to ancestors. The smoke was thick and the smell of incense was overpowering.

24

A good thing I didn't have any pages on me, too," Sahra told me. "The Greys started searching us going out. That woman Vancha tried to steal a little silver oil lamp. She'll spend all morning tomorrow being 'punished' by Jaul Barundandi."

"Does Barundandi's boss know what he does?"

"I don't think so. Why?"

"We could trick him into betraying himself. Get him tossed out."

"No. Barundandi is the devil we know. An honest man would be harder to manipulate."

"I loathe the man."

"That's because he's loathsome. Not unlike other men in similar positions of petty power. But we're not here to reform Taglios, Sleepy. We're here to find out how to release the Captured. And to torment our enemies when doing that doesn't jeopardize our primary mission. And we did a great job of that today. The Radisha was crushed by our messages."

Sahra told me what she had discovered. Then I told her about my own small triumph. "I got into the restricted stacks today. And I found what I think might be the original of one of the Annals we've got hidden in the Palace. It's in terrible shape but it's all there and it's still readable. And there may be more volumes. I only got through part of the restricted stack before I had to go help Baladitya find his slippers so his grandson could lead him home."

I had the book right there on the table. I patted it proudly. Sahra asked, "Won't it be missed?"

"I hope not. I replaced it with one of the moldy discards I've been saving."

Sahra squeezed my hand. "Good. Good. Things have gone well lately. Tobo, would you find Goblin? I have an idea to run past him."

I said, "I'll see how our guests are doing. Somebody might be ready to whisper confidences in my ear."

But only Swan wanted my ear and he did not have confidences in mind. In his way he was as incorrigible as One-Eye, yet he had a style that did not offend me. I do not think Swan had an evil bone in him. Like so many people, he was a victim of circumstance, struggling to keep his head up in the turbulence of the river of events.

Uncle Doj was displeased with his circumstances even though he was not a prisoner. "We can certainly get along without that book," I told him. "I doubt that I could read it, anyway. Mostly I want to make sure it doesn't get back to the Deceivers. What we really need is your knowledge."

Doj was a stubborn old man. He was not yet ready to make deals or to look for allies.

Before I left I asked, "Will it all die with you? Will you be the last Nyueng Bao to follow the Path? Thai Dei can't if he's buried under the glittering plain." I winked. I understood Doj better than he thought. His problem was not a conflict with his morality, it was a matter of control. He wanted to do everything his way, no strings.

He would come around if I kept reminding him of his mortality and his lack of a son or an apprentice. Nyueng Bao are famous for their stubbornness but even they will not sacrifice all their hopes and dreams rather than adjust.

I visited Narayan just long enough to offer a reminder that our interest did not lie in harming him. But the only reason we had for keeping the Daughter of Night healthy was our hope of his cooperation. "You can be stubborn for a while yet. We have several tasks to wrap up before you become our main interest and we concentrate on murdering your dreams."

That was my whole focus with each of our prisoners. Make them put their hopes and dreams on the line. Maybe I could weasel my way into history, as famous or infamous as Soulcatcher and Widowmaker, as Stormshadow and Longshadow, remembered forever as the Dreamkiller.

I had a vision of myself drifting through the night like Murgen, disembodied but dragging along a bottomless bag of black night into which I stuffed all the dreams I stole from restless sleepers. I was a real old-time rakshasa, there.

The Daughter of Night did not look up when I went to view her. She was in a cage Banh Do Trang used for keeping large animals of the deadliest sort. Sometimes leopards, but mostly tigers. A fully grown male tiger was worth a fortune in the apothecary market. She was shackled as well. The cats never were. In addition, I believe, a little opium and nightshade were used to season her food. Nobody wanted to underestimate her potential. Her family had a dire history. And she had a goddess on her shoulder.

Reason told me to kill her right now, before Kina wakened as much as she could. That would buy me the rest of my lifetime free of the end of the world. It would take the dark goddess generations to create another Daughter of Night.

Reason also told me that if the girl died, the Captured would spend the rest of time in those caverns under the glittering plain.

Reason told me, after a moment watching her, that she was not just ignoring me. She did not know I was there. Her mind was elsewhere. Which was not a comfortable feeling at all. If Kina could turn her loose, the way Murgen was loose. . . .

25

Master Santaraksita paused to tell me, "It was good of you to care for Baladitya yesterday, Dorabee. I had forgotten him in my eagerness to assemble the bhadrhalok. But you should be careful or his grandson will begin expecting you to walk the old man home for him. He tried it with me."

I did not look into his eyes, though I did want to see what was there. There was a tightness in his voice that told me he had something on his mind. But I had taken too many liberties with Dorabee already. He would not stare into the eyes of the priestly caste. "I but did the right thing, Master. Are we not taught to respect and aid our elders? If we do not when we are young, who will respect and aid us when we ourselves become frail?"

"Indeed. Nevertheless, you continue to amaze and intrigue me, Dorabee."

Uncomfortable, I tried to change the subject by inquiring, "Was the meeting of the bhadrhalok productive, Master?"

Santaraksita frowned, then smiled. "You're very subtle, Dorabee. No. Of course not. We're the bhadrhalok. We talk. We don't act." For a moment he mocked his own kind. "We'll still be debating what form our resistance should take when the Protector perishes of old age."

"Is it true what they say, Master? That she's four hundred years old, yet fresh as a bride?" I did not need to know, I just needed conversation to nurture Santaraksita's surprising interest in me.

"That seems to be the common belief, handed down from the northern mercenaries and those travelers the Radisha adopted."

"She must be a great sorceress indeed, then."

"Do I detect a note of jealousy?"

"Would we all not like to live forever?"

He looked at me oddly. "But we shall, Dorabee. This life is only a stage."

Wrong thing to say, Dorabee Dey. "I meant in this world. I find myself largely content to remain Dorabee Dey Banerjae."

Santaraksita frowned slightly but let it go. "How are your studies coming?"

"Wonderfully, Master. I'm especially fond of the historical texts. I'm discovering so many interesting facts."

"Excellent. Excellent. If there's anything I can do to help . . ."

I asked, "Is there a written Nyueng Bao language? Or was there ever?"

That took him from the blind side. "Nyueng Bao? I don't know. Why in the world would you—"

"Something I've seen a few times near where I live. Nobody knows what it means. The Nyueng Bao down there won't talk. But I never heard of them being literate."

He rested a hand on my shoulder for a moment. "I'll find out for you." His fingers seemed to be trembling. He murmured something unintelligible and hurried away.

26

Word was in that the Bhodi disciples were not happy with us for stealing their thunder at the Palace gate. I wondered what they would think when the news arrived about our behavior at Semchi. That seemed to be coming together perfectly for us. Unless Soulcatcher was thinking farther ahead than we could detect.

Murgen had Slink's party well on the way to the village. And moving faster than the group the Protector had sent to destroy the Bhodi Tree. That group outnumbered our brothers but did not expect any resistance. In a few days it would turn really nasty down there.

As the weather had here. Storm season had arrived. I had been delayed coming home by a ferocious thunderstorm that flooded some streets and sent down hail an inch in diameter. The kangali and other children went out and tried to gather up the ice, barking in pain every time a hailstone found unprotected skin. For a short while the air was almost tolerably cool. But then the storm moved on and the heat returned worse than it had been before. The stench of the city welled up. One storm was not enough to sluice it clean, only to turn everything over. In a few days the insects would be more miserable than ever before.

I hugged my burden and told myself I would not have to stay in this cesspool much longer.

One more to locate and I'll have everything I need from the library." My new acquisition lay open for public viewing. Of course no one could read it. Not even me. But I was confident that I now possessed another original of the three missing Annals. Perhaps the very first, since it was so alien. The other seemed to be inscribed in the same alphabet, much modified and somewhat like that used in the discarded volume I had rescued. If the language was the same, I would be able to figure it out eventually.

One-Eye cackled. "Yeah. Everything but somebody to translate that stuff for you. Everything but your new boyfriend." He insisted that Master Santaraksita was out to seduce me. And that Santaraksita would be brokenhearted if he succeeded and discovered that I was female.

"That's enough of that, you filthy old thing."

"Sacrifice for the cause, Little Girl." He started to offer some graphic advice. He had been drinking again. Or was drinking still.

Sahra arrived. She tossed a large bundle of pages my way. "Can it, One-Eye. Find Goblin. There's work to do." Of me she demanded, "Why do you put up with that?"

"He's harmless. And he's for sure too darned old to change. And if he's nagging me, he's not getting into something that's going to get us all killed."

"So you're sacrificing for the cause."

"Something like that. That was quick." Goblin had arrived. "What happened to One-Eye?"

"Taking a leak. What do I have to do now?"

Sahra said, "I can get into the Anger Chamber. The rest is up to you."

"You do this and you'll never be able to get back into the Palace. You know that, don't you?"

"What're we talking about?" I asked.

Sahra said, "I think we can kidnap the Radisha. With a little luck and a lot of help from Goblin and One-Eye."

"Goblin's right. You do that, we'd all better be a hundred miles away by the time the word gets out. I have a better idea. If we have to give away the fact that we can get inside the Palace, do it by sabotaging Soulcatcher. Get to one of her carpets, rig it to come apart under her when she's two hundred feet up and moving fast."

"I like the way you think, Sleepy. Put that on the list, Sahra. I want to be there. It'd be like the time the Howler flew into the side of the Tower at Charm. Man, he must've been going at least three times as fast as a horse could run when he hit that wall. Blauw! Hair, teeth and eyeballs all over the—"

"He walked away from that, you idiot." One-Eye was back. "He's out there under the plain with our guys right now." A unique odor suggested that One-Eye had taken a moment out to award himself some medicinal refreshment.

"Stop it. Now." Sahra was cranky tonight. "Our next step will be to neutralize Chandra Gokhale. We've already decided that. These other things we can worry about down the road."

I observed, "We'll need to freshen up our evacuation drill in case we need to get out of Taglios in a hurry. The more active we get, the more likely it becomes that something will go wrong. If it does, we'll have Soulcatcher breathing down our necks."

Goblin observed, "She isn't stupid, she's just lazy."

I asked Sahra, "Did she call in her shadows yet?"

"I don't know. I didn't hear anything."

Goblin grumbled. "What we really need is a formula for doing without sleep. For about a year. Let me see Minh Subredil's Ghanghesha."

Sahra sent Tobo to fetch the statue. The boy could be much less unpleasant when he was in a group.

Silence struck as Banh Do Trang rolled in, pushed by one of his own people. He smiled at a private joke. He enjoyed startling us. "One of my men tells me that we have a couple of outsiders caught in the confusion net. They appear to be harmless. An old man and a mute. Somebody will have to get them out and send them on their way without making them suspicious."

That news gave me a little chill but I did not suspect the truth till poor overworked Tobo and Goblin—the latter going along but staying out of sight while the boy led the intruders to safety—returned and Goblin reported, "I think your boyfriend followed you home, Sleepy."

"What?"

"There was this terrified old man who tried to impress Tobo with the fact that he was a librarian." A lot of Taglians *would* have been impressed. The ability to read was almost a sorcery in itself. "He called his sidekick Adoo. You told us—"

One-Eye began to howl. "The Little Girl's a regular heartbreaker! Damn, I'd give anything to be there when that old fool slides his hand into her pants and don't find what he's looking for."

I was embarrassed. I do not think I have been embarrassed about anything since the first time my uncle Rafi slipped his hand under my sari and did find what he was after. That darned fool Santaraksita! Why did he have to go complicating things like this?

"That's enough of that!" Sahra snapped. "There's supposed to be a meeting of the Privy Council tomorrow. I think we can use it to get to Gokhale. But I'll need to take Sawa and Shikhandini."

"Why?" I asked. I had no desire to go back inside the Palace ever again.

"That's great," One-Eye enthused. "You don't show at the library tomorrow, that old goat is gonna pine and whine and wonder what happened, if it's all his fault even though he knows there's no way you could know he tried to follow you home. You'll have your hook set, Little Girl. All you have to do is pull him in."

Sahra snapped, "I said—"

"Wait a minute. He may have a point. Suppose I do play Santaraksita's game? To the point where I get him to do my translations for me? We could even add him to our collection. I don't think he has much family. Why don't we take a closer look, see how long it might be before people wondered why he was missing."

"Oh, you're wicked, Little Girl," One-Eye said. "You're really wicked."

"You could find out someday, you keep riding me."

"About Gokhale?" Sahra asked.

"All right. Why are we taking me and Tobo both?"

"Tobo to put an idea into his head so he gets an itch he's going to have to go scratch. You to cover us. Just in case. I'll have Tobo carry his flute." Tobo's flute was a small version of the fire-projecting bamboo. "He can turn it over to you once we're inside." Tobo had carried that flute every time he had accompanied his mother into the Palace. We try to think ahead. "Also, I want to keep you fresh in Jaul Barundandi's mind. I'll definitely have to have you along when I snatch the Radisha. Goblin, what can you do with my Ghanghesha?"

No one else on earth would have dared hand the little wizard a straight line like that. But Sahra was Sahra. She did not have to pay the price.

I started to leave. I had other things to do. Tobo asked, "Is it all right if I show your Annals to Murgen? He wants to read them."

"You two starting to get along now?"

"I think so."

"Good. You can let him see them. Tell him not to be too critical. If he is, I won't come out there and dig him up."

27

Narayan seemed thoroughly puzzled by my continued interest. I do not believe he remembered me at all. But he now knew that I was female and had been the young man Sleepy that he had encountered, only rarely, ages ago.

"You've had time to reflect. Have you decided to help us yet?"

He looked at me with pure venom, yet without obvious personal hatred. I was just a particularly unpleasant obstacle delaying the inevitable triumph of his goddess. He had gotten his mind back into a rut.

"All right. I'll see you again tomorrow night. Your son Aridatha has a leave day coming up. We'll bring him around to visit you."

There was a guard watching the Daughter of Night. "What're you doing here, Kendo?"

"Keeping an eye on—"

"Go away. And don't come back. And spread the word. *Nobody* guards the Daughter of Night. She's too dangerous. Nobody even goes near her unless Sahra or I tell them to. And then they don't do it alone."

"She don't look—"

"She wouldn't, would she? Start hiking." I went to the cage. "How long would it take for your goddess to create all the right conditions for the birth of another like you? If I decide to kill you?"

The girl's gaze rose slowly. I wanted to cringe away from the power in her eyes but I held on. Maybe she should be getting even more opium than she was already.

"Reflect upon your value. And upon my power to destroy it." I felt puffed up. That was the kind of thing the devas, or lesser gods, blathered at one another on the fringes of the epics spun by the professional storytellers.

She glared. There was so much power in her eyes that I decided Kendo ought to spend a little time in private with Goblin and One-Eye, making sure he had not been taken in already.

"I think that without you there never will be a Year of the Skulls. And I *know* that you're still alive only because I want something from Narayan, who loves you like a father." Singh *was* her father, for all practical purposes. Croaker had been denied the chance by cruel Fortune. Or, more accurately, by the will of Kina.

"Keep well, dear." I left. I had a lot of reading to get done. And some writing if I got the chance. My days were always full and all too often they got confused. I decided to do things, then forgot. I told others to do things, then forgot that, too. I was beginning to look forward to the time when our successes—or sufficiently spectacular failures—forced us out of town. I could sneak off somewhere where nobody knew me and just loaf for a few months.

Or for the rest of my life if I wanted.

I had no trouble understanding why every year a few more of our brothers gave up and faded away. I only hoped a little notoriety would bring them back.

I studied the pages Sahra had brought out for me but the translation was difficult, the subject matter was uninspiring, and I was tired. I kept losing my concentration. I thought about Master Santaraksita. I thought about going back up to the Palace, armed. I thought about what Soulcatcher would do now that she knew she did not have us trapped inside the Thieves' Garden. I thought about getting old and being alone and had a suspicion that that fear might have something to do with why some brothers remained with the Company no matter what. They had no other family.

I have no other family.

I will not look back. I am not weak. I will not relax my self-control. I will persevere. I will triumph over myself and will conquer all adversity.

I fell asleep rereading my own recollections of what Murgen had reported about the Company's adventure on the glittering plain. I dreamed about the creatures he had encountered there. Were they the rakshasas and nagas of myth? Did they have anything to do with the shadows, or with the men who evidently created the shadows from hapless prisoners of war?

28

I have a bad feeling about this," I told Sahra as she and Tobo and I started the long walk. "You're sure the shadows are all off the streets?"

"Quit fussing, Sleepy. You're turning into an old woman. The streets are safe. The only monsters out here are human. We can handle those. You'll be safe in the Palace if you just stick to your character. Tobo will be safe as long as he remembers that he's not really Shikhandini and desperate for his mother to keep her job. It's in the nature of men like Jaul Barundandi that they do their bullying inside your head, not physically. They'll take 'no' for an answer. And I won't lose my job over it. My work is being noticed by others. Especially by Barundandi's wife. Now, get yourself into character. Tobo, you too. You particularly. I know Sleepy can do this when she concentrates on it."

Tobo was clad as a budding young woman, Minh Subredil's daughter, and I hoped we could get him back inside the warehouse unnoticed by Goblin and One-Eye, because they would ride him mercilessly. With the investment of a little artifice on his mother's part, Tobo made a very attractive young woman.

Jaul Barundandi thought so, too. Minh Subredil was the first worker called forward and Barundandi never bothered with his customary grumble about taking Sawa as part of the package.

Sawa had trouble keeping a straight face later when we found Barundandi's wife Narita waiting to pick women to work for her. One glance at Shiki was enough. Minh Subredil's family definitely belonged under her direct supervision.

Minh Subredil had done a good job of ingratiating herself with Narita. For the very good reason that Narita was in charge of cleaning those parts of the Palace of most immediate interest to us.

Sawa had not worked for Narita in the past. Subredil explained Sawa to Narita, who seemed more patient than she had the few times I had seen her before. Narita said, "I understand. There're plenty of simple things that need doing. The Radisha was particularly restless last night. These days when she has trouble sleeping, she breaks things and makes messes."

The woman actually sounded sympathetic. But the Taglian people loved their ruling family and seemed to feel that they deserved more room than the man on the street. Perhaps because of the burdens they bore, always in the past with maximum respect for *Rajadharma*.

Subredil maneuvered me into a spot whence I could observe well without being noticed. She and Narita brought me several brass treasures that needed cleaning. The ruling family had to be very fond of brass. Sawa cleaned tons of it. But Sawa could be trusted not to damage anything.

Shiki came to me and asked, "Will you take care of my flute for me, Aunt Sawa?" I took the instrument, studied it briefly, pasted on an idiot grin and tooted on the thing a few times. Just so everybody would know it was a real flute and not imagine that it might be a small fireball thrower, capable of making life both brief and painful for the first half-dozen people who got too close to a flautist in a bad temper.

Barundandi's wife asked Shiki, "You play the flute?"

"Yes, ma'am. But not very well."

"I was quite a skilled player when I was a girl . . ." She noticed her husband peeking in for the second time this morning and began to suspect he was interested in more than just the progress of the day's work. "Subredil, I don't think it's wise for you to bring your daughter here." And a moment later, she growled, "I'll be back in a minute. I have to talk to that man. I have to straighten him out."

The moment she stepped out, Minh Subredil moved with startling rapidity. She vanished into the Radisha's Anger Chamber. I had to admire her. Her mind never seemed clearer than when she was in a dangerous position. I suspected she actually enjoyed her role as a Palace menial. And the more dangerous the times, the more effective she seemed.

Despite a massive workload and Narita's frequent trips away to sabotage her husband's efforts to weasel in close to Shikhandini, or to draft Shiki into a different working group, in mid-afternoon we left the Radisha's personal suite for the gloomy chambers where the Privy Council assembled. There was a rumor that the Bhodi disciples were about to send another suicidal goof to the gateway. The Radisha wanted to forestall that somehow.

We were supposed to get the place ready for a Council session.

The Bhodi rumor had had its birth in the mind of Ky Sahra. It was supposed to be the device by which we could bring Shikhandini face-to-face with Chandra Gokhale.

We had almost two hours before the staffers appeared, the quiet little men who wrote everything down. Then the Purohita arrived, accompanied by the ecclesiastical members of the Privy Council. The Purohita did not deign to note our existence even though Shiki mistook him for Gokhale and batted her eyes till Subredil signed her off. I could hear the excuse that would come later: All old men looked alike.

Neither Arjuna Drupada nor Chandra Gokhale considered themselves old.

We continued our work, ignored. The folk of the Palace, particularly the inner circle, were lucky we had other things we wanted to do with our lives. Had we not cared about our own survival, we could have slaughtered scores of them. But getting rid of the Purohita would not mean much in the grand scheme. The senior priests would replace him with another old man just as nasty and narrow of mind before Drupada's bones got cold.

Chandra Gokhale came in and he did not overlook the help. Sahra must have gleaned a few suggestions from Willow Swan about what the old pervert liked, because he stopped dead, staring at Shikhandini like somebody had clubbed him between the eyes. Shiki had the role down perfectly. She was a shy virgin and a flirt at the same time, as though her maidenly heart had been smitten instantly. God apparently fashioned men so that they would swallow that sort of bait nine times out of ten.

Barundandi's timing was good. He came to move us out of the meeting chamber just as the Protector swooped in like some dark, angry eagle. Gokhale watched our departure with moon eyes. Before we completed our evacuation, he was whispering to one of his scribes.

Jaul Barundandi, unfortunately, had a sharp eye for some things. "Minh Subredil, I believe your daughter has charmed the Inspector-General of the Records."

Subredil appeared surprised. "Sir? No. That can't be. I won't let my child stumble into the trap that destroyed my mother and condemned me to this cruel life."

Sawa caught Subredil's arm. Apparently she had become frightened by that intense outburst, but in reality she squeezed, warning Subredil not to say anything that Barundandi might remember if Chandra Gokhale disappeared.

We might want to consider a change of plan. We did not want anyone to have any reason to connect anything outside with any of us.

Subredil's outburst faded. She became embarrassed and anxious to be elsewhere. "Shiki. Come on."

I was ready to kick Shikhandini's bottom myself. She was being a positive slut. But she did respond to her mother's command.

Sawa sort of settled down out of the way with the last of her dirty brass, in hopes of being overlooked while the Privy Council convened, but Jaul Barundandi was alert. "Minh Subredil. Bring your sister-in-law." He tried to flirt with Shikhandini. He got a look of disgust for his trouble.

Minh Subredil got me going, then went after her daughter. "What did you think you were doing in there?"

"I was just having fun. The man is a disgusting old pervert."

Softly, as though not meant for Barundandi's ears while the words really were, Subredil said, "Don't ever have fun like that again. Men like that will do whatever they like with you and there isn't anything anybody can do about it."

That warning was not all acting. The last thing we needed was one of the mighty dragging Shikhandini into a dark corner to do a little groping.

That was not supposed to happen. It was unthinkable, supposedly. And for ordinary people that was mostly true. But not so at a level where men began to believe that they existed outside the usual rules.

"Narita!" Barundandi called. "Where have you gotten to? That damned woman. She's slipped off to the kitchen again. Or she's gone somewhere to sneak a nap."

I heard the Radisha behind us, in the meeting chamber, but could not make out individual words. An angry voice responded. That had to be Soulcatcher. I wanted to be somewhere a little farther away. I started moving.

Sawa, of course, did things others did not always understand. Subredil grabbed hold and started to fuss. Barundandi told her, "Take this bunch to the kitchen, get something to eat. If Narita is there, tell her I want her."

The moment he was out of sight, I announced, "Sawa is going to wander off." Sawa was not completely happy with the pages Subredil kept bringing Sleepy. Subredil could not read them, worked in a rush and seemed incapable of collecting anything interesting.

I hoped I remembered the way. Even when you wear the yarn bracelet, the Palace is a confusing place and I had not roamed it since the days when the Captain was the Liberator and a great hero of the Taglian people. And even then, I had been only an occasional visitor.

As soon as I began to feel unsure, I got out a small piece of chalk and began to leave tiny marks in the Sangel alphabet. I had managed to learn a little of that language during our years in the far south but it had been a struggle. I hoped anyone who discovered the marks would not recognize what they were.

I did find the room where the old books were hidden. It was obvious that someone came there often. The dust was disturbed badly, which in itself would raise questions if discovered. I tried to drag out the book that looked the oldest. Darn, that thing was heavy. Once I got it open, I found that the pages were real stubborn about tearing. They were not paper at all, which never has been very common. I could tear them only one at a time. Which maybe explained why Subredil just grabbed whatever came easiest. She would not have time to pick and choose.

I worried that I had been away too long myself, convinced that Barundandi or his wife must have noticed that I was missing. I hoped it did not occur to them to wonder why Subredil was not making a scene because she had lost track of me.

Even so, I continued to tear pages until I had all I thought the three of us could carry away.

I hid everything in an unused room not far from the service postern, uncertain how we would recover it heading out, then took myself way down inside Sawa, almost to the point of incapacitating confusion.

They found me dirty and tearstained and still trying to find the way back to the meeting chamber, "they" being some of the other day workers. In moments I was reunited with Subredil and Shikhandini. I clung to my sister-in-law like a wood chip desperate to shed the embrace of a rushing flood.

Jaul Barundandi was not happy. "Minh Subredil, I accepted this woman here for your sake, out of kindness and charity. But lapses of this sort are not acceptable. No work got done while we were searching . . ." His voice trailed off. The Radisha and the Protector were headed our way, following a most unusual route. This was backstairs country. Which meant nothing whatsoever to Soulcatcher, of course. That woman had no sense of class or caste. There was the Protector and beneath the Protector there was everyone else.

Sawa just sort of folded up and squatted with her face in her lap. Subredil and Shikhandini and Jaul Barundandi partially tried to get out of the way, partially gawked. Shiki had not seen either woman before.

Sawa crossed her fingers out of sight in her lap. Subredil whispered prayers to Ghanghesha. Jaul Barundandi shivered in terror. Shikhandini stared with a teen's inability to feel appropriate fear.

The Radisha paid us no heed. She stamped past talking about ripping the guts out of Bhodi disciples. Her voice contained almost no emotional conviction. The Protector, though, slowed down and considered us all intently. For an instant I found myself almost overcome by the dread that she really could read minds. Then she went on and Jaul Barundandi ran along behind, forgetting us and Narita both because the Radisha barked some command back his way.

Sawa rose and whimpered, "I want to go home."

Subredil agreed that it was enough of a day.

Neither the Greys nor the Royal Guards were searching anyone. A good thing, too. I carried so much paper in my small clothes I could fake a normal walk for only a few dozen yards.

I got through my part of the evening meeting quickly and ran off to my own little corner so I could compare my newly acquired pages with those of the book I had stolen from the library that I thought was an exact copy—if not the genuine original—of the true first volume of the Annals of the Black Company. I was so cheerful I am sure One-Eye must have had great fun talking about me behind my back.

It did not occur to me to stick around to see how our temptation of Chandra Gokhale played out.

The story I got later was, Gokhale had a man try to follow Shiki home. When that man did not report back within a reasonable time—on account of he ran into Runmust and Iqbal Singh someplace he should not have been and ended up taking the long swim downriver—Gokhale headed for the joy house that specialized in serving him, his associates and those who shared their select but hardly rare tastes in pleasure. Riverwalker and several other brothers picked him up when he left the Palace. He was accompanied by two companions who would regret their wishes to ingratiate themselves with the Inspector-General by joining him in an evening of indulgence.

Murgen followed events closely, too. Knowing that he would do so, I felt at ease snuggling up with my new acquisitions.

It took me over an hour to conclude that what I had brought out today was indeed a later version of the first ever Annal and most of another hour to realize that I would not be able to winkle out the book's secrets without skilled help. Or a lot more time than I had.

Chandra Gokhale apparently died in that joy house. Likewise, his two companions. There were witnesses. People saw them strangled. Then a red rumel got left behind in the killers' haste to get away.

The Greys arrived almost immediately. They loaded the corpses into a cart, saying the Protector wanted Gokhale's back in the Palace instantly. But the Greys stopped being Greys moments after they left the pleasure house. Their course led them toward the river rather than toward the Palace. The extra bodies vanished into the flood.

A white crow dozing on a rooftop wakened when they started downhill. It stretched and followed them.

30

Murgen was there when Soulcatcher received the news. The report reached the Palace in a remarkably short time and was unusually complete. The Greys worked hard to please their mistress.

The party bringing Gokhale to the warehouse had not yet arrived.

Murgen had been asked to look around the Protector's quarters while he was there. We knew nothing about them. Nobody ever went into her suite. Not since Willow Swan had gone to his reward.

Murgen would have to be questioned about how she lived in private.

Soulcatcher did not retreat there, however. She went out looking for the Radisha right away.

The Radisha knew something had happened to Gokhale but she had not had detailed reports. The women settled in the receiving chamber of the Radisha's austere suite. Soulcatcher told what she knew. She used a very businesslike voice. It was said sometimes that the Protector was her most dangerous and least stable when she stopped being capricious and seemed calmest and most serious.

"It seems the Inspector-General shared some habits with Perhule Khoji. In fact, I'm now assured that his particular weakness was common amongst the senior men of his ministry."

"There were rumors."

"And you did nothing?"

"Chandra Gokhale's private amusements, loathsome as I found them personally, did not prevent his performing perfectly as Inspector-General of the Records. He was particularly adept at generating revenue."

"Indeed." Soulcatcher's businesslike manner wavered momentarily. Murgen would report his amusement at the thought she might actually have a moral opinion. "He was attacked in the same manner as Khoji was."

"Suggesting somebody might have a grudge against the ministry as a whole? Or that the Deceivers pick men of his particular weakness as ceremonial targets?"

"Deceivers didn't kill Gokhale. Of that I'm sure. This was done by the people who lured Swan out and killed him. *If* they killed him."

"If?" The Radisha was startled by the implication.

"We saw no corpse. Note that we have no body this time, either. Men disguised as our men were right there to haul the body away. That's two members of the Privy Council lost in less than a week. Organizationally, they were the most important. They made the machinery work. If the Great General was anywhere nearby, I'd predict that he would be their next target. That gaggle of priests means nothing. They do nothing. They control nothing. My sister proved that if they're killed, they can be replaced by other do-nothings within minutes. Nobody can replace Swan or Gokhale. The Greys are beginning to unravel already."

Murgen made a mental note to mention that Willow Swan might have been less a puppet than he led the world to believe.

"Why couldn't it be the Stranglers?" the Radisha asked.

"Because those people cut the head off that particular serpent the other day." She described events in the Thieves' Garden. Obviously, she had not bothered to share the news before. It was clear that the Protector considered the Princess a necessary but junior partner in her enterprise. "In a matter of days these people, whom we thought ruined forever, have cut the head off one enemy and have crippled the other seriously. There is a dangerous mind behind this."

Not dangerous at all. Not even that lucky. But a sufficiently paranoid mind will discern patterns and threats where only fortune has conspired. Soulcatcher was ever alert for evils as great as her own.

"We knew they couldn't remain in the darkness forever," the Radisha said. She corrected herself hastily. "*I* knew. The Captain reminded me often enough." She did not need to bring up the past and her belief in mistakes she had made. That devil was buried deep, hundreds of miles away. A much more immediate danger was right there in the room with her.

The Protector was a mistake she had abandoned hope of living long enough to correct. Blind to the consequences at the time, she had chosen to mount the tiger. Now her sole choice was to hang on for the rest of the ride.

Soulcatcher said, "We have to recall the Great General. If we can get his troops into the city before our enemies make their next move, we'll have the manpower to hunt them down. You should send the orders immediately. And once the courier is safely off, we should announce that the Great General is returning. Their special dislike for Mogaba should cause them to delay their other plans till they can gather him in as well."

"You think you know what they'll do?"

"I know what I'd do if I came down with the kind of sudden, burning ambition that seems to have taken them over. I wonder if there hasn't been some kind of coup or something?"

Exasperated, the Radisha demanded, "What will they do next?"

"I'll keep that to myself for now. Not that I don't trust you." Soulcatcher probably had abiding suspicions about herself. "I just want to make sure I've identified enough of a pattern to begin tapping into the workings of this new mind. I'm quite talented at that, you know."

The Radisha knew, to her own despair. She said nothing. Soulcatcher sat silently herself, as though waiting for the Princess to speak. But the Radisha had nothing to say.

The Protector mused, "I wonder who it could be? I knew the wizards of old. Neither one has the ambition or imagination or drive, even though both do have the hardness."

The Radisha made a squeak of sound. "The wizards?"

"The two little men. The day-and-night pair. They aren't much of anything but lucky."

"*They* survived?"

"I said they're lucky. Do you recall anyone who didn't go onto the plain who looked like a potential leader? I don't."

"I thought all those people were dead."

"As did I, in most cases. Our Great General claims to have seen most of their bodies personally. But the Great General identified them assuming that the two wizards had been killed first. Hmm. Here I had begun to be suspicious of him. Perhaps his only crime is that he's a fool. Can you think of anyone?"

"Not inside the Company I knew. But there was a Nyueng Bao who had something to do with the Standardbearer's wife. A priest of some sort. He seemed to be totally obsessed with weapons and the martial arts. I ran into him only a few times. And he's never been accounted for in any reports."

"A Master of the Path of the Sword? That would explain a lot. But I killed them all when I— Have you noticed how people keep turning up alive when there's every reason to believe that they're dead?"

An actual smile tried to gnaw its way out of the Radisha's mouth. The woman talking could be considered the mother of all those whose deaths had been celebrated prematurely. "There's sorcery afoot. Nothing should be any great surprise."

"You're right. You're absolutely right. And that's a blade that can have more than one edge." Soulcatcher rose to leave. Her voice changed, became cruel. "More than one edge. A Master of the Path of the Sword. It's been a long time since I visited those people. They may be able to tell me something useful." She stalked out of the room.

The Radisha remained motionless for several minutes, clearly troubled. Then she got up and went to her Anger Chamber. She settled herself there. The unseen spy went after the Protector. She, he discovered, had gone directly to the ramparts. She assembled her small, single-rider carpet, all the while arguing with herself in a dozen querulous voices.

He barely listened. He was too surprised and shocked. There was a white crow up there. It was watching the Protector, who remained unaware of Murgen's presence although, historically, she had been more sensitive to him than to any of the living except her sister. But the bird had no trouble seeing Murgen. It examined him with first one eye, then with the other. Then it winked deliberately. And then it launched itself into the night when the Protector's rookery took flight to accompany her on her travels.

But I *am the white crow!*

The disorientation was brief but as frightening as it had been years ago, when first Murgen had started stumbling around outside his flesh.

I said, "Better get Uncle Doj before we go any farther with this, Tobo." I spotted Kendo Cutter and Runmust. "You guys finally back? How did it go?"

"Perfect. Just like you planned it."

Sahra asked, "You have my present?"

"They're lugging him in now. He's still out cold."

"Drop him right here where I can chat with him when he comes around." Sahra had a wicked gleam in her eye.

I chuckled. "Soulcatcher thinks we're following some grand, carefully orchestrated master plan exquisitely fashioned by a great strategic mastermind. If she knew we were just stumbling around in the dark, hoping we stay lucky until we can open the way for the Captured—"

One-Eye barked, "You telling me you masterminds don't got a next step ready to go, Little Girl?"

"We have several." I did. "And I'm sure the next one hasn't ever occurred to Soulcatcher as being within the realm of possibility. I'm going to bring Master Santaraksita home for supper and give him a chance to sign up for the adventure of a lifetime."

"Heh-heh! I knew it."

Uncle Doj joined us. He was seriously peeved about the way he had been treated lately.

I told him, "One of our friends just reported a conversation between The Thousand Voices and the Radisha. The process of reasoning is beyond my imagination but The Thousand Voices has decided that all her troubles recently are the fault of a Master of the Path of the Sword who should've been killed a long time ago. When last seen, she was off to visit the folks at the Vinh Gao Ghang temple to ask about the man. You may be familiar with that temple."

Doj lost color. His sword hand trembled for an instant. His right eyelid twitched. He turned toward Sahra.

Sahra told him, "It's true. What can she learn there?"

"Speak the tongue of The People."

"No."

The Master of the Path of the Sword accepted what he could not control. You would have to say he was somewhat less than gracious about it, though, if you wanted to report the whole truth.

I said, "You still have a book we want. And you could tell us a great deal that we could use, I think."

He was a stubborn old man. He was determined not to let me stampede him into anything.

I said, "The Thousand Voices has sent for Mogaba. She means to have the army come dig us out. If I could, I'd like to get out of Taglios before she starts. But we have a lot to do and a lot to find out before we can go. Your help would be invaluable. As I keep reminding you, you have people under that plain, too. . . . Huh?"

"What? Sleepy?" Sahra said. "Goblin! See what's the matter with her!"

"I'm all right. I'm fine. I just had what you call an epiphany, I think. Listen. All the evidence indicates that Soulcatcher thinks the Captured are dead. Which would mean that she believes Longshadow is dead. *We* know he's not, which is why we're not worried right now. But if she doesn't know, why isn't she amazed that the world hasn't been overrun by shadows?"

I got a lot of blank looks for my trouble, even from the wizards.

I said, "Look, what it means is, it doesn't matter if Longshadow is dead or alive after all. As long as he stays inside the Shadowgate. There isn't a doomsday sword hanging over the world, certain to fall when the madman croaks. Somebody besides the cleverest wizards will survive."

The less clever wizards caught on then. They brightened up dramatically. Not that either had ever cared much what became of the world after they staggered out of it.

What to do about the Shadowmaster had never been a significant issue to us because there were always more immediate obstacles to overcome before he could become a major concern.

Sahra said as much. "If we can't open the way, there's no point in worrying about how we can keep it closed to those not in our favor."

"I wonder how the Shadowmasters did it? Brute force? The Black Company was still in the far north and the Lance of Passion was up there with them." I stared at Uncle Doj. Others began to do so, too. I wondered aloud, "Could it be that the great shame of the Nyueng Bao isn't nearly as ancient as I thought? Could it be that it just goes back a couple of generations? To about the time that the Shadowmasters appeared, practically manifesting themselves overnight?"

Uncle Doj closed his eyes. They stayed that way for a while. When the old priest opened them again, he glared at me. "Come walking with me, Stone Soldier."

Chandra Gokhale, Inspector-General of the Records and favorer of very young girls, chose that moment to groan. I told Doj, "Indulge me for a few minutes, Uncle. I have a guest to entertain. I promise not to take too long."

Goblin knelt beside the minister, patted his face gently, helped Gokhale to a sitting position. The Inspector-General began to puff up for a bluster storm. As his mouth opened, I leaned down to whisper, "Water sleeps."

Gokhale's head jerked around. In a moment he recalled where he had seen me before. Goblin told him, "All their days are numbered, buddy. And it looks like some of you got a few less days than some others do." Gokhale recognized him, too, though he was supposed to be dead. And when he remembered where he had seen Sahra before, he began to tremble.

Sahra asked, "Would you recall abusing Minh Subredil on several occasions? Subredil certainly remembers. What I think we'll do to requite that is to return it fivefold. The brothers will install you in a tiger cage in a moment. You'll be well treated otherwise. And in a few days maybe we'll bring in the Purohita to keep you company." She chuckled so wickedly I felt a chill. "For all the rest of their days, calling the Heaven and the Earth and the Day and the Night, like brothers, Chandra Gokhale and Arjuna Drupada."

Part of that was some Nyueng Bao formula I didn't understand. But I got the point. And so did Gokhale. He would be caged all the rest of his days with the man he most loathed.

Sahra chuckled again.

She made me nervous when she got like that.

32

I watched the old priest closely as we eased through the spell net surrounding the warehouse. He did not have a yarn amulet. His head twitched and jerked. His feet kept wanting to change direction but his will hacked a way through the illusions. Possibly that was a result of his training on the Path of the Sword. I recalled, though, that Lady had insisted he was a minor wizard.

"Where are we going, Uncle? And why are we going there?"

"We go where no Nyueng Bao ear will hear what I tell you. Old Nyueng Bao would label me a traitor. Young Nyueng Bao would call me a lying fool. Or worse."

And I? I was generally a proponent of the latter view whenever I heard him preaching about his path to inner peace through obsessively continuous preparation for combat. His philosophy had appealed only to a very few of Banh Do Trang's employees, all Nyueng Bao, all too young to have witnessed actual warfare. I understood that the Path of the Sword was not militaristic, but others had trouble grasping that fact.

"You want to maintain your image as an old stiff-neck who wouldn't be caught dead helping a subhuman *jengali* fall and break her skull."

It was too dark to tell but I thought he smiled. "That's an extreme way of stating it but it approximates the facts." His Taglian, never poor, improved now that he had no other audience.

"Are you overlooking the fact that every bit of darkness out here might harbor a bat or crow or rat, or even one of the Protector's shadows?"

"I have nothing to fear from those things. The Thousand Voices already knows everything I'm going to tell you."

But she might not want me to know, too.

We walked in silence for a long time.

Taglios seldom fails to amaze me. Doj cut across a wealthy section, where whole families fort up in estates surrounded by guarded walls. Their youths were out on Salara Road, which grew up ages ago to provide them with their diversions. Reason insisted that beggars ought to be plentiful where the wealth was concentrated, but that was not the case. The extremely poor were not allowed to offend the sight of the mighty with their presence.

There, as everywhere, odors assailed the nostrils but these scents were sandalwood, cloves and perfumes.

After that, Doj led me into the dark, crowded streets of a temple district. We stepped aside to let a band of Gunni acolytes pass. The boys were bullying the people living in the streets. I thought we might have trouble with them, too, which would have ended with them suffering a lot of pain, but a brake on their misbehavior saved them from its consequences. That arrived in the form of three Greys.

The Shadar do not disdain the caste system entirely but they do hold to the notion that the highest caste must include not just the priests and men qualified by birth to become priests, but also, certainly, any men of the Shadar faith. And that faith, which is an extremely heretical and Gunni-infected bastard offshoot of my own One True Faith, contains a strong strain of charity toward the weak and the unfortunate.

The Greys methodically applied their bamboo canes and invited the youths to take up any complaints with the Protector. The acolytes were smarter than they pretended. They got the hell out of there before the Greys used their whistles to invite all their friends to the caning.

All part of night in the city. Doj and I drifted onward.

Eventually he led me to a place called the Deer Park, which is an expanse of wilderness near the center of the city. It had been created by some despot of centuries past.

I told Doj, "I really don't need all this exercise." I wondered if he had some goofball plan to murder me and leave the body under the trees. But what would be the point?

Doj was Doj. With him, you never knew.

"I feel more comfortable here," he said. "But I never stay long. There is a company of rangers charged with keeping squatters out. They consider anyone not Taglian and high caste a squatter. This is good. This log has shaped itself to my posterior."

The log in question tripped me. I got back onto my feet and said, "I'm listening."

"Sit. This will take a while."

"Leave out the begats." Which was a Jaicuri Vehdna colloquialism having to do with difficulties memorizing scripture, which you have to do as a child. I meant, "Don't bother telling me whose fault it was and why they're such bloody villains for it. Just tell me what happened."

"Asking a storyteller not to embellish is like asking a fish to give up water."

"I do have to go to work tomorrow."

"As you will. You are aware, are you not, that the Free Companies of Khatovar and the roving bands of Stranglers who murder for the glory of Kina share a common ancestry?"

"There's enough suggestion in our recent Annals to allow for that interpretation," I admitted. Caution seemed indicated.

"My place amongst the Nyueng Bao would correspond roughly with yours as

Annalist of the Black Company. It includes, as well, the role of the priest in the Strangler band—whose secondary obligation is to maintain a sound oral history of the band. Over the centuries the *toog* have lost their respect for education."

My own studies suggested that a great deal of evolution had taken place in my Company during those same centuries. Probably a lot more than had been the case with the Deceiver bands. They had stayed inside one culture that had not changed a lot. Meanwhile, the Black Company kept moving into stranger and stranger lands, old soldiers being replaced by young foreigners who had no connection with the past and no idea that Khatovar even existed.

Doj seemed to echo my thoughts. "The Strangler bands are pale imitations of the original Free Companies. The Black Company retains the name and some of the memories, but you're philosophically much farther from the original than the Deceivers are. Your band is ignorant of its true antecedents and has been kept that way willfully, mainly through the manipulations of the goddess Kina, but also, to a lesser extent, by others who didn't want your Company to become what it had been in another time."

I waited. He did not volunteer to explain. Doj was difficult that way.

He did, I suppose, do something that was even harder for him. He told the truth about his own people. "Nyueng Bao are the almost pure-blooded descendants of the people of one of the Free Companies. One that chose not to go back."

"But the Black Company is supposed to be the only one that didn't go back. The Annals say—"

"They tell you only what those who recorded them knew. My ancestors arrived here after the Black Company finished laying the land to waste and moved on north, already having lost sight of its divine mission. Deserting in its own way, through ignorance of what it was supposed to be. By then it was already three generations old and had made no effort to maintain the purity of its blood. It had just fought the war which is the first that your Annalists remember and was almost completely destroyed. That seems to be the fate of the Black Company. To be reduced to a handful, then to reconstitute itself. Again and again. Losing something of its previous self each time."

"And the fate of your Company?" I noted that he did not mention a name. No matter, really. No name would mean anything to me.

"To sink ever deeper into ignorance itself. I know the truth. I know the secrets and the old ways. But I'm the last. Unlike other Companies, we brought our families with us. We were a late experiment. We had too much to lose. We deserted. We went and hid in the swamps. But we've kept our lineage pure. Almost."

"And the pilgrimages? The old people who died in Jaicur? Hong Tray? And the great, dark, terrible secret of the Nyueng Bao that Sahra worries about so much?"

"The Nyueng Bao have many dark secrets. All the Free Companies had dark secrets. We were instruments of the darkness. The Soldiers of Darkness. The Bone

Warriors charged with opening the way for Kina. Stone Soldiers warring for the honor of being remembered for all eternity by having our names written in golden letters in glittering stone. We failed because our ancestors were imperfect in their devotion. In every company there were those who were too weak to bring on the Year of the Skulls."

"The old people?"

"Ky Dam and Hong Tray. Ky Dam was the last elected Nyueng Bao captain. There was no one to take his place. Hong Tray was a witch with the curse of foresight. She was the last true priest. Priestess."

"Curse of foresight?"

"She never foresaw anything good."

I sensed that he did not want to get into that subject. I recalled that Hong Tray's final prophecy involved Murgen and Sahra, which certainly was an offense to all right-thinking Nyueng Bao—and was not yet a prophecy completely fulfilled, probably.

"The great sin of the Nyueng Bao?"

"You had that idea from Sahra, of course. And she, like all those born after the coming of the Shadowmasters, believes that 'sin' is what caused the Nyueng Bao to flee into the swamps. She believes wrongly. That flight involved no sin, but survival. The true black sin occurred within my own lifetime." His voice tightened up. He had strong feelings about this.

I waited.

"I was a small boy just taking my first small steps on the Path of the Sword when the stranger came. He was a personable man of middle years. His name was Ashutosh Yaksha. In the oldest form of the language Ashutosh meant something like Despair of the Wicked. Yaksha meant much the same as it does in Taglian today." Which was "good spirit." "People were prepared to believe he was a supernatural being because he had a white skin. A very pale, white skin, lighter than Goblin or Willow Swan, who sometimes get some sunlight. He wasn't an albino, though. He had normal eyes. His hair wasn't quite as blond as Swan's is. In sum, he was a magical creature to most Nyueng Bao. He spoke the language oddly but he did speak it. He said he wanted to study at the Vinh Gao Ghang temple, the fame of which had reached him far away.

"When pressed about his origins, he insisted that he hailed from 'The Land of Unknown Shadows, beneath the stars of the Noose.'"

"He claimed to have come off the glittering stone?"

"Not quite. That was never clear. There or beyond. No one pressed him hard. Not even Ky Dam or Hong Tray, though he troubled them. Very early we learned that Ashutosh was a powerful sorcerer. And in those days many of the older people still knew about the origins of the Nyueng Bao. It was feared that he might have been sent to summon us home. That proved to be untrue. For a long time Ashutosh seemed to be nothing but what he claimed, a student who wanted to absorb whatever wisdom had accumulated at the temple of Ghanghesha. Which had been a holy place since the Nyueng Bao first entered the swamp."

"But there's a but. Right? The man was a villain after all?"

"He was indeed. In fact, Ashutosh was the man you knew later as Shadowspinner. He was there to find our Key, sent by his teacher and mentor, whom you came to know as Longshadow. At a young age this man had stumbled across rumors that not all the Free Companies had returned to Khatovar. What he understood from that, that nobody else realized, was that each Company still outside must possess a talisman capable of opening and closing the Shadowgate. An ambitious man could use that talisman to recruit rakshasas he could send out to do evil for him. The power to kill becomes the ultimate power in the hands of a man who has no reservations about employing it."

"So this Ashutosh Yaksha found the Key?"

"He only assured himself that it existed. He wormed his way into the confidence of the senior priests. One day someone let something drop. Soon afterward, Ashutosh announced that he had received word that his teacher, mentor and spiritual father, Maricha Manthara Dhumraksha, impressed by his reports on the temple, had chosen to come visit. Dhumraksha turned out to be a tall, incredibly skinny man who always wore a mask, apparently because his face was deformed."

"You heard a name like Maricha Manthara Dhumraksha and you didn't suspect something?"

I could not see Doj in the darkness but I could feel his unhappy frown. He said, "I was a small child."

"And the Nyueng Bao aren't interested in anything not their own. Yes. I'm Vehdna, Uncle, but I recognize the names Manthara and Dhumraksha as those of legendary Gunni demons. Even though you walk amongst lesser beings, you might keep your ears open. That way, when a nasty *jengali* sorcerer pulls your leg, you'll at least have a clue."

Doj grunted. "He had a golden tongue, Dhumraksha did. When he discovered that each decade, as the custom was then, a band of the leading men undertook a pilgrimage south—"

"He invited himself along and tricked somebody into letting him examine the Key."

"Close. But not quite. Yes. You did guess correctly. The pilgrimage went to the very Shadowgate. The pilgrims would spend ten days there waiting for a sign. I don't believe anyone knew what that might be anymore. But the traditions had to be observed. The pilgrims, however, never took the actual Key with them. They carried a replica charged with a few simple spells meant to fool an inattentive thief. The real Key stayed home. The old men didn't really want a sign from the other side."

"Longshadow got in a hurry."

"He did. When the pilgrims arrived at the Shadowgate, they found Ashutosh

Yaksha and a half-dozen other sorcerers waiting. Several were fugitives from that northern realm of darkness where the Black Company was then in service. When Dhumraksha used the false key, his band found themselves under attack from the other side of the Shadowgate. Before the gateway could be stopped up, using the power of Longshadow's true name, three of the would-be Shadowmasters had perished. The one called the Howler, cruelly injured, had fled. The survivors quickly became the feuding, conquering monsters your brothers found in place when they arrived. And the same disaster caused the Mother of Night to reawaken and begin scheming toward a Year of the Skulls once more."

"And that's the great sin of the Nyueng Bao? Letting themselves be hoodwinked by sorcerers?"

"In those days there was little contact with the world outside the swamp. Banh Do Trang's family managed all outside trade. Once a decade a handful of the older men traveled to the Shadowgate. About as frequently, Gunni ascetics would enter the swamp hoping to purify their souls. These Gunni hermits were obviously crazy or they wouldn't have come into the swamps in the first place. They were always tolerated. And Ghanghesha found a home."

"Where does The Thousand Voices fit?"

"She learned the story from the Howler around the time we were trapped in Dejagore. Or soon afterward. She came to the temple soon after we returned, the best of us exhausted, our old men all dead, including our Captain and Speaker, and witch Hong Tray with them. There was no one but me left who knew everything—though Gota and Thai Dei knew some, and Sahra a little, they being of the family of Ky Dam and Hong Tray. The Thousand Voices went to the temple while I was away. She used her power to intimidate and torture the priests until they surrendered the mysterious object that had been given them for safekeeping ages ago. They didn't even know what it was anymore. They really can't be blamed but I can't help blaming them. And there you have it. All the secrets of the Nyueng Bao."

I doubted that. "I doubt that seriously. But it's a basis from which to work. Are you going to cooperate? If we get Narayan Singh to divulge what he did with the Key?"

"If you'll undertake a promise never to tell anyone what I told you here tonight."

"I swear it on the Annals." This was too easy. "I won't say a word to a soul." But I did not say anything about not writing it down.

I did not extract an oath from him.

Sometime, eventually, he would face the moral dilemma that had swallowed the Radisha once it seemed that the Company would fulfill its obligation to her and it was coming time for her to deliver on her own commitments. Once Uncle Doj had his own people out from under the glittering stone, his reliability as an ally would turn to smoke.

Easily dealt with when the time came, I thought. I told Doj, "I still have to work tomorrow. And it's a whole lot later now than it was an hour ago."

He rose, evidently relieved that I had not asked many questions. I did have a few in mind, such as why the Nyueng Bao had risked more frequent pilgrimages to the Shadowgate once the Shadowmasters were in power, adding women and children and old people to the entourage. So I asked anyway, while we were walking.

He told me, "The Shadowmasters permitted it. It added to their feelings of superiority. And it let us keep them thinking that we didn't have the real Key, that we were searching for it. Our own people believed that was what we were doing. Only Ky Dam and Hong Tray knew the whole truth. The Shadowmasters were hoping we'd find it for them."

"The Thousand Voices figured it out."

"Yes. Her crows went everywhere and heard everything."

"And in those days she had a very sneaky demon at her beck and call." I continued to pester him all the way back to the warehouse, cleverly trying to find his remaining secrets by coloring in more map around the blank places.

I did not fool him a bit.

Before I dragged off to bed, I visited Sahra, Murgen and Goblin one more time. "You people get all of that?"

"Most of it," Murgen said. "This weary old slave has been doing some other chores, too."

"Think he told the truth?"

"Mostly," Sahra admitted. "He told no lies that I noticed, but I don't think he told the whole truth."

"Well, of course not. He's Nyueng Bao right down to his twisted toe bones. And a wizard besides."

Before Sahra got indignant, Goblin told me, "There was a white crow out there with you."

"I saw it," I said. "I figured it was Murgen."

Murgen said, "It wasn't Murgen. I was there disembodied. Same as now."

"What was it, then? *Who* was it?"

"I don't know," Murgen replied.

I did not entirely believe him. Maybe it was a false intuition but I was sure he had a strong suspicion.

33

Master Santaraksita hardly waited till there were no eavesdroppers before he approached me. "Dorabee, your record is beginning to look bad. Two days ago you were late. Yesterday you didn't show up at all. This morning you don't look alert and ready for work."

I was not. I would have been testy with anyone else. In this case I barely noticed that his words were not spoken in a tone in keeping with their content. I sensed relief in him at my return and a lingering whiff of a fear that I would not. I lied. "I had a fever. I couldn't stay on my feet for more than few minutes at a time. I tried to come in but I was so weak I got lost for a while and eventually ended up just going home."

"Should you even be here today, then?" Changing course, sounding overly worried.

"I have a little more strength today. I have a lot of work to do. I really want to keep this job, Sri. None other would put me so close to so much wisdom."

"Where is home, Dorabee?" I had collected my broom. He was following me. Eyes were following us, some with a knowing look that told me Santaraksita may have pursued other young men in the past.

I was ready for this one because I knew he had tried to follow me. "I share a small room near the waterfront in the Sirada neighborhood with several friends from the army." A common situation throughout Taglios, where men outnumber women almost two to one because so many men have come in from the Territories, hoping to make their fortunes.

"Why didn't you go home when you came back, Dorabee?"

Oh-oh. "Sri?"

"Your mother, your brothers, your sisters, and their wives and husbands and children all still dwell in the same place where you lived as a child. They believed you were dead."

Oh, darn! He had gone to see them? The busybody. "I don't get along with those people, Sri." Which was an outright lie on behalf of Dorabee Dey Banerjae. The man I had known had been very close to his family. "When I came back from the Ki-aulune wars, I was so horribly changed that they wouldn't have recognized me. Had

I gone home, it wouldn't have been long before they found out things about me that would've caused them to disown me. I preferred to let them think Dorabee was dead. The boy they remembered no longer exists anyway."

I hoped he would interpret that according to his own wishful thinking.

He bit. "I understand."

"I'm grateful for your concern, Sri. If you will excuse me?" I went to work.

I worked briskly, deep in thought. What I needed to do required me to let myself be seduced. I had no experience along those lines, from either of the possible view-points. But the old men tell me I am clever, and after a while I thought I saw a way by which events could proceed as desired without Surendranath Santaraksita putting himself in a position of emotional or moral risk greater than he had when he tried to follow me home and I had to send Tobo out to rescue him. Which, of course, he did not know.

I had a weak spell toward mid-morning, at a point where old Baladitya could repay his small debt by being solicitous. By the time Master Santaraksita manufac-tured a reasonable excuse to put himself into my proximity, I had collected myself and was back at work.

A few hours later I contrived to throw up my lunch, then made a show of clean-ing up. I suffered dizzy spells later still. The last occurred after most of the librarians and copyists had gone home, despite the threat of further showers. The afternoon storm had not been as terrible as most. Taglians generally viewed that as a bad omen.

Santaraksita played his part perfectly. He was beside me before my spell was over. Nervously, he suggested, "You'd better quit now, Dorabee. You've put in more than your day's work. The rest will be here tomorrow. I'll walk along with you to make sure you're all right."

A relapse threatened as I began to protest that that was not necessary. So I said, "Thank you, Sri. Your generosity knows no bounds. What about Baladitya?" The old copyist's grandson had failed to show again.

"He's practically on our way. We'll just leave him off first." I tried to think of some small act or something I could say that would encourage Santaraksita's fantasy, but could not. That proved unnecessary, anyway. The man was determined to hook himself. All because I knew how to read.

Weird.

Riverwalker just happened to be hanging around outside when Master Santarak-sita, Baladitya and I left the library grounds. I made a little gesture to let him know we were going to do it. More signs and gestures along the way let him know that the old man should be rounded up as soon as Santaraksita and I left him. He was a witness who could say that the Master Librarian had been seen last in my company. And he might be useful.

Not far from the warehouse, I suffered another mild spell. Santaraksita put an arm around me to help. I drifted back into my safe place some and went on with the game. By now we were surrounded, at a distance, by Company brothers. "Just straight ahead," I told Santaraksita, who was becoming confused by the outer web of spells. "Just hold my hand."

Moments later a gentle tap at the base of the Master Librarian's skull let me step away from my uncomfortable role.

Here I'm known as Sleepy. I'm the Annalist of the Black Company. I brought you here to assist in the translation of material recorded by some of my earliest predecessors."

Santaraksita began to fuss. Kendo Cutter placed a hand over his mouth and nose so he could not breathe. After several such episodes, even a member of the priestly class recognized the connection between silence and unimpeded breathing.

I told him, "We have a pretty cruel reputation, Sri. And it's rightly deserved. No, I'm not Dorabee Dey Banerjae. Dorabee did die during the Kiaulune wars. Fighting on our side."

"What do you want?" In a shaky voice.

"Like I said, we need to translate some old books. Tobo, get the books from my worktable."

The boy went away grumbling about why was it always he who had to run and fetch.

Master Santaraksita was very put out when he discovered that some of what I wanted translated had been pilfered from his own restricted stacks. In fact, when I told him, "I want to start with this one," and showed him what I believed to be the earliest of the Annals, he lost some color.

"I'm doomed, Dorabee . . . I'm sorry, young man. Sleepy, was it?"

"Haw!" One-Eye bellowed, having appeared only moments before. "Did you ever go sniffing up the wrong tree. My little darling Sleepy, here, is all girl."

I smirked. "Darn! Here we go again, Sri. Now you have to get your mind around the fact that a *woman* can read. Ah. Here's Baladitya. You'll be working with him. Thank you, River. Did you run into any trouble?"

Santaraksita began to balk again. "I won't—"

Kendo silenced him again.

"You'll translate and you'll work hard at it, Sri. Or we won't feed you. We aren't the bhadrhalok. We quit talking about it a long time ago. We're doing it. It's just your misfortune to get caught up in it."

Sahra arrived. She was soaked. "It's raining again. I see you landed your fish." She collapsed into a chair, considered Surendranath Santaraksita. "I'm exhausted. My nerves were on edge all day. The Protector returned from the swamp at noon. She was in a totally foul mood. She had a huge argument with the Radisha, right in front of us."

"The Radisha stood up to her?"

"She did. She's reached her limit. Another Bhodi disciple came this morning but the Greys stopped him from burning himself. Then the Protector announced that she was going to take the night away from us by letting the shadows run loose from now on. That's when the Radisha started screaming."

Santaraksita looked so completely appalled by the implications of Sahra's revelations that I had to laugh. "No," he insisted. "It's not funny." Then we discovered that he was not really concerned about the shadows. "The Protector is going to clip my ears. At the very least. These books weren't supposed to be in the library at all. I was supposed to have destroyed them ages ago, but I couldn't do that to any book. Then I forgot about them. I should've locked them up somewhere."

"Why?" Sahra snapped. She did not get an answer.

I asked her, "Did you make any headway?"

"I didn't get a chance to pick up any pages. I did get into the Radisha's suite. I did eavesdrop on her and Soulcatcher. And I did pick up a little other information."

"For example?"

"For example, the Purohita and all the sacerdotal members of the Privy Council will be leaving the Palace tomorrow to attend a convocation of senior priests in preparation for this year's Druga Pavi."

The Druga Pavi is the biggest Gunni holiday of the Taglian year. Taglios, with all its numerous cults and countless minorities, boasted some holiday almost every day, but the Druga Pavi beggared all the rest.

"But that doesn't come up until after the end of the rainy season." I had a funny feeling about this.

"I got a premonition from it myself," Sahra admitted.

"River, take the Master and copyist and make sure they're as comfortable as we can make them here. Have Goblin provide them with chokers and make sure they understand how they work." I asked Sahra, "Did you happen to hear about this before or after Soulcatcher got back from terrorizing the swamp?"

"After, of course."

"Of course. She suspects something. Kendo. As soon as it's light out tomorrow, I want you to head for the Kernmi What. See what you can find out about this meeting without giving away how interested you are. If you see a lot of Greys or other Shadar around, don't bother. Just get back here with that word."

"Suppose this's a genuine opportunity?" Sahra asked.

"It'll stay genuine as long as they're outside the Palace. Won't it?"

"Maybe it would be best to just kill them. Put some flash buttons on the corpses. That would make Soulcatcher really mad."

"Wait. I'm having a thought. It might just be straight from *al-Shiel*." I waved a finger in the air as though counting musical beats. "Yes. That's it. We need to hope the Protector *is* trying to bait a trap with the Purohita." I explained my thinking.

"That's good," Sahra said. "But if we're going to make it work, you and Tobo will have to go inside with me."

"And I can't. There's no way I can miss work the day after Master Santaraksita disappears. Get Murgen. See if he was around the Palace today. Find out if there's a trap and where it's at. If Soulcatcher is going to be away, maybe you and Tobo can do it on your own."

"I don't want to belittle your genius, Sleepy, but this is something I've thought about a lot. Off and on for years. The possibility is partly why I keep trying to worm my way closer to the center of things. The truth is, it can't be managed by fewer than three people. I need Shiki and I need Sawa."

"Let me think." Sahra got Murgen's attention while I thought. Murgen seemed to be more alert and more interested in the outside world now, particularly where his wife and son were concerned. He must have begun to understand. "I've got it, Sahra! We can have Goblin be Sawa."

"Ain't no fucking way," Goblin said. He repeated himself four or five times in as many languages, just in case somebody missed his point. "What the fuck is the matter with you, woman?"

"You're as small as I am. We rub a little betel-nut juice on your face and hands, dress you up in my Sawa outfit, have Sahra sew your mouth shut so you can't shoot it off every time the urge hits you, nobody will know the difference. As long as you keep looking down, which is what Sawa mostly does."

"That may be a solution," Sahra said, ignoring Goblin's continued protests. "In fact, the more I think about it the better I like it. No disrespect meant but in a major pinch, Goblin would be a lot more useful than you would."

"I know. There you go. And I could go ahead and be Dorabee Dey besides. Isn't it wonderful?"

"Women," Goblin grumbled. "Can't live with them but they won't go away."

Sahra said, "You'd better start learning Sawa's quirks from Sleepy." To me she said, "There'll be plenty of work for Sawa. I made sure. And Narita is eager to get her back. Tobo, you need to get some sleep. Nobody's connected you with Gokhale but you'll still need to be alert."

"I really don't like going up there, Mom."

"You think I do? We all have—"

"Yes. I think you do. I think you keep going up there because you want the danger. I think it might be hard for you when you do have to stop taking risks. I think when that happens, we're all going to have to watch you close so you don't do something that might get us all killed along with you."

That was a kid who had been doing a lot of thinking. Maybe with a little help from one or more uncles. Sounded to me like he might be riding knee to knee with the truth, too.

34

I settled into a chair outside the cage where Narayan Singh was being kept. He was awake but he ignored me. I said, "The Daughter of Night still lives."

"I know that."

"You do? How?"

"I'd know if you'd harmed her."

"Then you need to know this. She isn't going to stay unharmed a whole lot longer. The only reason she's healthy now is that we want your cooperation. If we can't get it, then there's not much reason to keep on feeding her. Or you, either. Though I do intend to keep my word about taking care of you. Because I'd want you to see everything you value destroyed before you're allowed to die yourself. Which reminds me. Aridatha couldn't be with us tonight. His captain was concerned that there might be some unrest. Another Bhodi disciple planned to burn himself. So we'll have to wait until tomorrow night."

Narayan made a sound like a whispered moan. He did not want to have to acknowledge my existence, for existence, and mine in particular, was making him very unhappy. Which made me happy, though I had no personal grudge. My enmity was all very sanitary, very institutional, very much on behalf of my brothers who had been injured. And on behalf of my brothers who were imprisoned beneath the earth.

I suggested, "Maybe you should go to Kina for guidance."

Such a look he gave me. Narayan Singh had no sense of humor and did not recognize sarcasm when it struck from the grass and sank its fangs in his ankle.

I told him, "Just to recap: I don't have much patience left. I don't have much time left. We've leaped onto the tiger's back. The big catfight is coming."

Catfight. Universal male slang for a squabble amongst women.

Oh, really?

It had just occurred to me. We were all women in this fight. Sahra and I. The Radisha and Soulcatcher. Kina and the Daughter of Night. Uncle Doj was as close to a principal as any man was right now. And Narayan, though he was mainly the Daughter of Night's shadow.

Strange. Strange.

"Narayan, when the fur starts flying, I won't be much interested in looking out for your friend. But I'm definitely going to take care of you."

I started to leave.

"I can't do this thing." Singh's voice was almost inaudible.

"Work on it, Narayan. If you love the girl. If you don't want your goddess to have to start all over from scratch." I thought I had that much power. By killing the right people, I could lay Kina down to sleep for another age. And I would if I could not get my own brothers out of the ground.

I found Banh Do Trang awaiting me in the little corner where I worked and slept. He did not look well, which was not surprising. He was not too many years younger than Goblin and did not have Goblin's wondrous resources. "Can I be of any service, Uncle?"

"I understand Doj told you the story of our people." The best he could manage was a hoarse whisper.

"He told me *a* story. There're always doubts left behind when any Nyueng Bao shares a secret with me."

"Heh. Heh-heh. You're a bright young woman, Sleepy. Few illusions and no obvious obsessions. I think Doj was as honest with you as he could compel himself to be. Assuming he was honest with me when he consulted me afterward. He finally heard me when I told him that this's a new age. That that was what Hong Tray wanted to show us when she chose the *jengal* to become Sahra's husband. We're all lost children. We must join hands. That, too, is what Hong Tray wanted us to understand."

"She could've said so."

"She was Hong Tray. A seeress. A Nyueng Bao seeress. Would you have her issue blunt rescripts like the Radisha and Protector?"

"Absolutely."

Do Trang chuckled. Then he seemed to fall asleep.

Was that that? I wondered. "Uncle?"

"Uh? Oh? I'm sorry, young woman. Listen. I don't think anyone else has mentioned it. Maybe no one else but Gota and I have seen it. But there's a ghost in this place. We've seen it several times the past two nights."

"A ghost?" Was Murgen getting so strong people were starting to see him?

"It's a cold and evil thing, Sleepy. Like something that's happiest skulking around the mouths of graves or slithering through a mountain of bones. Like that vampire child in the tiger cage. You should be very wary of her. And I think I should find my way to bed. Before I fall asleep here and your friends begin to talk."

"If they're going to gossip about me, I can't think of anyone I'd rather have them connect me with."

"Someday when I'm young again. Next time around the Wheel."

"Good night, Uncle."

I thought I might read for a while but I fell asleep almost instantly. Sometime during the night I discovered that Do Trang's ghost did exist. I awakened, instantly alert, and saw a vaguely human shimmer standing nearby, evidently watching me. The old man had done a good job describing it, too. I wondered if it might not be Death Himself.

It went away as soon as it sensed my scrutiny.

I lay there trying to put it together. Murgen? Soulcatcher spying? An unknown? Or what it felt like, the girl in the tiger cage out for an ectoplasmic stroll?

I tried reason but was still too tired to stick with it long.

There was something wrong with the city. In addition to its extraordinarily clean smell. The rain had continued throughout most of the night. And in addition to the stunned looks on the faces of street-dwellers, who had survived their worst night yet. No. It was a sort of bated-breath feeling that got stronger as I approached the library. Maybe it was some sort of psychic phenomenon.

I stopped. The Captain used to say you had to trust your instincts. If it felt like something was wrong, then I should take time to figure out why I felt that way. I turned slowly.

No street poor here. But that was understandable. There were dead people around here. The survivors would be clinging to whatever shelter they could find, afraid the Greys would replace the shadows by day. But the Greys were absent, too. And traffic was lighter than it should be. And most of the tiny one-man stalls that sprawled out into the thoroughfare were not in evidence.

There was fear in the air. People expected something to happen. They had seen something that troubled them deeply. What that might be was not obvious, though. When I asked one of the merchants who was bold enough to be out, he ignored my question completely and tried to convince me that there was no way I could manage another day without a hammered-brass censer.

In a moment I decided he might be right. I paused to speak to another brass merchant whose space lay within eyeshot of the library. "Where is everyone this morning?" I asked, examining a long-spouted teapot sort of thing with no real utility.

A furtive shift of the merchant's eyes toward the library suggested there was substance to my premonitions. And whatever had spooked him had taken place quite recently. No Taglian neighborhood remains quiet and empty for long.

I seldom carry money but did have a few coins on me this morning. I bought the useless teapot. "A gift for my wife. For finally producing a son."

"You're not from around here, are you?" the brass smith asked.

"No. I'm from . . . Dejagore."

The man nodded to himself, as if that explained everything. When I started to move on, he murmured, "You don't want to go that way, Dejagoran."

"Ah?"

"Be in no hurry. Find a long way around that place."

I squinted at the library. I saw nothing unusual. The grounds appeared completely normal, though some men were working on the garden. "Ah." I continued forward only till I could slide into the mouth of an alley.

Why were there gardeners there? Only the Master Librarian ever brought them in.

I caught glimpses of something wheeling above the library. It drifted down to settle on the ironwork of the gate, above Adoo's head. I took it for a lone pigeon at first but when it folded its wings, I saw that it was a white crow. And a crow with a sharper eye than Adoo had. But Adoo was accustomed to posting himself in the gateway.

That constituted another warning sign.

The white crow looked right at me. And winked. Or maybe just blinked, but I preferred the implication of intelligence and conspiratorial camaraderie.

The crow dropped onto Adoo's shoulder. The startled gateman nearly jumped out of his sandals. The bird evidently said something. Adoo jumped again and tried to catch it. After he failed, he ran into the library. Moments later Shadar disguised as librarians and copyists rushed out and began trying to bring the crow down with stones. The bird got the heck out of there.

I followed its example, heading in another direction. I was more alert than I had been in years. What was going on? Why were they there? Obviously they were lying in wait. For me? Who else? But why? What had I done to give myself away?

Maybe nothing. Though failing to show up to be questioned would count as damning evidence. But I was not lunatic enough to try to bluff my way through whatever it was the Greys were trying to do.

The milk was spilt. No going back. But I did want to mourn the one volume of ancient Annals I had not yet been able to locate and pilfer.

All the way home I tried to reason out what had brought out the Greys. Surendranath Santaraksita had not been missing long enough to cause any official interest. In fact, some mornings the Master Librarian did not arrive until much later than this. I gave it up before I threw my brain out of joint. Murgen could go poking around down there. He could find the answer by eavesdropping.

Murgen was busy eavesdropping even though it was daytime. He was worried about Sahra and Tobo. And maybe even a little about Goblin. I found One-Eye, hung over but attentive, at the table where the mist engine resided. Mother Gota and Uncle Doj were there as well, tense and attentive themselves. Which told me that Sahra was determined to go ahead with our most daring stroke yet. To my amazement, One-Eye hustled over—in reality, a slow shuffle—and patted me on my back. "We heard you were coming in, Little Girl. We were scared shitless they were going to get you."

"What?"

"Murgen warned us there was a trap. He heard some of the Grey bosses talking about it when he was scouting to see what Sahra was headed into. The old bitch Soulcatcher herself was out there waiting for you. Well, not exactly you personally, just somebody who goes around stealing books that aren't supposed to be there in the first place."

"You've lost me good, old man. Start someplace where I can see a couple of landmarks."

"Somebody followed you and your boyfriend yesterday. Somebody more suspicious of him than of you. Evidently a part-time spy for the Protector."

We knew there were informants out there getting paid piecework rates. We tried not to be vulnerable to them.

"Also evidently with a boner for your boyfriend."

"One-Eye!"

"All right. For your boss. More or less literally. He went and told the Greys that this dirty old man was about to force perversions on one of the youths who worked for him. A few Greys went to the library and started poking around and asking questions and quickly discovered that some funds had gone missing, and Santaraksita as well, when they started dragging people out of bed and pulling them in. Then they discovered several books missing also, including some great rarities and even a couple that were supposed to have been removed from the library years ago but had not been. *That* got back to Catcher. She got her sweet little behind down there in about ten seconds and started threatening to eat people alive and hurting anybody whose looks she didn't like."

"And I almost walked into the middle of it." I mused, "How did they know the books were gone? I replaced them with discards." But maybe Master Santaraksita, if he was a crook, had been doing that, too.

If he had been corrupt, he had had me fooled.

We would have to talk.

"Near as Murgen could find out, Dorabee Dey Banerjae isn't suspected of anything worse than naïveté. Surendranath Santaraksita, though, is in deep shit. Soulcatcher is going to kill him one limb at a time and let him watch the crows eat them as they go. And after that she's going to get nasty." One-Eye grinned a grin in which just the one lonely tooth loomed. Not exactly a recommendation of his talents as the Company dental specialist.

"Say what you like about Soulcatcher, she doesn't put up with any corruption."

Which was just another black mark in her ledger as far as One-Eye was concerned.

"I'm safe," I said. "Here's food for thought. A white crow was waiting at the gate, possibly to warn me. It made a definite attempt to communicate. So what's the story with Sahra?"

"She's going ahead. That Jaul Barundandi is a real dimwit. He bought Goblin's feeble imitation of your Sawa character. Then he tried to get Tobo away from Sahra. Sahra threatened to tell his wife."

Minh Subredil was going to have trouble staying employed if she kept up the bad attitude.

"The cover team in place?"

"Little Girl, who's been doing this shit since before your great-grandmother was born?"

"You always check again. And keep on checking. Because sooner or later, you're going to save someone who overlooked something. Is the evacuation team operational?" Chances were good we were going to have to leave Taglios long before I wanted. Soulcatcher soon would be hunting us hard.

One-Eye said, "Ask Do Trang. He said he'd take care of it. You might find it interesting to note that Catcher dropped the watch on Arjana Drupada when the library jumped to the head of her list and she needed trustworthy people there."

"She doesn't have enough to go around?"

"Not that she trusts. Most of those she's had watching the Bhodi disciples so she can head them off before they pull any more suicide stunts."

"Then we have to hit Drupada—"

"Go teach your granny to suck eggs, Little Girl. Like I said, who was playing these games when Granny's mommy was still shitting her nappies?"

"Who's covering the warehouse, then?" Having so many things in the air meant that every brother had to be occupied somewhere. Soulcatcher was not alone in facing manpower limitations.

"You and me, Little Girl. Pooch and Spiff are around somewhere, being a mixture of sentries and couriers."

"You're sure Drupada is clean?"

"Murgen checks every half hour. Much as he'd rather be haunting his honey. Friend Arjana is clean. For now. But how long will it last? And Murgen's also been keeping an eye on Slink at Semchi. Checking him every couple of hours. Looks like that's going to happen today, too. Soulcatcher is going to shit. She's just going to shit rocks. We're going to do everything but stroll up and bite her on the tit today."

"Language, old man. Language."

Uncle Doj murmured something.

One-Eye hastened to the mist projector.

37

Despite her enthusiasm the night before, Sahra had been worried about having Goblin along, playing Sawa's role. The little man was not reliable. He was bound to do something. . . .

She did not give him enough credit. He had not survived so long by doing stupid things in tight places. He was determined to be more completely Sawa than ever I had played the role. He did nothing on his own. Minh Subredil guided him completely. But over his conservative role-playing he laid a glamour of disinterest. Jaul Barundandi and everyone else merely gave the idiot woman a glance and concentrated on Shiki, who appeared particularly attractive this morning. Who carried her flute hung on a thong around her neck. Anyone who tried to use force would suffer a cruel surprise.

The flute was not new but the Ghanghesha that Shiki carried was. Today even Sawa carried a statue of the god. Jaul Barundandi mocked Subredil. "When will you start carrying a Ghanghesha in each hand?" This was after he had been threatened because of Shiki and he was not feeling kindly.

Subredil bent and whispered to her Ghanghesha, something about pardoning Barundandi because at heart he was a good man who needed help finding his anchor within the light. Barundandi heard some of that. It disarmed him for a while.

He turned the madwoman and her companions over to his wife, who had developed an almost proprietary interest lately. Subredil, in particular, made her look good because she got so much work done.

Narita, too, noted the Ghanghesha. "If religious devotion will win you a better life next time around the Wheel, Subredil, you're headed for the priestly class for sure." Then the fat woman frowned. "But didn't you leave your Ghanghesha here yesterday?"

"Ah? Ah! Ah! I did? I thought I lost that one forever. I didn't know what had become of it. Where is it? Where is it?" She had prepared for this, though the Ghanghesha had been left behind intentionally.

"Easy. Easy." Subredil's love affair with her Ghanghesha amused everyone. "We took good care of it."

There was a lot of work scheduled for the day, which was good. It helped pass the time. Nothing else could be done till much later, and even then, luck would have to play a big part. Another dozen Ghangheshas would not have been out of place where the need for luck went.

During the noon break, over kitchen scraps, Subredil's party heard rumors of the Protector's rage over someone having stolen some books from the royal library. She was out there now, investigating personally.

Subredil shot warning looks at her companions. No questions. No worrying about the people they could not possibly help.

Later in the day there were more rumors. The Purohita and several members of the Privy Council, along with bodyguards and hangers-on, had been treated to a wholesale slaughter on the very steps of the Kernmi What, in what sounded like a full-scale military assault supported by heavy sorcery. Reports were vague and confused because everyone but the attackers had been trying to find somewhere safe to hide.

Subredil tried to take that into account but could not control her anger entirely. Kendo Cutter was too violent a man to have been in charge. And too devout a Vehdna. The Gunni were not going to be pleased about bloodshed happening on the very steps of a major temple.

There was much talk about the signs and portents thrown up as cover and diversion while the attackers faded away. There would be no doubt who had been responsible, nor even who was next on the list of the doomed. Any smoke cloud that did not declare "Water Sleeps" thundered "My Brother Unforgiven."

It had been rumored only for a day that the Great General had been summoned to Taglios to deal with the dead who refused to lie down. To the people in the street, it looked like the Company would be waiting.

Sahra was worried. Soulcatcher was sure to abandon the library when she heard about the attack. If she returned to the Palace extremely agitated, Sahra's operation might have to be abandoned because the sorceress would be too alert.

The Radisha stormed through not long after the news began to make the rounds. She was distraught. She headed directly for her Anger Chamber. Sawa looked up from the brasswork she was cleaning, just for an instant, apparently badly troubled. Subredil set her mop aside and went to see what was wrong. No one else paid them any attention.

Not much later, when Jaul Barundandi dropped in to see how the work was going and somehow got into an argument with Narita, Sawa wandered away when no one was looking. No one noticed right away because Sawa almost never did anything to be noticed and today she wore charms reinforcing that.

Shiki drifted closer to her mother. She looked pale and troubled and kept touching her flute. She whispered, "Shouldn't we be going?"

"It isn't time. Place your Ghanghesha." Shiki was supposed to have done that hours ago.

Rumor rushed through, pursued by uglier rumor still. The Protector had returned and she was in a frothing rage. She was visiting her shadows now. It was going to be another night of terror in the streets of Taglios.

The women started talking about the possible wisdom of finishing work before the Protector decided she had to see the Radisha. The Protector would not respect the privacy of the Princess. She made no secret of her contempt for Taglian custom. Even Narita seemed to hold the opinion that it would be best not to be where you could be seen when the Protector was in a mood.

At that point Shiki discovered that her aunt was missing.

"Damn it, Subredil!" Narita fumed. "You promised you'd watch her closer the last time this happened."

"I'm sorry, mistress. I became so frightened. She probably decided to go to the kitchen. That was what she was trying to do when she got lost last time."

Shiki was going already. Not more than a minute later, she called, "I found her, Mother."

When the rest of the women arrived, they found Sawa seated against a wall, brass lamp in her lap, unconscious, with vomit all over her. "Oh, no!" Subredil cried. "Not again." And in a whirlwind of nonsense and apparently vain efforts to get Sawa's attention, she got across the hint of a fear that Sawa might be pregnant after having been abused by one of the Palace staff.

Narita was away in seconds, fuming. Subredil and Shiki were right behind her, supporting Sawa between them, heading for the servants' postern. Nobody noticed that none of the women were carrying their Ghangheshas, not even the one that Subredil had forgotten the day before.

Because of the state Sawa was in, and the state Narita was in, and the imminent explosion of displeasure expected from the Protector, the women managed to draw their pay, then to escape without having to deal with Barundandi's kickback lieutenant. Again.

They were able to lay Sawa inside a covered ox cart not long after they got into the twisty streets downhill from the Palace. Subredil had to caution Shiki repeatedly against celebration.

E verything we did must have been seen by somebody," I told the gathered troops. "When word gets out that the Radisha has vanished, all those people are going to remember and try to help. Soulcatcher is supposed to have a knack for separating wheat from chaff."

"Also a knack for calling up the kind of supernatural assistance that can pick your particular trail out of a thousand," Willow Swan volunteered. He was present because he had agreed to take care of the Radisha. She was going to be in a state when she awakened and discovered that her demons had caught up with her at last.

Banh Do Trang wanted to know, "Are you going to flee or not?" The old man was at the edge of collapse. He had been working since before dawn.

"Can we?" I asked.

"You could go this instant if the situation became totally desperate. It will be a few hours yet before the barges are completely provisioned, however."

Nobody wanted to go, though. Not just yet. A lot of the men had developed ties. Everyone had unfinished business. That was life. The same situation had come up time and again over the course of the Company's history.

Sahra said, "You still haven't gotten Narayan to give you the Key."

"I'll talk to him. Is River back yet? No? What about Kendo? How about Pooch and Spiff?" We had people running all over on special assignments. Good old One-Eye had sent our last two men, the barely competent Pooch and Spiff, to assassinate Adoo the gateman because Murgen had been able to determine that it had been he who had caused all the excitement at the library. More, Adoo knew the general neighborhood where I lived.

One-Eye informed me, "Kendo Cutter is coming through the web right now. Arjana Drupada appears to be reasonably healthy for a man with a dozen knife wounds. Hang on."

Murgen was whispering something. It was thundering and hailing outside. I could not hear a word.

"It's started at Semchi, Murgen says. Slink hit them just as they were starting to pitch camp. Cut them off from their weapons."

"Darn!" I swore. "Darn-darn-darn!"

"What's the matter with you, Little Girl?"

"He should've waited until they tried to do something to the Bhodi Tree. This way, nobody will know why we jumped them."

"There's why you don't have you a man."

"What?"

"You ask too much. You sent Slink out there to kill some people. Unless you told him it's got to be a show, all our guys allowed to fight only left-handed or something, he's going to do it fast and dirty and with as little risk to our own guys as he can."

"I thought he understood—"

"Did you *assume*, Little Girl? At this late stage in your career? You, who's got to run a checklist on lacing your own boots?"

He had me. And he had me good. I tried to change the subject. "If we decide to evacuate, we're going to have to run somebody out there to warn Slink and tell him where to rendezvous."

"Don't try to change the subject."

I turned away. "Kendo. Does he need medical attention?"

"Drupada? He's not bleeding that much anymore."

"Then let's take him back to meet his new roommate." One-Eye catching me out had me feeling particularly evil. This seemed like a good time to take it out on the enemy. "The rest of you, take real good care of the Radisha. We don't want her coming up with a hangnail anybody can blame on us."

Cutter bobbed his head and muttered something under his breath.

"Hey, pervert!" I called to the Inspector-General of the Records. "I don't want you ever to say that the Black Company don't cater to its guests, so here's your very own human play toy. Maybe a little longer in the tooth than you prefer but it's only until the Protector gets around to rescuing you."

Kendo planted a boot in Drupada's behind and shoved. Into the cage the Purohita went. He and Gokhale backed off into opposite corners and glared at one another. Human nature being what it is, each man probably thought the other was responsible for his dismay.

I told Kendo, "Relax now. Get something to eat. Take a nap. But stay away from the girl."

"Hey, I got it the first time, Sleepy. And more so now she's started sleepwalking. So ease up."

"Give me a reason."

"Why don't we just skrag her?"

"Because we need Singh to help open the way through the Shadowgate. And he won't unless he feels confident that we'll be good to the Daughter of Night."

"I don't know any of the Captured that well. Don't feel like you've got to save them on my account."

"I feel like we have to save them on the Company's account, Kendo. Just the same as we'd be doing if it was you out there."

"Sure. Right." Kendo Cutter was one of those people who tended to look on the dark side no matter what.

"Get some rest." I went to talk with Narayan while I waited for Murgen to generate some report on what was happening inside the Palace.

I did not want to run away but knew it was very close to time for the Company to go. We had to see what Soulcatcher's reaction to the kidnapping would be. And we had to get Goblin out of the Palace.

If Soulcatcher did not come after us like a screaming monsoon storm, I was going to get really worried about what she was up to.

"I've had a real good day, thank you, Mr. Singh. A whole lot of planning and a little inspired improvisation fell into place all at once. Just one thing more could make the day perfect." I sniffed the air. It smelled like One-Eye and friends were cooking up a new batch. Probably so they could take a little something along when we had to run.

I kicked a bundle of hides of some kind over beside the bars of Singh's cage, settled myself. I caught him up on the latest gossip. Including, "None of your people seem to be worried about you two. Maybe you were just a little *too* secretive. Be kind of pathetic if the whole cult faded away because everyone just sat around waiting to find out what was going on."

"I've been told that I'm free to deal with you." There was no cringe to the man tonight. He had gotten a little backbone somewhere. "I'm prepared to discuss the object you seek if I receive absolute assurances that the Black Company will never do the Daughter of Night any harm."

"Never is an awful long time. You're out of luck." I got up. "Goblin's been wanting to work on her just forever. I'm going to let him pull a few fingers off now to show you we have no conscience or remorse where certain old enemies are concerned."

"I offered you what you asked."

"You offered me a delayed death warrant. If I agree to that kind of nonsense, ten years from now the blackhearted witch will start poisoning us and we'll be stuck with the disastrous choice of keeping our word and accepting destruction or breaking our word and seeing our reputation destroyed. I'm certain you don't know much northern mythology. There's an old religion up there that tells how a leading god allowed himself to be slain so his family would no longer be bound by a promise he made foolishly to an enemy, who wore it like a turtle's shell."

Narayan stared at me, cold as a cobra, waiting for me to crack. And I did, a little, because I bothered to explain. One-Eye has told me a hundred times that I should not explain. "I just don't want that artifact badly enough to commit my people to the level of vulnerability that you're asking. In particular, I won't undertake commitments for those of us who are buried. On the other hand, maybe you'd like to undertake commitments whereby, assuming you get out of this alive, you guarantee never to be a pain in the Company neck ever again. Whereby you agree to go to the Captain and the Lieutenant and beg their forgiveness for stealing their child."

The very suggestion appalled the living saint of the Deceivers. "She's the Child of Kina. The Daughter of Night. Those two are irrelevant."

"Evidently we don't have anything to talk about yet. I'll send you a few fingers for breakfast."

I went to see if Surendranath Santaraksita was being a good fellow and pursuing the tasks I had suggested he could use to help overcome the tedium of his captivity. To my surprise I found him hard at work, with old Baladitya assisting, translating what I had presumed to be the first volume of the lost Annals. They had a whole stack of sheets already done.

"Dorabee!" Master Santaraksita said. "Excellent. Your friend the foreigner keeps telling us we can't have any more real vellum when we're done with these last few sheets. He wants us to use those ridiculous bark books they still employ out in the swamps."

Before there were modern paper and vellum and parchment, there was bark. I do not know what kind of tree it came from, just that the inner bark was removed carefully, treated and pressed and used to write on. To make a book, you stacked the bark sheets, drilled a hole down through the upper-left-hand corner of the stack, then bound everything together with a cord or ribbon or length of very light chain. Banh Do Trang would favor bark because it was both cheap, traditional and hardier than animal products.

"I'll talk to him."

"There's nothing earthshaking in there, Dorabee."

"My name is Sleepy."

"Sleepy isn't a name. It's a disease, or a misfortune. I prefer Dorabee. I'll use Dorabee."

"Use whatever you like. I'll know who you're talking to." I read a couple of sheets. He was right. "This is tedious stuff. This looks like an account book."

"That's what it is, mainly. The things you want to know are just the things the writer assumes any reader of his own time would know already. He wasn't writing for the ages, or even for another generation. He was keeping track of horseshoe nails, lance shafts and saddles. All he has to say about their battle is that the lower-ranking officers and noncommissioned officers failed to demonstrate an adequate enthusiasm for appropriating weapons lost or abandoned by the defeated enemy, preferring to wait till the next dawn to begin gleaning. As a consequence, stragglers and the local peasantry managed to scavenge all the best."

"I notice he doesn't bother to name a single name, person or place." I had begun reading while the Master talked. I could listen and read at the same time even though I was a woman.

"He does give mileage and dates. The context suggests the appropriate systems of measure. It can be figured out. But what I've already started to wonder, Dorabee, is why we've all been deathly afraid of these people all our lives. This book gives us no reason to be afraid. This book is about a troop of crabby little men who marched off somewhere they didn't want to go for reasons they didn't understand, fully believing that their unstated mission would last only several weeks or, at most, a few months. Then they would be able to go home. But the months piled into years and the years into generations. And still they didn't really know."

The material also suggested we needed to revise our old belief that the Free Companies exploded into the world at the same time, in a vast orgy of fire and bloodshed. The only other company mentioned was noted to have returned years before the Black Company marched, and in fact, several senior Company noncoms had served as private soldiers in that earlier, unnamed band.

"I can see it," I grumbled. "We're going to translate these things, find out all sorts of things, and not be an inch closer to understanding anything."

Santaraksita said, "This's much more exciting than a meeting of the bhadrhalok, Dorabee."

Then Baladitya spoke for the first time. "Do we have to starve to death here, Dorabee?"

"Nobody's brought you anything to eat?"

"No."

"I'll just see about that. Don't be startled if you hear me shouting. I hope you enjoy fish and rice."

I took care of that, then hid in my corner for a while. I was feeling a little depressed after having seen Master Santaraksita's work. I suppose that sometimes I invest too much in my goals, then suffer a correspondingly huge disappointment when things do not work out.

Tobo woke me. "How can you sleep, Sleepy?"

"I guess I must be tired. What do you want?"

"The Protector has finally started to grumble about the Radisha. Dad wants you to come keep track yourself. So you don't have to record anything third-hand."

At the moment, my name felt entirely appropriate. I just wanted to lie down on my pallet and dream about finding another kind of life.

Trouble was, I had been doing this since I was fourteen. I did not know anything else. Unless Master Santaraksita was willing to let bygones be bygones and take me back at the library. Right after we buried Soulcatcher in a fifty-foot-deep hole we filled in with boiling lead.

I dragged a stool in between Sahra and One-Eye, leaned forward with my elbows on the table and stared into the mist where Murgen appeared to report when it suited him. One-Eye was fussing at Murgen even though Murgen was away. I said, "Anybody would think you were worried about Goblin, the way you're carrying on."

"Of course I'm worried about Goblin, Little Girl. The runt borrowed my transeidetic locuter before he went up there this morning. Not to mention he still owes me several thousands pais for . . . well, he owes me a bunch of money."

My recollection had it the other way around. One-Eye always owed everyone, even when he was doing well. And several thousand pais is not exactly a fortune, a pai being a tiny seed of such uniform weight that it is used as a measure for gems and precious metals. It takes almost two thousand of them to equal a northern ounce. Since One-Eye had not specified gold or silver, the standard assumption would be that he had meant coin-grade copper. In other words, not very much.

In other words still, he was worried about his best friend but he could not say so because he had a century-long history of reviling the man in public.

If there was any such magical instrument as a transeidetic locuter, One-Eye invented it an hour before he loaned it to Goblin.

He muttered, "That ugly little turd gets himself killed, I'm gonna strangle him. He can't leave me holding the bag on—" He realized he was thinking out loud.

Sahra and I both made mental notes to investigate the bag metaphor. It sounded like there were business plans afoot. Secret plans. Surprise, surprise.

Murgen materialized practically nose to nose with me. He murmured, "Soulcatcher is out of patience. A flock of crows just brought the news from Semchi. She's in a complete black mood. She says she's going into the Radisha's Anger Chamber after her if she doesn't come out in the next two minutes."

"How's Goblin?" One-Eye barked.

"Hiding," Murgen replied. "Waiting for sunrise." He was not going to try leaving during the night, the way we had planned originally. Soulcatcher had loosed her shadows, just to punish Taglios for irritating her. We had a few traps out, randomly distributed through likely neighborhoods, but I did not expect to catch anything. I figured our luck along those lines was about used up.

Goblin was armed with a shadow-repellent amulet left over from the Shadowmaster wars but did not know if it was any good anymore. Being bright and full of forethought, it had not occurred to any of us to test it on real shadows while we had some in stock.

You cannot think of everything.

But you should make the effort.

One of the Royal Guards actually tried to stop the Protector when her patience failed and she went to dig the Radisha out of her hideaway. He went down without a sound, stricken by a casual touch. He would recover eventually. The Protector was not feeling particularly vindictive. For the moment.

She crashed through the door of the Anger Chamber. And howled in frustration before the pieces finished falling. "Where is she?" The power of her rage wilted the onlookers.

A subassistant chamberlain, bowing almost double, continuing to bob and get lower, whined, "She was in there, O Great One!"

Someone else insisted, "We never saw her leave. She has to be in there."

From somewhere, echoing, almost as if coming from some distance in time as well as place, there was the sound of brief laughter.

Soulcatcher turned slowly, her stare a cruel spear. "Come closer. Tell me again." Her voice was compelling, chilling, terrible. She stared into one pair of eyes after another, making full use of the fear so many had that she could read the deepest secrets in their minds.

None of the Radisha's people changed their stories.

"Out of here. Out of this whole apartment. Something happened here. I want no distractions. I want nothing disturbed." She turned again, slowly, extending a sorceress's senses to feel the shape of the past. It was more difficult than she anticipated. She had been loafing for too long, falling out of practice and getting out of shape.

The remote laughter sounded again for an instant, seeming just a touch closer.

"You!" Soulcatcher snapped at a fat woman, one of the housekeepers. "What are you doing?"

"Ma'am?" Narita was barely able to croak her response. In a moment, she would lose control of her bladder.

"You just pushed something into your left sleeve. Something off the altar." A single white candle, almost consumed, still burned in the tiny shrine to ancestors. "Come here." Soulcatcher extended her gloved right hand.

Narita could not resist. She stepped toward the dark woman, so trim and evilly feminine in her leather. Idly, Narita hated her for maintaining that sleek body.

"Give it to me."

Reluctantly, Narita removed the Ghanghesha from her sleeve. She began to babble about not wanting her friend to get into trouble, making no sense at all, failing to realize that if she had not tried to conceal the Ghanghesha, the Protector would have overlooked it entirely.

Soulcatcher stared at the little clay figurine. "The cleaning woman. It belongs to the cleaning woman. Where is she?"

Far, mocking laughter.

"She's a day employee, ma'am. She comes in from outside."

"Where does she live?"

"I don't know, ma'am. I don't think anybody does. Nobody ever asked. It never mattered."

One of the other staffers offered, "She was a good worker."

Soulcatcher continued to examine the Ghanghesha. "Something's odd here. . . . Now it does matter. To me. Find out."

"How?"

"I don't care! Be creative! But do it." Soulcatcher hurled the clay figurine to the floor. Shards flew in every direction.

A wisp of a ghost of darkness curled up and stood like a rampant cobra a foot high for an instant. Then it struck. At the Protector.

The staffers squealed and began trampling one another, trying to get away. They had not seen a shadow before but they knew what a shadow could do.

The laughter was closer now, louder and lasting longer.

Soulcatcher offered a convincing squeal of surprise and fright, like a young woman who has just stepped on a snake. Her apparel and the handful of generalized protective spells that always surrounded her saved her from becoming a victim of her own cruelest weapon.

Even so, for a minute she was like a child swatting mosquitoes as the shadow enthusiastically strove to terminate their relationship. Failing to reclaim control of the shadow, Soulcatcher destroyed it. The necessity told her that a pretty clever mind had prepared it, probably hoping that she would be too angry to pay close attention for just that instant needed. . . .

"Woman! Come back here!" The Protector extended a hand in the direction Narita had fled. Somehow, a single strand of the woman's hair had become entwined through Soulcatcher's fingers. Those fingers shimmered momentarily. The air became charged. The other staffers whimpered and wished they had even had the nerve to try to run.

Narita reappeared slowly, taking short zombie steps. "Here!" Soulcatcher said. She pointed at a spot on the Anger Chamber floor. "The rest of you. Go away. Quickly." She did not have to add any encouragement. "Fat woman. Tell me everything about the creature who always carried the Ghanghesha."

"I've told you everything I know," Narita whined.

"No. You have not. Start talking. She may have kidnapped the Radisha."

Soulcatcher regretted mentioning that the instant the words left her helmet.

The laughter sounded like it was coming from just out in the hallway, a diabolic snickering. The Protector's head twitched toward that direction. She sensed no threat. It could wait a minute.

"Her name is Minh Subredil." It took Narita only another thirty seconds to relate everything she knew about Minh Subredil, her daughter Shikhandini and her sister-in-law Sawa.

"Thank you," Soulcatcher snarled. "You've been most unhelpful. And for that, I shall provide an appropriate reward." She gripped the fat woman's throat in her right hand, squeezed.

As Narita went limp, that laughter sounded once more. There might have been a word there, too. Ardath? Or perhaps Silath? Or might it have been . . . ? No matter. Soulcatcher would not listen to that, just to the mockery. She hurled herself toward the sound but when she burst into the hallway, there was nothing to see.

She started to call for Guards, for Greys, but recalled that she had just slain the one person other than herself who knew for sure that the Radisha had disappeared.

The Radisha had shut herself away from the world. *That* was all anybody really needed to know. The Princess could live forever right there in her Anger Chamber. She did not need to venture forth ever again. She had her good friend the Protector to handle the boring chores of managing her empire for her.

More laughter, apparently from nowhere and everywhere. Soulcatcher stamped away. This was not over yet.

* * *

A white crow dropped out of the murk near the ceiling of the hallway, flapped heavily, landed beside the fat woman. It held its beak poised beneath her nostrils momentarily, as though checking for breath. Then it flapped away suddenly, sharp ears having caught the sound of a stealthy footfall.

A shivering Jaul Barundandi eased into the chamber. He knelt beside the woman. He took her hand. He remained there, tears streaking his cheeks, until he heard the Protector returning, arguing with herself in a variety of voices.

What do you know about that?" I said to Sahra. "Narita tried to cover for you. And then Barundandi got all broken up about what happened to her."

Sahra waggled a finger. She was thinking. "Murgen. What do you know about that white crow?"

Murgen hesitated before responding. "Nothing." Which meant he was telling an approximate truth but he had some definite ideas. Sahra and I both knew him that well.

Sahra said, "Suppose you tell me what you think is going on, then."

Murgen faded away.

"What the heck is that?" I snapped at One-Eye. "You were supposed to rig this thing so he has to do what he's told."

"He does. Most of the time. He could be carrying out a previous instruction."

But the old fool sounded to me like he had no idea what Murgen was doing.

Soulcatcher worked quickly, then summoned the staff members who had been present when she had broken into the Anger Chamber. "The continuing excitement was too much for this poor woman. I've tried to resurrect her but her soul refuses to respond. She must be happy where she is now." There were no witnesses to contradict her, though remote laughter mocked her. "I did find the Radisha. She'd fallen asleep. She has retreated into the Anger Chamber and does not wish to be disturbed again. Not for a long time. I should have honored her wishes before. We would have avoided this disaster." She indicated the fat woman.

Even the staffers who had looked into the Anger Chamber earlier and had seen nothing had to admit that someone was inside now, moving around angrily, muttering the way the Radisha did and looking very much like the Radisha in glimpses caught through cracks in the poorly restored door.

The Protector suggested, "Let's all turn in for the night. Tomorrow we'll begin repairing the mess I made." She watched her audience intently, feeling for anyone who could cause trouble.

The staff departed. They were relieved just to be away from Soulcatcher.

Soulcatcher sat down and thought. There was no way to tell what was going through her mind till she began muttering in a committee of voices. Then it was clear that she was trying to work out the mechanics of the abduction. She seemed willing to give considerable weight to the possibility that the Radisha had stage-managed the whole thing herself.

A very suspicious woman, the Protector.

One by one she found and questioned each of the people who had dealt with Minh Subredil, Sawa and Shikhandini, beginning with Jaul Barundandi and finishing with Del Mukharjee, the man Barundandi usually trusted to collect the kickbacks from the outside workers. "You will cease that," the Protector informed Mukharjee. "You and anyone else involved. If it happens again, I will put you into a glass ball and hang you above the service postern with your whole body turned inside out. I'll add a couple of imps to feed on your entrails for the six months it will take you to die. Do you understand?"

Del Mukharjee understood the threat just fine. But he had no idea whatsoever why the Protector would want to interfere with his livelihood.

The Protector had a passion about corruption.

In time the Protector reasoned that three women had come into the Palace and three women had gone away again. It seemed very likely that the three who had departed were not the three who had entered. And no one the Radisha's size had gone out since.

Which meant that someone with some answers might still be inside.

Chuckling wickedly, Soulcatcher began to look for evidence that someone had slipped off into the untenanted wilds of the Palace.

Goblin was asleep on a dusty old bed. Occasionally his snores would turn to sneezes and snorts when too much dust got into his nostrils.

A squawk had him bouncing up so suddenly he almost collapsed from light-headedness. He spun around. He saw nothing. He heard soft laughter, then a bizarre, squawking voice that sounded almost familiar. "Wake up. Wake up. She is coming."

"Who's coming? Who's talking?"

There was no response. He did not feel any strong sorcerous presence. It was a puzzle.

Goblin had a good idea who might be coming, though. Not many women were likely to be hunting him here in the middle of the night.

He was ready. His little pack was carrying the two books Sleepy most wanted to save. Taking all three was physically impossible. His traps were set. All he had to do was move on into the now-empty part of the Palace that had been occupied by the Black Company back when its staff and leadership had been quartered there. There were ways to get out unnoticed. He and One-Eye had found them in olden times. The trouble was, he had no desire to be on the streets after dark, amulet or no.

Soulcatcher gave up most of her sense of touch when she chose to wrap every inch of her body in leather and helmet. She never noted the touch of or resistance of the strand of spider silk stretched across the corridor. But she did have a marvelously well-developed sense for personal danger. Before the Ghanghesha hit the floor, she was moving to defend herself. It was such reflexes that made it possible for creatures like her, her sister Lady, and the Howler, to have survived for so long. This time she had the proper controlling spells ready, hung about her, sparkling like spanking-new tools.

The shadow trapped inside the figurine barely got its bearings before it was attacked itself, seized and constrained, then twisted and crushed down into a whining, seething ball completely enclosed inside one of the Protector's gloved hands. A merry young voice called, "You'll have to do better than that."

Soulcatcher continued to move forward, amused by the idea of tossing the shadow back into someone's face. The trail began to grow indistinct, then disorienting. Experimentation showed her the cause was external. The corridor had been strewn with cobwebs of spells so subtle that even she might not have noticed had she just been hurrying along. "Oh, you clever devils. How long has this been here? Ah. A very long time indeed, I see. You were still in favor when you started this. Have you been hiding here all along? I certainly couldn't find you in the city if you never were out there."

In another voice entirely, she asked, "What have we here? It smells like somebody very frightened is hiding behind this door. And he didn't even bother to lock it. How stupid does he think I am?"

She shoved the door with her toe.

A clay Ghanghesha plummeted from its place atop the door. Soulcatcher giggled. She was even quicker to recapture this shadow, which she squeezed down inside her other hand. Then she pushed into the room.

There was no one there anymore. That was easy to sense. But there was a curious feel to the place. It demanded an investigation.

She generated a small light, stood in place, turned slowly while she read the history of the room for subtle clues. A great deal had happened there. Much of the recent history of the Black Company had been shaped in that room. It retained a strong smell of old fear she identified eventually with the long-dead Taglian court wizard, Smoke.

All this she debated with herself in a committee of argumentative voices. In the end, she seemed entertained. Most of the time life was a great entertainment for Soulcatcher.

"And what do we have here?" Something with inked characters on it peeped from beneath a dusty old bed where someone had been lying until minutes ago. Thoughtlessly, she reached for the object, opening her hand to grasp it. "Damn! That was stupid!" She wasted several minutes regaining control of the shadow. It was very agile this time. She stuffed it into the hand restraining the other. The two were extremely unhappy in there. One thing shadows seemed to hate more than the living was other shadows.

What Soulcatcher had found was a book with half the pages torn out. It was alone. "So this is what became of those. I was never quite sure who took them. I wonder if they got any use out of them?"

As she was about to depart, the Protector glanced at the damaged book once more. "Been taking these pages a few at a time. That would take a long time. Which means they've been coming in and out of the Palace for a long time. Which therefore suggests that the Radisha didn't engineer her own disappearance. Oh, well. She's gone. It amounts to the same thing. Let's catch our little rat and let him play with our little friends."

Unlike Soulcatcher, Goblin could not see in the dark. But he had the advantage of knowing where he was going. He did manage to stay ahead and did slide out of one of the old hidden exits. There was a little light outside from a fragment of moon peeking through scurrying young clouds trying to catch up with Mother Storm. Goblin laid the last Ghanghesha on the cobblestones in plain sight, then ran. The books on his back beat against him, pounding the breath out of him. He muttered something about the good news being that it was all downhill from here. The bad news was that it was dark out, there were shadows on the prowl, and he was not so sure about the quality of his fifteen-year-old amulet. He had to hope that in a city this vast, none of the handful of nightstalkers would cross his path while he was huffing and puffing and concentrating on staying ahead of Soulcatcher.

It did not occur to him that she might have recovered the shadows he had left in ambush, that they might be after him, too.

Soulcatcher stepped into the night close enough behind to glimpse a flicker of her quarry vanishing into the shadows between structures across the open area outside the Palace. She spied the abandoned Ghanghesha and several other small items that looked like they had been dropped in the rush to get away. She tossed her two shadows into the air and stomped her heel down on the clay figurine at the same time. This would set a pack of small deaths on the little man's heels.

By now, she was reasonably certain that she was chasing the wizard called Goblin.

She screamed. The pain in her heel was beyond anything she had ever experienced. As she collapsed, trying to will her throat to seal itself, she watched three ferociously bright balls of light streak into the night in pursuit of the shadows she had sent to claim Goblin. Still fighting the incredible pain, she produced a dagger and used its tip to dip another fireball out of her heel. Already it had eaten all the way to the bone and in, and had done some damage as high as her ankle—despite her normal protection.

"I'll be crippled," she snarled. "He lulled me. He set me up so I'd think this would be another easy shadowtrap." None of her voices were amused now. "Clever little bastard will pay for this."

The fallen fireball burned its way into the cobblestones. Still ignoring her pain, Soulcatcher tried to stand. She discovered that she was not going to be able to walk. She was, however, not losing any blood. The fireball had cauterized her wound. "My beloved sister, if you weren't already dead, I'd kill you for inventing those damned things."

Laughter echoed down off the ramparts of the Palace.

A flicker of white glided after Goblin.

"I think I'll kill *somebody* anyway." Soulcatcher made her way toward the Palace entrance on hands and knees, muttering continuously. She had isolated her pain in a remote corner of her mind and was now concentrating on being angry about what this odyssey was doing to her beautiful leather pants and gloves.

41

"Can you believe that?" I asked. "She was as mad about ruining her outfit as she was about losing Goblin and getting hurt."

One-Eye chuckled, immensely relieved because Goblin had gotten away. "I believe it."

"What? You, too?"

"It's a northern thing. Everything she wears is leather. You people are all goofy about stuff like that. She probably has to fly five thousand miles every time she wants a new pair of pants. Means she's really got to watch her waist and behind. Unlike some—hey! No punching! We're all on the same side here."

"Do you believe this little pervert?" I asked Sahra.

"You go ask Swan." One-Eye showed me his tooth. The one he was about to lose. "He'll tell you the woman's got her good points."

Sahra remained all business. "What are we going to do if she just pretends the Radisha is all right? How many people normally see the Princess? Not many, I know. And there's no Privy Council anymore. We've seen to them. Except for Mogaba."

"We've got to see about him, too," One-Eye grumbled.

"Let's not overreach. The Great General will be harder to take than the others were."

I mused, "She wouldn't actually have to keep the Radisha in hiding very long. Maybe two weeks, while she builds a new Council, handpicked to woof 'Yes, ma'am!' and 'How high?' when she tells them to jump."

One-Eye blew out a bushel of air. "She's right. Maybe we should've considered that."

I said, "I did consider it. Having the Radisha under our control looked like the best deal. We can trot her out any time Soulcatcher gets too bizarre. And Soulcatcher will realize that. She won't let temptation carry her too far. Not until she sorts us out."

"She will do everything she can to find and recover the Radisha," Sahra said. "I'm sure of that. Which means we need to hurry up and get out of the city."

I said, "I have one little thing to do before I go. Don't anybody wait on me. Murgen. Be a pal and put a little real effort into finding out about this other white crow."

I did not await his response. Now that Goblin seemed safe, I was eager to interview our newest prisoner.

Someone had taken some effort to make the Radisha comfortable. Nor had she been forced into a cage. Presumably, One-Eye had provided a sampler of choker spells.

I studied her while she remained unaware of my presence. She had had a formidable reputation when first the Company had come to Taglios. She had put up a good struggle, too, but the years had worn her down. She looked old and tired and defeated now.

I stepped forward. "Have they treated you well so far, Radisha?"

She showed me a weak smile. There was a twinkle both of anger and sarcasm in her eye.

"I know. It's not the Palace. But I've enjoyed worse. Including chains and no roof at all."

"And animal hides?"

"I've lived here for the last six years. You get used to it." It had been longer than that but I was not taking time to be precise.

"Why?"

"Water sleeps, Radisha. Water sleeps. You were expecting us. We had to come."

At that point it became completely real to her. Her eyes grew big. "I've seen you before."

"Many times. Lately, around the Palace. Once upon a time, long ago, around the Palace also, with the Standardbearer."

"You're the idiot."

"Am I? Perhaps one of us—"

She began to grow angry then.

I told her, "That won't help. But if you need to rage to feel better, consider this. The Protector is covering up your disappearance already. The one person who knew for sure—not counting us villains, of course—is dead already. There'll be more deaths. And you'll begin making the most outrageous pronouncements from the anonymity of your Anger Chamber. And in six months the Protector will be so solidly in control, behind her Greys and those who think they can profit from an alliance with her, that you won't matter anymore." As long as Soulcatcher could come to an accommodation with Mogaba.

I did not mention that.

The Radisha began to speak quite rudely of her ally.

I let her run for a while, then offered another slogan: "All their days are numbered."

"What the hell does that mean?"

"Sooner or later we're going to get everyone who injured us. You're right. It's not really sane. But it's the way we are. You've seen it happening lately. Only the Protector and the Great General are still running free. All their days are numbered."

The reality sank in a little deeper. She was a captive. She did not know where. She did not know what was going to happen. She did know that her captors were willing to pursue their grudges to insane lengths, just as they had promised they would before she made the mistake of letting herself be seduced by Soulcatcher's deadly promises.

"You have no designated heir, do you?"

The change of direction startled her. "What?"

"There isn't any clear-cut line of succession."

Again, "What?"

"At the moment I don't just hold you hostage, I have the entire future of Taglios and the Taglian Territories firmly under my thumb. You don't have a child. Your brother has no child."

"I'm too old for that now."

"Your brother isn't. And he is still alive."

I left her then, to think, her mouth hanging open.

I considered seeing Narayan Singh again, decided I would seem too eager. I was too tired, anyway. You do not treat with a Deceiver without full command of your faculties. Sleep was the lover whose arms I needed to wrap me up.

42

I was playing tonk with Spiff and JoJo and Kendo Cutter, an interesting mix. At least three of us took our religion somewhat seriously. JoJo's real name was Cho Dai Cho. He was Nyueng Bao and, in theory, One-Eye's bodyguard. One-Eye did not want a bodyguard. JoJo did not want to be a bodyguard. So they did not see much of one another, and the rest of us saw as little of JoJo as we did of Uncle Doj. JoJo complained, "You're just ganging up on the dumb swamp boy. I know."

I said, "Me get in cahoots with a heretic and an unbeliever?"

"You'll ambush them after you finish picking my bones."

I had been having an unusual run of luck.

Everybody resents it when their favorite mark gets lucky.

I said, "I can't get used to this not having to go to work." JoJo discarded a six I needed to fill to the inside of a five-card straight. "Maybe this is my day."

"Be a good time to get out and find you a man, then."

"Goblin. You're still alive. As mad as Soulcatcher was last night, I figured she would have you for a midnight snack before you got halfway home."

Goblin gave me his big frog grin. "She's gonna walk funny for a while. I couldn't believe she actually stomped on it." His grin faded. "I've been thinking. Maybe nailing her that way was a mistake. I could've led her somewhere where we could've got her in a crossfire—"

"She would've been looking for that. In fact, her suspecting something like that was probably one reason she didn't keep chasing you. You want to sit in?"

All three of my companions glowered. Goblin was not One-Eye but they did not trust him a bit. They knew with the confidence of ignorance that Goblin was just more clever when he cheated. The fact that his history was one of losing more than he won was just a part of the cover-up.

You might have noticed that the human animal is fond of forming and clinging to prejudices, remaining their steadfast curator in the face of all reason and contradiction.

"Not this time." Goblin could take a hint. He would also take them some other way sometime and laugh himself silly behind his hand. And it would serve them right. "Got work to do. I'm already getting complaints from everybody about a ghost that was all over the warehouse last night. Got to scope it out."

I had a losing hand. Or foot. I tossed it in. "He's making me feel guilty for loafing." I collected my winnings.

"You can't quit now," Kendo grumbled.

"You proved your point. Women can't play cards. I stay here much longer, I won't have a copper left to my name. Then you wouldn't get a birthday present this year."

"Didn't get one last year, either."

"I must've played tonk with you then, too. So many of you do it, I have a hard time keeping track of which ones of you guys keep beating up on me."

They all grumbled now.

Goblin said, "Maybe I can sit in, just for a hand or two."

"That's all right. You better help Sleepy. Or Sleepy can help you." The grumbling stopped till we were out of earshot.

Goblin chuckled. So did I. He said, "We ought to get married."

"I'm too old for you. See if Chandra Gokhale can fix you up."

"Aren't those two like a couple of starving rats?" Gokhale and Drupada were at one another constantly. Their squabbles had not yet devolved into anything physical only because they had been warned in the strongest of terms that the winner of any fight would be punished terribly.

"Maybe one of them will kill and eat the other one," I said. "If we're lucky."

"You're a dreamer, for sure."

"What's your opinion on this ghost?"

He shrugged.

"You know it's the girl, don't you?"

"I'm pretty sure."

"You think she's going through the same thing Murgen did when he started? Falling through time and everything?"

"I don't know. There's a difference. Nobody ever saw anything with Murgen."

"Can you stop her from doing it?"

"Spooking you out?"

"In the sense that I'm scared she'll go out and get help, sure."

"Ooh. I didn't think about that."

"Do think about it, Goblin. What about the white crow? Could she be the white crow?"

"I thought Murgen was the white crow."

He knew better. "Murgen's here, being Sahra's recon slave."

"It wouldn't be the first time Murgen was in the same place, looking at things from two different times."

"He tells me he can't remember being the crow."

"Maybe that's because he hasn't done it yet. Maybe it's a Murgen from next year or something."

I did not know what to say to that. That possibility had not occurred to me. And Murgen had done that sort of thing before.

"On the other hand, personally I don't think it's Murgen or the brat." He grinned his big toad grin. He knew I would stub my toe on that.

I did. "What? You little rat. Who is it, then?"

He shrugged. "I got a couple ideas but I'm not ready to talk about them yet. You got the Annals. All you need to follow my reasoning is right in there." He began giggling, pleased with himself for stumping the Annalist at her own game. So to speak. "Ha-ha." He spun around, dancing. "Let's go beat up on Narayan Singh. Whoa. Look who's here. Swan, you're too damned old to wear your hair that long. Unless you're going to comb it all up on top there to kind of cover the thin spot."

I held a finger above Goblin's dome, pointing down. He had not had a crop come in during my lifetime.

Swan said, "Kind of looks like your widow's peak is sagging back a little, too. Probably comes of banging your head on the bottoms of so many tables." Swan looked at me, an eyebrow raised. "He been in the ganja or something?"

"No. He just hasn't gotten over the fact that he went toe to toe with your girl-friend and came out ahead on points." Swan had suggested a good point indirectly, though. With hemp such a common weed, it was a wonder that Goblin and One-Eye had not gotten in on the entertainment side of that crop.

Goblin understood what I was thinking without me saying a word. He told me, "We don't have anything to do with it because it screws up your head."

"And that water-buffalo urine you brew back there doesn't?"

"That's pure medicine, Sleepy. You ought to try it. It's chock-full of stuff that's good for you."

"My diet is just fine, Goblin. Except for the fish and the rice."

"That's what I'm saying. We take up a collection, buy us a pig . . . never mind what Sahra says. There ain't nothing sweeter than some fatback and beans—"

Swan had invited himself to accompany us in our seventy-foot trek to Narayan's cage. He said, "I'll kick in on that myself. I haven't tasted bacon in over twenty years."

"Shit," Goblin said. "You're going to kick in? Man, you don't even have a name anymore. You're dead."

"I could run up to the Palace, dig around under my mattress. Times haven't been all bad for me."

"You won't marry me, Sleepy," Goblin said, "then you oughta marry Swan. He's got a hoard put back and he's too damned old to bother you with any of that man stuff. Narayan Singh. Get your skinny, shit-smelling ass up from there and talk to me."

Swan whispered, "Survival must be a real powerful drug."

"I expect it is when you're Goblin's age," I agreed.

"I guess it is at any age."

"Meaning?" I asked.

"Meaning, I guess, I should've headed back north a long time ago. I got nothing going for me here. I should've started moseying when Blade and Cordy went down. But I couldn't. And it wasn't just Soulcatcher twisting my arm."

"Umm?"

"I'm a loser. We were all losers. All three of us. We couldn't even make it as sol-diers in the old empire. We deserted. Blade got his ass thrown to the crocodiles for smarting off to the priests back in his home country. We never had no real start-up, any of us. Me and Cordy only headed on down here because once we got to run-ning, it took a long time to stop. Now I don't have my friends anymore, I don't have anybody to goose me into doing things."

I did not enlighten him about the health of Blade and Mather, who were among the Captured, but I did point out, "You can't be entirely inadequate. You've had some kind of commission or other from the Taglian throne practically since you got here."

"I'm an outsider. I make a great fall guy. Everybody knows who I am and everybody can recognize me. So the Protector or the Radisha puts me out front where I can take the heat for all their unpopular decisions."

"Now they'll need to find somebody else."

"Don't give me that look. I wouldn't join the Black Company if you promised to marry me and make me Captain, too. You guys got doom written all over you."

"What do you want?"

"Me? Since I don't got the stones or the young body to go home anymore—and home wouldn't be there when I showed up anyway—what I'd like to do is what we tried to do when we first came down here. Set me up a little brewery, spend my last few years making people's lives a little easier."

"I'm sure Goblin and One-Eye would be happy to take on a partner."

"Them two? No way. They'd drink up half the product. They'd get drunk and get in a fight and start throwing the barrels at each other—"

He had a point. "You have a point. Though they've shown considerable self-control lately."

"It helps you pay attention if your fuckup will get you killed. I'm always surprised by this guy." He meant Narayan Singh. "He looks like such a trivial little wart. There're ten thousand that look just like him out there on the streets right now and not one will ever do anything more important than starve to death."

"If I thought it would do any good, I'd starve this one to death, too. Narayan. I'm back. Are you going to talk to me today?"

Singh raised his eyes. He seemed serene, at peace. That could be said for Stranglers. They never had trouble with their consciences. "Good morning, young woman. Yes. We can talk. I took your advice. I went to the goddess. And she approved your petition. Frankly, I was surprised. She set down no special conditions for making a bargain. Other than that the lives and well-being of her chief agents remain unimpaired."

Swan was more taken aback than I was. "You got the right guy here, Sleepy?"

"I don't know. I figured they'd still try to weasel a little even after they couldn't stall anymore." This required a little thought. Or a lot of thought. And maybe some worry. "I'm definitely pleased, Narayan. Definitely. Where's the Key?"

Narayan smiled a smile almost as ugly as One-Eye's. "I'll take you to it."

"Aha," I murmured. "I see. The first shoe drops. Fine. When will you be ready to travel?"

"As soon as the girl recovers. You may have noticed she's been sick."

"Yes, I did. I thought it must be her time of the month." A horrible, *horrible* thought occurred to me. "She's not pregnant, is she?"

The look on Singh's face told me that notion was completely unthinkable to him.

"That's good. But it doesn't matter, Narayan. As long as we're conspiring together, Deceivers and Black Company, you two aren't going to be a team. It's a sad truth, Narayan Singh, but I just don't trust you. And her I wouldn't trust if she was in her grave."

He smiled like he knew a secret. "But you expect us to trust you."

"Based on the well-known fact that once it has sworn a thing, the Company always keeps its word. Yes." A slight exaggeration, of course.

Narayan glanced at Swan for just a second. He smiled again. "I guess that's just going to have to be good enough for me."

I pasted on my most scintillating false smile. "Wonderful. We're in business together. I'll get some people ready for an expedition. Do we have far to go?"

Smile. "Not far. Just a few days south of the city."

"Ha. The Grove of Doom. I should have guessed."

I led Swan away. I rejoined the fellows at the card table. "I want Singh's son brought in as soon as we can get him." It could not hurt to have a little extra ammunition.

43

I don't know what to do with myself, not having to work," Sahra told me. She and Tobo were huddled in front of the mist box, sharing what they could with Murgen. I was pleased to see mother and son getting along.

I suggested, "There's always work for those who want to put out the buttons that'll remind everyone about us after we're gone. There's always something that needs lugging down to the river."

"To paraphrase Goblin, I don't miss work so much I'm actually going to volunteer to do some. Was there something?"

"The guys just brought in Singh's son. Good-looking fellow. They also brought in a couple of rescripts they found posted on the official announcement pillars. Put up since the Radisha went into seclusion."

"What do they say?"

"Mainly that she's willing to pay some pretty big rewards for information leading to the apprehension of any member of the gang of vandals masquerading as members of the long defunct Black Company and causing public disorders."

"Will anybody believe that?"

"If she says it often enough. I don't care about her telling tall tales. I care about the reward offers. There're people out there who'd sell their mothers. She puts a couple of no-goods on the street throwing money around and bragging about how they cashed in, somebody who really knows something might decide to bet the long odds."

"Then why don't we just go? There isn't that much more we can do here anyway, is there?"

"We can get Mogaba."

"Let the world think that. Start a rumor. Start a bunch of rumors about the Great General *and* about the Radisha. While we evacuate. When are you leaving to get the Key?"

"I'm not sure. Soon. I'm stalling for time. So a message can get through to Slink."

Sahra nodded. She smiled. "Good thinking. Singh will have something up his sleeve."

Willow Swan suddenly invited himself to join us. "The girl is having some kind of a problem."

I scowled at him. Sahra did the same but was polite enough to ask, "The Daughter of Night? What kind of problem?"

"I think she's having a fit. A seizure, like."

"Perfect timing," I grumbled. At the same time, Sahra yelled for Tobo to get Goblin. I growled, "What were you doing anywhere near her, Swan?"

He showed some color and said, "Uh . . ."

"Aw, you dumb mudsucker! Lady did you in. You panted after her for years. Then you put the screws to a dozen million people by letting Lady's baby sister threaten to blow in your ear. Now you're going to let Lady's brat put a ring in your nose and make an even bigger idiot out of you? You really are stupid and pathetic, Swan!"

"I was just—"

"Thinking with something that isn't your brain. As though you're some dopey fifteen-year-old. This woman isn't some cute little virgin, Swan! She's worse than your worst nightmare. Come here."

He came. I moved suddenly, violently, the way I had wanted to do so many times with my uncles. The tip of my dagger penetrated the skin underneath his chin. "You really want to die a really stupid, humiliating, pointless death? Let me know. I'll arrange it. Without the rest of us having to pay the price again."

One-Eye's cackle filled the air. "Ain't she a wonder, Swan? You ought to think about her instead of your usual black widows." He was in Do Trang's spare wheelchair again but getting around under his own power.

"I could arrange something pointless and humiliating for you, too, old man."

He just laughed at me. "You invited this soldier Aridatha down here to meet his long-lost daddy, Sleepy. You ought to be dealing with him instead of here flirting with Swan."

He could be maddening at times. And he loved it. If he could find any kind of lever at all. . . . I told Swan, "You explain to One-Eye what you mean about the girl. One-Eye, deal with it. Solve it. Short of killing her. Singh won't give me the Key if we kill the skinny little . . . witch."

44

Darn. Aridatha Singh was almost enough to make me change my mind about swearing off men. He was gorgeous. Tall, well-proportioned, a beautiful smile that showed magnificent teeth even when he was under stress. His manners were perfect. He was a gentleman in every sense but condition of birth.

I told him, "Your mother must have been a marvel."

"Excuse me?"

"Nothing. Nothing. Around here, I'm called Sleepy. You're Aridatha. That's enough of an introduction."

"Who are you people? Why am I here?" He did not bluster or threaten. Amazing. Few Taglians ever recognized that as a waste of time.

"It isn't necessary for you to know who we are. You're here to meet a man who is also our prisoner. Don't mention the fact that you'll be released after your interview. He won't be. Come with me."

Moments later Aridatha Singh remarked, "You're a woman, aren't you?"

"I was the last time I checked. We're here. This is Narayan. Narayan! Get up! You have a visitor. Narayan, this is Aridatha. As promised."

Aridatha looked at me, trying to understand. Narayan stared at the son he had never seen and saw something there that made him melt, just for an instant. And I knew that I could reach him if I could keep it from looking like I was asking him to betray Kina.

I stepped back and waited for something to happen. Nothing did. Aridatha kept glancing back at me. Narayan just stared. Out of patience at last, I asked Narayan, "Shall I send people to collect Khaditya and Sugriva as well? And their children, too?"

This threatened Narayan and told Aridatha that he had been abducted because he belonged to a particular family. I recognized the instant the truth occurred to him. There was an entirely different look in his eyes when he glanced back at me again.

I said, "Not much good can be said about this man, from my point of view, but you can't call him a bad father. Fate never gave him the chance to be good or bad." Except to the girl, for whom he had done everything possible, to her complete indifference. "He's very loyal."

Aridatha realized that this was not about him at all. That he was a lever meant to get some kind of movement out of Narayan Singh. *The* Narayan Singh, the infamous chief of the Strangler cult.

Aridatha won my heart all over again when he squared up his shoulders, stepped forward and offered his father a formal greeting. There was no warmth in it but it was absolutely proper.

I watched them try to find some common ground, some point at which to start. And they found it quickly enough. We had not found any evidence, ever, to disdain Narayan Singh's affections for his Lily. Aridatha thought quite highly of his mother.

"The man's a piece of work, isn't he?"

I was startled. I had not heard a sound. But Riverwalker was behind me. River did not have much talent for lightfooting it. Which left me with the perfectly scary notion that Aridatha Singh really was having an effect on me. "Yes. He is. And I don't quite know why."

"Well, I'll tell you. He reminds me of Willow Swan. A bedrock-decent guy. Only smart. And still young enough to be unspoiled by life."

"River! You should hear yourself talk. You're halfway intelligent."

"Don't mention it in front of the guys. One-Eye will figure out why he can't cheat me at tonk more'n half the time." He considered Aridatha again. "Pretty, too. Better keep him away from your librarian. They'll elope on you."

Another broken heart. "You think? What kind of clues . . ."

"I don't know. I could be wrong."

"When does he have to be back? Can we keep him all night?"

"You figuring on testing him out?"

River did not usually rag me much, so I knew I had to be asking for it somehow. "No. Not that way. The villain in me came up with an idea. We introduce him to the Radisha before we turn him loose."

"Now you're matchmaking?"

"No. Now I'm showing a four-square guy that his ruler isn't in the Palace. He can make the rumors credible. Because he can tell the truth."

"Couldn't hurt."

"You keep an eye on those two here. I'll go talk to the Woman."

Riverwalker raised an eyebrow. Nobody but Swan used that term to describe the Radisha anymore. "You're picking up bad habits."

"Probably."

I found the Radisha lost inside herself. Not asleep, not meditating, just wandering around inside, probably feeling immensely guilty about having been relieved by her recent lack of stress. I felt a moment of compassion. She and her brother might be our foes but they were sound people at heart. *Rajadharma* had been bred into them.

"Ma'am?" She was due respect but I could not use princely titles. "I need to speak to you."

She raised her eyes slowly. They seemed to be knowing, caring eyes even in despair. "Were all of my household staff my enemies?"

"We didn't choose to become your enemies. And even today we honor and respect the royal office."

"You would, of course. To remind me of my folly. Like the Bhodi and their self-immolations."

"Our quarrel with you won't ever be as great as our quarrel with the Protector. We could never find a path to peace with her. You'd never unleash the *skildirsha* on the city. She would. And the depth of her evil is such that she doesn't see the wickedness in what she's doing."

"You're right. Do you have a name? If she was safely a few hundred years in the past, we might consider her a goddess. A power capable of smashing kingdoms out of whimsy, the way a child might kick over an anthill just to see the bugs scramble."

"I'm called Sleepy. I'm the Annalist of the Black Company. I'm also the villain who plans most of your misfortunes. This situation wasn't an intentional part of the master plan but the opportunity presented itself. Now it looks like we might've outmaneuvered ourselves."

The Radisha had become focused. "Go on."

"The Protector has chosen to cover up your disappearance. Officially you're in your Anger Chamber purifying yourself and asking the gods and your ancestors to calm your heart and give you wisdom in the coming troubled times. You have taken breaks to issue some fairly bewildering rescripts, though. My brothers brought back these two. My brothers are illiterate, so they couldn't select for content. But these are probably representative. I'll have more brought in if you like."

The Radisha read the announcement of rewards first. It was straightforward and sensible. "This must make you uncomfortable."

"It does."

"She doesn't have the money. What is this? A ten-percent reduction in the rice allowance? We don't have a rice ration. We don't need to ration rice."

"No, you don't. Though everybody who wants rice can't afford it. And some of us who would be happy to see the last of the stuff don't get to eat anything else."

"You know what this is?" The Radisha pounded her right forefinger against the rescript like she was trying to peck a hole through. "I'll bet. All those strange personalities. They don't just come out as voices. Or she was in an especially strange humor when she dictated these. She has those spells. When the voices seem to take over completely. They never last long."

Ah, I said to myself. This is an interesting tidbit, worth pursuing later. "Would you care to counter with something more sound? I don't have the manpower to cover the entire city but I can see that new rescripts are posted in the more important places."

"How do you prove they're genuine? Anyone can take a piece of treated *naada* and write something on it."

"I'm working on that. We have a guest, a highly respected soldier from one of the City Battalions. We brought him in to visit another prisoner. I thought he might pass the word that you're our prisoner, too."

"Interesting. You know what she'll do, don't you? Call your bluff. Produce an imitation or illusory version of me and challenge you to produce your Radisha. Which you won't do because you're not really interested in getting killed. Correct?"

"We can deal with that. The Protector has a serious handicap. Nobody believes anything she says. They've started thinking that way about you, too, because you're beginning to come across as her stooge. Why did you always have such a hateful and treacherous attitude toward the Company?"

"I'm not her stooge. You have no idea how many of her mad schemes I've managed to stifle."

I did not tell her that we did. I had her angry enough to talk, but prodded just a little more. "Why did you hate my brothers before they ever came down the river?"

"I didn't *hate*—"

"Maybe I chose the wrong word. There was something. The Annalists before me all sensed it and knew you'd turn on the Company as soon as you felt safe from the Shadowmasters. You weren't as obsessed as Smoke was but you shared his disease."

"I don't know. I've wondered about that a lot the last decade. It went away after I gave the order to turn on you. But Smoke and I weren't the only ones. The whole principality felt the same. There was a memory of a time before, when the Company—"

"There was no such time. Not that anybody bothered to record in the histories and documents of those days. The little I've been able to decipher of our own Annals from back then is dully routine. The only terrible battle I found came when the Company was three generations old. It took place not far from here and the Company lost. It was almost wiped out. Its three volumes of Annals fell into enemy hands. They've been in Taglian libraries ever since. From the moment the Company returned to Taglios, access to those has been denied us. All kinds of crazy things were done to keep us from getting to those books. People died because of those books. And from all I can see, the real secret that's hidden there, that had to be kept at all cost, was that nothing extraordinary happened during those early years. It was *not* an age of rapine and endless bloodshed."

"How could all the people of a dozen states remember something that never happened and become terrified that it was going to happen again?"

I shrugged. "I don't know. We'll ask Kina how she did it. Right before we kill her."

The Radisha's expression told me she was thinking she was not alone in her ability to believe the impossible.

I said, "You want to shake loose from your lunatic friend? You want to get off the hook with us? You want to get your brother back?" Presumably the possibility that the Prahbrindrah Drah still lived had grown significant in her recent thoughts.

The Radisha opened and closed her mouth several times. Never an attractive woman, age and present circumstances conspired to make her almost repulsive.

I should condemn? Time was doing no favors for me, either.

I said, "It can be managed. All of it."

"My brother is dead."

"No, he's not. No one outside the Company knows. Not even Soulcatcher. But the people she trapped out there under the plain are frozen in time. Sort of. I don't understand the mystic science involved. The point is, they're there, they're healthy, and they can be brought back out. I've just made a deal that will give us the Key we need to open the way."

"You can bring my brother back?"

"Cordy Mather, too."

The light was not good but I detected the rush of color to her neck. "There are no secrets from you people, are there?"

"Not many."

"What do you want from me?"

I never expected to be at this point with the Woman. Despite her down-to-earth, sensible, businesslike reputation. So I didn't have a ready answer. But I did manage to come up with a wish list quickly. "You could step out in public someplace where a whole lot of people would see you and recognize you and repudiate the Protector. You could exculpate the Black Company. You could fire the Great General. You could announce that you've been under Soulcatcher's evil spell for fifteen years but now you've finally made your escape. You could make us the good guys again."

"I don't know if I can do that. I've been afraid of the Black Company for too long. I'm still afraid."

"Water sleeps," I said. "What's the Protector done for you?"

The Radisha had no answer for that.

"We can bring back your brother. Think of the pressure that would take off you. *Rajadharma.*"

In a tightly controlled voice, the Radisha snapped, "Don't say that! That tears my entrails out and strangles me with them."

Exactly what I had wished on her a time or two when I was in a less forgiving mood.

Aridatha Singh looked at me oddly. "He wasn't anything like I thought Narayan Singh would be." Seeing his sovereign had not impressed him nearly so much as seeing his father had.

"Not many people are once you get to know them. River, you want to take this man back where you found him?" It was night, yes, but we still had those two protective amulets left over from the Shadowmaster wars. They definitely looked like they were still good. I wished we had another hundred but Goblin and One-Eye could not make them anymore. I am not sure why. They shared no trade secrets with me. I suppose they were just too old.

I worry a lot when I consider a future without them in it. And a future without One-Eye cannot be far away.

O Lord of Hosts, preserve him until the Captured are delivered and all our quarrels are resolved.

46

Men were charging everywhere around the warehouse. Some were continuing frenetic preparations for the Company's evacuation. Some were getting ready to accompany Narayan and me to the Grove of Doom to collect the Nyueng Bao Key. The Nyueng Bao, Do Trang's confederates and the handful still attached to the Company somehow, seemed to be doing a lot of nervous moving around just to be moving. They were scared and worried.

Banh Do Trang had suffered a stroke during the night. One-Eye's prognosis was not encouraging.

I told Goblin, "I'm not saying she had anything to do with it but Do Trang was the first one to realize that the girl was roaming around outside her flesh."

"He's just old, Sleepy. Nobody did it to him. You ask me, he's really way overdue. He hung on here because he cares about Sahra. She's all right now. It looks like her husband might actually be freed. And he's too old to run away. Soulcatcher is going to find this place eventually, once Mogaba arrives and starts searching. I wouldn't be surprised if Do Trang just decided that dying was the best thing he could do for everyone right now."

I did not want Do Trang to go, for all the reasons none of us like to see those close to us die, but also because he was, in his quiet way, the best friend the Company had had in generations.

Like everyone else, I tried to lose myself in work. I told Goblin, "Even if she's totally innocent, I want the girl fixed so she can't wander. Whatever you have to do short of permanently crippling or killing her."

Goblin sighed. Lately that was all he did when someone gave him more work. I guess he was too tired to squawk anymore.

"Where is One-Eye?"

"Uh—" Furtive look around. A whisper. "Don't say I said anything. I think he's trying to figure out how to take his equipment with us."

I shook my head and walked away.

Santaraksita and Baladitya called out to me. They had accepted their situation and were applying themselves with a will. The Master Librarian seemed particularly excited about facing a real academic challenge for the first time in years. He said, "Dorabee, in all the excitement I forgot to mention that I did get an answer to your question about a written Nyueng Bao language. There was one. And not only was there one, this oldest book is written in an antique dialect of that language. The others were recorded in an early Taglian dialect, although the original of the third volume does so employing the foreign alphabet instead of native characters."

"Which argues that the invader alphabet had well-defined phonetic values that at the time must have been more precise than those of the native script. Right?"

Santaraksita gawked. After a moment he said, "Dorabee, you never cease to amaze me. Absolutely correct."

"So have you discovered anything interesting?"

"The Black Company came off the plain, which was called Glittering Stone even then, and mostly minced around from one small principality to the next, squabbling internally over whether or not they were going to sacrifice themselves to bring on the Year of the Skulls. There was plenty of enthusiasm among the priests attached to the Company but not much among the soldiers. Many of those apparently volunteered as a way to escape something called The Land of Unknown Shadows, not because they wanted to bring on the end of the world."

"The Land of Unknown Shadows, eh? Anything else?"

"I've developed some very good information on the price of horseshoe nails four centuries ago and on the scarcity of several medicinal plants that are now found in every herb garden."

"Earthshaking stuff. Stay with it, Sri."

I meant to tell him he had to evacuate with the rest of us but decided not to upset him right away. He was having a good time. No point making him face a choice between abduction and being put to death just yet.

Uncle Doj materialized. "Do Trang wants to see you."

I followed him to the tiny room the old man had built for himself in a remote corner of the warehouse. On the way, Doj warned me that Do Trang was unable to speak. "He's already seen Sahra and Tobo. I think he was fond of you, too."

"We're going to get married in the next life. If the Gunni are right."

"I am ready to travel."

I stopped. "What?"

"I'm going with you to the Grove of Doom."

"You'd better not have some crazy idea about snatching the Key."

"I agreed to help. I'll help. I want to be there to make sure the Deceiver keeps his word. The Deceiver, Miss Sleepy. Deceiver. Also, I agreed to turn over that volume of the Books of the Dead. Its hiding place is on the way."

"Very well. The presence of Ash Wand will be a comfort to me and a vexation to my enemies."

Doj chuckled. "It will indeed."

"We won't be coming back here."

"I know. When we leave, I'll be carrying everything I wish to retain. You won't need to pretend with Do Trang. He knows his path. Do him the honor of an honest farewell."

I did more. I became all teary for the first time in my adult life. I rested my head on the old man's chest for a minute and whispered my thanks for his friendship and renewed my promise to see him in the next life. A small heresy but I do not think God has been monitoring me too closely.

Banh lifted a hand weakly and stroked my hair. And after that I got up and went away somewhere to be alone with my grief for a man who, it seemed, had never been that close, yet who was going to have a major impact on the rest of my life. I understood that after the tears stopped, I would never be quite the same Sleepy again. And that that was one legacy Do Trang wanted to leave behind.

The biggest problem I expected with the evacuation was one that came up every time the Company picked up and moved out after having been settled in one place for a long time. Roots had to be torn up. Ties had to be severed. Men had to abandon the lives they had created for themselves.

Some just would not go.

Some who did go would tell someone where they were headed.

The nominal strength of the Company was somewhat over two hundred people, a third of whom did not live in Taglios at all but maintained identities at scattered locations where they could aid brothers who were traveling. Overall, it was very much like what the Deceivers used to do. Partly that was intentional, because those people had spent centuries finding the safest ways.

Early on, couriers went out carrying code words to all our distant brothers to warn them that a time of trouble was coming. Nobody would be told what was happening, only warned that something was and that it was going to be big. Once that code word arrived, it would already be too late to drop out of anything.

Behind the couriers, eventually, would come the majority of the men, in driblets small enough not to attract attention, disguised a dozen ways, departing Taglios in what I considered their order of plausible risk. The last to leave town would be those with the heaviest entanglements. All the men would pass through a series of check-points and assembly points, each time being informed only of an immediate destination. The key hope, though, was that Soulcatcher would not begin to catch on until those who were going to go were well away.

Those who refused to go would be excused—if they remained loyal to the Company interests in the city. It would be useful to have a few agents on hand after the Company appeared to have gone.

That, too, was something the Deceivers had done for generations.

There would be flashy smoke shows. The demon Niassi would be much more prevalent, putting a damper on Grey efficiency. The men who stayed—I would not know who they were because I would be among the first to leave—would be expected to undertake what was supposed to look like a series of random assaults, break-ins and acts of vandalism that later would begin to appear to be part of a terror campaign meant to peak during the Druga Pavi. If Soulcatcher took the bait, she would spend her time preparing to ambush us there.

If not, every hour bought was an hour farther down the road my brothers would be before the Protector realized that we had done the unexpected again. And even then, I expected her to look in the wrong places for a long time.

48

My party was the first to leave Taglios. We went the morning Banh Do Trang died. With me went Narayan Singh, Willow Swan, the Radisha Drah, Mother Gota and Uncle Doj, Riverwalker, Iqbal Singh with his wife Suruvhija and two children and baby, and his brother Runmust. In addition, we had several goats with small packs and chickens tied to their backs, two donkeys, one or the other of which Gota rode much of the time, and an ox cart drawn by a beast we strove hard to keep looking sadder and scruffier than it really was. Most everyone adopted some form of disguise. The Shadar trimmed their hair and beards and the whole family adopted Vehdna dress. I stayed Vehdna but became a woman. The Radisha became a man. Uncle Doj and Willow Swan shaved their heads and became Bhodi disciples. Swan darkened himself with stain but there was no way to change his blue eyes. Gota had to do without Nyueng Bao fashions.

Narayan Singh remained exactly the same, virtually indistinguishable from thousands of others just like him.

We looked bizarre, but even stranger bands collected to share the rigors of the road. And we would collect together only when we camped. On the road we stretched out over half a mile, one Singh brother out front, the other in back, while River stayed fairly close to me. The brothers carried a pair of devices given them by Goblin and One-Eye. If Narayan, the Radisha or Swan strayed far from a line running between them, choke spells would begin constricting around their throats.

None of the three had been informed of that. We were all supposed to be friends and allies now. But I believe in trusting some of my friends more than others.

On the Rock Road that the Captain had had built between Taglios and Jaicur, we did not catch the eye at all. But a crowd like that, with a baby and an ox cart and regular Vehdna prayers and whatnot, is not swift. Nor did the season help. I became thoroughly sick of the rain.

The last time I traveled down the Rock Road I rode a giant black stallion that covered the distance between Taglios and Ghoja on the River Main in a day and a night without hurrying.

Four days after leaving the city we were still at least that long from the bridge at Ghoja, which would be our first dangerous bottleneck. In the afternoon Uncle Doj chose to announce that we had come as close as the road would carry us to the place where he had hidden the copy of the Book of the Dead.

"Aw, darn," I said. "I was hoping it would be way farther down the road. How are we going to explain having a book if we get stopped?"

Doj showed me his palms and a big smile. "I'm a priest. A missionary. Blame it on me." Despite the hardships, he was happy. "Come help me dig it up."

"What is this place?" I asked two hours later. We had come into something that might have come from one of Murgen's old nightmares about Kina. Twenty yards of woods formed a palisade all around it.

"It's a graveyard. During the chaos of the first Shadowlander invasion, before the Black Company came, possibly even before you were born, one of the Shadowlander armies used this as a camp, then as a burial ground. They planted the trees to conceal the tombs and monuments from enemy eyes." Noting my appalled expression, he added, "Down there they have different customs for dealing with the dead."

I knew that. I had been there. I had seen it. But never had I seen it so concentrated, nor exuding such an air of depression. "This is grim."

"A spell makes it seem that way. They thought they would come back and turn the place into a memorial after they won the war. They wanted to keep people away."

"I'm willing to go along with their wishes. This is too creepy for me."

"It's not that bad. Come on. This shouldn't take more than a few minutes."

It did, but not a lot longer. It was a matter of pulling the door away from one of the fancier tombs and digging out a bundle wrapped in several layers of oilskins.

"This is a place worth remembering," Doj said as we went away. "People around here won't come near it. People from farther away don't know about it. It's a good hideout."

"I can't wait."

"You'll love the Grove of Doom, too."

"I've been there. I didn't like it, either, but at the time I was too worried about Stranglers to be scared of ghosts or ancient goddesses."

"It's another good place to hide."

I am not suspicious by nature the way Soulcatcher is but I am suspicious occasionally. I am particularly suspicious of reticent old Nyueng Bao who suddenly turn chatty and helpful. "The Captain hid out there once," I said. "He didn't find the place congenial, either. What're you up to?"

"Up to? I don't understand."

"You understand perfectly, old man. Yesterday I was just another *jengali*, albeit one you had to tolerate. Today, suddenly, I'm getting unsolicited advice. I'm being offered the benefit of your accumulated wisdom, like I'm some kind of apprentice. You want me to take a turn carrying that?" He was, after all, an old man.

"As the pace and pressures have increased and events have taken unexpected— but usually favorable—twists, I've begun reflecting more intently on the wisdom of Hong Tray, on the foresight she showed, even upon her devilish sense of humor, and I believe I'm finally beginning to grasp the full significance of her prophecies."

"Or of mass quantities of bullfeathers. Tell it to Sahra and Murgen next time you see them. And put a little honest sentiment into your apologies."

My attempt to be unpleasant did not subdue him. That took the arrival of the afternoon rains, a little early, a lot heavy, supported by a truly ferocious fall of hail. Along the road, dashing out from under the trees where we had left our own party, a score of travelers tried to collect the ice before it melted. Taglians never see snow, and rainy-season storms provide the only time they ever see ice—unless they travel far down into what used to be the Shadowlands, to the higher elevations of the Dandha Presh.

Scavenging hailstones was a young people's game. The old folks pushed under the trees as far as they could get, wearing their rain gear. The baby would not stop crying. She did not like the thunder. Runmust and Iqbal tried to keep an eye on the children as well as to watch unknown travelers closely. They were convinced that anyone met on the road might be an enemy spy. Which seemed a perfectly sensible attitude to me.

Riverwalker prowled, cursing the rain. That also seemed a perfectly sensible attitude.

Uncle Doj did a fine job of not drawing attention to his burden. He settled beside Gota. She began to gripe but without her usual enthusiasm.

I sat down near the Radisha. We were calling her Tadjik these days. I said, "Have you begun to understand why your brother found life on the road so appealing?"

"I trust you're being sarcastic?"

"Not entirely. What was the worst crisis you faced today? Your feet get wet?"

She grunted. She got the point.

"I believe it was the politics he resented. The fact that no matter what he considered doing, there were always a hundred selfish men who wanted to subvert his vision for their own profit."

"You knew him?" the Radisha asked.

"Not well. Not to philosophize with. But he wasn't a man who kept his views secret."

"My brother? Being away must've changed him a lot more than I thought it could, then. He never revealed his inner self while he lived in the Palace. That would have been too risky."

"His power was more secure out there. He didn't have to please anyone but the Liberator. His men came to love him. They would've followed him anywhere. Which got most of them killed when you turned on the Company."

"He's *really* alive? You aren't just manipulating me for your own ends?"

"Of course I am. Manipulating you, that is. But it *is* true that he's alive. All the Captured are. That's why we left Taglios even though we had your side on the run. We want our brothers out before we do anything more."

I heard a whisper. "Sister. Sister."

"What?"

The Radisha had not spoken. She eyed me inquisitively. "I didn't say it."

I glanced around apprehensively, saw nothing. "Must just be the rain in the leaves."

"Uhm." The Radisha was not convinced, either.

Hard to believe. I really missed Goblin and One-Eye.

I found Uncle Doj again. "Lady insisted that you're a minor wizard. If you have any talent at all, please use it to see if we're being watched or followed." Once Soulcatcher started looking for us outside Taglios, it should not take long for her crows and shadows to find us.

Uncle Doj grunted noncommittally.

49

Real fear found us the morning after next, just when it seemed we had every reason to be positive. We had made good time the day before, there were no crows around yet, and it looked like we would reach the Grove of Doom before the afternoon rains, which meant we could complete our business there and get clear before night fell. I was happy.

A band of horsemen appeared on the road south of us, headed our way. As they drew nearer, it became evident that they were uniformly clad. "What should we do?" River asked.

"Just hope they aren't looking for us. Keep moving." They showed no interest in travelers ahead of us, though they forced everyone off the road. They were not galloping but were not dawdling, either.

Uncle Doj drifted nearer the donkey not carrying Gota. Ash Wand lay hidden amidst the clutter of tent and tent poles that formed that animal's burden. Several precious fireball projectors were among the bamboo tent poles, too.

We had very few of those left now. We would have no more until we fetched Lady out of the ground. Goblin and One-Eye could not create them themselves—though Goblin admitted privately that the opposite would have been the case even just ten years ago.

They were too old for almost anything that required flexible thought and, especially, physical dexterity. The mist projector was, in all probability, the last great contribution they would make. And most of the nonmagical construction on that had been accomplished using Tobo's young hands.

I caught a glint of polished steel from the horsemen. "Left side of the road," I told River. "I want everybody over there when we have to get out of their way."

But I spoke too late. Point-man Iqbal had already jumped off to the right. "I hope he has sense enough to get back across after they pass by."

"He isn't stupid, Sleepy."

"He's out here with us, isn't he?"

"That's a fact."

The band of horsemen turned out to be what I expected: the forerunners of a much larger troop which, in turn, proved to be the vanguard of the Third Territorial Division of the Taglian Army.

The Third Territorial Division was the Great General's personal formation. Which meant that God had chosen to bring us face-to-face with Mogaba.

I tried not to worry about what sort of practical joke God was contemplating. Only He knows His own heart. I just made sure my whole crowd was on the left side of the road. I got us loosened up even more. Then I worried about which of us might be recognizable by Mogaba or any veterans who had been around long enough to recall the Kiaulune and Shadowmaster wars.

None of us were memorable. Few of us went back far enough to have crossed paths with the Great General. That is, except Uncle Doj, Mother Gota, Willow Swan . . . right! And Narayan Singh! Narayan had been a close ally of the Great General in the days before the last Shadowmaster war. Those two had had their wicked heads together innumerable times.

"I will need to alter my appearance."

"What?" The skinny little Deceiver had materialized beside me, startling me. If he could sneak up like that . . .

"This will be the Great General, Mogaba. Not so? And he might recognize me even though it has been years since last we stood face-to-face."

"You astonish me," I admitted.

"I do what the goddess desires."

"Of course." There is no God but God. Yet every day I had to deal with a goddess whose impact on my life was more tangible. There were times when I had to struggle hard not to think. In Forgiveness He is Like the Earth. "Suppose you just borrow some clothing and get rid of your turban?" Though doing nothing struck me as the perfect solution with him. As noted before, Narayan Singh resembled the majority of the poor male Gunni population. I thought Mogaba would have trouble recognizing him even if they had been lovers. Unless Narayan gave himself away. And how could he do that? He was the Master Deceiver, the living saint of the cult.

"That might work."

Singh drifted away. I watched him, suddenly suspicious. He could not be unaware of his own natural anonymity. Therefore he must be trying to create a predisposed pattern of thought inside my mind.

I wished I could just cut his throat. I did not like what he did to my thinking. I could easily become obsessed with concerns about what he was really doing. But we needed him. We could not collect the Key without him. Even Uncle Doj did not know exactly what we were seeking. He had never actually seen, or even known about, the Key before it was stolen. I hoped he would recognize it if he saw it.

I might spend a little time thinking how we could get around my having given him such solid guarantees that he was willing to travel with us and trust us not to murder the Daughter of Night while they were separated.

The cavalry finished clattering past. They had paid us no heed, since we had not insisted on getting in their way. Behind them a few hundred yards came the first battalion of infantry, as neat, clean and impressive as Mogaba could keep them while on the march. I received several offers of temporary marriage but otherwise the soldiers were indifferent to our presence. The Third Territorial was a well-disciplined, professional division, an extension of Mogaba's will and character, nothing like the gangs of ragged outcasts that constituted the Company.

We were a military nil anyway. We could not get together and fight our weight in lepers today, let alone deal with formations like the Third Territorial. Croaker's heart would be broken when we dragged him out of the ground.

My optimism began to fade. With the soldiers hogging the road, we traveled much slower. The landmarks showing the way to the Grove of Doom were in sight but still hours away. The cart and the animals could not be pushed on muddy ground.

I began to watch for a place to sit out the rain, though I did not recall any good site from previous visits to the area. Uncle Doj was no help when I asked. He told me, "There is no significant cover closer than the grove."

"Someone should go scout that."

"You have reason for concern?"

"We're dealing with Deceivers." I did not mention that Slink and the band from Semchi were supposed to meet us there. Doj did not need to know. And Slink might have gotten slowed down if he had to duck around Mogaba's army and patrols.

"I'll go. When I can leave without arousing curiosity."

"Take Swan. He's the most likely to give us away." The Radisha was a risk, too, though thus far she had shown no inclination to yell for help. But Riverwalker was close enough to grab her by the throat if she even took a deep breath.

She was not stupid. If she intended to betray us, she meant to wait till she could manage it with some chance of surviving the attempt.

Uncle Doj and Willow Swan managed to drift away without attracting attention, though Uncle had to go without Ash Wand. I joined River and the Radisha. I noted, "This country is a lot more developed than it used to be." When I was young, most of the land between Taglios and Ghoja was deserted. Villages were small and poor and supported themselves on minimal tracts of land. There were no independent farms in those days. Now the latter seemed to be everywhere, founded by confident and independence-minded veterans or by refugees from the tortured lands that once lay prostrate under the heels of the Shadowmasters. Many of the new farms crowded right up to the road right-of-way. They made getting off the road difficult at times.

The force moving north numbered about ten thousand, men enough to occupy miles and miles of roadway even without the train and camp followers coming on behind. Soon it was obvious we would not reach the Grove of Doom before the rains came and might not get there before nightfall.

Given any choice at all, I did not want to be anywhere near the place after dark. I had gone in there by night once before, ages ago, as part of a Company raid meant to capture Narayan and the Daughter of Night. We murdered a lot of their friends but those two had gotten away. I remembered only the fear and the cold and the way the grove seemed to have a soul of its own that was more alien than the soul of a spider. Murgen once said that being in that place at night was as bad as walking through one of Kina's dreams. Though of this world, it had a powerful otherworldly taint.

I tried to ask Narayan about it. Why had his predecessors chosen that particular grove as their most holy place? How had it been different from other groves of those times, when humanity's impact on the face of the earth had been so much less?

"Why do you wish to know, Annalist?" Singh was suspicious of my interest.

"Because I'm naturally curious. Aren't you ever curious about how things came to be and why people do the things they do?"

"I serve the goddess."

I waited. Evidently he deemed that an adequate explanation. Being somewhat religious myself, I could encompass it even though I did not find it satisfying.

I offered a snort of disgust. Narayan responded with a smirk. "*She* is real," he said.

"She is the darkness."

"You see her handiwork around you every day."

Not true. "Untrue, little man. But if she ever gets loose, I think we will." This discussion had become terribly uncomfortable suddenly. It put me in the position of admitting the existence of a god other than my god, which my religion insisted was impossible. "There is no God but God."

Narayan smirked.

Mogaba did the one good thing he had ever done for me. By turning up in person he saved me the rigorous and embarrassing mental gymnastics necessary to reconfigure Kina as a fallen angel thrown down into the pit. I knew it could be done. Elements of Kina myth could be hammered into conformity with the tenets of the only true religion, given a quick coat of blackwash, and I would have completed a course of religious acrobatics elegant enough to spark the pride of my childhood teachers.

Mogaba and his staff traveled three quarters of the way toward the rear of the column. The Great General was mounted, which was a surprise. He was never a rider before. The greater surprise, though, was the nature of his steed.

It was one of the sorcerously bred black stallions the Company had brought down from the north. I had thought they were all dead. I had not seen one since the Kiaulune wars. This one not only was not dead, it was in outstanding health. Despite its age. It also appeared bored by the business of travel.

"Don't gape," Riverwalker told me. "People get curious about why other people are curious."

"I think we can afford to stare some. Mogaba will feel like he deserves it." Mogaba looked every bit the Great General and mighty warrior. He was tall and perfectly proportioned, well-muscled, well-clad, well-groomed. But for the dust of silver in his hair, he looked little older than he had been when first I saw him, right after the Company captured Jaicur from Stormshadow. He had had no hair then, having preferred to shave his head. He seemed in a good humor, not a condition I had associated with him in the past, when all his schemes had come to frustration as the Captain just seemed to bumble around and do the one thing that would undo all his efforts.

As the Great General came abreast, his mount suddenly snorted and tossed its head, then shied slightly, as though it had stirred up a snake. Mogaba cursed, although he was never in any danger of losing his seat.

Laughter dropped out of the sky. And a white crow fell right behind it, alighting precariously atop the pole carried by the Great General's personal standardbearer.

Cursing still, Mogaba failed to note that his steed turned its head to watch me as I passed.

The darned thing winked.

I had been recognized. The beast must be the very one I had ridden so long ago, for so many hundreds of miles.

I began to get nervous.

Someone amongst Mogaba's personal guard launched an arrow at the crow. It missed. It fell not far from Runmust, who shouted angrily before he thought. Now the Great General vented his spleen upon the archer.

The horse continued to watch me. I fought an urge to run. Maybe I could get through this yet. . . .

The white crow squawked something that might have been words but were just racket to me. Mogaba's mount jumped enough to freshen the well of vituperation. It faced forward and began to trot. The ultimate effect was to divert attention from us southbound scrubs.

Everybody but Iqbal's Suruvhija stared at the ground and walked a little faster. Soon we were past the worst danger. I drifted over beside Swan, who was still so nervous he stuttered when he tried to crack a joke about pigeons coming to roost on the Great General while he was still alive.

Laughter passed overhead. The crow, up high, was almost indistinguishable against the gathering clouds. I wished I had someone along who could advise me about that thing.

For a generation, crows have not been good omens for the Company. But this one seemed to have done us a favor.

Could it be Murgen from another time?

Murgen would be watching, I was sure, but that crow had no way to communicate. So maybe so. . . .

If so, this encounter would have been an adventure for him, too, what with him knowing that if we got caught, his chances for resurrection plummeted to zero.

The passages of the Great General held us up long enough that we could not leave the road unremarked until after the rains began falling hard enough to conceal our movements from everyone except someone extremely close by. We left the road unnoticed then. Our travel formation collapsed into a miserable pack. Only Narayan Singh showed real eagerness to get to the grove. And he did not hurry. Not often long on empathy, I found myself pitying Iqbal's children.

Swan pointed out, "It'd be to Singh's advantage to get us there just after night falls."

"Darkness always comes."

"Uhn?"

"A Deceiver aphorism. Darkness is their time. And darkness always comes."

"You don't seem particularly bothered." He was hard to hear. The rainfall was that heavy.

"I'm bothered, buddy. I've been here before. It isn't what you'd call a good place." I could not state that fact with sufficient emphasis. The Grove of Doom was the heart of darkness, a spawning ground for all hopelessness and despair. It gnawed at your soul. Unless you were a believer, apparently. It never seemed to trouble those for whom it was a holy place.

"Places are natural, Sleepy. People are good and evil."

"You'll change your mind after you get there."

"I got a sneaking suspicion I'm gonna drown first. Do we got to be out in this?"

"You find a roof, I'll be glad to get under it." Big thunder had begun fencing with swords of lightning. There would be hail before long. I wished I had a better hat. Maybe one of those huge woven-bamboo things Nyueng Bao farmers wear in the rice paddies.

I could just make out Riverwalker and the Radisha. I followed them hoping they were following someone they could see. I hoped we did not have anyone get disoriented and lost. Not tonight. I hoped the guys from Semchi were where they were supposed to be.

Iqbal appeared in the gloom as the hail began to fall. He bent over to try to ease the sting of the missiles. I did the same. It did not help much.

Iqbal shouted, "Left, down the hill. There's a stand of little evergreens. Better than nothing at all."

Swan and I dashed that way. The hailstones kept getting bigger and more numerous as the thunder got louder and the lightning closer. But the air was cooling down.

There is a bright side to everything.

I slipped, fell, rolled, found the trees the hard way, by sliding in amongst them. Uncle Doj and Gota, River and the Radisha were in there already. Iqbal was an optimist. *I* would not have called those darned things trees. They were bushes suffering from overweening ambition. Not a one was ten feet tall and you had to get down on your belly in the damp and needles to enjoy their shelter. But their branches did break the fall of the hailstones, which rattled and roared through the foliage. I started to ask about the animals but then heard the goats bleating.

I felt a little guilty. I do not like animals much. I had been shirking my share of their caretaking.

Hailstones dribbled down through the branches and rolled in from outside. Swan picked up a huge example, brushed it off, showed it to me, grinned and popped it into his mouth.

"This is the life," I said. "When you're with the Black Company, every day is a paradise on earth."

Swan said, "This would be a superb recruiting tool."

As those things always do, the storm went away. We crawled out and counted heads and discovered that not even Narayan Singh had gone missing. The living saint of the Stranglers did *not* want to leave us behind. That book really was important to him.

The rain dwindled to a drizzle. We clambered out of the muck, many communing bluntly with their preferred gods while we formed up. We did not spread out much now, except for Uncle Doj, who managed to disappear into a landscape with almost no cover.

Over the next hour we ran into several landmarks I recognized from Croaker's and Murgen's Annals. I kept an eye out for Slink and his companions. I did not see them. I hoped that was a good omen rather than a bad.

The later it got, the more peachy it seemed to Narayan Singh. I was afraid he would curse us all by betraying a genuine smile. I considered mentioning his children's names just to let him know he was weighing on my mind.

My divination skills were flawless. It was dusk when we reached the grove. We were all miserable. The baby would not stop crying. I was developing a blister from walking in wet boots. With the possible exception of Narayan, not a soul amongst us remained mission-oriented. Everybody just wanted to drop somewhere while somebody else got a fire going so we could dry out and get something to eat.

Narayan insisted that we press on to the Deceiver temple in the heart of the grove. "It'll be dry there," he promised.

His proposal aroused no enthusiasm. Though we were barely inside its boundary, the smell of the Grove surrounded us. It was not a pleasant odor. I wondered how much worse it was back in the heyday of the Deceivers, when they murdered people there often and in some numbers.

The place possessed strong psychic character, an eerieness, a creepiness. Gunni would blame that on Kina because this was one of the places where a fragment of her dismembered body had fallen, or something such. Despite the fact that Kina was also supposed to be bound in enchanted sleep somewhere on or under or beyond the plain of glittering stone. Gunni do not have ghosts. We Vehdna do. Nyueng Bao do. For me, the grove was haunted by the souls of all the victims who died there for Kina's pleasure or glory or whatever reason Stranglers kill.

Had I mentioned it, Narayan or one of the more devout Gunni would have brought up the matter of rakshasas, those malignant demons, those evil night-rangers jealous of men and gods alike. Rakshasas might pretend to be the spirit of someone who had passed on, merely as a tool for tormenting the living.

Uncle Doj said, "Like it or not, Narayan is right. We should move into the best shelter available. We would be no less safe there than here. And we would be free of this pestilential drizzle." The rain just would not go away.

I considered him. He was old and worn out and had less reason to want to move on than any of us younger folks. He must have a reason to want to go on. He must know something.

Doj always did. Getting him to share it was the big trick.

I was in charge. Time for an unpopular decision. "We'll go ahead."

Grumble grumble grumble.

The temple projected a presence more powerful than that of the Grove. I had no trouble locating it without being able to see it. Walking close behind, Swan asked me, "How come you never tore this place down when you were on top?"

I did not understand his question. Narayan, just ahead of me, overheard it and did understand. "They tried. More than once. We rebuilt it when no one was watching." He launched a rambling rant about how his goddess had watched over the builders. It sounded like a recruiting speech. He kept it up until Runmust swatted him with a bamboo pole.

It was one of *those* poles, too, though Narayan did not know. The grove was a very dark place, perfect for an ambush by shadows. Runmust was not going to go quietly.

I could not help wondering what evils Soulcatcher was up to now that she had complete freedom to work her will upon Taglios.

I hoped the people who stayed behind completed their missions, particularly those tasked to penetrate the Palace again. Jaul Barundandi had to be recruited and brought in too deep to run before his rage subsided sufficiently for reason to re-assert itself.

The baby continued to cry, burrowing into her mother's breast without looking for nourishment. The noise worried everyone. Anyone who wished to visit misfortune upon us would have no trouble tracking us. We would be unlikely to hear them sneaking up, because of the crying and the sound of drizzle falling from branch to branch in the waterlogged trees. River and the Company Singhs kept their hands on their weapons. Uncle Doj had recovered Ash Wand and was keeping it handy despite the risk of rust.

The animals were as thrilled as the infant was. The goats bleated and dragged their feet. The donkeys kept getting stubborn, but Mother Gota knew a trick or three for getting balky beasts of burden moving. A considerable ration of pain was involved.

The rain never ended.

Narayan Singh took the lead. He knew the way. He was home.

I felt the dread temple loom before us although I could not see it. Narayan's sandals whispered as they scattered soggy leaves. I listened intently but heard nothing new until Willow Swan started muttering, nagging himself for having followed up on the one original idea he had ever had. If he had ignored it, he could be rocking beside a fireplace in his own home, listening to his own grandkids cry, instead of tramping through the blue miseries on yet one more mystery quest where the best he could look forward to was to stay alive longer than the people dragging him around. Then he asked me, "Sleepy, you ever consider throwing in with that little turd?"

Somewhere, an owl screamed.

"Which one? And why?"

"Narayan. Bring on the Year of the Skulls. Then we could all finally sit back and relax and not have to slog around in the rain and shit anymore."

"No. I haven't."

The owl screamed again. It sounded frustrated.

What sounded like crow laughter answered it, taunting.

"But that's what the Company set out to do in the first place, isn't it? To bring on the end of the world?"

"A handful of the senior people did, apparently. But not the guys who actually had to do the work. There's a chance they didn't have any idea what it was all about. That they marched because staying home might be a less pleasant option."

"Some things never change. I know that story by heart. Careful. These steps are slicker than greased owl shit."

He had heard the birds conversing, too. That was a northern saying that lost something in translation.

Rain or no, the goats and donkeys flat refused to move any nearer the Deceiver shrine, at least until a light took life inside the temple doorway. That came from a single feeble oil lamp, but in the darkness it seemed almost bright.

Swan observed, "Narayan knows right where to look, don't he?"

"I'm watching him. Every minute." For what good keeping a close eye on a Deceiver would do.

To tell the truth, I was counting on Uncle Doj. Doj would be much harder to trick. He was an old trickster himself. As a trickmaster, I needed to stick to what I knew, which was designing wicked plots and writing about them after they ran their course.

Something flapped overhead as I entered the temple. Owl or crow, I did not turn quickly enough to discover the truth. I did tell Runmust and Iqbal, "Keep a close watch while I check this out. Doj. Swan. Come with me. You know more about this place than anyone else."

Below, River and Gota swore vilely as they strove to keep the goats under control. Iqbal's sons had fallen asleep where they stood, indifferent to the ongoing rain.

Narayan blocked my advance just steps inside the temple. "Not until I complete the rituals of sanctification. Otherwise you'll defile the holy place."

It was not my holy place. I did not care if I defiled it. In fact, that sounded like an amusement to be indulged—just before I had the place torn down yet again and this time plowed under. But I did have to get along. For the moment. "Doj. Keep an

eye on him. Runmust. You, too." He could pick the living saint off with his bamboo
if the Deceiver tried to be clever.

"We have an understanding," Narayan reminded me. He seemed troubled. And
not by me. He kept poking around like he was looking for something that was supposed to be there but just was not.

"You make sure you hold up your end, little man." I stepped back outside, into
a drizzle that had become more of a heavy, falling mist.

"Sleepy," Iqbal whispered from the base of the steps. "Check what I found."

I barely heard him. The baby continued to crank. Long-suffering Suruvhija
rocked her and hummed a lullaby. She was not much more than a girl herself and, I
suspected, not very bright. I could not imagine any woman being happy with her life,
but Suruvhija seemed content to go where Iqbal led. A breeze stirred the branches of
the grove. "What?" Of course I could not see. I descended the temple steps into the
damp, chilly darkness.

"Here." He shoved something into my hands.

Pieces of cloth. Fine cloth, like silk, six or seven pieces, each with a weight in one
corner.

I smiled into the face of the night. I snickered. My faith in God was restored.
The demon had betrayed her children again. Slink had gotten to the grove in time.
Slink had been sneakier than any Deceiver. Slink had done his job. He was out there
somewhere right now, covering us, ready to offer Narayan another horrible surprise. I felt much more confident when I went back inside and yelled at Narayan,
"Get your skinny ass moving, Singh. We've got women and children freezing out
here."

Narayan was not a happy living saint. Whatever he was looking for, under cover
of fortifying the temple against the defiling presence of unbelievers, just was not
there to be found.

I was tempted to toss him the captured rumels. I forbore. That would only
make him angry and tempt him to go back on his agreement. I did tell him, "You've
had time enough to sanctify the whole darned woods against the presence of non-
believers, don't you think? You forget how miserable it is out here?"

"You should cultivate patience, Annalist. It's an extremely useful trait in both
our chosen careers." I forbore mentioning that we had been patient enough to get
him tucked into our trick bag. Then his exasperation surfaced for a moment. He
hurled something to the floor. He was not out of control by much but it was the
first time I ever saw him less than perfectly composed when he was supposed to
be the master of the situation. He whispered something as he beckoned me. I do
believe he took his goddess's name in vain.

This new version of the temple was scarcely a shadow of what Croaker and Lady
had survived. The present idol was wooden, not more than five feet tall and unfinished. The offerings before it were all old and feeble. The temple as a whole did not

possess the sinister, grim air of a place where many lives had been sacrificed. These were lean times for Deceivers.

Narayan persisted in his search. I could not bring myself to break his heart by telling him the friends he expected to meet must have fallen foul of the friends I'd hoped to meet. You need to keep a certain amount of mystery in any relationship.

I said, "Tell me where it's all right to spread out and where you'd rather we didn't and I'll see that we do our best to honor your wishes."

Narayan looked at me like I'd just sprouted an extra head. I told him, "I've been thinking a lot lately. We're probably going to be working together for a while. It'd make things easier for everybody if we all made the effort to respect one another's customs and philosophies."

Narayan scooted off. He began the process of laying a fire and of telling people where they could homestead. The temple was not that big inside. There would not be much room to spread out there.

Singh would not turn his back on me.

"You spooked him good," Riverwalker told me. "He'll spend the whole night with his back to the wall, trying to stay awake."

"I hope my snoring helps. Iqbal, don't do that." The fool had actually started helping Mother Gota set up to do some cooking. That old woman was a menace around a cook fire. She was already under a ban throughout the Company. She could boil water and give it a taste to gag you.

Iqbal grinned a grin that told the world he needed to consult One-Eye about his teeth. "We're setting this up for me."

"All right." Much better. Much much better.

After she finished helping Iqbal, the old woman helped milk the goats. Now I understood how Narayan felt. Maybe I should keep my back to a wall and watch my dozing, too.

Gota was not even complaining.

And Uncle Doj had stayed outside, presumably to enjoy the refreshing weather and cheerful woods.

52

It was dry in that wicked temple but it never got warm. I do not believe a brush-fire could have routed the chill that inhabited that place, that gnawed into your bones and soul like an ancient and ugly spiritual rheumatism. Even Narayan Singh felt it. He hunched over the fire, twitching, as though he expected a blow from behind at any minute. He muttered something about his faith having been tested enough.

I do not belong to an empathetic and compassionate brotherhood. Those who offend us must look forward to moments of extreme discomfort, should God in His magnanimity see fit to present us with the opportunity to provide it. And our antipathy toward Narayan Singh was so old it had become ritual. So it was not with any commiseration that I told him, "We're prepared to make the exchange. Our First Book of the Dead for your Key."

His head came up. He stared at me directly, the true Narayan behind the masked Narayan considering me coldly. Wariness took life in the corners of his eyes. "How could—"

"Never mind. We have it. A swap was the deal. And we're ready to swap now."

Calculation began to replace caution. I would have bet a handsome sum he was assessing his chances of murdering us in our sleep so he would not have to keep his side of the bargain.

"It would be, perhaps, a less elegant solution than mass murder, Narayan, but why not just do the deal the way we agreed?" I shivered. The temple seemed to be getting colder, if that was possible. "In fact, I'll give you a bonus. Once you hand over the Key, you can go. Away. Free. As long as you vow not to screw with the Black Company anymore." A vow he would make in an instant, I was sure, such vows being worth the bark they are written on when they spring from the mouths of Deceivers. Kina would not expect him to keep faith with an unbeliever.

"A truly generous offer, Annalist," Singh replied. Suspiciously. "Let me sleep on it."

"By all means." I snapped my fingers. Iqbal and Runmust broke out the shackles. "Put the goatbells on him tonight, too." We had several of those, to go with several goats. Once attached to Narayan's shackles, they made a racket whenever he moved. He was a stealthmaster, but not master enough to keep the bells from betraying him. "But don't be surprised if I don't feel as generous when light and warmth return to the world. Darkness always comes, but the sun also rises."

I had my blanket around me already. I pulled it tighter and lay down, squirmed a little in a vain attempt to get comfortable, then fell into the sort of evil-haunted dreams apparently experienced by anyone who passes the night in the Grove of Doom.

I was aware that I was dreaming. And I was familiar with the dreamscapes, though I had never visited them myself. Both Lady and Murgen had written about them. The visual elements did not trouble me terribly. But nothing had prepared me for the stench, which was the stink of thousand-week-old battlefields, worse than any stench I remembered from the siege of Jaicur. Countless crows had come to banquet there.

After a while I began to feel another presence, far off but approaching, and I was afraid, not wanting to come face-to-face with Narayan's dreadful goddess. I wanted to run but did not know how. Murgen had drawn upon years of experience when he eluded Kina.

Then I realized I was not being stalked. This presence was not inimical. In fact, it was more aware of me than I of it. It was amused by my discomfort.

Murgen?

'Tis I, my apprentice. I thought you'd dream here tonight. I was right. I like being right. It's one of the joys of bachelorhood I had forgotten until I became a haunt.

I don't think Sahra would appreciate—

Of course not. Forget that. I don't have time. There're things you should know and I won't be able to reach you again directly until you enter the dark roads on the glittering plain. Listen.

I "listened."

Life in Taglios was proceeding normally. The scandal at the royal library and disappearance of the chief librarian had been played into a major distraction by the Protector. Soulcatcher was more interested in consolidating her position than in rooting out remnants of the Black Company. After all these years she still did not take us as seriously as we wanted. Or she was completely confident that she could root us out and exterminate us any time she felt like bothering.

That being a possibility, Murgen's advice was sound. We should keep moving fast while that option was available.

The best news was that Jaul Barundandi had shown an eager willingness to attach himself to the cause in hopes of avenging his wife. His initial assignment, to be carried out only if he was confident he could manage without getting caught or leaving evidence, was to penetrate the Protector's quarters and steal, destroy, or somehow incapacitate the magical carpets she had stolen from the Howler. If those could be denied her, our position would improve dramatically. He was also to recruit allies—without telling them that he was helping the Black Company. The ancient hysterical prejudice remained potent.

It sounded wonderful but I counted on nothing. Men driven solely by a need for revenge are flawed tools at best. If he let the obsession consume him, he would be lost to us before he could do any of the quiet, long-term things that make an inside man such a treasure.

The bad news was bad indeed.

The main party, traveling by water, had passed through the delta and was now ascending the Naghir River, meaning, it was way ahead of us in terms of time still needed to reach the Shadowgate.

One-Eye had suffered a stroke two nights earlier, during a drunken knock-down-drag-out with his best friend Goblin.

Death did not claim him. Goblin's swift intercession had prevented that. But now he suffered from a mild paralysis and the sort of perplexing speech problems that sometimes come after a stroke. The latter made it difficult for One-Eye to communicate to Goblin what Goblin needed to know to cope with the problem. The words One-Eye wanted to say or write were not the words that came out.

A problem that is maddening enough for the ordinary Annalist, coping only with time constraints and native stupidity.

You cannot prepare yourself enough. The inevitable is always a shock when it lowers its evil wing.

As if responding to a great joke, the circling crows rattled with dark, mocking laughter. The skulls in the bonefield grinned, enjoying the grand joke, too.

There were more minor bits of news. Once Murgen exhausted his store, I asked, *Can you reach Slink if he's here? Can you put a thought into his empty head?*

Possibly.

Try. With this.

My idea amused Murgen. He hurried off to haunt Slink's certain-to-be-strange dreams. The crows scattered, as though there was nothing interesting keeping them around anymore.

I continued to people the place of nightmare, hoping I would not become a regular, as had befallen Lady and Murgen. I wondered if Lady still went there, making her interment that much more a session in hell.

A crow landed high up in a barren tree, against the face of what passed for a sun in that place. I could not distinguish it but it seemed different from the other crows.

Sister, sister. I am with you always.

Terror reached down inside me and squeezed my heart with a fist of iron. I shot bolt upright. Panic and confusion swamped me as I grabbed for my weapons.

Doj stared at me from beyond the fire. "Nightmares?"

I shivered in the cold. "Yes."

"They're the bad side of staying here. But you can learn to shut them out."

"I know what to do about them. Get away from this godforsaken place as soon as I can. Tomorrow. Early. Right after the Deceiver turns over the Key and you authenticate it."

I thought I heard faint crow laughter in the night outside.

I took my turn on watch. I discovered that I was not the only one with problem dreams. Everyone slept poorly, including Narayan. Iqbal's baby never stopped whimpering. The goats and donkeys, though not allowed inside, also bleated and snorted and whimpered all night long.

The Grove of Doom is just plain a Bad Place. No way around that. Some things *are* black and white.

Morning was not much more pleasant than night had been. And even before breakfast, Narayan tried to sneak away. Riverwalker showed remarkable restraint in bringing him back still able to walk.

"You were going to run out on me now?" I demanded. I had a good idea what he really had in mind but did not want him to suspect I knew what had become of the friends he had expected to rescue him. "I thought you wanted that book back."

He shrugged.

"I had a dream last night. And it wasn't a good dream. It took me places I didn't want to go, with beings I didn't want to see. But it was a true dream. I came away with the certainty that neither of us has any chance of getting what we want if we don't fulfill our ends of our bargain. So I'm here to tell you I'm playing it straight up, the Book of the Dead for the Key."

Narayan betrayed a flicker of annoyance at my mention of a dream. No doubt he had hoped for divine guidance and had failed to receive it last night. "I just wanted to look for something I left here last time I visited."

"The Key?"

"No. A personal trinket." He squatted beside the cook fire, where Mother Gota and Suruvhija were preparing rice. The Radisha, to the amazement of all, was trying to help. Or, better put, was trying to learn what was being done so she could help at another time. Neither woman offered the Princess's status any special respect. Gota snarled and complained at the Radisha exactly as she would have done with the rest of us.

I watched Narayan eat. He used chopsticks. I had not noticed that before. Paranoid me, I searched my memory, trying to remember if Singh had used the customary wooden spoon in the past. Uncle Doj, like all Nyueng Bao, used chopsticks. And he claimed they constituted some of his deadliest weapons.

I was going to go crazy if I did not get Narayan out of my life for a while.

He smiled as though he was reading my mind. I think maybe he put too much faith in my word on behalf of the Company. "Show me the book, Annalist."

I looked around. "Doj?"

The man appeared in the temple doorway. What was he up to in there? "Yes?"

"The Master Deceiver wishes to see the Book of the Dead."

"As you wish." He descended the leaf-strewn outer steps, rummaged through one of the donkey packs, came up with the oilskin package we had retrieved from the Shadowlander tomb. He presented it to the Deceiver with a bow and a flourish, stepped back and crossed his arms. I noted that in some mystic manner, Ash Wand had found its way onto his back. I recalled that Doj's adopted family bore Narayan Singh and the Strangler cult an abiding grudge. Deceivers had murdered To Tan, the son of Sahra's brother Thai Dei. Thai Dei lay buried beneath glittering stone with the Captured.

Uncle Doj had offered no promises to Narayan Singh.

I wondered if Singh knew all that. Most of it, probably, though the subject never arose in his presence.

I noted, also, that without plan or signal, my other companions had placed themselves so that we were surrounded by armed men. Only Swan seemed unsure of his role. "Settle and have some rice," I told him.

"I *hate* rice, Sleepy."

"We're going places where there'll be a little more variety. I hope. I've eaten rice till it's coming out my ears, too."

Narayan opened the oilskins reverently, set them aside one by one, ready to be reused. The book he revealed was big and ugly but not much distinguished it from volumes I saw every day when I was Dorabee Dey Banerjae. Nothing branded it the most holy, most sacred text of the darkest cult in the world.

Narayan opened it. The writing inside was completely inelegant, erratic, disorganized and sloppy. The Daughter of Night had begun inscribing it when she was four. As Narayan turned the pages I saw that the girl was a fast learner. Her hand improved rapidly. I saw, too, that she had written in the same script used to record the first volume of the Annals. Were both in the same language?

Where was Master Santaraksita when I needed him?

Out on the Naghir with Sahra and One-Eye. No doubt complaining about the accommodations and the lack of fine dining. Too bad, old man. I have the same problems here.

"Satisfied that it's genuine?" I asked.

Narayan could not deny it.

"So I've lived up to my half of the bargain. I have, in fact, made every effort to facilitate it. The game is back to you now."

"You have nothing to lose, Annalist. I still wonder how I would get away from here alive."

"I won't do anything to keep you from leaving. If revenge is absolutely necessary, it'll be that much sweeter down the road." Narayan tried to read my true intentions. He was incapable of accepting anything at face value. "On the other hand, there's no way you'll go anywhere if you don't produce the Key. And we'll know if you try to pass off a substitute." I looked at Doj.

Narayan did the same. Then he settled into an attitude of prayer and sealed his eyes.

Kina may have responded. The grove did turn icy cold. A sudden breeze brought a ghost of the odor from the place of the bones.

Singh shuddered, opened his eyes. "I have to go into the temple. Alone."

"Wouldn't be a back way out of there, would there?"

Singh smiled softly. "Would it do me any good if there were?"

"Not this time. Your only way out of here is not to be a Deceiver."

"So be it. There'll be no Year of the Skulls if I don't take a chance."

"Let him go," I told Doj, who stood between Narayan and the temple. River and Runmust, I noted, now had bamboo in hand, in case the little man made a break.

H e's been in there a long time," River complained.

"But he's still there," Doj assured us. "The Key must be well hidden."

Or not there anymore, I did not say. "What're we looking at here?" I asked Doj. "I'm not clear on what this Key is. Is it another lance head?" The Lance of Passion had opened the plain to Croaker, then had ushered the Captured to their doom.

"I've only heard it described. It's a strangely shaped hammer. He's about to come out."

Narayan appeared. He seemed changed, invigorated, frightened. Riverwalker gestured with his bamboo. Runmust raised his slowly. Singh knew what those poles could do. He had no chance if he tried to run now.

He carried what looked like a cast-iron war hammer, old, rusty, and ugly, with the head all chipped and cracked. Narayan made it seem heavier than it looked.

"Doj?" I asked. "What do you think?"

"Fits the description, Annalist. Except for the head being all cracked."

Singh said, "I dropped it. It cracked when it hit the temple floor."

"Feel it, Doj. If there's any power there, you ought to be able to tell."

Doj did as I said once Singh surrendered the hammer. The Nyueng Bao seemed startled by its weight. "This must be it, Annalist."

"Take your book and start running, Deceiver. Before temptation makes me forget my promises."

Narayan clutched the book but did not move. He stared at Suruvhija and the baby.

Suruvhija was using a red silk scarf to dab spit-up off the infant's chin.

Fools! Idiots!

While we were getting ready to travel, one of Iqbal's kids—the older boy—noticed a particularly deep flaw in the head of the hammer. The rest of us had been too busy congratulating ourselves and deciding what the Company would do once we brought the Captured forth from the plain. The boy got his father's attention. Iqbal summoned Runmust and me.

Being old folks, it took us a while to see what the boy meant. Us having bad eyes and all.

"Looks like gold in there."

"That would explain the weight. Doj. Come here. You ever hear anything about this hammer being gold inside?"

Iqbal began prying with a knife. A fragment of iron fell away.

"No," Doj said. "Don't damage it any more."

"Everybody calm down. It's still the Key. Doj, study it. Carefully. I don't want all the years and all the crap we went through to go to waste now. What?" Weapons had begun to appear.

"Look who's here," Swan said. "Where did those guys come from?"

Slink and his band had arrived. I exchanged looks with Slink. He shrugged. "Gave us the slip."

"I'm not surprised. We screwed up here. He knew somebody was out there." Suruvhija still had the red scarf draped over her shoulder. "Folks, we need to get traveling. We want to get across the bridge at Ghoja before the Protector starts looking for us." From the beginning I had pretended that getting across that bridge would give us a running chance.

I told Slink, "You guys did a great job at Semchi."

"Could've been better. If I'd thought about it, I'd've waited till they damaged the Bhodi Tree. Then we'd have been heroes instead of just bandits."

I shrugged. "Next time. Swan, tell that goat we're going to eat it if it don't start cooperating."

"You promise?"

"I promise we'll get some real food when we get to Jaicur."

55

Our crossing at Ghoja was another grand anticlimax.

We all worked ourselves into a state of nerves before we reached the bottleneck. I sent Slink forward to scout and did not believe a word, emotionally, when he reported the only attention being paid anyone went to those few travelers who argued about paying a two-copper pais toll for use of the bridge. These tightwads were commended to the old ford downstream from the bridge. A ford that was impassable because this was the rainy season. Traffic was heavy. The soldiers assigned to watch the bridge were too busy loafing and playing cards to harass wayfarers.

Some part of me was determined to expect the worst.

Ghoja had grown into a small town serving those who traveled the Rock Road, which was one of the Black Company's lasting legacies. The Captain had had the highway paved from Taglios to Jaicur during his preparations for invading the Shadowlands. Prisoners of war had provided the labor. More recently, Mogaba had used convicts to extend the road southwestward, adding tributaries, to connect the cities and territories newly taken under Taglian protection.

Once we were safely over the Main, I began to ponder our next steps. I gathered everyone. "Is there any way we could forge a rescript ordering the garrison here to arrest Narayan if he crosses the bridge?"

Doj told me, "You're too optimistic. If he's going south, he's already ahead of us."

Swan added, "Not to mention that if he fell into the Protector's hands, she'd find out everything he knows about you."

"The voice of an expert heard."

"I didn't take the job voluntarily."

"All right. She could, yes. He knows where we're headed. And why. And that we have the Key. But what does he know about the other bunch? If he doesn't get caught, won't he try to intercept them so he can do something about getting the Daughter of Night away from them?"

No one found any cause to disagree.

"I suggest we remind one another of that occasionally, so it gets said sometime when Murgen is around to hear it." Sahra never promised to spare Narayan's ragged old hide. Maybe she could ambush him and take back that unfinished first Book of the Dead.

Swan pointed out, "That crow is still following us."

A small but lofty fortification overlooked the bridge and ford from the south bank. The bird was up top watching us. It had not moved since our crossing. Maybe it wanted to rest its bones, too.

River whispered, "We still have one bamboo pole with crow-killing balls in it."

"Leave it alone. It doesn't seem to mean any harm. For now, anyway." I was sure it had tried to communicate several times. "We can take it out if anything changes."

At Ghoja we heard nothing but the traditional grumbling about those in charge. Rumors concerning events in Taglios seemed so exaggerated that no one believed a tenth of anything they heard. Later, after we reached Jaicur and were taking it easy for a while, the temper of rumor began to change. It now carried a subtle vibration suggesting the great spider at the heart of the web had begun to stir. It would be a long time before any concrete news caught up but the general consensus was that we should get going right now and not dawdle along the way.

Runmust discovered that a man answering Narayan's description had been seen lurking in the vicinity of the shop operated by his now-pseudonymous offspring, Sugriva. "The man does have a weakness. Should we kill Sugriva while we're here?"

"He's never done anything to us."

"His father did. It would be a reminder to him."

"He doesn't need reminding. If Narayan is so dim that he thinks we're done with him now, let him. Just let me be there to see the look on his face when we catch him again."

Narayan had stood out in Jaicur because the city was still very nearly a military encampment. People would remember us as well, if asked during the next few weeks.

I roamed around looking for my childhood a few times but nothing that I remembered, people or places, good or evil, remained. That past survived nowhere but within my mind. Which was the one place I wished that it could die.

The practical rules of Company field operations resemble those obeyed by stage magicians. We would prefer our audience saw nothing at all but we do realize that invisibility is impractical. So we try to show the watcher something other than what he is looking for. Thus the goats and donkeys. And, south of Jaicur, all new looks and identities for everybody, with the enlarged party breaking up into two independently traveling "families," plus a group of failed southern fortune-hunters dragging home in despair and defeat after having had their spirits crushed by the Taglian experience. There were quite a few men of the latter sort around. They had to be watched. Many were not above taking advantage of weaker parties if they thought they could manage it. The roads were not patrolled anymore. The Protector did not care if they were safe.

Doj and Swan, Gota and I formed the advance party. We looked weak but that old man was worth four or five ordinary mortals. We had only one scrape. It was over in seconds. Several blood trails led off into the brush. Doj had chosen to leave no one dead.

The land became less hospitable and rose steadily. In clear air it was possible to look ahead and catch the faintest glimpse of the peaks of the Dandha Presh, still many days' journey south of us. The paved road ended alongside an abandoned work camp. "They must've run out of prisoners," Swan observed. The camp had been stripped of everything portable.

"What they ran out of is enemies Soulcatcher thought were worth an investment in a road. She could always find people she doesn't like and use them up in an engineering project." And she had done so on the western route, which was being followed by the rest of the Company. They would have paved footing all the way to Charandaprash. Their road, and the waterways serving it, had remained under construction until just a few years ago, when the Protector evidently decided the Kiaulune wars really were over, that it was not necessary to make life easy for the Great General and his men, and bullied the Radisha into no longer spending the money.

I wondered what the Radisha's perspective would be. I suspected she had believed she was in charge right up to the moment we disappeared her. Then she had begun getting an education, here amongst her faithful subjects.

We reached Lake Tanji, which I love. The lake is a vast sprawl of icy indigo beauty. When I was a lot younger, we fought our deadliest encounter with the things that had given the Shadowmasters their names there. More than a decade later you could still see places where rock had melted. If you went exploring some of the narrow gulches scarring the hillsides, you could find clutches of human bones that had come back to the surface with time.

"This is a place of dark memory," Doj remarked. He had been here for that battle, too. And so had Gota, who had stopped complaining long enough to deal with her memories also.

She really did have a lot of pain these days.

The white crow streaked overhead. It dropped down the slope ahead, vanished into the ragged foliage of a tall mountain pine. We saw that bird almost every day now. There was no doubt it was following us. Swan swore that it had tried to strike up a conversation with him once when he was out in the brush relieving himself.

When I asked what it wanted, he said, "Hey, I got the hell out of there, Sleepy. I've got problems enough. I don't need to get known as a guy who gossips with birds, too."

"It might've had something interesting to say."

"Without a doubt. And if it *really* wants to tell somebody something badly enough, it'll come talk to you."

Right now Swan looked down the slope and said, "It's hiding from something."

"But not from us." I looked back up the slope. The ground appeared untouched up there. There was no sign of other travelers. Below me, downhill, the meandering track appeared occasionally upon the slope and along the shore, both of which were deserted. This was no longer a popular route. "I could retire beside that lake," I told Swan.

"Must not be the best place or somebody would've beaten you to it."

He had a point. This country was far emptier now than it had been twenty years ago. Then there had been villages around the lake.

"There you go," Swan said, looking back.

"What?" I looked. It took a moment. "Oh. The bird?"

"Not just a bird. A crow. The regular kind of crow."

"Your eyes are better than mine. Ignore it. If we don't pay it any special attention, it shouldn't have any reason to concentrate on us." My heartbeat was rising, though.

Maybe it was just a feral crow and had nothing to do with Soulcatcher. Crows are not fastidious about their dining.

Or maybe the Protector had, at last, begun looking for us outside of Taglios.

White crow in hiding, black crow in the air, searching. What did it mean?

Not much we could do about it, whatever. Though Uncle Doj had a calculating eye whenever he looked up at the black crow.

It lost interest after a while. It went away. I told the others, "That shouldn't be a problem. Crows are smart, for birds, but one by itself can't remember a lot of instructions or carry much information back. If it is one of hers." We had to assume that it was. Crows were much less common than they used to be. Those remaining always seemed to be under Soulcatcher's control. Her control was probably why they were dying out.

If this one *was* a scout for the Protector, it would be days yet before it could report.

Doj observed, "If it was suspicious, we can expect to have shadows around in a few days."

That would be Soulcatcher's best means of scouting us. Shadows traveled faster than crows, could be given much more complex instructions and could bring back far more information. But could Soulcatcher control them so far away? The original Shadowmasters had had major difficulties managing their pets over long distances.

We passed along the shores of Lake Tanji. Each of us seized an opportunity to bathe in the icy water. The old road then led us on to the Plain of Charandaprash, where the Black Company had won one of its greatest triumphs and the Great General had suffered his most humiliating defeat—through no fault of his own. Though a capricious history would not recall the blame due his cowardly master, Longshadow. Wreckage from that battle still lay scattered across the slopes. A small garrison watched over the approaches to the pass through the Dandha Presh. It showed no interest in clearing any mess or, even, in monitoring traffic. Nobody looked my group over. Nobody asked questions. We were assessed an unofficial toll and warned that the donkey might find the footing treacherous in the high pass because there was still ice on the rocks up there. We did learn that there had been heavier traffic than usual lately. That told me that Sahra's group had encountered no insuperable difficulties and was ahead of us, as it should be, even with all the old men and reluctant companions.

The mountains were far colder and more barren than the highlands we had crossed. I wondered how the Radisha was handling it, about her thoughts concerning the empire she had acquired, mostly thanks to the Company. Doubtless her eyes had been opened some.

They needed a lot of opening. She had spent most of her life cooped up inside the Palace.

The white crow turned up every few days but its darker kinfolk did not. Maybe the Protector was preoccupied elsewhere.

I wished I had Murgen's talent for leaving his body. I had not had so much as a good dream since leaving the Grove of Doom. I knew exactly as little as everyone else. And that was extremely frustrating after having had easy access to secrets from afar for so long.

Nights in the mountains get really cold. I told Swan I was tempted to take up his suggestion that we go off somewhere and set up housekeeping in our own tavern and brewery. When it got really cold, a few lesser sins did not seem to matter.

The timing of events in Taglios is uncertain because the principal reporter, Murgen, had maintained such a casual relationship with the concept for the last decade and a half. But his sketchy descriptions of events in the city following our departure are of more than passing interest.

At first the Protector suspected nothing. The stay-behinds planted smoke buttons and started rumors but with a declining enthusiasm the Taglian peoples began to sense. At the same time, though, the populace developed an abiding suspicion that the Protector had done away with the reigning Princess. The people became less tractable by the hour.

The arrival of the Great General and his forces guaranteed the peace. Moreover, it freed the Protector to go hunting enemies instead of spending her time making sure her friends remained intimidated enough to continue supporting her. In just days she found the Nyueng Bao warehouse on the waterfront, empty now except for a few cages occupied by missing members of the Privy Council, none of whom were in shape to resume their duties. An armamentarium of booby traps came with the prodigal ministers, of course, but none of those were clever enough to inconvenience Soulcatcher herself. Quite a few Greys were not so fortunate. The Protector took rather a heartless view of those who did fall victim to the Company legacy. "Better to get the dimwits winnowed out now, when the broader risk is minimal," she told Mogaba. The Great General's attitude complemented hers precisely.

Questions asked in the neighborhood produced no information of substance, however vigorously they were put. The Nyueng Bao merchants had been careful to maintain a veil around themselves and their businesses. They had even employed the magical in their quest for greater anonymity. Wisps of confusion spells persisted yet.

"I smell those two wizards," Soulcatcher muttered. "But you promised me that they were dead, didn't you, Great General?"

"I saw them die myself."

"You'd better hope you don't irritate *me* so much you don't survive to see them die again, for real." Her voice was that of a spoiled child.

The Great General did not respond. If Soulcatcher frightened him, he showed no sign. Neither did he betray any anger. He waited, reasonably confident that he was too valuable to become the victim of an evil caprice. Perhaps, in his heart of hearts, he thought the Protector was not equally valuable.

"There's no trace of them," Soulcatcher mumbled later, in a voice academically cool. "They're gone. Yet the impression of their presence persists, as bold as a bucket of blood thrown against a wall."

"Illusion," Mogaba said. "I'm sure you'd find a hundred instances in the Black Company Annals of where they drew an enemy's eye in one direction while they moved in another. Or made someone believe their numbers were far greater than they actually were."

"You'd find as many instances in my diaries. If I bothered to keep any. I don't, because books are nothing but repositories for those lies the author wants his reader to believe." The voice she used now was the antithesis of academic. It was that of a man who knew, from painful experience, that education just taught people sneakier ways to rob you. "They aren't here anymore but they may have left spies."

"Of course they did. It's doctrine. But you'll have a hell of a time finding them. They won't be people anyone else would suspect."

Jaul Barundandi and two of his assistants laid out a dinner while the Protector and her champion talked. Their presence attracted no notice. Paranoid though she was, Soulcatcher paid little heed to the furniture. Every staffer had been interrogated in the hours following the Radisha's disappearance and no inside accomplices had been found.

The Protector was not unaware that she was not as beloved of the staff as the Radisha had been. But she was not troubled. No mundane attacker had any genuine hope of penetrating her personal defenses. And these days she had no peer in this world. Sheer perversity and protracted elusiveness had put her in a position to elect herself queen of the world. If she wanted to bother.

Someday, when she got her head organized, she was going to have to think about that.

Halfway through a rare meal Soulcatcher paused in mid-chew. She told Mogaba, "Find me a Nyueng Bao. Any Nyueng Bao. Right now. Right away."

The lean black man showed no emotion as he rose. "May I ask why?"

"Their headquarters was inside a Nyueng Bao warehouse. Nyueng Bao have been associated with the Company since the fighting at Dejagore. The last Annalist married one of them. He had a child by her. The association may be more than historical happenstance." She knew a great deal more about Nyueng Bao than she was willing to share, of course.

Mogaba inclined his upper body in a ghost of a bow. Mostly he was comfortable working with Soulcatcher. Mostly he approved of her thinking. He went in search of someone who could catch him a couple of swamp monkeys.

The servants hovered around the Protector, perfectly attentive. Idly, she noted that these three were among the same half dozen who struggled to make her life easier wherever she happened to be in the Palace. In fact, one or more always followed her on her exploratory safaris into the maze of abandoned corridors that made up the majority of the Palace, just in case she needed something. Lately they had brought life into her personal quarters, which for so long had been as chill and barren and dusty as the empty sectors.

It was their nature. It was bred into them. They must serve. Without the Radisha to fulfill their need for a master, they had had to turn to her.

Mogaba was away hours longer than she liked. When the man did deign to return, her voice of choice was spoiled-brat querulous. "Where have you been? What took you so long?"

"I've been demonstrating how hard it is to catch the wind. There are no Nyueng Bao anywhere in the city. The last time anyone can remember seeing any of them was the day before yesterday, in the morning. They were going aboard a barge that later headed downriver, toward the swamps. Evidently the swamp people have been leaving Taglios since *before* the Radisha disappeared and you hurt your heel."

Soulcatcher growled. She did not want to be reminded that she had been tricked. The heel itself was reminder enough.

"The Nyueng Bao are a stubborn people."

"Famous for it," Mogaba agreed.

"I've visited them twice before. Each time they failed to appreciate my full message. I suppose I'll have to go preach to them again. And round up any fugitives they've taken in." It was an obvious conclusion, that the Company survivors had retreated into the swamps. The Nyueng Bao had taken in fugitives before. And supportive evidence was available if the Protector cared to dig. The barges carrying the majority of the Company had gone downriver. You had to go down into the delta to get to the Naghir River, which was the principal navigable waterway leading into the south.

Soulcatcher popped up. She rushed out with the bounce and enthusiasm of a teenager. Mogaba settled down to contemplate the remains of his meal, which had not yet been cleared away. One of the servants murmured, "We thought you might wish to continue, sir. Should you prefer otherwise, we will clear away instantly."

Mogaba looked up into a bland face that projected eagerness to serve. Nevertheless, he had a momentary impression that the man was measuring his back for a dagger.

"Take it away. I'm not hungry."

"As you wish, sir. Girish, take the leftovers to the charity postern. Make certain the beggars there know that the Protector is thinking of them."

Mogaba watched the servants depart. He wondered what had given him the impression that that man was insincere. The truth supposedly lay in a man's deeds, and that one never behaved as anything less than a totally devoted servant.

S oulcatcher stamped into her personal suite. The more she thought about the Nyueng Bao, the more enraged she became. What would it take to teach those people? That seemed like something they could work out between them before the sun came up. A night of shadow-terror ought, at the very least, to put them into a mood to pay attention.

Soulcatcher understood herself better than outsiders believed she did. She wondered why she was in so foul a temper, which seemed to go beyond her usual caprice and irritability. She belched, hammered her chest with a fist to loosen another burp. Maybe it was the spicy food. She sensed bad heartburn coming. She felt a little light-headed, too.

She climbed to the parapet where she kept the only two flying carpets left in the world. That could be reached only by the route she followed. She would go down there and make those swamp monkeys pay for the heartburn, too. Dinner had been a Nyueng Bao ethnic specialty consisting of big, ugly mushrooms, uglier eels, and unidentifiable vegetables in a blisteringly spicy sauce, served upon a bed of rice. It had been a favorite of the Radisha's, served often. The kitchens had not changed their routines, because the Protector did not care about the menu.

The Protector belched again. The growing heartburn seared her insides.

She jumped on the larger carpet. It creaked under her weight. She ordered it to head downriver. Fast.

A few miles out, four hundred feet above the rooftops, streaking faster than a racing pigeon, sabotaged frame members under the carpet began to snap. Once the first went, the stress became too much for the others. The carpet disintegrated in seconds.

A burst of light flared, bright enough to be seen by half the city. The last thing Soulcatcher saw, as she arced toward the surface of the river, was a huge circle of characters declaring "Water Sleeps."

Just before the flash leaped through his window, a bemused Mogaba discovered a folded, sealed letter on his spartan cot. Belching, glad he had eaten no more of that spicy food, he broke the wax and read "My brother unforgiven." Then the unexpected lightning grabbed his attention. He read the slogan in the sky, too. All the labor he had invested in learning to read over the past few years was to be rewarded thus?

What now? If the Protector was gone? Pretend she was in hiding, too, and make the deceit a double veil?

He belched again, settled down on his cot. He did not feel well at all. That was a baffling new feeling for him. He never got sick.

58

A chatty youngster of native stock and a more than customarily ambitious disposition interviewed us at the military control point we encountered at the southern end of the pass. He was not yet old enough to be pompously officious but he would get there. Personally, he seemed more interested in foreign news than in contraband or wanted men. "What's going on up north?" he wanted to know. "We've seen a lot of refugees lately." He examined our meager possessions without ever looking inside anything.

Gota and Doj rattled at one another in Nyueng Bao and pretended not to understand the young man's accented Taglian. I shrugged and responded in Jaicuri at first, which is close enough to Taglian for the two peoples to understand one another most of the time, but here it only frustrated the young official. I had no desire to stand around gossiping with a functionary. "I do not know about others. We have had nothing but decades of misfortune and suffering. We heard there were opportunities down here so we abandoned the Land of Our Sorrows and came."

The official assumed I meant a particular country, as I had hoped, rather than recognizing that the Land of Our Sorrows was the Vehdna way of describing where a convert lived before he became acquainted with God.

"You say there are many others doing the same as us?" I tried to sound troubled.

"Recently, yes. Which is why I feared something might be afoot."

He feared for the stability of the empire to which he had attached himself. I could not resist a prank. "There were rumors that the Black Company had surfaced in Taglios and was warring with the Protector. But there are always crazy stories about the Black Company. They never mean anything. And they had nothing to do with our decision."

The young man became more unhappy. He passed us through without further interest. I did not bother commending him but he was the only official we had encountered since leaving Taglios who was making a serious effort to perform his duties. And he was doing it only in hopes of getting ahead.

I never had to bring out the richly complex legend I have invented for our foursome, in which Swan was my second husband, Gota the mother of my deceased first spouse and Doj her cousin, all of us survivors of the wars. The story would have played in any region where there had been any extended fighting. Splatchcobbled family survival teams were not at all uncommon.

I complained, "I worked on weaving us a history all the way down here and I never got to use it. Not once. Nobody's doing their job."

Doj smiled and winked and vanished into the broken ground beside the road, off to reclaim the weapons we had hidden before approaching the checkpoint.

"Somebody should do something about that," Swan declared. "Next vice-regal subofficer I see, I'll march right up and give him a piece of my mind. We all pay taxes. We have a right to expect more effort from our officials."

Gota woke up long enough to call Swan an idiot in Taglian and Nyueng Bao. She told him he ought to shut up before even the God of Fools renounced him. Then she closed her eyes and resumed snoring. Gota had begun to concern me. She had shown less life every day for the past few months. Doj seemed to think she believed she no longer had anything to live for.

Maybe Sahra could get her going again. We should be joining up with the others before long. Maybe Sahra could get her excited about rescuing Thai Dei and the Captured.

I was troubled about consequences. All these years I had striven toward the undertaking we would launch before long, and now, for the first time, I had begun to wonder what success might really mean. Those people buried out there never were paragons of sanity and righteousness. They had had almost two decades to ferment in their own juices. They were unlikely to entertain much brotherly love toward the rest of the world.

And then there was the guardian demon Shivetya and, somewhere, the enchanted and enchained thing worshipped by Narayan Singh and the Daughter of Night. Not to mention the mysteries and dangers of the plain itself. And all the perils we did not yet know.

Only Swan had any experience of that. He had nothing positive to report. Nor had Murgen at any time over the years, though his experiences had been dramatically different from Swan's. Murgen had experienced the glittering plain in two worlds at once. Swan seemed to have experienced the version in our world in sharper focus. Even after so many years he could describe particular landmarks in exquisite detail.

"How come you never talked about this before?"

"I never hid it, Sleepy. But there just don't seem to be much percentage in volunteering anything in this world. If I admit anything I know about that place, *next* thing I'll know is, good old Willow Swan is elected to go back up there as the guide for a gang of invaders guaranteed to irritate the shit out of whatever spirits haunt the place. Am I right? Or am I right?"

"You aren't as stupid as you let on. I thought you didn't see any spirits."

"Not the way Murgen claimed he saw them but that don't mean I didn't feel them creeping around. You'll find out. You try to sleep at night when you feel hungry shadows calling you from a few feet away. It's like being inside a zoo with all the predators in the world slavering just the other side of the bars. Bars that you can't see and can't even feel and so have no way of knowing if they're trustworthy. And all this jabber ain't doing my nerves any good at all, neither, Sleepy."

"We may never have to go up there, Swan—if the Key we've got is a fake or isn't any good anymore. Then there won't be anything we can do but maybe set up your brewery and pretend we never heard of the Protector or the Radisha or the Black Company."

"Be still, my heart. You know goddamn well that thing's going to be the true Key. Your god, my gods, somebody's gods have got a boner for Willow Swan and they're gonna keep making sure that whatever happens, it's gonna be the worst possible thing and it's gonna happen to me. I oughta run out on you now. I oughta turn you in to the nearest royal official. Only that would let Soulcatcher know that I'm still alive. Then she'd get real nasty, asking me why I didn't turn you in three, four months ago."

"Not to mention you'd probably get yourself dead long before you could unearth an official who cared enough to listen to you."

"There's that, too."

Doj came back with the weapons. We passed them around, resumed traveling. Swan continued eloquently describing himself as the firstborn son of Misfortune. He went through these spells of high drama.

A half mile down the road we encountered a small peasants' market. A few old folks and youngsters who could not contribute much on the farm waited to take advantage of travelers still shaking from the miseries of the mountains. Fresh foods in season were their hot sellers but they retailed gossip at no charge as long as you contributed a few snippets of your own. They found doings beyond the Dandha Presh particularly intriguing.

I asked a young girl, who looked like she could be the little sister of the customs official back up the road, "Do you remember many of the people who came through here? My father was supposed to have come down ahead of us, to find us a place to settle." I proceeded to describe Narayan Singh in detail.

The child was a lighthearted thing, without a care or concern. Chances were she did not recall what she had eaten for breakfast. She did not remember Narayan but went off to find someone who might.

"Where was she when I was young enough to get married?" Swan grumbled. "She'll be pretty when she's older and she doesn't have a brain in her head to complicate things."

"Buy her. Bring her along. Raise her up right."

"I'm not as pretty as I used to be."

I tried to think of someone who was. Not even Sahra qualified.

I waited. Swan muttered. Doj and Gota wandered around, Uncle swapping tales and Mother examining the wares for sale. Except for the produce, those were feeble. She did acquire a scrawny chicken. The one positive of our travel team was that there were no Gunni or Shadar to complicate mealtime. Only Gota, who kept trying to do the cooking. Maybe I could murder the chicken in her sleep and get it roasted before she woke up.

The girl brought a very old man. He was no help, either. He seemed interested only in telling me what he thought I wanted to hear. But it did seem possible that Narayan had come through the pass some time before we had.

I hoped Murgen was on the job and had alerted the others to the possibilities.

Doj and Gota headed on down the road before I finished with the locals, surprised that my command of the language was adequate to the task. Evidently Gota was tired of riding. The donkey certainly could use the break.

"Is that a pet?" the small girl asked.

"It's a donkey," I said, really astonished that I had been having so little trouble communicating. They had donkeys down here, did they not?

"I know that. I meant the bird."

"Huh! Well." The white crow was perched on the donkey's pack. It winked. It laughed. It said, "Sister, sister," and flapped into the air, then glided on down the mountain.

Swan said, "I was just thinking I found an upside to this trip. It's not raining down here."

"Maybe I'll see if they'll let *me* have the child. In exchange for your strong back."

"We're getting a little too domestic here, Goodwife . . . Sleepy? Didn't you ever have a real name?"

"Anyanyadir, the Lost Princess of Jaicur. But even now my wicked stepmother has discovered that I still live and has summoned the princes of the rakshasas to bargain with them for my murder. Hey! I'm kidding. I'm Sleepy. And you've known me practically since I started being Sleepy, off and on. So just let it be."

Once we cleared the mountains, it was no long journey to the site of Kiaulune. Incredible destruction had been wrought there during the Shadowmaster wars, then during the Kiaulune wars between the Radisha and those who chose to keep faith with the Black Company. A pity most of the wreckage had been cleared away even before Soulcatcher decided she could declare victory and go north to claim her new place as Protector of All the Taglias. The Radisha should have seen it at its worst, to understand what she had wrought by betraying her contract with the Company. But the worst now existed only in the memories of survivors. The once-clamorous valley now boasted a sizable town and a checkerboard of new farms peopled by a mixture of natives, former prisoners of war and deserters from every conceivable faction. Peace had broken out and was being enthusiastically exploited on the presumption that it could not possibly last.

The transition from the old Kiaulune, once called Shadowcatch, and the new, simply called the New Town, saw one thing remain unchanged. Over there on the far slope of the valley, miles and miles away, beyond the crumbled, brush-strewn ruins of once-mighty Overlook, where the land quickly changed from rich green to almost barren brown, was the dreaded thing called the Shadowgate. It did not stand out but I felt its call. I told my companions, "We have to be careful not to get in a hurry now. Haste could be deadly."

The Shadowgate was not just the only way we could get up onto the plain to go free the Captured, it was also the only portal through which the shadows imprisoned up there could escape and begin treating the whole world the way their cousins had the destitute of Taglios. And that gate was in tender shape. The Shadowmasters had injured and weakened it badly when gaining access to the shadows they enslaved.

"We're in complete agreement on that," Uncle Doj replied. "All the lore emphasizes the need for caution."

There had been some disagreement between us lately. He had resumed his romance with the idea of the Company Annalist becoming his understudy in the peculiar role he played among the Nyueng Bao. The Company Annalist who had no great interest in the job but Doj was one of those people who just have grave difficulties getting their minds around the concept "No!"

"That's new," I said, indicating a small structure a quarter mile below the Shadowgate, beside the road. "And I don't like its looks." It was hard to tell from so far but the structure looked like a small fortification built of stone salvaged from the rubble of Overlook.

Doj grunted. "A potential complication."

Swan observed, "We keep standing around looking like spies, somebody's going to get unpleasant with us."

A point not without substance, although those in charge seemed awfully lax. It was obvious that trouble had not visited in a while. Quite probably not since the Black Company left. "Somebody—probably named me, because I'm the only one here who looks like what she says she is—will have to go scout around." The original plan had been for everybody to camp in the barrens not far downhill from where that new structure now stood.

I was troubled. Someone should have been watching for us to come out of the mountains. I hoped that was just Sahra's oversight. She had been married to the Company for an age but never did learn to think like a soldier. If nobody offered good advice, or she chose to ignore the advice she was given because, like many civilians, she could not grasp why all the little horsepuckey things have to be done, she might not have thought it important to watch for us.

I prayed it was as simple as that.

Nobody demanded that I give them the role of scout. Poor me. More sore feet while the rest of them loafed around in the shade of young pines.

The white crow materialized minutes after I turned the knee of a hill and the others were out of sight. It swooped at me and squawked. It swooped at me again. I tried to swat it like it was some huge, really annoying bug. It laughed and came back, now squawking what sounded like words.

I got it. Finally. The bird wanted me to follow it. "Lead on, fell harbinger, never forgetting that I'm not Gunni and therefore hobbled by no holy ban against eating meat." I had enjoyed, if that is the proper word, crow stew several times during the lowest lows of my military career.

The crow had only my interests at heart. It led me straight to a large tent village on a hillside overlooking the near outskirts of the New Town. Our people had to be only some of the refugees housed there but Sahra's hand was obvious everywhere. The layout was neat and orderly and clean. Exactly as the Captain's rules insisted, though those are honored mainly in the breech when he is not around.

I suffered an immediate conflict. Charge ahead to see everyone I had missed for months? Or run back and collect my traveling companions? Once I started grabbing, it might be hours before—

My choice got made for me. Tobo spotted me.

My first warning was a shout. "Sleepy!" A mass of churning arms and legs charged in from the left and collected me in a totally unexpected hug.

I wriggled loose. "You've grown." A lot. He was taller than me now. And his voice had deepened. "You won't be able to be Shiki anymore. The great men of Taglios will be brokenhearted."

"Goblin says it's time I start breaking the girls' hearts, anyway." There was not much doubt that he would have the power to do that. He was going to be a handsome man who had no lack of confidence.

Uncharacteristically, I slipped an arm around his waist and walked down toward where other familiar faces had begun to appear. "How was your journey?"

"Mostly kind of fun, except when they made me study, which was about all the time. Sri Surendranath is worse than Goblin but he says I could be a scholar. So Mother always backs them up whenever anybody wants to make me study. But we got to see a lot of neat things. There was this temple in Praiphurbed that was completely covered with carvings of people doing it all different ways—oh, I'm sorry." He reddened.

Tobo had a mental image of me as a sort of chaste nun. And most of my adult life would not contradict that view. But I am not against interpersonal adventures, I am just not interested myself. Probably because, Swan insists, I have not yet run into the man whose animal presence completely overwhelms my intellectual reluctance. Swan being a leading authority in his own mind.

He keeps volunteering. Who knows? Maybe someday I will become curious enough to experiment, just to find out if I can be touched without running away to my place to hide.

Now the others were wishing me welcome with a sincerity that set another place inside me, a small, warm place, all aglow. My comrades. My brothers. All kinds of rattle and chatter inundated me. Now we were going to do something. Now we were going to get somewhere. Now we were going to kick some ass if we had to. Sleepy was here to figure it all out and tell everybody where and when to stick the knife.

"God knows all the secrets and all the jokes," I said, "and I wish He'd share the secret of the joke that explains why He created such a scruffy bunch of hired killers." I used a little finger to get rid of a tear before anybody realized that it was not raining. "You guys look pretty fat for having been on the road so long."

Somebody said, "Shit, we been here waiting for you for a whole fuckin' month. Some of us. The slowest ones got here last week."

"How's One-Eye doing?" I asked as Sahra wriggled through the throng.

"He's fucked up," a voice volunteered. "How'd you know . . . ?"

I exchanged hugs with Sahra. She said, "We were starting to worry." A question clung to the edge of her statement.

"Tobo. Your grandmother and Uncle Doj are waiting in the woods back up the road. Run up and tell them to come on down."

"Where're the rest?" somebody demanded.

"Swan is with them. The rest are behind us somewhere. We broke up into three groups after we reached the highlands. There were crows around. We didn't want to give them anything obvious to watch."

"We did the same thing after we left the barges," Sahra told me. "Did you see many crows? We saw only a few. They might not have been the Protector's."

"The white one keeps turning up."

"We saw it, too. Are you hungry?"

"You kidding? I've been eating your mother's cooking since we left Jaicur." I looked around. People were watching who were not Black Company. They might only be refugees, too, but the enthusiasm of my reception was sure to cause talk.

Sahra laughed. It sounded more like the laughter of relief than that of good humor. "How is Mother?"

"I think there's something wrong, Sahra. She's stopped being nasty, bitter old Ky Gota. Most of the time she's lost inside herself. And those times when she is completely aware, she almost has manners."

"In here." Sahra lifted a tent flap. It was the largest tent in the encampment. "And Uncle Doj?"

"A step slower but still Uncle Doj. He wants me to turn Nyueng Bao and be his apprentice. Like I have a lot of free time being Murgen's apprentice. He says it's just because he doesn't have anybody else to pass his responsibilities on to. Whatever they are. He seems to think I should sign on before he tells me what for."

"Did you get the Key?"

"We did. Uncle Doj has it in his pack. But Singh got away. Not unexpectedly. Did he turn up here? We picked up rumors along the way that gave me the idea that he was ahead of us and gaining ground. You do still have the girl?"

Sahra nodded. "But she's a handful. I think bringing her south again put her in closer touch with Kina. Common sense tells me we should break our promise and kill her." She settled on a cushion. "I'm glad you're here. I'm completely worn out. Keeping these people under control when there's so little for them to do . . . it's a miracle that we haven't had any major incidents. . . . I bought a farm."

"You what?"

"I bought a farm. Not far from the Shadowgate. They tell me the soil is lousy, but it's a place where most of the men can stay out of sight and keep out of trouble and even stay busy building housing or working the ground so we'll eventually be self-supporting. Half the gang is over there now. Most of these guys here would be, too, except that Murgen said you were going to arrive today. You made good time. We didn't expect you for several more hours."

"Does that mean you're all caught up on what's going on in the world outside?"

"I have a particularly talented husband who doesn't always share everything with me. And I don't always share him with the others. And we both probably shouldn't be that way. There're a thousand things we need to talk about, Sleepy. I don't know where to start. So why not just with, how are you?"

The brotherhood had to begin moving.

Goblin burst into the tent uninvited and gasped out the news that Murgen said my feted arrival had caught the eyes of official informants and had aroused the suspicions of the local authorities. Those folks had been disinclined to investigate the refugee camp before only due to a complete lack of ambition. I sent Kendo and a dozen men to secure the southern end of the pass through the Dandha Presh, both to guarantee a favorable welcome for those coming down behind me and to help keep anyone from strolling off northward with news about where we were. I sent several small teams off to capture senior officers and officials before they could become organized. There was no real, fixed, solid governmental structure here because the Protector favored the rule of limited anarchy.

It was obvious that these former Shadowlands, despite their proximity to the glittering plain, were no more than an afterthought to the powers in Taglios. The troubles in the region had been settled with a vengeance. The Great General had won the reputation he had desired. There were few troops and no officials of any renown here now. It looked like a safe, remote province suitable for rusticating human embarrassments deemed not worth exterminating.

Even so, regionwide, there were many more of them than there were of us and we were out of battle practice ourselves. Brains, speed and ferocity would have to sustain us till we gathered the whole clan and completed preparations to follow the road up the south side of the valley.

"So, now you've had your power fix and you've got time to talk, how the hell are you, Sleepy?" Goblin asked. He looked exhausted.

"Worn to the bone from traveling but still full of vinegar. It's nice to talk to somebody where I don't have to lean over backwards to look them in the eye."

"Walk in the goddamn door talking that shit. I knew there was a reason I didn't miss you."

"You say the sweetest things. How's One-Eye?"

"Getting better. Having Gota here will hurry it up. But he's never going to be completely right. He's going to be slow and shaky and have spells where he'll have trouble remembering what he's doing. And he'll always have trouble communicating, especially when he's excited."

I nodded, took a deep breath, said, "And it's going to happen again, isn't it?"

"It could. It often does. It doesn't have to, though." He rubbed his forehead. "Headache. I need some sleep. You can drive yourself crazy trying to deal with something like this."

"If you need sleep, you'd better get it now. Things are starting to happen. We'll need you fresh when it gets exciting."

"I knew there was another reason I didn't miss you. You haven't been here long enough to blow your nose and already people and things are flying all over, getting ready to beat each other in the head."

"It's my perky personality. Think I should visit One-Eye?"

"Up to you. But he'll be heartbroken if you don't. He's probably already all bent out of shape because you came and saw me first."

I asked how to find One-Eye and left Goblin. I noted that refugees not associated with the Company were sneaking out of the camp. There were signs of excitement over in the New Town, too.

Gota, Doj and Swan were nearing the camp from the uphill side. Tobo larked around them like an excited pup. I wondered where Swan would stand once the real excitement started. He would stay neutral as long as he could, probably.

"You look better than I expected," I told One-Eye, who was actually doing something when I ducked into his tent. "That spear? I thought you lost it ages ago." The weapon in question was an elaborately carved and decorated artifact of extreme magical potency that he had begun crafting back during the siege of Jaicur. Its designated target then had been the Shadowmaster Shadowspinner. Later, he had continued improving it so he could use it against Longshadow. That spear was so darkly beautiful that it seemed a sin to use it just to kill someone.

One-Eye took his time collecting himself. He looked up at me. There was less of him than there was when last I had seen him, and even then he had been just a shell of the One-Eye I remembered from when I was young.

"No."

Just that one word. None of the usual creative invective or accusations and insults. He did not want to embarrass himself. The results of the stroke were more crippling emotionally than physically. He had been master of his surroundings for two hundred years, far beyond the dreams of men, but now he could not count on being able to speak a complete, coherent sentence.

"I'm here. I've got the Key. And things have begun to happen already."

One-Eye nodded slowly. I hope he understood. There had been a woman in Jaicur, she was a hundred nineteen when she died, they said. In all my years I never saw her do anything but sit in a chair and drool. She understood nothing anyone said to her. She had to be changed like a baby. She had to be fed like a baby. I did not want that to happen to One-Eye. He was old and cantankerous and a major pain more often than not, but he was a fixture of my universe. He was my brother.

"That other woman. That married one. She does not have the fire." His words were a ghost of speech. When he talked, his hands shook too badly to hold his tools.

"She's afraid to succeed."

"And afraid not to. You are busy, Little Girl." He beamed because he had gotten that out without much trouble. "You do what you must. But I have to talk to you again. Soon. Before this happens to me again." He spoke slowly and with great care. "You are the one." He was tiring, so great was his mental effort. He beckoned me closer, murmured, "Soldiers live. And wonder why."

Someone threw the tent flap back. Brilliant light burst inside. I knew it was Gota without being able to see. Her odor preceded her. "Try not to make him talk too much. He's worn out."

"I have seen this problem before." Cold, yet civil. More animated than she had been for some time but still not the caustic, frequently irrational Gota of last year. "I will be of more value here." Her accent was much less heavy than usual. "Go kill someone, Stone Soldier."

"Been a while since anybody called me that."

Gota bowed mockingly as she waddled past. "Bone Warrior. Soldier of Darkness, go forth and conjure the Children of the Dead from the Land of Unknown Shadows. All Evil Dies There an Endless Death."

I stepped outside, baffled. What was that all about?

Behind me, "Calling the Heaven and the Earth and the Day and the Night."

I thought I had heard that formula before but could not recall the place or the context. Surely it was sometime when a person of the Nyueng Bao conviction was being particularly cryptic.

The excitement had increased. Someone had stolen some horses already . . . had *acquired* them. Let us not leap too far with our conclusions. Several riders were charging around, unguided by any rational plan. Something should have been in place for a situation like this. I grumbled, "This's what happens when nobody wants to take charge. You three men! Get over here! What in the name of God are you doing?"

After listening to their hemming and hawing, I gave some orders. They galloped off with messages. I murmured, "There is no God but God. God is the Almighty, Boundless in Mercy. Show Mercy unto me, O Lord of the Seasons. Let mine enemies be even more confused than my friends." I felt like I was inside the eye of a storm of screwups.

My fault? All I did was show up. If I was likely to have that effect, someone should have met me away from witnesses and led me to Sahra's farm. That might have given us time to get into shape, with nobody the wiser.

We really had very little formal organization, no declared chain of command, and no established table of responsibility. We had no real policies other than fixed enmities and an emotional commitment to release the Captured. We had deteriorated into little more than a glorified bandit gang and I was embarrassed. It was partly my fault.

I rubbed my behind. I had a distinct feeling the Captain was going to catch up on years' worth of chew-outs. I could make all the excuses I wanted about only being a stand-in for Murgen while he was buried, but I had been chosen as his understudy. And the Annalist is often the Standardbearer, too, and the Standardbearer is generally designated because those in command think he is capable of becoming Lieutenant and possibly, eventually, Captain. Which meant that Murgen had seen something in me a long time ago and the Old Man had not found cause to disagree with him. And I had done nothing with that but have a good time designing torments for our enemies while a woman who was not a pledged member of the Company assumed most of its leadership by default. Sahra's courage and intelligence and determination were beyond reproach but her skills as a soldier and commander were less so. She meant well but she did not understand strategies not designed around her own needs and desires. She wanted to resurrect the Captured, of course, but not for the benefit of the Black Company. She wanted her husband back. To Sahra, the Company was just a means of achieving her ends.

We were about to pay the price of my reluctance to step forward and serve the interests of the Company.

We were hardly more than the gang of thugs the Protector claimed us to be. I was willing to bet that any determined resistance we encountered hereabouts was likely to shatter what little family spirit the Company had left. We would have to pay for forgetting who and what we were. And my anger, mainly at myself, made me seem twice life-size. I stomped around screaming and foaming at the mouth and before long had bullied everyone into doing something useful.

And then a sorry bunch of ragamuffins trudged out of the New Town and headed for the refugee camp like a reluctant flock of geese, honking and straggling all over. They numbered about fifty and carried weapons. The steel was more impressive than the soldiers carrying it. The local armorer did his job well. Whoever trained recruits did not. They were more pathetic than my gang. And my guys had the advantage of having knocked people over the head before and so had little reluctance to hurt someone again. Particularly if that someone threatened them.

"Tobo. Go get Goblin."

The boy eyed the approaching disorder. "I can handle that clusterfuck, Sleepy. One-Eye and Goblin have been teaching me their tricks."

Scary idea, a frenetic teenager with their skills and their lunatic lack of responsibility. "That might well be. You might be a god. But I didn't tell you to handle it. I told you to go get Goblin. So move it."

Red anger flooded his face but he went. If I had been his mother, he would have argued until the wave of southerners rolled over us.

I walked toward the soldiers, painfully conscious that I still wore the rags I had had on since the day we sneaked out of Taglios. Nor was I equipped with anything remarkable in the way of weapons. I carried a stubby little sword that never had been much use for anything but chopping wood. I was always at my best as the kind of soldier who stands off at a distance and plinks the enemy when he is not looking.

I found a suitable spot and waited, arms crossed.

61

No grand effort had been made to train these troops or clothe them well. Which reflected the Protector's disdain for petty detail. What threat could the fledgling Taglian empire possibly face out here at the edge of beyond, anyway? There were no threats from beyond the borders.

The officer leading the pack was overweight, which also told me something about the local military. Peace had persisted for a decade but times were not yet so favorable that this country could support many fat men.

Huffing and puffing, the officer could not speak first. I told him, "Thank you for coming. It shows initiative and a mind capable of recognizing the inevitable swiftly. Have your men stack their weapons over there. Assuming everything goes the way it should, we'll be able to let them go home in two or three days."

The officer gulped some more air while he strove to understand what he was hearing. Evidently this little person had some mad notion that she had the upper hand. Though he had no way of telling if I was he, she or it.

I allowed the rags at my throat to fall open long enough for him to see the Black Company medallion I wore as a pendant on a silver chain. "Water sleeps," I told him, sure rumor had had plenty of time to carry that slogan to the ends of the empire.

Though I failed to intimidate him into ordering his men to disarm instantly, I did buy a few moments for the rest of the gang to gather. And a grim-looking band of cutthroats they were. Goblin and Tobo came down to stand beside me. Sahra shouted at her son from somewhere behind us but he ignored her. He had decided he was one of the big boys now and that stinking Goblin kept encouraging his fantasies.

I said, "I suggest you disarm. What's your name? What's your rank? If you don't get rid of the weapons, a lot of people will get hurt and most of them are going to be you. It doesn't have to be that way. If you cooperate."

The fat young man gulped air. I do not know what he had expected. This was not it. I was not it. I expect he was used to bullying refugees too battered by fate to even consider resisting another humiliation.

Goblin cackled. "Here's your chance, kid. Show us what you got."

"Here's one I've been practicing when nobody was around." Tobo kept on talking but in a whisper so soft I could not make out the words. In a few seconds I did not care about the words, anyway. Tobo began turning into something that was no gangly teenage boy. Tobo began turning into something I did not want to be around.

The kid was a shapeshifter? Impossible. That stuff took ages to master.

At first I thought he was going to become some mythical being, a troll, an ogre, or some misshapen and befanged creature still essentially human in shape, but he went on to become something insectoid, mantislike but big and really ugly and really smelly and getting bigger and uglier and smellier by the second.

I realized I did not smell so good myself. Which is usually a clue that you smell pretty awful to those around you, since you are not normally aware of your own odor.

Like most of what he saw from his teachers, Tobo was presenting an illusion, not undergoing a true transformation. But the southerners did not know that.

I was part of an illusion of my own. Goblin's huge grin told me who was behind the little practical joke, too. He was not too far over the top with it, either, so I might not have noticed had I not been alerted by what was happening with Tobo.

I seemed to be becoming some more-traditional nightmare. Something like what you might expect to see if for generations they had been saying that the Black Company was made up of guys who ate their own young when they could not roast yours.

"Have your men stack their weapons. Before this gets out of hand."

Tobo made a clacking noise with his mouth parts. He sidled forward, rotating his bug head oddly as he considered where to start munching. The officer seemed to understand instinctively that predators take the fat ones first. He discarded his weapons where he stood, having no inclination to get any closer to Tobo.

I said, "Men, you might help these fellows dispose of their tools." My own people were as stunned as the native soldiers were. I was stunned myself but remained plenty scared enough to take advantage while we retained the upper hand psychologically. I went around to the other side of the soldiers, putting them between horrors. Horrors they were not yet sure were entirely illusions. Sorcerers conjured some pretty nasty creatures sometimes. Or so I have heard.

That must be true. My brothers had told me about the ones they had seen. The Annals told me about more.

The southerners began to give up their weapons. Spiff or Wart or somebody remembered to make them lie down on their bellies. Once a handful got it started, the rest found themselves short on the will to resist, too.

Sahra could not hold back anymore. She tied into Goblin. "What are you doing to my son, you crazy old man! I told you I don't want him playing with—"

A *Ssss!* and a *Clack!* erupted from Tobo. A claw on the tip of a very long limb snipped at Sahra's nose.

The kid was going to be sorry about that stunt later.

Uncle Doj hustled up. "Not now, Sahra. Not here." He pulled her away. His grip evidently caused her considerable distress. Her anger did not subside but her voice did. The last thing I heard her say was something unflattering about her grandmother, Hong Tray.

I said, "Goblin, enough with the show. I can't talk to this man if I look like a rakshasa's mother."

"It ain't me, Sleepy. I'm just here to watch. Take it up with Tobo." He sounded as innocent as a baby.

Tobo was preoccupied, having altogether too much fun playing the scary monster. I told Goblin, "You're going to be teaching him that stuff, you'd better put some time into getting across the concept of self-discipline, too. Not to mention, you need to teach him not to bullshit people. I know who's doing what to whom here, Goblin. Stop it."

I was not disappointed to discover that Tobo had some talent. It was almost inevitable, actually. It was in his blood. What troubled me was the time of life when Goblin and, presumably, One-Eye had chosen to lure his talent into the open. In my opinion, Tobo was at exactly the wrong age to become all-powerful. If no one controlled him while he learned to rule himself, he could become another perpetual adolescent chaotic like Soulcatcher.

"All part of the program, Sleepy. But you need to understand that he's already more mature and more responsible than you or his mother want to admit. He's not a baby. You have to remember that most of what you see in him is him showing you what he thinks you expect to see. He's a good kid, Sleepy. He'll be all right if you and Sahra don't mother him to death. And right now he's at an age when you have to back off and let him stub his toes or regret it later."

"Child-rearing advice from a bachelor?"

"Even a bachelor can be smart enough to know when the child-rearing part is over. Sleepy, this boy has a big, hybrid talent. Be good to him. He's the future of the Black Company. And that's what that old Nyueng Bao granny woman foresaw when she first saw Murgen and Sahra together, back during the siege."

"Marvelous reasoning, old man. And your choice of time to bring that to my attention is typically, impeccably inconvenient. I've got fifty prisoners to deal with. I've got a pudgy little new boyfriend here and I need to convince him that he ought to help me talk his fellow captains into cooperating with us. What I don't have is time to deal with the difficult side of Tobo's adolescence. Pay attention. In case you haven't noticed, we're no longer a secret. The Kiaulune wars have started up again. I wouldn't be surprised if Soulcatcher herself didn't turn up someday. Now get me out of this imaginary ugly suit so I can do whatever I have to do."

"Oh, you're so forceful!" Goblin made the illusion go away. He made the one surrounding the boy fade, too. Tobo seemed surprised that he could be overruled so easily, but the little wizard softened the blow to his ego by immediately engaging him in a technical critique of what he had accomplished.

I was impressed by what I had seen. But Tobo as the future of the Company? That made me real uncomfortable, despite its questionable reassurance that the Company did have a future.

62

I stirred the fat officer with a toe. "Come on. Hop up here. We need to talk. Spiff, let the rest of these people sit up as soon as their weapons are cleared away. I'll probably let them go home in a little while. Goblin, you want to go face the music with Sahra? Get that out of the way so it isn't just waiting for a bad time to blow up on us?"

The fat officer got his feet under him. He looked very, very unhappy, which I could understand. This was not his best day. I took hold of his arm. "Let's you and me take a walk."

"You're a woman."

"Don't let it go to your head. Do you have a name? How about a rank or title?"

He offered a regional name about a paragraph long, filled with the unmanageable clicks that mess up a language otherwise already unfit for the normal human tongue. As proof of my assertion, I offer my inability to manage it at much more than a pidgin level despite having spent years in the area.

I picked out what sounded like it identified his personal place in the genealogy of a nation. "I can call you Suvrin, then?" He winced. I got it after a moment. Suvrin was a diminutive. No doubt he had not been called that by anyone but his mother for twenty years.

Oh, well. I had a sword. He did not.

"Suvrin, you've probably heard rumors to the effect that we're not nice people. I want to put your mind at ease. Everything you've ever heard is true. But this time we're not here to loot and pillage and rape the livestock the way we did last time. We're really just passing through, we hope with minimal dislocation for everybody, both us and you. What I need from you, assuming you'd rather cooperate than lie in a grave being walked on by some replacement who will, is a bit of official assistance aimed at hurrying us on our way. Have I been going too fast for you?"

"No. I speak your language well."

"That's not what I—never mind. Here's what's happening. We're going to go up on the glittering plain—"

"Why?" Pure fear filled his voice. He and his ancestors had lived in terror of the plain since the coming of the Shadowmasters.

I offered a bit of nonsense. "For the same reason the chicken crossed the road. To get to the other side."

Suvrin found that concept so novel he could think of no response.

I continued, "It'll take us a while to get ready. We have to assemble provisions and equipment. We have to scout some things. And not all of our people have arrived yet. I'd just as soon not fight a war at the same time. So I want you to tell me how to avoid that."

Suvrin offered an inarticulate grumble.

"What's that?"

"I never wanted to be in the army. My father's doing. He wanted me away from the family, someplace where I couldn't embarrass him, but he also wanted me doing something he felt to be in keeping with the family dignity. He thought if I was a soldier, there'd be nothing I could mess up. We had no enemies who could embarrass me."

"Stuff happens. Your father should know that. He's lived long enough to have a grown-up son."

"You don't know my father."

"You might be surprised. I've met plenty just like him. Probably some that were way worse. There's nothing new in this world, Suvrin. And that includes all kinds of people. How many more soldiers are there around here? How many all told on this side of the mountains? Do any of them have any special loyalty to Taglios? Will they abandon Taglios if the pass is closed?" The Territories south of the Dandha Presh were vast but weak. Longshadow had exploited them mercilessly for more than a generation, then the Shadowmaster and Kiaulune wars had devastated them.

"Uh . . ." He wriggled but not hard. Just enough to satisfy his self-image.

We spent the remainder of the day together. Suvrin made the transitions from grudging prisoner to nervous accomplice to helpful ally. He was easily led, overresponding to modest praise and expressions of gratitude. My guess was that he had not had many nice things said to him during his young life. And he was scared to death that I would demolish him the instant he did fail to cooperate.

We sent the rest of the soldiers home as soon as our men stripped the New Town armory. Most of the weapons stored there looked like they had been picked up off old battlefields and treated with contempt ever since by the armorer whose work I had so much admired earlier.

I found the man and drafted him. He was a prima donna, a master with an artist's attitude. I figured One-Eye could tame him.

Suvrin accompanied me when I went across to the farm Sahra had acquired. Poor leader though he was, Suvrin really was in charge of all the armed forces in the Kiaulune region. Which said very little for the quality of his men or for the wisdom and commitment of his superiors. But I decided to keep him handy. He was useful as a symbol, if nothing else.

When I went across I insisted that everyone else make the move, too. I wanted everyone not out on picket duty or patrol in one place so we could respond quickly, in strength, to any threat.

I told Suvrin, "I've neutralized the whole province except for that little fort below the Shadowgate. Right?" That stronghold had sealed its gate. The men inside would not respond to the messenger I sent.

Suvrin nodded. He was having second thoughts, too late.

"Will they leave if you tell them to go?"

"No. They're foreigners. Left by the Great General to keep the road to the Shadowgate closed."

"How many?"

"Fourteen."

"Good soldiers?"

Embarrassed, "Much better than mine." Which might only mean that they could march in step.

"Tell me about their fort. How are they set for water and provisions?"

The fat man hemmed and hawed.

"Suvrin, Suvrin. You have to think about this."

"Uh . . ."

"You can't get in any deeper than you already are. You can only do your best to get back out. Too many people have seen you cooperating already. I'm sorry, buddy. You're stuck." I fought sliding into the character of Vajra the Naga, seductive as it was. It was so blessedly useful.

Suvrin made a sound suspiciously like a whimper.

"Courage, Cousin Suvrin. We live with it every day. All you can do is put on a death's-head grin and tug on their beards and yank out their tail feathers. Here we go. This looks like the place." A poorly built structure had loomed out of the darkness. Light leaked out through the roof and walls both. I wondered why they bothered. Maybe it was still under construction. I could make out the vague shapes of tents beyond it.

Something stirred on the rooftree as I pulled the door hanging aside so Suvrin could enter. The white crow. A soft chuckle came from the bird. "Sister, sister. Taglios begins to waken." The thing took wing. I watched it fade in the light of a rising fragment of moon. That had been pretty clear.

I shrugged and went inside. I could worry about the white crow next week, once I finally got a chance to go to bed. "Are any of you guys aware that we're at war? That under similar circumstances every army since the dawn of time has put out sentries to watch for people sneaking up?"

Several dozen faces watched me blandly. Goblin asked, "You didn't see anybody?"

"There's nothing out there to see, old man."

"Ah. And you got here alive, too." Which remark left me to understand that there were dire traps out there, held in abeyance only by the alert decision-making of sentries I not only overlooked but whose presence I never suspected.

"All I can say to that is, somebody must have taken a bath sometime since the turn of the century." The same could not be said for most of the crowd inside that shelter. Which might be the reason the roof and walls were so porous. "This is my new friend, Suvrin. He was the captain of the local garrison. I blew in his ear and he decided he wanted to help us so we would go away before the Protector shows up and makes life tough for everybody."

Somebody in back said, "You could blow in mine and—ow! What the fuck you hit me for, Willow?"

Vajra the Naga said, "Knock it off. Swan, keep your hands to yourself. Vigan, I don't want to hear your mouth again. You should know better. What've you guys done to get ready to knock over that tower over by the Shadowgate?"

Nobody said a word.

"You guys obviously did something while you were waiting around." I gestured at our surroundings. "You managed to build a house. Badly. Or a barracks. But you didn't do anything else? There're no scouts out? No planning got done? No preparations got made? Was there something going on that I haven't heard about yet?"

Goblin sidled up. In an uncharacteristic tone he murmured, "Don't press these issues. Now isn't the time. Just tell people what to do and send them out to do it."

I trust the little wizard's wisdom occasionally. "Sit down. Here's what we'll do. Dig out whatever fireball launchers we have left. Vigan, pick ten men. Carry the heaviest launcher yourself. The others can carry lighter ones. If there aren't enough to go around, bring bows. We'll go take care of this right now. Vigan, choose your team."

The man who had made the mistake of irritating me rose. In a surly tone he named his helpers. Chances were all of them had irritated him sometime recently. It rolls downhill.

In the few minutes it took Vigan to get ready, I had the others tell me things they thought I ought to know.

63

I had the men encircle the little fort. We carried torches and made no effort to sneak. Per instructions, Vigan carried the heaviest piece of bamboo. It had an interior diameter of three inches. He told me, "There's supposed to be only a couple, three balls left in this one."

"That ought to be enough. Right here should be fine." A good archer with a strong bow might cause us trouble but those were exceedingly rare in modern Taglian armies. Mogaba was a warrior. He believed real men got in close, where they could get splattered with each other's blood when they fought. It was a blind spot we had exploited more than once during the Kiaulune wars and would exploit again until he figured it out.

Goblin shuffled into position behind us. Tobo did, too. They said nothing, which must have been a trial for the boy. He talked in his sleep.

"What do I do?" Vigan asked.

"Let them have one. Through the stonework right above the gate." Louder, I said, "Stand fast. Nobody do anything until I tell you."

The first two times Vigan turned his hand release crank, nothing happened.

"Is it empty?" I asked.

"It's not supposed to be."

Goblin advised, "Try again, then. It's been over ten years since it was used. Maybe it just needs to be loosened up."

I mused, "I'll bet nobody's bothered to keep the mechanism clean. And you folks wondered why I wanted to hire an armorer. Go ahead. Crank it again. Carefully, so you don't lose your aim."

Whack! Crackle-crackle-crackle-sizzle! into the distance. The fireball ripped right through the little fortification's two outside walls and whatever lay between them. Stone steamed and ran. The scarlet ball wobbled through the air for several miles more, gave up the last of its momentum, gradually darkened as it drifted to earth beyond the ruins of Overlook.

"Move to the left a few yards, drop your aiming point five feet, then do it again."

Vigan was having fun now. There was a bounce to his step as he moved to his new position. This time it took only one extra turn of the crank to get the fireball launched.

A blistering, lime-colored ball ripped through the fortification. It hit something significant inside. It had almost no energy left when it appeared on the far side.

A gout of steam blew out the top of the tower. "Must've gotten a water barrel," I said. Water and the fireballs made a wicked combination resulting in storms of superheated steam. "Suvrin, where are you?" Two fireballs should have gotten their attention inside, should have gotten the survivors to thinking. Now I could begin placing my shots. "Suvrin! Have you ever been inside that rockpile?"

The fat man came forward reluctantly. When he was close by me, his face was in the light. The garrison inside would remember him. He wanted to lie to me, too, I could see. But he did not have the courage. "Yes."

"What's the layout? It doesn't look like it could be that complicated."

"It isn't. Animals and storage on the ground floor. They can pile up stuff behind the gate so you can't knock it in. They live on the second floor. It's just one big room. There's a stove for cooking and pallets for sleeping and racks of weapons and that's about it."

"And the roof is basically just a fighting platform, right? Wait a minute, Vigan. Don't spend any more fireballs than we have to. Let them think for a while now. Maybe they'll give up. They know I didn't hurt Suvrin's men. Tobo, circle around and tell all the men that if they have to launch a fireball, we need it to go through the second level. Preferably low. They'll probably get down on the floor when death starts coming through."

"Can I shoot one of those things, Sleepy?"

"Get the message out first." I watched him scoot off. He did not expose himself unnecessarily. Faces could be seen occasionally behind the archers' embrasures over yonder. A couple of arrows had come out and fallen harmlessly. I told Goblin, "If anybody had been paying attention, we'd have the place mapped down to the last cot and table and we'd know exactly where to aim every fireball to get the best effect."

"You're absolutely right again. Just as you always are. Be quiet for a second. There's something going on here. Those men aren't as scared as they should be."

As he spoke, I glimpsed a face peeking over the parapet. A moment later the white crow plummeted out of the night. It knocked the leather helmet off the soldier.

I yelled, "Everybody wake up! They're about to pull something!"

Goblin had started muttering already. He was doing something odd with his fingers.

Men jumped up atop the little fort. Each had something in hand, ready to throw. A half-dozen fireballs squirted their way without my approval. One grenadier went down but not before he launched his missile.

Glass, I saw. Same type One-Eye had used to make firebombs, years ago. We still had a few of those, too. But throwing firebombs at us out here would be pointless. We were too far away to be reached.

"Aim low!" I yelled. "Shadows coming!" That was not a shout that had been heard for an age but it was one the veterans remembered and could respond to without ever thinking.

Goblin was already wobbling across the slope in as near a sprint as his old bones could manage, still muttering and wiggling his fingers. Pink sparks leaped between his fingers and slithered around amongst his few remaining hairs. He grabbed a skinny little bamboo pole from one of the men. It had been painted with black stripes, meaning that its dedicated purpose was use against shadows.

Fireballs flew. Some peppered the fortress. Some dove after the shadows that spilled out of the breaking glass containers. Suvrin began whimpering behind me. I told him, "Don't run. They'll get you for sure. They love a fleeing victim."

There was a lot of screaming inside the fortress. Fireballs streaking through had found human targets. In their way, the fireballs were almost as bad as the killing shadows.

One of my men began shrieking when a shadow found him. But he was the only one. Goblin's spell helped some. The quick use of fireballs helped more.

Goblin began loosing fireballs from the pole he had snagged but sent them racing northward instead of toward the stubborn little fort. He quit after only a few tries. He came back to me. "They've done their job, those brave boys in there. They got their warning away." He was as sour as a lemon slice under the tongue.

"So I take it Soulcatcher didn't die when she hit the water." I had heard the news from Taglios only up to the part where the Protector's carpet had fallen apart in midair, with her streaking along four hundred feet above the river. The break coming at that point had not been because anyone was trying to make things particularly dramatic, it was just because there was too much going on to have a lot of time left for catching up. Especially where Murgen was concerned. Murgen seemed to be employed full time easing Sahra's frights and concerns.

"She was one of the Ten Who Were Taken, Sleepy. Those people don't hurt easy. Hell, she survived having her head cut off. She carried it around in a box for about fifteen years."

I grunted. Sometimes it was hard to remember that Soulcatcher was much more than just an unpleasant, distant senior official. "They likely to have any more surprises in there?" I meant the question for Suvrin but Goblin answered.

"If they did, they would've used them. You thinking about going in after them?"

"Oh, heck no! Somebody might get hurt. Somebody besides them. Suvrin, go over there and tell them if they surrender in the next half hour, I'll let them go. If they don't, I'll kill them all before the hour is up."

The fat man started to protest. Vigan poked his behind with the tip of a dagger. I told Suvrin, "If they do anything to you, I'll avenge you."

"That's a big weight off my heart."

Goblin asked, "How are you going to avenge anybody? Considering you're not going to go in there after them."

"That's what we have wizards for. This looks like a wonderful opportunity for you to give Tobo some on-the-job training."

"Am I surprised? Not hardly. For a hundred years it's been, 'What do we do now?' 'I don't know. Let's let Goblin handle it.' I oughta just take a hike and let you figure it out for yourself."

"I'm tired. I'm going to sit down here and rest my eyes until Suvrin gets back."

I heard Goblin tell Vigan to put another heavyweight fireball into the corner of the fortification, along the length of the wall so all its energy would be spent devouring the pale limestone. There was a solid *thump!* swiftly followed by the smell of superheated limestone. As I drifted away, Goblin muttered something about burning them out.

64

The surface of the river was not friendly when Soulcatcher hit it but neither was the impact like hitting stone from the same altitude. Her fall had been long enough to allow her time to prepare for the landing.

Even so, the collision was brutal enough to extract her consciousness temporarily. But she had prepared for that, too, between curses. When consciousness returned she was drifting downriver with the flood, head above the surface. It being the rainy season, the river was high and the current brisk. It took a great effort to complete the swim to the south bank. By the time she crawled out of the flood and collapsed, she was a half-dozen miles downstream from where she had gone in, which was outside the city proper, in a domain best known for its jackals, of both the two- and four-legged varieties. It was said that leopards still hunted there at night, the occasional crocodile could be found along the shore, and it was not that many years since a tiger had come visiting from down the river.

The Protector experienced no difficulties with any mad or hungry thing. A hundred crows perched around her, standing guard. Others flapped about in the darkness until squadrons of bats had gathered. Birds and bats together discouraged the scavengers and predators till Soulcatcher awakened and in a fit of pique, sent an entire band of jackals racing away with their pelts aflame.

She stumbled toward home, regaining strength slowly, muttering about growing old and less resilient. A tremor entered the voice she chose to inveigh against the predations of time.

Eventually she reached the home of a moneylender, where she commandeered transportation back to the Palace. She arrived there somewhat after the breakfast hour in a temper so foul that the entire staff made a point of becoming invisible. Only the Great General came to inquire after her well-being. And he went away when she started snarling and snapping.

Though she reveled in her paranoia, Soulcatcher did not suspect that her accident had been anything else until she examined her remaining carpet preparatory to another effort to fly off to entertain the Nyueng Bao. Then she discovered that the light wooden-frame members on which the carpet was stretched had been weakened by strategic saw cuts.

The who and probable why became clear within seconds. She sent out a summons to Jaul Barundandi and his associates.

Surprise. Barundandi was nowhere to be found. He had been called out of the Palace for a family emergency, he had said, just moments after her return. So the Greys reported when told to investigate.

"What an amazing coincidence. Find him. Find the men he worked with regularly. We have a great deal to discuss."

Greys scattered. One bold captain, however, remained behind to report, "Rumor in the city says the Bhodi intend to resume their self-immolations. They want the Radisha to come out and address their concerns personally."

The news did not improve Soulcatcher's temper. "Ask them if they would like me to donate the naphtha they need. I'm feeling particularly charitable today. Also ask them if they can hold off starting long enough for the carpenters to put up grandstands so more of the Radisha's good subjects can enjoy the entertainment. I don't care what those lunatics do. Get out of here! Find that Barundandi slug!" The voice she used was informed with a potent lunacy.

Jaul Barundandi's luck was mixed. He managed to avoid the attentions of the bats and crows and shadows the Protector released when the Greys had no immediate success in locating him, but an informer eventually betrayed him when the reward for his capture grew large enough. The lie was that he had attacked and severely wounded the Radisha, that only the Protector's swift intercession with her most powerful sorcery had saved the Princess's life. The Radisha's situation remained grave.

The Taglian people loved their Radisha. Jaul Barundandi discovered that he had no friends but his accomplices and it was one of those who betrayed him in exchange for a partial reward (the Grey officers pocketing the bulk) and a running start.

Jaul Barundandi suffered terrible torments and tried hard to cooperate so the pain would stop but he could tell the Protector nothing that she wanted to know. So she had him put into a cage and hung fifteen feet above the place where the Bhodi disciples generally chose to give up their lives and issued a rescript encouraging passersby to throw stones. It was her intent that he hang there indefinitely, his suffering neverending, but sometime during the first night, somehow, someone managed to toss him a piece of poisoned fruit while leaving his betrayer and a murdered Grey below, each with a piece of paper in his mouth bearing the characters for "Water Sleeps." Crows savaged both corpses before they were discovered.

It was the last time Black Company tokens would be seen but their appearance was sufficient to provoke the Protector almost beyond reason. For days the still-loyal remnants of the Greys remained extremely busy making arrests, most of them of people unable to guess what they had done to irk Soulcatcher.

She never did get to the Nyueng Bao swamp despite having made necessary repairs to her remaining carpet. Taglios became more fractious by the hour. She had to devote her entire attention to keeping the city tamed.

Then came the faithful and tattered little shadow that had made its way through mountains and forests, over lakes and rivers and plains, in order to bring her news of what was happening in the nethermost south.

Soulcatcher screamed a scream of rage so potent that the entire city became informed of it instantly. Immigrants began to rehearse the wisdom of a return to the provinces.

The Great General and two of his staff officers broke through the door to the Protector's apartment, certain she needed rescuing. Instead, they found her pacing furiously and debating herself in half a dozen voices. "They have the Key. They must have the Key. They must have murdered the Deceiver. Maybe they made an alliance with Kina. Why would they go down there? Why would they go onto the plain after what happened to the last group? What keeps pulling them out there? I've read their Annals. There's nothing in those. What do they know? The Land of Unknown Shadows? They cannot have developed an entirely new and independent oral tradition since they served me in the north. If it's important one of them will record it. Why? Why? What do they know that I don't?"

Soulcatcher became aware of Mogaba and his men. The latter looked around nervously, trying to figure out where the voices were coming from. When Soulcatcher became excited, those seemed to come from everywhere at once.

"You. Have you caught me any terrorists yet?"

"No. Nor shall I unless an angry family member comes forward because he thinks it would be a good way to get even. There won't be more than a handful left here and those probably don't know each other. I gather, from what I overheard, that they've gone back to Shadowcatch." He had worked for the Shadowmaster Longshadow. He could not get out of the habit of calling Kiaulune by the name given it by his previous employer.

"Exactly. We're back where we were fifteen years ago. Only now they have the Radisha and the Key." Her tone left no doubt she placed the blame entirely on him.

Mogaba was not bothered. Not immediately. He was accustomed to being blamed for the shortcomings of others and he did not believe the remnants of the Black Company could offer any real threat any time soon. They had been beaten down too thoroughly and had been away from it too long. They were more military than the Deceivers only inside their own fantasies. Even the comic-opera functionaries down there ought to be able to wear them down and bury them eventually. They would find no aid or sympathy in the Shadowlands. The people down there really did remember the Black Company's last visit. "The Key? What is that?"

"A means of passing through the Shadowgate unharmed. A talisman that makes it possible to travel on the plain." Her voice had become pedantic. Now it became angry. "I possessed that talisman at one time. Long ago I used it to go up there and explore. Longshadow would have been unmanned had he known. More unmanned than the eunuch he already was. But it disappeared in the early excitement around Kiaulune. I suspect that Kina clouded my mind while the Deceiver Singh stole both it and my sister's darling daughter. I can't imagine why that rabble would want to go onto the plain after the previous disaster but if it's something they want to do, it's something I want to prevent. Prepare for a journey."

"We can't leave Taglios unsupervised for as long as it would take us to travel all the way to Shadowcatch. We don't have the stallion anymore, even if it could carry double."

Soulcatcher was baffled. "What?"

"The black stallion from the north. The one I've been using all these years. It's vanished. It broke down its stall and ran off. I told you that last month." She did not recall that, obviously.

"We'll fly."

"But—" Mogaba hated flying. In the days when he had been Longshadow's general he had had to fly with the Howler almost daily. He still loathed those times. "I thought the larger carpet was the one that was destroyed."

"The small one will carry both of us. It'll be hard work. I'll have to rest a lot. But we'll still be able to get down there and back before these people know we're gone and try to take advantage. A week for the round trip. Ten days at the outside."

The Great General had a few dozen reservations but kept them behind his teeth. The Protector was worse than Longshadow had been about suffering opinions she did not want to hear.

Soulcatcher said, "We'll adopt disguises once we get there and go among them. I want you to keep an eye out for a hammer, so by so, made of cast iron but far heavier than it ought to be."

Mogaba bowed slightly. He said nothing about how difficult it would be for either of them to blend in with the crowd they would be chasing.

Soulcatcher told him, "Prepare your men. They'll have to keep Taglios under control for a couple of weeks."

Mogaba withdrew, saying nothing about the proposed time changing already. In his position it was necessary to do a lot of saying nothing.

The Protector watched him go, amused. He did not conceal his thinking nearly as well as he believed. But she was ancient in her wickedness and had studied the dark side of humanity so thoroughly that she could almost read minds.

The little fortress settled in upon itself slowly, as though made of wax only slightly overheated. As soon as I fell asleep and could not interfere, Goblin handed the magical siege work over to Tobo, who did a creditable job of rooting the enemy survivors out of their shelter. The wicked little thing had been taking lessons a lot longer than he and his teachers would admit.

The garrison was bringing out its dead and wounded when a shout awakened me. I sat up. Morning had begun to arrive. And the world had changed.

"What's Spiff's problem?" I asked.

One of my veterans had recognized one of theirs.

The devil himself arrived to explain. "The guy in charge. That's Khusavir Pete, Sleepy. You remember, we thought he was killed when the Bahrata Battalion got wiped out in the ambush at Kushkhoshi."

"I remember." And I recalled something that Spiff did not know, a fact I shared only with Murgen, who had been the ghost in the rushes while the slaughter was taking place. Khusavir Pete, at that time a sworn brother of the Company, had led our largest surviving force of allies into a trap that efficiently took us out of the Kiaulune wars. Khusavir Pete had cut a deal. Khusavir Pete had betrayed his own brothers.

Khusavir Pete was high on my list of people I wanted to meet again, though until just now I had been the only one who knew that he had survived and that his treachery had been rewarded with a high post, money and a new name. But just seeing him had some of the men figuring it out fast.

"You should've asked her to change your face, too," I told him when they flung him down bleeding in front of me. "Though you've had a better run than you probably expected when she turned you." I held his eyes with mine. What he saw convinced him it would not be worth his trouble to deny anything. Vajra the Naga had come out to play.

More and more of the men gathered around, most of them not getting it until I explained how Khusavir Pete had been seduced by Soulcatcher into betraying and helping destroy more than five hundred of our brothers and allies. Would-be greetings quickly became imaginative suggestions of ways whereby we might reduce the traitor's life expectancy. I let the man listen until some of the troops tried to lay hands on. Then I told Goblin, "Hide him somewhere. We may have a use for him yet."

T he excitement was over. I had indulged in a decent meal. My attitude much improved, I took the opportunity to renew my acquaintance with Master Surendranath Santaraksita. "This life seems to agree with you," I told him as I arrived. "You look better now than you did when we left the city." And that was true.

"Dorabee? Lad, I thought you were dead. Despite their endless assurances." He leaned closer and confided, "They aren't all honest men, your comrades."

"By some chance did Goblin and One-Eye offer to teach you to play tonk?"

The librarian managed to look a little sheepish.

"Not to play with them is a lesson everyone has to learn."

Sheepishness transformed into impishness. "I think I taught them a little something, too. Card tricks were one of my hobbies when I was younger."

I had to laugh at the idea of those two villains getting taken themselves. "Have you discovered anything that would be useful to me?"

"I've read every word in every book we brought along, including all of your company's modern chronicles written in languages known to me. I found nothing remarkable. I have been amusing myself by trying to work backward into the chronicles I can't read by comparing materials repeated in more than one language."

Murgen had done a lot of that. He had had a thing about copying stuff over, in cleaner drafts, and one of his great projects had been to revise Lady's and the Captain's Annals for accuracy, based on evidence provided by other witnesses, while rendering them into modern Taglian. We have all done that to our predecessors, some, so that every recent volume of the Annals is really an unwilling collaboration.

I said, "We drag a lot of books around, don't we?"

"Like snails, carrying your history on your back."

"It's who we are. Cute image, though. Doesn't all that study get dull after a while?"

"The boy keeps me sharp."

"Boy?"

"Tobo. He's a brilliant student. Even more amazing than you were."

"Tobo?"

"I know. Who would expect it of a Nyueng Bao? You're destroying all my pre-conceptions, Dorabee."

"Mine are taking a beating, too." Tobo? Either Santaraksita had an unsuspected talent for inspiring students or Tobo had suffered an epiphany and had become miraculously motivated. "You sure it's Tobo and not a changeling?"

The demon himself popped in. "Sleepy. Runmust and Riverwalker and them are on their way over. Good morning, Master Santaraksita." Tobo actually seemed excited to be there. "I don't have any other duties right now. Oh, Sleepy, Dad wants to talk to you."

"Where?" Things had been happening too fast. There had been no chance to catch up with Murgen.

"Goblin's tent. Everybody but Mom thought that would be the safest place to keep him."

I had no trouble picturing Sahra being irritated about not being able to share the occasional private moment with her husband.

When I ducked out, the young man and the old were already settling with a book. I glared a warning at Santaraksita which, it developed, was both wasted and unnecessary.

G oblin was not home. Of course not. He was working his way through a long list of jobs bestowed upon him by me. Chuckle.

I found it hard to credit the possibility that one human being could make so huge a mess in a space so constricted. The inside of Goblin's tent was barely wider than either of us was tall and twice as deep. At its peak it was tall enough for me to stand up with two inches to spare. What looked like a milkmaid's stool, undoubt-edly stolen, constituted the wizard's entire suite of furniture. A ragged burrow of blankets betrayed where he slept. The rest of the space was occupied by a random jumble, mostly stuff that looked like it had been discarded by a procession of pre-vious owners. There was no obvious theme to the collection.

It had to be stuff he had acquired since his arrival here. Sahra would never have allowed him space on a barge for such junk.

The mist projector stood at the head of Goblin's smelly bedding, tilted precari-ously, leaking water. "If this is the safest place to keep that darned thing, then the whole Company is mad with delusions of adequacy."

A whisper came from the mist projector. I got down close to it, which offered me an opportunity to become intimately aware of the aroma permanently associated with Goblin's bedding, some pieces of which must have been with him since he was in diapers. "What?"

Murgen's strongest effort was barely audible. "More water. You need to add more water or there won't be any mist much longer."

I started to drag the evidence out of the tent.

Anger gave Murgen a little more voice. "No, dammit! Bring the water to me, don't take me to the water. If you suffer from a compulsion to drag me around, at least wait until after you water me. And don't waste time. I'm going to lose my anchor here in a few minutes."

Finding a gallon of water turned out to be a challenging experience.

What took you so damned long?"

"Bit of an adventure coming up with the water. Seems it never occurred to any of these morons that we need to have some handy somewhere. Just in case the royal army decides to camp between us and the creek where we've been getting it, which is almost a mile away. I just unleashed several geniuses on the problem. How am I supposed to put this in here?"

"There's a cork in the rear. It might be of some use to you to start doing readings from the Annals. Like they do in temples. The way I used to do sometimes. Pick something situationally appropriate. 'In those days the Company was in service' and so on, so they have examples of why it might be useful to haul water up the hill before you have to use it, and such like. These are grown men. You can't just bully them into doing the right things. But if you start reading to them, they'll have heard tell of other times when the Annalist did that and they'll recall it was always right before the big shitstorm moved in. You'll get their attention."

"Tobo said you want to talk to me."

"I need to catch you up on what's going on elsewhere. And I want to make suggestions about your preparations for the plain, one of which is to listen to Willow Swan but the most critical of which is, you're going to have to upgrade discipline. The plain is deadly. Even worse than the Plain of Fear, which you don't remember. You can't ignore the rules and stay alive there. One idea would be for you not to burn or bury the man who was killed by the shadow last night. Make every survivor look at him and think about what *will* happen to all of you if even one of you screws up up there. Read them the passages chronicling our adventures. Have Swan bear witness."

"I could just bring a handful of reliables in to get you."

"You could. But the rest of the world wouldn't be very nice to the men you leave behind. Right now there's a shadow heading north to tell Soulcatcher where you are. She may know enough already to figure out what you're trying to do. She definitely doesn't want her sister and Croaker on the loose and nursing a grudge. She'll get here as fast as she can. And aside from Soulcatcher, there's Narayan Singh. He retains Kina's countenance, so he's extremely hard to trace but I do catch glimpses occasionally. He's on this side of the Dandha Presh and he's probably not far away. He wants to recapture the Daughter of Night and reunite her with the book you traded for the Key. Which, by the way, you should take away from Uncle Doj before he becomes overly tempted to try something on his own. And so Goblin can study it."

"Uhm?" He was a gush of information this morning, all of it carefully rehearsed.

"There's more to the Key than you see right away. I have a feeling the Deceiver overlooked something. Doj keeps picking at it, trying to find out what's inside the iron. We should find out more about it before we trust it. And we need to find out fast. It won't be all that long before that shadow gets to Taglios."

"River and Runmust are coming in. They're halfway responsible people. I'll turn some of the work over to them as soon as they're rested up. Then I can worry about—"

"Worry about it now. Let Swan sergeant for you. He's experienced and he's got no choice but to throw in with us now. Catcher will never believe that he didn't betray her."

"I hadn't thought of that."

"You don't have to do everything yourself, Sleepy. If you're going to take charge, you need to learn to tell people what needs doing, then get out of the way and let them do it. You keep hanging over their shoulders nagging like somebody's mother, you aren't going to get much cooperation. You seduced that fat boy yet?"

"What?"

"That local-yokel captain. The one who couldn't keep in step if you painted his feet different colors. You got him wrapped up yet?"

"You're zigging when I'm zagging. You lost me completely."

"Let me draw you a picture. You forget to tell him Catcher is going to stop by. You get him to make a deal. He keeps his job. He helps us out so he can get us out of his hair. When he isn't looking, you fix him up so when the shitstorm starts, he don't have no choice but to take his chances with us."

"I have him wrapped up, then. Seventy percent."

"Hey. Blow in his ear. Throw a liplock on his love muscle. Do whatever you have to. If Catcher loses him, she won't ever trust anybody else down here, either."

Goblin used almost the same language as Murgen had when I stopped to visit again. He found Murgen's advice fully excellent. "Grab fat boy by his prong and never let go. Give him a little squeeze once in a while to keep him smiling."

"I've probably said it before. You're one cynical mud-sucker."

"It's all those years of watching out for One-Eye that done it to me. I was a sweet, innocent young thing when I joined this outfit. Not unlike yourself."

"You were born wicked and cynical."

Goblin chuckled. "How much stuff do you think you need to collect before we go up the hill? How long do you think it'll take?"

"It won't take forever if Suvrin cooperates."

"Never, ever, forget that you don't have long. I can't emphasize that enough. Soulcatcher is coming. You've never seen her when she's all worked up."

"The Kiaulune wars don't count?" He must have seen something extreme. He was determined to pound the point home.

"The Kiaulune wars don't count. She was just entertaining herself with those."

I forced myself to make the visit I had been avoiding.

The Daughter of Night wore ankle shackles. She resided inside an iron cage heavily impregnated with spells that caused ever-increasing agony as their victim moved farther away. She could escape but that would hurt. If she pushed it hard enough, she would die.

It appeared that every possible step had been taken to keep her under control. Except the lethal step reason urged me to take. I had no more motive for keeping her alive—except that I had given my word.

The men all took turns being exposed to her, in pairs, at mealtimes and such. Sahra had not been lax. She appreciated the danger the girl represented.

My first glimpse left me stricken with envy. Despite her disadvantages, she had kept herself beautiful, looking much like her mother in a fresher body. But something infinitely older and darker looked out through her pretty blue eyes. For a moment she struck me not as the Daughter of Night, but as the darkness itself.

She did have plenty of time to commune with her spiritual mother.

She smiled as though aware of the serpents of dark temptation slithering the black corridors of my mind. I wanted to bed her. I wanted to murder her. I wanted to run away, begging for mercy. It took an exercise of will to remind myself that Kina and her children were not evil in the sense that northerners or even my Vehdna co-religionists understood evil.

Nevertheless . . . she was the darkness.

I stepped back, tossed the tent flap open so my ally, daylight, could come inside. The girl lost her smile. She backed to the far side of her cage. I could think of nothing to say. There was really nothing we could say to one another. I had no inclination to gloat and little news of the world outside to report, which might motivate her to do something besides wait.

She had her spiritual mother's patience, that was sure.

A blow from behind rocked me. I clawed at my stubby little sword.

White wings mussed my nattily arranged hair. Talons dug into my shoulder. The Daughter of Night stared at the white crow and revealed real emotion for the first time in a long time. Her confidence wavered. Fear leaked through. She pressed back against the bars behind her.

"Have you two met?" I asked.

The crow said something like, "Wawk! Wiranda!"

The girl began to shake. If possible, she became even paler. Her jaw seemed clenched so tight her teeth ought to be cracking. I made a mental note to discuss this with Murgen. He knew something about the crow.

What could rattle the girl so badly?

The crow laughed. It whispered, "Sister, sister," and launched itself back into the sunlight, where it startled some passing brother into a fit of curses.

I stared at the girl, watched the inner steel reassert itself. Her gaze met mine. I felt the fear within her evaporate. I was nothing to her, less than an insect, certainly less than a stubbed toe at the beginning of her long trek across the ages.

Shuddering, I broke eye contact.

That was a scary kid.

66

Our days began before sunrise. They ended after sunset. They included a great deal of training and exercise of the sort that had been let slide for too long. Tobo worked with almost fanatic devotion to improve his skills as an illusionist. I insisted upon daily readings from the Annals in an effort to reinforce the depth and continuity of brotherhood that were so much the foundation of what the Company was. There was resistance at first, of course, but the message sank in at a pace not unrelated to a growing realization that we were going to go up onto the glittering plain—really!—or were going to die here in front of the Shadowgate when Soul-catcher chose to write our final chapter.

The renewed training paid dividends quickly. Eight days after we reduced the fort below the Shadowgate, another mob like Suvrin's, but much larger, trudged in out of the country west of the New Town. Thanks to Murgen, we had plenty of warning. With Tobo and Goblin assisting, we sprang a classic Company ambush using illusions and nuisance spells that confused and disorganized a force that had had almost no idea what it was doing already. We hit fast and hard and mercilessly and the threat evaporated in a matter of minutes. In fact, the relief force fell apart so fast we could not take as many prisoners as I wanted, though we did round up most of the officers. Suvrin generously identified those he recognized.

Suvrin was practically an apprentice Company man by now, so desperate was he to belong to something and to gain the approval of those around him. I felt halfway guilty exploiting him the way I did.

The prisoners we did take became involuntary laborers in our preparations for the future. Most jumped on the opportunity because I promised to release those who did work hard before we went up onto the plain. Those who failed to work hard would go along as porters. Somehow a rumor got started amongst the prisoners that human sacrifice might be involved in what we were going to be doing once we passed the Shadowgate.

I found Goblin in with One-Eye, whose recovery seemed to have been sped by Gota's presence. Possibly because he needed to be well enough to get away from her and her cooking. I do not know. They had the Key laid out on a small table between them. Doj, Tobo and Gota watched. Even Mother Gota kept her mouth shut.

Sahra was conspicuously absent.

She was carrying her snit over Tobo too far. I expect there was more to it than what she admitted, though. A big part would center on her fear of the near future.

"Right there," One-Eye said just as I leaned forward to see what Goblin was doing. The little bald man had a light hammer and a chisel. He tapped the chisel. A piece of iron flipped off the Key. This had been going on for a while, evidently, because about half the iron was gone, revealing something made of gold. I was so surprised at the wizard's lack of greed that I almost forgot to worry about what they were doing to the Key.

I opened my mouth. Without looking up, One-Eye told me, "Don't shit your knickers yet, Little Girl. We ain't hurting a thing. The Key is this thing inside. This golden hammer. You want to bend down a little closer? Maybe you can read what's inscribed on it."

I bent. I scanned the characters made visible by removal of the iron. "Looks like the same alphabet as the first book of the Annals." Not to mention the first Book of the Dead. Which I did not mention.

Goblin used the tip of his chisel to indicate a prominent symbol that appeared in several places. "Doj says he saw this sign at the temple in the Grove of Doom."

"It should be there." I knew that one. Master Santaraksita had taught me its meaning. "It's the personal sign of the goddess. Her personal chop, if you want." I did not name a name. I suggested, "Don't speak the name. Not in any of its forms. In the presence of this thing, that would be guaranteed to attract her attention." Everyone stared at me. I asked, "You didn't do that already, did you? No? Uncle, you don't know what this thing might really be, do you?" I had an intuition it was something Narayan Singh might never have surrendered had he been aware that it was in his possession. I thought it might exist solely so that the priest who carried it could obtain the attention of his goddess instantly. Even in my own religion, people had had a much more immediate and scary relationship with the godhead in ancient times. The scriptures told us so. But no such golden hammer played any part in the Kina mythology, insofar as I could recall. Curious. Maybe Master Santaraksita could tell me more.

Goblin continued chipping away. I continued watching. The process went faster as each fragment fell.

"That isn't any hammer," I said. "That's a kind of pickax. It's a Deceiver cult thing. And older than dirt. It has to be something of huge religious significance." I suggested, "Show it to the girl. See how she responds."

"You're as close to a Kina expert as we've got, Sleepy. What could it be?"

"There's actually a name for that kind of tool but I can't remember what it is. Every Deceiver band had a pickax like this. Not made out of gold, though. They used them in the burial ceremonies after their murders. To break the bones of their victims so they would fold up into a smaller wad. Sometimes they used them to help dig graves. All with the appropriate ceremonies aimed at pleasing Kina, of course. I really do think somebody should show this to the Daughter of Night and see what she says."

It seemed like a thousand pairs of eyes were staring at me, waiting for me to volunteer. I told them, "I'm not doing it. I'm going to bed."

All those eyes kept right on staring. I had put myself in charge. This was something nobody but the guy in charge ought to handle.

"All right. Uncle. Tobo. Goblin. You back me up on this. That child has talents we can't guess at yet." I had been warned that she still tried to walk away from her flesh at night, despite all the constraints surrounding her. She was both her mothers' daughter and there was no telling what might happen when she had to suffer too much stress.

Tobo protested. "I don't like to be around her. She gives me the creeps."

Goblin beat me to it. "Kid, she gives everybody the creeps. She's the creepiest thing I've run into in a hundred fifty years. Get used to it. Deal with it. It's part of the job. Which they say you were born to do and which you did ask for."

Curious. Goblin the mentor and instructor seemed much more articulate than Goblin the want-to-be-layabout and slacker.

The little wizard suggested, "You carry the Key. You're young and strong."

The Daughter of Night did not look up when we entered the tent. Perhaps she was not aware of us. She seemed to be meditating. Possibly communing with the Dark Mother. Goblin kicked the bars of her cage, which rattled nicely and shed a shower of rust. "Well, look at her. Cute."

"What?" I asked.

"She's been working some kind of spell on the iron. It's rusting away a thousand times faster than it ought to. Clever girl. Only—"

The clever girl looked up. Our eyes met. Something behind hers chilled me to the bone. "Only what?" I asked.

"Only every spell holding her and controlling her has that cage for an anchor, Anything that happens to it will happen to her. Look at her skin."

I saw what he meant. The Daughter of Night was not exactly rusty herself but did look spotty and frayed at the surface.

Her gaze shifted to Uncle, Goblin, Tobo . . . and she gasped, like she was seeing the boy for the first time. She rose slowly, drifted toward the bars, gaze locked with his. Then a little frown danced across her brow. Her gaze darted down to Tobo's burden.

Her mouth opened and, I swear, a sound like the angry bellow of an elephant rolled out. Her eyes grew huge. She lunged forward. Her shackles gave way. The bars of the cage creaked and let fall another shower of rust. They bent but did not give. She thrust an arm through in a desperate effort to reach the Key. Little bits of skin blackened and fell off her. And still she was beautiful.

I observed, "I guess we can safely say the thing does hold some significance for the Deceivers."

"You could say so," Goblin admitted. The girl's whole arm had begun to look like it had been badly burned.

"So let's take it away and see what else we can find out. And get the cage reinforced and her shackles replaced. Tobo!" The boy kept staring at the girl like he was seeing *her* for the first time. "Don't tell me he just fell in love. I couldn't handle it if we had to worry about that in addition to everything else."

"No," Uncle Doj reassured me. "Not love, I think. But the future, just maybe."

Although I tried to insist, he would not expand upon that remark. He was still Uncle Doj, the mystery priest of the Nyueng Bao.

67

Things came together nicely after the defeat of the relief column. Murgen said nobody else was likely to challenge us without help from beyond the mountains. Which help, unfortunately, was on the way already. Soulcatcher was airborne and lurching southward in small, erratic leaps that, nevertheless, were bringing her closer faster than any animal could do—even one of those magical stallions from the Tower at Charm—but still definitely very feebly for a flying carpet. Once upon a time the Howler could conquer the miles between Overlook and Taglios in a single night.

Soulcatcher had to rest several hours for every hour she spent aloft. Even so, she was on her way. And the impact of the news on the troops was electric. With only days left, or possibly only hours, everyone buckled down and put their back into it. I saw very little slacking, little wasted effort, and some very serious concentration when it came to honing military skills.

Suvrin was right in there with the troops, drilling his behind off. Literally. Though he had been with us only a short time, he had begun to lose weight and show signs of shaping up. He approached me soon after Murgen and Goblin began issuing regular reports about Soulcatcher's progress. "I want to stay with you, ma'am," he told me.

"You what?" I was surprised.

"I'm not sure I want to be part of the Black Company but I do know for sure that I don't want to be here when the Protector shows up. She has a reputation for seldom letting herself be swayed by the facts. The futility of me having resisted you won't impress her."

"You're right about that. If you shirked because you would've gotten killed doing what she expected, she'll arrange it so you get dead anyway. In a less pleasant way, if possible. All right, Suvrin. You've kept your word and you've been a good worker."

He winced. "You understand what 'Suvrin' actually means?"

"Junior, essentially. But you're stuck with it now. Most people in the Company don't go by their birth names. Even most of the men who go by regular names don't go by their real ones. They're all getting away from their past. And you will be, too."

He grimaced.

"Report to Master Santaraksita. Until I find something else for you, your job will be to assist him. Old Baladitya is no use at all. He's worse than Santaraksita, who keeps getting farther and farther behind in his packing because he keeps getting distracted by his books." Santaraksita had managed to acquire several antique volumes locally that had, miraculously, survived the countless disasters that had beset the region these past several decades.

Suvrin bowed. "Thank you." There was a fresh bounce in his step as he walked away.

I suspected he and Master Santaraksita might have a lot in common. Heck, Suvrin could even read.

Tobo materialized. "My father says to tell you that Soulcatcher has reached Charandaprash. And that she's decided to rest there before she crosses the Dandha Presh."

"A few more hours' grace. Excellent. Means there's a good chance there won't be anything left here for her to find but our tracks. How are you getting along with your mother? Did you make any effort at all?"

"Dad also says he wants you to post somebody with a warning horn that can be sounded once the Protector gets dangerously close. And he says you should pull in the pickets watching the pass now, just in case Soulcatcher changes her mind about taking some time off."

That was a good idea.

Runmust and Riverwalker made the mistake of being close enough to be seen. I sent them to go bring the scouts home. "Tobo, you can't ignore your mother. You'll end up getting along with her worse than she gets along with your grandmother."

"Sleepy . . . why can't she just let me grow up?"

"Because you're her baby, you idiot! Don't you understand that? When you're twice as old as One-Eye you'll *still* be her baby. The only baby that cruel fate hasn't gobbled down. You do remember that your mother had other children and she lost them?"

"Uh . . . yeah."

"I've never had children. I never want to have children. In part because I can see how horrible it would be to see my own flesh and blood die and not be able to do anything to prevent it. Family is supposed to be extremely important to you Nyueng Bao. I want you to drop whatever you're doing. Right now. Go over and sit on that boulder. Spend two hours not thinking about anything but what it must have meant to your mother to see your brother and sister die. Think about how badly she must not want to go through that again. Think about what it must be like to be her after everything else she's had to go through. You're a smart kid. You can figure it out."

When you are around people long enough you get a feel for how they react. I could see his first petulant inclination was to remind me that I had been younger than he was now when I attached myself to Bucket and the Company, which had little to do with the argument at hand but which was the sort of tool you grab when you are that age.

"If you intend to say something, make sure it makes sense before you do. Because if you can't think logically and argue logically, then there isn't much hope that you'll have any success with the sorcery, no matter how talented you are. I know. I know. From everything you've seen, the bigger the wizards are, the crazier they are. But within the boundaries of their insanity, every one of them is rigorously, mathematically rational. The entire power of their minds serves their insanity. When they stumble it's because they let emotions or wishful thinking get in the way."

"All right. I surrender. I'll sit on the damned rock until it hatches. Oh, Dad also said to tell you that Narayan Singh is somewhere close by. He can sense the Deceiver but he can't pinpoint him. Kina is protecting him with her dreams. Dad says you should ask the white crow to look for him. If you can find it and get it to sit still long enough."

"Crowhunter. Maybe I'll call myself that. It sounds more glamorous than Sleepy."

"Tobo sounds more glamorous than Sleepy." Tobo headed for the boulder and settled in an approved attitude. I hoped I had planted seeds that would take root and sprout while he was trying to think of everything else but.

"At least you get to change your name when you grow up. . . ." Stupid. Anytime I feel like it I can tell everyone to call me whatever strikes my fancy.

Crowhunter gave up her name. She was a failure. The white monster was nowhere to be found. So I went and spent some time with Sahra even though she did not welcome me right away. We recalled old days, hard times, her husband's lack of perfection, till I thought she was relaxed enough to actually listen to what I had to say about Tobo.

The villain himself scored a coup by showing up with an olive branch at the perfect time. I elected to remove myself while things were going well. I hoped the peace would last but did not count on forever.

I would settle for one halcyon week. In a week we would know if it was possible to resurrect the Captured. In a week we would either be dead on the glittering plain or ready to return as a force of ultimate destruction. Or maybe . . .

68

The warning horn sounded deep in the night, when even those who were stuck with guard duty were at their most sluggish. But the man on horn duty was married to his job. He kept blowing and blowing. In minutes our entire encampment was seething. And I was out there with my heart in my throat, striding along, making sure the chaos was only apparent, not real. Everyone remained calm and focused. There was no panic. I was pleased. Even a little training and discipline are better than none.

I ducked into Goblin's tent. Sahra and Tobo were there already and not at one another's throats. I must have gotten through to the kid. I should keep after them both. In my copious free time. I bent close to the mist projector. "What's the word?"

Murgen whispered, "Soulcatcher is airborne and moving south. She plans to arrive shortly after sunrise. She has a good idea where you are. During her rest time she sent a shadow down to scout your position. She didn't learn a lot more. The shadow didn't dare get close enough to eavesdrop. She plans to don one of her disguises and infiltrate your camp so she can find out what you're really up to. From the beginning, she's operated under the assumption that we're dead out here. Even though she didn't kill us directly when she trapped us. She flew out of there believing we'd be dead in just a few days. I expect learning that Croaker and Lady are still alive is going to be the kind of shock that ruins her whole century."

"How fast is she moving? Strike that. You said she'd get here just after sunrise. Is Mogaba with her?" That would make a big difference in how fresh she would be when when she arrived. Which would determine the shape of what I started doing now.

"No. If she manages to get in among you and unearths all the answers to the questions she has, she'll smash you, scatter you, grab the Key, then go back for the Great General." Murgen sneered when he used Mogaba's title. The fact that we never beat him once, heads up, during the Kiaulune wars, did nothing to ease our contempt for him as a deserter and traitor.

"Warn me if she does anything unexpected. Sahra, have you checked on your mother?"

"Briefly. Doj and JoJo are helping her and One-Eye. I think she was a little delirious. She kept muttering about a noose and a land of unknown shadows and calling the heaven and earth and the day and the night."

"All evil dies there an endless death."

"That, too. What is it?"

"I don't know. A phrase I picked up somewhere. It has to do with the plain but I don't know what. Doj might be able to tell you. He promised to be cooperative and forthcoming but since I passed on his offer to make me his apprentice, that hasn't materialized. My fault as much as his, probably. I haven't taken time to press him. I have work to do." I ducked out.

The excitement had become more rigorously organized. There were torches and lanterns to light the road to the Shadowgate. A band of our bravest were up near the gate already, arranging more lighting and fine-tuning the colored powders used as road marks. Loaded animals were beginning to line up. Likewise a train of carts. Babies cried, children whined, a dog barked without pause. Sounds of men slipping through the darkness beyond the light came from all around. Prisoners who had been sure we meant to drag them onto the plain to become human sacrifices were being chivied toward the New Town. Some of the harder men had wanted to use them as bearers instead of the animals, disposing of them as their usefulness ended. I had demurred. They would become obstinate and obstreperous after the first few died and we would not be able to eat them after we ate up the consumables they carried. Not that the majority of us would eat flesh anyway. But those who could would from the beginning.

I spied Willow Swan strolling through the mob. He spun off orders like a drill instructor. I approached him. "Gone nostalgic for the good old days when you were the boss Grey?"

"A true genius, whose name we won't bring up in present company, sent all the master sergeants to make preparations at the Shadowgate. She didn't detail anybody to keep things moving down here."

The unnamed genius had to admit that he was right. River, Runmust, Spiff, all the men I had known the longest and trusted the most, were up there or somewhere out in the darkness. I guess I just assumed Sahra and I could handle everything else. Forgetting that I would be sprinting around making decisions for everyone who could not make up their minds for themselves. "Thanks. If I don't get a better offer by my fortieth birthday, I'll marry you yet."

Swan made a halfhearted effort to click his heels. "So. How old are you today?"

"Seventeen."

"That's about what I guessed. With maybe another twenty years of experience, plus wear and tear."

"It's tough being a teenager today. Just ask Tobo. Nobody's *ever* had it as awful as he does."

He chuckled. "Speaking of kids, who's handling the Daughter of Night? Which I don't want to be me."

"Darn! I figured Goblin and Doj for that. But Goblin's tied up helping keep track of Soulcatcher, and Doj has Gota and One-Eye to worry about. Thanks for reminding me." I headed back toward Goblin's tent. "Hey, Short Wart! Leave it to Tobo and Sahra a while. We got to get the Daughter of Night loaded up."

Goblin came out muttering, surveyed the excitement, grumbled, "All right. Let's get at it. Only, how come the fuck we never gave her a name? So what if she don't want one. She don't want to live in no cage, either. Even Booboo would be easier than calling her Daughter of Night all the time. Whoa! What the fuck is that?" He stared past me, downhill.

I turned, saw a pair of red eyes bobbing in the darkness, coming closer fast. I grabbed for my sword. Then I frowned as I heard the hoofbeats. Then I said, "Hey, buddy! Is that you? What the heck are you doing here? I thought you had yourself a job working for the traitor."

The old black stallion stepped close, lowered its head to nuzzle the hair beside my right ear. I hugged it around the neck. We had been friends once upon a time but I had not thought we were so close that it would desert Mogaba and track me down over hundreds of miles once it discovered that I was still alive. The creatures had been created to serve the Lady of the Tower but were supposed to be used to passing from one secondary master to another. This one had been Murgen's before it had become mine, then I had lost it.

"You ought to get out of here," I told it. "Your timing's really lousy. Soulcatcher is going to be all over us in just a few hours. If we're not already up there on that plain."

The horse surveyed my companions and what it could see of the Company, shuddered. Then, turning its gaze on Swan, the stallion managed a very human snort.

I patted its neck. "I'm not sure I don't agree with you, but Willow does have his redeeming qualities. He just keeps them well hidden. Go ahead and tag along if you want. I'm not riding. Not without a saddle."

Swan chuckled. "So much for the conquering Vehdna horsemen whose pride disdained both saddles and stirrups."

"Admitting no shortcomings of my own, I still have to observe that most of those proud horsemen were over six feet tall."

"I'll find you a ladder. And promise never to say a word about how those proud conquerors fared as soon as they ran into cavalry who did favor saddles and stirrups."

"Bite him, buddy."

To my amazement, the stallion snorted and nipped at Willow's shoulder. Swan leaped back. "You always did have a temper and bad manners, half-ass."

"Might be the company."

"Far be it from me to interfere with your sparking, Crowhunter," Goblin said, "but I thought you had a notion to do something with Booboo."

"Sarcastic, eavesdropping mudsucker. I did, didn't I? And I overlooked our old pal Khusavir Pete, too. I haven't checked in on him lately, either. Is he still healthy?" The horse nuzzled me again. I patted its neck. Maybe it felt more nostalgic about our good old days than I did.

"I can check. You definitely overlooked him in your master plan."

"Oh, no, I didn't. Not a bit. I have a very special mission cooked up specially for Khusavir Pete. And if he pulls it off, not only will he get to stay alive, I'll forgive everything he did at Kushkhoshi."

Somebody shouted. A scarlet fireball blistered across the night. It missed its target. It did not miss a tent, however. Then another tent after that, then the crude wooden barracks the men had built while they were waiting for me to arrive. All three began to smolder.

"That was Narayan Singh," Willow Swan said, stating what two-score people had seen during the carmine instant. "And he had Booboo—"

"Can it, Swan." I started yelling at everyone nearby, trying to organize a pursuit.

Goblin told me, "Calm down, Sleepy. All we need to do is wait till she starts screaming, then go pick her up."

I had forgotten the incredible array of control spells attached to the Daughter of Night. Her pain would increase geometrically as she moved farther away from her cage. Then at some distance known only to Goblin and One-Eye, choke spells would kick in and tighten rapidly. Narayan could take her away from us but only at the cost of killing her. Unless . . .

I asked.

"The spells have to be taken off from outside. She could be her mother and sister, the Shadowmasters and the Ten Who Were Taken all rolled into one and she'd still have to have somebody else help her get loose."

"All right. Then we'll wait for the screams."

There were no screams. Not then or ever.

Murgen looked hard. He could find no sign. Kina was dreaming strongly, protecting her own. Goblin remained adamant that they had to be close by, that there was no way the Daughter of Night had shed her connection to her cage.

I told Swan, "Then you gather up some men and drag that cage up to the Shadowgate. We'll *make* her follow us."

The warning horn sounded again. Soulcatcher had crossed the summit. She was on our side of the Dandha Presh. There were hints of light in the east.

It was time to leave.

69

A brutal argument was under way aboard Soulcatcher's carpet as she approached her destination, skimming the rocks, the sun's blinding fires behind her. Part of her wanted to forget about assuming a disguise and infiltrating the enemy. That part wanted to arrive as a killing storm, destroying everything and everyone that was not Soulcatcher. But by doing that she would expose herself to the counterefforts of people who had shown themselves very resourceful in the past. Innovation was one of the more irksome traditions of the Black Company.

She grounded the carpet and stepped off, concealed it using a minor spell. Then she crept toward the Company encampment, a few yards at a time, until she found a good hiding place where she could undertake the illusion creations and modest shapechanges that would render her unrecognizable. That work required total concentration.

Back in the brush, not far from where she had set down, Uncle Doj crept forward and after having used his small wizard's skills to make sure there were no booby traps, demolished Soulcatcher's flying carpet in a straightforward, no-nonsense manner using a hatchet. He might be old and a step slower, but he was still very quick and very sneaky. He was almost all the way back to the Shadowgate when Soulcatcher appeared, looking the epitome of scruffy young manhood.

A white crow, balanced precariously in a bit of rain-hungry brush, observed her passage. When she could no longer glance back and see anything damning, the bird flapped into the place where she had changed and started going through the clothing and whatnot she had left behind. The bird kept making noises like it was talking to itself.

Soulcatcher entered the encampment where she had expected to find the remnants of the Black Company. It was empty. But up ahead she saw a long column already beyond the Shadowgate. One man with a sword across his back had not passed through the gate yet but he was moving swiftly, and a number of people were waiting for him just on the other side.

They did have the Key! And they had used the damned thing! She should have gotten here faster! She should have attacked! Dammit, everyone knew subtlety was no good with these people. Hey! They had to have known that she was coming.

There was no other explanation for this. They had known she was coming and they knew where she was now and . . .

The first fireball was so accurately directed that it would have taken her head off if she had not been getting down already. In another moment the damned things were streaking in from several different sources. They set brush afire and shattered rocks. She got down on her stomach and crawled. Before she worried about her dignity, she had to get away from the focal point of the fire. Unfortunately, her efforts did not seem to matter. The assassins seemed to know exactly where she was and her disguise did not fool them for an instant.

As a swarm of fireballs closed in, she flung herself into a deep hole that had been a cesspit not that long ago. No matter. Right now shelter was priceless. Now the snipers could not get her without coming out of hiding and coming to her.

She took advantage of the respite to engineer, prepare and launch a counterattack. That involved a lot of color and fire and boiling, oily explosions, none of which did much harm because her surviving attackers had fled through the Shadowgate as soon as she went into the pit.

She climbed out. Nothing happened. She glared up the hill. So. Even the snipers were beyond the Shadowgate now. Nearly a dozen people were standing around there, waiting to see what she would do. She calmed herself. She could not let them goad her into doing something stupid. The Shadowgate was in extremely delicate shape. One angry, thoughtless move on her part might damage it beyond repair.

She conquered the rage that threatened to conquer her. She was ancient in her wickedness. Time was an intimate ally. She knew how to abide.

She limped uphill, urging her anger to bleed off in movement, with an ease no normal being could manage.

The slope immediately below the Shadowgate was covered with swaths and patches of colored chalk. A carefully marked safe path passed through. Soulcatcher did not yield to temptation and try to follow it. There was a chance that they had forgotten that she had gone this way before. Or perhaps they refused to believe she could recall that in those days the safe path had entered the Shadowgate eight feet farther west, just beyond that rusty, twisted iron cage lying on its side as though it was exhausted and dying. She waved a finger. "Naughty, naughty."

Willow Swan—damn his treacherous, should-be-dead bones!—and the Nyueng Bao family stared back impassively. The pale-faced little wizard Goblin smirked, obviously remembering whose fault it was that she could no longer walk normally. And the ugly little woman smiled evilly. She said, "I wasn't *trying* to suck you in, Sweet Stuff. I *did* suck you in." She lifted a hand and raised a middle finger in a sign obviously learned from a northerner. "Water sleeps, Protector."

What the hell did that mean?

70

No human being can jump as high as Soulcatcher did. Nevertheless, she managed to get her heels ten feet off the ground a gnat's breath before the fireball ripped through the air where she had stood. I should have kept my big darned mouth shut. Gloating will do you in every time. How many stories and sagas are there where the hero survives because his captor insists on wasting time bragging and gloating before the execution? Add another one to the roll, where Company Annalist Sleepy does the incredibly dumb deed and leaves the target not quite relaxed enough.

Of course, she was *fast*. Epically fast. Poor old Khusavir Pete only got off two more fireballs before Soulcatcher got to him where we had left him chained.

It did not play out the way I hoped, only the way I expected. Now Khusavir Pete would have a hard time repaying any debt he still owed us.

I caught a glimpse of motion, the white crow plunging like a striking hawk. It pulled out and glided away. I murmured to myself, "Sister, sister." I was beginning to read the messages.

"Come here, Tobo." He was carrying the Key. He was supposed to be up at the head of the column but had hung back so he could watch the fireworks. He was the only one of us who did not have the sense to be frightened. Because he was not up where he belonged, all progress had come to a halt above us. He wore a hangdog look as he approached. He expected to be chastised. And he would be, later. "Hold up the Key."

"But won't that—"

"The Company isn't a debating club, Tobo. Show her the Key. Today."

He hoisted the Key overhead angrily. The morning sunlight blazed off the golden pick.

Soulcatcher did not show much excitement. But I had not meant the demonstration for her benefit, really. I wanted Narayan Singh to know what he had let slip through his fingers.

It was the Key, of course, but it was also some ancient and holy relic of Kina's Strangler cult. In their glory days every Deceiver company priest had carried a replica. I muttered, "You win some, you lose some, Narayan. In the excitement you got the girl back. But I've got this. And I can carry it. You've got the Daughter of Night and you can take her anywhere you want to. If you can carry her and her cage." Goblin and One-Eye had crafted a masterpiece of wicked sorcery. She could not even escape by destroying the cage. Whatever happened to it would happen to her.

I was not pleased about having to leave the cage behind but the Shadowgate had been decidedly stubborn in resisting its passage. That could have been overcome by sheer muscle power but I had not been able to get enough men onto it fast enough to force it through before the fireballs started flying.

Good luck, Baby Darkness, dragging all that iron around whilst you pursue your wickedness.

I hoped Singh had left the Book of the Dead hidden on the other side of the Dandha Presh so it would be a long time before the girl and it embraced one another. Long enough for me to get where I wanted to go and accomplish what I wanted to accomplish.

"That's good, Tobo. Now get back up front and get this mob moving. Swan. Tell me about the camping circles. And give me your best guess about how soon we're likely to run into trouble because of breaks in the protection of the road."

"I don't remember them ever being more than a few hours apart. And although we used them as camping places, I think that they were actually crossroads. That's easier to tell at night." Ominously, he added, "You'll see. Everything is different at night."

I did not like the sound of that.

I was still in the rear guard and only halfway to the crest when Soulcatcher found out what had happened to her flying carpet. The sound of her anger reached us despite the dampening effect of whatever barrier stood between us and the rest of the world. The earth shivered at the same time.

Uncle Doj was not far away, standing at the edge of the road, watching for evidence of his success. I said, "She seems displeased with the prospect of having to walk home." My friend the horse stood behind me, looking over my shoulder. It made a sound that could have passed for a snicker if it had not been a horse making it.

Doj indulged in a rare smile. He was thoroughly pleased with himself.

Willow Swan asked me, "What did you do now?"

"Not me. Doj. He totally obliterated her means of transport. She's on her own two hooves, now. She's a hundred miles from her only friend. And Goblin's already fixed up one of her feet so she can't run or dance."

"What you're telling me, then, is that you've created another Limper."

He was old enough to remember that nemesis of the Company. I could not contradict him. I did lose my smile. I had read those Annals often because they had been recorded by the Captain himself when he was young. "Nah, I don't think so. Soulcatcher doesn't have the concentrated venom and nearly divine malice that possessed the Limper. She doesn't get obsessed the way he did. She's more chaos walking while he was malevolence incarnate."

I showed Swan my crossed fingers. "I'd better dash up front and pretend that I know what I'm doing. Tobo?"

"He went ahead without you," Doj said. "You upset him."

I noted that the column had resumed moving, which meant that Tobo was on the plain already, carrying the Key like a protective talisman.

I needed to give a lot of thought to the fact that that artifact, evidently considered a holy of holies by the Stranglers, may actually have been brought off the plain into my world by the ancestors of the Nyueng Bao. I had to spend some thought on what the Key might mean to the last informed priest of the Nyueng Bao.

71

Something beside the road caught my attention just before I reached the crest and got my first close look at the glittering plain. It was a small frog, mostly black but with stripes and whorls of dark green upon its back. It had eyes the color of fresh blood. It clung to a slightly tilted slab of grey-black rock. It wanted to go somewhere, anywhere, but its right hind leg was injured and when it tried to jump, it just sort of spun around in place. "Where the heck did that come from? There isn't supposed to be anything alive up here." I had been looking forward to having the clouds of flies that followed the animals get thinned out when they buzzed out beyond the safe zones and encountered killer shadows.

Swan said, "It won't be alive for long. The white crow dropped it. I think it was bringing it along for a snack." He pointed.

At the white crow. Bolder than ever, the bird had made itself at home on the back of my friend the mystic stallion. The horse seemed content with the situation. Perhaps even a little smug when it looked at me.

"I just remembered," Swan said. "For what it's worth. Last time we came up here Croaker made everybody who belonged to the Company touch their badges and amulets to the black stripe that runs down the middle of the road. Right after he touched the stripe with the lancehead on the standard. Maybe none of that amounts to anything. But I'm a superstitious kind of guy and I'd be more comfortable—"

"You're right. So be quiet. I recently reread everything Murgen had to say about his trip and he thought it might be a good idea, too. Tobo! Hold up!" I did not believe the boy would actually hear me over the clatter generated by the column but did expect that people would pass the word. I looked at the hapless frog once more and marveled that the crow was smart enough to let it go. Then I hastened to overtake our fledgling wizard.

The column stopped. Tobo had gotten my message. He had chosen not to ignore it. Maybe he had caught something from the white crow.

His mother and grandmother both were right there with him where he waited, making sure he did sensible things. He was exasperated by the delay. He was already far ahead of everyone but Sahra and Gota. . . .

Ah! As I recalled, Murgen had had the same trouble with the Lance of Passion.

My first glimpse of the plain awed me. Its immensity was indescribable. It was as flat as a table forever. It was grey on grey on grey, with the road just barely darker. There was no doubt whatsoever that this was all one vast artifact.

"Hang on, Tobo. Don't go any farther," I called. "We almost forgot something. You need to take the Key and touch it to the black stripe that runs down the middle of the road."

"What black stripe?"

Swan said, "It doesn't show up nearly as well this time. But it's there if you look." It was. I found it. "Come back this way. You can see it back here."

Tobo backtracked reluctantly. Maybe I should have Gota carry the Key. She could not move fast enough to outrun the rest of us.

I stared on, beyond Tobo, feeling a faint touch of that passion to hurry myself. I was getting close to my brothers now. . . . Dark-grey clouds were beginning to gather down there. Murgen had mentioned a nearly permanent overcast that, nevertheless, did not always seem to have been around during his nights. I could make out no hint of the ruined fortress that was supposed to be a few days ahead of us. I did see plenty of the standing stones that were one of the outstanding features of the plain.

"I see it!" Tobo shouted, pointing downward. The little idiot swung the pickax, burying the point in the road surface.

The earth shuddered.

This was no devastating quake like those some of us recalled from years ago, when half the Shadowlands had been laid waste. It was just strong enough to be sensed and set tongues wagging and animals protesting.

The morning sun must have touched the plain oddly, somehow, because all the standing stones began to sparkle. People oohed and aahed. I said, "I guess this is why they call it glittering stone."

Swan demurred. "I don't think so. But I could be wrong. Don't forget what I said about the Company badges."

"I haven't forgotten."

Tobo pried the pick out of the road's surface. The earth shifted again, as gently as before. When I joined him he was staring downward, baffled. "It healed itself, Sleepy."

"What?"

"When I hit it the pick went in sort of like the road was soft. And when I yanked it back out, the hole healed itself."

Swan remarked, "The center stripe is getting easier to see."

He was right. Maybe that was because of the brightening sunlight.

The ground trembled again. Behind me, voices changed tone, becoming frightened as well as awed. I glanced back.

A huge mushroom of dark rouge dust with black filigree highlights running through it boiled up from whence we had come. Its topmost surface seemed almost solid but as it rose and moved, the pieces of junk riding on it fell off.

Goblin burst into laughter so wicked it must have carried for miles. "Somebody got into my treasure trove. I hope she learned a really painful lesson." I was close enough for him to add a whispered, "I wish it could be fatal but there's not much chance of that."

"Probably not."

"I'll settle for crippling her other leg."

I said, "Sahra, there's something I need you to do. You remember Murgen telling us how he kept getting ahead of everyone when he came up here? Tobo has been doing the same thing. Try to slow him down."

Sahra sighed wearily. She nodded. "I'll stop him." She seemed apathetic, though.

"I don't want him stopped, I just want him slowed down enough so everyone else can keep up. This could be important later." I decided the two of us needed to have a long talk in private, the way we used to do before everything got so busy. It was obvious that she needed to get some things out where they could be lined up and swatted down and pushed away from her long enough for her heart to heal.

She did need healing. And for that she had no one to blame but herself. She did not want to accept the world as it was. She seemed worn out from fighting it. And in those ways she had begun to look very much like her mother.

I told her, "Put a leash on him if that's what it takes."

Tobo glowered at me. I ignored him. I made a brief speech suggesting anyone who carried a Black Company badge should press it to the road's surface right where Tobo had wounded it. The public readings aloud I had been doing had included Murgen's adventures on the plain. Nobody questioned my suggestion or refused to accept it. The column began moving again, slowly, as we found ways to bless, if only secondarily, the animals and those who did not have Company badges. I stayed in place and said something positive to everyone who passed by. I was amazed at the number of women and children and noncombatants in general who had managed to attach themselves to the band without me really noticing. The Captain would be appalled.

Uncle Doj was last to go by. That troubled me vaguely. A Nyueng Bao to the rear, more Nyueng Bao to the front, with the foremost a half-breed . . . But the whole Company was a miscegenation. There were only two men in this whole crowd who had belonged to the Company when it had arrived from the north. Goblin and One-Eye. One-Eye was almost spent and Goblin was doing his determined best, quietly, to pass on as many skills as he could to Tobo before the inevitable began to overhaul him as well.

I walked past the slow-moving file, intent on getting back up near the point so I could be among the first to see anything new. I did not see or feel any particular mission in anyone I passed. It seemed that a quiet despair informed everyone. These were not good signs. This meant the euphoria of our minor successes had collapsed. Most of these people realized that they had become refugees.

Swan told me, "We have an expression up north, 'going from the frying pan into the fire.' Seems like about what we've done here."

"Really?"

"We got away from Soulcatcher. But now what?"

"Now we march on until we find our buried brothers. Then we break them out."

"You're not really as simple as you pretend, are you?"

"No, I'm not. But I do like to let people know that things aren't always as difficult as they want to make them." I glanced around to see who might overhear. "I have the same doubts everyone else has, Swan. My feet are on this path as much because I don't know what else to do as they are out of high ideals. Sometimes I look at my life and it seems pretty pathetic. I've spent more than a decade conspiring and committing crimes so I can go dig up some old bones in order to find somebody who can tell me what to do."

"Surrender to the Will of the Night."

"What?"

"Sounds like something Narayan Singh would say, doesn't it? In my great-grandfather's time it was the slogan of the Lady's supporters. They believed that peace, prosperity and security would result inevitably if all power could be concentrated in the hands of the right strong-willed person. And it did turn out that way, more or less. In principalities that did 'Surrender to the Will of the Night,' particularly near the core of the empire, there were generations of peace and prosperity. Plague, pestilence and famine were uncommon. Warfare was a curiosity going on far, far away. Criminals were hunted down with a ferocity that overawed all but the completely crazy ones. But there was always bad trouble along the frontiers. The Lady's minions, the Ten Who

Were Taken, all wanted to build sub-empires of their own, which never lacked for external enemies. And they all had their own ancient feuds with one another. Hell, even peace and prosperity create enemies. If you're doing all right, there's always somebody who wants to take it away from you."

"I never pictured you as a philosopher, Swan."

"Oh, I'm a wonder after you get to know me."

"I'm sure you are. What are you trying to tell me?"

"I don't know. Killing time jacking my jaw. Making the trip go faster. Or maybe just reminding you that you shouldn't get too distressed about the vagaries of human nature. I've been getting my roots ripped out and my life overturned and a boot in my butt propelling me into an unknown future, blindfolded, for so long now that I *am* getting philosophical about it. I enjoy the moment. In a different context I do Surrender to the Will of the Night."

Despite my religious upbringing, I have never cherished a fatalistic approach to life. Surrender to the Will of the Night? Put my life in the hands of God? God is Great, God is Good, God is Merciful, there is no God but God. This we are taught. But the Bhodi philosophers may be right when they tell us that homage to the gods is best served when seconded by human endeavor.

"Going to get dark after a while," Swan reminded me.

"That's one of those things I've been trying to avoid thinking about," I confessed. "But Narayan Singh was right. Darkness always comes."

And when it did, we would find out just how wonderful a talisman our Key was.

"Have you noticed how the pillars keep on glittering even though the sky has started to look like it's going to rain?"

"I have." Murgen never mentioned this one phenomenon. I wondered if we had not done something never done before. "Did this happen last time you were up here?"

"No. There was a lot of glitter when we had direct sunlight but none that seemed like it was self-generated."

"Uhm. And was it this cold?" It had been getting chillier all day.

"I recall a sort of highland chill. Nothing intolerable. Whoa. Sounds like party time."

A whoop and holler had broken out at the head of the column. I could not determine a cause visually, being of the short persuasion. "What is it?"

"The kid's stopped. Looks like he's found something."

72

What Tobo had found were the remains of the Nar, Sindawe, who had been one of our best officers in the old days and, possibly, the villain Mogaba's brother. Certainly those two had been as close as brothers until the siege of Jaicur, when Mogaba chose to usurp command of the Company. "Clear away from him, people," I growled. "Give the experts room to take a look." The experts being Goblin, who dropped to his knees and scooted around the corpse slowly, moving his head up and down, murmuring some sort of cantrips, touching absolutely nothing until he was certain there was no danger. I dropped to one knee myself.

"He got a lot farther than I would've expected," Goblin said.

"He was tougher than rawhide. Was it shadows?" The body had that look.

"Yes." Goblin pushed gently. The corpse rolled slightly. "Nothing left here. He's a dried-out mummy."

A voice from behind me said, "Search him, you retard. He might've been carrying a message."

I glanced back. One-Eye stood behind me, leaning on an ugly black cane. The effort had him shivering. Or maybe that was just the cold air. He had been riding one of the donkeys, tied into place so he would not fall if he dozed off, which he did a lot these days.

I suggested, "Move him over to the side of the road. We need to keep this crowd moving. We have about eight more miles to go before we stop for the night." I pulled that eight out of the air but it was a fact that we needed to keep moving. We were better prepared for this evolution than our predecessors had been but our resources remained limited. "Swan, when a mule with a tent comes along, cut it out of line."

"Uhm?"

"We need to make a travois. To bring the body."

Every face within earshot went blank.

"We're still the Black Company. We still don't leave our own behind." Which was never strictly true but you do have to serve an ideal the best you can, lest it become debased. A law as ancient as coinage itself says bad money will drive out good. The same is true of principles, ethics and rules of conduct. If you always do the easier thing, then you cannot possibly remain steadfast when it becomes necessary to take a difficult stand. You must do what you know to be right. And you do know. Ninety-nine times out of a hundred you do know and you are just making excuses because the right thing is so hard, or just inconvenient.

"Here's his badge," Goblin said, producing a beautifully crafted silver skull in which the one ruby eye seemed to glow with an inner life. Sindawe had made that himself. It was an exquisite piece from talented hands. "You want to take it?"

That was the custom, gradually developed since the adoption of the badges under Soulcatcher's suzerainty back when the Captain was just a young tagalong with a quill pen. The badges of the fallen were passed down to interested newcomers, who were expected to learn their lineage and thus keep the names alive.

It is immortality of a sort.

I jumped. Sahra made a startled noise. I recalled that something similar had happened to Murgen last time. Although in that case, only he had sensed it. I thought. Maybe I ought to consult him. An entire squad of soldiers had been assigned to tend and transport the mist projector as delicately as was humanly possible. Even Tobo was under orders to match his pace to that manageable by the crew moving our most valuable resource.

Tobo had not done a good job of conforming.

Carts creaked past. Pack animals shied away from Sindawe's remains but never so far they risked straying from the safety of the road. I had begun to suspect that they could sense the danger better than I could because I had to rely entirely upon intellect for my own salvation. Only the black stallion seemed unmoved by Sindawe's fate.

The white crow seemed very much interested in the corpse. I had the feeling Sindawe was someone it knew and mourned. Ridiculous, of course. Unless that was Murgen inside there, as someone had suggested, trapped outside his own time.

Master Santaraksita came along, leading a donkey. Baladitya the copyist bestrode the beast. He studied a book as he rode, completely out of touch with his surroundings. Perhaps that was because he could not see them. Or he did not believe in the world outside his books. He had the lead rope of another donkey tied to his wrist. That poor beast staggered under a load consisting mostly of books and the tools of the librarian's trade. Among the books were some of the Annals, on loan, including those that I had salvaged from the library.

Santaraksita pulled out of line. "This is so absolutely exciting, Dorabee. Having adventures at my age. Being pursued through ancient, eldritch, living artifacts by terrible sorcerers and unearthly powers. It's like stepping into the pages of the old *Vedas.*"

"I'm glad you're enjoying it so much. This man used to be one of our brothers. His adventure caught up with him about fourteen years ago."

"And he's still in one piece?"

"Nothing lives on the plain unless it has the plain's countenance. Even including the flies and carrion eaters you'd expect to find around a corpse anywhere."

"But there are crows here." He indicated birds circling at a distance. I had not noticed them because they were making no sounds and there were only a few of them in the air. As many as a dozen more perched atop the stone columns. The nearest of those were now just a few hundred yards ahead.

"They're not here to feast," I said. "They're the Protector's eyes. They run to her and repeat whatever we do. If they touch down after dark, they'll end up just as dead as Sindawe did. Hey, Swan. Right now, up and down the column, pass the word. Nobody does anything to bother those crows. It might break holes in the protection the road gives against the shadows."

"You're determined to put me on Catcher's shit list, aren't you?"

"What?"

"She doesn't know I'm not dead, does she? Those crows are going to put the finger on me."

I laughed. "Soulcatcher's displeasure shouldn't worry you right now. She can't get to you."

"You never know." He went off to tell everybody I wanted those watchcrows treated like favored pets.

"A strange and intriguing man," Santaraksita observed.

"Strange, anyway. But he's a foreigner."

"We're all foreigners here, Dorabee."

That was true. Very true. I could close my eyes and still be overwhelmed by the strangeness of the plain. In fact, I felt that more strongly when I was not looking at it. When my eyes were closed it seemed as aware of me as I was aware of it.

Once we got Sindawe loaded I continued walking beside Master Santaraksita. The librarian was every bit as excited as he claimed. Everything was a wonder to him. Except the weather. "Is it always this cold here, Dorabee?"

"It's not even winter yet." He knew about snow only by repute. Ice he knew as something that fell from the sky during the ferocious storms of the rainy season. "It could get a lot colder. I don't know. Swan says he don't recall it being this chilly the last time he was up here but that was at a different time of year and the circumstances of the incursion were different." I was willing to bet that seldom in its history had the plain ever experienced the crying of a colicky baby or the barking of a dog. One of the children had sneaked the dog along and now it was too late to change anyone's mind.

"How long will we be up here?"

"Ah. The question nobody's had the nerve to ask. You're more familiar with the early Annals than I am anymore. You've had months and months to study them while I haven't had time to keep my own up to date. What did they tell you about the plain?"

"Nothing."

"Not who built it? Not why? By implication Kina is involved somehow. So are the Free Companies of Khatovar and the golem demon Shivetya. At least we think the thing in the fortress up ahead is the demon who's supposed to stand guard over Kina's resting place. Not very effectively, apparently, because the ancient king Rhaydreynak drove the Deceivers of his time into the same caverns where Soulcatcher trapped the Captured. And we know that the Books of the Dead are down there somewhere. We know that Uncle Doj says—without offering any convincing evidence—the Nyueng Bao are the descendants of another Free Company, but we also know that Uncle and Mother Gota sometimes mention things that aren't part of the usual lore."

"Dorabee?"

Santaraksita I found wore that expression he always put on when I surprised him. I grinned, told him, "I rehearse all this every day, twenty times a day. I just don't usually do it out loud. I believe I was hoping you would add something to the mix. Is there anything? By direct experience we know that it takes three days to get to the fortress. I assume that stronghold is located at the heart of the plain. We know there's a network of protected roads and circles where those roads intersect. Where roads exist there must be someplace to go. To me that says there must be at least one more Shadowgate somewhere." I looked up. "You think?"

"You bet our survival on the *possibility* that there's another way off the plain?"

"Yep. We didn't have anywhere left to run back there."

There was that look again.

Suvrin, plodding along and listening in silence, had that look, too.

I said, "Although I've been surrounded by Gunni all my life, I'm still unfamiliar with the more obscure legendry. And I know even less about that of the older, less well-known, non-proselytizing cults. What do you know about The Land of Unknown Shadows? It seems to be tied in with aphorisms like 'All Evil Dies There an Endless Death' and 'Calling the Heaven and the Earth and the Day and the Night.' "

"The last one is easy, Dorabee. That's an invocation of the Supreme Being. You might also hear it as the formula 'Calling the Earth and the Wind and the Sea and the Sky,' or even 'Calling Yesterday and Today and Tonight and Tomorrow.' You spout those off thoughtlessly because they're easy and you have to deliver a certain number of prayers every day. I'm sure Vehdna who actually keep up with their prayers take the same shortcuts."

Twinges of guilt. My duties of faith had suffered abominably the past six months. "Are you sure?"

"No. But it sure sounded good, didn't it? Easy! You asked about Gunni. I could be wrong in a different religious context."

"Of course. How about Bone Warrior, Stone Soldier, or Soldier of Darkness?"

"Excuse me? Dorabee?"

"Never mind. Unless something related occurs to you. I'd better trot up the line and get Tobo slowed down again."

As I passed the black stallion and white crow, the latter chuckled and whispered that "Sister, sister" phrase again. The bird had heard the entire conversation. Chances were that it was not Murgen, nor was it Soulcatcher's creature, but still, it was extremely interested in the doings of the Black Company, to the point of trying to give warnings. It seemed quite pleased that we were headed south and were unable to turn back.

Behind me, Master Santaraksita's group paused. He and Baladitya studied the face of the first stone column, where golden characters still sparked occasionally.

It is immortality of a sort.

73

The people of the former Shadowlands clung to the best cover available while they watched Nemesis cross their country in a slow and angry progression toward the pass through the Dandha Presh. In more than one place Soulcatcher's appearance gave rise to the rumor that Khadi had been reborne and was walking through the world again.

She always did love a good practical joke.

What the witnesses saw seemed to be the goddess in her most terrible aspect. She was naked except for a girdle of dried penises and a necklace of babies' skulls. Her skin was a polished-mahogany black. She was hairless everywhere. She had vampire fangs and an extra pair of arms. She seemed about ten feet tall. What she did not seem was happy. People stayed out of her way.

She was not alone. In her wake came an equally naked woman as white as Soulcatcher was dark. She was five and a half feet tall. Even covered with cuts and bruises and dirt, she was attractive. Her face was empty of all expression but her eyes burned with patient hatred. She wore only one item of ornamentation, a shoulder harness to which a cable ten feet long had been attached. That cable connected her to the rusty iron cage floating in the air behind her. The cage enclosed a skinny old man who had suffered several severe injuries, including a broken leg and some bad burns. The girl was compelled to tow the cage. She never spoke, even when the monster encouraged her with a switch. Possibly she had lost the faculty.

Narayan Singh had been the unfortunate who triggered Goblin's booby trap, not its beloved intended.

The Deceiver shared the cage with a large bound book. He was too weak to keep it closed. Wind toyed with its pages. Once in a while the breeze showed its vicious side and yanked a page away from the book's tired binding.

Sometimes delirious, Narayan thought he was in the hands of his goddess, either being punished for some forgotten transgression or transported to Paradise. And perhaps he was right. It did not occur to Soulcatcher to wonder what use she had for him alive. Not that she was taking any special trouble to keep him that way. Nor did the Daughter of Night seem particularly concerned about his fate.

74

I managed to overtake Tobo before he sped through the crossroads' circle. "We're stopping here," I told him, hanging onto his shoulder.

He looked at me like he was trying to remember who I was.

"Back up to the circle."

"All right. You don't have to be so pushy."

"Good. The real you is back. Yes. I do. No one else seems to be able to restrain you." As we stepped into the circle, I told him, "There should be a . . . yes. Right here." There was a hole in the roadway surface, four inches deep and as big around as my wrist. "Put the handle of the pickax in that."

"Why?"

"If the shadows can get inside the protected areas, that's the direction they'll come from. Come on. Do it. We've got a ton of work to do if we're going to set up a safe camp." There were too many of us to get everyone inside the circle. That meant some would have to overnight on the road, not a practice encouraged by Murgen.

I wanted only the calmest personalities back there. Murgen guaranteed that every night on the plain would be some kind of adventure.

Suvrin found me trying to get Iqbal and his family moved toward the heart of the circle. The animals were hobbled there. And I had a feeling that the plain really did not like being trampled upon by things with such hard feet. "What is it, Suvrin?"

"Master Santaraksita would like to see you at your earliest convenience." He grinned like he was having a wonderful time.

"Suvrin, have you been getting into the ganja or something?"

"I'm just happy. I missed the Protector's state visit. Therefore I'm all right until sometime that's still far off yet. I'm on the greatest adventure of my life, going places no one of my generation would have thought possible even a few weeks ago. It won't last. It just plain won't last. The way my luck runs. But I'm for damned sure having fun now. Except my feet hurt."

"Welcome to the Black Company. Get used to it. Bunions should be our seal, not a fire-breathing skull. Did anyone learn anything useful today?"

"My guess would be that Master Santaraksita might have come up with something. Else why would he bother to send me to find you?"

"You got bold and sarky fast once you got up here."

"I've always thought I'm more likable when I'm not afraid."

I glanced around. I wondered if stupid ought not to be in there somewhere, too. "Show me where the old boy is."

Suvrin had the chatters. Bad, for him. "He's a wonder, isn't he?"

"Santaraksita? I don't know about that. He's something. Keep an eye out that you don't accidentally find his hand fishing around in your pants."

Suvrin had made camp for himself and the older men right at the edge of the circle, on its eastern side. Santaraksita had to have picked the spot. It was directly opposite the nearest standing stone. The librarian was seated Gunnistyle, cross-legged, as near the edge as he dared get, staring at the pillar. "Is that you, Dorabee? Come sit with me."

I overcame a burst of impatience, settled. I was out of shape for that. The Company continued its northern habits—using chairs and stools and whatnot—even though we now had only two Old Crew souls left. Such is inertia. "What are we looking for, Master?" It was obvious he was watching the standing stone.

"Let's see if you're as bright as I believe you are."

There was a challenge I could not ignore. I stared at the column and waited for truth to declare itself.

A group of the characters on the pillar brightened momentarily. That had nothing to do with the light of the setting sun, which had begun creeping in under the edge of the clouds. That was painting everything bloody. After a while I told

Santaraksita, "It seems to be illuminating groups of characters according to some pattern."

"Mainly in reading order, I think."

"Down? And to the left?"

"Reading downward in columns isn't uncommon in the temple literature of antiquity. Some inks dried quite slowly. If you wrote in horizontal lines, you sometimes smeared your earlier work. Writing downward in columns right to left suggests to me left-handedness. Possibly those who placed the stellae were mostly left-handed."

It struck me that writing whatever way was convenient for you personally could lead to a lot of confusion. I said so.

"Absolutely, Dorabee. Deciphering classical writing is always a challenge. Particularly if the ancient copyists had time on their hands and were inclined to play pranks. I've seen manuscripts put together so that they could be read both horizontally and vertically and each way tells a different story. Definitely the work of someone who had no worries about his next meal. Today's formal rules have been around for only a few generations. They were agreed upon simply so we could read one another's work. And they still haven't penetrated the lay population to any depth."

Most of that I knew already. But he needed his moments of pedantry to feel complete. They cost me nothing. "And what do we have here?"

"I'm not sure. My eyes aren't sharp enough to pick up everything. But the characters on the stone closely resemble those in your oldest book and I've been able to discern a few simple words." He showed me what he had written down. It was not enough to make sense of anything.

"Mostly I think we're looking at names. Possibly arranged in a holy scripture sort of way. Maybe a roll-call-of-the-ancestors kind of thing."

"It is immortality of a sort."

"Perhaps. Certainly you can find similarly conceived monuments in almost every older city. Iron was a popular material for those who considered themselves truly rich and historically significant. Generally, though, they were erected to celebrate individuals, notably kings and conquerers, who wanted following generations to know all about them."

"And every one of those I've ever seen was a complete puzzle to the people living around it now. Thus, a feeble immortality of a sort."

"And there's the point. We'll all achieve our immortality in the next world, however we may conceive that, but we all want to be remembered in this one. I suppose so that when the newly dead arrive in heaven, they'll already know who we are. And, yes, even though I am a devout, practicing Gunni, I'm very cynical about what humanity brings to the religious experience."

"I'm always intrigued by your thinking, Master Santaraksita, but in today's circumstances I just don't have time to sit around musing on humanity's innumerable foibles. Nor even those of God. Or the gods, if you prefer."

Santaraksita chuckled. "Do you find it amusing to see our roles thus reversed?" A few months in the real world had done wonders for his attitude. He accepted his situation and tried to learn from it. I considered accusing him of being a Bhodi fellow traveler.

"I fear I'm much less of a thinker than you like to believe, Master. I've never had time for it. I'm probably really more of a parrot than anything."

"And I suspect that surviving in your trade eventually leaves everyone more philosophical than you want to admit, Dorabee."

"Or more brutal. None of these men were ever sterling subjects."

Santaraksita shrugged. "You remain a wonder, whether or not you wish to be one." He made a gesture to indicate the standing stone. "Well, there you have it. It may say something. Or it may just be remembering the otherwise unheralded whose ashes nourished weeds. Or it may even be trying to communicate, since some of the characters seem to have changed." His tone became one of intense interest as he completed his last sentence. "Dorabee, the inscription doesn't remain constant. I must have a closer look at one of those stellae."

"Don't even think about it. You'd probably be dead before you got to it. And would get the rest of us dead, too."

He pouted.

"This's the dangerous part of the adventure," I told him. "This's the part that leaves us no room for innovation or deviation or expressing our personalities. You've seen Sindawe. No better or stronger man ever lived. That was nothing he deserved. Whenever you feel creative, you just go look on that travois. Then take another look. Gah! It smells like the inside of a stable here already. A little breeze wouldn't hurt." As long as it blew away from me.

The animals were all crowded together and surrounded so they could not do something stupid like wander out of the protective circle. And herbivores tend to generate vast quantities of by-product.

"All right. All right. I don't make a habit of doing what's stupid, Dorabee." He grinned.

"Really? What about how you got here?"

"Maybe it's a hobby." He could laugh at himself. "There's stupid and stupid. None of those boulders is going to make my pebble turn into a standing stone."

"I'm not sure if that's a compliment or an insult. Just keep an eye on the rock and let me know if it says anything interesting." It occurred to me to wonder if these pillars were related to the pillars the Company had found in the place called the Plain of Fear, long before my time. Those stones had even walked and talked—unless the

Captain exaggerated even worse than I thought. "Whoa! Look there. Right along the edge of the road. That's a shadow, being sneaky. It's already dark enough for them to start moving around."

It was time I started moving around, making sure everyone remained calm. The shadows could not reach us if no one did anything stupid. But they might try to provoke a panic, the way hunters will try to scare up game.

Despite the numbers and the animals and my own pessimism, nothing went wrong. Goblin and I made repeated rounds of the circle and the tailback running north up the protected road. We found everyone in a mood to be cooperative. I suppose that had something to do with the shadows clinging to the surface of our invisible protection and oozing around like evil leeches. Nothing focuses the attention like the proximity of a bad death.

"There are other ways in and out of this circle besides the one we came in and the one we're going to use tomorrow," I told Goblin. "How come we can't see them?"

"I don't know. Maybe it's magic. Maybe you ought to ask One-Eye."

"Why him?"

"You've been around long enough that you should've discovered the truth. He knows everything. Just ask. He'll tell you." Evidently he was less worried about his friend. He was back to picking on One-Eye.

"You know, you're right. I haven't had much chance to talk to him but I did notice that he's going all-out to be a pain. Why don't we go wake him up, tell him he's in charge, and get ourselves some shut-eye?" Which is what we did, with slight modifications, after we made sure there was a watch rotation for every potential entry into the circle, whether it could be seen or not. With help from Gota and Uncle Doj, One-Eye was still capable of contributing a little something to his own protection. Not that he was willing to admit that.

I believe Goblin went off and whispered something to Tobo, too, after we went our respective ways.

I had just gotten comfortable on my nice rock bed when Sahra invited herself over for a chat. I really was tired and uncharitable. When I sensed her presence, I just wanted her to go away. And she did not stay long.

She said, "Murgen wanted to talk to you but I told him you were exhausted and needed to rest. He wanted me to warn you that your dreams may be particularly vivid and probably confusing. He said just don't go anywhere and don't panic. I have to go tell Goblin and One-Eye and Uncle and some others and have them spread the word to everyone else. Rest easy." She patted my hand, letting me know we were still friends. I grunted and closed my eyes.

Murgen was right. Night on the glittering plain was another adventure entirely. The landmarks were similar but seemed to be ghosts of their daytime selves. And the sky was not to be trusted.

The plain itself was still all shades of grey but now with some sort of implied illumination that left all the angles and edges clearly defined. Once when I glanced upward I saw a full moon and the sky crowded with stars, then only moments later, the overcast was back and there was nothing to be seen at all. The characters inscribed on the standing stones all seemed busy, which was not something Murgen had noted during his own visit. I watched for a moment, recognizing individual characters but no words. Nevertheless, I had an epiphany I would have to pass on to Master Santaraksita in the morning. The inscriptions on the pillars did begin at the upper right and read downward. For the first column. The second column read from the bottom upward. Then the third read back down. And so on.

I became more interested in the things moving amongst the pillars, though. There were some big shadows out there, things with a presence potent enough to terrify and scatter the little shadows radiating hunger as they crawled over the surface of our protection. The big ones would not come closer. They had about them an air of infinite, wicked patience that left me convinced they would be out there waiting if it took a thousand years for one of us to screw up and open a gap in our protection.

In dream, all roads leading into the circle were equally well-defined. Each was a glimmering ruler stroke running off to glowing domes in the distance. Of all those roads and domes, though, only those on our north-south trace seemed to be fully alive. Either the road knew what we wanted to do or it knew what it wanted us to do.

In an instant I was amazed, bewildered, terrified, exultant, having realized that in order to see what I was seeing, I would have to be at least a dozen feet above my normal height of eye. Which meant that I had to go outside my skin, the way Murgen did, and while I had wished for the ability a thousand times and the view was engrossing, the risks were none I cared to face when the opportunity was real. I sped a prayer heavenward. God needs to be reminded. I was totally, ecstatically, happy being Sleepy, without one shred of mystical talent. Really. If it was necessary that somebody in my gang do this sort of thing, Goblin or One-Eye or Uncle Doj or almost anyone else could have the magic, sparing only Tobo, despite him being the prophesied future of the Company. Tobo was still a little too short on self-discipline to be handed any more capabilities.

The presence of the small shadows was kind of like that of a flock of pigeons. They were not silent on that ghostworld level but they did not try to communicate unless with one another. It took me only moments to shut them out.

The skies above were more troublesome. Each time I lifted my gaze I saw that some dramatic change had occurred. Sometimes there was an impenetrable overcast, sometimes a wild starfield and a full moon. Once there were fewer stars and an extra moon. Once a distinct constellation hung right over the road south. It conformed exactly to Murgen's description of a constellation called the Noose. Hitherto I had always suspected the Noose to have been a fabrication on Mother Gota's part.

Then, just beyond the golden pickax, I spied a strapping trio of the uglies Murgen had reported meeting in that very spot his first night on the glittering plain. Were they yakshas? Rakshasas? I tried to shoehorn them into Gunni or even Kina's mythology but just could not make them fit. There would be plenty of room, though, I did not doubt. The Gunni are more flexible in matters of doctrine than are we Vehdna. We are taught that intolerance is our gift of faith. Gunni flexibility is just one more reason they will all suffer the eternal fires. The idolators.

God is Great. God is Merciful. In Forgiveness He is Like the Earth. But He can become a tad mean-spirited with unbelievers.

I tried desperately to recall Murgen's report of his encounter with these dream creatures. Nothing came forward despite the fact that I had been the one who had written it all down. I could not for certain recall if his night visitors had been identical to these. These were humanoid and human-size but definitely lacking human features. Possibly they wore masks in the guise of beasts. Judging from their frenetic gestures, they wanted me to follow them somewhere. I seemed to recall something similar having happened during Murgen's episode. He had refused. So did I, although I did drift toward them and did attempt to engage them in conversation.

I did not, of course, have a knack for generating sound without a body or tools. And they did not speak any language I knew, so the whole business was an exercise in futility.

They became extremely frustrated. They seemed to think that I was playing games. They finally stamped away, obviously possessed by a big anger.

"Murgen, I don't know where you are. But you're going to have to spend some time clueing me in here."

The ugly people were gone. No skin off my nose. Now maybe I could get some sleep. Some real sleep, without all these too-real dreams and awful, improbable skies.

It started to rain, which told me which sky was the true sky and paramount above the me that lay twitching fitfully as the cold drops began to make themselves felt. There was no way to get in out of it. There was no way to erect tents or other shelters on the plain. In fact, the matter of weather had not arisen during our planning sessions. I do not know why, though it seems that there is always something big that you overlook, something to which every planner on the team turns a blind eye. Then, when the breakdown or failure comes, you cannot figure out how you overlooked the obvious.

Somehow we must have concluded that there was no weather on the plain. Maybe because Murgen's Annals did not recall any. But somebody should have noticed that the Captured made this journey at a different time of year. Somebody should have realized that that was sure to have some impact. Somebody probably named me.

It had been cool already when the rain began to fall. It grew chillier fast. Crabbily, I got up and helped cover stuff to protect it, helped get out means for recovering some of the water, then confiscated a piece of tenting and another blanket, rolled up and went back to sleep, ignoring the rain. It was only a persistent drizzle and when you are exhausted, nothing but sleep matters much.

I found Murgen waiting when I got home to dreamland. "You seem surprised. I told you I'd see you on the plain."

"You did. But I don't need it to be right now. Right now I need to sleep."

"You are. You'll wake up as refreshed as if you hadn't dreamed at all."

"I don't want to be drifting around loose from my body, either."

"Then don't."

"I can control it?"

"You can. Just decide not to do it. It's pretty basic. Most people manage it instinctively. Ask around tomorrow. See how many of these people even recall being loose from their flesh."

"It's something everybody does?"

"Up here. It's something everybody can do. If they want. Most don't want it so emphatically that they don't even recognize that the opportunity is there. Which doesn't matter. It's not why I'm here."

"It matters a bunch to me. That stuff is scary. I'm just a simple low-class city brat—"

"Cancel the old whine-and-toe shuffle, Sleepy. You're wasting time. I probably know as much about you as you know about yourself. There're things you need to know."

"I'm listening."

"Till now you've dealt with the plain well enough by letting the Annals guide you. Stick with the rules you've already made and you won't have any trouble. Don't dawdle. You didn't bring enough water—even if you slaughter your animals as you go, the way you planned. There's ice here that you can melt but if you waste time getting here, you'll end up having to kill more animals than you want. And take good care of them while they're still alive. Don't let them get so thirsty they start charging around looking for water and go busting through your protection. That'll heal itself but it does take time. The shadows won't give you time."

"Then we're safe from the break that killed Sindawe and some of the others?"

"Yes. You'll find Bucket tomorrow. I warn you now so you'll have time to prepare yourself."

I was prepared already. I had been prepared for a long time. Actually seeing Bucket dead would be difficult but I would get past it. "Tell me what I should do now that I'm here."

"You're doing it. Just don't do it slowly."

"Should I split the group? Send a strike force forward?"

"That wouldn't be wise. You wouldn't be able to manage whichever group you weren't with. And that'll be the one where somebody screws up and gets us all killed."

"You, too?"

"There's nobody else who can get me out if you fail. There isn't even anyone else out there who knows that we're alive."

"The Daughter of Night and Narayan Singh know. Probably." They had overheard enough to figure it out, certainly.

"Which means Soulcatcher does too, now. But you know, I don't really see those people developing an interest in raising the dead. Not to mention that now the Shadowgate can only be opened from this side. This is the last cast of the dice, Sleepy. And it's for everything."

I did not remind Murgen that Narayan Singh and his ward had a very strong interest in resurrecting someone who was practically his grave-mate. He was right about the Shadowgate, assuming there were no more Keys outside. "How did I know you were going to say something like that?"

He gave me the smile that probably won Sahra's heart.

I told him, "You should go see Sahra."

"I already have. That's why I was so late getting around to you."

"What can I say? Oh. I saw those creatures . . . the . . ." I did not know what they were called, so I tried to describe them.

"The Washane, the Washene and the Washone, collectively referred to as the Nef. They're dreamwalkers, too."

"Too?"

"I'm a dreamwalker. You can see me but only with your mind's eye. In some way that you remember me. The Nef are out here all the time. They may be trapped, or they may no longer have bodies to go back to. I've never been able to tell. They want to communicate so badly—because they want something badly—but don't seem capable of learning how. They're from one of the other worlds. If they no longer have bodies they may even be skinwalkers, so be very careful around them."

"The . . . duh . . . what are you blathering about?"

"Oh. We haven't talked about any of that yet, have we?"

"Any of what?"

"I really thought you'd figure most of it out by reading between the lines. The Companies had to come from somewhere and it would be hard to scratch out a living on a tabletop of bare stone. So they must have come from somewhere else. Somewhere very else, since the plain isn't so big you can't walk around it and discover that there's nowhere for armies to come from. The land just gets colder and more inhospitable."

"I'm real thick, boss. You should've drawn me some pictures."

"I wasn't keen on having anyone outside know. I didn't want anybody getting scared to come get me."

"You're my brother."

He ignored me. "I haven't slept here, so I have a lot of time on my hands. I've used some of it exploring. There are sixteen Shadowgates, Sleepy. And fifteen of them open onto places that aren't our world. Or did at one time. Most of them are dead now and in my state, I can't see what used to be on the other side without actually going out there. And I don't have the eggs to do that, because I like my own world just fine and I don't want to take a chance of getting trapped any farther away from it than I already am.

"Only four of the gates are still alive. And the one to our world is so badly hurt that it probably won't last many generations more."

I was lost. Completely. I was prepared for none of this. And yet he was right when he hinted that there were bells I should have heard ringing. "What does all that have to do with Kina? It isn't in her legend anywhere. In fact, what does it even have to do with us? It's not in *our* legend anywhere."

"Yes it is, Sleepy. The truth is just so old that time has totally distorted it. Examine Gunni mythology. There's a lot there about other planes, other realms of reality, different heavens and whatnot. Those stories go way back before the coming of the Free Companies, a thousand years or more. Near as I've been able to find out, when the first Free Company came off the plain, almost six hundred years ago, that event marked the first time our Shadowgate had been used in at least eight centuries. That's a lot of time for truth to mutate."

"Whoa. Whoa. You're starting to imply things I can't quite get my mind around."

"You'd better open it up and spread it out wide, Sleepy, because there's a whole lot more. And I doubt I've discovered even a tenth of it."

I have a dark, cynical, untrusting side that at times even doubts the motives of my closest friends. "Why is it that none of this ever got mentioned until now? This isn't fresh news to you, is it?"

"No. It isn't. But I told you, I want out of here. Badly. I chose not to pass on any information that might handicap you."

"Handicap me? What the heck are you talking about?"

"Kina and the Captured aren't the only things sleeping up here. There're also a lot of truths that would shake the foundations of our world. Truths I have no trouble imagining wholesale slaughters and holy wars arising to suppress. Truths I have no trouble seeing getting my family and the Company obliterated, they're so threatening."

"I'm trying to open my mind but I'm having trouble. I feel like I'm about to plunge into an abyss."

"Just hang on. I've been out here forever and I still have trouble with it. I think the way to start is, I should outline the history of the plain."

"Yes. Why don't you do that? That might be interesting."

"You still have that edge on your tongue, don't you? Maybe Swan is right and what you really need is a good . . . all right. All right. Listen closely. The plain was created so far back in antiquity that nobody on any of the worlds has any idea who built it, how, or why, though you have to believe that it was meant to be a pathway between the worlds."

"Why the shadows and standing stones and—"

"I can't tell you anything if I'm not the one doing the talking."

"Sorry."

"In the beginning there was the plain. Just the plain, with its network of roads that have to be walked a certain way to get to other worlds. For example, every traveler has to enter the great circle at the center of the plain before he can leave the plain again. Back then there were no shadows, no Shadowgates, no standing stones, no great fortress inside the great circle, no caverns beneath the stone, no sleeping gods, no Captured, no Books of the Dead. There was nothing but the plain. The crossroads of worlds. Or possibly of time. One rogue school of thought insists the gates all open into the same world but at times which are separated by tens of thousands of years.

"At some time still in unimaginable antiquity, human nature asserted itself and would-be conquerers began to charge back and forth across the plain. During a period of exhaustion the wise men of a dozen worlds combined to make the first modifications to the plain. They built a fortress in the great circle and garrisoned it with a race of created immortal guardians whose task it would be to prevent armies from passing from world to world.

"Then we pass to the edge of proto-history, the age now recalled poorly as it is distorted in Gunni myth.

"Those driven to conquer will try to do so, whatever the obstacles. Kina apparently started out as your run-of-the-mill, dark-lord type that arises every few centuries, as Lady's first husband was, only she was another in a line and association of many such, some of whom are now recalled as gods because of the impact they had on their times. The whole cabal decided to beef Kina up until she could overcome the 'demons' on the plain. In the process she did become what, for want of a better descriptive, we would have to call a god. And she behaved every bit as badly as her associates should have expected, with results more or less like those recalled in the mythology. Once Kina was asleep, her associates opened the maze of caverns under the plain and buried her way down deep somewhere. Then they created Shivetya, the Steadfast Guardian, to keep watch. Or they conscripted a surviving demon of the same name and strengthened him and bound him to do the job, if you prefer a less common version of the story. Then, apparently too exhausted to recover their greatness, they faded away. So Kina came out on top even if she ended up imprisoned."

"Why didn't they just kill her? That's something I've never understood about these squabbles amongst the gods. There's only one version of the Kina myth where her enemies do anything but just tuck her in. And in that one, even after she's all chopped up and scattered around, they leave the pieces alive and trying to get back together."

"My guess would be she had some kind of deadman spell that entwined the fates of the other gods with her own. Those people wouldn't have trusted one another for a second. All of them would have had some protective mechanism like Longshadow used when he tied his fate into the well-being of the Shadowgate."

"But the Shadowgate doesn't depend on his health anymore. Not as long as he stays inside."

"I was just posing an example, Sleepy. Let's stick to the history of the plain. What followed Kina's downfall isn't documented at all, but more conquerers came and went and further efforts were made to dissuade them while keeping the plain open for commerce. The gates and Keys were created. One world gathered its sorcerers and had them steal the souls of millions of prisoners of war, creating the shadows and endowing them with a bitter hatred of everything living. They meant to close down the plain entirely. Which naturally led some other race to create the shields that protect the circles and roads. Nobody knows for sure how or when the standing stones began to appear but they're the most recent addition to the plain, probably put out by the precursors of the multiple-worlds' religious movement that produced the Free Companies. I understand that the stones aren't quarried, they're created things. They're immune to the shadows and indifferent to the protective shields but they're attuned to the various Keys carried away during the Free Companies' age."

"It's too much to grasp. It'll take a long time to digest. Kina is real, though?"

"Absolutely. Buried right down here under me somewhere. I've never been tempted to go look for her. I wouldn't want to accidentally cut her loose. I don't know how I could manage that but I definitely don't want to find out the hard way."

"What about Rhaydreynak and the Books of the Dead? Where do they fit?" Rhaydreynak's war on the cult of Kina antedated the appearance of the Free Companies by several centuries supposedly, yet there were scary similarities suggesting shared origins.

"The rise of the Free Companies is actually one of the least well known despite its being closest in time. There were many Companies over several hundred years. They came from several different worlds and went off into several more, representing almost as many different sects of Kina worshippers. Most seem to have been sent out to explore, not conquer or to serve as mercenaries or even to bring on the Year of the Skulls. What their true mission seems to have been was to determine which world should be awarded the honor of being sacrificed in order to bring on the Year of the Skulls."

"Then a bunch of worlds decided to gang up on ours?"

"Kina spanned many worlds. Her deviltry was almost universal, apparently."

"And we lost the toss and got to bury her in ours?"

"You're not in our world anymore, Sleepy. This's the in-between. Where you are depends on what gate you walk out. And these days you have only one choice. Its Shadowgate lies straight ahead, on the far side of the plain. It's as if the plain itself is closing down the alternate ways."

"I don't get it. Why would it do that? And how?"

"Sometimes its seems like the plain itself is alive, Sleepy. Or at least that it can think."

"Is it where we came from? Is it where the Captain spent most of his life trying to go?"

"No. The Company can't go back to Khatovar. Croaker will never reach the promised land. That Shadowgate is dead. The world where you're headed is very much like our own. To other worlds it's known by a name that translates into Taglian somewhat vaguely as The Land of Unknown Shadows."

Without thinking I responded, "All Evil Dies There an Endless Death."

"What?" Startled. "Yes. How did you know? They were the people who committed the murders that produced the shadows."

"I heard it somewhere. From a Nyueng Bao."

"Yes. Nyueng Bao De Duang. In current Nyueng Bao usage that means some-thing like 'The Chosen Children' colloquially and nothing whatsoever that's sensible literally. In the days when their forebears were sent out from The Land of Unknown Shadows it meant, roughly, 'the Children of the Dead.'"

"You've been busy," I observed.

"Hardly, considering how long I've been trapped here. Try it for a decade, Sleepy. You won't have to put up with any of the distractions you complain about when you aren't getting everything you want to do done."

"No kidding? Seems to me I'm all of a sudden having to work even while I'm sleeping."

"Not for long. Whoever has control of that mist-making thing is trying to get me to answer him. Why don't you sneak around there and smash that sucker so I don't have to get dragged into it every time somebody wants my view on how to crack a walnut or whatever else the crisis of the moment happens to be."

"Not hardly, former boss. I'm carrying a whole bag of nuts myself."

"You would—" Murgen departed as though yanked away.

I could have sworn I heard the laughter of an eavesdropping white crow.

77

How come you're so crabby?" Willow Swan demanded when I snapped at him for no good reason. "Rag time again already?"

I blushed. Me, after twenty years among the crudest men on two hooves. "No, jerk. I didn't sleep very well last night."

"*What?*"

It exploded out of him like the shriek of a stomped rat.

"I didn't sleep well last night."

"Oh, yeah. Not our sweet little Sleepy. Guys, anybody, Ro, River, whoever, you want to step up and remind us about the Roar in the Rain last night?"

Riverwalker told me, "Boss, your snoring made more noise than a tiger in heat. We had people get up and move back up the road toward home to get away from the racket. There were people wanted to strangle you or at least put your head in a sack. I bet if anybody else knew what the hell we were doing and where we were going, you'd be on that travois with General Sindawe."

"But I'm such a sweet, delicate flower. I couldn't possibly snore." I had been accused of the crime before but only jokingly, never with such passion.

River snorted. "Swan decided not to marry you."

"I'm stricken. I'll see if One-Eye doesn't have a cure."

"A cure? The man can't even take care of himself."

I scrounged up something to eat. It was barely worth the effort and definitely not filling. We would be on short rations for a long time. Before I finished what morning preparations were possible for me, the forward elements were already moving. The general mood was more relaxed. We had survived the night. And yesterday we had shoved it to the Protector real good.

The relaxation ended when we found Bucket's remains.

Big Bucket, real name Cato Dahlia, once a thief, once an officer of the Black Company, was almost a father to me. He never said and I never asked but I suspect he knew I was female all along. He was very unpleasant to some of my male relatives, way back when.

You did not want to be the object when Bucket got angry.

I managed not to break down. I had had a long time to get used to the idea that he was gone, though there was always some small, irrational hope that Murgen was wrong, that death had overlooked him and he was buried with the Captured.

The men put Bucket on the travois with Sindawe without having to be told.

I tagged along and became entranced by one of those unaccountably irrelevant trains of thought that often take shape at such times.

We had left a truly nasty mess where we had spent the night, particularly in the line of animal waste. Likely the Captured had done the same during their passage along this same road. However, other than the odd corpse, there was no sign that they had passed through. There were no dung piles now, no gnawed, discarded bones, no vegetable waste, no ashes from charcoal braziers, nothing. Only human bodies lasted and they became thoroughly desiccated.

I would have to take it up with Murgen. Meantime, it was a mental exercise that would keep me from dwelling upon Bucket.

We trudged on southward. The rain came and went, never more than a drizzle, though sometimes the wind brought it stinging in from a sharp angle. I shivered a lot and worried about it getting cold enough to sleet or snow. No other evil found us. Eventually I spied the vague silhouette of our initial destination, that mysterious central fortress.

The wind began to blow steadily.

Some of the men complained about the cold. Some complained about the wet. Quite a few complained about the menu, and a handful insisted on complaining about all the complaining. I sensed few positive feelings concerning what we were doing.

I felt very much alone, almost abandoned, the whole day long despite well-meant efforts from Swan, Sahra and quite a few others. Only Uncle Doj did not bother because even at this late date he remained piqued because I would not enlist as his apprentice. He continued his emotional machinations. Several times I caught myself retreating into my away place and had to remind me that I did not need to go there now. None of those people could hurt me anymore. Not if I did not let them. I controlled their reality. They survived only in my memory. . . .

Even that is immortality of a sort.

We Vehdna believe in ghosts. And we believe in evil. I wondered if the Gunni might not be onto something after all. For them the pain inspired by the departure of loved ones is less personal and far more fatalistic and is accepted as a necessary stage of life that does not end with this one transformation.

If the Gunni, by some bizarre and remote practical joke of the divine, happen to be in possession of a more accurate theology, I must have been a bad, bad girl in a previous life. I sure hope I had fun. . . . Forgive me, O Lord of the Hours, Who Art Merciful and Compassionate. I have sinned in my heart. Thou Art God. There Can Be No Other.

There were flakes of snow in the air whenever the wind took to loafing. Then each time it found renewed ambition it hurled tiny flecks of ice that stung my face and hands. Though it sounded fearful, the level of grumbling never reached suggestions of mutiny. Willow Swan trotted up and down the column gossiping and dropping reminders that we had nowhere to go but straight ahead. The weather did not hamper him at all. He seemed to find it invigorating. He kept telling everyone how wonderful it would be once we got some real snow, say, four or five feet. The world would look better then, yes sir! He guaranteed it. He grew up in stuff like that and it made a real man out of you.

With equal frequency I overheard some advice—the fulfillment of which was physically impossible for anyone not some select variety of worm—as often the people cried out, offering up impassioned pleas to One-Eye, Goblin, even Tobo, to fill Swan's mouth with quick-setting mortar.

"Are you having fun?" I asked him.

"Oh, yeah. And they're not blaming you for anything, either."

His boyish grin told me he was not being some kind of unwanted hero. He was playing games with me, too.

All northerners seemed to have that capacity for play. Even the Captain and Lady, sometimes, had shown signs with one another. And One-Eye and Goblin . . . the little black wizard's stroke may have been a godsend. I could not imagine those two missing an opportunity for screwing up as grand as this one was if they were both in excellent health.

When I suggested something of the sort to Swan he failed to understand. Once I explained, he observed, "You're missing the point, Sleepy. Unless they're *extremely* drunk, those two won't do anything dangerous to anybody but themselves. I'm on the outside and I recognized that twenty years ago. How could you miss it?"

"You're right. And I do know that. I'm just looking for things to go wrong. I get gloomy when I try to prepare myself for the worst. How come you're so cheerful?"

"Right up ahead. Another day. Two, maximum. I get to say hi to my old buddies, Cordy and Blade."

I looked at him askance. Could he be the only one of us more excited than frightened by the possibilities inherent in releasing the Captured? Only one of those people had not spent the past fifteen years trapped inside his own mind. And I was not convinced that Murgen was not working overtime to maintain a false facade of sanity. The others . . . I did not doubt that quite a few would come forth stark, raving mad. Nor did the rest.

Nowhere was that fear more evident than in the Radisha.

"Tadjik," had remained almost invisible since she had rejoined us this side of the Dandha Presh. Though Riverwalker and Runmust stayed close, she needed no watching and made few demands. She stayed to herself, cloaked in brooding. The farther we moved from Taglios, the nearer we approached her brother, the more withdrawn she became. On the road, after the Grove of Doom, we had become almost sisterly. But the pendulum had been swinging the other way ever since Jaicur and we had not exchanged a hundred words a week this side of the mountains. That did not please me. I enjoyed her company, conversation and slashing wit.

Even Master Santaraksita had had no luck drawing her out lately, though she had developed an affection for his scholarly drollery. Between them, the pair could gut and flense a fool's argument faster than a master butcher ever cleaned a chicken.

I mentioned the problem to Willow Swan.

"I'll bet it's not her brother that's bothering her. He wouldn't be the biggest thing, anyway. I'd guess she's down about not being able to go back. Ever since she realized we're probably on a one-wayer here, she's been in a black depression."

"Uhm?"

"It's *Rajadharma*. That's not just a handy propaganda slogan for her, Sleepy. She takes being the ruler of Taglios seriously. You got her strolling on down here, month after month, seeing what the Protector did in her name. You have to understand that she's going to be upset about the way she let herself get used. And then she has to face the fact that she'll probably never get a chance to do anything about it. She's not that hard to understand."

But he had been close to her for thirty years. "We're going back."

"Oh, sure. And on the one chance in a zillion that we really do, who's going to have an army waiting? Can you say Soulcatcher?"

"Sure. And I can also say she'll forget us in six months. She'll find a more interesting game to play."

"And can you say 'Water sleeps?' So can Soulcatcher, Sleepy. You don't know her. Nobody does—except maybe Lady, a little. But I got closer than most for a while. Not exactly by choice, but there I was. I tried to pay attention, for what good it would do me. She isn't entirely inhuman and she isn't as vain and heedless as she might want the world to think. Bottom line, you need to keep one critical fact firmly in mind when you're thinking about Soulcatcher. And that is that she's still alive in a world where her deadliest enemy was the Lady of the Tower. Remembering that in her time Lady made the Shadowmasters look like unschooled bullies."

"You're really wound today, aren't you?"

"Just stating the facts."

"Here's one of your own right back. Water sleeps. The woman who used to be the Lady of the Tower will be back on her feet in another few days."

"You'd better ask Murgen if he thinks she'll want to bother getting up. I'll bet you it's not this cold where she's at." The breeze on the plain had begun to gnaw both deeply and relentlessly.

I did not disagree even though he knew the truth. He might not remember but he must have helped Soulcatcher move the Captured into the ice caverns where they lay imprisoned.

A murder of crows appeared from the north, fighting the wind. They had very little to say to one another. They circled a few times, then fought for altitude and rode the breeze toward Mama. They would not have much to report.

We began to find more bodies, sometimes in twos and threes. A fair number of the Captured had not been caught at all. I recalled Murgen's report that almost half the party made a break for the world after Soulcatcher got loose. Here they were. I did not remember most of them. They were Taglian or Jaicuri rather than Old Crew, mostly, which meant they had enlisted while I was up north on Murgen's behalf.

We came upon Suyen Dinh Duc, Bucket's Nyueng Bao bodyguard. Duc's body had been prepared neatly for ceremonial farewells. That Bucket had paused in the midst of terror to honor one of the quietest and most unobtrusive of the Nyueng Bao companions spoke volumes about the character of my adopted father—and that of Duc. Bucket had refused to accept protection. He did not want a bodyguard. And Suyen Dinh Duc had refused to go away. He had felt called by a power far superior to Bucket's will. I believe they became friends when nobody was looking.

I began to shed the tears that had not come when we had found Bucket himself.

Willow Swan and Suvrin tried to comfort me. Both were uneasy with the effort, not quite knowing if hugging would be acceptable. It sure would have been but I did not know how to let them know without saying it. That would have embarrassed me too much.

Sahra provided the comfort as the Nyueng Bao gathered to honor one of their own.

Swan woofed. The white crow had landed on his left shoulder and pecked at his ear. It studied the dead man with one eye and the rest of us with the other.

Uncle Doj observed, "Your friend was supremely confident that someone would come this way again, Annalist. He left Duc in the attitude called 'In Respect of Patient Repose,' which we do when a proper funeral has to be delayed. Neither gods nor devils disturb the dead while they lie so disposed."

I sniffled. "Water sleeps, Uncle. Bucket believed. He knew we'd come."

Bucket's belief had been stronger than mine. Mine barely survived the Kiaulune wars. Without Sahra's relentless desire to resurrect Murgen I would not have come through the times of despair. I would not have become strong enough to endure when Sahra's own time of doubt came upon her.

Now we were here, with nowhere to go but forward. I dried my eyes. "We don't have time to stand around talking. Our resources are painfully finite. Let's load him up—"

Doj interrupted. "We would prefer to leave him as he is, where he is, till we can send him off with the appropriate ceremonies."

"And those would be—"

"What?"

"I haven't seen many dead Nyueng Bao since the siege of Jaicur. You people do a good job of dancing around death. But I have seen a few of your tribe dead and there wasn't any obviously necessary funeral ritual. Some got burned on the ghats as though they were Gunni. I saw one man buried in the ground, as if he were Vehdna. I've even seen a corpse rubbed with bad-smelling unguents, then wrapped like a mummy and hung head-down from a high tree branch."

Doj said, "Each funeral would have been appropriate to the person and situation, I'm sure. What's done with the flesh isn't critical. The ceremonies are intended to ease the soul's transition to its new state. They're absolutely essential. If they're not observed, the dead man's spirit may be compelled to wander the earth indefinitely."

"As ghosts? Or dreamwalkers?"

Doj seemed startled. "Uh? Ghosts? A restless spirit that wants to finish tasks interrupted by death. They can't, so they just keep going."

Although Vehdna ghosts are wicked spirits cursed to wander by God Himself, I had no trouble following Doj's notion. "Then we'll leave him here. You want to stand beside him? To make sure he stays safe from traffic?" Bucket had placed Duc at the edge of the road so he would not be disturbed by the terrified fugitives back then.

"How did he die?" Swan asked. Then he squawked. The white crow had nipped his ear again.

Everybody turned to stare at Swan. "What do you mean?" I asked.

"Look, if a shadow got Duc and somebody tried to lay him out proper, that layer-outer would be here dead as a wedge, too. Right? So he must've died some other way, before——" A dim lamp seemed to come alive inside his head.

"Catcher did it!" the crow said. It was crow caw but the words were clear. "Haw! Haw! Catcher did it!"

The Nyueng Bao began to press in on Swan.

"Catcher did it," I reminded them. "Probably with a booby-trap spell. By the time Duc reached this point, she would've been ten miles ahead of anybody on foot. She was mounted, remember. From what I remember about Duc, he probably saw the trap as Bucket tripped it and jumped in the way."

Gota pointed out, "The Protector could not have left a booby trap to kill Duc if she had not been released." Her Taglian was the best I had ever heard it. The anger in her eyes said she wanted no mistake to be made.

Sahra whispered, "Suyen Dinh Duc was a second cousin to my father."

I said, "We've been through this before, people. We can't exonerate Willow Swan but we can forgive him if we recall the circumstances he faced. Do any of you really think you can get the best of the Protector, face-to-face? No hands? But some of you think so in your heart." Few Nyueng Bao lacked for arrogant self-confidence. "Here's your challenge. Run back and prove it. The Shadowgate will let you out. Soul-catcher is on foot. She's crippled. You can catch up fast. Can you ask for any more?" I paused. "What? No takers? Then lay off Swan."

The white crow cawed mockingly.

I saw a few thoughtful, sheepish faces but Gota's was not one of them. Gota had never been wrong in her life—except that one time when she had thought she might be wrong.

Swan let it roll off. As he had done for years. He had learned from the strictest instructress. He did suggest, "You said we need to keep rolling, Sleepy. Although I guess we meat-eaters can start on the vegetarians after their stories run out."

"Carry the Key, Tobo. Thank you, Sahra."

Sahra turned away. "Mother, stay with Tobo. Don't let him walk any faster·than you do."

Ky Gota grumbled something under her breath and turned away from us. She followed Tobo. Her rolling waddle could be deceptive when she was in a hurry. She overhauled the boy, grabbed hold of his shirt. Off they went, the old woman's mouth going steadily. No gambler by nature, still I would have bet that she was fuming about what foul mortals the rest of us be.

I observed, "Ky Gota appears to have found herself."

Not one of the Nyueng Bao found any reason to celebrate that eventuation.

A mile later we came across the only animal remains that we would ever find from the earlier expedition. They were piled in a heap, bones and shredded dry flesh so intertangled there was no telling how many beasts there had been or why they had gathered together, in life or in death. The whole grim mess appeared to have been subsiding into the surface of the plain slowly. Given another decade, it would be gone.

79

The ugly dreamwalkers returned after dark. They were more energetic in their efforts tonight. The rain returned, too. It was more energetic and was accompanied by thunder and lightning that made sleeping difficult. As did the cold rainwater, all of which seemed determined to collect inside the circle where we were camped. The stone did not appear to slope but water sure behaved as though it did. The animals drank their fill. Likewise, the human members of the band. Runmust and Riverwalker directed everyone to fill waterbags and top off canteens. And as soon as someone raised his voice to bless our good fortune, the first snowflakes began to fall.

What sleep I did manage was not pleasant. A full-blown tumult was underway in the ghostworld and it spilled over into my dreams. Then Iqbal's daughter decided this would be a wonderful time to cry all night. Which got the dog started howling. Or maybe that happened the other way around.

Shadows swarmed over the face of our protection. They were more interested in us than they had been in the interlopers of Murgen's time. He told me so himself.

The shadows remembered ages past. I was able to eavesdrop on their dreams.

On their nightmares. All they remembered were horrors from a time when men resembling Nyueng Bao tortured them to death in wholesale lots while sorcerers great and small spanked the demented souls until, when they were released eventually, they were so filled with hatred of every living thing that even a creature as slight as a roach was subject to instant attack, with great ferocity. Some shadows, already evilly predatory by nature, became so wicked they even attacked and devoured other shadows.

There had been millions so victimized. And the only virtue in their creators was that they manufactured the horrors from invaders who arrived in countless waves from a world where an insane sorcerer-king had elevated himself to near-godhood, then had set out to take full mastery of all the sixteen worlds.

Uncounted tens of thousands of corpses littered the glittering plain before the shadows stemmed that tide. Scores of the monsters escaped into neighboring worlds. They spread terror and havoc until the gates could be modified to prevent their passage. For centuries no traffic crossed the plain. Then came another age of halfhearted commerce, once some genius devised the protection now shielding the roads and circles.

The shadows saw everything. They remembered everything. They saw and remembered the missionaries of Kina, who had fled my own world at the pinnacle of Rhaydreynak's fury. In every world they reached, the goddess's dark song fell upon a few eager ears, even amongst the children of those who had created the shadows.

Commerce on a plain so constrained and dangerous perforce remained light. It took determined people to hazard the crossing. Traffic peaked when the world we recalled as Khatovar launched a flurry of expeditions to other worlds to determine which would be best suited to host the cosmic ceremony called the Year of the Skulls.

Followers of Kina from other worlds joined that quest. Companies marched and countermarched. They argued and squabbled. They accomplished very little. Eventually a consensus took shape. The sacrifice ought to be the world that had treated the Children of Kina so abominably in the first place. Rhaydreynak's descendants should reap what he had sown.

The companies sent out were not swarms of fanatics. The plain was dangerous. Few men wanted to cross it. Most of the soldiers were conscripts, or minor criminals under the rule of a few dedicated priests. They were not expected to return. It became the custom for the conscripts' families to hold a wake for their Bone Warriors or Stone Soldiers before they departed—even though the priests always promised they would be back in a matter of months.

The few who did return usually came back so drained and changed, so bitter and hard, they came to be known as Soldiers of Darkness.

Kina's religion was never popular anywhere it took root. Always a minority cult, it lost what power it did have as generations passed and the early fervor faded into the inevitable, tedious rule of functionaries. One world after another abandoned Kina and turned away from the plain. Dark Ages took shape everywhere. One gate after another failed and was not restored. Those that did not fail fell into disuse. The worlds were old, worn, tired, desperately in need of renewal. The ancestors of the Nyueng Bao may have been the last large party to travel from one world to another. They seemed to have been Kina-worshippers fleeing persecution at a time when the rest of their people had become insanely xenophobic and determined to expunge all alien influences. The ancestors of the Nyueng Bao, the Children of the Dead, had vowed to return to their Land of Unknown Shadows in blazing triumph. But, of course, because they were safe on the far side of the plain, their descendants soon forgot who and what they were. Only a handful of priests remembered, not entirely correctly.

A voice that did not speak aloud tickled my consciousness. *Sister, sister*, it said. I saw nothing, felt only that featherweight touch. But it was enough to spin my soul sideways and toss it into another place where, when I caught my spiritual breath, the stench of decay filled my nostrils. A sea of bones surrounded me. Unknown tides stirred its surface.

There was something wrong with my eyes. My vision was warped and doubled. I raised a hand to rub them . . . and saw white feathers.

No! Impossible! I could not be following Murgen's path. I could not be losing my moorings in time. I would not stand for it! I willed myself—

Caw! Not from my beak.

A black shape popped into sight in front of me, wings spread, slowing. Talons reached toward me.

I spun, hurled myself off the dead branch where I had been perched. And was sorry instantly.

I found myself just yards from a face five feet tall. It boasted more fangs than a shark does teeth. It was darker than midnight. The odor of its breath was the stench of decaying flesh.

The triumphant grin on those wicked ebony lips faded as I evaded the swat of a gigantic, clawed hand. I, Sleepy, was in a trousers-soiling panic but something else was inside the bird with me. And it was having fun. *Sister, sister, that was close. The bitch is getting sneakier. But she will never surprise me. She cannot. Nor will she understand that she cannot.*

Who is "me?"

The exercise was over. I was in my body on the plain, in the rain, shuddering while my mind's eye observed the capering dreamwalkers. I examined what I had experienced and concluded that I had been given a message, which was that Kina knew we were coming. The dreaming goddess had been pretending quiescence of recent decades. She knew patience intimately, by all its secret names. And I may have been given another message as well.

Kina still was the Mother of Deceit. Quite possibly nothing I had learned recently was entirely or even partially true if Kina had found a way to wander the shadowed reaches of my mind. I had no doubt that she could. She had managed to inform entire generations and regions with a hysterical fear of the Black Company before the advent of the Old Crew.

I swear I sensed her amusement over having quickened in me a deeper and more abiding distrust of everything around me.

Suvrin wakened me early. He sounded glum. I could not see his face in the darkness. "Trouble, Sleepy," he whispered. And I have to give him credit. He was first to realize the implications of the fact that it was snowing. But then, he had seen more of the white stuff than any of us but Swan. And Willow had been away from it long enough to turn into an old man.

I wanted to moan and groan but that would have done no good and we needed to get a handle on the situation right away. "Good thinking," I told him. "Thanks. Go around in that direction and wake up the sergeants. I'll circle around to the left." Despite my nightmares, I felt rested.

The snowfall in no way recognized the presence of the protection shielding our campsite. Which meant the boundaries were no longer obvious. I sensed a heightened killing lust amongst the shadows. They had seen this before. It would be snack time if anyone started running around nervously.

We had One-Eye and Goblin on our side. Tobo, too. They could winkle out the whereabouts of the boundaries.

But they needed a little light to do the job.

One by one I made sure everyone wakened and understood the gravity of the situation, especially the mothers. I made sure everyone understood that no one should move around until daylight.

Wonder of wonders, nobody did anything stupid. Once there was light enough, the wizards started drawing lines in the snow.

I arranged for teams to enforce the boundaries.

Everything went so well I was feeling smug before it turned time to go. Then I discovered that it was going to be a long day—which, of course, I should have known instinctively.

This next leg of the journey had taken the Captured only a few hours. It would take us far longer. The shattered fortress could not be discerned behind the falling snow. The old, old men would have to mark out every step before it could be taken, walking to either side of Tobo and the Key, keeping him centered on the road—but never getting ahead of him. Just in case.

A quarter mile along I was worrying about time already. We had too many mouths and too few supplies. Harsh rationing was in place. These people had to be gotten across the plain fast, excepting those of us who would bring out the Captured.

"This's getting out of hand!" Goblin yelled. "If it gets any heavier, we're up Shit Creek."

He was right. If this snowfall turned into a blizzard, we were going to have no other worries. If it worsened much, we were going to die out here and make Soulcatcher the happiest girl in the world.

She probably was anyway, now that she had had time to reflect on the fact that there was no one left able to dispute her in any whim she cared to indulge. Water sleeps? So what. Those days were over.

Not while I was still standing, they were not.

Swan joined me for breakfast. "How's my wife this morning?"

"Frigid." Darn! Open mouth, insert boot with manure veneer.

Swan grinned. "I've known that for years. Isn't this something? There's more than an inch already."

"It's something, all right. Unfortunately, I don't encourage myself to use the kind of language needed to describe it. Most of these people have never seen snow. Watch out for somebody to do something stupid. In fact, you might stick close to the Radisha. I don't want her getting hurt because somebody doesn't use his head."

"All right. Did you dream last night?"

"Of course I did. I got to meet Kina right up close, too."

"I saw lights on the road to the east of us."

That got my attention. "Really?"

"In my dream. They were just witchlights. Maybe the plain's own memories, or something. There wasn't anything there when I went to look."

"Getting bold in your old age, are you?"

"It just sort of happened. I wouldn't have done it if I'd thought about it."

"Did I snore again last night?"

"You solidified your grasp on the all-time women's championship. You're ready to compete at the next level."

"Must have something to do with the dreaming."

Sahra drifted up. She looked grim. She did not like what was happening even a little, the snow or the way we had to cope with it. But she bit her tongue. She understood that it was now too late to be a fussy mom. Like it or not, her boy was carrying us all right now.

One-Eye limped along using a staff somebody had made for him from one of the smaller bamboo weapons. I did not know if it was still armed. Very likely so, he being One-Eye. He told me, "I'm not going to last at this, Little Girl. But I'll go as long as I can."

"Show Tobo what to do and let him take over as soon as he's got it. Let Gota carry the pickax and you get up on the horse. Advise from there."

The old man just nodded instead of finding some reason to argue, betraying his true weakness. Goblin scowled at me, though, assuming he was going to get a large ration of unsolicited counsel. But he shrugged off the temptation to debate.

"Tobo. Hold up. You really understand what we have to do today?"

"I've got it, Sleepy."

"Then give your grandmother the Key. Where is that horse buddy of mine? Get up here, you. Carry One-Eye." I noted that the white crow had left the beast's back. In fact, the bird was nowhere to be seen. "Up you go, old man."

"Who you calling old, Little Girl?" One-Eye drew himself up as tall as he got.

"You, so old you've gotten shorter than me. Get your tail up there. I really want to get there today." I offered Goblin a hard look, just in case he got a notion to try poking sticks in the spokes. He just looked back blankly. Or maybe blandly.

Spoiled brat, me. I got my way. The ruined fortress loomed out of weakly falling snow around what felt like noon. Once Tobo got the hang of discovering the boundaries well enough to keep up with Goblin, the band began moving at a pace limited only by Mother Gota's capacities. And she seemed taken by a sudden urge to hasten toward whatever destiny awaited whoever arrived with the Key.

My natural pessimism went almost entirely unrewarded. Had Iqbal's boys not discovered the wonders of snowballs, I would have had nothing to complain about at all. Even then I would have been entertained had not a few wild volleys of missiles not strayed my way.

We arrived at the chasm Murgen had mentioned, a tear in the face of the plain rent by powers almost unimaginable. The earthquake responsible had been felt as far away as Taglios. It had flattened whole cities this side of the Dandha Presh. I wondered if it had wrought as much destruction in the other worlds connected to the plain.

I also wondered if the quake had been natural in origin. Had it been caused by some premature effort of Kina's to rise and shine?

"Swan! Willow Swan! Get up here."

Mother Gota had halted at the lip of the chasm simply because there was no way for her to go forward. The rest of the mob crowded up behind the leaders because, naturally, everyone wanted to see. I snapped, "Make a hole, people! Make a hole. Let the man get up here." I stared at the wrecked fortress. Shattered was too strong a description but its state of disrepair went way beyond neglect, too. I supposed if the original golem garrison were still around, it would be in perfect condition and right now the whole crew would be outside dusting off the snow patches attached to every little roughness of the stone.

Swan grumbled, "You need to make up your mind, darling. You want me to look out for the Radisha or—"

"Never mind. I don't have time. I'm cold and I'm cranky and I want to change that. Look at this crack. Is this the way it was before? Because even though it's pretty impressive, it's nowhere as huge as Murgen made me think it would be. Everybody but Iqbal's baby can skip across this."

Swan studied the gap in the plain.

Immediately evident to any eye was the fact that there were no sharp edges. The stone seemed to have softened and oozed like taffy.

"No. It wasn't like this at all. It looks like it's been healing, it's not a quarter as wide as it was. I bet in another generation there won't even be a scar."

"So the plain can heal itself. But not so things that were added later." I indicated the fortress. "Except for the spells protecting the roads."

"Apparently."

"Start moving across. Swan, stick with Tobo and Gota. Nobody else has any idea where to go from here. There you are," I answered an impatient *caw!* from above. If I kind of squinted and looked sideways, I could make out the white crow perched on the battlements, looking down.

Still muttering to himself, though somewhat good-naturedly, Swan stepped across the crack, slipped, fell, skidded, got up exercising a string of out-of-shape northern expletives. Everyone else laughed.

I summoned Runmust and Riverwalker. "I want you two to figure out how to get the animals and carts across. Draft Suvrin if you want. He claims he's had some minor experience in practical engineering. And keep reminding everyone that if they remain calm and cooperative, we'll all get to sleep in a warm, dry place tonight." Well, maybe dry. Warm was probably too much to expect.

Uncle Doj and Tobo helped Mother Gota across. Sahra followed. Several other Nyueng Bao followed her. That made an awful lot of Nyueng Bao concentrated in one place suddenly. My paranoia began to quiver and narrow its eyes suspiciously.

I said, "Goblin. One-Eye. Come along. Slink? Where are you? Come with us." Slink I could count on to be quick and deadly and as morally reluctant as a spear when I pointed and said, "Kill!"

Uncle Doj did not fail to note the fact that even now I trusted him only incompletely. He seemed both irked and amused. He told me, "There isn't anything for our people here, Annalist. This is all for Tobo's benefit."

"That's good. That's good. I wouldn't want the future of the Company to be placed in the slightest risk."

Doj frowned, disappointed by my sarcasm. "I have not won your heart yet, Stone Soldier?"

"How could you? You keep calling me names and won't even explain."

"All will become clear. I fear."

"Of course. Once we reach the Land of Unknown Shadows. Right? You'd better hope there aren't any half-truths or outright cover-ups in your doctrine. 'All Evil Dies There an Endless Death.' It could still be true."

Doj responded with a baleful look but it seemed neither angry nor calculating. I said, "Swan. Show us the way."

81

I think this's as far as I can take you," Swan told me. He spoke slowly, as though having trouble sorting out his thoughts. "I don't get it. Stuff keeps going away. I know I was farther inside than this. I know all the things we did. But when I try to remember anything specific, I lose everything between the time I got to this point until sometime during the gallop back. Stuff comes to me all the time when I'm not trying. I do remember that. Maybe Catcher messed up my brain somehow."

"There's an all-time understatement," Goblin muttered.

Swan ignored Goblin. He complained, "We were actually off the plain before I realized that we were the only ones who would be coming out."

I was not sure I believed that but it did not matter now. I grunted, suggested, "How about you make a guess? Maybe your soul will remember what your brain can't."

"First you need to get some light in here."

"What do I have wizards for?" I asked the gloom. "Certainly not anything useful or practical like providing a light. They wouldn't need one. They can see in the dark."

Goblin muttered something unflattering about the sort of woman who indulges in sarcasm. He told Swan, "Sit down and let me look at your head."

"Let me!" Tobo enthused at the same time. "Let me try to make a light. I can do this one." He did not wait for permission. Filaments of lemon and silver light crawled over his upraised hands, swift and eager. The darkness surrounding us retreated, I thought reluctantly.

"Wow!" I said. "Look at him."

"He has the strength and enthusiasm of youth," One-Eye conceded. I glanced back. He was still astride the black stallion, wearing a smug look but obviously exhausted. The white crow was perched in front of him. It studied Tobo with one eye while considering our surroundings with the other. It seemed amused. Then One-Eye began to chuckle.

Tobo squealed in surprise. "Wait! Stop! Goblin! What's happening?"

The worms of light were snaking up his arms. They would not respond to his insistence that they desist. He started slapping himself. One-Eye and Goblin began to laugh.

Meantime, the two of them had done something to Swan to clarify his mind. The man looked like he had just sucked down a tall, frosty mug of self-confident recollection.

Sahra saw nothing funny in Tobo's situation. She screamed at the wizards to do something. She was almost incoherent. Which betrayed how much stress she inflicted upon herself.

Doj told her, "He isn't in any danger, Sahra. He just let himself get distracted. It happens. It's part of learning," or words to that effect, several times, before Sahra calmed down and began to look defiant and sheepish at the same time.

Goblin told Tobo, "I'll take it till you get your concentration back." And in a moment there was light enough to see the walls of the huge chamber. Someone who is skilled at something always makes it look easy. The little bald wizard was no exception. He told One-Eye, "Help Swan keep his head clear."

I thought the place looked like a nice change from sleeping out in the weather. I wished there was fuel we could burn to heat it.

"Whither now?" I asked Swan. For some time I had been silently regretting not having caught Murgen while I was dreaming so I could have gotten reliable directions.

The white crow squawked and launched itself, leaving One-Eye cursing because it had swatted him in the face with its wings.

I was starting to understand the beast. "Somebody see where it goes. One of you sorcerer geniuses want to send a light with it?" Tobo had received control of his light again and had it working in good form but it took all his attention to manage it. I hoped he outgrew this more-confidence-than-sense stage before he took a really big bite of disaster.

Uncle Doj trailed the crow at a dignified pace. I supposed I ought to contribute something more than executive decisions, so I followed him. A ball of leprous green light from behind overtook me and made a nest in my tangled hair. My scalp began to itch. I had a suspicion One-Eye might be sneering at my personal hygiene, which, I confess, sometimes became the victim of a negligent attitude. Sort of. "This'll teach me to take my darn helmet off," I grumbled. I refused to allow him to flash me his smug, toothless grin by not looking back.

I had not been wearing an actual helmet. God save me, that would have been cold. I had been wearing a leather helmet liner, which had kept my ears from getting frostbitten. Barely. Winter. It was one of those things the planning team had not foreseen.

I hurried past Doj, who was startled when he saw my hair. Then he grinned as big as ever I had seen him do. I tossed him a bloodthirsty scowl. Unfortunately, to do so I had to turn around far enough to see One-Eye and Goblin suddenly stop exchanging handslaps and snickers. Even Sahra turned slightly sideways to conceal her amusement. All right. So suddenly I am the clown princess of the Company, eh? We would see. Those two would . . .

I realized that they had lured me into accepting their system of thought. Before long I would be setting traps so I could get even first.

The crow cawed. It was down on the cold stone floor. It danced back and forth, suddenly impatient. Its talons clicked softly. I dropped to my knees. It let me get almost within touching distance before it flopped farther into the darkness.

More light took life behind us as people and animals came inside, making the predictable racket. Every new arrival had to know what was going on.

The crow became a silhouette if I lowered my head and looked at it with my cheek against the floor.

I told Doj, "There's light coming from somewhere. This must be where the Captured got into the inner fortress." I got down on my belly. There was a definite gap in a wall of stone so dark it seemed unseeable even in the available light. I could not make out anything on the other side.

Doj got down and placed his own cheek on the floor. "Indeed."

I called, "We need some more light over here. And maybe some tools. River. Runmust. Have those people start setting up some kind of camp. And see what you can do about shutting out the cold." That would be difficult. There were several large gaps in the outside wall.

Goblin and One-Eye stopped grinning like fools and came forward dressed in their business faces. They kept Tobo right there with them, determined to teach him their trade quickly, hands-on.

With more light it was easier to see what the bird meant me to see, which had to be the crack Soulcatcher had sealed after working her wicked spells on the Captured. "There any spells or booby traps here?" I asked.

"The Little Girl's a genius," One-Eye grumbled. His speech had grown a little slurred. He needed rest badly. "The bird strutted through and didn't go up in smoke. Right? That suggest anything?"

"No spells," Goblin said. "Don't mind him. He's just cranky because him and Gota haven't had no privacy for a week."

"I'm gonna fit you out for all the privacy you'll need for a couple of eons, Runt Man. I'm gonna plant your wrinkled old ass—"

"Enough! Let's see if we can make the hole any bigger."

The crow made impatient noises on the other side. It had to have some connection with the Captured even if it was not Murgen operating from some lost corner of time. Certainly I hoped it was not Murgen from the future. That would imply a less than successful effort on our part now.

I grumbled and snarled. I stamped back and forth while half a dozen men expanded the hole, every one of them grousing about the shortage of light. I did not contribute much as a human candle, either. Maybe the thing in my hair was Goblin and One-Eye offering commentary on how bright I was. Though I doubted that after only two hundred years they could yet have developed that much cleverness and subtlety.

A larger and larger crowd piled up behind me. "River," I growled, "I said you should have these people do something useful. Tobo, get back from there. You want a boulder to fall on your head?"

A voice behind me suggested, "You ought to get more light on it so you can see if you need to do any shoring."

I turned. "Slink?"

"There were miners in my family."

"Then you're as near an expert as we've got."

One-Eye jabbed a thumb at Goblin. "The dwarf here has sapper experience. He helped undermine the walls at Tember." His face split in an ugly grin.

Goblin squeaked, a definite clue that "Tember" was an episode he did not recall fondly. I did not remember any mention of a Tember in the Annals. Reason suggested that the referenced event must have taken place long before Croaker became Annalist, which he had done at an early age.

Two of Croaker's more immediate predecessors, Miller Ladora and Kanwas Scar, had been so lax in their duties that little is known about their time—other than what their successors have reconstructed from oral tradition and the memories of survivors. It was during that era that Croaker, Otto and Hagop joined the band. Croaker says little about those days himself.

"Am I to take it, then, that I shouldn't invest unlimited faith in Goblin's engineering skills?"

One-Eye cawed like a crow. "As an engineer our bitty buddy makes a wonderful lumberjack. Things fall down wherever he goes."

Goblin growled like a mastiff issuing a warning.

"See, this here skinny little bald-egg genius sold the Old Man the notion of sneaking into this burg Tember by tunneling under its walls. Deep down. Because the earth was soft. It'd be easy." One-Eye snorted as he talked, his laughter barely under control. "And he was right. It *was* easy. When his tunnel caved in, the wall fell down. And the rest of us charged through the gap and sorted them Temberinos out."

Goblin grumbled, "And about five days later somebody remembered the miners."

"Somebody was just plain damned lucky he had a friend as good as me to dig him out. The Old Man just wanted to put up a gravestone."

Goblin growled some more. "Not so. And the real truth is, the tunnel never would've collapsed if this two-legged, overripe dog turd hadn't been playing one of his stupid games. You know, I almost forgot. I never did pay you back for that. You should've never brought it up, you human prune. Damn! You almost went and died on me before I got you paid off. I *knew* you were up to no good. You had that stroke on purpose, didn't you?"

"Of course I did, you nitwit. Every chance I get, I try to die just so's you can't backstab me no more. You want to be that way? I saved your ass and you want to be that way? Ain't no fool like an old fool. Bring it on, you hairless little toady frog. I maybe slowed down a step the last couple years but I'm still three steps faster and ten torches brighter than any lily-white—"

"Boys!" I snapped. "Children! We have work to do here." They must have driven the whole Company crazy when they were young and had the energy to keep it up all the time. "As of this moment, all the slates are clean of anything that happened before I was born. Just open me a hole so I can go see what we have to do next."

The two wizards did not stop growling and muttering and threatening and trying to sabotage one another in small ways but they did lend their claimed expertise to the effort to open the gap.

82

Once the opening had been expanded enough to use, there was a brief debate about who would use it first. The accord was universal: "Not me." But when I squatted down to duckwalk forward into the shadows, in hopes I could get a look at what might eat me a few seconds before its jaws snapped shut, several gentlemen turned all noble and chivalrous. I suspect it was significant that two of them, Swan and Suvrin, were not Company brothers.

Goblin grumbled, "All right. All right. Now you're making us look bad. All of you, get out of the way." He bustled forward.

He did not have to duck.

I did, just slightly, as I followed him through.

I did not *need* anyone to be noble or chivalrous or to go in before me.

"There is no God but God," I muttered. "His Works are Vast and Mysterious." I was five steps inside and had just bumped into Goblin, who had stopped to stare as well. "I presume that's the golem demon Shivetya."

"Or his ugly little brother."

Murgen had not kept me posted on the golem's state. At last report it had been just a single earth tremor short of plunging into a bottomless abyss, still nailed to a huge wooden throne by means of a number of silver daggers. I observed, "It appears the plain has been healing itself in here, too." I eased forward.

There was still a vertiginous abyss. I had to close my eyes momentarily while I regained my equilibrium. Shivetya remained poised over it but the gap clearly was narrower than Murgen had described. In closing, the surface had pushed the wooden throne upward somewhat. Shivetya was no longer in momentary peril of falling. It looked like a few decades would see him lying there with his nose pressed into healed stone, the overturned throne on top of him still.

Willow Swan invited himself to join me. He said, "That thing hasn't moved since last time."

I countered, "Thought you couldn't remember anything."

"Whatever the short farts did, it seems to be working. I recognize things when I see them."

Goblin told Swan, "Considering what could still happen if Shivetya starts jumping around, holding still seems like a pretty good idea. Don't you think?"

"Could you hold still for fifteen years?"

I said, "He's held still a lot longer than that, Swan. He's been nailed to that throne for hundreds of years. Or even thousands. He has to have been nailed down since before Deceivers fleeing Rhaydreynak came here on their way to other worlds and hid the Books of the Dead." That observation got me some looks, particularly from Master Santaraksita. I had not yet shared the tales I had gleaned from Murgen. "Else he would've stomped them good at the time. They would've looked like the kind of thing he was put here to guard against. I think."

"Who nailed him down?" Goblin asked.

"I don't know."

"Might be a handy piece of information. You'd want to keep an eye on a guy who could do that kind of thing."

"I would," Swan agreed. He grinned nervously.

"It's listening," I said. I moved along the edge of the abyss several steps, squatted. From there I could see the demon's eyes. They were open a crack. I could also see that there were three of them instead of two, the third being in the center of the forehead above and between the other two. This point had not come up before, though it was the sort of thing you would expect of a Gunni-style demon.

The oversight became self-explanatory as soon as the demon sensed my scrutiny. The third eye closed and vanished.

I asked Swan, "That throne look like it's solidly wedged?"

"Yeah. Why?"

"Just wondering if we could move it without losing it down that crack."

"I'm no engineer but it looks to me like you'd really have to work at it to dump it down there now. Obviously, it could go. One really stupid move . . . it's a hell of a deep hole. But . . ."

The curious kept piling up behind us. Their chatter was becoming annoying. Every single whisper turned into a gaggle of echoes that made the place seem more haunted than it was. "Everybody be quiet. I can't hear myself think." I must have sounded nastier than I intended. People shut up. And gawked. I asked, "Does anyone see a way to get that thing turned right side up and pushed back away from the gap?"

"How come you'd want to do that?" One-Eye asked. "Quit shoving, Junior."

Suvrin asked, "Using equipment we have on hand?"

"Yes. And it would have to get done today. I want the majority of these people back on the road south at first light tomorrow."

"That means using brute force. Right now. Some of us would have to get on the other side of the fissure and lift the top of the throne enough so people and animals on this side could get the leverage to pull it on up. Using ropes."

Swan said, "You try to stand it up the way it is there, the bottom end will just slide off the edge. Then it's a grand ride off to the entrails of the earth."

"How come you'd want to do that?" One-Eye demanded again. I ignored him again.

I concentrated on the argument spreading outward from Suvrin and Swan. I let it run for several minutes. Then I announced, "Suvrin seems to be the only one here with a positive view. So he's in charge. Suvrin, draft anybody you want. Help yourself to any resources you need. Sit Shivetya back up for me. You hear that, Steadfast Guardian? Gentlemen, if you have any ideas, feel free to share them with Mr. Suvrin."

Suvrin said, "I can't . . . I don't . . . I shouldn't . . . I guess the first thing we'd better do is get a solid idea of how much weight we're dealing with. And we'll have to rig up some way to get across the gap. Mr. Swan, you handle that. Young Mr. Tobo, I understand you're skilled at mathematics. Suppose you help me calculate how much mass we're dealing with here?"

Tobo grinned and headed for the throne, not at all intimidated by the demon.

"One adjustment," I said. "I need Swan with me. He's been here before. Runmust, you and Iqbal figure out how to get across. Willow. Come with me."

Out of earshot of the others, Swan asked, "What's going on?"

"I didn't want to remind anybody that the Company got this far once before. Somebody might recall a grudge against the man who made it impossible for our predecessors to go any farther."

"Oh. Thanks. I guess." He glanced at the clot of Nyueng Bao. Mother Gota continued to nurture her grudge. She had a son somewhere down under this stone.

"I may just have a strange perspective. I do believe all of us should accept responsibility for our actions but I'm not sure we ever understand why we do some things. Do you know why you cut Soulcatcher loose? I'd bet you've spent the odd minute here and there trying to figure that out."

"You'd win. Except it'd be more like the odd year here and there. And I still can't explain it. She did something to me, somehow. Just with her eyes. All the way across the plain. Probably manipulating my feelings about her sister. When the time came it seemed like the right thing to do. I never had a doubt until it was all over and we were on the run."

"And she kept her word."

He understood. "She gave me everything her eyes promised. Everything I could never have from the sister I really wanted. Whatever her failings, Soulcatcher keeps her word."

"Sometimes we get what we want and find out that it wasn't what we needed."

"No shit. Story of my life, Sleepy."

"Around fifty people came onto the plain. Two of you got away. Thirteen died on the road, trying. The rest are still out here somewhere. And you helped put them where they are. So I'm going to need you to show me. Are you still blind in the memory or have you started to remember?"

"Oh, those spells took. It's coming back. But not necessarily organized the same way that it happened. So bear with me when I seem a little confused."

"I understand." I kept an eye on the others as we talked. Sahra seemed to be putting herself under a lot of unnecessary stress. Doj looked ferociously ready to seize the day should an opportunity pop up. Gota was nagging One-Eye about something while keeping one grim eye aimed Swan's way. Goblin was trying to get the mist projector set up amidst a jostling crowd. I noted, "There seems to be more light than Murgen reported."

"Tons more. And it's warmer, too. If I was allowed a guess, mine would be that it has something to do with the healing that's going on."

I did feel overdressed for the indoor weather. It was not hot but it was warmer than the plain outside and there was no wind biting.

"Where are the Captured?"

"There was a stairway over there. We must have gone a mile down into the earth."

"You carried thirty-five unconscious people down there and got back in time to get away from the evening shadows? Without killing yourself?"

"Catcher did most of it. She has a spell that makes things float through the air. We roped the people together and pulled them along like a string of sausages. She did the pulling, actually. I stayed on the uphill end. More or less. At first. Because the stair has some twists and turns. We had trouble getting them around the corners. But a lot less trouble than if we'd carried them one at a time."

I nodded. I knew of other instances when Catcher had used the same sorcery. Seemed like a handy one to have. We could use it right here, right now, to hoist my future buddy Shivetya.

Curious. Once upon a time Murgen said that name meant "Deathless," although more recently I had been given the meaning "Steadfast Guardian." But I had been provided with whole new sets of creation myths and whatnot, too.

I fought off an urge to charge off and plunge down the stairway right then. I hustled back to talk it over with the others. Most of the crowd were preoccupied with an effort to get Shivetya's throne turned right side up by the power of talking about it. Suvrin told me, "It's a way to keep warm." And a way to work off some tension, no doubt. I heard plenty of traditional-style grumbling questioning the intelligence of any leader who wanted to play around with something like that great ugly thing over there on that throne.

I gathered everyone interested. "Swan knows the way down to the caverns. His memory is getting better all the time." Goblin and One-Eye preened. I gave them no chance to congratulate themselves publicly. "I'm going down there to scout. I want the rest of you to get camp set up. I want you to work out specifically how we'll divide up tomorrow so the majority can scoot on across the plain to safety." We had discussed this time and again—how we could break up the party, leaving the minimum number of people with the maximum stores to bring out the Captured while the rest moved on to, it was hoped, a more congenial clime.

Doj's position, so perfectly rational, was that we should ignore the Captured until we had crossed the plain, had gotten ourselves established in the Land of Unknown Shadows, and were capable of mounting a more thoroughly prepared and supplied expedition. But none of us knew what we would face at that end of this passage, and way too many of us were emotionally incapable of walking away from our brothers again now that we were this close.

I should have gotten more information out of Murgen while we still had some flexibility. Time was winnowing our options rapidly.

Sahra's response to Uncle's repeating his suggestion was blistering enough to melt lead. She might be reluctant to have her husband back but she was not going to delay any crisis.

Swan leaned over my shoulder and whispered, "If you hang around here waiting for all these people to agree on something, we're going to get very old and very hungry before anything happens."

The man had a point. A definite point.

I got my daily constitutional in before we reached the stairway. I began to appreciate just how vast the hall at the heart of that fortress was. My party dwindled into the distance. I observed, "This thing has got to be a mile across."

"Almost exactly. It's a few yards under, according to Soulcatcher. I don't know why. I wish we had a torch. I saw patterns in the flooring last time I was here, when there wasn't quite so much dust, but she wouldn't let me waste time looking at them."

There was a lot of dust. There had been none outside. The plain tolerated nothing alien except the corpses of invaders, evidently. Even here, we had yet to discover any sign of the animals or equipment that had accompanied the Captured south.

"How much farther?"

"Almost there. Watch for a drop-off."

"A drop-off?"

"A step down. It's only about eighteen inches but you could break a leg if it surprises you. I turned an ankle last time."

We found the drop-off. I stopped to look back once I stepped down. All sorts of genius was being invested in the assignments I had given. Closer, Sahra and the Radisha and several others to whom I had not given specific assignments had decided to follow me. I said, "You're right. It does look like there're some kind of inlays. If we have time, maybe we can take a closer look." I considered the edge of the stone. "This curves. And it's polished."

"That part of the floor is a circle. And it's almost exactly one-eightieth of the diameter of the plain. According to Soulcatcher. The raised part where the demon's throne used to sit is one-eightieth the size of this."

"That's probably got to mean something. It have anything to do with the Captured?"

"Not that I'm aware of."

"Then we'll worry about it later."

"The stairs start over here."

They did indeed, right next to the wall. The crack in the floor had extended clear through that. The wall's partial collapse had filled the gap there, then the material from the wall had been pushed back up as the fissure healed itself.

The stairs simply started. There was a rectangular hole in the floor. Steps went down, roughly paralleling the outer wall, away from the crack in the floor, which had healed almost completely. There was no handrail.

Twenty steps down we reached a landing eight feet by eight. The descending steps led off from our right. This flight appeared to go downward forever. Faint light crept up it, just strong enough so you could see where to put your feet.

Sahra and the Radisha had caught up close enough that I could hear them talking without being able to pick up specific words. Both women sounded frightened by the immediate future.

I could sympathize. I was nervous about achieving my life's ambition myself. Just a little.

"You want to go first?" Swan asked. He lacked considerable enthusiasm, I thought.

"Are there booby traps or something?"

"No. She probably wanted to, just in case somebody passed this way someday, just for the sheer mean fun of it, but there wasn't enough time. She piddled around so much, for so long, I didn't really believe we'd ever get away. I'm sure we wouldn't have if she hadn't been who she was. She spun spells that chased the shadows away. She'd been in there before. And she'd practiced."

"There it is!"

"What?"

"Nothing. Just remembering something." Stupid me. All those years I wondered how Swan and Soulcatcher had found time to bury the Captured without getting gobbled up by shadows and I had overlooked the obvious, the fact that Soulcatcher was a major sorceress and already had some experience manipulating shadows. You can be screamingly blind to the obvious if you don't realize that you have not opened up all the doors of your mind.

Forgive me, O Lord of the Hours. Be Merciful. Be Compassionate. I shall close the borders of my soul as soon as my brothers are free.

At this point Swan had no incentive to steer me into danger. I started downstairs.

The architects, engineers and stonemasons responsible had not been determined to achieve geometric perfection. Though this portion of the stairwell continued downward in a specific general direction, it tended to meander from side to side of a straight line. Nor were the steps of a uniform height. The builders had been thoughtful enough to provide landings every little way, though. I had a feeling those would seem to be miles apart once I started climbing up again.

"If we have to bring One-Eye down here, we're going to have to carry him back up. He won't survive the climb otherwise."

"You might want to organize what you're going to do before we go down there, then."

"I can't decide what has to be done until I see what I'm dealing with."

"You might call up your genie in a bottle. Get him to tell you."

"He's never said much about the place where he's at. Not since he's been in there himself. It's like he's constrained against that. I dreamed about it a few times but I don't know how accurate my dreams were."

Swan groaned. "I really didn't want to make this trek."

"Will it be that bad?"

"Not going down. But heading the other way is likely to change your attitude."

"I don't know. I'm beginning to get a little winded just going in this direction."

"Then slow down. A few minutes isn't going to make a difference. Not after all these years."

He was right. And wrong. There was no rush for the Captured. But for us, with our limited resources, time was destined to become critical.

Swan continued, "You need to slow down, Sleepy. Really. It's going to get a little bit hairy in a minute."

He was absolutely right. But he understated the case dramatically.

The stairwell did a meander to the right. It caught up with the chasm caused by the earthquakes that had occurred during the reign of the Shadowmasters.

There was only half a stairway there. It hung in the face of a cliff. That left a whole lot of down on my right-hand side. And it was down that was entirely too well illuminated by a reddish-orange light that may have come from the stone itself, since there seemed to be no other obvious source. Though I did have trouble opening my eyes wide enough to look. Wraithlike wisps of vapor wobbled upward from somewhere down below. The air seemed warmer. I asked, "We're not heading into Hell itself, are we?" Some Vehdna believe *al-Shiel* is a place where wicked souls will burn for all eternity.

Swan understood. "Not your Hell. But I'd guess it's Hell enough for them that're trapped down there."

I stopped on the remains of a landing. The steps narrowed to two feet just below me. By leaning out slightly I could see clearly that the stairwell had been constructed inside a larger bore at least twenty feet in diameter. The shaft had been filled with a stone darker than that through which it had been cut. Maybe the bore had needed to be that big so Kina could be dragged down below. I asked, "Can you imagine what an engineering project this must have been?"

"People with plenty of slaves aren't daunted by big projects. What's the matter?"

"I have a problem with heights. This next part is going to take a lot of prayer and some outside encouragement. I want you to go first. I want you to go slow. And I want you to stay where I can touch you. I believe in meeting my fears eyeball to eyeball but if it gets bad and I feel like I might freeze up, I want to be able to close my eyes and keep going." I was astounded by how calm and reasonable my voice sounded.

"I understand. The real problem then is, who's going to keep his eyes open for me? Whoa! Don't panic, Sleepy. I was joking! I can handle it. Really."

It was not the worst thing I ever dealt with. I never abandoned rational thought. But it was difficult. Even when Swan promised me that an unseen protective barrier existed on the abyssal side and demonstrated its presence, the animal inside me wanted to get the heck out of there and go someplace where the ground was flat and green, there was a sky overhead, and there might even be a few trees.

Swan assured me that I was missing one heck of a view, especially as we approached the lower end of the gap, where the light was brighter, revealing churning mists way below, mists that concealed the depths of the abyss. I kept my eyes closed until we were back into a closed cavern again.

I had started counting steps up top so I could get an idea of how deep we went but I lost count while I was pretending to be a fly crawling on a wall. I was too busy being terrified. But it did seem like we had traveled a long way horizontally as well as downward.

Almost immediately after I had that thought, the stair turned left, then left again. The orange-red light faded away. The stair made a couple more quick turns into a total darkness, which aroused whole new species of terrors. But nothing bit me and nothing came to steal my soul.

Then there was light again, growing so subtly I was never really aware of first noticing it. It had a golden cast to it but was extremely cold. And as soon as I was aware of it, I knew we were approaching our destination.

The stairwell passed right through a natural cavern. At one time that had been sealed off but the quakes had toppled the responsible masonry walls. I asked, "We here?"

"Almost. Careful climbing over the stones. They aren't very stable."

"What's that?"

"What?"

"That sound."

We listened. After a while, Swan said, "I think it's wind. Sometimes there was a breeze when we were down here before."

"Wind? A mile underground?"

"Don't ask me to explain it. It just is. You want to go first this time?"

"Yes."

"I thought you would."

84

Golden caverns where old men sat beside the way, frozen in time, immortal but unable to move an eyelid. Madmen they, some covered with fairy webs of ice as though a thousand winter spiders had spun threads of frozen water. Above, an enchanted forest of icicles grew downward from the cavern roof.

So Murgen described it once upon a time, decades ago. The description remained apt, though the light was not as golden as I expected and the delicate filigrees of ice were denser and more complex. The old men seated against the walls, caught up in the webs, were not the wide-eyed madmen of Murgen's visions, though. They were dead. Or asleep. I did not see one open eye. Nor did I see one face I recognized.

"Willow. Who are these people?" The bitter wind continued to rush through the cavern, which was a dozen feet high and nearly as wide, with a relatively flat floor, side to side. It sloped with the length of the cavern. It looked like ancient, frozen mud covered with a pelt of fine frost fur. Water had run through the cavern in some epoch before the coming of men.

"These ones? I don't know. They were here when we came down."

I leaned closer but was careful not to touch. "These caves are natural."

"They have that look."

"Then they've been down here all along. They were here before the plain was built."

"Possibly. Probably."

"And whoever buried Kina knew about them. So did the Deceivers chased here by Rhaydreynak. Hunh! This one is definitely deceased. Naturally mummified but definitely gone." The corpse was all dried out. Bare bone showed at a folded knee and tattered elbow. "These others? Who knows? Maybe the right sorcery could get them up and running around like Iqbal's kids."

"Why would we get them up? We're here to get the guys that me and Catcher buried. Right? They're on up there." He pointed upslope, where the light was even less golden, becoming almost an icy blue.

The light was not bright. Not nearly so much so as in the vision I had experienced. Maybe it was more a psychic witchlight than a physical one, more suited to the dreamwalker's eye. I mused, "They might be able to tell us something interesting."

"I'll tell you something interesting," Swan muttered to himself. In a normal voice, for my benefit, he said, "I don't think so. At least I don't think it would be anything any of us would want to hear. Catcher took extreme pains to avoid even touching them. Getting the captives past without disturbing them was the hardest work we did."

I bent to examine another of the old men. He did not look like he belonged to any race I knew. "They must be from one of the other worlds."

"Maybe. There's a saying where I grew up: 'Let sleeping dogs lie.' Sounds like exquisitely appropriate advice. We don't know why they were put down here."

"I have no intention of releasing any deviltry but our own. These men here aren't the same as those."

"There were several different groups last time. I doubt that that's changed. I got the feeling that they were dumped here at different times. See how much less ice there is around these guys? Makes me think it takes centuries to accumulate."

"Ow!"

"What?"

"I banged my head on this damned rock icicle thing."

"Hmm. I must've *over*looked it somehow."

"Get smart and I'll punch you in the kneecap, Lofty. Does it feel like it's colder in here than it ought to be?" It was not my imagination and not the icy wind, either.

"Always." His grin had gone away. "It's them. I think. Starting to realize somebody's here. It keeps building up. It can get on your nerves if you pay any attention to it."

I could feel the growth of whatever it was. Insanity becoming palpable, I suppose. That was the impression, anyway.

"How come we're able to move around in here?" I asked. "Why aren't *we* frozen?"

"We'd probably end up that way if we stayed long enough to fall asleep. These people all had to be unconscious when they were brought down here."

"Really?" We were up where there was less ice. The frost on the floor still betrayed the tracks left by Soulcatcher and Willow Swan years ago. The old men here were different. They resembled Nyueng Bao, except for one, who had been tall, thin and extremely pale. "But they don't stay asleep?" Several pairs of open eyes seemed to track me. I hoped it was my imagination, stimulated by the spookiness of the cave. I never actually saw any movement.

Footsteps.

I jumped hip-high to a short elephant before I realized that it had to be Sahra and the Radisha and whoever else had decided not to participate in all those exciting projects that were underway upstairs. "Go keep those people from stomping in here and messing everything up. I'll get an idea of the layout and try to figure out what we'll have to do."

Swan scowled and growled and grunted, then minced carefully back down the slight slope toward the stairwell. He talked to himself all the way. And I did not blame him. Even I thought nothing ever went right for him.

I took a step in the direction the old footprints led. My boots went out from under me. I hit hard, then slid downhill until I caught up with Swan, who did a convincing job of acting amused after he stopped me. "You all right?"

"Bruised my side. Hurt my wrist."

"I shoulda told you. That floor can be pretty slippery where there's a lot of frost."

"You're lucky I don't swear."

"Uhm?"

"You forgot on purpose. You're as bad as One-Eye or Goblin."

"Did I just hear my name taken in vain?" One-Eye's voice, punctuated by rasping panting more suitable to a lunger, came from the shadows down where the stair intercepted the cavern.

"God is Great, God is Good. God is the All-Knowing and All-Merciful. His Plan is Hidden but Just." And save me from the Mystery of His Plan because all I ever get is the Misery of His Plan. "What is *he* doing down here?" I asked Swan. "I know. I'll leave him behind. I know I'm definitely not going to carry him up out of here just so he doesn't suffer another stroke from the effort. Hit him over the head when he isn't looking." I began moving deeper into the cave again. "I'm going to try this one more time." Beneath my breath I continued my conversation with God. As usual, He did not trouble Himself to defend His Works to me. My fault for being a woman.

I nearly missed the transition from the ancient Nyueng Bao types to Company men because the first few modern bodies belonged to Nyueng Bao bodyguards. I halted only when I reached and recognized a Nyueng Bao bodyguard named Pham Quang. I studied him for a moment.

I backed up carefully.

When you looked for it, the boundary was evident. My brothers and their allies had several centuries' less frost accumulation upon them. They had only just begun to develop the delicate webbings that encased the older bodies. That seemed awfully fast, actually, considering how long some of the others must have been buried. Possibly Soulcatcher had indulged in a little artistry during her visit.

Interspersed with my brothers were several bodies so ancient that they had become completely cocooned. I intuited them as bodies only because the chrysalises slumped just like the Captured did.

A thought. It might be worthwhile having One-Eye along after all. Down here Soulcatcher might have taken time to set a trap or two, just for the devil of it.

The Nar generals Isi and Ochiba sat against the cave wall opposite Pham Quang. Ochiba's eyes were open. They did not move but did seem fixed on me. I hunkered down, got as close as I could without touching him.

Those brown pools were moist. There was no dust on their surfaces, nor any frost. They had opened quite recently.

A chill crawled down my spine. A very creepy feeling came over me. I felt like I was walking among the dead. In the far north, whence Swan came carrying travelers' tales, some religions supposedly pictured Hell as a cold place. My imagination, running with the terror that my brothers' situation sparked, had no trouble picturing this cave as a suburb of Hell.

I rose carefully and moved away from Ochiba. Now the cave floor was almost perfectly level. My brothers were not crowded together. The rest seemed to be scattered along the next several hundred feet, not all immediately visible because of a turn in the cave. A few old cocoon men were interspersed with them. "I see the Lance!" I announced. Which was wonderful. Now we could split into two parties and have both retain their capacity for accessing the plain.

My voice echoed like there was a chorus of me all talking at the same time. Hitherto, Swan and I had tried to speak softly. The echoes had been little more than ghostly whispers although extremely busy even at that level.

"Keep it down," One-Eye said. "What are you doing, Little Girl? You don't have any idea what you're dealing with here." He had gotten past Swan somehow and was headed my way. He was awfully damned spry for a two-hundred-year-old stroke victim. This business had him truly excited.

That left me suspicious. But I had no time to try reasoning out what angle the man might have.

I looked into another pair of eyes, these belonging to a long, bony, pallid man who had to be the sorcerer Longshadow. Longshadow was a prisoner of the Company. He had been brought along because neither Croaker nor Lady trusted anyone else to guard him and he could not be exterminated because the health of the Shadowgate, insofar as they had known, was dependent upon his continued well-being. And well that they had been so distrustful. It would be a much different and more terrible world if the Shadowmaster had been left behind to tinker at whatever wickedness took his fancy. Soulcatcher's evil was capricious and unfocused. Longshadow's malice and insanity were deep and abiding.

That insanity stared out of his eyes right then. On my mental checklist I made a tick that meant this one would stay right where he was. Others might have plans for him but they were not in charge. If we could work out how to strengthen our world's Shadowgate, maybe we could even execute him.

I continued moving, working my silent triage, constantly bemused because there were so many faces that I did not recognize. A lot of men who had enlisted while I was away from the center of the action. "Oh, darn!"

"What?" One-Eye was only a few steps behind me, gaining ground fast. His voice seemed to rattle as it echoed.

"It's Wheezer. The stasis didn't take for him."

One-Eye grunted, evidently indifferent. Old Wheezer came from the same tribe One-Eye did, although Wheezer was more than a century younger than the wizard. There had never been any affection between them. "He had a better run than he deserved." Wheezer had been old and dying of consumption when he joined the Company during its passage southward, decades ago. And he had continued to survive despite his infirmities and despite all the trials the Company had endured.

"Here're Candles and Cletus. They're gone, too. And a couple of Nyueng Bao and two Shadar I don't recognize. Something happened here. This makes seven dead men, all in a clump."

"Don't move, Little Girl. Don't touch anything before I have a chance to look it over."

I froze. It was time to acknowledge his expertise.

85

I haven't found them yet!" I snapped at Sahra and the Radisha. "I don't want to go any farther if One-Eye can't assure me that I'm not going to kill somebody just by being here." Against all advice, those two had pushed as far forward as I would let them go. I could understand that they wanted to see their husbands and brothers and boyfriends, but they ought to have sense enough to restrain themselves until we knew what we could and could not do without risking harm to those very husbands and brothers and boyfriends.

Sahra gave me a sharp, hurt look.

"Sorry," I said, insincerely. "Come on. Think. You can see that the stasis down here didn't work for everyone. Swan. How far up this tunnel do we have to go?" I could see a scatter of eight recumbent forms between myself and the curve, none of whom were immediately recognizable as the Captain, Lady, Murgen, Thai Dei, Cordy Mather or Blade. "From where we stand now, roughly eleven people still aren't accounted for."

"I don't remember," Swan grumped. Bass echoes chased one another around the cavern. They were worse with my higher-pitched voice, though.

"Memory spell wearing off?"

"I don't think so. This feels more like something I never knew. I'm still a whole lot confused about what went on down here."

One big problem was that none of us really knew exactly how many Captured there were. Swan was the best witness because he had ridden with them, but he had not kept track, other than of key people. Murgen never had been any help because after he had become one of the Captured, he had apparently become unable to explore the immediate vicinity where he was confined.

"We need to get Murgen awake first thing. Nobody else will know all the names and faces." It seemed probable that some of the people I did not recognize just were not part of the Company. "One-Eye. Figure out how to wake these people up. As soon as I find Murgen, I want to get him into talking condition. Can I go ahead?" Squabbling echoes reminded me to keep my voice down.

Crabbily, One-Eye responded, "Yes. Just don't touch anybody. Or even anything that you don't recognize. And stop trying to rush me."

"*Can* you bring them out of stasis?"

"I don't know yet, do I? I've been too damned busy answering dumb questions. Leave me alone long enough and I might figure it out, though."

Tempers were getting short and manners were becoming frayed. I sighed, rubbed my forehead and temples because I had begun to develop a headache, listened to the sounds of more people descending the stair. "Willow, see if you can keep those fools out of here till One-Eye's ready." I looked ahead without eagerness. Not only did the cavern turn to the right, it steepened. The water-polished floor was covered with frost. The footing was going to be treacherous.

"Caw!"

The white crow was up there somewhere. It had been announcing itself repeatedly, sounding more impatient every time.

I moved forward carefully. When I reached the steeper floor, I knelt and brushed the frost away to improve the footing. I told Sahra and the Radisha, "If you *have* to follow me, you'd better be even more careful than I am."

They insisted. They were careful. Not one of us slipped and went flailing back down the slope. "Here's Longo and Sparkle," I said. "And that wad definitely looks like the Howler."

In fact, that wad definitely was that crippled little Master Sorcerer. He had been one of the Lady's henchmen in the far north, then our enemy down here. He had become a prisoner of war along with his ally Longshadow, and Lady must have foreseen some use for him or she would not have kept him alive. But he was not likely to get released while I was in charge. In his way, he was crazier than Soulcatcher.

The crow chided me for taking so long.

The Howler was awake. His will was such that he could move his eyes, though nothing more was within his capacity. One glimpse of the madness within those dark orbs and I knew that *this* man could not be permitted to make it back to the world. "Be very careful around this one," I said. "Or he'll nail you as surely as Soulcatcher nailed Swan. One-Eye. Howler is awake. He can move his eyes."

One-Eye repeated my warning, absentmindedly. "Don't get too close to him."

The crow began to nag. Its voice gave birth to a particularly annoying generation of echoes.

"Ah. Radisha. Here's your brother. And he seems to be in pretty good shape. No! Don't touch! That's probably what contaminated the stasis spells protecting the dead men. You'll just have to be patient, same as the rest of us."

She made a sound like a low growl.

The icy cave ceiling above us made creaking sounds that added to the volleys of echoes.

I continued, "It's hard. I know it's hard. But right now patience is the best tool we have for getting them out of here safely." Once I was sure she would restrain herself I resumed inching forward. The white crow cawed impatiently. Out loud I thought, "I do believe I'll wring that thing's neck."

The Radisha reminded me, "You'll build bad kharma. You might come back as a crow or parrot in your next life."

"One of the beauties of being Vehdna is that you don't have a next life to worry about. And God, the All-Powerful, the Merciful, has no love at all for crows. Except to use as plagues upon the unrighteous. Does anybody know if Master Santaraksita planned to come down here?" My organizational skills had vanished because of my own eagerness to reach the Captured. It occurred to me only now that the scholar's knowledge might prove especially useful here—if he could connect anything in this cave to known myth.

I got no answer. "I'll send for him if I have to. Ah. Sahra, here's your honey. *Don't touch!*" I said that a little too loudly. The echoes got very boisterous. Several small icicles broke loose from the ceiling. They shattered with an almost metallic tinkle when they struck the floor.

The crow spoke, very distinctly, "Come here!"

And I, having finally figured it out, told it, "If your manners don't improve dramatically, you might not get out of here at all."

The bird was strutting back and forth nervously in front of Croaker and Lady. Soulcatcher had left those two snuggled up together, arranged so that the Captain had one arm around Lady's waist while she held his other hand with both of hers in her lap. Additional delicate touches suggested that Soulcatcher's wicked sense of play had peaked for this bit of still life.

If Catcher had left any booby traps at all, this was where they would be. "One-Eye. I need help." Any traps that existed were beyond me.

Lady's eyes were open. There was no dust on them. She was angry. And the white crow wanted to tell me all about it.

"Patience," I counseled, close to becoming impatient myself. "Swan. One-Eye. Come on up here." Swan arrived first despite coming from farther away. I asked, "You recall anything special she did with these two? Any little bit of sneakiness?"

"No. I wouldn't worry about it. By the time she laid them out, she was worried about what might happen next. That's the way she is. When she's starting something, it's her whole world and she has no doubts about any part of it. But the closer she comes to getting finished, the more trouble she has keeping her confidence up."

"Nice to know that she's human." I did not mean a word of that. "One-Eye. Look for booby traps around here. And make up your mind. Tell me if you can bring these people back, darn it!" My headache had not gotten any better. But, thank the God of Mercies, it had grown no worse.

Another icicle fell.

"I know. I know. I heard you the first time you asked." He grumbled something about wishing he knew a way to charm me up a better love life.

I stared past Croaker and Lady. The cavern went on. Pale light barely illuminated it. There was no gold in that at all now. A touch of silver, a touch of grey, a lot of blue ice. In fact, the sedimentary rock seemed to give way to actual ice now, ahead. "Willow. Did Catcher go up there when you were here?"

He checked where I was looking. "No. But she could have during an earlier visit."

Someone had traveled in that direction recently, in cavern scales of time. There were still clear tracks in the frost. And I suspected that I would not enjoy the journey once I began to follow them. But I would do so. I had no choice. I had failed elsewhere by letting Narayan and the Daughter of Night get away. That Kina undoubtedly supplied them with a subtle boost did not sufficiently signify. I should have been better prepared. "One-Eye. Talk to me. Can you resurrect these people or not?"

"If you'd stop barking for five minutes I could probably figure that out."

"Take your time, sweetness. It'll take us a while to starve." That ice up there must have been what Swan had meant when he mentioned ice on the plain.

You've had all the fool-around time I'm willing to give you," I told One-Eye. "Can you do it? Yes or no. Right now."

"The shape I'm in, I need more rest." His speech was slow and slurred and had taken on an odd rhythm that made following him difficult. He was right, of course. *All* of us needed rest. But we also needed to finish our business and get off the plain. Hunger was a reality already. It was not going to go away. I feared it might become a companion as intimate and dreaded as it had been during the siege of Jaicur.

I had decided, already, that I would adopt Uncle Doj's suggested strategy. We would recover only a few people now. We would return for the others later. But that meant making cruel choices. Somebody would end up hating me no matter what I did. If I was really clever, I would find some good old-fashioned Goblinlike way of spreading the blame all around me. Those tagged to wait could not hate everybody.

And there went some good old-fashioned wishful thinking, Sleepy. We were talking about human beings. If there is any way to be contrary, unreasonable and obnoxious, human beings are sure to find and pursue it. With verve and enthusiasm at whatever might be the most inconvenient time.

86

Is anybody at all still up topside?" I demanded. I had settled down for a short nap when the timing had seemed appropriate and that had turned into a long nap that might have become a permanent nap had not so many people been around to keep me from drifting too far away. I dreamed while I was out, I knew that, but I remembered none of it. The smell of Kina remained strong in my nostrils, so I knew where I must have gone, though.

One-Eye was seated beside me, apparently assisting me with my snoring. A worried Goblin appeared, checking to make certain his best friend did not drift too far into sleep. Beyond me, Mother Gota had become engrossed in a protracted debate with the white crow. That must have been a classic dialog to disinterested listeners.

Goblin murmured, "From now on, don't make any sudden movements, Sleepy. Always look around you. Always make sure that you're not going to damage any of our friends."

I heard Tobo talking rapidly, softly, in a businesslike voice. I could not distinguish his words. Somewhere Uncle Doj rattled away, too. "What's happening?"

"We've started waking them up. It's not as complicated as we feared it might be but it takes time and care, and the people we bring out aren't going to be any use to us after they waken—if you had any plans along those lines. One-Eye worked it all out before he collapsed." The little wizard sounded grimmer suddenly.

"Collapsed? One-Eye collapsed? Was it just exhaustion?" I hoped.

"I don't know. I don't want to know. Yet. For now, I'm just going to let him rest. Right down on the edge of the stasis. Or even into it if I think that's necessary. Once his body regains its strength, I'll bring him out and see how bad it really was." He did not sound optimistic.

I said, "If we had to we could leave him here, in stasis, till we could give him proper treatment." Which reminded me. "You're not just getting everyone up, are you? There's no way we can nurse and feed the whole crowd." Surely the Captured would not be able to take care of themselves after fifteen years of just sitting around, stasis or not. They might even be as weak and unskilled as babies and have to learn everything all over again.

"No, Sleepy. We're going to do five people. That's all."

"Uhm. Good. Hey! Where the heck did the standard go? It was right over there. I'm the Standardbearer. I have to keep track—"

"I had it moved over by the gap to the stair. So somebody going that way can take it upstairs. Will you quit fussing? That's Sahra's specialty."

"Speaking of Sahra— Tobo! Where do you think you're going?" While I was talking with Goblin, the boy had slipped past and headed up the cave.

"I was just gonna go see what's up there."

"No. You're just gonna stay right here and help your uncle and Goblin take care of your father, the Captain and the Lieutenant."

He gave me a black look. Despite everything, he still had those moments when he was just a boy. He put on a pouty face that made me grin.

Willow Swan came up behind me. "I've got a problem, Sleepy."

"Which would be?"

"I can't find Cordy. Cordy Mather. Not anywhere."

From the corner of my eye I noted that the Radisha had overheard. She rose slowly from a squat in front of her brother, looked our way. She said nothing nor did anything otherwise that might betray an interest. It was not common knowledge that she and Mather had enjoyed an intimate relationship.

"You're sure?"

"I'm sure."

"You did bring him down here?"

"Absolutely."

I grunted. There was one other absentee whose nonpresence I had been willing to ignore until some rational excuse for her disappearance arose. The shapeshifter Lisa Bowalk, unable to shed the guise of a black panther, had gone up onto the plain as a prisoner but was not now to be found among the dead above or the Captured down below.

Lisa Bowalk had been possessed of a towering hatred for the Company, and particularly for One-Eye because it was One-Eye's fault that she had become trapped in the feline shape. I had to ask. "What about the panther, Willow? It's not around here anywhere, either."

"What panther? Oh. I remember. I don't know." He was looking around like he thought he might spot his old friend Mather hiding behind a stalagmite. "I remember we had to leave her upstairs because we couldn't get her cage around the first turn in the stair. I mean, it would have gone if Catcher and I didn't have anything else to mess with, but we couldn't manage it and the rest of the string both. So Catcher decided to leave the cage up there for later. I don't know what happened when later came. I don't remember much of anything that happened after we came down here. Maybe One-Eye should give me another dose of that memory spell." He tugged on and twisted the ends of his hair, girl-style, and stared down the slope. "I know I left Cordy right down there, just a little above Blade, where it seemed like the floor would be more comfortable."

"Right down there" was the downhill edge of the clot of seven dead men. There had to be a connection. "Goblin, what's the story? Are we going to wake these people up or not?" Me, ignoring everything he had said earlier.

Goblin responded with a sneer that turned into one of his big toad grins. "I've already got Murgen out."

"But I wanted him down here where I could ask questions."

"I mean I've got him out of stasis, bimbo-brain. He's right over there. I'm working on the Captain and Lady now. Tobo and Doj have been doing prelims on Thai Dei and the Prahbrindrah Drah."

Exactly according to my expectations. With the latter two men included entirely for political reasons. Neither was likely to contribute much to the Company's glory or survival.

I moved down to where Murgen lay snoring. The echoing racket and the melting ice webs were the only changes I saw. I squatted. "Anybody think to bring blankets down?" I had not. I am what you would have to call disorganized when it comes to present-tense operations. It had not occurred to me to bring spare clothing or blankets or gear. But I sure can plan bloodshed and general mayhem real well.

There were treasure chambers down here somewhere, though. I had glimpsed several in my dreams. There might be something useful there—if we could find them.

My stomach growled. I was getting hungry. The rumble reminded me that it would not be long before our situation became desperate.

Murgen's eyes opened. He tried to form an expression, a smile for Sahra, but the effort was too much for him. His gaze shifted to me. A whisper struggled through his lips. "The Books. Get . . . the Daughter . . ." His eyes closed again.

It was true. The Captured were not going to jump up and dance tarantellas when they were liberated.

Murgen's message was clear. The Books of the Dead were down here. Something had to be done before the Daughter of Night got another chance to begin copying them. And I had no doubt that she would manage that, despite Soulcatcher. She had Kina backing her up.

"I'll take care of it." I did not have a ghost of a notion how I would manage that, though.

87

The rescue was running smoothly, like a well-greased siege engine missing only a few minor parts. Goblin had Murgen and Croaker headed toward the surface aboard makeshift litters.

Croaker had not said a word, nor had he made any effort to do so, even though he had been awake and aware. He stared at me for a long time. I had no idea what was going on inside his head. I just hoped he was sane.

Before he departed, Murgen did give my hand a small squeeze. I hoped that was an expression of gratitude or encouragement.

I was not at all happy about his being unable to provide information or advice. I had not thought much about what role I would play after the Captured were wakened. I had operated on the unspoken assumption, more or less, that I would retire to my Annals—or even farther, to the Standardbearer job, if Murgen wanted to be Annalist again.

More and more people kept coming downstairs even though I had tried to send word up to warn everyone that they faced a horrible climb going in the other direction.

The white crow continued to curse and jabber semicoherently until it lost its voice. I was concerned about Lady. She had managed that feathery spy quite well for a long time, never giving herself away even when she did try to clue me in, but now she seemed to be losing control. Of herself. I assured her repeatedly that she would go upstairs as soon as I had bearers capable of getting her there. Doj, Sahra and Gota had Thai Dei ready to travel. I gave them the go-ahead. One-Eye would follow him, then Lady would go. The Prahbrindrah Drah would be the last, this time.

Tobo seemed fascinated by his father, apparently because he could not quite believe that the man was real in a fleshy sense. Circumstances had kept his parents separate almost since his conception.

The boy started to tag along after the rest of the family. I called out, "Tobo, stay down here. You have a job to do. See about your dad after we get Lady and the Prince moved out. Hello, Suvrin. Why're you down here?"

"Curiosity. Sri Santaraksita's curiosity. He insisted that he had to see the caverns. He drove me crazy reminding me how storied they are in religious legend. He couldn't be this close to something like that and not explore it personally."

"I see." I noticed the old librarian now. He was working his way up the line of old men, examining each and murmuring to himself. Occasionally he would bounce up and down in excitement. Swan had gone back to make him keep his hands to himself. He wanted to finger and sniff every bit of ancient metal and cloth. He seemed to have trouble understanding that those old men were still alive but very vulnerable.

"Swan. Bring him up here." I did want the benefit of his expertise just a while ago. In a softer voice, I told Suvrin, "You're the one who's going to carry him back upstairs if he can't make it on his own. And I'll be right behind you, giving encouragement by poking you with a spear."

Suvrin seemed to have thought about the climb already. He was not looking forward to it, either. "The man has no concept—"

I interrupted. "What about Shivetya?"

"He's back right side up and safely away from the pit. I can't say he seemed particularly grateful, though."

"He say or do something?"

"No. It was his expression. And that was probably because we dropped him on his nose once. In think I'd have trouble being grateful for a pop in the snoot myself."

Santaraksita was puffing when he joined us. He was excited. "We're walking the actual roads of myth, Dorabee! I have begun begging the Lords of Light to let me live long enough to report my adventures to the bhadrhalok!"

"Who will call you a liar over and over again. Sri, you know the Right People don't become involved in actual adventures. All of you, follow me now. We're going to have another actual adventure traveling into mythology." I headed on up the steepening slope.

I soon discovered that someone had gone this way before me. At first I suspected Tobo had gotten farther than I had thought. Then I decided that the disturbances in the frost were too old for that, so concluded that Soulcatcher must have gone back this way, just to see what she could see.

Back there, small side caves entered the main cavern, few of them large enough to permit passage of an adult body. The main cave dwindled in diameter. We had to hunch down, then we had to crawl. Whoever had gone before us had done the same.

"Do you know what you're doing?" Swan asked. "Do you know where you're going?"

"Of course I do." Leadership tip: Sound confident even when you have no idea. Just do not make a habit of it. They will find you out.

I had been through here in my dreams. But only sort of, evidently, because every few feet I ran into some detail I did not recall from those nightmares. And then we stumbled onto something that was far more than a mere detail.

The sole of a boot nearly smacked me in the face because I was concentrating on trying to decipher the story encrypted in the frost on the cave floor. That was the story of someone who had been moving wildly, maybe in a panic. Not only had the frost been rubbed away, in places the stone itself was bruised or chipped.

"I think I've found Mather, Willow." It was one of those odd moments when you discover the trivial. I noticed that Cordy Mather really needed to have his boots resoled. I did not immediately wonder how a man's leg could stick out like that, with the toe pointing halfway upward above horizontal while the man himself was lying on his stomach. "We'd better stop right here and take a good look. I don't see the man doing this to himself."

Swan said, "I'll get Goblin. Don't do anything till he gets here."

"Don't sweat it. I'm fond of my hide. If I lose it, I'll miss out on our honeymoon." I drew my sword, for what good that might do, then raised up slowly till the top of my head bumped the cavern roof.

Cordy Mather had crawled over a hump in the floor. And something fatal had happened to him before he could get all of himself onto the downward side.

Suvrin eased up beside me. Inexplicably, I found myself painfully aware of him as a masculine presence. Luckily, he was even less interpersonally adept than I was. He failed to notice my flustered and uncomfortable reaction.

Odd. The urge was not something I would pursue, certainly. I just wondered why I sometimes suffered these sudden, random impulses, some of which were extremely difficult to resist. Ninety-nine percent of the time I did not so much as *think* about the possibility of combining myself, a man and a bed in a search for adventure.

Maybe I should not have been teasing Swan.

Suvrin said, "That sure doesn't look very appetizing. What do you think happened?"

"I'm not even going to guess. I'm just going to sit here and wait for the expert to show up."

"May I look?" Santaraksita asked.

Suvrin scooted back. He discovered that the older man was too broad to pass by him there. So we all had to retreat twenty yards so Santaraksita could get past us in turn. I admonished him repeatedly not to go farther forward than I had. "I definitely don't want to have to drag you out of here." Though I will grant that the man was a great deal leaner now than when I had worked for him. "And because you want to get home to tell the bhadrhalok all about this."

"You were right about them, Dorabee. They won't believe a word I say. And not only because they're the Right People but because Surendranath Santaraksita never had an adventure in his life. He never had the urge until this adventure had him."

"Rich men have dreams. Poor men die to make them come true."

"You persist in amazing me, Dorabee. Who are you quoting?"

"V.T.C. Ghosh. He was an acolyte of B.B. Mukerjee, one of the six Bhomparan disciples of Sondhel Ghose the Janaka."

Santaraksita's face lit right up. "Dorabee! You are a marvel indeed. A wonder of wonders. The pupil begins to exceed the master. What was your source? I don't recall ever having read of a Ghosh or a Mukerjee featured in the Janaka school."

I snickered like a prankster kid. "That's because I was pulling your leg. I made it up, Sri." And that seemed to leave him even more amazed.

Goblin broke it up. "Swan says you found a dead man."

"Yes. It looks like Cordy Mather from this end. I didn't see his face, though. I wasn't going to move anything anywhere until we had a good idea what happened to him. I'd rather it didn't happen to me."

Goblin grunted. "Pudgeman, you want to back down here so I can get past you? This tunnel gets pretty tight, don't it? Watch out you don't let your chubby butt plug it up. For how come do you want to go slithering around back here, anyway, Sleepy?"

"Because if I keep going this way far enough I'll get to the place where the Deceivers concealed the original Books of the Dead."

Goblin gave me a funny look but took my word for it. I talked to ghosts in mist machines. Birds talked to me. A talking bird was following me right now, at a distance. At the moment it did not have much to say because its throat was sore but it did manage to rip out a curse or two whenever it had to dodge somebody's flailing feet. "That's interesting."

"I thought so."

"Ah. Yeah. It's not sorcery, though. It's your basic mechanical booby trap. Springloaded. Stabs you with a poisoned pin. There're probably twenty more between here and where you want to go. What do you think Mather was trying to do?"

"If he woke up and found himself down here and didn't know where he was or what had happened to him, he might have panicked and taken off and just went in the wrong direction. I bet it's his fault all those guys back there are dead. He probably tried to wake them up."

Goblin grunted again. "There. That's disarmed. I'd better go ahead and see what else is waiting. But first we need to get Mather pulled back so you all can get past him."

"If you can weasel past him so can I."

"Yeah, you can. But what about your boyfriend and your sugar daddy? They've got a little more pork on them." He grunted and cursed softly as he fought Mather's remains back over the hump in the floor. I noticed, for the first time, that the echoes were different in this more confined space, jammed with bodies. They were almost nonexistent.

88

I do not believe it was miles to where the Deceivers of antiquity concealed their treasures and relics but my body believed that before we got there. Goblin disarmed another dozen traps and found several more that had fallen victim to time. The underground wind whimpered and whined as it rushed past us in the tight places. It sucked the warmth right out of me. But it did not dissuade me. I went where I wanted to go. And was hungry enough to eat a camel when I got there.

It had been a long, long time since breakfast. I had a dread feeling it could be longer still before supper.

"It feels like a temple, doesn't it?" Suvrin asked. He was less troubled than the rest of us. Though raised nearer this place than anyone else, he was less intimate with the legends of the Dark Mother. He stopped staring at the three lecterns and the huge books they bore long enough to turn to me and whisper, "Here." He offered me a bit of crumbling flax cake from the pouch he wore at the small of his back.

"You must have read my mind."

"You talk to yourself a lot. I don't think you realize you're doing it." I did not. It was a bad habit that needed breaking right now. "I heard you when we were crawling through the tunnel."

That had been a private discourse with my God. An internal dialog, I had thought. The subject of food had come up. And here was food. So maybe the All-Merciful was on the job after all.

"Thanks. Goblin. You feel any tricks or traps in here?" There were echoes again, though with a different timbre. We were inside a large chamber. The floor and walls were all ice that had been cut and polished by the flow of frigid water. I presumed the invisible ceiling was the same. The place did have a feel of the holy to it—even though that was the holiness of darkness.

"No traps that I can sense. I'd think they'd leave that sort of stuff outside, don't you?" He sounded like he wanted to convince himself.

"You're asking me to define the psychology of those who worship devils and rakshasas? Vehdna priests would guarantee you that there's nothing so foul or evil as to be beyond the capacity of those most accursed of unbelievers." I thought they would guarantee it. If they had heard of the Stranglers. I had not heard of them before I became attached to the Company.

Suvrin said, "Sri, I don't think you should—"

Master Santaraksita had recognized the ancient books as something remarkable and just could not resist going up for an up-close look. I agreed with Suvrin. "Master! Don't go charging—"

The noise sounded something like someone ripping tent canvas for half a second, then popped like the crack of a whip. Master Santaraksita left the floor of the unholy chapel, folded around his middle, and flew at the rest of us in an arc that admitted only slight acquaintance with gravity. Suvrin tried to catch him. Goblin tried to duck. Santaraksita bounced Suvrin sideways and ricocheted into me. The lot of us ended up in a breathless tangle of arms and legs.

The white crow had something uncomplimentary to say about that.

"You and me and a stew pot, critter," I gasped when I got my breath back. I snagged Goblin's leg. "No more traps, eh? They'd leave that sort of thing out in the caverns, eh? What the devil was *that*, then?"

"That was a magical booby trap, woman. And a damned fine example of its kind, too. It remained undetectable until Santaraksita tripped it."

"Sri? Are you injured?" I asked.

"Only my pride, Dorabee," he puffed. "Only my pride. It'll take me a week to get my wind back, though." He rolled off Suvrin, got onto his hands and knees. He had a definite green look to him.

"You've enjoyed a cheap lesson, then," I told him. "Don't rush into something when you don't know what you're rushing into."

"You'd think I'd know that after this last year, wouldn't you?"

"You might think, yes."

"Don't anybody ask how Junior is doing," Suvrin grumbled. "He couldn't possibly get hurt."

"We knew you'd be fine," Goblin told him. "As long as he landed on your head." The little wizard limped forward. As he neared the point where Santaraksita had gone airborne, he became very cautious. He extended a single finger forward one slow inch at a time.

A smaller piece of cloth ripped. Goblin spun around, his arm flung backward. He staggered a couple of steps before he fell to his knees not far from me.

"After all this time he finally recognizes the natural order of things."

Goblin shook his hand the way you do when you burn your fingers. "Damn, that smarts. That's a *good* spell. It's got real pop. Don't do that!"

Suvrin had decided to throw a chunk of ice.

On its way back, the missile parted Suvrin's hair. It then hit the cavern wall and showered the white crow with fragments of ice. The bird had a word to say about that. It followed up with a few more. I began to wonder if Lady had lost track of the fact that she was not, herself, the white crow, and in fact, was just a passenger making use of the albino's eyes.

Goblin stuck his injured finger in his mouth, squatted down and considered the chamber for a while. I squatted, too, after taking time out to keep Suvrin and Master Santaraksita from making even greater nuisances of themselves.

Swan slithered into the chamber, disturbing the crow. The bird said nothing, though. It just sidled away and looked put out about all existence. Swan settled beside me. "Wow. Kind of impressive even though it's simple."

"Those are the original Books of the Dead. Supposedly almost as old as Kina herself."

"So why is everybody just sitting here?"

"Goblin's trying to figure how to get to them." I told him what had happened.

"Damn. I always miss the best stuff. Hey, Junior! Run up there and show us your flying trick again."

"Master Santaraksita did the flying, Mr. Swan." Suvrin needed to work on his sense of humor. He did not own a proper Black Company attitude.

I asked, "Why not try it yourself, Willow? Take a run at the books."

"You promise to let me land on you?"

"No. But I'll blow you a kiss as you fly by."

"It'd probably help if you people would shut up," Goblin said. He rose. "But by being blindingly, blisteringly brilliant I've worked it out anyway, already, in spite of you all. We get to the lecterns by using the golden pickax as a passkey. *That* was why Narayan Singh was so upset when he saw what we had."

"Tobo still has the pick," I said. A minute later I said, "Don't everybody stumble all over each other offering to go get him."

"Let's just go together and all be equally miserable," Goblin suggested. "That's what the Black Company is all about. Sharing the good times along with the bad."

"You trying to con me into thinking that this is one of the good times?" I asked, crawling into the cave right behind him.

"Nobody wants to kill us today. Nobody's trying. That sounds like a good time to me."

He had a point. A definite point.

Maybe my Company attitude needed attention, too.

Behind me, Suvrin grumbled about starting to feel like a gopher. I glanced back. Swan had had an attack of good sense and decided to bring up the rear, thereby making sure that Master Santaraksita did not stay behind and tinker with things that might cause a change in Goblin's opinion about this being one of the good times.

W here did he go?" I mused aloud. People were still working in the cave of the ancients, getting Lady and the Prahbrindrah Drah ready to go upstairs. But

Tobo was not among them. "He wouldn't just run upstairs, would he?" He had the energy of youth but nobody was so energetic they would just charge into that climb on impulse.

While I tromped around muttering and looking for the kid, Goblin did the obvious and questioned witnesses. He got an answer before I finished building up a good mad. "Sleepy. He left."

"Surprise, surprise . . . what?" That was not all of it. The little wizard was upset. "He turned right when he left, Sleepy."

"He . . . oh." Now I did have a good mad worked up. A booming, head-throbbing, want-to-make-somebody-pay, real bad mad. "That idiot! That moron! That darned fool! I'll cut his legs off! Let's see if we can catch him."

Right was downward. Right was deeper into the earth and time, deeper into despair and darkness. Right could only be the road to the resting place of the Mother of Night.

As I started out, with intent to turn right, I collected the standard. The white crow shrieked approval. Goblin sneered, "You're going to be sorry before you go down a hundred steps, Sleepy."

I was tempted to abandon the darned thing before we had gone that far. It was too long to be dragging around in a stairwell.

89

T his stair has no bottom," I told Goblin. We were puffing badly despite the direction we were headed. We had passed openings into other caves the stairwell had pierced. Each appeared to have been visited by human beings sometime in the past. We discovered both treasures and boneyards. I suspected Sri Santaraksita, Baladitya and I could not live long enough just to catalog all the mysteries buried beneath the plain. And every darned unknown ancient thing I glimpsed in passing called to me like the sirens of legend.

But Tobo was still ahead of us and seemed deaf to our calling. Perhaps just as we did not waste time and breath responding to Suvrin and Santaraksita, who kept calling down to us from ever farther behind. It was my devout hope they would be smitten by good sense and abandon the pursuit.

Goblin did not respond to my remarks. He had no breath left over.

I asked, "Can't you use some kind of spell to slow him down or knock him out? I'm worried. He really can't be so far ahead that he can't hear us. Darn!" I had gotten tangled with the standard. Again.

Goblin just shook his head and kept moving. "He can't hear." Puff-puff. "But he don't know that he can't hear."

Enough said. There *was* a bottom to the stair. And the Queen of Deceit was napping down there, with just a whisper of awareness left for manipulating a cocky, know-it-all boy who had a touch of talent and had taken possession of an instrument that could become a nasty weapon in the hands of those who would disarm her and have her slumber continue never-ending.

After a while we had to slow down. The unnatural light faded until it became too weak to provide a reliable forecast of our footing. The occasional breezes rising past us were no longer cold. And they had begun to bear traces of a familiar, repugnant odor.

When Goblin caught that smell he slowed way down, worked hard on regaining his breath before he had to suck that stench down in its full potency. "Been a while since I've come face-to-face with a god," he said. "I don't know if I've got what it takes to wrangle one anymore."

"And what would that be? I never realized that I was in the company of an experienced god-wrangler."

"It takes youth. It takes confidence. It takes brashness. Most of all, it takes a huge ration of stupidity and a lot of luck."

"Then why don't we just sit down here and let those sterling qualities carry Tobo through? Though I confess I'm a little nervous about his supply of luck."

"I'm tempted, Sleepy. Sorely and sincerely. He needs the lesson." Troubled, perhaps even a little frightened, he continued, "But he's got the pickax and the Company needs him. He's the future. Me and One-Eye are today and yesterday." He started picking up the pace again, which meant a rapid heightening of the intensity of my skirmish with the standard.

"What do you mean, he's the future?"

"Nobody lives forever, Sleepy."

The burst of speed did not last. We encountered a mist that complicated the hazards of darkness. The visibility turned nil and the footing became particularly treacherous for a short person trying to drag a long pole down a tight and unpredictable stairway. The moist air was heavier than anything I had experienced since the fogs above the corpse-choked flood that had surrounded Jaicur during the siege.

A chilling shriek came from far back up the stair. My mind flooded with images of horrors pouncing gleefully upon Suvrin and Master Santaraksita.

The shriek continued, approaching faster than any human being could possibly descend that stairway. "What the hell is that?" Goblin snapped.

"I don't—" The shrieking stopped. At the same time, I stepped down and there was no more down to step. I staggered, betrayed by the darkness. The Lance banged into overhead and wall. We had reached another landing, I assumed, until I felt around with my toes and the standard and could find no more edge. "What do you have over there?" I asked.

"Steps behind me. A wall to the right that goes forward about six feet, then ends. All level floor."

"I've got a wall on the left that just keeps going on and a level floor. Gah!" Something slammed into my back. I had only an instant of warning, the sound of wings violently flapping as a large bird tried to stop before it hit.

The white crow cursed as it landed on the floor. It flopped around for a moment, then started climbing me. That would have been a sight, I am sure, had there been any light to reveal it.

I fought down an impulse to bat the creature into the darkness. I hoped it was here to help. "Tobo!"

My voice rolled away into the distance, then came back in a series of echoes. The heavy air seemed to load those up with despair.

The boy did not answer but he did move. Or something moved. I heard a rustle from less than twenty feet away.

"Goblin. Talk to me about this."

"We've been blinded. By sorcery. There's light out there. I'm working on getting our sight back. Give me your hand. Let's stick together."

The crow murmured, "Sister, sister. Walk straight ahead. Look bold. You will pass through the darkness." Its diction had improved dramatically over the past year. Maybe that was because we were so much closer to the force manipulating the bird.

I felt around for Goblin, grabbed hold, pulled, dropped the standard, picked it up and pulled again. "All right. I'm ready."

That crow knew what it was talking about. After a half dozen steps we transited into a lighted ice cavern. Make that comparatively lighted. Dim, grey-blue light leaked in through translucent walls as though it was high noon just on the other side of a few feet of ice. Much more light radiated from the vicinity of the woman asleep on a bier at the center of the vast chamber, some seventy feet away. Tobo stood halfway between us and it, looking backward, completely surprised to see us there and equally baffled as to where there might be.

"Don't you move, boy," Goblin snapped. "Don't you even take a deep breath until I tell you it's safe to do so."

The form on the bier was a little fuzzy, as though surrounded by heat shimmer. And in spite of that, I *knew* the woman lying there was the most beautiful creature in the world. I knew that I loved her more than life itself, that I wanted to rush over there and drink deeply of those perfect lips.

The white crow sneezed in my ear.

That certainly took the edge off the mood.

"Where have we seen all this before?" Goblin asked, voice dripping sarcasm. "She must be awfully weak or she'd pluck something better from our minds than a replay of an old Sleeping Beauty fairy tale. There isn't a castle built like this anywhere south of the Sea of Torments."

"A castle? What? What castle?" The word for castle did not exist in Taglian or Jaicuri. I knew it meant a kind of fortress only because I had spent so much time exploring the Annals.

"We seem to be inside the keep of an abandoned castle. There're dormant rose creepers all over the place. There're tons of cobwebs. In the middle of everything is a beautiful blonde woman lying in an open casket. She just begs to be kissed and brought back to life. The part that always gets ignored, and that our ungracious hostess has overlooked here, is that the bitch in the story almost certainly was a vampire."

"That isn't what I see." Carefully, detail by detail, I described the ice cave and the absolutely not blonde woman I saw lying upon a bier at its center. While I spoke, Goblin finally worked some subtle spell on Tobo that kept him too confused to move.

Goblin asked, "Do you remember your mother, Sleepy?"

"I vaguely recall a woman who might have been. She died when I was little. Nobody talked about her." We did not need to go into this. We had work to do right here, right now. I hoped he got that message from my tone and expression.

"What do you want to bet that what you're seeing is an idealized vision of your mother charged up with a whole lot of sexual come-hither."

I did not argue. That might be. He knew the artifices of darkness. I did keep moving forward slowly, closing in on Tobo.

"Which would mean that up close and quickly, she doesn't have a real good connection with what's outside her." Two decades ago it had become clear that Kina did not think or work well in real time, that she did best when she applied her influence over years rather than minutes. "I'm too old to be snared by temptations of the flesh and you're too unsexed and undefined." He grinned weakly. "The kid, on the other hand, is at that age. I'd give a toe or two to see what he sees. Ruff!" He gestured. Tobo collapsed like a wet sock. "Grab the hammer. Hang onto it hard. Don't get any closer to her than you absolutely have to. Drag Tobo back to the doorway." He sounded old and hollow and possessed by a despair that he did not want to share.

"What's going on, Goblin? Talk to me." This was a situation where we ought not to keep dangers to ourselves.

"We're face-to-face with the great manipulator who's been disfiguring our lives for twenty-five years. She's very slow but she's far more dangerous than anything we've faced before."

"I know that." But my reaction was elation. My spirits soared. All my hidden doubts, kept so carefully submerged for so long, now seemed trivial, even silly. This lovely creature was no god. Not like my God is God. Forgive me my weakness and my doubts, O Lord of Hosts. The Darkness is everywhere, and dwells within us all. Forgive me now, when the hour of my death stares me in the face.

In Forgiveness He is Like the Earth.

I grabbed hold of Tobo's arm and yanked him upright. I clutched him as tightly as I gripped the standard. He would not break away easily. Disoriented, he did not struggle when I pulled him back from the sleeping form.

I averted my eyes. She was beauty incarnate. To gaze upon her was to love her. To love her was to dedicate oneself to her will, to lose oneself within her. O Lord of the Hours, watch over and guard me in the presence of the spawn of *al-Shiel*.

"I need the pickax, Tobo." I tried not to think about why I wanted that unholy tool. At this distance Kina might be able to pluck that right out of my mind.

Moving slowly, Tobo removed the pick from under his shirt and handed it over. "Got it!" I told Goblin.

"Then get going!"

As I started to do that, Suvrin and Santaraksita, gasping violently, stumbled into the light. Both froze, staring at Kina. In soft awe, Suvrin declared, "Holy shit! She's gorgeous!"

Master Santaraksita seemed to be experiencing some confusion as he stared.

Suvrin started forward, drooling. I popped him in the funny bone with the dull end of the pick head. That not only got his attention, it relaxed his overwhelming interest in Kina. "Mother of Deceivers," I told him. "Mistress of Illusion. Turn around. Get the boy out of here. Take him back to his mother. Sri, don't make me hurt you, too."

Something like a bit of mist rose from and hovered over the sleeping woman's mouth. For an instant it seemed vaguely man-shaped, which reminded me of *afrits*, the unhappy ghosts of murdered men. Millions of such devils could be at Kina's beck.

"Run, goddamnit!" Goblin said.

"Run," the crow told me.

I did not run. I got hold of Santaraksita and started pulling.

Goblin was talking to himself, something about wishing he had had the good sense to steal One-Eye's spear if he was going to get himself into something like this.

"Goblin!" I heaved the standard. It was not my intent that it do so, but it stood straight up and bounced a couple of times on its butt before it tipped forward and fell into the little wizard's eager hands. He turned with it as the illusions surrounding Kina evaporated.

90

If Kina was ever human, if any of the countless forms of myth regarding her creation indeed resembled fact, a lot of work had gone into making her big and ugly.

She is the Mother of Deceivers, Sleepy. The Mother of Deceivers. That great
hideous form covered with pustules from which infant skulls suppurated could no
more be the true aspect of Kina than the sleeping beauties had been.

The stench of old death became powerful.

I stared at the body, now lying upon the icy floor. It was the dark purple-black
of the death-dancer of my dreams but it dwarfed Shivetya. It was naked. Its perfect
female proportions distracted from the ten thousand scars that marred its skin. It
did not move, not even to breathe.

Another feather of vapor rose from one huge nostril.

"Get the fuck out of here!" Goblin shrieked. He jerked to the right suddenly, the
Lance of Passion darting toward some target I could not see. The Lance's head
burned like it was covered by flickering alcohol flames.

A huge, unheard scream tore at my mind. Suvrin and Master Santaraksita
moaned. Tobo squealed. The white crow unleashed a random stream of obsceni-
ties. I am sure I contributed to the chorus. As I kicked and punched the others to
get them going, I realized that my throat was raw.

Goblin whirled back to his left, thrusting at the wisp of mist that had left Kina's
nostril a moment before.

Once again pale blue fire surrounded the head of the Lance. This time it ran a
foot up the shaft before it faded. This time the Lance's head betrayed penstrokes of
dark ruby glow along its edges.

Another wisp of the essence of Kina rose from her nose.

There was no darkness or mist hiding the entrance now. Kina's focus was elsewhere. Suvrin and Santaraksita were on the stair already, wasting breath babbling
about what they had seen. I slugged Tobo upside the head with all the force I could
muster. "Get out of here!"

When he opened his mouth to argue, I popped him again. I did not want to
hear it. I did not want to hear anything. Not even a divine revelation. It could wait.
"Goblin! Get your sorry butt in motion. We're out of the way."

The third wisp impaled itself upon the Lance's head. This time the fire crept two yards up the shaft, though it did not seem to affect the wood directly. However, this time the Lance's head became so hot that shaft wood in contact with it began to smolder.

Goblin started to back down but another wisp rose and drifted faster than he moved, getting between him and the stair. He thrust at it a few times but each time he did, it drifted out of reach. It continued to control his path of retreat.

I am no sorceress. Despite a life spent in the proximity of wizards and witch women and whatnot, I have no idea how their minds work when they are involved with their craft. So I will never be clear on what thought process led Goblin to make his decision. But from having known the man most of my life, I have to conclude that he did what he did because he believed it was the most effective thing that he could do.

Having failed to skewer the wisp, having noted that a second had appeared and had begun to circle him from the opposite direction, the frog-faced little man just whirled, lowered the head of the Lance and charged Kina. He let out a great mad bellow and drove the weapon through the flesh of an arm and into her ribs below her right breast. And just before the weapon struck home, one wisp flung itself in front, trying to block the thrust. The Lance's head was ablaze when it pierced demonic flesh.

The second wisp set Goblin aflame.

Even screaming, telling me to get out, Goblin continued to heave against the Lance, driving it deeper into Kina, possibly in some mad, wild hope of penetrating her black heart.

The blue flame feasted on Goblin's flesh. He let go of the Lance, threw himself to the icy floor, rolled around violently, slapping at himself. Nothing helped. He began to melt like an overheated candle.

He screamed and screamed.

On that psychic level where I had sensed her moments earlier, Kina also screamed and screamed and screamed. Suvrin and Santaraksita screamed. Tobo screamed. I screamed and staggered into the stairwell, retreating despite the urging of that mad part of me that wanted to go back and help Goblin. And there could have been no greater madness than that. The Destroyer ruled the cavern of her imprisonment.

Goblin had struck a fierce blow but in truth, its impact was no greater than the nip of a wolf cub at the ear of a dozing tiger. I knew that. And I knew that the cub, caught, was trying to buy time for the rest of its pack.

I gasped, "Tobo, go ahead as fast as you can. Tell the others." He was younger, he was faster, he could get there long before I could.

He was the future.

I would try to keep anything from coming up the stair behind him.

The screaming continued down below, from both sources. Goblin was being more stubborn than ever he had been with One-Eye.

We climbed as fast as Master Santaraksita could manage. I stayed behind the other two, already ready to turn and put the unholy pickax between us and any pursuit. I was convinced that the power of that talisman would shield us.

Darkness no longer inhabited the stair. Visibility was much better than it had been when we came down. So good, in fact, that had there been no landings to break up the line of sight, we would have been able to look up the stairs for a mile.

I was gasping for breath and fighting leg cramps before the screaming stopped. Suvrin had collapsed once already, losing what little his stomach contained. Master Santaraksita seemed the hardiest of us now, without a complaint to his name, though he was so pale I feared his heart would betray him before long.

As we fought for breath I stared downward, listening to the ominous silence. "God is Great." Gasp. "There is no God but God." Gasp. "In Mercy He is Like the Earth." Gasp. "He Walks with Us in All Our Hours." Gasp. "O Lord of Creation, I Acknowledge that I am Your Child."

Master Santaraksita had enough spare breath to chide, "He's going to get bored and find something else to do if you don't get to the point, Dorabee."

"How's this?" Gasp. "Help!"

"Better. Much better. Suvrin! Get up."

The white crow arrowed up the stairwell, nearly bowled me over landing on my shoulder. I did make the process more difficult by trying to duck the arriving bird. It lashed my face with flapping wings. "Climb," it said. "Slowly, without panic. Steadily. I will watch behind you."

We climbed for five or ten days. Hunger nagged me. Terror and lack of sleep made me see things that were not there. I did not look back for fear of seeing something terrible closing in. We moved slower and slower as the effort devoured our energies and will, and our capacity for recovery. It became a major trek and an act of ultimate will to climb from one landing to the next. Then we began resting between landings, though neither Suvrin nor Santaraksita ever suggested it.

The crow told me, "Stop and sleep."

No one argued. There are limits to how far and hard terror can drive anyone. We found ours. I collapsed so fast I later claimed I heard my first snore before I hit the stone of the landing. I was only vaguely aware of the crow launching itself into the darkness, headed downward again.

91

S leepy?"

My soul wanted to leap up and flail around in terror. My flesh was incapable and quite possibly indifferent. I was so stiff and I hurt so much that I just could not move.

My mind still worked fine. It ran as sparkling swift as a mountain stream. "Huh?" I continued trying to get the muscles unlocked.

"Easy. It's Willow. Just open your eyes. You're safe."

"What're you doing way down here?"

"Way down where?"

"Uh—"

"You're one landing downstairs from the cave of the ancients."

I kept trying to get up. Muscle by muscle my body gradually yielded to my will. I looked around, vision foggy. Suvrin and Master Santaraksita were still asleep.

Swan said, "They were tired, guaranteed. I heard you snoring all the way up in the cave."

Twinge of fear. "Where's Tobo?"

"He went on up top. Everyone went. I made them go. I stayed in case. . . . The crow told me not to come down. But what's one landing? You think you can get moving again? I can't carry anybody. I can barely keep going myself."

"I can manage one flight. Up to the cave. That's far enough for now."

"The cave?"

"I still have something to do there."

"Are you sure you want to go out of your way?"

"I'm sure, Willow." I could tell it was a matter of life or death. For a whole world. Or maybe for multiple worlds. But why be melodramatic? "Can you get these two moving again? And headed toward the top?" I did not think Master Santaraksita could bear seeing what I intended to do next.

"I'll get them moving. But I'm sticking with you."

"That won't be necessary."

"Yes, it will. You can hardly stand up."

"I'll work it out."

"You go right ahead and talk. It'll get the kinks out of your jaw. But I'm staying."

I stared at him hard for some time. He did not back down. Neither did he betray any motive but concern for a brother he suspected of failing to be in her right mind. I closed my eyes for half a minute, then opened them to peer down the stairs. "God was listening."

Swan was working on Suvrin. The Shadowlander officer had his eyes open but seemed unable to move. He murmured, "I must be alive. Otherwise I wouldn't hurt so much." Panic flooded his eyes. "*Did* we get away?"

I said, "We're getting away. We've still got a long way to climb."

"Goblin's dead," Swan said. "The crow told me when it came up to get something to eat."

"Where is that thing?"

"Down there. Watching."

I felt a chill. Paranoia touched me. There had been a connection between Lady and Kina ever since Narayan Singh and Kina had used Lady as a vessel to produce the Daughter of Night. That had created a connection, a connection Lady had hammered into place cleverly, unbreakably, so that she could steal power from the goddess indefinitely. "Forgive me, O Lord. Drive these infidel thoughts from my heart."

Swan said, "Huh?"

"Nothing, part of the ongoing dialog between me and my God. Suvrin! Sweety. You ready to do some jumping jacks?"

Suvrin offered me an old-fashioned, storm-cloud glower. "Smack her, Swan. At a time like this, cheerful ought to be against the laws of heaven and earth."

"You'll be cheerful in a minute, too. As soon as you figure out that you're still alive."

"Humph!" He began to help Swan waken Master Santaraksita.

Upright now, I did a few small exercises to loosen up even more.

"Ah, Dorabee," Santaraksita said softly. "I have survived another adventure with you."

"I've got God on my side."

"Excellent. Do keep him there. I don't think I can survive another of your adventures without divine assistance."

"You'll outlive me, Sri."

"Perhaps. Probably, if I do get out of this and I don't tempt fate ever again. You, you'll probably graduate to snake-dancing with cobras."

"Sri?"

"I've decided. I don't want to be an adventurer anymore, Dorabee. I'm too old for it. It's time to wrap myself up in a cozy library again. This just hurts too much. Ow! Young man—"

Swan grinned. He was not that much younger than the librarian. "Let's get going, old-timer. You keep lying around here and whatever adventure you found down there is going to catch up and have you all over again."

A possibility that posed a fine motivation for us all.

When we finally got moving again, I brought up the rear. Swan wrangled my companions. I gripped the golden pickax so tightly my knuckles ached.

Goblin was dead.

That did not seem possible.

Goblin was a fixture. A permanent fixture. A cornerstone. Without its Goblin, there could be no Black Company. . . . You are mad, Sleepy. The family will not cease to exist simply because one member, unexpectedly, has been plucked out by evil fortune. Life would not end because of Goblin's absence. It would just get a lot harder. I seemed to hear Goblin whisper, "He is the future."

"Sleepy. Snap out of it."

"Huh?"

Swan said, "We're at the cave. You two. Keep climbing. We'll catch up with you."

Suvrin started to ask. I shook my head, pointed upward. "Go. Now. And don't look back." I waited until I saw Suvrin actually guide Master Santaraksita over the tumbled stones and onto the stairs. "We'll catch up."

"What's that?" Swan asked. He cupped an ear.

"I don't hear anything."

He shrugged. "It's gone now. Something from upstairs."

We entered the cavern of the ancients. The wonder had been polished off it by the trampling about of a horde of Company people. I was amazed that they had managed without damaging any more of the sleepers. As it was, almost all the wondrous ice webbing and cocooning had broken up and collapsed. A few stalactites had fallen from the ceiling. "How did that happen?"

Swan frowned. "During the earthquake."

"Earthquake? What earthquake?"

"You didn't . . . there was one hell of a shake. I can't say exactly how long ago. Probably when you were all the way down. It's hard to tell time in here."

"No lie. Oh, yuck." I had discovered why the white crow had all that energy. It had been dining on one of my dead brothers.

Some evil part of me tossed up the thought that I could follow the bird's example. Another part wondered what would happen if Croaker found out. That man was obsessed with the holy state of Company brotherhood.

"You never know what you'll do until you're in the ring with the bull, do you?"

"What?"

"A proverb from back home. Means that actually facing the reality is never quite like preparing to face the reality. You never really know what you'll do until you get there."

I passed the rest of the Captured, not meeting any open eyes. I wondered if they could hear. I offered up some reassurances that sounded feeble even to me. The cavern shrank. When it came time to get down and crawl, I crawled. I told Swan, "Maybe it's good, you being here after all. I'm starting to have little dizzy spells."

"You hear anything?"

I listened. This time I did hear something. "Sounds like somebody singing. A marching song? Something full of 'yo-ho-ho's.' " What the devil?

"Down here? We have dwarfs, too?"

"Dwarfs?"

"Mythical creatures. Like short people with big beards and permanent bad tempers. They lived underground, like nagas, only supposedly big on mining and metalworking. If they ever did exist, they died out a long time ago."

The singing was getting louder. "Let's get this handled before somebody interrupts."

92

The pessimist in me was sure I would not be able to pull it off. If nothing else, the earthquake Swan mentioned would in some way have sealed the chamber of unholy books off from the rest of the world. If the chamber was not sealed off, then I would trip the only booby trap that Goblin had overlooked. If Goblin had not overlooked any booby traps, then the pickax would not be a protective key, it would be a trigger igniting the thousand secret sorceries protecting the books.

"Sleepy, do you know you talk to yourself when you're worried about stuff?"

"What?"

"You're crawling along there muttering about all the bad things that're going to happen. You keep on and you're going to convince me."

That was twice. I had to get that under control. I did not use to do that.

The place where the Books of the Dead were hidden had not changed visibly. The pessimist in me worked hard to find a dangerous difference, though.

Swan finally asked, "Are you going to study on it till we pass out from hunger? Or are you going to go ahead and do something?"

"I always was a better planner than a doer, Willow." I sucked in a peck of frigid air, took the pickax out of my waistband, intoned, "O Lord of Heaven and Earth, let there be no password that has to go with this."

"Right behind you, boss," Swan said, making a joke as he nudged me forward. "Don't be shy now."

Of course not. That would belittle Goblin's sacrifice and memory.

I realized that my breathing had turned to rapid, shallow panting as I reached the point where Master Santaraksita had achieved flight. I held the pick in front of me with both hands, muscles protesting its weight, squeezing it so tight I feared I would leave my fingerprints etched upon it permanently.

A tingling began in my hands. It crept up my arms as I eased forward. My skin crawled and I developed severe goose bumps. I said, "You'd better hold onto me, Willow." In case I needed yanking back. "In case you need the connection to the pick." The shield was not rejecting me. Not yet.

Swan rested his hands on my shoulders an instant before the tingling reached my body. I began to shiver. Suddenly I had the chills and shakes of an autumn sickness.

"Woo!" Swan said. "This feels weird."

"It gets weirder," I promised. "I've got one of those agues where the chill goes all the way to the marrow."

"Uh . . . yeah. I'm getting there, too. Toss in some joint aches, too. Come on. Let's get that fire started and warm ourselves."

Would fire be enough?

Once we moved forward another ten feet, the miseries stopped getting worse. The tingling on the outside faded. I told Swan, "I think it's safe to let go now."

"You should have seen your hair. It started dancing around when we were halfway through. It lasted only a couple of steps but it was a sight."

"I'll bet." My hair was a sight anyway, usually. I did not offer it nearly enough attention and I had not had it trimmed in months. "Got anything to start a fire with?"

"You don't? You didn't prepare for this? You knew it had to be done and you didn't bring—"

"All right, we'll use mine. I just don't have much tinder left. Didn't want to use mine up when I could use yours."

"Thanks a lot. You're getting as bad as those two nasty old men." Chagrined, he recalled that one of the nasty old men he meant had just completed his tenure with the Company.

"I learned from the best. Listen. I've been thinking about this. Even if we are past all the traps, the books themselves might be dangerous. Considering the way the brains of wizards work, it's probably not a smart thing to peek inside at the pages. One look at the writings and you're likely to spend the rest of your life standing there reading—even if you don't recognize a word—out loud. I recall reading about a spell that worked that way, once."

"So what do we do?"

"You notice that all three books are open? We'll have to come at them from underneath and tip the covers shut. So that they end up face-down. Even then we might want to handle them with our eyes shut when we go burn them. I've read about grimoires that had rakshasas bound into their covers." Although nothing as exciting as that ever turned up in the library where I had worked.

"A talking book that can read itself to me. That's what I need."

"I thought Soulcatcher made you learn how to read when you were the king of the Greys."

"She did. That don't mean I *want* to read. Reading is bloody hard work."

"I thought managing a brewery was hard work. You never shied away from that." Being shorter, I took the job of sneaking up on the three lecterns. I used extreme caution. They might have been great actors but I was soon convinced that they could not see me coming.

"I like making beer. I don't like reading."

He should have been the one getting ready to burn books, then. I was suffering a crisis of conscience as troublesome as any of my crises of faith. I loved books. I believed in books. As a rule I did not believe in destroying books because their contents were disagreeable. But these books contained the dark, secret patterns for bringing on the end of the world. The end of many worlds, actually, for if the Year of the Skulls successfully sacrificed my world, others connected to the glittering plain must follow.

This was not a crisis that needed immediate resolution. I had my answers worked out already, which was why I was on hands and knees under the lecterns while suffering verbal abuse from an infidel who had no use for my god *or* for the Deceivers' merciless Destroyer. I tipped the covers of the books shut while wondering if there was still some way the Children of Night could get to me.

"The covers appear to be blank," Swan said.

"You're looking at the backs of the books. I'm closing them so they're face-down. Remember?"

"Hold it." He held up a finger, cocked an ear.

"Echoes."

"Uhm. Somebody's out there."

I listened harder. "Singing again. I wish they wouldn't sing. Nobody in the band but Sahra can carry a tune in a bucket with a lid on it. You can come on up here now. I think it's safe."

"You *think*?"

"I'm still alive."

"I don't know if that's necessarily a recommendation. You're too sour and bitter for the monsters to eat. I, on the other hand—"

"You, on the other hand, are plain lucky that my god forbids me to reveal that the only thing interested in eating you would be the kind of beetle that flourishes on a diet of livestock by-product. Right there looks like a good place to start a fire."

Swan was up beside me now. "There" was some kind of large brazier-looking thing that still had a few charcoal remnants in it. It was made of hammered brass in a style common to most of the cultures of this end of the world.

"You want me to tear a few pages out for tinder?"

"No, I don't want you to tear pages out. Weren't you listening when I told you the books might make you want to read them?"

"I was listening. Sometimes I don't hear very well, though."

"Like most of the human race." I *was* prepared. In minutes I had a small fire burning. I lifted one of the books carefully, making sure it faced away from Swan and me. I fanned its pages out slightly and set it down in the flames, spine upward. I burned the last volume first. Just in case.

Something might interfere. I wanted the first volume destroyed to be one the Daughter of Night had not yet seen. The first book, which she had copied parts of several times and might have partially memorized, I would burn last.

The book caught fire eventually but did not burn well. It produced a nasty-smelling dark smoke that filled the cavern and forced Swan and me to get down on our stomachs on the icy floor.

The underground wind did carry some of the smoke away. The rest was no longer overwhelming when I consigned the second book to the flames.

While waiting to add the final book to the fire, I brooded about why Kina was doing nothing to resist this blow to her hopes for resurrection. I could only pray that Goblin's sacrifice had hurt her so badly she could not look outside herself yet. I could only pray that I was not a victim of some grand deceit. Maybe these books were decoys. Maybe I was doing exactly what Kina had planned for me to do.

There were doubts. Always.

"You're muttering to yourself again."

"Uhn." I possessed not so much as the faintest hope that Goblin's death had put Kina out of the misery of the world permanently.

"This feels so nice," I said. "I could go to sleep right here." And I did so, promptly.

Good old Willow's sense of duty, or self-preservation, or something, kept him going. He got the last Book of the Dead into the fire for me before he, too, settled down for a nap.

93

The singing soldiers proved to be Runmust, Iqbal and Riverwalker. They had come to rescue the rest of us when Tobo reached them with news of the disaster that had befallen us down below. They had found us by following the smoke. "At the risk of finding myself goaded into employing unseemly language, how is it that I find *anyone* singing? How is it that you haven't taken the road to The Land of the Unknown Shadows? I believe I was pretty insistent on the necessity for that."

Runmust and Iqbal giggled like they were younger than Tobo and knew a dirty joke. Riverwalker managed to maintain a more sober demeanor. Barely. "You're tired and hungry, so we don't blame you for being cranky, Sleepy. Let's do something about that. Settle down and have a snack." He could not restrain a big, goofy grin as he rummaged in his pack.

I exchanged glances with Swan. I asked, "You have any clue what's going on here?"

"Maybe there's a stage of starvation where you get lightheaded and silly."

"I suppose Jaicur could have been an exception."

Riverwalker produced something the shape and color of a puffball mushroom but a good eight inches in diameter. It looked heavier than a mushroom that size ought to be.

"What the hell is that?" Swan asked. River had several more in his pack. And his henchmen had brought packs, too.

Riverwalker produced a knife and began slicing. "A gift from our demon friend, Shivetya. Evidently after a day of reflection he decided we deserved a payoff for saving his big ugly ass. Eat." He offered me an end slice an inch thick. "You'll like it."

Swan started eating before I did. I had an ounce of paranoia left. He leaned my way. "Tastes like pork. Heh-heh-heh." Then he had no time for joking. He began wolfing the material, which looked exactly the same all the way through.

It had a heavy, almost cheesy texture. When I surrendered to the inevitable and bit into it, my salivary system responded with a flood. The experience of taste was so sharp it was almost painful. There was nothing comparable in my memory. A touch of ginger, a touch of cinnamon, lemons, sweetness, the scent of candied violets. . . . After the first shock a sense of well-being gradually spread outward from my mouth, and again from my stomach soon after the first mouthfuls hit bottom.

"More," Swan said.

Riverwalker surrendered another slice.

"More," I agreed, and bit into another slice myself. It might be poison but if it was, it was the sweetest poison God ever permitted. "Shivetya really gave you this?"

"About a ton. Almost literally. Fit for man and beast. Even the baby likes it."

Iqbal and Runmust found that news hilarious. Swan snickered, too, though he could not possibly have any idea what the joke might be. In fact, I found that assertion rather amusing myself. Heck, everything was amusing. I had begun to feel relaxed and confident. My aches and pains no longer formed the center of my consciousness. They had become mere annoyances way out on the edge of awareness.

"Continue."

Iqbal squealed, "He grew them. These nasty lumps developed all over him, like big-ass boils, only when they popped, out came these things."

Under more normal circumstances that idea and the images it engendered would have seemed repulsive. I grunted, took another wonderful mouthful, pictured the creation process, caught myself in the midst of a fit of giggles. I regained control, though that took an effort. "So it finally decided to communicate?"

"Sort of. When we left, it was trying to manage some kind of dialog with Doj. It didn't seem to be working all that well, though."

Swan sighed. "I haven't felt this relaxed and positive since Cordy and I used to go fishing when we were kids. This's the way we felt lying beside the creek in the shade, never really caring if we got a bite while we shared our daydreams or just watched clouds scoot overhead."

Even the recollection of his friend's fate did not break his mood entirely.

I understood what he was trying to communicate even though I had had no special friend with whom to share the rare, golden moments of childhood. I had had no childhood. I felt really good myself. I said, "This whatever-it-is is great stuff. River. You seen any side effects yet?"

"It's damned near impossible to stop yourself if you get the giggles."

"I'll try not to get started. Wow! I feel like I could whip twice my weight in wolves right now. Why don't we get going?"

Nobody took the opportunity to mention that me whipping twice my weight in wolves might entail me fighting only the back half of one of the monsters. Iqbal and Runmust continued to giggle over some shared joke of long ago.

"Boys," I said, pointing. "That way. Don't touch anything. Keep going. We're going to go back upstairs."

Dang me, I kept getting silly ideas. And every one of them made me want to start laughing. Riverwalker told me, "We found out that if we sing it helps us keep our minds on business." A big grin spread across his face. He began humming one of the filthier marching songs. It concerned the business that seems to be on the minds of most men most of the time.

I hummed along and got everybody started moving.

Foul-smelling smoke from roasted books filled the cavern. It seemed even stronger in the stairwell. Some of it drifted downward.

Kina was not yet aware, I was sure. She would have done *something* if she had known. But she would not remain ignorant forever.

I hoped we could get ourselves well on the road before she recovered enough to assimulate the truth. Her dreams were deadly enough.

I settled my behind onto the rise in the floor near the entrance to the stairwell. I sat there dully wondering why the excavation had been started way out here on the periphery. I did not concern myself about it much, though. I ate again. "This stuff could get addictive." And not because it made me feel happy and silly but because it took away aches and pains and every inclination to sleep. I could sit there knowing my body was at its physical limits without having to endure all the suffering associated with that state. And my mind remained particularly alert and useful because I was not preoccupied with the miseries plaguing my flesh.

Swan grunted his agreement. He did not seem to have been rendered as cheerful as the rest of us. Although, come to think of it, I was not doing much whistling or singing myself.

My mood improved after I had eaten again, though.

In one of his more lucid moments Riverwalker suggested, "We shouldn't waste any more time than we have to, Sleepy. The rest should all be gone by now but they went away hoping that you and the standard would catch up."

"If Tobo hasn't already told them, I've got some bad news about that."

"The boy said nothing about the standard. He may not have had a chance. Everybody was so shocked about Goblin and so worried about how to keep One-Eye from finding out. . . ."

"Goblin drove the Lance into Kina's body. It's still there. You know me. I'm completely hooked by the Company mystique. I believe that besides the Annals, the standard is the most important symbol we have. It goes all the way back to Khatovar. It ties the generations together. I'd understand if somebody wanted to go back after it. But that somebody isn't going to be me. Not in this decade."

That good feeling was moving through me again. I rose. Swan helped me step up to the higher floor level. "Hello!"

Riverwalker chuckled. "I wondered how long it would take you to notice."

The crack in the floor was almost gone.

I went and looked. It seemed to be as deep as ever but now was nowhere more than a foot wide. "How did it heal so fast?" I assumed our presence had been a catalyst. Glancing around the crack toward the demon's throne, I noticed Doj and Tobo hurrying our way. Shivetya's eyes were open. He was watching. "I thought you said everybody had left."

"The earthquake did it." River ignored the presence of Doj and Tobo.

Swan said, "It's the latest thing in home repairs. Go down there and stab that thing again, maybe the plain will heal up completely."

"Might get the clockwork running again," Doj said, having overheard our conversation as he arrived.

"Clockwork?"

Doj did a little hop. "This floor is a huge circle. It's a one-eightieth-scale representation of the plain as a whole, with a complete travel chart inlaid. It rides on stone rollers and was capable of turning before the Thousand Voices got curious and broke it."

"Interesting. I take it your chat with the demon proceeded informatively."

Doj grunted assent. "But slowly. That was the big problem. Just figuring out that communication has to be managed *very* slowly. I think that would carry over physically, too. That if he decided to stand up—if he could—it might take hours. But as the Steadfast Guardian, he never had to move fast. He controlled the whole plain from here, using the charts in the floors and the clockwork mechanisms."

Never had I seen Doj so straightforward and animated. The knowledge bug must have bitten him, along with its kissing cousin that makes the newly illuminated want to share with everyone. And that was not like Doj at all. Nor like any other Nyueng Bao of my experience. Only Mother Gota and Tobo ever chattered— and between them they revealed less than Uncle Doj on a particularly reticent day.

Doj continued, "He says his original reason for being created was to manage the machinery that saw that travelers got where they wanted to go. Over time there were battles upon the plain, wars between the worlds, this fortress was built around him, and at every stage he was saddled with additional duties. Sleepy, the creature is half as old as time itself. He actually witnessed the battle between Kina and the demons when the Lords of Light fought the Lords of Darkness. It was the first great war between the worlds, it did take place here on the plain, and none of the myths have got it close to right."

That was interesting and I said so. But I refused to allow the past's allure to seduce me right now.

"I must confess a grand temptation to create a permanent camp here," Doj enthused. "It will take lifetimes to recover and record everything. He's seen so much! He remembers the Children of the Dead, Sleepy. To him the passing of the Nyueng Bao De Duang happened just yesterday. We need only to keep him convinced that we should have his help."

I looked questions at each of my companions. Riverwalker finally volunteered, "He's got to have been stuffing himself with the demon food." Meaning he thought Doj was out of character a few leagues, too. "Several others also went through big changes when they overindulged."

"That much I understood already. Tobo. Have you undergone a complete character shift, too?" He had not said a word. That was remarkable. He had an opinion about everything.

"He scared the crap out of me, Sleepy."

"He? Who?"

"The demon. The monster. Shivetya. He looked inside my head. He talked to me there. I think he did it to my father, too. For years and years, maybe. In the Annals? When Dad thought Kina or the Protector were manipulating him? I'm betting that lots of times it was really Shivetya."

"That could be. That really could be."

The world is infested with superhuman *things* that toy with the destinies of individuals and nations. Gunni priests have been claiming that for a hundred generations. The gods were banging elbows with each other, stirring the cauldron. But none of those gods were my God, the True God, the Almighty, Who seemed to have elected to elevate Himself above the fray.

I needed the solace of my kind of priest. And there were none nearer than five hundred miles.

"How many stories are there about this place?" I asked Doj. "And how many of them are true?"

"I suspect we haven't yet heard one out of ten," the old swordmaster replied. He grinned. He was enjoying himself. "And I wouldn't be surprised if most of them are true. Can you sense it? This fortress, this plain, they're many things at the same time. Until recently I believed it had to be the Land of Unknown Shadows. As your Captain believed that it had to be Khatovar. But it's only a pathway to other places. And Shivetya, the Steadfast Guardian, is many things, too. Including, I think, infinitely weary of being everything that he's had to be."

Tobo was so anxious to interject his own thoughts that he danced around like a little boy with a desperate need to pee. He announced, "Shivetya wants to die, Sleepy. But he can't. Not as long as Kina is still alive. And she's immortal."

"He's got a problem then, doesn't he?"

Swan had an idea. "He could divide up that life span and offer it to us. I'd take him up on it. I could use another couple thousand years. After I get away from this kind of life."

I moved us closer to the demon as we talked. My natural pessimism and sourness evidently reasserted itself, though I never stopped feeling younger and happier and more energetic than I had for ages. I just stopped giggling with the rest of them. I asked, "Where's your mother, Tobo?"

His good humor waned momentarily. "She went with Granny Gota."

A glance at Doj made me suspect that there had been a sharp encounter between Sahra the mother and men willing to accept her son as one of them. This was Nyueng Bao stubbornness again, from two directions. On this one the Troll must have sided with her grandson and Doj.

I changed the subject. "All right. You two claim you've been in Shivetya's mind. Or maybe he's been in yours. Whichever, tell me what he wants." I did not believe the demon was being helpful out of the goodness of his ancient heart. He could not be. He was a demon, accursed of God whether he was a creature of light or of shadow. To a demon we adventurers had to be as brief and transient as individual honeybees would be to us—though, like the bees, we might be able to make ourselves obnoxious for a short while.

Doj said, "He wants what anyone in his position would want. That seems obvious."

Tobo interjected, "He also wants loose, Sleepy. He's been pinned that way for a long time. The plain keeps changing because he can't get out to stop anybody."

"What's he going to do if we pluck the daggers out of his limbs? Will he go on being our pal? Or will he start busting heads?"

Doj and Tobo exchanged uncertain glances. So. They had not spent much time worrying about that.

I said, "I see. Well, he may be the sweetest guy on God's green earth but he stays right where he is for now. A few weeks or months more shouldn't make much difference to him. How the heck did he manage to get himself nailed to his chair?"

"Somebody tricked him," Tobo said.

Surprise, surprise. "You think so?"

It seemed there was a lot more light now than there had been when I was headed in the other direction with Swan. Or maybe my eyes had adapted to the interior of the fortress. I could make out the designs in the floor clearly. All the features of the plain could be found there except for the standing stones with their glittering gold characters. And those might have been represented by certain shadowy discolorations I was unable to examine more closely. There were even tiny points that seemed to be moving, which almost certainly meant something if one knew how to read them.

Shivetya's throne rested atop a circular elevation positioned at the heart of an intermediate raised circle just over twenty yards across. Doj assured me that that was roughly one-eightieth the diameter of the biggest circle and that that was an eightieth of the diameter of the entire plain. The smaller circle, I noted, also boasted its representation of the plain—in much less obvious detail. Presumably, Shivetya could sit his throne and, turning, could see the whole of his kingdom. If he needed more information, he could step down to the next level, where everything was portrayed in a scale eighty times finer.

The implications of the quality of the magical engineering involved in creating all this began to seep through. I was intimidated thoroughly. The builders must have been of godlike power. They had to have been as far beyond the greatest wizards known to me as those were beyond no-talents like me. I was sure that Lady and Longshadow, Soulcatcher and Howler, would have little more grasp of the forces and principles involved than I did.

I stepped in front of Shivetya. The demon's eyes remained open. I felt him touch me lightly, inside. For some reason my thoughts turned to mountainous highlands and places where the snow never melted. To old things, slow things. To silence and stone. My brain had no better way of interpreting the actuality of what Shivetya was.

I kept reminding myself that the demon antedated the oldest history of my world. And I sensed what Tobo had mentioned, Shivetya's quiet, calm desire not to grow any older. He had a very Gunni sort of desire to find his way into a nirvana as an antidote to the infinite tedium and pain of *being*.

I tried talking to the demon. I tried exchanging thoughts. That was a frightening experience even though I was filled with the confidence and good feeling that came from the gift food Shivetya had provided. I did not want to share my mind even with an immortal golem who could not possibly have any genuine comprehension of the things it contained or of why those troubled me so.

S leepy?"

"Huh?" I jumped up. I felt good enough to do that. I felt as good as I should have back in my teens, had I never had a need to feel sorry for myself. The healing properties of the demon's gift continued to work their magic.

Swan said, "We all fell asleep. I don't know for how long. I don't even know how."

I looked at the demon. It had not moved. No surprise there. But the white crow was perched on its shoulder. As soon as it recognized that I was alert, it launched itself toward me. I threw up an arm. The bird settled on my wrist as though I were a falconer. In a voice almost too slow to follow, it said, "This will be my voice. It is trained and its mind is not cluttered with thoughts and beliefs that will get in the way."

Marvelous. I wondered what Lady would think. If Shivetya took over, she would be deaf and blind until we brought her back from her enchanted sleep.

"This will be my voice now."

I understood the repetition to be a response to my flutter of unspoken curiosity.
"I understand."

"I will aid you in your quest. In return, you will destroy the Drin, Kina. Then you will release me."

I understood that he meant for me to release him from life and obligation, not just from that throne.

"I would if I had the power."

"You have the power. You have always had the power."

"What does that mean?" I recognized a cryptic, sorcerer-type pronouncement when I heard one.

"You will understand when it is time to understand. Now it is time for you to depart, Stone Soldier. Go. Become Deathwalker."

"What the devil does that mean?" I squeaked. So did several of my companions, all of whom were awake now and most of whom were gobbling demon food while eavesdropping.

The floor started moving, at first almost imperceptibly. Quickly I noted that only the part immediately around the throne, that had healed itself completely, was involved. I now knew that all the damage, including the earthquake so violent it had been felt as far away as Taglios, had been initiated entirely by Soulcatcher during an ill-conceived experiment. She had discovered the "machinery" and in her willful, damn-the-consequences way, had begun tinkering just to see what would happen. I knew that as fully as if I had been there as an eyewitness, because an actual eyewitness had given me his memories.

I knew everything Soulcatcher had done during her several visits to the fortress, in a time when Longshadow believed he was the total master of the Shadowgate and did not believe that others would dare approach it even if they did possess a workable key.

I now knew many things as if I had lived them. Some were things I was not eager to know. A few concerned questions I had had for years, offering answers that I could share with Master Santaraksita. But mostly it was just stuff I was likely to find useful if I was going to become what Shivetya hoped I would.

A startled bluebottle of speculation buzzed through my mind. I checked to see if I had an answer. But I had no memories of what might have become of the Key that would have been necessary if, indeed, Longshadow, as Maricha Manthara Dhumraksha, with his student Ashutosh Yaksha, had come to our world from the Land of Unknown Shadows.

And for sure, I did not get any relief from my fear of heights.

An instant after the floor stopped turning, the white crow launched itself upward. And darned if I did not launch myself right after it—though not through any wish of my own.

My companions rose behind me. In their surprise and fright several dropped weapons and possessions and, probably, body contents. Only Tobo seemed to find unanticipated flight to be a positive experience.

Runmust and Iqbal sealed their eyes and belched rapid prayers to their false vision of God. I spoke my mind to the God Who Is God, reminding Him to be merciful. Riverwalker addressed impassioned appeals to his heathen deities. Doj and Swan said nothing at all, Swan because he had fainted.

Tobo babbled in delight, informing everyone how wonderful the experience was, look here, look there, the vast expanse of the chamber stretches out below us like the plain itself. . . .

We passed through a hole in the ceiling and into the colder air of the real plain. It was dusk out there, the sky still crimson over the western horizon but already deep indigo directly ahead. The stars of the Noose shone palely in front of us. As we descended toward the surface, I found nerve enough to glance back. The fortress stood silhouetted against the northern sky, on its outside in worse shape now than when we had arrived. All our clutter, everything dropped during our ascension or that we had had no time to grab, now flew along right behind us.

For a while I watched eagerly for the standard to join the flock. My hopes were disappointed. It did not appear.

In retrospect I cannot see why I should have hoped otherwise.

Now Tobo pretended he was a bird. By experimenting he discovered that he could use his arms to direct his flight, to rise and fall somewhat, to speed up and slow down slightly. He never shut up for a instant, loving every moment, continuously admonishing the rest of us to enjoy the adventure, because none of us would ever have the chance to experience anything like this again.

"Wisdom from the mouths of infants," Doj announced. Then he threw up.

They were both right.

95

Our flight ended where the rest of the band was camped at the last circle before the southwest road reached our destination Shadowgate. Flying definitely offered the advantage of speed. We outflew the white crow, arriving less than two hours after our toes departed solid stone. That Shivetya fellow was a handy friend to have.

I tried to see what lay beyond the edge of the plain but it was just too dark. There might have been one or two small points of light out there. It was hard to tell.

We descended feetfirst, evidently immune to shadows. I had sensed several of those pacing us but they had shown no inclination to get too close. Which left me admiring Shivetya's power even more, for those things were little more than bundles of hatred and hunger to kill.

We passed through the top of the shielding protecting our brethren without compromising it. The whole band watched our arrival in disbelief. Tobo managed to direct himself toward his mother and accomplished a somersault before he touched down. I did not exactly get down and hug the stone surface but I was glad the ordeal was over. The Singh brothers rushed around looking for family. So did Doj, who ignored Sahra and went directly to Gota. Gota was not in good spirits and possibly was in ill health. I could not tell much more about anyone in the feeble light available from a changeable moon. Gota did not offer any complaint or criticism.

Swan stuck with me.

As soon as he convinced himself that it was safe to open his eyes, Riverwalker began bustling around being a busybody, devoutly determined to make sure everyone and everything conformed to whatever rules he happened to recall at the moment. I frowned, shook my head, but did not interfere. We all need our rituals to help us get by.

"Sahra," I asked, "how are they?" I meant those we had brought out of the caverns, because I had a suspicion that Gota's state meant nothing good and I did not want to hear what I feared it did mean.

Sahra could not feel friendly. She blamed me because she had discovered her baby strolling through the sky. Never mind that he had come down safely and could not stop raving about the experience.

What a fall from a great height might do to a body never occurred to him. But it certainly did to Sahra.

"No change in the Captured. One-Eye went into a funk when he heard about Goblin and hasn't spoken since. Mother isn't sure if it's emotional withdrawal or he had another stroke. What worries her is the possibility that he doesn't want to live anymore."

"Who would he fight with?" I did not mean to belittle, though it came out sounding that way.

Sahra showed me an instant of pique but did not reveal her thoughts. "Mother can be a handful."

"Probably what got them together in the first place." I made no mention of the fact that I feared Gota would not be with us much longer. The Troll had to be around eighty. "I'll go talk to him."

"He's asleep. It can wait."

"In the morning, then. Are we still in touch with Murgen?"

The light was good enough to reveal Sahra's anger. Perhaps she was right. I had not had my feet on the ground two minutes and already I wanted to use her husband. But she managed the emotion. We had worked together for a long time now, early on with her usually being the stronger one, only occasionally with me taking the lead role. We always managed without sharp words. We always managed because we knew we had somewhere to go and we had to collaborate to get there. These days I took charge most of the time but she could do so when it was appropriate.

Only she was just about where she wanted to get to now, was she not? She had Murgen out of the ground. She would not need to go on with her role once he was up and around. Unless he was not the man she wanted him to be. In which case she would have to contrive a new Sahra all over again.

I am sure that had her on edge more than ever. Neither she nor Murgen were the people they had been. None of us were. There were going to be some difficulties adjusting, possibly some major difficulties.

I anticipated big problems with Lady and the Captain.

Sahra said, "I've done my best to keep the mist projector working but I haven't been able to make contact since we left that fortress. He doesn't seem to be willing to leave his body anymore. And I can't get that to wake up more than it already is." So she was also afraid that the rescue might have been a mistake, that we might have hurt Murgen instead of saving him. Upbeat, hopefully, she said, "Maybe Tobo can help."

I wondered what had become of the tough, focused, dedicated Sahra who had been Minh Subredil. I tried to reassure this Sahra. "Murgen will be fine." Shivetya had given me the knowledge we needed to reanimate the Captured. "But we have to get him off the plain before we can wake him all the way up. Same for the others."

Riverwalker returned from his tour. "The demon food is going fast here, Sleepy.

There's enough to get us off the plain and have a couple meals more but then we're on our own. We either eat the dog and the horses or we scrounge up something locally fast."

"Ah, well. We knew that going in. We're better off than we expected to be. Did anybody think to steal anything valuable while we were there?"

That comment got me blank looks. Then I realized that it was possible no one else had noticed the treasures I had discovered while chasing Tobo into the deeps of the earth. The boy would have said something if he had seen anything. He could not shut up.

Swan told me, "It'll be harvest time when we get there."

"What?"

He shrugged. "I just know."

So he might. "Everybody listen up. Get all the rest you can tonight. I want to get up and move out early tomorrow. And nobody knows what we'll run into at the end of the road."

Somebody grumbled something about if I wanted him to sleep, why did I not shut up and let him get to work?

I could not keep my eyes open myself, although it had not been that long since I had wakened by Shivetya's throne. In fact, my mind seemed to be shutting down. I said, "Forget everything else. I'm going to take my own advice. Where's a place I can wrap my blanket around me and lie down before I collapse?"

The only open space was back at the tail end of the Company. All my flying companions except Tobo had to migrate back there. I had planned to eat before I slept but exhaustion overwhelmed me before I swallowed my third bite of demon's food. My final reflection concerned whether God could overlook one of the Faithful accepting a gift from one of the Damned.

An interesting exercise. God knows all. Therefore, God knew what Shivetya was doing and allowed him to do it. Therefore, it must be God's will that we benefit from the demon's generosity. It would be a sin to defy God's will.

96

I dreamed strange dreams.

Of course I did. Was not Shivetya in my mind? Was I not in the haunted place of glittering stone?

Stone remembered. And stone wanted me to know.

I was in another place, then, in a time not my own. I was Shivetya as the demon experienced the world, everywhere at once, a pale imitation of God. I could be everywhere at once because by staring at the floor surrounding my throne, I connected with my realm as a whole. We became one knowledge, the singer and the song.

Men were moving across my face, a large band. I knew time differently from mortals but I understood that it had been ages since this had happened last. Mortals did not cross me anymore. Not often. Never in numbers like this.

There was enough Sleepy there for me to recognize Shivetya's memory of the coming of the Captured, before they stumbled into Soulcatcher's trap. Why would the demon want me to see this? I knew this story. Murgen had shared it with me several times, to make sure it got recorded in the Annals just the way he wanted.

There was no solid feeling of a personality surrounding me, yet I felt a mild pressure to abandon curiosity, to turn outward from questions, to cease being a viewpoint, to let the flower unfold. I should have paid more attention to Uncle Doj. The ability to abandon the self would have been a useful talent at a time like this.

Time was different for the demon, definitely. But he tried to accommodate the ephemeral mortal, to get to the point, to provide the information he thought I would find useful.

I watched the whole adventure, including the great and desperate escape that had devoured Bucket and had allowed Willow the chance to remain in the story as a pawn of wickedness. And I did not understand immediately because at first I observed only the finer details of a story already known in outline.

I was not completely stupid. I caught on. The question had occurred to me before but had not been critical. Now I just needed to reclaim enough self to recall that I had asked it.

The question was, what had become of the one member of that expedition for whom there was still no account? The incredibly dangerous apprentice shapeshifter Lisa Deale Bowalk, trapped in the form of a black leopard, had been carried onto the plain in a cage, as had the prisoners Longshadow and Howler. She had vanished during the excitement. Murgen never discovered what had become of her. That he mentioned.

I learned the truth. According to Shivetya.

Not every trivial detail became entirely clear. Shivetya had trouble focusing that tightly in time. But it seemed that Bowalk's cage had gotten damaged in the panicky rush to escape by brothers of the Company unfortunate enough not to be included amongst the Captured.

Panic mothers panic. The great, wicked cat caught the fever. Her violence was sufficient to complete the demolition of her cage. She ripped her way out, injuring herself in the process. She fled on three legs, carrying her left front paw elevated, allowing it to touch stone only when absolutely necessary. She whined horribly when she did. Nevertheless, she covered ground fast. She traveled nearly thirty miles before nightfall—but had chosen a direction at random and apparently did not recognize that she was not headed toward home until it was too late to change her mind.

She chose a road and ran. And in the night one small, clever shadow caught up, just short of the end of that road. It did what untamed shadows always do. It attacked. I found the result difficult to believe. The shadow hurt the panther but did not kill her. She fought it and won. And stumbled onward. And before a more powerful shadow could overtake and finish her, she staggered through a derelict Shadowgate and became invisible to Shivetya. Which meant that she was last seen alive entering a world neither our own nor the Land of Unknown Shadows. I hoped that that crippled gate had finished her, or that it had injured her beyond recovery, because she was possessed of a hatred as dark as that which impelled the shadows, but hers was a hatred much more narrowly directed. And the Company was its object.

The fragment of Sleepy-self never entirely subsumed into the Shivetya overview wondered what the Captain would think when he learned that Bowalk had reached Khatovar by accident when it was supposed to be impossible for the Company to get there by intent.

The Sleepy-self did not see why this news was important enough for Shivetya to have hijacked my dreams, but significant it must be.

Significant, too, must be the Nef, the dreamwalkers, that Murgen had named the Washene, the Washane and the Washone.

I became more Shivetya, pulling away from the point experience of tracking the shapechanger. I became more one with the demon while the demon became more one with the plain, more purely a manifestation of the will of the great engine. I enjoyed flickers of memories of golden ages of peace, prosperity and enlightenment that had reached across silent stone to many worlds. I witnessed the passage of a hundred conquerers. I saw portions of the most ancient wars now recalled in the Gunni and

Deceiver religions, and even in my own, for being Shivetya and embracing all times at the same time, I could not help but see that the war in Heaven, which was supposed to have occurred soon after God created the earth and the sky, and which ended with the Adversary being cast down into a pit, could be an echo of the same divine struggle other religions remembered according to their own predilections.

Before the war of the gods, there was the plain. And before the plain, there was the Nef. The plain, the great machine, eventually imagined Shivetya as its Steadfast Guardian and servant. In turn, the demon imagined the Washene, the Washane and the Washone in the likeness of the Nef. These dreamwalking ghosts of the builders were Shivetya's gods. They existed independently of his mind but not of his existence. They would perish if he perished. And they had had no desire to be called into being in the first instance.

Bizarre. I was caught amongst the personifications of aspects of religion in which I could not believe. Here were facts my faith forbid me to accept. Acceptance would damn me forever.

Cruel, cruel tricks of the Adversary. I had been gifted with a mind that wanted to explore, to find out, to know. And I had been gifted with faith. And now I had been gifted with information that put fact and faith into conflict. I had not been gifted with a priest's slippery dexterity when it came to reconciling the philosophically irreconcilable.

But perhaps that was not necessary. Truth and reality seemed to be protean on the plain. There were too many different stories about Kina, Shivetya and the fortress in the middle. Maybe every story was true at least part of the time.

There was an intellectual exercise of a sacerdotal magnitude. What if my beliefs were completely valid—but only part of the time and only where I was located myself? What then? How could that be? What could that mean?

It meant unpleasant times in the afterlife if I persisted in relaxing my vigilance against heresies. It might be difficult for a woman to achieve Paradise but it would be no trouble at all for her to win a place in *al-Shiel*.

97

"That must have been one kick-ass nightmare," Willow Swan told me, kneeling beside me, having just shaken my shoulder to waken me. "Not only were you snoring, you were grunting and squeaking and carrying on a conversation with yourself in three different languages."

"I'm a woman of many talents. Everybody says so." I shook my head groggily. "What time is it? It's still dark."

"Another talent emerges. I can't get anything past the old girl."

I grumbled, "The priests and the holy books tell us that God created man in His own image but I've read a lot of holy books—including those of the idolators—and not once have I found any other evidence that He had a sense of humor, let alone is the kind of person who would try to make jokes before the sun even came up. You're a sick man, Willow Swan. What's going on?"

"Last night you said we'd have to start early. So Sahra thought you meant we should be ready to go as soon as there's light enough to see. So we can get off the plain with plenty of daylight to spare."

"Sahra is a wise woman. Wake me up when she's ready to go."

"I think right now would be a good time to get up, then."

I raised my hands. It was just light enough to see them. "Gather 'round, people." Once a reasonable crowd had done so I explained that each of us who had stayed behind in the fortress had been given knowledge that would help us in times to come. "Shivetya seems very interested in our success. He tried to give us what he believed would be useful tools. But he's very slow and has his own demonic perspectives and doesn't know how to explain anything clearly. So it's extremely likely that there is a lot we know that we won't know we know until something makes us think of it. Be patient with us. We'll probably be a little strange for a while. I'm having trouble getting used to the reeducated me and I live here. New knowledge pops up every time I turn around. Right now, though, I just want to get off this plain. Our resources are *still* limited. We have to establish ourselves as fast as we can."

Those faces I could discern revealed fear of the future. Somewhere the dog whined. Iqbal's baby whimpered momentarily as Suruvhija shifted her from one nipple to the other. In my consideration, that child ought to have been weaned by now but I knew I had no justification for my opinion. None of my babies have been born yet. And it is getting a little late to bring them in.

People waited for me to tell them something informative. The more thoughtful now wondered what new troubles awaited us since we had actually made it this far. Swan could be right. It could be harvest season in the Land of Unknown Shadows. And it could also be the season for scalping foreigners.

I was troubled myself but had been faced with the unknown so often that I had calluses on that breed of fear. I knew perfectly well it would do me no good to fuss and worry when I had no idea what lay ahead. But worry I would, anyway. Even when knowledge contracted while I slept assured me that we would not encounter disasters once we shifted off the plain.

I had planned to offer a rousing speech but quickly discarded that notion. No one was interested. Not even me. "Is everybody ready? Then let's go."

Getting started took less time than I expected. Most of my brothers had not stopped to hear me say what they anticipated would be the same old same old. They had gone on getting ready to roll. I told Swan, "I guess 'In those days the Company . . .' works a lot better after supper and a hard day's work."

"Does for me. Works even better when I've had something to drink. And it's a kick-ass wowser after I've gone to bed."

I walked with Sahra for a while, renewing our acquaintance, easing the strain between us. She remained tense, though. It would not be that long before she had to deal with her husband in the flesh for the first time in a decade and a half. I did not know how to make that easier for her.

Then I walked with the Radisha for an hour. She, too, was in an unsettled mood. It had been even longer since she had had to deal with her brother in all but the most remote capacities. She was a realist, however. "There's nothing I can lose to him, is there? I've lost it all already. First to the Protector, through my own blindness. Then you stole me away from Taglios and robbed me of even the hope of reclaiming my place."

"Bet you something, Princess. Bet you that you're already being remembered as the mother of a golden age." That actually seemed a reasonable prediction. The past always seems better when the present consists of clabbered misery. "Even without the Protector back in the capital yet. Once we're established, the first mission I mean to launch will be to get word back to Taglios that you and your brother are both alive, you're really angry, and you're going to come back."

"We all must dream," the woman told me.

"You don't *want* to go back?"

"Do you recall the taunt you laid before me every day? *Rajadharma*?"

"Sure."

"What I may want is of no importance. What my brother might want does not signify, either. He's had his adventures. Now I've had mine. *Rajadharma* constrains us more surely than could the stoutest chain. *Rajadharma* will call us back across the uncounted leagues as long as we continue to breathe, through the impossible places, past all the deadly perils and improbable beings. You reminded me again and again of my obligation. Perhaps by doing so, you created a monster fit to battle the beast who displaced me. *Rajadharma* has become my vice, Sleepy. It has become my irrational compulsion. I continue to follow you only because reason insists that even though this path leads me farther from Taglios today, it is the shortest road to my destiny."

"I'll help where I can." I did not commit the Company, though. I still had the Captain and Lieutenant to waken and deal with. I started to move on. I wanted to visit with Master Santaraksita for a while and lose myself, perhaps, in an interplay of intellectual speculation. The librarian's horizons were much broader these days.

"Sleepy."

"Radisha?"

"Has the Black Company extracted sufficient revenge?"

We had taken away everything but the love of her people. And she was not a bad woman. "In my eyes you're just one small gesture short of redemption. I want you to apologize to the Captain once he recovers enough to understand what's happening."

Her lips tightened. She and her brother did not let themselves be slaves to considerations of station or caste, but still, apology to a foreign mercenary? "If I must, I must. My options are limited."

"Water sleeps, Radisha." I joined Suvrin and Master Santaraksita, taking a few minutes to visit with the black stallion on the way there. It carried One-Eye, who was breathing but otherwise did not look much better than a corpse. I hoped he was just sleeping an old man's sleep. The horse seemed bored. I suppose it was tired of adventures.

"Master. Suvrin. By some chance do you two suffer any memories you didn't have before we came to the plain?"

They did indeed, Santaraksita more so than Suvrin. Shivetya's gifts seemed shaped for each individual. Master Santaraksita proceeded to relate yet another version of the Kina myth and of Shivetya's relationship to the Queen of Death and Terror. This one assumed the point of view of the demon. It did not say much that was new, just shifted the relative importance of various characters and, laterally, blamed Kina for the passing of the last few builders.

Kina remained a black-hearted villain in this version, while Shivetya became one of the great unsung heroes, deserving of a much higher standing in myth. Which could be true. He had no standing at all. Nobody outside the plain had ever heard of him. I suggested, "When you get back to Taglios now, Master, you can establish a mighty reputation by explaining the myths in the words of a being who lived through their creation."

Santaraksita smiled sourly. "You know better, Dorabee. Mythology is one area where nobody wants to know the absolute truth because time has forged great symbols from raw materials supplied by ancient events. Prosaic distortions of fact metamorphose into perceived truths of the soul."

He had a point. In religion, precise truth has almost no currency. True believers will kill and destroy to defend their inaccurate beliefs.

And *that* is a truth upon which you can rely.

98

I raised my head carefully to peer over the edge of the plain at the Land of Unknown Shadows. Willow Swan snaked up on my right. He did the same. Riverwalker copied him on my left. River said, "I'll be damned."

I agreed. "No doubt about it. Doj. Gota. Come and look. Will somebody bring One-Eye up?" The little man had started talking about an hour ago. He did appear to be in touch with the real world at least part of the time.

I beckoned the white crow. That darned thing was going to give us away if it kept circling.

"To who?" Swan asked. "I don't see anybody." Obviously, I was thinking out loud again. Swan weaseled sideways so Doj could crawl up beside me.

Doj rose up. He froze. After fifteen seconds he harrumphed.

Gota said it. "Is the same place we left. You got us turned around, you fool Stone Soldier."

At first glimpse it was identical. Only, "Look to the right. There isn't any Overlook. And never was. And Kiaulune isn't the New City." I never saw Kiaulune before it became Shadowcatch but doubted these ruins resembled that old city much, either. "Get Suvrin. He might know."

I continued to stare. The more I did so, the more differences stood out. Doj said it. "The hand of mankind rested more lightly here. And men went away a long time ago." It was only the shape of the land that was identical.

"Back about the time of the earthquakes, you suppose?" What would have been hardscrabble farmland in my world here looked like better soil that had been abandoned for twenty years. It was overgrown by brush and brambles and cedars but no truly sizable trees were yet evident except those that grew in orderly rows and those so distant they painted the foothills of the Dandha Presh a deep green that was almost black.

Suvrin arrived. I offered a few questions. He told me, "It does look like they say Kiaulune did before the Shadowmasters came. When my grandparents were children. The city didn't start growing until Longshadow decided to build Overlook. Only, I don't see anything down there now but ruins."

"Look at the Shadowgate. It's in better shape than our own." But not in good repair by any standard. The quakes had taken their bites. "You can tell where it is." That was a weight off my shoulders. I had anticipated fighting starvation while we fussed with strings and colored powders in an effort to survey the only safe pathway through.

Several men carried One-Eye up and set him down amongst us. They silhouetted themselves above the skyline doing so. My grumbling did no good. On the other hand, no bloodthirsty hordes materialized below the Shadowgate, so it was possible that we were not yet betrayed.

"One-Eye. Do you sense anything down there?"

I did not know if he would respond. He seemed to be asleep again. His chin rested on his chest. People gave him room because it was in these moments he began to ply his cane. After a few seconds, though, he lifted his chin, opened his eyes, murmured, "A place where I can rest." The wind that was always with us on the plain almost stole his words away. "A place where all evil dies an endless death. No wickedness stirs down there, Little Girl."

One-Eye's remarks excited everyone who had witnessed his most recent episode. Half a dozen more men exposed their silhouettes to anyone watching from below. Still others seemed to think we ought to trudge right on down there in a big, disorderly mob, right now.

"Kendo!" I called. "Slink! I want you each to take six men out through the gate. Fully armed, including bamboo. Slink, take the right side of the road. You take the left, Kendo. You'll be covering the rest of us as we come out. River, you're the reserve. Take ten men and wait just inside the Shadowgate. You'll stay there and become the rear guard if nothing bothers them."

Training and discipline took over. A superior standard of both are among the Company's most potent tools. Properly employed, they become our deadliest tools. We try to inculcate discipline from a recruit's first day, right alongside a healthy distrust of everyone on the outside. We try to pound into his very bones what he needs to do in every situation.

The slope from the edge of the plain to the Shadowgate seemed to stretch for miles. I felt bone-naked descending it without the standard. Tobo, carrying the golden pickax, had to take my place. I told him, "Don't get too fond of the job, kid. It may be all I have if we get the Captain and the Lieutenant back. And I won't even have that if your dad wants all of his old jobs back."

Experiment quickly proved no key but the pick was needed to leave the plain. The Shadowgate did tickle and tingle, though.

The first thing I noticed outside was a powerful mixture of sagey and piney smells. There had been few odors on the plain. Then I noticed the incredible warmth. This world was much warmer than the plain was. It was early autumn here . . . as promised, Willow. As promised.

Kendo and Slink kept their squads moving, screening our advance. More and more people passed through the gate. I got myself hoisted onto the black stallion so I could see better. Which meant that somebody had to carry One-Eye. I told Sahra, "Let's head for those ruins." I was about to add something about shelter being easier to find there when Kendo Cutter shouted.

I looked where he pointed. It took a sharp eye to see them. The old men coming uphill slowly wore robes almost exactly the same color as the road and the earth behind them. There were five of them. They were bent and moved slowly.

"We did give ourselves away up there. And somebody was watching. Doj!"

Waste of breath. The Swordmaster was headed downhill already. Tobo and Gota were right behind him, which did nothing for Sahra's nerves. I rushed forward, caught the boy. "You stay back."

"But, Sleepy!"

"You want to debate it with Runmust and Iqbal?"

He did not want to argue with the large Shadar gentlemen.

I did not want to argue with the Troll. I let her go. She might be more intimidating than Doj, anyway. He was just one old man with a sword. She was a vicious old woman with a virulent tongue.

I checked my battered old shortsword. That was going to perform wonders if they climbed over Uncle Doj. Then I headed downhill myself. Sahra accompanied me.

The old men in brown looked at Doj and Gota. Doj and Gota looked at them. Those five men looked like they had been cast in the same mold, being nearly as wide as they were tall and very long in the tooth.

One of the natives said something rapid in a liquid tongue. The cadence was unusual but the words sounded vaguely familiar. I did catch the phrase "Children of the Dead." Doj replied at length in Nyueng Bao, which included the formulas "The Land of Unknown Shadows" and "All Evil Dies There an Endless Death." The old men seemed hugely puzzled by Doj's accent but recognized those phrases well enough to become visibly agitated. I could not tell if that was a positive sign or not.

Mother Gota began muttering the incantation that included "Calling the Heaven and the Earth and the Day and the Night," and that excited the old men even more.

Sahra told me, "Evidently the language has changed a great deal since the Children of the Dead ran away."

It took me a moment to understand that she was translating what Doj had said in an aside to Gota.

There was a stream of chatter from the old men, all apparently in the form of pointed questions that Doj could not answer.

Sahra said, "They seem to be extremely worried about someone they keep calling 'that devil-dog Merika Montera.' Also about a pupil of this monster, a supposed future Grandmaster. Apparently the two were driven into exile together."

"Merika Montera would be Longshadow. We know there was a time when he used the name Maricha Manthara Dhumraksha. He sent an agent named Ashutosh Yaksha to live among the Nyueng Bao in an effort to find and steal the Key that we've brought with us. The golden pickax."

Uncle Doj chided, "Sleepy, these old men don't speak Taglian or Dejagoran, but there's still a chance that they might recognize our version of names they fear and hate just a whole hell of a lot. Right now they're clamoring for answers about one Achoes Tosiak-shah. It sounds like Longshadow and Shadowspinner, before they were exiled, were the last of a race of outsider sorcerers who enslaved these people's forefathers—through their ability to manipulate killer shadows they summoned from the plain."

"Wouldn't you know? They brought their business with them. Tell these guys whatever they need to know. Tell them the truth. Tell them who we are and what we intend to do. And what we've already done to their buddies Longshadow and Shadowspinner."

"We might be wise to find out a little more about them before we become completely candid."

"I wouldn't expect you to break any lifetime habits."

Doj nodded slightly, betraying the slightest smile. He faced the old men and began talking. I found that my Nyueng Bao was improving. I had no trouble isolating "Stone Soldiers" and "Soldiers of Darkness" in his monologue. Native faces kept turning my way, always more surprised.

Sahra told me, "They're monks of some sort. They've been watching for a long time. Watching is what their order does. In case the Shadowmasters try to return. They did not expect anyone to come for real."

"They especially didn't expect women, eh?"

"That amazes them. And Swan worries them. Their ancestors' experiences with white devils were not positive."

Then, of course, the white crow swooped and landed on my shoulder. And the great black stallion, with its prune of a rider, came down to stick its nose in. And as the chatter picked up, still well-seasoned with "Stone Soldier" and "Soldier of Darkness" and "Steadfast Guardian," the rest of the band drifted forward, impelled by curiosity.

First thing I knew, Tobo was right there beside me, along with Runmust, Iqbal and Suruvhija and all their offspring, the dog, and ever-increasing jabber about what should we do with the Captured, where were we going to set up camp. . . .

"You hearing these questions?" I asked Doj.

"I hear them. I think we're going to be granted this whole valley. For the time being. While they send messages to the Court of All Seasons and the File of Nine. We'll have more important visitors eventually. Until then—as I understand them—we can set down anywhere we want. The dialect is a little tricky, though, so be careful."

Dozens of veteran eyes scanned the valley for defensible positions. It took no effort to identify them. They were the same as those we recalled from the Kiaulune wars.

I wondered if all the connected worlds would be equally familiar physically.

I indicated my choice. No one demurred. Runmust and the Singhs hurried off to survey the site, accompanied by a dozen men armed for anything. The five old monks did not protest. Mostly they seemed bemused and amazed.

So it was that the Black Company reached the Land of Unknown Shadows instead of fabled Khatovar. There it was that the Company settled and rested and recovered. There it was that I filled book after book with words when I was not planning or leading expeditions to rescue the rest of my captured brothers, and even that devil-dog Merika Montera so he would be available for another, rather less pleasant encounter with justice than the one that had driven him into exile. The grandchildren of his former slaves feared him not at all.

I won him a stay, at Lady's request, so he could help with Tobo's schooling. The stay was good for as long as he did that job satisfactorily and not for a moment more. The old monks, as tight of lip as their cousin Doj, agreed that Tobo had to be trained but would not reveal their reasoning even to me.

At one time the Land of the Unknown Shadows had suffered many lean, pale bonesacks just like Longshadow. They were invaders from another world. They had brought no wives with them. Time did not love them.

And thus it was. And thus it was.

Soldiers live. And wonder why.

One-Eye survived another four years, suffering strokes, yet recovering slowly every time. Seldom did he leave the house we built for him and Gota. Mostly he tinkered with his black spear while Gota hovered around and fussed. He fussed right back and never stopped worrying about Tobo's education.

Once again Tobo was smothered in parents both real and surrogate.

He studied with One-Eye, he studied with Lady, he studied with Longshadow and Master Santaraksita, with the Radisha and the Prahbrindrah Drah, and with the masters of our adoptive world. He studied hard and well and much, much more than he wanted. He was very talented. He was what his great-grandmother Hong Tray had foreseen.

The Captured all returned to us, except for those who died beneath the plain, but even the best of them—Murgen, Lady, the Captain—were strange and deeply changed. Fey. But we were changed as well, by life, so that those of us they remembered at all were almost alien to them.

A new order came into being.

It had to be.

Someday we will cross the plain again.

Water sleeps.

For now, I just rest. And indulge myself in writing, in remembering the fallen, in considering the strange twists life takes, in considering what plan God must have if the good are condemned to die young while the wicked prosper, if righteous men can commit deep evil while bad men demonstrate unexpected streaks of humanity.

Soldiers live. And wonder why.

99

The Great General started south through the Dandha Presh moments after the Protector abandoned him so she could make more speed. Consequently he met Soulcatcher on the southern side of the summit just a week later. She talked to herself continuously in a committee of voices while she was awake and gibbered in tongues during her brief bouts of sleep. Mogaba thought the Daughter of Night seemed smugly pleased in the moment before she collapsed from exhaustion.

"Kill them," Mogaba urged the moment he had Soulcatcher's ear and a bit of privacy. "Those two can be nothing but trouble and there's no way you can profit from keeping them around."

"Possibly true." The Protector's voice was a sly one. "But if I'm clever enough I can use the girl to tap into Kina's power the way my sister did."

"If there's one thing I've learned from a life noteworthy for its regiments of disappointments, it's that you can't rely on cleverness. You're a powerful woman now.

Kill them while you can. Kill them before they find a way to turn the tables. You don't need to become any stronger. There's no one in this world capable of challenging you."

"There's always someone, Mogaba."

"Kill them. They sure won't waste a second on you."

Soulcatcher approached the Daughter of Night, who had not moved since her collapse. "My dear sweet niece wouldn't harm me." The voice she chose could have been that of a naive fourteen-year-old responding to the charge that her twenty-five-year-old lover was interested in only one thing. Then she laughed cruelly, kicked the Daughter of Night viciously. "You even think about it, bitch, and I'll roast and eat you one limb at a time. And still make sure you live long enough to see your mother die first."

The Great General neither moved nor made any remark. His face betrayed nothing, not even to Soulcatcher's acute eye. But in his sinking heart he understood that yet again he had allied himself with complete and unpredictable insanity. And yet again he had no option but to ride the tiger. He observed, "Perhaps we should give thought to how to guard our minds against intrusion by the Queen of Terror and Darkness."

"I'm ahead of you, General. I'm the professional." This voice was that of a self-important little mouse of a functionary. It became that of a self-confident woman being conversational, the voice Mogaba suspected was Soulcatcher's own. It resembled closely the voice of her sister, Lady. "For the last week I've had nothing to do but nurture the blisters on my feet and think. I conceived marvelous new torments to practice upon the Black Company—too late to enjoy them. Isn't that the way it always goes? You always think of the perfect comeback about an hour too late for it to do any good? I suppose I'll find other enemies and my innovation won't be wasted. Most of the time, though, I considered how best to circumvent Kina's power." She did not fear naming the goddess directly. "We can do it."

The Daughter of Night stirred slightly. Her shoulders tightened. She glanced up for an instant. She looked a little uncertain, a little troubled.

For the first time since her birth she was completely out of touch with her soul-mother. She had been out of touch for several days. Something was wrong. Something was terribly wrong.

Soulcatcher eyed Narayan Singh. That old man was not much use anymore. She could test her new torments on him once she had him back in Taglios, before a suitable audience.

"General, if I get caught up in one of those byways that distract me so often, I want you to nudge me back to the business at hand. Which will be empire building. And, in my spare time, the creation of a new flying carpet. I think I know enough of the Howler's secrets to manage. This past week has forced me to admit to myself that I have no innate fondness for exercise."

Soulcatcher prodded the Daughter of Night again, then settled on a rotten log and removed her boots. "Mogaba, don't ever tell anyone that you've seen the world's greatest sorceress stumped for a way to handle something as trivial as blisters."

Narayan Singh, who had been snoring fitfully, suddenly rose up and gripped the bars of his cage, his face contorted in terror, its butternut color all but gone. "Water sleeps!" he screamed. "Thi Kim! Thi Kim is coming!" Then he collapsed, unconscious again, though his body continued to spasm.

Soulcatcher growled softly. "Water sleeps? We'll see what the dead can do." They were all gone this time. It was her world now. "What else did he say?"

"Something that sounded like a Nyueng Bao name."

"Uhm. Yes. But not a name. Something about death. Or a murder. Thi Kim. Coming. Hmm. Maybe a nickname? Murder walker? I should learn the language better."

The Daughter of Night, she noted, was shaking more than Singh.

The wind whines and howls through fangs of ice. It races furiously around the nameless fortress but tonight neither the lightning nor the storm has any power to disturb. The creature on the wooden throne is relaxed. He will rest comfortably through a night of years for the first time in a long millennium. The silver daggers are no inconvenience at all.

Shivetya sleeps and dreams dreams of immortality's end.

Fury crackles between the standing stones. Shadows flee. Shadows hide. Shadows huddle in terror.

Immortality is threatened.

SOLDIERS LIVE

BOOK FOUR
of
GLITTERING STONE

For Russell Galen, #40, at a quarter century.
It hasn't been a perfect marriage, but close enough
to keep me smiling. Let's see if we can't make it to silver.
(Diamond? Whatever a 50th anniversary is.)

An Abode of Ravens:
When No Men Died

Four years passed and no one died.

Not of violence or hazard of the calling, anyway. Otto and Hagop did pass on within days of each other, of natural causes associated with aging, last year. A few weeks ago one Tam Duc, recruit in training, perished of the overconfident exuberance of youth. He fell into a crevasse while he and his lance brothers were riding their blankets down the long slick slope of the Tien Myuen glacier. There were a few others. But not a one by an unfriendly hand.

Four years has to be a record, though not the sort often recalled in these Annals. That much peace is impossible to believe.

Peace that prolonged becomes increasingly seductive.

Many of us are old and tired and retain no youthful fire in the belly. But us old farts are not in charge anymore. And though we were prepared to forget horror, horror was not as accomodating toward us.

In those days the Company was in service to its own name. We recognized no master. We counted the warlords of Hsien as our allies. They feared us. We were supernatural, many recalled from the dead, the ultimate Stone Soldiers. They dreaded the chance that we might take sides in their squabbles over the bones of Hsien, that once-mighty empire the Nyueng Bao recall as the Land of Unknown Shadows.

The more idealistic warlords have hopes of us. The mysterious File of Nine provide arms and money and let us recruit because they hope we can be manipulated into helping them restore the golden age that existed before the Shadowmasters enslaved their world so cruelly that its people still call themselves the Children of the Dead.

There is no chance we will participate. But we permit them the hope, the illusion. We have to get strong. We have a mission of our own.

By standing still we have caused the blossoming of a city. A once-chaotic encampment has become ordered and has acquired names, Outpost or the Bridgehead among those who came from beyond the plain and what translates as Abode of Ravens amongst the Children of the Dead. The place keeps growing. It has generated scores of permanent structures. It is in the processing of acquiring a wall. The main street is being paved with cobblestones.

Sleepy likes to keep everyone busy. She cannot stand a loafer. The Children of the Dead will inherit a treasure when we finally go away.

An Abode of Ravens:
When the Baobhas Sang

Boom! Boom! Somebody hammered on my door. I glanced at Lady. She had stayed up late last night and so had fallen asleep while studying this evening. She was determined to discover all the secrets of Hsien magic and to help Tobo harness the startlingly plentiful supernatural manifestations of this world. Not that Tobo needed much help anymore.

This world has more real phantoms and marvellous beings hiding in the bushes and behind the rocks and trees and on the edge of night than any twenty generations of our own frightened peasants could imagine. They gravitate toward Tobo as though he is some sort of nightside messiah. Or amusing pet, maybe.

Boom! Boom! I would have to get off my butt myself. That looked like a long, hard trek over there.

Boom! Boom! "Come on, Croaker! Wake up!" The door swung inward as my visitor invited himself inside. The very devil of my thoughts.

"Tobo . . ."

"Didn't you hear the baobhas singing?"

"I heard a racket. Your friends are always kicking up a fuss about something. I don't pay any attention anymore."

"When the baobhas sing it means somebody is going to die. And there's been a cold wind off the plain all day and Big Ears and Golden-Eye have been extremely nervous and . . . it's One-Eye, sir. I just went over to talk to him. He looks like he'd had another stroke."

"Shit. Let me get my bag." No surprise, One-Eye suffering a stroke. That old fart has been trying to sneak out on us for years. Most of the vinegar went out of him back when we lost Goblin.

"Hurry!"

The kid loved that old shit-disturber. Sometimes it seemed like One-Eye was what he wanted to be when he grew up. In fact, it seemed Tobo venerated everybody but his own mother, though the friction between them diminished as he aged. He had matured considerably since my latest resurrection.

"I'm hurrying as fast as I can, Your Grace. This old body doesn't have the spring it did in the olden days."

"Physician, heal thyself."

"Believe me, kid, I would if I could. If I had my druthers I'd be twenty-three years old for the rest of my life. Which would last another three thousand years."

"That wind off the plain. It has Uncle worried, too."

"Doj is always worried about something. What does your father say?"

"He and Mom are still at Khang Phi visiting Master Santaraksita."

At a tender twenty Tobo is already the most powerful sorcerer in all this world. Lady says he might possibly become a match for her in her prime. Scary. But he has parents he calls Mom and Dad still. He has friends he treats like people, not objects. He accords his teachers respect and honor instead of devouring them just to prove that he is stronger. His mother raised him well, despite having done so in the environment of the Black Company. And despite his innate rebellious streak. I hope he will remain a decent human being once he comes into his full powers.

My wife does not believe that is possible. She is a pessimist about character. She insists that power corrupts. Inevitably. She has only her own history by which to judge. And she sees only the dark side of everything. Even so, she remains one of Tobo's teachers. Because, despite her bleak outlook, she retains the silly romantic streak that brought her here with me.

I did not try to keep up with the boy. Time definitely has slowed me. And has left me with an ache for every one of the thousands of miles this battered old corpse has trudged. And it has equipped me with an old man's talent for straying off the subject.

The boy never stopped chattering about the Black Hounds, fees, hobs and hobyahs and other creatures of the night that I have never seen. Which is all right.

The few he has brought around have all been ugly, smelly, surly and all too eager to copulate with humans of any sex or sexuality. The Children of the Dead claim that yielding is not a good idea. So far discipline has held.

The evening *was* chill. Both moons were up. Little Boy was full. The sky was totally clear except for a circling owl being pestered by what appeared to be a brace of night-flying rooks. One of those, in turn, had some smaller black bird skipping along behind it, darting in and out as it prosecuted reprisals for some corvine trangression. Or just for the hell of it, the way my sister-in-law would do.

Likely none of the flyers were actual birds.

A huge something loomed beyond the nearest house. It made snorting noises and shuffled away. What I made out looked vaguely like the head of a giant duck. The earliest of the conquering Shadowmasters had possessed a bizarre turn of humor. This big, slow, goofy thing was a killer. Among the worst of the others were a giant beaver, a crocodile with eight legs and a pair of arms and many variations of the themes of killer cattle, horses and ponies, most of which spend their daytimes hiding underwater.

The most bizarre beings were created by the nameless Shadowmaster now recalled as the First One or the Master of Time. His raw material had consisted of shadows off the glittering plain, which in Hsien are known as the Host of the Unforgiven Dead. It seems appropriate that Hsien be called the Land of Unknown Shadows.

A long feline roar ripped the night. That would be Big Ears or his sister Cat Sith. By the time I reached One-Eye's place the Black Hounds had begun to vocalize, too.

One-Eye's house was scarcely a year old. The little wizard's friends raised it after they completed their own places. Before that One-Eye and his girlfriend, Tobo's grandmother Gota, lived in an ugly, smelly little stick-and-mud hut. The new place was of mortared stone. It had a first-rate thatch roof above its four large rooms, one of which concealed a still. One-Eye might be too old and feeble to weasel his way into the local black market but I am sure he will continue distilling strong spirits till the moment his own spirit departs his wizened flesh. The man is dedicated.

Gota kept the house spotless via the ancient device of bullying her daughter Sahra into doing the housework. Gota, still called the Troll by the old hands, was as feeble as One-Eye. They were a matched pair in their passion for potent beverages. When One-Eye gave up the ghost he would be drawing a gill of the hard stuff for his honey.

Tobo poked his head back outside. "Hurry up!"

"Know who you're talking to, boy? The former military dictator of all the Taglias."

The boy grinned, no more impressed than anyone else is these days. "Used to be" is not worth the breeze on which it is scribbled.

I tend to philosophize about that, probably a little too much. Once upon a time I was nothing and had no ambition to be anything more. Circumstance conspired to put immense power into my hands. I could have ripped the guts out of half a world had that been my inclination. But I let other obsessions drive me. So I am here on the far side of the circle, where I started, scraping wounds, setting bones and scribbling histories nobody is likely to read. Only now I am a lot older and crankier. I have buried all the friends of my youth except One-Eye. . . .

I ducked into the old wizard's house.

The heat was ferocious. One-Eye and Gota had trouble keeping warm even in summer. Though summers in southern Hsien seldom become hot.

I stared. "You sure he's in trouble?"

Tobo said, "He tried to tell me something. I didn't understand so I came for you. I was afraid." Him. Afraid.

One-Eye was seated in a rickety chair he had built for himself. He was motionless but things stirred in the corners of the room, usually only visible at the edge of my eye. Snail shells cluttered the floor. Tobo's father, Murgen, calls them brownies after little folk recalled from his youth. There had to be twenty different races of them around, from no bigger than a thumb to half a man high. They really did do work when nobody was looking. That drove Sleepy crazy. It meant she had to work harder to think up chores to keep the Company's villains out of trouble.

An overpowering stench pervaded One-Eye's house. It came from the mash for his still.

The devil himself looked like a shrunken head the shrinker had not bothered to separate from its body. One-Eye was a little bit of a thing. Even in his prime he had not been big. At two hundred and some years old, with both legs and most of one arm in the grave, he looked more like a shriveled monkey than a human being.

I said, "I hear tell you're trying to get some attention again, old man." I knelt. One-Eye's one eye opened. It focused on me. Time had been kind in that respect. His vision remained good.

He opened his toothless mouth. At first nothing came out. He tried to raise a mahogany spider of a hand. He did not have the strength.

Tobo shuffled his feet and muttered at the things in the corners. There are ten thousand strange things infesting Hsien and he knows every one by name. And they all worship him. For me this intersection with the hidden world has been the most troubling development of our stay in the Land of Unknown Shadows.

I liked them better when they were still unknown.

Outside Skryker or Black Shuck or another Black Hound began raising a racket. Others replied. The uproar moved southward, toward the Shadowgate. I willed Tobo to go investigate.

He stayed put, all questions and nags. He was about to become a major pain in the ass. "How's your grandmother?" I asked. Preemptive strike. "Why don't you check?" Gota was not in the room. Usually she was, determinedly trying to do for One-Eye even though she had grown as feeble as he was.

One-Eye made a noise, moved his head, tried to raise that hand again. He saw the boy leave the room. His mouth opened. He managed to force out words in little bursts. "Croaker. This is the . . . last. . . . She's done. I feel it. Coming. Finally."

I did not argue with him, did not question him. My error. We had been through similar scenes a half dozen times. His strokes were never quite fatal. It seemed fate had some last role for him in the grand design.

Whatever, he had to work his way through his standard soliloquy. He had to warn me against hubris because he could not get it into his head that not only am I no longer the Liberator, the military dictator of all the Taglias; I have abdicated claim to captaincy of the Black Company. The Captivity did not leave me rational enough for that task. Nor had my understudy, Murgen, come through sufficiently unscathed. The burden now rests upon Sleepy's sturdy little shoulders.

And One-Eye had to ask me to look out for Gota and Tobo. Over and over he would remind me to watch out for Goblin's wicked tricks even though we had lost Goblin years ago.

I suspect that, should there be any afterlife at all, those two will meet up about six seconds after One-Eye croaks and they will pick up their feud right where they left it in life. In fact, I am a little surprised Goblin has not been around haunting One-Eye. He threatened to often enough.

Maybe Goblin just cannot find him. Some of the Nyueng Bao say they feel lost because the shades of their ancestors cannot find them to watch over them and give advice inside their dreams.

Kina cannot find us, either, apparently. Lady has not had a bad dream in years. Or maybe Goblin killed her.

One-Eye beckoned with one desiccated finger. "Closer."

Kneeling in front of him, opening my kit, I was about as close as I could get. I took his wrist. His pulse was weak and rapid and irregular. I did not get the impression that he had suffered a stroke.

He murmured, "I am not. A fool. Who doesn't know. When he is. And what. Has happened. You *listen*! You watch out. For Goblin. Little Girl. And Tobo. Didn't see him dead. Left him with. Mother of Deceit."

"Shit!" That never occurred to me. I was not there. I was still one of the Captured when Goblin stuck the sleeping Goddess with the standard. Only Tobo and Sleepy had witnessed that. And anything they knew had to be suspect. Kina was the Queen of Deceivers. "A good idea, old man. Now, what do I have to do to get you to get up and fetch me a drink?"

Then I started as something that looked like a small black rabbit peeked at me from under One-Eye's chair. This was a new one. I could call Tobo. He would know what it was. There are uncounted varieties of the things, huge and small, some gentle and many definitely not. They just gravitate toward Tobo. In only a few cases, generally involving the most disagreeable sorts, has he taken Lady's advice and bound them to his personal service.

The Children of the Dead worry about Tobo. Having suffered a few hundred years under the heels of the Shadowmasters they are paranoid about outsider sorcerers.

So far the warlords have remained reasonable. None of them want to spark the ire of the Soldiers of Darkness. That might cause the Company to align itself with a rival. Status quo and balance of force are cherished and jealously nurtured by the File of Nine. Terrible chaos followed the expulsion of the last Shadowmaster. None of the warlords want the chaos to return, though what Hsien has now resembles nothing so much as lightly organized anarchy. But not a one is willing to yield a minimum of power to another authority, either.

One-Eye grinned, revealing dark gums. "Not going to. Trick me. Captain."

"I'm not the Captain anymore. I'm retired. I'm just an old man who pushes paper as an excuse to keep hanging around with the living. Sleepy is the boss."

"Still. Management."

"I'm about to manage your scruffy old ass. . . ." I trailed off. His eye had closed. He made a statement by beginning to snore.

Another hoot and holler arose outside, some close by, more far away toward the Shadowgate. The snail shells creaked and rustled and, though I never saw a one touched by anything, rocked and spun around. Then I heard the distant bray of a horn.

I rose and retreated, not turning my back. One-Eye's lone remaining pleasure—other than staying drunk—was tripping the unwary with his cane.

Tobo reappeared. He looked ghastly. "Captain . . . Croaker. Sir. I misunderstood what he tried to tell me."

"What?"

"It wasn't him. It was Nana Gota."

An Abode of Ravens:
A Labor of Love

Tobo's grandmother, Ky Gota, had died happy. As happy as the Troll could die, which was drunker than three owls drowned in a wine cask. She had enjoyed a vast quantity of extremely high-potency product before she went. I told the boy, "If it's any consolation she probably didn't know a thing." Although the evidence suggested she knew exactly what was happening.

I did not fool him. "She knew it was coming. The Greylings were here." Something behind the still chittered softly in reponse to the sound of his voice. Like the baobhas, the greylings are a harbinger of death. One of a great many in Hsien. Some of the things that had been howling in the wilderness earlier would have been, too.

I said the things you say to the young. "It was probably a blessing. She was in constant pain and there was nothing I could do for her anymore." The old woman's body had been a torment to her for as long as I had known her. Her last few years had been hell.

For a moment Tobo looked like a sad little boy who wanted to bury his face in his mother's skirt and shed some tears. Then he was a young man whose control was complete again. "She did live a long life and a fulfilled one, no matter how much she complained. The family owes One-Eye for that."

Complain she had, often and loudly, to everyone about everything and everyone else. I had been fortunate enough to miss much of the Gota era by having gotten myself buried alive for a decade and a half. Such a clever man am I. "Speaking of family, you'll have to find Doj. And you'd better send word to your mother. And as soon as you can you'll need to let us know about funeral arrangements." Nyueng Bao funerary customs seem almost whimsical. Sometimes they bury their dead, sometimes they burn them, sometimes they wrap them and hang them in trees. The rules are unclear.

"Doj will make the arrangements. I'm sure the Community will demand something traditional. In which case my place is somewhere out of the way."

The Community consists of those Nyueng Bao associated with the Black Company who have not enlisted formally and who have not yet disappeared into the mysterious reaches of the Land of Unknown Shadows.

"No doubt." The Community are proud of Tobo but custom demands that they look down on him for his mixed blood and lack of respect for tradition. "Others will need to know, too. This'll be a time of great ceremony. Your grandmother is the first female from our world to pass away over here. Unless you count the white crow." Old Gota seemed much less formidable in death.

Tobo's thoughts were moving obliquely to mine. "There'll be another crow, Captain. There'll always be another crow. They feel at home around the Black Company." Which is why the Children of the Dead call our town the Abode of Ravens. There *are* always crows, real or unknown.

"They used to stay fat."

The unknown shadows were all around us now. I could see them easily myself, though seldom clearly and seldom for more than an instant. Moments of intense emotion draw them out of the shells where Tobo taught them to hide.

A renewed racket arose outside. The little darknesses stirred excitedly, then scattered, somehow disappearing without ever revealing what they were. Tobo said, "The dreamwalkers must be hanging around on the other side of the Shadowgate again."

I did not think so. This evening's racket was different.

An articulate cry came from the room where we had left One-Eye. So the old man had been faking his snooze after all. "I'd better see what he wants. You get Doj."

Y ou don't believe it." The old man was agitated now. He was angry enough to speak clearly, without much huffing and puffing. He threw up a hand. One wrinkled, twisted ebony digit pointed at something only he could see. "The doom is coming, Croaker. Soon. Maybe even tonight." Something outside howled as if to strengthen his argument but he did not hear it.

The hand fell. It rested for several seconds. Then it rose again, one digit indicating an ornate black spear resting on pegs above the doorway. "It's done." He had been crafting that death tool for a generation. Its magical power was strong enough for me to sense whenever I considered it directly. Normally I am deaf, dumb and blind in that area. I married my own personal consultant. "You run into. Goblin. Give him. The spear."

"I should just hand it over?"

"My hat, too." One-Eye showed me a toothless grin. For the entirety of my time with the Company he had worn the biggest, ugliest, dirtiest, most disreputable black felt hat imaginable. "But you got. To do it. Right." So. He still had one practical joke to pull even though it would be on a dead man and he would be dead himself long before it could happen.

There was a scratch at the door. Someone entered without awaiting invitation.

I looked up. Doj, the old swordmaster and priest of the Nyueng Bao Community. Associated with the Company but not of it for twenty-five years now. I do not entirely trust him even after so long. I seem to be the only doubter left, though.

Doj said, "The boy said Gota . . ."

I gestured. "Back there."

He nodded understanding. I would focus on One-Eye because I could do nothing for the dead. Nor all that much for One-Eye, I feared. Doj asked, "Where is Thai Dei?"

"At Khang Phi, I assume. With Murgen and Sahra."

He grunted. "I'll send someone."

"Let Tobo send some of his pets." That would get some of them out from under foot—and have the additional consequence of reminding the File of Nine, the master council of warlords, that the Stone Soldiers enjoy unusual resources. If they could detect those entities at all.

Doj paused at the doorway to the back. "There's something wrong with those things tonight. They're like monkeys when there's a leopard on the prowl."

Monkeys we know well. The rock apes haunting the ruins lying where Kiaulune stands in our own world are as pesky and numerous as a plague of locusts. They are smart enough and deft enough to get into anything not locked up magically. And they are fearless. And Tobo is too soft of heart to employ his supernatural friends in a swift educational strike.

Doj vanished through the doorway. He remained spry although he was older than Gota. He still ran through his fencing rituals every morning. I knew by direct observation that he could defeat all but a handful of his disciples using practice swords. I suspect the handful would be surprised unpleasantly if the duel ever involved real steel.

Tobo is the only one as talented as Doj. But Tobo can do anything, always with grace and usually with ridiculous ease. Tobo is the child we all think we deserve.

I chuckled.

One-Eye murmured, "What?"

"Just thinking how my baby grew up."

"That's funny?"

"Like a broken broom handle pounded up the shit chute."

"You should. Learn to appreciate. Cosmic. Practical jokes."

"I . . ."

The cosmos was spared my rancor. The street door opened to someone even less formal than Uncle Doj. Willow Swan invited himself inside. "Shut it quick!" I snapped. "That moonlight shining off the top of your head is blinding me." I could not resist. I recalled him when he was a young man with beautiful long blond hair, a pretty face and a poorly disguised lust for my woman.

Swan said, "Sleepy sent me. There're rumors."

"Stay with One-Eye. I'll deliver the news myself."

Swan bent forward. "He breathing?"

With his eye shut One-Eye looked dead. Which meant he was laying back in the weeds hoping to get somebody with his cane. He would remain a vicious little shit till the moment he did stop breathing.

"He's fine. For now. Just stay with him. And holler if anything changes." I put my things back in my bag. My knees creaked as I rose. I could not manage that without putting some of my weight on One-Eye's chair. The gods are cruel. They should let the flesh age at the rate the spirit does. Sure, some people would die of old age in a week. But the keepers would hang around forever. And I would not have all these aches and pains. Either way.

I limped as I left One-Eye's house. My feet hurt.

Things scurried everywhere but where I was looking. Moonlight did not help a bit.

The Grove of Doom:
Night Songs

The drums had begun at sunset, softly, a dark whispering promise of a shadow of all night falling. Now they roared boldly. True night had come. There was not even a sliver of moon. The flickering light of a hundred fires set shadows dancing. It appeared that the trees had pulled up their roots to participate. A hundred frenzied disciples of the Mother of Night capered with them, their passion building.

A hundred bound prisoners shivered and wept and fouled themselves, fear unmanning some who had believed themselves heroic. Their pleas fell upon unhearing ears.

A looming darkness emerged from the night, dragged by prisoners straining at cables in the hopeless hope that by pleasing their captors they might yet survive. Twenty feet tall, the shape proved to be a statue of a woman as black and glistening as polished ebony. It had four arms. It had rubies for eyes and crystal fangs for teeth. It wore a necklace of skulls. It wore another necklace of severed penises. Each taloned hand clutched a symbol of her power over humanity. The prisoners saw only the noose.

The beat of the drums grew more swift. Their volume rose. The Children of Kina began to sing a dark hymn. Those prisoners who were devout began to pray to their own favored gods.

A skinny old man watched from the steps of the temple at the heart of the Grove of Doom. He was seated. He no longer stood unless he had to. His right leg had been broken and the bone improperly set. Walking was difficult and painful. Even standing was a chore.

A tangle of scaffolding rose behind him. The temple was undergoing restoration. Again.

Standing over him, unable to remain still, was a beautiful young woman. The old man feared her excitement was sensual, almost sexual. That should not be. She was the Daughter of Night. She did not exist to serve her own senses.

"I feel it, Narayan!" she enthused. "The imminence is there. This is going to reconnect me with my mother."

"Perhaps." The old man was not convinced. There had been no connection with the Goddess for four years. He was troubled. His faith was being tested. Again. And this child had grown up far too headstrong and independent. "Or it may just bring the wrath of the Protector down on our heads." He went no farther. The argument had been running from the moment that she had used some of her raw, completely untrained magical talent to blind their keepers for the moments they had needed to escape the Protector's custody three years ago.

The girl's face hardened. For a moment it took on the dread implacability apparent on the face of the idol. As she always did when the matter of the Protector came up, she said, "She'll regret mistreating us, Narayan. Her punishment won't be forgotten for a thousand years."

Narayan had grown old being persecuted. It was the natural order of his existence. He sought always to make sure that his cult survived the wrath of its enemies. The Daughter of Night was young and powerful and possessed all of youth's impetuosity and disbelief in its own mortality. She was the child of a Goddess! That Goddess's ruling age was about to break upon the world, changing everything. In the new order the Daughter of Night would herself become a Goddess. What reason had she to fear? That madwoman in Taglios was nothing!

Invincibility and caution, they were forever at loggerheads, yet were forever inseparable.

The Daughter of Night did believe with all her heart and soul that she was the spiritual child of a Goddess. She had to. But she had been born of man and woman. A flake of humanity remained as a stain upon her heart. She had to have *somebody*.

Her movements became more pronounced and more sensual, less controlled.

Narayan grimaced. She must not forge an interior connection between pleasure and death. The Goddess was a destroyer in one avatar but lives taken in her name were not taken for reasons so slight. Kina would not countenance her Daughter yielding to hedonism. If she did there would be punishments, no doubt falling heaviest upon Narayan Singh.

The priests were ready. They dragged weeping prisoners forward to fulfill the crowning purpose of their lives, their parts in the rites that would reconsecrate Kina's temple. The second rite would strive to contact the Goddess, who lay bound in enchanted sleep, so that once again the Daughter of Night would be blessed with the Dark Mother's wisdom and far-seeing vision.

All things that needed doing. But Narayan Singh, the living saint of the Deceivers, the great hero of the Strangler cult, was not a happy man. Control had drifted too far away. The girl had begun altering the cult to reflect her own inner landscape. He feared the chance that one of their arguments would not heal afterward. That had happened with his real children. He had sworn an oath to Kina that he would bring the girl up right, that they both would see her bring on the Year of the Skulls. But if she continued growing ever more headstrong and self-serving . . .

She could restrain herself no longer. She hurried down the steps. She plucked a strangling scarf from the hands of one of the priests.

What Narayan saw in the girl's face then he had seen only one place before, in his wife's face, in her passion, so long ago that it seemed to have happened during an earlier turn around the Wheel of Life.

Saddened, he realized that when the next rite started she would throw herself into the torture of the victims. In her state she might become too involved and spill their blood, which would be an offense the Goddess would never excuse.

He was becoming extremely troubled, was Narayan Singh.

And then he became more troubled still as his wandering eye caught sight of a crow in the crotch of a tree almost directly behind the deadly rite. Worse, that crow noticed him noticing it. It flung itself into the air with a mocking cry. A hundred crow voices immediately answered from all over the grove.

The Protector *knew*!

Narayan yelled at the girl. Attention much too focused, she did not hear him.

Agony ripped through his leg as he climbed to his feet. How soon would the soldiers arrive? How would he ever run again? How would he keep the Goddess's hope alive when his flesh had grown so frail and his faith had worn so threadbare?

5

An Abode of Ravens:
Headquarters

Outpost was a quiet city of broad lanes and white walls. We had adopted the native custom of whitewashing everything but the thatch and decorative vegetation.

On holidays some locals even painted each other white. White had been a great symbol of resistance to the Shadowmasters in times gone by.

Our city was artificial and military, all straight lines, cleanliness and quiet. Except at night, if Tobo's friends got to brawling amongst themselves. By day, noise was confined to the training fields where the latest bunch of native would-be adventurers were learning the Black Company way of doing business. I was remote from all that except for patching up training mishaps. No one from my era was involved anymore. Like One-Eye I am a relic of a distant age, a living icon of the history that makes up so much of the unique social adhesive we used to hold the Company together. They rolled me out on special occasions and had me give sermons that began, "In those days the Company was in service to . . ."

It was a spooky night, the two moons illuminating everything while casting conflicting shadows. And Tobo's pets were increasingly disturbed about something. I began to catch straightforward glimpses of some when they became too distracted to work at staying out of sight. In most cases I was sorry.

The uproar up toward the Shadowgate rose and fell. There were lights up there now, too. A couple of fireballs flew just before I reached my destination. I began to feel uneasy myself.

Headquarters was a two-story sprawl at the center of town. Sleepy had filled it with assistants and associates and functionaries who kept track of every horseshoe nail and every grain of rice. She had turned command into a bureaucratic exercise. And I did not like it. Of course. Because I was a cranky old man who remembered how things used to be in the good old days when we did things the right way. My way.

I do not think I have lost my sense of humor, though. I see the irony in having turned into my own grandfather.

I have stepped aside. I have passed the torch to someone younger, more energetic and tactically brighter than I ever was. But I have not abandoned my right to
be involved, to contribute, to criticize and, particularly, to complain. It is a job
somebody has to do. So I exasperate the younger people sometimes. Which is good
for them. It builds character.

I strode through the ground-floor busywork Sleepy uses to shield herself from
the world. Day or night there was a crew on duty, counting those arrowheads and
grains of rice. I should remind her to get out into the world once in a while. Putting
up barriers will not protect her from her demons because they are all inside her
already.

I was almost old enough to get away with talk like that.

Irritation crossed her dry, dusky, almost sexless face when I walked in. She was at
her prayers. I do not understand that. Despite everything she has been through, much
of which puts the lie to Vehdna doctrine, she persists in her faith.

"I'll wait till you're done."

The fact that I had caught her was what irritated her. The fact that she needed
to believe even in the face of the evidence was what embarrassed her.

She rose, folded her prayer rug. "How bad is he this time?"

"Rumor got it wrong. It wasn't One-Eye. It was Gota. And she's gone. But One-
Eye is in a pickle about something else he thinks is going to happen. About which he
was less than vague. Tobo's friends are being more than normally weird so it's entirely possible it isn't One-Eye's imagination."

"I'd better send someone after Sahra."

"Tobo is taking care of it."

Sleepy considered me steadily. She may be short but she has presence and self-
confidence. "What's on your mind?"

"I'm feeling some of what One-Eye is. Or maybe I just naturally can't stand a
prolonged peace."

"Lady nagging you about going home again?"

"No. Murgen's last communion with Shivetya has her worried." To say the least.
Modern history had turned cruel back in our home world. The Deceiver cult has
rebounded in our absence, making converts by the hundred. At the same time Soulcatcher tormented the Taglian Territories in a mad and mainly fruitless effort to
root out her enemies, most of whom were imaginary until she and Mogaba created
them through their zeal. "She hasn't said so but I'm pretty sure she's afraid Booboo
is manipulating Soulcatcher somehow."

Sleepy could not stifle a smile. "Booboo?"

"Your fault. I picked it up from something you wrote."

"She's your daughter."

"We have to call her something."

"I can't believe you two never picked a name."

"She was born before . . ." I like "Chana." It was good enough for my grandmother. Lady would have demurred. It sounded too much like Kina.

And although Booboo might be a nightmare stalking, Booboo was *Lady's* daughter and in the land where she had grown up mothers always named the daughters. Always. When the time was right.

This time will never be right. This child denies us both. She stipulates that our flesh quickened her flesh but she is animated by an absolute conviction that she is the spiritual daughter of the Goddess Kina. She is the Daughter of Night. Her sole purpose for existing is to precipitate the Year of the Skulls, that great human disaster that will free her slumbering soulmother so she can resume working her wickedness upon the world. Or upon the worlds, actually, as we had discovered once my quest for the Company's ancient origins had led us to the time-wracked fortress on the plain of glittering stone lying between our world and the Land of Unknown Shadows.

Silence stretched between us. Sleepy had been Annalist a long time. She had come to the Company young. Its traditions meant a great deal to her. Consequently she remained unfailingly courteous to her predecessors. But internally, I am sure, she was impatient with us old farts. Particularly with me. She never knew me well. And I was always taking up time wanting to know what was going on. I have begun putting too much emphasis on detail now that I do not have much to do but write.

I told her, "I don't offer advice unless you ask."

That startled her.

"Trick I learned from Soulcatcher. Makes people think you're reading their minds. She's much better at it."

"I'm sure she is. She's had all that time to practice." She puffed air out of expanded cheeks. "It's been a week since we've talked. Let's see. Nothing to report from Shivetya. Murgen's been at Khang Phi with Sahra so he hasn't been in touch with the golem. Reports from the men working on the plain say they're suffering from recurring premonitions of disaster."

"Really? They said it that way?" She had her pontifical moments.

"Roughly."

"What's the traffic situation?"

"There is none." She looked puzzled. The plain had seen no one cross for generations before the Company managed the passage. The last, before us, had been the Shadowmasters who had fled the Land of Unknown Shadows for our world back before I was born.

"Wrong question. I guess. How're you coming with preparations for our return?"

"That a personal or professional question?" Everything was business with Sleepy. I do not recall ever having seen her relax. Sometimes that worried me. Something in her past, hinted at in her own Annals, had left her convinced that that was the only way she could be safe.

"Both." I wished I could tell Lady that we would be going home soon. She had no love for the Land of Unknown Shadows.

I am sure she will not enjoy the future wherever we go. It is an absolute certainty that the times to come will not be good. I do not believe she understands that yet. Not in her heart.

Even she can be naive about some things.

"The short answer is that we can probably put a reinforced company across as early as next month. If we can acquire the Shadowgate knowledge."

Crossing the plain is a major undertaking because you have to carry with you everything you will need for a week. Up there there is nothing to eat but glittering stone. Stone remembers but stone has little nutritional value.

"Are you going too?"

"I'm going to send scouts and spies, no matter what. We can use the home Shadowgate as long as we only put through a few men at a time."

"You won't take Shivetya's word?"

"The demon has his own agenda."

She would know. She had been in direct communion with that Steadfast Guardian.

What I knew of the golem's designs made me concerned for Lady. Shivetya, that ancient entity, created to manage and watch over the plain—which was an artifact itself—wanted to die. He could not do so while Kina survived. One of his tasks was to ensure that the sleeping Goddess did not awaken and escape her imprisonment.

When Kina ceased to exist, my wife's tenuous grasp on those magical powers critical to her sense of self-worth and identity would perish with her. What powers Lady boasted, she possessed only because she had found a way to steal from the Goddess. She was a complete parasite.

I said, "And you, believing the Company dictum that we have no friends outside, don't value his friendship."

"Oh, he's perfectly marvelous, Croaker. He saved my life. But he didn't do it because I'm cute and I jiggle in the right places when I run."

She was not cute. I could not imagine her jiggling, either. This was a woman who had gotten away with pretending to be a boy for years. There was nothing feminine about her. Nor anything masculine, either. She was not a sexual being at all, though for a while there had been rumors that she and Swan had become a midnight item.

It turned out purely platonic.

"I'll reserve comment. You've surprised me before."

"Captain!"

Took her a while, sometimes, to understand when someone was joking. Or even being sarcastic, though she had a tongue like a razor herself.

She realized I was ribbing her. "I see. Then let me surprise you one more time by asking your advice."

"Oh-oh. You'll have them sharpening their skates in hell."

"Howler and Longshadow. I've got to make decisions."

"File of Nine nagging you again?" The File of Nine—"File" from military usage—was a council of warlords, their identities kept secret, who formed the nearest thing to a real ruling body in Hsien. The monarchy and aristocracy of record were little more than decorative and, in the main, too intimate with poverty to accomplish much if the inclination existed.

The File of Nine had only limited power. Their existence barely assured that near-anarchy did not devolve into complete chaos. The Nine would have been more effective had they not prized their anonymity more than their implied power.

"Them and the Court of All Seasons. The Noble Judges really want Longshadow." The imperial court of Hsien—consisting of aristocrats with less real world power than the File of Nine but enjoying more a demonstrative moral authority—were obsessively interested in gaining possession of Longshadow. Being an old cynic I tended to suspect them of less than moral ambitions. But we had few dealings with them. Their seat, Quang Ninh City, was much too far away.

The one thing the peoples of Hsien held in common, every noble and every peasant, every priest and every warlord, was an implacable and ugly thirst for revenge upon the Shadowmaster invaders of yesteryear. Longshadow, still trapped in stasis underneath the glittering plain, represented the last possible opportunity to extract that cathartic vengeance. Longshadow's value in our dealings with the Children of the Dead was phenomenally disproportionate.

Hatreds seldom are constrained to rational scales.

Sleepy continued, "And hardly a day goes by that I don't hear from some lesser warlord begging me to bring Longshadow in. The way they all volunteer to take charge of him leaves me nurturing the sneaking suspicion that most of them aren't quite as idealistically motivated as the File of Nine and the Court of All Seasons."

"No doubt. He'd be a handy tool for anybody who wanted to adjust the power balance. If anyone was fool enough to believe he could manage a puppet Shadowmaster." No world lacks its villains so self-confident that they don't believe they can get the best end of a bargain with the darkness. I married one of those. I am not sure she has learned her lesson yet. "Has anyone offered to fix our Shadowgate?"

"The Court is actually willing to give us someone. The trouble with that is that they don't actually have anyone equipped with the skills to make the needed fixes. Chances are, no one has those skills. But the knowledge exists in records stored at Khang Phi."

"So why don't we? . . ."

"We're working on it. Meantime, the Court do seem to believe in us. And they absolutely do want some kind of revenge before all of Longshadow's surviving victims have been claimed by age."

"And what about the Howler?"

"Tobo wants him. Says he can handle him now."

"Does anybody else think so?" I meant Lady. "Or is he overconfident?"

Sleepy shrugged. "There's nobody telling me they've got anything more they can teach him." She meant Lady, too, and did not mean that Tobo suffered from a teen attitude. Tobo had no trouble taking advice or instruction when either of those did not originate with his mother.

I asked anyway. "Not even Lady?"

"She, I think, might be holding out on him."

"You can bet on it." I married the woman but I don't have many illusions about her. She would be thrilled to go back to her old wicked ways. Life with me and the Company has not been anything like happily ever after. Reality has a way of slow-roasting romance. Though we get along well enough. "She can't be any other way. Get her to tell you about her first husband. You'll marvel that she came out as sane as she did." I marveled every day. Right before I gave in to my astonishment that the woman really had given up everything to ride off with me. Well, something. She had not had much at the time and her prospects had been grim. "What the hell is that?"

"Alarm horns." Sleepy bolted out of her seat. She was spry for a woman treading hard on the heels of middle age. On the other hand, of course, she was so short she did not have a lot of real getting up to do. "I didn't order any drills."

She had an ugly habit of doing that. Only the traitor Mogaba, when he had been with us, had had as determined an attitude about preparedness.

Sleepy was too serious about everything.

Tobo's unknown shadows began raising their biggest uproar yet.

"Come on!" Sleepy snapped. "Why aren't you armed?" She was. She always was, although I never have seen her use a weapon more substantial than guile.

"I'm retired. I'm a paper pusher these days."

"I don't see you wearing a tombstone for a hat."

"I had an attitude problem once upon a time, myself, but . . ."

"Speaking of which. I want a reading in the officers' mess before lights out. Something that tells us all about the wages of indolence and the neglect of readiness. Or about the fate of ordinary mercenaries." She was in brisk motion, headed for the main exit, overtaking staffers who were not dawdling themselves. "Make a hole, people. Make a hole. Coming through."

Outside, people were pointing and babbling. The moonlight and a lot of fire betrayed a pillar of black, oily smoke boiling up from just below the gate to the glittering plain. I stated the obvious. "Something's happened." Clever me.

"Suvrin's up there. He has a level head."

Suvrin was a solid young officer with maybe just a tad of worship for his captain. You could be confident that neither accidents nor stupid mistakes would happen on Suvrin's watch.

Runners gathered, ready to carry Sleepy's instructions. She gave the only order she could till we knew more. Be alert. Even though to a man we believed that there was no way major trouble could come at us from off the plain.

The thing that you know to be true is the lie that will kill you.

An Abode of Ravens:
Suvrin's News

Suvrin did not arrive until after midnight. By then even our dullards understood that there was significance to the agitation of the hidden folk and the crows whose presence gave our settlement its local name. Arms had been issued. Men with fireball poles now perched on every rooftop. Tobo had warned his supernatural friends to stay out of town lest taut human nerves snap and cause them harm.

Everyone of stature available gathered to await Suvrin's report. A couple of sub-alterns took turns running up to the headquarters' roof to check the progress of the torches descending the long scarp from the Shadowgate. Local boys, they seemed to feel that their great adventure had begun at last.

They were fools.

An adventure is somebody else slogging through the mud and snow while suffering from trench foot, ringworm, dysentery and starvation, being chased by people with their hearts set on murder or more. I have been there. I have done that, playing both parts. I do not recommend it. Be content with a nice farm or shop. Make lots of babies and bring them up to be good people.

If the new blood remain blind to reality after we move out I guarantee that their naivete will not long survive their first encounter with my sister-in-law, Soulcatcher.

Suvrin finally arrived, accompanied by the runner Sleepy had sent to meet him. He seemed surprised by the size of the assembly awaiting him.

"Get up front and talk," Sleepy told him. Always direct and to the point, my successor.

Silence fell. Suvrin looked around nervously. He was short, dark, slightly pudgy.

His family had been minor nobility. Sleepy had taken him prisoner of war four years ago, just before the Company climbed onto the glittering plain, headed this way. Now he commanded an infantry battalion and seemed destined for bigger things because the Company was growing. He told us, "Something came through the Shadowgate."

Jabber jabber, question question.

"I don't know what. One of my men came to tell me he thought he'd seen something sneaking around in the rocks on the other side of the gate. I went to look. After four years of nothing happening I assumed it would be just a shadow or one of the Nef. The dreamwalkers visit us all the time. I was wrong. I never got a good look at the thing but it seemed to be a large animal, black and extremely fast. Not as big as Big Ears or Cat Sith but definitely faster. It was able to pass through the Shadowgate without help."

I felt a chill. I tried to reject my immediate suspicion. It was not possible. Nevertheless, I said, "Forvalaka."

"Tobo, where are you?" Sleepy demanded.

"Here." He sat with several Children of the Dead, officers in training.

"Find this thing. Catch it. If it's what Croaker said, I want you to kill it."

"That'll be easier said than done. It's already squabbled with the Black Hounds. They backed off. They're just trying to keep track of it now."

"Then kill it, Tobo." There was no "try to" or "do whatever you can" with this Captain.

I told him, "Ask Lady to help you. She knows those things. But before anybody does anything, we need to set up some kind of protection for One-Eye." If it was a shapeshifting, man-eating werepanther from our homeworld, it could be only one monster. And that creature hated One-Eye with the deepest and most abiding passion imaginable because One-Eye had slain the only wizard capable of helping it regain its human form.

"You think it really is Lisa Bowalk?" Sleepy asked.

"I get that feeling. But you told me it escaped from the plain through the Khatovar gate. And it couldn't get back."

Sleepy shrugged. "That's what Shivetya showed me. It's possible that I just assumed it couldn't get back onto the plain."

"Or maybe it made new friends out there."

The little woman spun, barked, "Suvrin?"

Suvrin understood. "I left them on maximum alert."

I said, "Tobo will have to check the seals on the gate. We don't want it leaking shadows because whatever it was broke through." Though the boy would not be able to do much to stem a real flood. That honor would have to go to his hidden folk friends. Lack of technical knowledge about Shadowgates was the main reason we continued to reside in the Land of Unknown Shadows.

"I understand that, Croaker. Can I get to work here?"

I was underfoot. Being considered useless is irksome. That condition was familiar to most of us whom Soulcatcher had beguiled and captured and managed to leave buried for fifteen years. Our Company had changed during our slumber. Even Lady and Murgen, who had maintained tenuous connections with the outside world, found themselves marginalized now. Murgen did not mind.

The culture of the Company has become quite alien. Almost no northern flavor remains. Just a few little quirks, in how things are done, and my own proud legacy, an interest in hygiene that is completely foreign to these climes.

These southerners did not enjoy a proper terror of the forvalaka. They insisted on picturing it as just another spooky nightstalker like Big Ears or Paddlefoot, which they consider essentially harmless. Near as I can tell they appear harmless only because their victims seldom survive to report any contrary facts.

A reading from the First Book of Croaker," I told the assembly. It was after midnight. There had been no uproar for a while. The Shadowgate was not leaking the Unforgiven Dead. Tobo was trying to pinpoint the intruder but was having difficulties. It was moving around a lot, scouting, plainly unsure how it should view the fact that it had fallen right in among us. "In those days the Company was in service to the Syndic of Beryl."

I told them about another forvalaka, long ago and far away and way more cruel than this one ever could be. I wanted them to worry.

An Abode of Ravens:
Night Visitor

Lady and I sat up with One-Eye. Gota had been laid out in the same room. Candles surrounded her. "I see no obvious change in the woman."

"Croaker! Hush!"

"I hear a difference, though. She hasn't complained about anything since we got here."

Playing deaf, One-Eye took a long drink of his product, closed his eye, nodded off. Lady whispered, "It's probably best if he naps."

"Not very lively bait."

"Carrion's good enough to draw this thing. What it wants to kill really only exists inside itself. One-Eye is just its symbol." She rubbed her eyes.

I winced. She looked so old, my love. Grey hair. Wrinkles. Jowls developing. Broadening in the beam. The deterioration had been swift since Sleepy rescued us.

Lucky for me there was no mirror handy. I really do not like to look at that fat, old, bald guy who goes around claiming to be Croaker.

The shadows in the room were restless. They made me nervous. From the beginning of our association with Taglios, shadows have been cause for terror. A shadow in motion meant death could have hold of you any moment. Those sad but cruel monsters off the plain had been the lethal instruments by which the Shadowmasters had earned their fame and had enforced their wills. But here, in the Land of Unknown Shadows, the hidden folk who lurked in the dark were shy but not ordinarily unfriendly—if treated with respect. And even those manifestations owning a history of wickedness and malice now worshipped Tobo and harmed no mortal closely associated with the Company. Unless that mortal was dim enough to irk Tobo somehow.

Tobo lived as much in the world of the hidden folk as he did in ours.

In the distance the spectral cat Big Ears again mouthed his unique call. Native legend says only the creature's prospective victims ever hear that chilling cry. A couple of the Black Hounds bayed. Legend suggests you do not want to hear their voices, either. Interviews with locals lead me to believe that before Tobo arrived only ignorant peasants really believed in most such perils of the night and the wild. Educated folk at Khang Phi and Quang Ninh had been stunned by what the boy had summoned from the shadows.

I glanced at the spear above the door. One-Eye had worked on that for decades. It was as much work of art as weapon. "Hon. Didn't One-Eye start crafting that spear because of Bowalk?"

She paused in her knitting, stared up at the spear, mused, "Seems to me Murgen wrote that One-Eye intended to use it on one of the Shadowmasters but ended up sticking Bowalk with it instead. During the siege. Or was that? . . ."

My knees creaked as I rose. "Whatever. Just in case." I took the spear down. "Damn. It's heavy."

"If the monster does get this far, try to keep in mind that we'd rather catch it than kill it."

"I know. It was my bright idea." The wisdom of which I had begun to doubt. I thought it might be interesting to see what would happen if we could force it to change back into the woman it had been before it had become fixed in its cat shape. I wanted to ask her questions about Khatovar.

Always assuming that the invader was the dread forvalaka, Lisa Daele Bowalk.

I sat down again. "Sleepy says she's ready to send spies and scouts across."

"Uhm?"

"We've been avoiding the facts a long time." This was hard. It had taken me an age to work up to it. "The girl . . . Our child . . ."

"Booboo?"

"You, too?"

"We have to call her something. The Daughter of Night is so unwieldy. Booboo works without being an emotional calthrop."

"We have to make some decisions."

"She'll . . ."

Black Hounds, Cat Sith, Big Ears and numerous other hidden folk began to give voice. I said, "That's inside the wall."

"Headed this way." She set her knitting aside.

One-Eye's head rose.

The door exploded inward before I finished turning to face it.

A plank floated toward me in slow motion, slapped me across the belly hard enough to set me down on the floor on my butt. Something huge and black with blazing angry eyes followed the board but lost interest in me in midleap. Still falling backward onto my back I scored its flank with One-Eye's spear. Flesh parted. Rib bones appeared. I tried to thrust on into the beast's belly but did not have enough leverage. It screamed but could not alter its momentum.

Burning pain seared deep into my left shoulder, not three inches from the side of my neck. The forvalaka was not responsible, though. Friendly fire was. My sweet wife had discharged a fireball projector while I was between her and her target. There was plenty of fire left, though, when that ball, its flight path altered, clipped the panther's tail two inches from its root.

The monster's scream continued. It flung its head back while still airborne. Its whole frame was in the position heralds call rampant.

It hit One-Eye.

The old man made no obvious effort to defend himself. His chair went over. It shattered into kindling wood. One-Eye skidded along the dirt floor. The forvalaka ploughed into Gota, tipping the table on which she had been laid out. Lady loosed another fireball. It missed. I fought to get around onto my hands and knees, then to get the head of the spear up, between me and the monster. It fought for its footing while trying to turn at the same time. It slammed into the far wall. I got my feet under me, started to stumble around.

Lady missed again.

"No!" I shrieked. My feet tangled. I came close to landing on my face again. I tried to do three things at once and, naturally, did none of them well. I wanted to get hold of One-Eye, I wanted to get my spearhead back up, I wanted to get the hell out of that house.

Lady did not miss again. But this fireball was a puny one, a near dud. It hit the monster right between the eyes. And just ricocheted off, taking a few square inches of skin along with it, leaving a patch of skull bone exposed.

The forvalaka screamed again.

Then One-Eye's still blew up. Which is what I had expected from the moment Lady's fireball had gone through the wall.

Taglios:
Trouble Follows

Mogaba knew there was trouble seconds after he left his rooms, so austerely furnished in shabby regrets. Palace staffers pushed to the sides of the corridors as he passed. Without exception they were scuttling away from the Privy Council Chamber. They must have heard rumors that had not yet reached his ears. Rumors they were sure would displease the Protector, which meant that, soon, someone would be making life unpleasant for someone else and these people hoped to be well out of the way before he started.

"Pride," he said, in a normal, conversational voice to a young Grey runner trying to ease past without attracting notice. "Pride is what did me in."

"Yes, sir." Color drained from the young Shadar's face. He did not yet have a beard to hide behind. "I mean, no sir. I'm sorry. . . ."

Mogaba was gone, indifferent to the apprentice soldier. Similar incidents occurred each time he passed through the Palace. He spoke to almost everyone. Those who had watched the habit develop understood that he was talking to himself and did not expect any reply. He was pursuing a running debate with his own guilts and ghosts—unless he was spouting proverbs and aphorisms, most of the meanings fairly obvious but a few convolute and obscure. He was particularly fond of "Fortune smiles. And then betrays." He just could not get into bed comfortably with the truth that he had made that bed himself. He still had difficulty separating "ought to be" from "the way things really are." He was no fool, though. He knew he had problems.

He was certain that he had a much more solid grip on reality than did his employer, though.

Soulcatcher, however, took the view that she was a virtual free agent and refused to be wedded to any particular reality. She believed in creating her own by making her imaginings come true.

Some were quite mad. Few, however, lasted beyond the heated moment of conception.

Mogaba heard crows arguing ahead. Crows infested the Palace these days. Soulcatcher was fond of crows. She allowed no one to harass or harm them. Of late bats had made a claim on her affections as well.

When the crows became vocal the few servants still around started moving much faster. Unhappy crows meant unhappy news. Unhappy news was guaranteed to produce an extremely unhappy Protector. When Soulcatcher was unhappy she did not care who suffered the consequences. But someone surely would.

Mogaba stepped into the council chamber and waited. She would talk to him when she was ready. Ghopal Singh of the Greys and Aridatha Singh of the City Battalions—no relation: Singh was the most common surname in Taglios—were there already. Which meant that Soulcatcher must have been haranguing them about their failure to root out enough enemies, again, before the bad news arrived.

Mogaba exchanged glances with both men. As he believed himself to be, they were good men trapped by impossible circumstances. Ghopal had a flair for enforcing the law. Aridatha was equally talented at keeping the peace without enraging the populace. Both men managed despite Soulcatcher, who loved both chaos and despotism and inflicted each with verve and ferocity, driven by the dictates of whimsy.

The woman seemed to materialize suddenly. It was a talent she used to disconcert lesser beings. A lesser man than Mogaba might have been numbed by the sight of her. The woman had a body the wonders of which seemed highlighted rather than concealed by the tight black leather she wore. Nature had blessed her with superb raw materials. Her vanity had driven her, over the centuries, to keep making improvements through cosmetic sorceries.

"I'm not happy," Soulcatcher announced. Her voice was petulant, that of a spoiled child. Today her look was younger than usual, as though she wanted to spark every young man's fantasy. Although the preening crow on the tall chair back behind her was a distraction once she settled.

"May I ask why?" Mogaba asked. His voice was calm, untroubled. Life in the Palace at Taglios consisted of a disorganized stumble from crisis to crisis. He no longer became emotionally involved. Soulcatcher would turn on him someday. He had made his peace with that already. He would face it calmly when it came. He deserved no better.

"There is a huge Deceiver festival being celebrated in the Grove of Doom. Right now. Tonight." This voice was cool, calm, rational. Masculine. You got used to the changes after a while. Mogaba seldom noticed anymore. Aridatha Singh, only recently promoted, still found the unpredictable chorus disconcerting. Singh was a sound officer and good soldier. Mogaba hoped he lasted long enough to become accustomed to the Protector's quirks. Aridatha deserved better than he was likely to get.

"That's definitely not good news," Mogaba agreed. "Seems I recall you wanting to harvest the timber there while obliterating every last trace of the holy place. Selvas Gupta talked you out of it. Said it would set a bad precedent." Gupta had had secret encouragement from the Great General, who had not cared to waste manpower and time clearing a forest. But Mogaba loathed Selvas Gupta and his smugly holy attitude of superiority.

Gupta was the current Purohita, or official court chaplain and religious adviser. Purohita was a post that had been forced upon the Radisha Drah twenty years earlier by the priesthoods at a time when the princess had been too weak to defy them. Soulcatcher had not yet abolished it. But she had little patience with the men who occupied it.

Selvas Gupta had been Purohita for a year, which incumbency exceeded that of all his predecessors since the establishment of the Protectorate.

Mogaba was confident that slimy little snake Gupta would not last out the week.

Soulcatcher gave him a look which offered the impression that she was peering deep inside him, sorting his secrets and motives. Having paused just long enough to suggest that she was not being fooled, she said, "Get me a new Purohita. Kill the old one if he argues about it." She had an ancient custom of being unpleasant toward priests who disappointed her. Which ran in the family. Her sister had slain hundreds in a single massacre a generation earlier. The exemplary demonstrations of both sisters, however, never seemed sufficient to convince the survivors that they ought to abandon their scheming. They were stubborn. It seemed likely that Taglios would come up short of priests before it ran short of conspiracies.

The crow hopped down onto Soulcatcher's shoulder. She lifted gloved fingers to offer it some tidbit.

"Did you have a response in mind? Something involving my colleagues?" Mogaba nodded toward the Singhs in turn. He suffered little jealousy of either man and did respect each for his abilities. Time and persistent adversity had ground the rough edges off of his once potent sense of self-appreciation.

"These gentlemen were here already, regarding another matter, when the news from the Grove arrived." She offered the crow another morsel.

Mogaba's eyes narrowed the tiniest fraction. He was not to be made privy to that matter?

But he was. Soulcatcher used a cackling crone's voice. "The Greys found several slogans painted on walls today." The crow cawed. Elsewhere, other crows began squabbling.

"Not uncommon," Mogaba replied. "Every idiot with a brush, a pot of paint and enough education to string five characters together seems to be compelled to say something if he discovers a blank piece of wall."

"These were slogans from the past." This was the voice the Protector used when she was focused entirely on business. It was a male voice. A voice like Mogaba imagined his own to be. "Three said '*Rajadharma.*'"

"I've heard the Bhodi cult is making a comeback, too."

Ghopal Singh added, "Two said '*Water Sleeps.*' That's not Bhodi. And they weren't stray graffiti left over from four years ago."

A thrill, half fear, half excitement, coursed through Mogaba. He stared at the Protector. She said, "I want to know who's doing it. I want to know why they've decided to do it right now."

Mogaba thought both Singhs looked cautiously pleased, as though glad to have potential real enemies to chase instead of just irritating people who would otherwise remain indifferent to the Palace.

The Grove of Doom was outside the city. Everything outside was Mogaba's province. He asked, "Was there some particular action you wished me to take in regard to the Deceivers?"

Soulcatcher smiled. When she did that, just that way, every minute of her many centuries shone through. "Nothing. Not a thing. They're scattering already. I'll let you know when. It'll be when they're not ready." This voice was cold but was filled with her evil smile. Mogaba wondered if the Singhs knew how seldom anyone saw the Protector without her mask. It meant that she meant to involve them in her schemes too deeply for them to escape the association.

Mogaba nodded like a dutiful servant. It was all a game to the Protector. Or possibly several games. Maybe making a game of it was how you survived spiritually in a world where everyone else was ephemeral.

Soulcatcher said, "I want you to help catch rats. There's a shortage of carrion. My babies are going hungry." She offered her black-winged spy another treat. This one suspiciously resembled a human eyeball.

9

An Abode of Ravens:
The Invalid

"A m I still alive?" I did not need to ask. I was. Pain was a dead giveaway. Every square inch of me hurt.

"Don't move." That was Tobo. "Or you'll wish you hadn't."

I already wished I did not have to breathe. "Burns?"

"Lots of burns. Lots of banging around, too."

Murgen's voice said, "You look like they whipped your ass with a forty-pound ugly stick, then slow-roasted what was left over an open pit."

"I thought you were at Khang Phi."

"We came home."

Tobo said, "We kept you unconscious for four days."

"How is Lady?"

Murgen told me, "She's in the other bed. In a lot better shape than you."

"She ought to be. I didn't shoot *her*. The cat get her tongue?"

"She's asleep."

"What about One-Eye?"

Tobo's response was barely audible. "One-Eye didn't make it, Croaker."

After a while, Murgen asked, "You all right?"

"He was the last."

"Last? Last what?"

"The last one who was here when I joined. The Company." I was the real Old Man now. "What happened to his spear? I've got to have his spear in order to finish this."

"What spear?" Murgen asked.

Tobo knew what spear. "I have it at my place."

"Was it damaged by the fire?"

"Not much. Why?"

"I'm going to kill that thing. Like we should have a long time ago. You don't let that spear out of your sight. I've got to have it. But right now I'm going to sleep for a while some more." I had to go where the pain was not, just for a time. I had known One-Eye would leave us someday. I thought I was ready for that. I was wrong.

His passing meant more than just the end of an old friend. It marked the end of an age.

Tobo said something about the spear. I did not catch it. And the darkness came back before I remembered to ask what had become of the forvalaka. If Lady had caught or killed it I had gotten myself worked up for nothing. . . . But I guess I knew it could not be that easy.

There were dreams. I remembered everyone who had gone before me. I remembered the places and times. Cold places, hot places, weird places, always stressful times, swollen with unhappiness, pain and fear. Some died. Some did not. It makes no sense when you try to figure it out. Soldiers live. And wonder why.

Oh, it's a soldier's life for me. Oh, the adventure and glory!

It took me longer to recuperate than it had that time I almost got killed outside Dejagore. Even with Tobo applying his own best healing spells, learned from One-Eye, and urging his edge-of-the-eye friends to help as well. Some of those were supposed to be able to bring a fossil back to life. I felt like a fossil, like I had not enjoyed the advantage of the stasis that had frozen the others while we were prisoners under the plain. There was a lot of confusion inside me. I could no longer figure out how old I am. My best guess is fifty-six, give or take a few years, plus all that time underneath the earth. And fifty-six years, brother, was a pretty damned good run—particularly for a guy in my racket. I ought to appreciate every second, including all the misery.

Soldiers live. And wonder why.

An Abode of Ravens:
Recovery

Two months had passed. I felt ten years older but I was up and around—and moving like a zombie. I had indeed been roasted well-done by a jet of almost pure alcohol blowing through the hole that had been drilled by Lady's errant fireball. Everybody kept telling me how much the gods must love me, that I had no business being alive. That had I not been turned the way I was, with the forvalaka positioned perfectly to absorb a lot of the blast, there would not have been much left of me but bones.

I was not entirely convinced that that might not have been the better outcome.

Persistent pain does little to buoy one's optimism or elevate one's mood. I began to develop a certain sympathy for Mother Gota's perspective.

I did manage a smile when Lady began to rub me down with healing unguents. "Silver linings," she told me.

"Oh, yes indeed. Yes indeed."

"Would you look at that? Maybe you're not as old as you think."

"It's all your fault, wench."

"Sleepy's worried about you wanting to avenge One-Eye."

"I know." I did not have to be told. I had had to put up with people like me when I was Captain.

"Maybe you should tone it down."

"It's got to be done. It's going to be done. Sleepy's got to understand that." Sleepy is all business. Her world does not include much leeway for emotional indulgence.

She thinks I just want to use One-Eye's death as an excuse to visit the Khatovar Shadowgate, basing her judgment on the fact that I had tramped through Hell for a decade trying to get to that place.

The woman is hard to fool. But she can also get fixed on one idea to the exclusion of other possibilities.

"She doesn't want to make any more enemies."

"More? We don't have any. Not out here. They may not like us much but they all kiss our asses. They're scared to death of us. And they get more scared every time another White Lady or Blue Man or *wichtlin* or whatnot lumbers out of folklore and joins Tobo's entourage."

"Uhn. Is that the spot? I saw something Tobo called a *wowsey* with the Black Hounds yesterday." That is my honey. She can see those things clearly, even over here. "It's as big as a hippo but looks like a beetle with a lizard's head. A lizard with big teeth. To quote Swan, 'It looks like it fell out of the ugly tree and hit every single branch on the way down.'"

Willow Swan seemed to be cultivating a new image as a churlish but colorful old man.

Somebody has to step in and take One-Eye's place. Though I was sort of thinking about picking up the stick myself.

"What do we know about the forvalaka?" I asked. I had avoided asking for specifics before. I knew the damned thing got away. That was all I needed to know until I was prepared mentally to start planning the conclusion of its tale.

"It left its tail behind. It suffered severe burns and several deep wounds and I blinded it partially with my last fireball. It lost several teeth. Tobo has created a number of fetishes using those and bits of flesh torn off by the Black Hounds while it was fleeing toward the Shadowgate."

"But it did have what it takes to get back to Khatovar."

"It did."

"Then it's going to be as hard to kill as the Limper was."

"Not anymore. Not with what Tobo has."

"He had your help?"

"I'm ancient in the ways of wickedness. Am I not? Didn't you write something like that a time or two?"

"Especially after I got to know you. . . . Ouch! Well . . . as long as you're a bad girl like you're being a bad girl right now. . . ." I do not recall if I did write the exact words she claimed but I know I recorded those approximate sentiments many years ago. Without exaggerating. "I'm going to go after it."

"I know." She did not argue. They were humoring me. They wanted to keep me quiet. Sleepy was involved in touchy negotiations with the File of Nine. The Court of All Seasons and the monks of Khang Phi were behind us already. The warlords of the File remain unconvinced that it would be wise to give us what we want even though the Company has grown to the point where it has become a serious burden on Hsien's economy. And poses a threat, if the notion of conquest happens to take root. I, myself, do not see one warlord, or even a cabal of warlords, out there, who would stand much more chance than smoke in a high wind if the notion did take us. Most of the warlords are clear on that, too.

They still want Maricha Manthara Dhumraksha—our Shadowmaster Longshadow—desperately. Their hunger for revenge borders on racial obsession.

They are not forthcoming about the evils Longshadow visited upon their forbears but we have our sources inside Khang Phi. Longshadow's cruelties had been as capricious as any wickedness of Soulcatcher's but far more terrible for their victims. The need to haul the Shadowmaster up before a tribunal colored every consideration of the warlords, the legal and noble courts, even the several spiritual traditions of Hsien. Maricha Manthara Dhumraksha was the one thing they all agreed upon. Nor did I ever sense a hint of a chance some rogue would try to acquire control of Longshadow in an effort to amplify his own power.

Sleepy did not want a short-tempered, foulmouthed but still influential former Captain stumbling around being sarcastic and opinionated while she was trying to wring the one last concession she wanted out of the File of Nine. She was confident that our years of good behavior would tilt the scale. And if it did not, well, she was the kind of planner who always had a secondary scheme in motion. In fact, she was that wonderful kind of villain for whom the public and obvious scheme might well be only a tertiary effort meant primarily as a smoke screen. Our Sleepy was one wicked little girl.

There are no great sorcerers in the Land of Unknown Shadows. "All Evil Dies There an Endless Death" means that they have persecuted the talented since the flight of the Shadowmasters. But Hsien does not lack or disdain knowledge. There are several huge monasteries—of which Khang Phi is the greatest—dedicated to the preservation of knowledge. The monks do not sort it into good and evil knowledge, nor do they make moral judgments. They take the position that no knowledge is evil until someone chooses to do evil with it.

Even though it has been engineered to wreak havoc upon the human body, a sword is strictly inert metal until someone chooses to pick it up and strike. Or chooses not to do so.

There are, of course, a thousand sophistries spewed by those who wish to deny individuals the opportunity to choose. Which is an arrogant presumption of a divine scale.

This is what happens when you get old. You start thinking. Worse, you start telling everybody what you think.

Sleepy was nervous lest I express an unfortunate opinion to one of the Nine, whereupon, in high dudgeon, the offended party would abandon all sensibility and self-interest and deny to us forever the knowledge we need to repair the Shadowgate opening on our native world. She misapprehends my ability to evoke the unfriendly response.

Before the werepanther came I might have stumbled. I might have expressed an actual opinion to a member of the File, some of whom are amongst the most reprehensible generals I have ever encountered. I doubt that, given the opportunity to rule unchallenged, many of them would be more enlightened than the hated Shadowmasters.

People are strange. The Children of the Dead are among the strangest.

I will not upset anyone. I will be diligently supportive of any policy Sleepy sets. I want to leave this Land of Unknown Shadows. I have things to accomplish before I hand these Annals over for the last time. Settling up with Lisa Daele Bowalk is just one. There is the Great General, Mogaba, the darkest traitor ever to stain the Company's history. There is Narayan Singh. For Lady, there is Narayan and Soulcatcher. For both of us there is our child. Our wicked, wicked child.

I asked, "Is there anything besides Longshadow we could offer the File of Nine? Sweeten it just enough to make them move over beside Khang Phi and the Court of All Seasons?"

My sweetie shrugged. "I can't imagine what." She smiled enigmatically. "But it may not matter."

I did not pay sufficient attention. Sometimes I overlook the new truths. These days my Company is managed by sly children and devious old women, not straightforward stalwarts like myself and the men of my time.

An Abode of Ravens:
Exercise Session

As soon as I healed enough I asked Uncle Doj to let me resume the martial arts exercises I had given up many years ago. "Why are you interested now?" he asked. Sometimes I think he is more suspicious of me than I am of him.

"Because I have time. And the need. I'm as weak as a puppy. I want to get my strength back."

"You chased me away when I offered."

"I didn't have time then. And you were so much more abrasive."

"Ha." He smiled. "You're too kind."

"You're right. But I'm a prince."

"A Prince of Darkness, Stone Soldier." He knew that would get my goat. "But a lucky prince." The old fart indulged in a smirk. "Several of your contemporaries have approached me recently, also motivated by anticipation of those hardships that can no longer be that far ahead."

"Good." Did he know something I did not? Probably a lot. "When and where?"

His grin became evil, revealing bad teeth. Which made me wonder if Sleepy had found anybody to fill the dentistry vacancy left by One-Eye's passing. The old fool had not bothered taking on apprentices.

"When" was the crack of dawn and "where" was the unpaved street outside Doj's small house, which he shared with Tobo's uncle Thai Dei and several bachelor officers of local origin. My fellow victims were Willow Swan, the brothers Loftus and Cletus, who remain the Company's principal architects and engineers, and the exiled ruling prince and princess of Taglios, the Prahbrindrah Drah and his sister the Radisha Drah. Those are not names, they are titles. Even after decades I do not know their personal designations. And they show no inclination to share.

"Where's your pal Blade?" I asked Swan. For a while Blade had been Sleepy's military envoy to the File of Nine, but I had heard that he had been recalled after One-Eye's death. I had not seen him around, though.

"Old Blade's got too much on his plate for anything like this."

Loftus and Cletus both grumbled under their breaths but did not clarify. I had not seen much of them lately, either. I supposed they were working themselves to death building a city from scratch. Suvrin, who arrived just in time to hear what they mumbled, nodded vigorously. "She's going to work us all till there's nothing but grease spots left." I am not sure about Suvrin. I have no trouble imagining him going around endlessly repeating the silent mantra, "Every day in every way I am going to become a better soldier."

"Well, old Blade never was real ambitious," Swan replied. "Except when it came to carving up priests." He seemed to know what he was talking about even if it was not obvious to me.

Clete said, "If we're getting the straight shit from Shivetya there'll be a whole new crop in need of culling when we get home."

The Prahbrindrah Drah and his sister edged closer, eager for hard news from home. Sleepy took no trouble to keep them posted. She did not have much of a diplomatic streak. I had best remind her that she will need their amity once we are back across the plain.

They were not handsome, those two. And the Radisha looked more like the Prince's mother than his sister. But he had been under the ground with me while she rode the Taglian tiger and tried not to lose its reins to Soulcatcher. They strove to remain unobtrusive here, the Prince because he had been our active enemy in the field, the Princess because she had turned on us at the very last moment of our victory over the last Shadowmasters.

Sleepy fixed her for that.

Technically, the Radisha was our prisoner. Sleepy had abducted her. She and her brother will become tools of the Company once Sleepy stages our return. Everyone agrees. But I suspect that the royals have reservations.

"*Rajadharma.*" I said, bowing slightly. I could not resist the taunt, reminding them both that by attempting to betray us they had ended up failing to fulfill their duty to their subjects.

"Liberator." The Radisha returned a tiny bow. I swear, the woman gets homelier by the month. "You appear to be healing well."

"I've got a knack for coming back. But my bounce sure ain't as fast or as high as it used to be. Guess it's old age creeping up." I lied and told her, "You're looking well yourself. You both are. What have you been doing? I haven't seen you for a while."

The Prahbrindrah Drah said nothing. He remained inscrutable. He had been quiet and unexpressive since our resurrection. We had gotten along well, once. But times change. Neither of us were the men we had been during the Shadowmaster wars.

"You're lying like a snake's belly," the Radisha told me. "I'm old and I'm ugly and I'm still ashamed of myself. . . . But you're telling the lie my soul wants to hear. Forget *rajadharma*, though. That accusation has no power to hurt me anymore. From outside. I still crucify myself. I know what I did. At the time I thought it was the right thing. The Protector manipulated me using my sense of *rajadharma*. Once we get back there you'll see us in a different light."

Rajadharma means the ruler's obligation to serve the ruled. When the word is thrown into a ruler's face, or is used as an epithet, it is a savage accusation of failure.

The Radisha is a hard, stubborn little woman. Unfortunately, she will have to get the better of a hard, stubborn, crazy, almost supremely powerful sorceress if she wants to fulfill her expectations for herself.

I glanced at her brother. The Prince's expression had not changed but I sensed that he thought he appreciated the difficulties more fully than his sister did.

Uncle Doj whacked something with a practice sword. The loud crack ended our chatter. "Your canes, please. On the count, commence the Crane Kada." He did not bother to explain what that was to the new guy.

Maybe two decades ago I had observed and briefly joined the Nyueng Bao exercises. Murgen was Annalist then. He had had Gota, Doj and his wife Sahra's brother, Thai Dei, living with him. Doj expected me to remember.

About all I recalled of the Crane Kada was that it constituted the first and simplest of a dozen slow-motion dances incorporating all the formal steps and strokes of Doj's school of fencing. The old priest led from up front, his back to his pupils. Although he was the eldest of us all, he moved with a precision and grace that verged on beauty. But when Thai Dei and Tobo joined us briefly, later, both outshone the old man. It was hard not to stop just to appreciate Tobo's mastery.

The boy made me feel clumsy and inept just standing still.

Everything came so easily for him.

He had all the talents and skills he could possibly need. If any question remained, it concerned his character. A lot of good people had worked hard to make sure that he became a virtuous and upright man. Which he did appear to be. But he was a blade not yet tested. True temptation had not yet whispered in his ear.

I missed a step badly, stumbled. Uncle Doj laid his cane across the seat of my trousers as vigorously as if I had been an adolescent. His face remained bland but I suspected that he had wanted to do that for a long time.

I tried to concentrate.

Glittering Stone:
Steadfast Guardian

The being on the huge wooden throne in the heart of the fortress at the center of the stone plain is a construct. Possibly he was created by the gods, who fought their wars upon that plain. Or perhaps his creators were the builders who constructed the plain—if they were not gods themselves. Opinions vary. Stories abound. The demon Shivetya himself is not disposed to be unstinting with the facts, or is, at best, inconsistent in their distribution. He has shown his latest chronicler several conflicting versions of ancient events. Old Baladitya has abandoned all hope of establishing an exact truth and, instead, seeks the deeper range of meaning underpinning what the golem does reveal. Baladitya understands that in addition to being foreign territory the past is, as history, a hall of mirrors that reflect the needs of souls observing from the present. Absolute fact serves the hungers of only a few disconnected people. Symbol and faith serve the rest.

Baladitya's Company career duplicates his prior life. He writes things down. When he was a copyist at the Taglian Royal Library he wrote things down. Now, nominally, he is a prisoner of war. Chances are he has forgotten that. In reality he is freer today to pursue his own interests than ever he was at the library.

The old scholar lives and works around the demon's feet. Which has to be as close to personal heaven as a Gunni historian can imagine. If the historian does not remain too determinedly wedded to Gunni religious doctrine.

Shivetya's motives for refusing categorical declarations may stem from bitterness about his lot. By his own admission he has met most of the gods face-to-face. His recollections concerning them are even less flattering than those spicing most of Gunni mythology, where few of the gods are extolled as role models. Almost without exception the Gunni deities are cruel and selfish and untouched by any celestial sense of rajadharma.

A tall black man stepped into the light cast by Baladitya's lamps. "Learned anything exciting today, old-timer?" The copyist's fuel expenses are prodigal. He is indulged.

The old man did not respond. He is almost deaf. He exploits his infirmity to its limits. Not even Blade insists that he share routine camp chores any longer.

Blade asked again but the copyist's nose remained close to the page on which he was writing. His penmanship is swift and precise. Blade cannot decipher the complicated ecclesiastical alphabet, except for some of those characters it shares with the only slightly simpler common script. Blade looked up into the golem's eye. That appeared to be about the size of a roc's egg. The adjective "baleful" fit it well. Not even naive old Baladitya has ever proposed that the demon be delivered from the restraint guaranteed by the daggers nailing its limbs to the throne. Neither has the demon ever encouraged anyone to release it. It has endured for thousands of years. It has the patience of stone.

Blade tried another approach. "I've had a runner come from the Abode of Ravens." He prefers the native name for the Company's base. It is so much more dramatic than Outpost or Bridgehead and Blade is a dramatic man fond of dramatic gestures. "The Captain says she expects to acquire the needed Shadowgate knowledge shortly. Something is about to break loose in Khang Phi. She wants me to get cracking getting more treasure brought up. She wants you to finish finding everything out. She'll be moving soon."

The copyist grunted. "He's easily bored, you know."

"What?" Blade was startled, then angry. The old man had not heard a word.

"Our host." The old man did not lift his eyes from the page. It would take them too long to readjust. "He's easily bored." Baladitya cared nothing about the Company's plans. Baladitya was in paradise.

"You'd think we'd be a change that would distract him."

"He's been distracted by mortals a thousand times before. He's still here. None of those people are, except those remembered in stone." The plain itself, though older and vastly slower than Shivetya, might have a mind of its own. Stone remembers. And stone weeps. "Their very empires have been forgotten. How much chance is there that this time will be different?"

Baladitya sounded a little empty. Not unreasonable, Blade thought, considering the fact that he looked into the time abyss represented by the demon all the time. Talk about vanity and chasing after wind!

"Yet he's helping us. More or less."

"Only because he believes we're the last mayflies he'll see. Excepting the Children of Night when they raise up their Dark Mother. He's convinced that we're his last chance to escape."

"And all we got to do to get his help is skrag the nasty Goddess, then put his ass away for the long night." The demon's gaze seemed to drill right through him. "Nothing to it. Piece of cake, as Goblin used to say. Though the saying doesn't make any literal sense." Blade lifted his fingers to his eyebrow in a salute to the demon. Whose eyes seemed to be smouldering now.

"God killing. That should be perfect work for you."

Blade was unsure if Baladitya had spoken or Shivetya had entered his mind. He did not like what the observation implied. It echoed too closely Sleepy's thinking, which is why his posh job in Khang Phi is gone and he has charge of operations on the plain, having abandoned banquets and down mattresses for iron rations and a bed of cold and silent stone shared only with unhappy, withered dreams, a crazy scholar, miscellaneous thieves and a house-sized lunatic demon half as old as time.

All his adult life Blade has been driven by a hatred for religion. He has an especial abhorrence for its retailers. Considering his current whereabouts and present occupation it seems likely that he should have restrained his impulse to share his opinions.

Blade could have sworn that, for an instant, a smile played across the demon's features.

Blade chose not to comment.

He is a man of few words. He believes there is little point to speech. He believes the golem eavesdrops on his thoughts. Unless it has become so bored with ephemerals that it no longer pays attention.

That hint of amusement again. Blade's speculation is not valid. He should know better. Shivetya is interested in every breath every brother of the Black Company takes. Shivetya has anointed these men as the death-givers.

"You need anything?" Blade asked the old man, resting a hand on his shoulder briefly. "Before I head down below?" The contact is entirely contrived. But Baladitya cares nothing about the touch, genuine or not.

Baladitya lifted his pen from his right hand with his left, flexed his fingers. "I suppose I should eat something. I can't recall when last I put fuel on the fire."

"I'll see that you get something." The something was sure to be rice and spice and golem manna. If there was anything Blade regretted about his life, it was having lived most of it in a part of the world where a majority of the population include a vegetarian diet within their religion and those who do not mainly eat fish or chicken. Blade is ready to start at whichever end of a spit-roast pig and not stop until he reaches the other.

Blade's command, the thieves, the Company pathfinders, includes twenty-six of the outfit's brightest and most trusted youngsters, all Children of the Dead. They need to be both smart and trustworthy because Sleepy wants to exploit the treasures in the caverns beneath the plain and because they really have to understand that the plain itself will not forgive them if they do the wrong thing. Shivetya has extended his favor. Shivetya sees everything and knows everything inside the gates of his universe. Shivetya is the soul of the plain. No one comes or goes without Shivetya's countenance, or at least his indifference. And in the unlikely event that Shivetya remained indifferent to an unauthorized theft, there was nowhere for a thief to run but back to the Shadowgate opening on the Land of Unknown Shadows. That was the only Shadowgate under control and functioning properly. That was the only Shadowgate not certain to kill the thief.

It was a long stroll across the great circle surrounding the crude throne. That floor is anything but crude. It is an exact one-eightieth scale representation of the plain outside, less the memorial pillars that were added in a later age by men who failed to possess even mythologized recollections of the builders. Hundreds of manhours have gone into clearing the accumulated dirt and dust off its surface so Shivetya can more clearly discern every detail of his kingdom. Shivetya's throne rests upon a raised wheel one-eightieth the size of this.

Decades ago, Soulcatcher's tampering triggered an earthquake that battered the fortress and split its floor into a vast crevasse. Outside the plain the disaster destroyed cities and killed thousands. Today the only memorial of what had been a gap in the floor a dozen yards wide and thousands of feet deep is a red stripe meandering past the throne. It dwindles every day. As does Shivetya, the mechanism ruling the plain heals itself.

The great circular model of the plain rises half a yard above the rest of the floor, which exists at the level of the plain outside.

Blade dropped off the edge of the wheel. He strode to a hole in the floor, the head of stairs leading down. They descend for miles, through caverns natural and created. The sleeping Goddess Kina lies at the deepest level, patiently awaiting the Year of the Skulls and the beginning of the Khadi Cycle, the destruction of the world. The *wounded* Goddess Kina.

Shadows stirred along the nearby wall. Blade froze. Who? No way that could be his people. Or, *what*?

Fear speared through Blade. Shadows in motion often presaged cruel, screaming death. Had those things found a way into the fortress? Their merciless feasting was not a horror he cared to witness ever again. And in particular he did not want to be the main course.

"The Nef," Blade told himself as three humanoid shapes emerged from the darkness. He recognized them despite never having seen them before. Hardly anyone did, outside of dreams. Or maybe nightmares. The Nef were incredibly ugly.

Though they might have been wearing masks. The several descriptions available did not agree except as to ugliness. He counted them off. "The Washane. The Washene. The Washone." Names Shivetya had given Sleepy years ago. What did they mean? Did they mean anything at all? "How did they get in here?" The answer might be critical. Killer shadows might exploit the same opening.

As the Nef always did, they tried to communicate something. In the past their efforts inevitably failed. But this time their appeal seemed obvious. They did not want Blade to go down those stairs.

Sleepy, Master Santaraksita, and others who have been in contact with Shivetya believe that the Nef are artificial reproductions of the beings who created the plain. Shivetya brought them into existence because he longed for a connection with something approximating those whose artifice had wrought the great engine and its pathways between the worlds, because he was lonely.

Shivetya has lost his will to live. If he should perish, whatever he has created himself will go with him. The Nef are not yet prepared to embrace oblivion, despite the endless horror and tedium existence upon the plain imposes.

Blade spread his hands at his sides in a gesture of helplessness. "You guys need to polish your communication skills." Not a sound came from the Nef but their growing frustration became palpable. Which had been a constant from the first time anyone had dreamt of them.

Blade stared. He did try to understand. He considered the ironies of the Black Company's adventure across the glittering plain. He was an atheist himself. His journey had brought him face-to-face with a complete ecology of supernatural entities. And Tobo and Sleepy, whom he considered reliable witnesses otherwise, claimed actually to have seen the grim Goddess Kina who, myth suggested, lay imprisoned a mile beneath his feet.

Sleepy, of course, faced her crises of faith. A devout Vehdna monotheist, she never, ever encountered any worldly sustenance for her beliefs. Though supportive evidence is thin, the Gunni religion only creaks badly under the burden of the knowledge we have unearthed. The Gunni are polytheists accustomed to having their gods assume countless aspects and avatars, shapes and disguises. So much so that, in some myths, those gods seem to be murdering or cuckolding themselves. The Gunni have the flexibility to look at every discovery, as Master Santaraksita has, and declare new information to be just another way of proclaiming the same old divine truths.

God is god, whatever his name. Blade has seen those sentiments inlaid in the wall tiles in several places in Khang Phi.

Whenever anyone strays far from Shivetya, a ball of earthy brown glow tags along. It hovers above and behind one shoulder or another. The ball does not shed much light but in what otherwise would be utter darkness they are sufficient.

They are the golem's doing. Shivetya has powers he has forgotten how to use. He might be a small god himself if he was not nailed to his ancient throne.

Blade descended nearly a thousand steps before he encountered anyone headed upward. This soldier carried a heavy pack. "Sergeant Vanh."

The soldier grunted. Already he was winded. No one made more than one trip a day. Blade gave Vanh the bad news because he might not run into him again for days. "Had a message from the Captain. We have to step it up. She's almost ready to move."

Vanh mumbled the sorts of things soldiers always do. He continued his climb. Blade wondered how Sleepy planned to haul off the mountain of treasure already accumulated up top. It was, for sure, enough to finance a pretty good war.

Another thousand steps downward, repeating his message several times. He left the stair at the level everyone called the Cave of the Ancients because of the old men interred there. Blade always stopped to visit his friend Cordy Mather. It was a ritual of respect. Cordy was dead. Most of the others confined in the cave remained alive, enmeshed in stasis spells. Somehow, during the long Captivity, Mather had shed the spells confining him. And success had cost him his life. He had not been able to find his way out.

Most of the old men in the cave meant nothing to Blade or the Company. Only Shivetya knew who they were or why they had been interred. Certainly they had irked someone armed with the power to confine them. Several corpses, though, had been Company brothers when still alive. Several others had been captives before Soulcatcher buried the Company. Death had found them because, evidently, Cordy Mather had tried to wake them up. Touching the Captured without sorcerous precautions inevitably caused the death of the touched.

Blade resisted the urge to kick the sorcerer Longshadow. That madman was a commodity of incalculable worth in the Land of Unknown Shadows. The Company had grown strong and wealthy because of him. It continued to prosper. "How you doing, Shadowmaster? Looks like you'll be here a while yet." Blade assumed the sorcerer could not hear him. He could not recall having heard anything when he was under the enchantment himself. He could not recall having been aware in any way, though Murgen said there were times when it looked like the Captured were aware of their surroundings. "They haven't pushed the bidding high enough yet. I hate to admit it but you really are a popular guy. In your own special way." Not a generous or forgiving or even empathetic man, Blade stood with hands on hips staring down at Longshadow. The sorcerer looked like a skeleton barely covered by diseased skin. His face was locked into a scream. Blade told him, "They still say, 'All Evil Dies There an Endless Death.' Especially when they're talking about you."

Not far from Longshadow is the Company's other insane sorcerer prisoner, the Howler. This one presents a greater temptation. Blade saw no value whatsoever to keeping Howler alive. The little shit has a history of treachery that goes way, way back and a character unlikely to change because of this confinement. He survived a similar Captivity before. That one endured for centuries.

Tobo did not need to learn any of the Howler's evil crap. And Tobo's education was the only excuse Blade had heard for letting the little ragbag live.

Blade paid his deepest respects to Mather. Cordy was a good friend for a long time. Blade owes Cordy his life. He wished the evil fortune had befallen him. Cordy wanted to live. Blade believes he is proceeding on inertia.

B lade continued his descent into the earth, past the treasure caverns that were being looted to finance the Company's homegoing, it was hoped on a spectacularly memorable scale.

Blade is not much given to emotional vapors or seizures of fear. He has a cool enough head to have survived for years as a Company agent inside Longshadow's camp. But as he moved deeper into the earth he began to twitch and sweat. His pace slackened. He passed the last known cavern. Nothing lay below that but the ultimate enemy, the Mother of Night herself. She was the enemy who would still be waiting once all the other, lesser adversaries had been brushed aside or extinguished.

To Kina, the Black Company is an annoying buzz in the ear, a mosquito that has gotten away with taking a sip or two of blood and has not had the good sense to get the hell away.

Blade slowed again. The light following him kept weakening. Where once he could see clearly twenty steps ahead now he could see only ten, the farther four seeming to be behind the face of a thickening black fog. Here the darkness seemed almost alive. Here the darkness felt as though it was under much greater pressure, the way water seemed to exert more as you swam deeper beneath its surface.

Blade found it harder to breathe. He forced himself to do so, deeply and rapidly, then went on, against the insistence of instinct. A silver chalice took form in the fog, just five steps below. It stood about a foot tall, a simple tall cup made of noble metal. Blade had placed it there. It marked the lowest step he had yet been able to reach.

Now each step downward seemed to take place against the resistance of liquid tar. Each step brought the darkness crushing in harder. The light from behind was too weak to reach even one step beyond the chalice.

Blade makes this effort frequently. He accounts it exercise for his will and courage. Each descent he manages to make it as far as the chalice mostly by being angry that he cannot push past it.

This time he tried something different. He threw a handful of coins collected from one of the treasure caves. His arm had no strength but gravity had not lost its power nor had sound been devoured by the darkness. The coins tinkled away down the stairwell. But not for long. After a moment it sounded like they were rolling around on a floor. Then they were silent. Then a tiny little voice from far, far away cried, "Help."

The Land of Unknown Shadows: Traveling Hsien

The physical geography of the Land of Unknown Shadows closely recollects that of our own world. The essential differences stem from the impact of man.

The moral and cultural topographies of the worlds are completely different, though. Even the Nyueng Bao still have trouble making any real connection here—despite the fact that they and the Children of the Dead share common ancestors. But the Nyueng Bao escaped Maricha Manthara Dhumraksha and his kin centuries ago, then developed as a cultural island constantly washed by alien waves.

Hsien proper spans roughly the same territories as what were known as the Shadowlands at home when things were going well for the Shadowmasters. The farther reaches of Hsien, that none of us have visited, are more heavily populated than our own. In olden times every town here boasted its kernel of resistance to the Shadowmasters. Few of those groups communicated because of travel restrictions imposed by the master race. Still, when the uprising did come there were local champions enough to ensure success.

The flight of the last Shadowmasters left a power vacuum. The resistance chieftains anointed themselves to fill it. Hsien remains in the custody of their descendants, scores of warlords in constant conflict, few of whom ever get any stronger. Any who appear to be gaining strength are torn apart by their neighbors.

The File of Nine is an anonymous, loose assembly of senior warlords, supposedly drawn one each from the nine provinces of Hsien. This is not true and never has been—though few outside the Nine know it. That is just one more fiction helping keep the current state of chaos alive.

Popularly, the File of Nine is seen as a cabal of secret masters who control everything. The File of Nine would love that to be true but, in reality, they have very little power. Their situation leaves them with few tools they can use to enforce their will. Any real effort to impose anything would betray their identities. So they mostly issue bulls and pretend to speak for Hsien. Sometimes people listen. And sometimes they listen to the monks of Khang Phi. Or to the Court of All Seasons. So each must be wooed.

The Black Company is feared mainly because it is a joker in the warlord deck. It has no local allegiance. It could jump any direction for any alien reason. Worse, it is reputed to include powerful wizards assisting skilled soldiers led by competent commanders and sergeants, none of whom are at all handicapped by excesses of empathy or compassion.

What popularity the Company enjoys essentially arises from its capacity to deliver the last Shadowmaster to the justice of Hsien. And among peasants, from the fact that nervous warlords have reined in their squabbles amongst themselves considerably while they have this unpredictable monster crouched, growing rapidly, to their south.

All the lords and leaders of Hsien, in the last, would prefer that the Company went away. Our presence places too much strain on the state of things as they are and always have been.

I attached myself to the deputation headed for Khang Phi even though I was not yet completely recovered. I would never be one-hundred percent again. I had some blurring in my right eye. I had acquired some truly intimidating burn scars. I would never regain the full range of motion in the fingers of my right hand. But I was convinced that I could be an asset in our negotiations for the Shadowgate secrets.

Only Sahra agreed with me. But Sahra is our foreign minister. Only she has the patience and tact to deal with such fractious folk as the File of Nine—part of whose problem with us is that our women do more than cook and lie on their backs.

Of course, of Lady, Sleepy, Sahra and the Radisha I suspect only Sahra can heat water without burning it. And she may have forgotten how by now.

The Company on the move, bound for the intellectual heart of Hsien, was a terror to behold, judging by the response of peasants along the way. And that despite the fact that our party, guards included, numbered just twenty-one. Human souls.

Tobo's shadowy friends surrounded and paced us, in such numbers that it was impossible for them to remain unseen all the time. Old fears and superstitions exploded in our wake, then terror ran ahead far faster than we could travel. People scattered when we approached. It made no difference that Tobo's night pals were well-behaved. Superstition completely outweighed any practical evidence.

Had we been more numerous we would not have gotten past Khang Phi's gate. Even there, among supposed intellectuals, the fear of the Unknown Shadows was thick enough to slice.

Sahra had had to agree, long ago, that neither Lady nor One-Eye nor Tobo would enter the Repose of Knowledge. The monks were particularly paranoid about sorcerers. Hitherto it had suited Sleepy to comply with their wishes. And none of those three were part of our party when we arrived at the Lower Gate of Khang Phi.

There was a strange young woman in our midst. She used the name Shikhandini, Shiki for short. She could easily arouse almost any man who did not know she was Tobo in disguise. Nobody bothered to tell me what or why but Sahra was up to something. Tobo was, obviously, an extra card she wanted tucked up her sleeve. Moreover, she suspected several of the Nine of harboring evil ambitions which would soon flower.

What? Men of power possessed of secret agendas? No! That does not seem possible.

Khang Phi is a center of learning and spirituality. It is a repository for knowledge and wisdom. It is extremely ancient. It survived the Shadowmasters. It commands the respect of all the Children of the Dead, throughout the Land of Unknown Shadows. It is neutral ground, a part of no warlord's demesne. Travelers bound toward Khang Phi, or returning home therefrom, are in theory immune.

Theory and practice are sometimes at variance. Therefore we never let Sahra travel without obvious protection.

Khang Phi is built against the face of a mountain. It rises a thousand whitewashed feet into the bellies of permanent clouds. The topmost structures cannot be seen from below.

At the same site in our world a barren cliff broods over the southern entrance to the only good pass through the mountains known as the Dandha Presh.

A life misspent making war left me wondering if the place had not begun its existence as a fortress. It certainly commanded that end of the pass. I looked for the fields necessary to sustain its population. And they were there, clinging to the sides of the mountains in terraces like stairsteps for splay-legged giants. Ancient peoples carried the soil in from leagues away, a basket at a time, generation after generation. No doubt the work goes on today.

Master Santaraksita, Murgen and Thai Dei met us outside the ornate Lower Gate. I had not seen them for a long time, though Murgen and Thai Dei attended the funeral ceremonies for Gota and One-Eye. I missed then because I was unconscious at the time. Fat old Master Santaraksita never went anywhere anymore. That elderly scholar was content to end his days in Khang Phi, pretending to be the Company's agent. Here he was among his own kind. Here he had found a thousand intellectual challenges. Here he had found people as eager to learn from him as he was eager to learn from them. He was a man who had come home.

He welcomed Sleepy with open arms. "Dorabee! At last." He insisted on calling her Dorabee because it was the first name he had known her by. "You *must* let me show you the master library while you're here! It absolutely beggars that pimple we managed in Taglios." He surveyed the rest of us. Merriment deserted him. Sleepy had brought the ugly boys along. The kind of guys he believed would use books for firewood on a chilly night. Guys like me, who bore scars and were missing fingers and teeth and had skin colors the likes of which were never seen in the Land of Unknown Shadows.

Sleepy told him, "I didn't come for a holiday back in the stacks, Sri. One way or another I've got to get that Shadowgate information. The news I'm getting from the other side isn't encouraging. I need to get the Company back into action before it's too late."

Santaraksita nodded, looked around for eavesdroppers, winked and nodded again.

Willow Swan leaned back, looked up, asked me, "Think you can make it to the top?"

"Give me a few days." Actually, I am in better shape now than I was that evil night. I have lost a lot of weight and have put on muscle.

I still get winded easily, though.

Swan said, "Lie all you want, old man." He dismounted, handed his reins to one of the youngsters beginning to swarm around. They were all boys between eight and twelve, all as silent as if they had had their vocal cords cut. They all wore identical pale brown robes. Parents unable to provide for them had donated them to Khang Phi as infants. These had surpassed a particular milestone on their path to becoming monks. We were unlikely to see anyone younger.

Swan picked up a stone two inches in diameter. "I'm going to throw this when we get up top. I want to watch it fall."

Parts of Swan never grew up. He still skips stones across ponds and rivers. He tried to teach me the art coming to Khang Phi. My hand and fingers will no longer conform to the shape of a proper skipping stone. There is a lot they cannot accomplish anymore. Managing a pen while writing is chore enough.

I miss One-Eye.

"Just don't bomp some asshole warlord on the noggin. Most of them don't like us much already." They were afraid of us. And they could find no way to manipulate us. They kept giving us provisions and letting us recruit in hopes we will go away eventually. Leaving Longshadow behind. We did not inform them that local financing would not be needed to underwrite our campaign beyond the plain.

After four hundred years it has become a given: You keep everybody outside just a little bit nervous. And you do not tell them anything they do not need to know.

Longshadow. Maricha Manthara Dhumraksha. He has several other names here as well. None indicate popularity. As long as we have the ability to deliver him in chains the warlords will tolerate almost anything. Twenty generations of ancestors cry out for justice.

I suspect Longshadow's wickedness has grown with the retelling, thereby making giants of the heroes who drove him out.

Though they are soldiers themselves the warlords do not understand us. They fail to recognize the fact that they are soldiers of a different breed, drawn on by a smaller destiny.

The Land of Unknown Shadows: Khang Phi

Swan and I stood looking out a window outside the conference hall where we would engage the File of Nine in negotiations. Eventually. It took them a while to sneak into Khang Phi, then change their disguises so their identities would remain unknown. We saw nothing below but mist. Swan did not waste his stone. I said, "I thought I was back in shape. I was wrong. I ache all over."

Swan said, "They say some people here go their whole lives without ever moving more than a floor or two after they finish their apprenticeship and get their assignments."

"Kind of people that balance out you and me," I said. Swan had not traveled as far as I had but at a world's remove an extra few thousand miles does not seem important. I tried to make out the rocky ground we had traversed approaching Khang Phi. The mist just seemed darker when I looked down.

"Thinking about taking the easy way back down?" Swan asked.

"No. I'm thinking being isolated like this might leave you with a very limited worldview." Not to mention the impact of the scarcity of females in Khang Phi. The few there are belong to an order of celibate nuns who care for the donated infants, the very old and the very sick. The rest of the population consists of monks, all of whom were donated and all of whom are sworn to chastity, too. The more fanatic brothers render themselves physically incapable of yielding to temptation. Which makes most of my brothers shudder and consider them more bizarre than Tobo's shadowy friends. No soldier likes the thought of losing his best friend and favorite toy.

"A narrow view can be as much a strength as a weakness, Liberator," a voice observed from behind us. We turned. Sleepy's friend, Surendranath Santaraksita, was joining us. The scholar has gone native, adopting local garb and assuming the Khang Phi haircut—which is no hair at all—but only a deaf and blind man would take him for a local monk. His skin is more brown and less translucent than that of any native and his features are shaped more like mine and Swan's. "That mist and their narrowness of vision allows the monks to avoid forming worldly attachments. Thus their neutrality remains beyond reproach."

I did not mention Khang Phi's one-time role as an apologist for and collaborator with the reign of the Shadowmasters. That embarrassing dab of history was being expunged by the acids of time and relentless lie.

Santaraksita was happy. He was convinced that in this place learned men did not have to prostitute themselves to temporal powers in order to remain scholars. He believed even the File of Nine deferred to the wisdom of the eldest monks. He was unable to see that if the Nine acquired more power Khang Phi's relationship to the File would soon lapse into subservience. Master Santaraksita is brilliant but naive.

"How's that?" I asked him.

"These monks are so innocent of the world that they don't try to impose anything on it."

"Yet the File of Nine presume to speak from here." The File enjoy issuing bulls which are, more often than not, ignored by the population and warlords.

"They will, yes. The Elders want them to. In hopes that a little wisdom will rub off before their power becomes more than symbolic."

I said nothing about leading horses to water. I made no observations concerning the wisdom of backing a cabal of secret masters in preference to one strongman or the remnant aristocracy of the Court of All Seasons. I did admit, "It does look like they're trying to do what's best for Hsien. But I don't trust anybody who'll bet their pot on guys who hide behind masks." No need to tell him the File have no secrets from us. Little that they do or discuss goes unremarked by Tobo's familiars. None of their identities are secrets to us.

We operate on the assumption that both the File and the other warlords have placed spies among our recruits. Which explains why there is little resistance to our recruiting amongst the Children of the Dead.

It is not difficult to identify most of the spies. Sleepy shows them what she wants them to see. Being a spiteful, vengeful little witch, I am sure she plans to use those spies cruelly at some later time.

She worries me. She has her own old hatreds to redress but their objects escaped life unpunished a long time ago. But there is always the chance she might choose somebody else to take the heat, which would not be to the Company's advantage.

I asked Santaraksita, "What did you want?"

"Nothing special." His face went coolly neutral. He is Sleepy's friend. I make him uncomfortable. He has read my Annals. Despite what Sleepy has dragged him through he cannot yet come to grips with the cruel realities of our sort of life. I am sure that he will not go home with us. "I did hope to see Dorabee again before you went into conference. It could be important."

"I don't know what happened to her. Shiki's missing, too. They were supposed to meet us here." Local mores made it impossible for women to share quarters with men. Even Sahra has to room separately from Murgen, though they are legally married. And Shikhandini's presence saddled Sahra with special obligations. She wanted the holy men distracted but not to the point where they went berserk. Just enough, maybe, so they would give way on a subtle point or two. Though distraction would not be Shiki's principal mission.

Master Santaraksita wrung his hands briefly, then folded his arms. His hands disappeared into the sleeves of his robe. He was worried. I looked closer. He knew something. I glanced at Swan. Swan shrugged.

Murgen and Thai Dei puffed into the room. Murgen demanded, "Where are they?" Thai Dei looked worried but said nothing. He would not. The man seldom says anything. It was a pity his sister could not learn from his example.

Thai Dei knew something, too.

"Haven't shown yet," Swan said.

"The File of Nine will be angry," I added. "Are Sleepy and Sahra dealing some kind of game?"

Santaraksita backed away nervously. "The Unknowns aren't here yet, either."

My companions were a diverse bunch. Once Sleepy arrived we would include five races. Six counting Santaraksita as one of us. Sleepy believes our sheer diversity intimidates the File of Nine.

Sleepy entertains other notions even more strange.

I do not know why she thought cowing them would mean anything. All we needed from them was their permission to research the knowledge needed to mend and manipulate Shadowgates. The monks of Khang Phi were willing to share that knowledge. The stronger we grow the more eagerly the monks want us gone. They are more frightened of the heresies we propagate than they are of any armies we might bring back later.

The latter dread keeps the warlords awake at night. But they do want us gone, too, because the stronger we grow here the more real and immediate a threat do they perceive. And I do not blame them for thinking that way. I would do so myself, in their boots. The entirety of human experiences argues on behalf of suspicion of strangers laden with weapons.

The womenfolk made their advent. Willow Swan spread his arms wide and declaimed dramatically, "Where have you been?" He struck a second pose and tried the line another way. Then he went with a third. Making fun.

Sahra told Thai Dei, "Your daughter kept flirting with the acolytes we encountered along the way."

I glanced at Shiki, frowned. The girl seemed almost ethereal, not at all vampish. I blinked but the fuzzy quality did not go away. I blamed my damaged eye. The girl seemed more a distracted ghost than a boy in disguise having fun with a role.

In Hsien's eyes Thai Dei passed as Shiki's father because it was well known that Sahra had just the one son. Her brother, Thai Dei, has managed to remain so obscure that even at the Abode of Ravens the locals never raise a question about the fact that the seldom-seen Shikhandini would have had to have been born while her father was buried beneath the plain. Nor did anyone seem much inclined to ask what had become of the girl's mother. She could be dismissed with a few vague, angry mutters.

Shiki was always empty-headed, always in minor trouble, always considered a threat only to the equilibrium of young men's minds.

Shiki solidified. She pouted. She said, "I wasn't flirting, Father. I was just talking." Her words should have been argumentative but just sounded flat, rote.

"You were told not to speak to the monks. That's the law here."

"But Father . . ."

The act never stopped once it started. There might be watchers. But it *was* an act. And a pretty good one, at least to those of us unaccustomed to dealing with very young women.

Master Santaraksita kept whispering to Sleepy. He must have said something she wanted to hear because her face lit up like a beacon. She did not bother to report to the Annalist, though. These Captains are all alike. Always playing their hands close to their chest. Except for me, of course. I was a paragon of openness in my time.

Thai Dei and his daughter continued to squabble till he issued some loud *diktat* in heated Nyueng Bao that left her sulking and silent.

The Land of Unknown Shadows:
The Secret Masters

An old, old monk opened the door to the meeting chamber. The task was a great chore for him. He beckoned with one frail hand.

This was my first visit to Khang Phi but I knew him by his robes, which were dark orange edged with black. They distinguished him as one of the four or five eldest of Khang Phi. His presence made it clear that Khang Phi's monks were deeply interested in this meeting's outcome. Otherwise some midlevel sixty-year-old would have handled the door and then would have hung on to manage the acolytes who were supposed to attend to the comfort of both us and the Nine. Master Santaraksita smiled. Maybe he had had something to do with this meeting having been invested with importance.

Sahra approached the old man. She bowed, murmured a few words. He responded. They knew one another and he did not disdain her for her sex. The monks might be wiser than I had thought.

We soon learned that she had asked if everyone could reduce the ceremony that attends all functions of the Children of the Dead. Formalities imbue every occasion with elaborate ritual. People must not have had much that was practical to do during the reign of the Shadowmasters.

We barbarians do not know the proper forms. The Children of the Dead hoist their noses around us—then sigh in relief because uncomfortable business gets handled quickly when the Black Company is on the far side of the carpet.

Our host scowled at Shikhandini. He was old and bitter and narrow. But! Behold! Not so old and bitter and narrow that a shimmering smile from a beautiful girl would not put a momentary twinkle in his eye. Never that old.

From earliest times our enemies have accused us of fighting dirty, of dealing in trickery and treachery. And they are right. Absolutely right. We are shameless. And this was about as dirty as we could get, having Tobo vamp these old men. They knew women only in the most academic fashion. It was easier than plinking blind men with arrows.

It was all so effortless. Shiki just seemed to float around, not quite all there, not paying much attention, showing none of the enjoyment I expected of Tobo. I mean, what man his age does not enjoy making fools of wise old men? Everything I knew about Tobo suggested he would enjoy that more than most.

I was getting curious. What was going on?

Sleepy claimed the kid was along because she wanted a wizard handy. Just in case. Being paranoid. Having been made that way by lifetimes of treachery from outside. And Khang Phi law would keep Tobo out if he came as himself.

She wanted me to believe.

There would be more. Much, much more. I understand the sneaky little witch better than she suspects. And I approve, thoroughly.

"Move," Sleepy said. She was uncomfortable in Khang Phi. The place is infested with the trappings of strange religions.

The chamber we entered undoubtedly served some high ceremonial purpose when not on loan to the File of Nine. That end where the warlords waited could pass for an altar and its associated clutter. The warlords had seated themselves above us, in front of the possible altar, where five large stone seats were in place permanently. Seven of the Nine were on hand. Chairs had been dragged in for the surplus pair, presumably the junior members of the quorum. All seven wore masks and disguises, which seems to be customary with secret masters—and here possibly a legacy of the Shadowmasters who had found masks and disguises very fashionable. In this case that was a waste of effort. But they did not need to know that. Not right away.

Lady has a talent for rooting out true names and identities. She learned in a deadly school. She has taught Tobo some of her tricks. He unearthed the identities of the members of the File, using his supernatural friends. Knowing who we might find, in the event we developed a corporate inclination to surprise somebody, should prove to be a valuable bargaining tool.

Sahra had dealt with the File before. They were accustomed to her impatience with ceremony. They paid attention when she stepped forward.

Master Santaraksita trailed her by three paces. He would serve as a specialist translator. Though the Children of the Dead and the Nyueng Bao spoke the same language in times past, separation and circumstance have conspired to make misunderstandings common. Santaraksita would have to point out those instances when the parties were using the same word with different meanings.

Sleepy moved a few steps forward but stayed closer to the rest of us than to the warlords.

Sleepy started humming. She was determined to appear cheerful despite being surrounded by unrepentant heathens.

Sahra stepped forward again. She asked, "Are the File ready to stop objecting to the Company gaining the knowledge we need to repair Shadowgates? You have to understand that we won't leave Hsien without it. We're still prepared to turn over the criminal Dhumraksha." The same offer had been before the File all along. They wanted something more but never articulated it—though supernatural espionage revealed that they hoped to gain our support in establishing a much stronger File position. Only they did not dare suggest that themselves before the witnesses that always exist when negotiations take place in Khang Phi.

The masks faced Sahra's way. None of the Unknowns responded. You could sense their exasperation. Lately they had begun to believe, on no creditable evidence, that they had some power over us. Probably because we had not gotten into the sort of pissing contest with any of our neighbors that would have demonstrated the lethal inequalities between their forces and ours. We would devour most of the local armies.

Sleepy stepped past Santaraksita, took position beside Sahra. In passable local dialect she said, "I am Captain of the Black Company. I will speak." Facing a warlord wearing a mask surmounted by a crane's head, she continued, "Tran Thi Kim-Thoa, you are Last Entered of the File." The warlords stirred. "You are young. Possibly you know no one whose life and pain would regain meaning if Maricha Manthara Dhumraksha came back here to atone for his sins. I understand that. Youth is always impatient with the pasts of its elders—even when that past crushes down upon youth's shoulders."

She paused.

Seven silk-clad butts shifted nervously, filling an extended silence with soft rustles. All us Company people grinned, baring our fangs. Exactly like those rock apes around Outpost, trying to intimidate one another.

Sleepy had named the newest of the Nine. His identity would be no secret to the other eight. They had chosen him when last there was an opening in their circle. He would be ignorant of their identities—unless some of the older warlords had chosen to reveal themselves. Each warlord normally knew only those elected to the File after themselves. By naming the Last Entered, Sleepy offered another threat while endangering just the one Unknown.

Sleepy beckoned. "Croaker." I stepped forward. "This is Croaker. He was Captain before me and Dictator to All the Taglias. Croaker, before us we have Tran Huu Dung and six others of the File of Nine." She did not specify this Tran's position in the File. His name caused another stir, though.

She beckoned Swan. "This is Willow Swan, a longtime associate of the Black Company. Willow, I present Tran Huu Nhan and six others of the File of Nine. Tran is a common patronym in Hsien. There are a lot of Trans among the Nine, none of them related by blood."

The next name she offered, after introducing Willow Swan, was Tran Huu Nhang. I began to wonder how they kept themselves sorted out. Maybe by weight. Several of the File carried some surplus poundage.

When Sleepy named the last of the Trans of the File, Tran Lan-Anh, their spokesman, the First, interrupted her with a request for time to confer. Sleepy bowed, offered him no further provocation. We knew that he was Pham Thi Ly of Ghu Phi, an excellent general with a good reputation among his troops, a believer in a unified Hsien, but old enough to have lost his zest for struggle. By the slightest of nods Sleepy let him know that his identity was no secret, either.

Sleepy announced, "We have no interest in coming back to Hsien once we return to the plain." As though that was some dear secret we had held clutched close to our hearts forever. Any spy among us would have reported that we just wanted to go home. "Like the Nyueng Bao who fled to our world, we came here only because we had no choice." Doj would not have accepted her assessment of Nyueng Bao history, brief as it might be. In his eye his immigrant ancestors had been a band of adventurers similar to the forebrethren of the Black Company, who had gone forth from Khatovar. "We're strong now. We're ready to go home. Our enemies there will cringe, unmanned by the news of our coming."

I did not believe that for an instant. Soulcatcher would be pleased to see us. A good squabble would relieve the tedium of her daily grind. Being an all-powerful ruler actually takes most of the fun out of life. In the heyday of her dark empire, my wife had made that discovery, too. Management trivia consumes you.

Lady hated it enough to walk away. But misses it now.

Sleepy said, "We lack only the knowledge to repair our Shadowgate, so that our world isn't overrun by the Host of the Unforgiven Dead."

Our spokespeople never fail to harp on that point. It remains central to every statement of our purpose. We would wear the Nine down. They would give in so they would not have to hear about it anymore. They were, however, extremely paranoid about the risk of another otherworld invasion.

If they were hard asses they could try to outstubborn us, hoping we would give up, go home, and have our Shadowgate fall apart behind us. That would end our threat permanently.

The power of the File lies in the anonymity of its members. When warlords get together to plot they are restrained by the possibility that among them is one of the Nine. The File publishes any schemes it uncovers, thereby focusing the wrath of warlords not included in the plan. It is a clumsy system but it has kept conflict limited for generations by making it difficult to forge alliances.

Sleepy could expose the File. If they were betrayed, chaos would come baying right behind. Few warlords like having their ambitions held in check—though restraints had to be imposed on all those other villains.

The Unknowns did not like being bullied, either. Those whose names had been betrayed soon grew so angry the elder monk placed himself between parties as a reminder of where we were.

Being an old soldier, I began a swift inventory of resources available for a fight if some warlord was dim enough to force one. I was not reassured. Our greatest asset was missing.

Where did Shiki go? When did she go? Why?

I needed to keep a closer eye on my surroundings. An oversight this big could turn fatal.

One masked warlord bounded out of his chair. He yipped and slapped his buttocks. We gaped. Silence fell. The man began to gather his dignity. A trill of faint high-pitched laughter sparkled in the silence. Something with humming diamond wings darted about too fast to be made out clearly. It left the room before anybody could react.

Sahra observed, "Most of the Hidden Realm will follow us when we leave. Possibly so much of it that Hsien will no longer be the Land of Unknown Shadows."

Master Santaraksita murmured in her ear. That irked the warlords and the old referee elder, too. The monk was particularly unhappy because the ladies kept spinning those implied threats. But he was cautious. The Company was up to something new. This was frightening. Had the outsiders run out of patience? All Hsien nurtures some fears of the sleeping tiger of the Abode of Ravens. And we make a point of encouraging them.

When I looked around again there was Shikhandini. How? . . .

I studied her, expecting to see some deviltry suggested by her stance or expression. There was nothing there. The kid was stone cold indifferent.

Sahra waved Santaraksita away. He scurried over to Sleepy, murmured some more. Sleepy nodded but did not do anything else. That left the old scholar looking like he was about to panic.

Shiki's disappearance and reappearance made it more obvious than ever that there was something going on. Obvious to the former Captain, anyway. And the former Captain had been told nothing beforehand.

The ladies were into one of their schemes. And that would be the real reason they wanted Shiki along. Shiki brought an awesome array of weapons into the game.

And they had had me convinced that they just wanted the magic handy in case somebody suffered an impulse to be unpleasant, which happens all too frequently when we are around.

The Radisha and the Prahbrindrah Drah still mourn their treacherous impulses.

I told Swan, "This business was a lot more fun when I was the one scheming and being mysterious."

The First of the File said, "Will you do us the courtesy of withdrawing for a moment, Captain? Ambassador? I believe a consensus may be within reach."

While we waited in the antechamber, Swan asked, "Why did he bother asking us to leave? After what happened? Does he really think we won't know what's going on in there?" Things moved in the corners of my vision. Strings of shadow snaked over the walls until I tried to look at them directly. Then, of course, nothing was visible.

"Possibly he didn't catch all the implications." Like the fact that something would be eavesdropping on every word he spoke until the Black Company left the Land of Unknown Shadows. At this late date anything he tried to pull together would be a complete wasted effort.

"Let's go," Sleepy said. "Move out. Croaker. Swan. Quit jacking your jaws and get moving."

"Moving where?" I asked.

"Downstairs. Home. Get going."

"But . . ." This was not what I expected. A good Black Company trick ends up with lots of fire and bloodshed, the vast majority of both not inflicted upon us.

Sleepy growled. It was a pure animal sound. "If I'm going to be Captain I'm going to be Captain. I'm not going to discuss or debate or request preapproval from the old folks. Get moving."

She had a point. I had made it a few times myself, in my day. I had to set an example.

I went.

"Good luck," Sleepy told Sahra. She strode toward the nearest stairwell. I followed. Presumably better trained by Sleepy's predecessor, the others were clattering down those ancient stairs already. Only Sahra and Master Santaraksita remained behind, though Shiki did hover around Sahra briefly, as though interested in a parting hug.

"Interesting," Sleepy observed. "It's such a good mimic that it almost forgets itself."

She was talking to herself, not to the Captain-Emeritus. He no longer needed an explanation. He had seen this stuff before. The ladies were going to take the information that we needed. Santaraksita had located it and had tagged it and now our own people were in the process of collecting it. Tobo was somewhere else, hard at work. One of his spooky friends was masquerading as Shikhandini.

All of which meant that Sleepy was better prepared to travel than I had supposed.

You miss so much when you are laid up.

Things continued to stir in the corners. Movements persisted at the edge of my vision. Always there was nothing to be seen when I looked directly.

Nevertheless . . .

Khang Phi had been conquered. That unvanquishable fortress of enlightenment had been taken and its occupants did not yet know. Most might never find out—assuming the real Shikhandini successfully completed the real mission given to Tobo by Sleepy and Sahra.

Hard to imagine becoming badly winded by running downhill. I managed. Those stairs went down forever, much farther than when I had gone up at a more leisurely pace. I began to develop cramps. Behind me Sahra and Sleepy kept right on barking and mocking and pushing like they were not almost as old as me.

I spent a lot of time wondering what had compelled me to come along. I was too old for this shit. The Annals did not need to record every little detail. I could have done this One-Eye's way. "They went to Khang Phi and got the knowledge we needed to fix the Shadowgates."

Some deep-voiced bell bonged far above. No one had enough breath to explain but no explanation was needed. An alarm was being sounded.

Our fault?

Who else? Though I could imagine scenarios where the File of Nine might be guilty of trying to snuff the Company brain trust.

It did not matter. I reminded myself that Khang Phi is bereft of arms. That the monks abhor violence. That they always yield to strength, then seduce it with reason and wisdom.

Yes, sometimes it does take a while.

I did not feel reassured. I spend too much time hanging around with guys like me.

The air began to whisper and rustle, like a gentle breeze in a time of falling leaves. The sound started in the dimness far below. It rose toward us, met and passed us before I had any real chance to become afraid. I had a brief impression of passing two-dimensional, black, transparent forms accompanied by a touch of cold and a whiff of old mold, then autumn was gone on to adventures far above.

At times the stairway passed behind the outer face of Khang Phi. Windows presented themselves then. Each was filled with an exquisite view of grey mist. Shapes moved within the greyness, never defined. They did not need definition for me to know that I had no interest in making the acquaintance of anything that did not mind having a thousand feet of wet air beneath its toes.

Several times I saw Shikhandini drift downward or rise through the fog. Once she saw me watching, paused, smiled and showed three slim fingers in a delicate wave.

The genuine Tobo was not shy any digits.

What I did not see during our entire descent was even one member of the Khang Phi community. They all had business elsewhere when we passed by.

"How much farther?" I panted, thinking it was a good thing I had lost all that weight while I was recuperating.

I got no answer. No one wanted to waste the breath.

It proved to be much farther than I had hoped. It always is when you are running away.

Ten Finger Shikhandini was waiting with the horses and the rest of our gang when we stumbled out of the unguarded Lower Gate. Animals and escort were ready to travel. All we had to do was mount up and go.

Tobo would sustain the Shiki role till we were home again. The Children of the Dead did not need to know that he was she.

Tobo told his mother, "Sri Santaraksita refused to come."

"I didn't think he would. That's all right. He did his part. He'll be happier here after we're gone."

Sleepy agreed. "He's found his paradise."

"Excuse me," I gasped. It had taken me three tries and a boost from a helpful escort to get myself into the saddle. "What did we just do?"

"We committed robbery," Sleepy told me. "We went in there pretending we were going to appeal to the File of Nine yet one more time. We got them all twisted out of shape by naming some of their names, so they had nothing else on their minds while we stole the books containing the information we need to get home safely."

"They still don't know," Tobo said. "They're still looking the other way. But that won't last. The doppelgangers I left behind will fall apart before long. Those things can't keep their minds on business."

"Quit jawing and ride, then," Sleepy grumbled. I swear. The woman was Annalist for fifteen years. She ought to have a better appreciation of the Annalist's needs.

The mist surrounded us and seemed to move with us, unnaturally dense. Tobo's work, probably. Shapes moved out there but did not come too close. Until I looked back.

Khang Phi had vanished already. It might be a thousand miles away or might never have existed at all. Instead I saw things I would rather not, including several of the Black Hounds, big as ponies, with high, massive shoulders like those of hyenas. For an instant, as they began to lose color and focus, an even larger beast with a head like a leopard's, but green, loomed out of the mist between them. Cat Sith. It, too, wobbled away from reality, like an exaggerated case of heat shimmer fading. The gleam of its exposed teeth was the last to go.

With Tobo's help we evaporated into the landscape ourselves.

Wastelands:
Night's Children

Narayan Singh released his grip on his *rumel*, the consecrated killing scarf of a Strangler. His hands had become two aching, arthritic claws. Tears filled his eyes. He was glad the darkness hid them from the girl. "I never took an animal before," he whispered, drawing away from the cooling carcass of the dog.

The Daughter of Night did not respond. She had to concentrate hard to use her crude talents to misdirect the bats and owls searching for them. The hunt had been on for weeks. Scores of converts had been taken. The rest had scattered in time-honored fashion. They would come together again after the hunters lost interest. And the hunters did lose interest in them before long. But this time the Witch of Taglios seemed determined to collar the Daughter of Night and the living saint of the Deceivers.

The girl relaxed, sighed. "I think they've moved off to the south." Her whisper contained no note of triumph.

"This should be the last dog." Narayan felt no sense of accomplishment, either. He reached out, touched the girl lightly. She didn't shake him off. "They've never used dogs before." He was tired. Tired of running, tired of pain.

"What's happened, Narayan? What's changed? Why won't my mother answer me? I did everything right. But I still can't feel her out there."

Maybe she was not there anymore, the heretical side of Narayan thought. "Maybe she can't. She has enemies among the gods as well as among men. One of those may be . . ."

The girl's hand covered his mouth. He held his breath. Some owls had hearing acute enough to catch his wheezing—should they catch the girl off guard.

The hand withdrew. "It's turned away. How do we reach her, Narayan?"

"I wish I knew, child. I wish I knew. I'm worn out. I need someone to tell me what to do. When you were little I thought you'd be queen of the world by now. That we would've passed through the Year of the Skulls and Kina's triumph and I would be enjoying the rewards of my persistent faith."

"Don't you start, too."

"Start?"

"Wavering. Doubting. I need you to be my rock, Narayan. Always, when everything else turns to filth in my hands, there's been the granite of Papa Narayan."

For once she seemed not to be manipulating him.

They huddled, prisoners of despair. The night, once Kina's own, now belonged to the Protector and her minions. Yet they were compelled to travel under cloak of darkness. By day they were too easily recognized, she with her pale, pale skin and he with his physical impairments. The reward for their capture was great and the country folk were always poor.

Their flight had led them southward, toward the uninhabited wastelands clinging to the northern foothills of the Dandha Presh. Peopled lands were far too dangerous right now. Every hand was against them there. Yet there was no promise the wastelands would be any friendlier. Out there it might be easier for the hunters to track them.

Narayan mused, "Perhaps we should go into exile until the Protector forgets us." She would. Her passions were furiously intense but never lasted.

The girl did not reply. She stared at the stars, possibly looking for a sign. Narayan's proposition was impossible and they both knew it. They had been touched by the Goddess. They must do her work. They must fulfill their destinies, however unhappy the road. They must bring on the Year of the Skulls, however much suffering they must endure themselves. Paradise lay beyond the pale of affliction.

"Narayan. Look. The sky in the south."

The old Deceiver raised his eyes. He saw what she meant immediately. One small patch of sky, due south, very low, rippled and shimmered. When that stopped for half a minute an alien constellation shone through.

"The Noose," Singh whispered. "It isn't possible."

"What?"

"The constellation is called the Noose. We shouldn't be able to see it." Not from this world. Narayan knew of it only because he had been a prisoner of the Black Company at a time when the constellation had been the subject of intense discussion. It had some connection with the glittering plain. Beneath which Kina lay imprisoned. "Maybe that's our sign." He was ready to grasp any straw. He dragged his weary frame upright, tucked his crutch under his arm. "South it is, then. Where we can travel by day because there'll be no one to spot us."

The girl said, "I don't want to travel anymore, Narayan." But she got up, too. Travel was what they did, day after month after year, because only by remaining in motion could they evade the evils that would prevent them from fulfilling their holy destinies.

An owl called from somewhere far away. Narayan ignored it. He was, for the thousandth time, reflecting on the change of fortune that had befallen them so swiftly, after life had gone so well for several years. His whole life had been that way, one wild swing after another. If he could cling to the tatters of his faith, if he could persevere, soon enough fortune would smile on him again. He was the living saint. His tests and trials had to be measured accordingly.

But he was so tired. And he hurt so much.

He tried not to wonder why there was no sense whatsoever of Kina's presence in the world anymore. He tried to concentrate his whole will upon covering the next painful hundred yards. With that victory in hand he could concentrate on conquering the hundred yards that followed.

The Land of Unknown Shadows: The Abode of Ravens

It took Tobo ten days to teach himself everything he needed to become a master Shadowgate tinkerer. Those ten days seemed much longer for some of us because the File of Nine, defying the express wishes of the Elders of Khang Phi and the lords of the Court of All Seasons, issued a bull declaring the Black Company to be the enemy of the Children of the Dead. It encouraged all warlords to gather their forces and march against us.

That trouble was slow developing. The warlords who were our neighbors knew too much about us to try anything. Those who were farther away were willing to wait until someone else moved first. Most never bothered to call in their troops. And, characteristic of Hsien's politics, the stream of volunteers, of money and materials helping us become an ever greater threat to the Children of the Dead, never slackened.

Tobo finished work on the Hsien-end Shadowgate fourteen days after our return from Khang Phi. Despite the war clouds, Sleepy was in no hurry. Sahra assured her that it would be months before anyone got started our way—if they ever did at all. She claimed the warlords could not possibly agree that quickly and move that fast. No need to hurry. Haste causes mistakes. Mistakes come back to haunt you every time.

Y ou do a good job, you're guaranteed gonna have to pay for it," I told Suvrin. The young Shadowlander had just been informed of his latest honor: He was going to cross the glittering plain to scout and to repair our home Shadowgate. Right after Tobo trained him. Tobo would not go himself because he did not want to be separated from his pets. Filled with low cunning, I asked, "How are your writing skills?"

He stared at me for several seconds, eyes big and brown and round in a big round, brown face. "No. I don't think so. I like it in the Company. But I don't plan to spend my life here. This is a learning experience. This is training. But I won't become a lord of mercenaries."

He surprised me, in several ways. I never heard anyone describe their Company time quite that way, though many do join up fully intending to desert just as soon as they are safely away from the trouble that had them on the run. Nor had I noticed, ever, anyone grasp so quickly what it could mean, in the long run, to be approached about becoming the apprentice Annalist.

A stint as Annalist could be a step toward becoming Captain someday.

I was teasing, mostly, but Sleepy did think a lot of Suvrin. The suggestion might not be a joke to her.

"Have fun on the other side. And be careful. You can't be careful enough where Soulcatcher is involved." I went on and on. His patient blank expression and glazed eyes told me he had heard it all before. I stopped. "And you'll hear it all a hundred times more before you go. The Old Woman'll probably write it all down in a scroll you'll have to take along and read before breakfast every morning."

Suvrin put on a febble, insincere smile. "The Old Woman?"

"Thought I'd try it out. I have a feeling it isn't going to work."

"I think you can count on that."

I didn't expect to cross paths with Suvrin again this side of the plain. I was wrong. Only minutes after we parted it occurred to me that it might be useful if I sat in on the Shadowgate training.

It occurred to me that I ought to ask the Captain's permission. I was able to resist the temptation.

Lady decided it might be good if she extended her own education, too.

The Land of Unknown Shadows:
Due South

Campfires burned on the far slopes, opposite Outpost. Those pesky rock apes had emigrated. The flocks of crows were expanding. Choosers of the slain, I heard them called somewhere. The File of Nine had pulled a half-ass army together far faster than our bemused foreign minister had believed possible.

"At last," I said to Murgen, as he and I shared a newly discovered jar of skull-buster. "To One-Eye." The stuff just kept turning up. We were doing our best to make sure it did not fall into the hands of the soldiers. In their hands strong drink was likely to cause indiscipline. "Your old lady talked like it'd be next year before they tried anything. If they ever got anything going at all."

The advent of unfriendly forces had been no surprise, of course. Not with Tobo handling intelligence.

"To One-Eye. She has been known to err, Captain." He was starting to slur already. The boy could not hold his liquor. "Upon rare occasions."

"Rare occasions."

Murgen hoisted his cup in a salute. "To One-Eye." Then he shook his head. "I do love that woman, Captain."

"Uhm." Oh-oh. I hoped we did not get maudlin here. But I understood his problem. She got old. We spent fifteen years in stasis, not aging a minute. A little payoff from the gods for doing us so dirty the rest of the time, maybe. But Sahra, who meant more to Murgen than life itself, who was the mother of his son, had not been one of the Captured.

Which had been lucky for us. Because she had dedicated herself to freeing Murgen. And eventually she succeeded. And freed me and my wife and most of the Captured as well. But Sahra had grown and had changed and had aged more than those fifteen years. And their son had grown up. And even now, four years after our resurrection, Murgen still had not adjusted completely.

"You can get by," I told him. "Bless One-Eye. Put it all out of your mind. Exist in the now. Don't worry about the then. That's what I do." In terms of experience my wife had been ancient centuries before I was born. "You did get to be the ghost that rode around with her and shared her life, even if you couldn't touch her." I live with ten thousand ghosts from my wife's past, few of whom ever got discussed. She just did not want to talk about her olden days.

Murgen grunted, mumbled something about One-Eye. He was having trouble understanding me even though I was articulating with especial precision. He asked, "You never were much of a drinker, were you, Captain?"

"No. But I've always been a good soldier. I've always done what's got to be done."

"I gotcha."

We were outside, of course, watching shooting stars and the constellations of fires that marked the enemy encampment. There seemed to be an awful lot of those fires. More than the reported numbers deserved. Some genius of a warlord was playing games.

"They're not going to come," Murgen said. "They're just going to sit there. It's all for the benefit of the Nine. It's showmanship."

I blessed One-Eye and took another drink, wondered if Murgen was repeating his wife's assumption or his son's. I cocked my head in favor of my left eye. My night vision is questionable even when I am sober.

Murgen said, "I don't think you can imagine the level of fear over there right now. The boy does something to terrorize them every night. He hasn't hurt a louse on one of their heads yet but they're not stupid. They get the message."

You got the Black Hounds strolling through your camp, eating out of your cookpots, or maybe pissing in them, and you have dozens of lesser night things pulling up tent pegs and starting fires and stealing your boots and treasures, you have troubles that will effect morale for sure. The soldiers will not believe the stories you tell to soothe them, however clever you think you are.

"The thing is, if the leadership decides there'll be war, they'll come." I knew. I have been with the Company forever. I have seen men fight under incredibly bad conditions. And, admittedly, I have seen men lose heart when conditions seemed ideal. "To One-Eye. He was a big part of the glue that held us together."

"One-Eye. You know the Fourth Battalion's going up tonight?"

"Up?"

"To the plain. They're probably moving out right now."

"Suvrin can't possibly have the Shadowgate ready to go yet."

Murgen shrugged. "I'm just saying what I heard. Sahra telling Tobo. She got it from Sleepy."

Once again the Annalist had not been included in the planning and decision-making. The Annalist was irked. In a former life he had gained a lot of experience planning campaigns and managing large groups of fractious people. The Annalist can contribute still.

In a moment of clarity I understood why I was being left out. Because of the thing that killed One-Eye. Its punishment was unimportant to Sleepy. She did not want to waste time and resources on it. Particularly the time needed to argue with me and those who felt the way I do.

I mused. "Maybe I shouldn't try to avenge One-Eye."

Murgen didn't mind an unexplained shift in topic. He was listening more closely to his own soul, anyway. He did say, "What're you talking about? It's got to be done."

So he agreed with me. It occurred to me that he had known One-Eye longer than anyone else but me. I still thought of him as the new kid sometimes because he was almost the last man to join us while we were still in service to the Lady, in that other world so far away and so long ago that there were moments when I almost waxed nostalgic for those bad old days.

"Here's one more to One-Eye. And I want to know when we're going to start racking up some good old days."

"They're in there, Captain. Here and there. They just don't stick out."

I remembered one or two. But that only got me started thinking about what might have been. About Booboo. And when I mix strong spirits with thoughts of my daughter the weather turns maudlin every time. And we see more and more of that weather as I get older.

"You got any idea what Sleepy's strategy is?" I asked. She would have one. Scheming and planning is supposedly her long suit. Long enough for her to have outwitted the Radisha and my sister-in-law.

"Not a clue. I knew more about what was going on when I was a ghost."

"You don't go out of body anymore?"

"I'm cured. At least in this world."

Not good, I feared. His loose attachment to his flesh had been the Company's most potent weapon for years. What would we do if we could no longer see what was happening in places we were not at?

You do get spoiled fast.

Something chittered in the darkness. For a moment I thought it was mocking me. But then a huge fireball rolled up into the night across the valley. The unseen thing's amusement was at the expense of the soldiers over there.

"This jar's gone empty," I grumbled, leaning back and shaking a last drop into the back of my mouth. "I'm going to go see if I can't make another one turn up where we found this one."

Glittering Stone:
Sneak Away

Doj nodded slightly as Lady and I rode past his place. When I glanced back a minute later he was in the street with several Nyueng Bao henchmen. He was wearing his sword, Ash Wand. Up ahead, Thai Dei, Murgen's brother-in-law and bodyguard, strolled along the street. He was armed, too. If he was moving, Murgen would be, too.

I kept a wary watch behind. This had to be done before Sleepy caught on. Before she could issue orders forbidding it. I would not defy direct orders.

She and Sahra were down in the valley. Tran Huu Nhang had come out under a flag of truce. I had a feeling he would announce that the File of Nine had decided to accept reality. They would never admit it but their army had been defeated without stepping onto the field of battle. It was evaporating. The private soldiers were unwilling to endure the persistent attentions of the Unknown Shadows.

It was all pretty amusing—unless you were one of the Nine determined to make a reputation for the File, or you were a crow with hopes of getting fat. Amusing but handy. I was tired of waiting for a chance to slip away. My need to settle with the Bowalk monster had grown pretty powerful, though I hid it well. I have a number of obsessions that I do not let show.

Officially, the Eleventh Battalion was rotating up to guard the Shadowgate. In reality, the Eleventh would be started through to the fortress at the heart of the plain, after nightfall. My gang would be up there much earlier, swiftly moving beyond any hope of Sleepy turning us around. Tobo would cover our backtrail.

I made a sign I hoped would be seen and passed along. We needed to move faster. Sleepy is a resourceful little witch. If there was any way to beat me out of this she might have it figured out already.

It did seem like she was out there by herself on the Bowalk question. One-Eye had a lot more friends dead than he had had while he was alive.

Tobo was at the Shadowgate. But he was supposed to be keeping an eye on his mother and the Captain. Before I could say anything, though, he told me, "They're safe. The meet is a face-saving scheme by the Nine. They've realized what they did was stupid. There'll be a lot of ceremony but no admission of anything, like even that they've got an army over there that wanted to do us evil, and before they're done they'll give Mom a bull that grants the Company permission to find and use the Shadowgate secrets." He grinned, a kid excited. "I don't think they've been getting enough sleep."

"And why are you here?"

"I have family going through. Don't I?"

Of course he did. I was on edge. "Let's keep moving, people." With Nyueng Bao, old Company hands, my wife and whatnot, I would have just over forty people joining my hunt. For a while. If it dragged on I might not be able to hold them together.

Tobo told me, "Make camp at the first circle. Even if it seems like you can cover a lot more ground before it gets dark." He told Lady, "It's important. Keep him in check. The first circle. So I can catch up when I get away."

Willow Swan called, "Hey, Croaker. If you stand right here and look just right out of the side of your eye, you can see the Nef. In broad daylight."

Swan was on the other side of the Hsien Shadowgate. His voice had a dampened, distant quality.

I gave him my best scowl. "Don't forget plain discipline." Shivetya might be our ally and the soul of the plain but there were perils up there even he could not master. The Unforgiven Dead were as hungry for life as ever. Only the roads and circles were safe. Extreme care had to be taken to avoid piercing the protective boundaries. Their master spells would repair them if you did. But you would not be alive to enjoy the result. All that would be left of you was a desiccated husk that had taken a while dying, screaming all the way.

Lately there seemed to be less shadow activity than in the past. Possibly Shivetya had found a way to control them. Maybe even to destroy them. They were a later accretion. He had no use for them. He would love to be rid of them.

Which would be as wonderful for those sad but deadly monsters as it would be for us. They would achieve the release of death at least. A release Shivetya understood. It was a release he yearned for himself.

I started barking at people. "Let's get that equipment out and moving! Where are those mules? I thought I sent them up here last week." When a lot of people agree with you, you can move a lot of material without drawing much attention. I started work on this as soon as I was sure Sleepy did not intend to pursue it herself.

"Calm down," Tobo told me. And I did. Stunned. Because a kid was saying it to a veteran. And was right. "Come here. Lady, you too." He stepped away from the road, to a rudely made wooden box balanced precariously atop a jagged boulder.

"This same rock is over on the home side," I said. "Your father had a bunker right over there where that bush is. What have you got?"

The box contained what looked like four black glass cylinders a foot long, two inches in diameter, equipped with a metal handle on one end.

"These are keys. Like the Lance of Passion was. The kind you need to get on and off the plain. I made new ones. It's not hard if you have the specifications. Blade has one key. Suvrin has two. One is in place in this gate here. We'll take it away when we leave. Two more are with a couple of the battalion commanders who went up already. You're going to take two with you. Just in case."

He handed me one cylinder and gave the other to Lady. Mine seemed heavier than an object its size ought to be. The handle was silver. I asked, "You just drop it into the hole in the plain, right?"

"Exactly. Remember your repair lessons?" He faced Lady when he asked that. I did sit in on the classes but my wife had gotten a lot better understanding of the process. It would have to be a major emergency before we counted on me doing anything even vaguely related to sorcery.

A stream of mules and men passed through the Shadowgate. Each got checked by a sergeant who must have spent his formative years at Sleepy's headquarters. He wanted to make note of every man, every animal, every fireball thrower and other major item of equipment or weaponry. The Nyueng Bao, not really belonging to the Company, were rude to him. I went over and was rude myself. "You're gumming up the works, Sergeant. Go away. Or I'll ask Tobo to sic one of the Black Hounds on you."

The pack was not far off. Nobody could see them, of course, but they made plenty of racket when they quarreled among themselves. And that never stopped.

My threat had the desired effect. The keeper of inventories departed so fast there was almost a whoosh. He would file an official complaint. But that would end up far down the list of my delinquencies.

Tobo overtook me. Most of my gang were through now. The kid bowed to his father, formally polite. He and Murgen had a mutual problem. Neither knew quite how to bridge the gap left by Murgen having been buried during most of the years Tobo was growing up.

The boy told me, in a voice his father was intended to hear, "You'd better push it now. Mom just got word of what you're doing. She'll keep her mouth shut for Gota's sake. For now. But when she hears that Dad is in on it she's going to boil over and head straight for the Captain."

I gave Murgen an ugly look. Didn't tell the old lady you were going out with the guys, eh?

How did Tobo know what his mother had just found out?

The kid snapped his fingers, made a series of hand gestures, said something obscure, apparently to empty air.

A pair of shadows raced across the slope, slanting down from the southwest.

They headed straight toward us. I saw nothing to cast them. Then, suddenly, I had a face full of flapping wings, weights on my shoulders and what felt like dragon's talons trying to rip the meat off my collarbones.

Ravens.

"They only look like crows," Tobo said. "Don't ever forget that they're not."

I shuddered. I have lived with this stuff all around me, decade after decade, but being exposed to it has not made it any less creepy.

Tobo told me. "At my request they've agreed to assume this shape. They'll be your eyes and ears wherever you have to operate without me. They won't have the strategic range you were used to with Dad but they can cover a few hundred miles, fast, and they'll give you a strong tactical advantage. Besides scouting they can carry messages. Be sure to frame those carefully, clearly, without ambiguity, and try to keep them short. Give them an absolutely crystal clear address. Name names and make sure they know who the names belong to."

I turned my head right and left, caught glimpses from the sides of my eyes. It was disconcerting, having those cruel beaks so close. The eyes are the first things the Choosers of the Slain go for on the battlefield.

One bird was black, the other white. They were bigger than the local breed of raven. And the white one had not gotten the shape quite right. It looked like one of its parents had been a startled pigeon instead of a crow.

"If it turns out that I can't catch up and you need to get in touch, they can find me easily."

I am sure I looked grim.

Grinning, Tobo told me, "And I thought they'd go great with your costume. Mom told me you always had ravens on your shoulders when you did Widowmaker, years ago."

I sighed. "Those were real crows. And they belonged to Soulcatcher. The two of us had a sort of understanding in those days. Enemy of my enemy kind of thing."

"You did bring the Widowmaker armor with you, didn't you? And One-Eye's spear? You know you won't be able to come back for anything you leave behind."

"Yes, yes. I have it." This Widowmaker costume armor was not the same outfit that I had worn decades ago. That had gotten lost during Sleepy and Sahra's Kiaulune wars. Soulcatcher probably had it in her trophy chamber. This armor, though mainly for show, came from Hsien's finest armories and had a distinct native flavor. Its black, chitinous lacquer surface boasted inlays of gold and silver symbols that Hsien associated with sorcery and evil and darkness. Some reproduced arcane characters of power once associated with the Shadowmasters. Others went back to an age when Hsien's now-extinct Kina cult was sending out Deceiver companies on crusade. All those symbols were scary, at least in the world where first they had been imagined.

Lady's reconstituted Lifetaker armor was uglier than mine. The stuff on its exterior was less clearly defined and much more creepy because she had insisted on being involved in its design and creation. The inside of her head is filled with spiders.

She did not get any pretend-to-be Choosers of the Slain. She got several ornate little teak boxes and a thin stack of sheets of the strange rice paper preferred by the monks of Khang Phi.

"You have to go. I'll see that they don't send a messenger to order you back."

I grunted. Except for Uncle Doj, who paused to murmur with Tobo, I was the last of my gang through the Hsien Shadowgate. Lady squeezed my hand when I joined her on the risky side. She said, "We're off, darling. Again." She seemed excited.

"Again." I could not recall ever being excited by moving out.

Murgen asked, "You want to show the standard now?"

"Not until we're on the plain itself. We're renegades here. Let's don't make Sleepy look small." I had an idea, then. If I could come up with some material . . . we could run up the old Company standard. From before we adopted Soulcatcher's firebreathing skull.

"Good," Doj told me, stepping through the gate. "A bit of wisdom. That's really good."

I began the climb to the plain somewhat numbed by the realization that I was the only living member of the company who recalled our original banner. It had been no more cheerful than today's was but it had been a lot busier. A field of scarlet with nine hanged men in black and six yellow daggers in the upper left and lower right quadrants, respectively, while the upper right quandrant featured a shattered skull and the lower left boasted a bird astride a severed head. It might have been a raven. Or an eagle.

There was nothing in the Annals to suggest when or why that banner had been adopted.

Glittering Stone:
Mystic Roads

Different stars tonight," Willow Swan said, lying back, staring at the sky.

"Different everything," Murgen replied. "Find me Little Boy or the Dragon's Eye."

There was no moon. There is always a moon up in the Land of Unknown Shadows.

The sky on the plain . . . is changeable. It may not boast the same constellation two nights running.

The weather is usually benign. Cold, of course. But seldom rainy, or worse. In my experience. But I was not concerned about rain or snow. Shadow weather worried me.

The sixteen Shadowgates are equally spaced around the perimeter of the plain. From each a road of stone of a different color from the plain runs inward to the nameless fortress like a spoke in a wagon wheel. I had seen only two of the roads. One was darker than the surrounding plain, the other slightly lighter. At six-mile intervals along the spokes there were large circles of appropriately shaded material. Those got used as campgrounds though that might not have been their original function. The plain has changed with the ages. Man cannot leave anything alone. The roads were once just mystical routes between worlds. Now they are the only safety out there when the sun sets. When darkness falls the killer shadows leave their hiding places. As we gagged down our rough supper the little light glowing from charcoal fires revealed dozens of black stains oozing over the invisible dome protecting the circle.

"The Slugs of Doom," Murgen said through a mouthful of bread, waving at a nearby shadow. "Much better than the Host of the Unforgiven Dead."

"The man's suddenly developing a sense of humor," Cletus said. "This worries me."

His brother Loftus said, "Be afraid, people. Very afraid. The End Days are upon us."

"You saying it's bad jokes going to bring on the Year of the Skulls?"

I observed, "If that was the case we'd've been dead twenty years ago and the only thing you'd see up there is Kina's ugly face."

"Speaking of ugly." Lady pointed.

We had staked our few square feet of turf at the edge of the circle, where the road to the heart of the plain departed it. I had placed the key given to me by Tobo in the socket in the stone where circle and road came together. Every circle had the sockets. The key sealed the road off. It would keep shadows who got past the protective barriers anywhere else from being able to get us.

"The Nef," Murgen said.

The three creatures at the barrier were plain for everyone to see. They were bipedal but their heads were dissimilar masses of ugliness other Annalists have said they hoped were masks. I could see why—though, seeing them, I got a powerful sense of déjà vu. Maybe I ran into them in a dream. I must have had a few while I was buried. I said, "You know these guys, Murgen. See if you can talk to them."

"Yeah. And after I do that I'll fly off to the sun." No one had yet managed to communicate with the Nef, though it was obvious the creatures desperately wanted to talk. We were so alien to each other that communication was impossible.

"We must be getting a better grasp. We're seeing them when we're awake. We are awake, aren't we?" Historically, the Nef appeared only in dreams. Only in the past year did guards at the Shadowgate report catching glimpses the way troops elsewhere made sightings of Tobo's pets.

Murgen ambled over warily. I observed. But I also started keeping an eye on my ravens. Until nightfall they had been almost somnolent, entirely indifferent to the world. The appearance of shadows on the barrier turned them restless, even bellicose. They hissed and coughed and produced a whole range of uncorvine noises. Some form of communication was going on because the shadows responded—though, clearly, not the way the ravens wanted.

The Unknown Shadows of Hsien did share a common ancestry with the Host of the Unforgiven Dead.

Murgen marveled, "I think I'm actually getting what they're trying to tell me."

"What's that?" My wife, I noticed, was watching the Nef intently. Could they be making sense to her, too? But she had no previous experience with the dreamwalkers. Unless while she was a sort of dreamwalker herself, while we were buried.

No, it had to be those three. They had studied us long enough to figure out how to get through. Maybe.

Murgen said, "They want us not to keep heading toward the center of the plain. They're saying we should take the other road."

"Based on what's in the Annals, I'd say they've been trying to get us to do something besides what we want from the first time anybody dreamed them. They're just never able to make themselves clear."

"That would've been me," Murgen said. "And you're right. What I've never figured out, though, is whether they're trying to save us trouble or are pushing their own agenda. It seems to work out both ways."

The tiniest hiss escaped my black raven. A warning. I turned. Uncle Doj had appeared behind Murgen, two steps back, fully armed, staring at the Nef. After watching them for a minute he drifted around the circle to the right, not quite a quarter of the way. Then he shuffled back and forth, squatted, rose up on his toes.

Then Lady went over there. She checked the view from multiple angles herself. "There is a ghost of a road, Croaker." She came back, dug out the key Tobo had given her. I walked back with her. A socket for the key had appeared in the stone surface when no one was watching. It was not there earlier. I had done a one-hundred percent walkaround of the perimeter before we settled down.

Doj said, "The boy told me not to let you waste time trying to make time. Perhaps this is why."

"Murgen. You know about shortcuts and side roads on the plain?"

"They're supposed to exist. Sleepy saw them."

Vaguely, now, I recalled something from my own first passage across the plain.

Lady wanted to plug in her key. I held her back. I said, "All right. If you feel comfortable. Doj? What do you think? Is it safe?" He was as near a real wizard as we had here.

"It doesn't feel wrong."

Not exactly a ringing endorsement. But good enough.

Lady lowered the key into place. In moments the ghost road became more substantial, began to give the impression of a golden glow that was not quite there when you tried to see it. My shoulder ornaments were not pleased. They hissed and spat and retreated to the far side of the circle, where they got into a squabble with something large and dark oozing across the surface of our protection.

Murgen said, "I think they want to enter the circle, Captain. I think they want to cut across."

"Yeah?" The auxiliary road was now more plainly seen than the main way. I mused, "We could hike straight across to the first circle right behind the Khatovar Shadowgate." I went and started getting my gear together.

Doj told me, "Not before morning. Tobo told you that we have to stay here overnight."

I glanced around. Obviously, the only way I would get anybody moving again tonight would be by making myself extremely unpopular.

Khatovar had been there for ages. It would be there after the sun came up. My interest in Lisa Daele Bowalk went back farther than my interest in that place, to a city called Juniper, before she made the acquaintance of a Taken known as Shapeshifter. Justice delayed a few hours more would not set the universe wobbling.

I sighed, dropped my stuff. I shrugged. "After breakfast, then."

"Let them go through," Lady said.

"The Nef? You kidding?"

"Doj and I can handle them."

Interesting, her confidence. But it was misplaced. She knew nothing about the Nef. Unless she had met them in her dreams.

I moved people away from potential trouble, creating a clear path. "Everyone ready? Pull the key, then, Murgen." It would be intriguing to see if the plain would let him.

Doj swung Ash Wand around in front of him, exposed eight inches of blade.

The key came out of its seat. Murgen jumped back. The Nef leapt into the circle. And streaked straight across, to the side road. They hit it and never looked back.

"That's definitely weird," Willow Swan said. The dreamwalkers were in a hurry but nobody dwindles that fast. Nor, normally, do they grow transparent as they go. "Slid right back into dreamland."

I wondered, "You suppose I would've slid into dreamland if I'd tried that road?" The road itself began to fade.

Nobody disagreed. Doj mused, "Tobo did say to stay put."

M iddle of the night. Something wakened me. Felt like a tiny earthquake. The stars above were dancing. After another jiggle they settled down. And were no longer the stars that had been up there when I laid down. This was a different sky altogether.

T hat way!" Doj insisted. It was morning, we were up and Doj insisted on head-ing back the way we had come.

"The fortress is that way."

"We don't want to go to the fortress," Lady reminded me. "We want to go to Khatovar."

"Which isn't back that way . . . is it?" Tobo had not caught up. I was not thrilled about that.

Willow Swan suggested, "You can go look, Croaker. It wouldn't take that long."

I was tired of arguing, particularly in front of a crowd. I did not want my right to lead to become more questionable than it was already. We all possessed guilty hearts. Me more than any because I bought the Company mystique more than any. "I'll take Swan's advice." I pointed here, there, choosing companions. "You guys get to go with me. Mount up. Let's go."

So we were off to the mule races.

I don't believe it." I did not. Could not. My eyes had to be liars.

Lying at the rim of the glittering plain I stared down at another landscape with topography resembling that at Kiaulune and at the Abode of Ravens. But here there was no bustling, recovering Kiaulune. There was no fallen castle Overlook, formerly equipped with towers from which Longshadow could look down onto the glittering plain and see what was coming to get him. Nor was there a whitewashed army town with neat ranks of fields on the slopes below it. This country was feral. This country was much more damp than the other two. Wild brush and scraggly trees advanced to within yards of the crippled Shadowgate. The works around that were the only recognizable human handiwork visible, and they were in ruins.

"Stay low," Doj advised when I started to rise, which would silhouette me above the skyline. I knew better than that. People who do know better generally get skragged that one time they forget or let something slide. Which is why we pound it in and pound it in and pound it in. "That jungle doesn't mean that there aren't eyes watching."

"You're right. I almost did a stupid. Anybody want to guess how old that scrub down there is? I'd say between fifteen and twenty with a bet that it's a lot closer to twenty."

Murgen wondered, "What difference does it make?"

"The forvalaka broke through this Shadowgate about nineteen years ago. She got away. Soulcatcher was too busy burying our asses to chase her, shadows did get after her. . . ."

"Oh. Yeah. She didn't go out alone when she went."

"That's my guess. Shadows got out behind her and wiped out everything we can see from here."

Murgen grunted. Lady nodded, as did Doj. They saw it the same.

Khatovar. My destination for an age. My obsession. Destroyed because we had not had the good sense to cut a young woman's throat in a place now long ago and far away.

The quality of mercy has left me a great, sour role in the theater of my own despair.

Though it is true that it had not seemed important at the time, and we were real busy trying to get out of there with our asses still attached.

Taglios:
The Great General

Mogaba leaned back, smiling. "I can't help wishing Narayan Singh continued luck." Relaxed, content, for the first time in years, he found life good. The Protector was in the provinces indulging her passion for religious persecution. Therefore, she was not around the Palace making life miserable for those who actually hauled on the reins, riding the tiger whilst trying to keep the mundane work of government simmering.

His mention of the living saint made Aridatha Singh flinch. It was subtle but the reaction was there. And it was unique. Other Singhs did not react to the name, other than with an obligatory curse, perhaps. This demanded further examination.

Mogaba asked, "Any trouble out there?"

Aridatha said, "It's quiet. You have the Protector out of town, making no ridiculous demands, things settle down. People get too busy making a living to act up."

Ghopal was less upbeat. The Greys were out in the streets and alleys every day. "Graffiti keeps turning up more and more. 'Water Sleeps' most often."

"And?" Murgen asked. His voice was soft but intense, his eyes narrow.

"The other traditional taunts are all there. 'All Their Days Are Numbered.' 'Rajadharma.'"

"And?" Mogaba seemed to have shifted characters the way Soulcatcher did. Perhaps he was aping her style.

"That one, too. 'My Brother Unforgiven.'"

That harsh indictment again. That accusation which always disturbed the incomplete slumber of the part of him guilty about betraying the Black Company to advance his own ambitions. No good had come of it. His life had become enslaved by it. His punishment was to move from one villain to another, always serving wickedness, like a loose woman passing from man to man down a long decline.

Aridatha Singh, eager to move away from talk about Narayan Singh and the Deceivers, interjected, "One of my officers reported a new one yesterday. 'Thi Kim is coming.'"

"Thi Kim? What is that? Or who?"

Ghopal observed, "It sounds Nyueng Bao."

"We don't see much of those people these days."

"Since somebody snatched the Radisha right out of the Palace . . ." Ghopal stopped. Mogaba had begun to darken again, though that failure belonged to the Greys, not to the army. He had been in the territories at the time.

"So. All the old slogans. But the Company all fled through the Shadowgate. And perished on the other side because they never came back."

Ghopal knew little about the world outside his own narrow, filthy streets. "Maybe some of them did survive and we just don't know about it."

"No. They didn't. We would've heard. The Protector's had people down there harvesting shadows since they left." People who had been lured into her service by cruelly false promises to teach them her ways and make them captains in her great, unrevealed enterprise.

None of those collaborators survived long. Shadows were clever and persistent. Quite a few found ways to escape from novices long enough to destroy their tormenters and be destroyed themselves.

Soulcatcher made sure conditions for disaster remained ripe.

Mogaba closed his eyes, leaned back again, steepled his dark fingers. "I've enjoyed not having the Protector around." Getting those words out casually was difficult. His throat was tight. His chest felt like a huge weight was pressing in on it. He was afraid. Soulcatcher terrified him. And for that he hated her. And for that he loathed himself. He was Mogaba, the Great General, the purest, smartest, strongest of the Nar warriors produced by Gea-Xle. For him fear was supposed to be a tool by which he managed the weak. He was not supposed to know it personally.

Silently, within, Mogaba repeated his warrior's mantras, knowing habits ingrained since birth would hold the fear at bay.

Ghopal Singh was a functionary. Very good at managing the Greys but not a natural conspirator. That was one attribute that had recommended him to the Protector. He did not apprehend the message lurking on the edges of the Great General's statement. Aridatha Singh, in some ways, was as naive as he was handsome. But he did understand that Mogaba was sneaking up on something that could be a great watershed in all their lives.

Mogaba had championed Aridatha's elevation because of his naivete concerning the complex motives of others and because of his enthusiastic idealism. Rajadharma was a lever that Mogaba was sure would move Aridatha Singh.

Aridatha peered around nervously. He had heard the old saying that in the Palace the very walls have ears.

Mogaba leaned forward, lit a cheap tallow candle from a lamp and took the fire to a stoneware bowl filled with a dark liquid. Ghopal held his tongue even though the animal product offended him religiously.

The bowl's contents proved to be flammable, though they produced more unpleasant black smoke than they did flame or light. The smoke spread out across the ceiling, then crept down the walls and flowed out the doors. Its progress was marked by squeaks and chitterings and an occasional complaint from an unseen crow.

Mogaba said, "We may have to get down on the floor for a few minutes, till the smoke thins out."

Aridatha whispered, "Are you really proposing what I think you're proposing?"

Mogaba murmured, "You may not have the same reasons I do but I think we'd all be better off if the Protector no longer held her position. Particularly the Taglian people. What do you think?"

Mogaba had expected Aridatha to agree easily. The soldier believed in his obligation to the people he served. And he did nod.

Ghopal Singh was his main worry. Ghopal had no obvious reason to want change. The Greys were all members of the Shadar religion, traditionally with little influence in government. Their alliance with the Protector had given them power out of proportion to their numbers. They would be reluctant to lose that power.

Ghopal glanced around nervously, completely failing to note Mogaba's intense examination. He blurted, though in a whisper, "She has to go. The Greys have believed that for a long time. The Year of the Skulls couldn't be much more terrible than what we've suffered from her. But we don't know how to get rid of her. She's too powerful. And too smart."

Mogaba relaxed. So the Greys were *not* enamored of their benefactor. Interesting. Excellent.

"But we'll never get rid of her. She always knows what everyone around her is thinking. And we'll never be able not to think about it because we'll be so scared. She'll sniff it out in about ten seconds. Really, we're walking dead men now, just for having considered it."

"Then get your family out of town now," Mogaba told him. It was Soulcatcher's habit to exterminate her enemies root and branch. "I've been giving this a lot of thought. I think that the only way it could be managed would be to have everything in place and strike before she has a chance to look around and pick up clues. We might engineer it so that she arrives exhausted. That might give us the edge we need."

Aridatha mused, "Whatever it is, it will have to be sudden and massive and a complete surprise."

"She'll begin to suspect," Ghopal said. "There are too many people loyal to her, because without her they'll be dead themselves. They'll warn her."

"Not if we don't get carried away. If just us three know what's happening. We're in charge. We can give any orders we want. People won't question us. There's trouble on the streets and it's getting worse. People will expect us to do something about it. Plenty of others hate the Protector. They'll feel free to act up while she's away. That gives us an excuse to do almost anything we want. If we mainly use people whose loyalty to the Protector is absolute, letting them do most of the work and carry the messages, there's no reason she should suspect anything until it's too late."

Ghopal looked at him like he was whistling in the dark. Maybe he was. Mogaba said, "I've opened my mouth here. I've committed myself. And I have nowhere to run." They were natives. They could vanish into the territories. There was nowhere he could hide. And a return to Gea-Xle had been out of the question for twenty-five years. The Nar back home knew all about what he had done.

Aridatha mused, "Then every day in every way we should do our jobs to the utmost on the Protector's behalf—until we create a rattrap we can close like this." He clapped his hands.

"We'll only get one chance," Mogaba said. "Five seconds after we fail we'll all be praying for death." He waited a moment during which he checked the smoke. Its usefulness was almost exhausted. "Are you in?"

Both Singhs nodded but neither showed an unbound eagerness. The truth was, it was a poor bet that any of them would survive this adventure.

Mogaba sat in his quarters staring out at a full moon. He wondered if it had been too easy. Were the Singhs genuinely interested in ridding Taglios of the Protector? Or had they just played along, sensing that he was the more deadly threat at the moment?

If they were not committed he would learn the truth only when Soulcatcher sank her teeth into his throat.

He was going to be an intimate acquaintance of fear for a long time to come.

22

Khatovar:
Invasion

Swan volunteered to slither down to the Shadowgate with me. I demurred. "I think I'll take my sweetheart. We don't get many chances to get away together." And she would have a steadier hand than I would when it came to working on the Shadowgate. Which, even from the head of the slope, could be seen to need restoration.

After examining the Shadowgate from a closer vantage, I told my beloved, "Bowalk really tore it up getting through."

"She had shadows gnawing on her. According to what Sleepy says Shivetya showed her. Tell me you'd be gentle and not slam the door if you had those things after you."

"I don't even want to think about it. Are we safe? Is anything out there watching?"

"I don't know."

"What?"

"I have a little power here on the plain. A dim one-hundredth of what used to be. But outside the Shadowgates I might as well be deaf, dumb and blind. All I can do is pretend."

"So Kina is alive, then?"

"Possibly. If I'm not just tapping Shivetya or some residual, ambient power. The plain is a place of many strange energies. They leak in from the different worlds."

"But you believe you're bleeding Kina again. Don't you?"

"If I am, she's not just sleeping, she's in a coma."

"There!"

"There what?"

"I thought I saw something move."

"That was just the breeze stirring the branches."

"You think so? I'm not inclined to take chances."

The sarky witch said, "You stand guard. I'll work on the gate."

If she did I could not tell. She was less active than I would have been.

*   *   *

We were through. Into Khatovar. I did not feel like I had found my way into paradise. I did not feel like I had come home. I felt the letdown I had expected almost from the moment I had become aware that my lust to find Khatovar had been imposed upon me from without. Khadi's Gate was a wasteland.

Clete and Loftus started laying out a camp close enough to the gate that we could make a quick getaway if that became necessary. I was still at the gate itself, surveying this world where the Black Company had been born.

Definitely the disappointment I had anticipated. Maybe even worse.

Something stirred the hair on the back of my neck. I turned. I saw nothing but had a distinct feeling that something had just come through the Shadowgate.

I caught movement in the edge of my vision. Something dark. A shape both large and ugly.

One of the Black Hounds.

The back of my neck went cool again. Then again.

Maybe Tobo was coming after all.

The darker of my two ravens settled onto a nearby boulder. After a shower of hisses directed nowhere in particular, it cocked a big yellow eye my way and said, "There are no occupied human dwellings within fifty miles. The ruins of a city lie under the trees below the rocky prominence to the northeast. There are signs that humans visit it occasionally."

I gaped. That damned bird was better-spoken than most of my companions. But before I could strike up a conversation, it took to the air again.

So there were people in this world. But the closest were at least three days away.

The promontory the bird mentioned was the place where the fortress Overlook had stood in our own world. The ruins likely occupied the same site as Kiaulune.

Another chill on the neck. The Unknown Shadows continued to come through.

I went down to camp. The engineer brothers were old but efficient. It was livable right now—as long as we got no rain.

The rain would be along before long. It was clear it rained often here.

Fires were burning. Somebody had killed a wild pig. It smelled heavenly, roasting. Shelters were going up. Sentries were out. Uncle Doj had appointed himself sergeant of the guard and was making a circuit of the four guardposts.

I waited till Murgen found something to occupy him, beckoned Swan and Lady. "Let's think about what we do now." I looked my wife in the eye. She understood what I wanted to know. She shook her head.

There was no Khatovaran source of magical power she could parasitize.

I grumped, "I didn't expect towers of pearl and ruby beside streets of gold, but this is ridiculous." I checked Doj and Murgen. They showed no interest in us yet.

"Sour grapes." Swan sneered, heading straight for the critical point. "That's a whole world out there. Damned near empty, it looks like. How do you expect to find one insane killer monster?"

"I got to thinking about that while I was standing up there looking at all this. Amongst other things. And I think I've had an evil epiphany."

Lady contributed to the Annals and tried to keep up with her successors. She shook her head, said, "There isn't much in what she wrote."

Swan glanced around. Nobody was close. In a soft voice he said, "She hasn't been writing the histories since you came back, has she?"

I asked, "What's that mean?"

"Over the years Tobo and Suvrin and some of their cronies have visited most of the Shadowgates. They visited the Khatovar gate several times."

"How do you know?"

"I sneak around. I listen when I'm not supposed to hear. I know Suvrin and Tobo came out here while you were wounded. Just the two of them. And later, while we were in Khang Phi, Suvrin went out again. Alone."

"Then I'm right. We've been jobbed. How come you didn't mention this before?"

"It had to do with Khatovar. I figured you were behind whatever was going on."

Lady made a growling, chuckling sound that told me she had a handle on the truth. "That devious little witch. You really think so?"

Swan asked, "What am I missing?"

I told him, "I think we're out here raiding Khatovar not because I'm so damned clever but because Sleepy wants us old farts out from under foot when she breaks out into the homeworld. I'll bet the whole damned force is moving right now. And Sleepy won't have a single one of us asking questions or giving advice or trying to do things our own way."

Swan took a while to think about it. Then he took a while to look around at the gang who had elected to defy the command authority to pursue revenge on One-Eye's killer. He said, "Either she is *really* an astute little bitch or we've been around so many sneaky people so long that we see machinations everywhere we look."

"Tobo knew," I said. Tobo had to be part of it. He let his father and Uncle Doj come out here. . . . "You know, I'm so paranoid I'm going to put a guard on the gate from the other side. And I'll fill them up with lies about how a demon in the guise of one of our people might try to sabotage the gate so we can't get back out of Khatovar."

Neither Lady nor Swan argued. Swan did remark. "You *are* paranoid. You think Sahra would let Sleepy get away with leaving Thai Dei, Murgen and Doj trapped out here?"

"I think it's a mad universe. I think almost anything somebody can imagine happening can happen. Even the cruelest, blackest sin."

Lady asked, "And what do you intend to do about it?"

"I'm going to kill the forvalaka."

Swan said, "Murgen's noticed that something's going on. He's headed this way."

"I'm going to play the game. Tobo sent a bunch of his pets through after us. Let's make sure they can't get back out unless we let them go. We'll use them to find Bowalk. Then we'll kill her."

Glittering Stone:
Fortress with No Name

Sleepy reached the fortress at the heart of the plain by the expedient of refusing to be steered elsewhere. Shivetya's helpful shortcuts were not going to divert her from examining the root of her scheme for conquest.

There was one temporal power greater than the greatest sorcery. Greed. And she owned the wellspring of a flood of what the greedy held most dear: gold. Not to mention silver and gems and pearls.

For thousands of years fugitives from many worlds had hidden their treasures in the caverns beneath Shivetya's throne. Who knew why? Possibly Shivetya. But Shivetya would not tell tales—unless they advanced his cause. Shivetya had the mind and soul of an immortal spider. Shivetya had no remorse, no compassion, knew only his task and his will to end it. He was the Company's ally but he was not the Company's friend. He would destroy the Company instantly if that suited an altered purpose and he was in a position to do so.

Sleepy meant to cover her back.

She approached Baladitya. "Where's Blade?"

Baladitya had begun gushing discoveries he had made since being handed his mission. Sleepy felt a twinge of guilt. She remembered Baladitya's kind of excitement, long ago and far away. But being responsible for thousands of people, pursuing a timetable with very little slippage built in, left no opportunity for simple pleasures. That made her cranky and curt, sometimes.

"He's down below. He doesn't come up much anymore."

Irked, Sleepy looked around for someone young enough to gallop a mile down into the earth. She spied Tobo and Sahra arguing. Not exactly unusual. But not so frequently lately. They had been butting heads since Tobo entered puberty.

One of Tobo's djinn could get down there faster than the youngest pair of legs. "Tobo!" Sleepy beckoned.

Exasperation flashed across the boy's face. Everyone wanted something from him.

He did respond. He showed no defiance. He never did. His calm half-caste face settled into perfect nonexpression. Nor did his stance in any way betray what he might be thinking. Sleepy seldom saw anyone so inscrutable. And yet he was so young.

He just stood waiting for her to tell him what she wanted.

"Blade is down below somewhere. Send one of your messengers to tell him I want him up here."

"Can't do it."

"Why not?"

"I don't have any here. I've explained before. The Unknown Shadows hate the plain. It's very difficult to get them to come up here. Most of those who do come refuse to have anything to do with people. I don't want them to have anything to do with people. It puts them in a bad temper every time. You have a whole regiment cluttering up the place. There must be a man somewhere who doesn't have something else to do."

Sarcastic infidel. There were twelve hundred men cooling their heels around the fortress, waiting to lead the treasure train, doing nothing useful in the interim. "I was looking for something a little faster." Once the Company was on the barren plain, even with Shivetya working wonders, there was little time to waste.

There had been no good news from Suvrin, either. Tobo should have gone with him. Or Doj or Lady, at the very least. Someone better equipped to deal with the Unknown Shadows. But at the very least there should have been word that a bridgehead had been established.

Baladitya said, "Then you'd better go down there yourself. Because he isn't going to respond to any lesser authority."

"What? Why?"

"Because he hears voices calling him. He's trying to figure out what to answer them."

"Darn!" Sleepy broke out in what, for her, was a blistering blue streak. "That wrangle-franging mudsucker! I'm going to . . ."

Tobo and Baladitya grinned. Sleepy shut up. She remembered times when her Company brothers would get her going to see just how creative she would be in avoiding use of common profanity. She muttered, "I should've written you people the way you really are. Not you, Baladitya. You're actually a human being." She glared at Tobo. "You I'm beginning to wonder about."

"For a nonbeliever," Baladitya said, of himself.

"Yes. Well. There're more of you lost souls than there are those of us who know the Truth. I must be God's Beacon in the Land of Our Sorrows."

Baladitya frowned, then caught on. Sleepy was actually poking fun at her religion's attitude toward those outside it, all the unbelievers who made up the population of the Land of Our Sorrows. Which, in an earlier age, when the Vehdna were more numerous and more enthusiastic about rescuing the infidel from damnation, had been called the Realm of War.

Only Believers lived inside the Realm of Peace.

Sleepy snapped, "Tobo, stop trying to sneak away. You're going down there with me. Just in case he really is hearing voices."

"That sounds to me like a real good reason for everybody else to stay away."

"Tobo."

"Right behind you, Captain. Ain't nobody gonna sneak up on your back."

Sleepy growled. She never got used to the informality and irreverence, though it had been a firm fixture of Company culture since long before her advent.

The soldiers mocked everything and bitched about the rest. Yet the work got done.

Sleepy conscripted a half dozen more companions while hurrying to the stairway down. All from Hsien. She marveled at the results of her relentless training regimen. Many who had joined the Company had been the dregs of the Land of Unknown Shadows, criminals and fugitives, bandits and deserters from the forces of the warlords, and fools who thought a turn with the Soldiers of Darkness would be a great adventure. Sleek, strong and confident, they put on a show now, after months of intense preparation. The clash of steel, probably closer than they anticipated, would be their final tempering.

Sleepy's descent led her past dozens of men still carrying treasure toward the surface. From behind her Tobo asked, "You sure you aren't overdoing the tomb robbing? We've already got enough to make the whole mob rich." A fact not lost on some recruits of less than unstained provenance. But temptation was easy to resist when you knew only your Captain could get you off the plain alive and that the Unknown Shadows would hound you pitilessly if you tried anything after you were off.

"We can't beat the Protector with eight thousand men, Tobo. We need secret weapons and force multipliers. Gold fills both roles."

Sometimes Tobo was troubled by his Captain. At some point, during her copious free time, she had gotten too close to a library centered around military theory. At times she tended to regurgitate notions like "strategic center of gravity" and "force multipliers" just when that would leave her listeners uncomfortable and concerned.

Tobo was also concerned because the old folks, the veterans, Croaker and Lady and the others, approved. That meant that *he* was not getting it.

"We'll take time out here," Sleepy said when they reached the level of the ice caverns where the Captured had been held. "You men," she said to those she had had follow, "I want four of you to take a couple of sleepers up top. Longshadow and the Howler. Howler is going to travel with us. With Tobo. A work party will take Longshadow to Hsien for trial. You two. Stay with us."

The ice caverns seemed timeless, changeless. Frost soon obscured the smaller signs of any traffic. The dead could not be told from the enchanted except on close examination by someone who was knowledgeable.

Sleepy continued, "You men don't go in there until we call you. You even breathe on those things sometimes, somebody dies." Which, upon close examination, could be seen to have happened before. The corpses included several of the Captured as well as a handful of the mystery ancients whose presence Shivetya had yet to explain.

There was a great deal the demon would not share.

Sleepy told Tobo, "We want these two to go upstairs without them waking up."

"I have to break stasis. Otherwise they'll die as soon as we touch them."

"I understand that. But I want them kept in a condition where they can't cause trouble. There won't be anybody there to control Longshadow if he wakes up all the way."

"Let me do my job."

Touchy. Sleepy posted herself between the boy wizard and the cavern entrance in case curiosity overcame the good sense of the soldiers. She marveled at how quickly the ice reasserted itself, at how delicately cobweblike some of the structures around the sleeping old men were. Beyond Howler, now, there was little evidence of the trampling the place had taken when the Captured were released. The cavern floor tilted upward back there, turned, and the cave itself got tight enough to force an explorer to crawl. If you went back far enough you reached a place where the most holy relics of the Deceiver cult had been hidden during an ancient persecution. The Company had destroyed them, giving particular attention to the powerful Books of the Dead.

S leepy was quiet for a long time after she sent the two sleeping sorcerers to the surface. She and Tobo and two young Bone Warriors resumed their descent into the earth. Sleepy had two things on her mind: The first was the identity of the source of the pale blue light leaking through the ice of the cavern of the old men, to illuminate the human hoard, and second, "What is the center of gravity of the Taglian empire?" She was more interested in the latter. The former was just a curiosity. It did not matter. Probably just the light of another world.

"Soulcatcher," Tobo replied. "You don't have to think about that. If you kill the Protector you're left facing a big snake with no head. The Radisha and the

Prahbrindrah Drah step up and announce themselves and the whole thing is over with." He made it sound simple.

"Except for hunting down the Great General."

"And Narayan Singh. And the Daughter of Night. But the Protector is the only part we can't manage using the Black Hounds."

Sleepy did not miss the way his voice went hollow when he mentioned the Daughter of Night. He had met the witch when she was the Company's prisoner, before the flight to the Land of Unknown Shadows. Sleepy had not failed to notice the impact the girl had had then.

The Captain missed very little. And forgot nothing. And seldom made an error.

But setting up the old folks to put themselves out of the way, so they would not be peering over her shoulder, proved to be an error of the first order.

The Captain found Blade standing in front of a wall of blackness, rigid, a lantern dangling from his left hand. It was obvious that he had spent a lot of time there. Empty fuel containers littered the steps. The contents of those containers had been meant for Baladitya and the rangers mining the treasure hoards.

The Captain was irked. "Blade! What? . . ."

Blade gestured for silence. He whispered, "Listen."

"For what?"

"Just listen." And when Sleepy had just about exhausted her store of patience, he added, "For that."

She heard it plainly, though remote, weak, echoing. A cry of, "Help."

Tobo heard it, too. He jumped. "Captain . . ."

"Summon your Cat Sith. Or one of the Black Hounds."

"I can't do that." He would not tell her that he had exceeded his instructions by sending most of the Unknown Shadows to help Croaker and Lady.

"Why not?"

"They'd refuse to come down here."

"Compel them."

"I can't. They're partners, not slaves."

Sleepy grumbled to herself about damnation and consorting with demons.

"You can't go any farther than this," Blade said, answering a question that had not been asked. "I've tried a thousand times. There isn't enough willpower in the Company to move another step downward. I can't even throw one of these oil jars."

Sleepy asked, "Are any of them full?"

"Over there."

Sleepy picked up three full pots. She dropped two at Blade's feet, told him, "Step back." The oil from the broken jars could not be intimidated by a supernatural darkness. "Now light it."

"What?"

"Set it on fire."

With considerable reluctance Blade tilted his lantern and let a few drops of burning oil spill.

The stairwell filled with flame.

"Damn!" Tobo squealed. "What did you do that for?"

"Can you see now?" Sleepy had an arm up to shield her face from the heat.

The blackness had not been able to overpower the flames.

Tobo told her, "Just two more steps down there's a floor. With coins scattered around on it."

Sleepy lowered her arm. She stepped past Blade. Tobo followed. Stunned, Blade again tried to push forward. He staggered. There was none of the resistance he expected.

Why not, suddenly?

Blade was sure there would have been no change had he started a fire himself. "Captain, I'd be very careful."

The darkness had been waiting.

"Help!"

The voice was louder and more insistent. And clear enough to be recognized.

Tobo echoed Blade. "Captain, be very careful indeed. This isn't possible. The man has to be dead."

"Help!"

Goblin's plaints sounded increasingly urgent.

Khatovar:
The Unholy Land

We had been in the holy land of my imagination for four days. Nothing had been gained. Something had been lost. An old Company hand named Spiff was dead. Likewise, Cho Dai Cho, alias JoJo, the Nyueng Bao who had been One-Eye's indifferent bodyguard for so long.

Shadows had gotten them the first night. Killer shadows that had escaped the glittering plain after the forvalaka's breakout had damaged the Khatovar Shadowgate. Shadows that had depopulated this part of Khatovar.

Once we knew they were there we had little trouble luring and destroying them. We had had plenty of experience. But the alarm method was awfully unpleasant.

It could have been worse. The fact of regional devastation had inspired everyone to a higher state of readiness.

During subsequent nights we eliminated a total of nine shadows. I hoped that augured well for the rest of this world. I hoped they were now that uncommon.

The Black Hounds helped destroy the shadows. They hated their undomesticated cousins from the plain. And feared them greatly. Though these shadows seemed much less aggressive than those we had encountered in the past.

They ranged afar, too, and found no living people south of Khatovar's equivalent of the Dandha Presh. Of the forvalaka they found little sign, either. Its trail, though, they were able to uncover. Apparently it was so plain my ravens suspected that it had been left that way on purpose.

"You really want to cross those mountains again?" Swan asked.

Lady remarked, "He looks exhausted already, doesn't he? And we haven't walked a foot."

I admitted, "This would be a great time to have one of those flying carpets."

"There're a lot of things we could use. Several of the black stallions from Charm would be handy. So would a hundred more fireball throwers. You wouldn't steal Sleepy's horse."

"Well, I couldn't, could I? It's the last one left. She'd notice it was missing."

"But she isn't missing you and me and the rest of these droppings beneath the roost of the rooks of dim wittedness."

"That's a cute image," Swan said. "Here come the lead birds of the flock." Murgen. Thai Dei and Uncle Doj were approaching. Like the rest of the band they wanted to know, "What now?" and I had promised to tell them this afternoon.

Murgen asked, "So what're we going to do, boss?"

"Go get it. We can't stay here. The shadows wiped out almost all the game."

They just kill. They will kill bugs if the passion takes them. Large animals they overlook only when they have the opportunity to suck the life out of something human.

Murgen asked, "You think that's why she didn't hang around here?"

Only part of it. "She does have to eat." A glance around told me the fire in their bellies for revenge no longer burned so hot.

Doj said, "But there is food here. And it's not that hard to find. I've seen wild pigs and a species of miniature deer that I didn't recognize. I've seen rabbits and several kinds of smaller rodents. I'd say there was food enough if she wanted it. I'd also say the shadows haven't been active here for a long time. Otherwise I wouldn't have seen the animals I have. The monster had to be rejoining her allies. And the shadows had to be sent. To spy on us."

I said, "Do go on."

"I've considered several alternate frames for the evidence. Maybe it does add up to nothing more than the surface picture. A raid by an insane monstrosity. But I think that is just too simple. I feel there has to be more. Insanity and revenge as motives don't seem adequate. But if she's working with someone local . . ."

I had been supposing almost from the moment I broke out of my coma. I did not have enough information to support my guesswork, though.

I grunted.

"The monster had to know she would be pursued. The Soldiers of Darkness have that reputation. And they've tried to kill her before, with much weaker provocation."

"And Goblin also tried to help her, as I recall. Which she repaid by turning on him before he could do her any good."

Doj continued, "She had to get through two Shadowgates to reach Hsien. Which she knew, somehow, was where One-Eye could be found. Both Shadowgates, as far as she knew, were damaged. So even if she was safe on the roads she could expect to be vulnerable at the gates. But she didn't get hurt. And then the distance between the gates would be a long one if she got no help from Shivetya. We have no reason to believe he helped her. On its face it looks like it would've been too long and too dangerous and too hungry a journey if One-Eye's murder was all she hoped to accomplish and could expect no help managing it."

I turned to Lady, then looked back to Doj. He was as smart as I was. "I see. Of course she couldn't have managed without help. With the shadows and, especially, with food. She had no chance to feed while she was in Hsien. The Hounds were after her all the time."

Lady chipped in, "Then she had help from helpers who expected a sizable payback. What might that be?"

"How about the same thing we worked for four years to dig out of the Land of Unknown Shadows?" Murgen said. "The secrets of the Shadowgates."

Heads nodded. I asked, "How would they know? And why would they want it? To stop this gate from leaking? Didn't Shivetya say they always repair themselves to that level? Tobo and Suvrin never found any that were open, did they?" I assumed Doj would be familiar with Tobo's adventures.

All eyes were on me. Murgen suggested, "This is Khatovar. Source of the Free Companies."

"More than four hundred years ago. Closer to five, now. They might not even remember."

"Probably not."

"And they must have some knowledge of Shadowgates. They got Bowalk through this one, in and out of Hsien, then back through here again. Without destroying anything."

Lady said, "Another thing we can infer is that someone here knows something about controlling shadows."

"We can?"

"Implicit in the fact that Bowalk made it to Hsien and back again. As well as in the fact that we should've had more shadows to deal with here if a horde did break out and devastate the world when Bowalk came through the gate the first time. There's game, Doj says. If those were feral shadows we destroyed they would've killed all the game. Those things were here to watch us."

I growled. "Damn! Murgen. All that time at Khang Phi. You ever hear tell of any Shadowmasters that never were accounted for? We're not going to have to butt heads with Longshadow's long-lost mom, are we?"

"They're accounted for. Any that turn up here would have to be home grown." Which was possible. Two of the three we had destroyed in our world were exactly that. One had been one of the Lady's henchwomen believed dead but gone fugitive instead.

Continued talk led to the notion that we might have been lured to Khatovar specifically so we could be stripped of whatever knowledge we might possess.

Even now Lady remained a tremendous repository of arcane information.

I went off alone with my raven companions. One I told to take the Unknown Shadows out scouting, ranging as far as necessary to find the nearest natives. The other I sent to find Tobo. It carried a detailed and honest report, just as if Sleepy had sent us to Khatovar and expected regular communiqués.

I hoped Tobo might have some useful suggestions. I hoped he knew more about Khatovar than he had pretended.

N either Lady nor I could sleep. The white raven had not taken long to find people. An army was headed our way, though it was still on the far side of the mountains. The forvalaka was there, accompanying a family of wizards who, according to reports from Tobo, were the uncontested overlords of modern Khatovar.

Tobo's source was indirect. He had consulted the scholar Baladitya, who took our questions to the demon Shivetya. Shivetya then tacitly acknowledged his ability to monitor events in the worlds connected to the glittering plain.

The rulers of Khatovar were a sprawling, brawling, turbulent clan of wizards known as the Voroshk, which was simply their family name. The founding father's talented blood had bred true. And often. He had been a man of immense appetites. There were several hundred Voroshk today. Their regime was cruel. Its sole purpose was to further enrich and empower the Family. Following the disaster caused by the forvalaka's breakthrough into Khatovar, the Voroshk had learned to manage the shadows. It would be the Voroshk who had sent the shadows we had destroyed.

Kina, or Khadi, was no longer worshipped in the world bearing the name that meant Khadi's Gate. The Voroshk had exterminated the Children of Kina.

Nevertheless, once each year, sometime during the time when the Deceivers would have celebrated their Festival of Lights, somebody managed to strangle a member of the Family and get away.

Chances were good that the Voroshk knew their history well enough to recall that the Free Companies of Khatovar had gone out as missionaries on behalf of the Mother of Night. They might well dread the Queen of Darkness's return.

M y own supernatural allies were under instruction to avoid notice except in instances where Khatovar's shadows could be picked off without risk of our secret strength being revealed.

Her face against my chest, Lady murmured, "These Voroshk sound like bad people, hon. As bad as any you've run into before."

"Including you?"

"Nobody's as bad as me. But you need to worry about this. There's a whole family of them. And they don't squabble amongst themselves. Much. Even when I had the Ten on their shortest rein they were always trying to stab each other in the back."

There was a message there, under her teasing. I held her and told her, "I'll retreat to the plain rather than risk the confrontation. We can always sneak back here some other time." But I would not be happy if I had to let Bowalk get away yet again.

I drifted off wondering about the minds of the Voroshk. Wondering about this mysterious world that had sent our forbrethren out so long ago, on a crusade that had gotten lost. Were the Voroshk unwitting pawns of Kina? Could they be yet another device by which the Dark Mother might try to bring on the Year of the Skulls?

"No," Lady said when I suggested it aloud. "We know whose role that is."

"Don't want to think about Booboo, hon. Just want to go to sleep."

25

Glittering Stone:
The Revenant

Goblin denied nothing. "She kept me alive somehow. She intended to use me. But she never did anything to me. I spent most of the time sleeping. Dreaming ugly dreams. Probably her dreams."

The little wizard's voice was barely a whisper. It husked. He seemed permanently on the verge of tears. The irrepressible spirit that had made him the Goblin of old seemed to have fled.

His audience did nothing to make him welcome or feel wanted. He was not welcome or wanted. He had spent four years sleeping with the Queen of Night, the Mother of Deceivers.

"She lives in the bleakest place you can imagine. It's all death and corruption."

"And madness," Sahra added without looking up from the trousers she was mending.

Tobo asked, "Where's the Lance?"

Goblin had been asked before. The Lance of Passion was the soul of the Company. As much as the Annals did, it tied past and present together. It went all the way back to the Company's departure from Khatovar. It had symbolic power and real power. It was a Shadowgate key. And it was capable of causing a Goddess terrible pain.

Goblin sighed. "There's nothing but the head left. Inside her, from when I stabbed her. She made it migrate through her flesh. She's taken it into her womb."

The Captain, obviously uncomfortable with this heathen talk, snapped, "Would any of you infidels care to explain that? Tobo?"

"I don't know anything about religion, Captain. Not the practical stuff, anyway."

"Anybody?"

None of the infidels had a thought.

Sleepy had a few. One was that Kina was not a real Goddess. Kina was just an incredibly powerful monster. All the Gunni Gods and Goddesses were nothing but powerful monsters. There was only one God. . . . She continued staring at Goblin, wondering if he was worth believing, wondering if the best course was just to kill him. The silence stretched. Goblin remained immensely uncomfortable. As he should be, considering the circumstances and his limited ability to explain what had happened to him.

There was no way anyone would ever trust him.

The Captain said, "I have a thought, Tobo."

Silence stretched again as the boy waited on her and she waited for him to ask what her thought was. Grown-up silliness.

Sahra said, "Why don't we have Goblin go help Croaker with Khatovar? He'll be more comfortable with his old friends, anyway."

Sleepy gave her a dirty look. Then Tobo did the same. Sahra smiled, bit the thread she was using, put her needle away. "That's done, then."

Goblin's froglike face had lost the little color that had survived his time underground. It lost all expression. The man within was trying hard to remain unreadable. In trying he gave away the fact that he did not want to join the expedition to Khatovar.

Maybe he just dreaded facing the forvalaka again.

"I think that's a wonderful idea," the Captain said. Coldly. "Croaker sent a raven whining for help. He has all those unpredictable soldiers and sorcerers headed his way. Goblin. You can still cut it, can't you? Sorcery-wise? You haven't lost the knack?"

The sad little wizard shook his head slowly. "I don't know. I'd have to try. Not that I would be any good against a real talent even on my best day. I never was."

"It's decided. You'll take the Khatovar road. Everyone else. We're done here. We're moving out. Tobo, find the Chu Ming brothers. They're going to go with Goblin."

The news that movement was imminent spread quickly. The remaining troops were glad to hear it. They had stayed here in this uncomfortable, frightening place far too long while the higher-ups fussed about nothing. Rations were growing short, despite all the years of preparation.

26

Khatovar:
Hunkered Down

I returned from consultations with the white raven. "They've reached the down-hill side of the pass."

Lady observed, "They're moving fast, then."

"They've begun to wonder if we suspect something. They've begun to wonder why so few of their shadow scouts come back and why the few that do never came close to us. So they left their infantry and heavy cavalry and artillery behind in an effort to get here before we can do a lot to get ready if we do expect trouble. The bird tells me they're also preparing some sort of surprise but it couldn't get close enough to find out what."

Swan grumbled, "I don't understand why they weren't just sitting here waiting for us."

"Probably because there's not much here to eat, it's a long way from where things are happening and they couldn't know when we'd arrive. Or even if we would. They have an empire up north to keep in line. And if they were camped out here, chances are we'd just not bother to come off the plain. Also, I would imagine that they really expected us to follow the forvalaka once we understood what had happened here. So they could trap us north of the Dandha Presh. In familiar territory, closer to home. Which I would've run into if I didn't have the Blacks Hounds and whatnot to go scouting.

"On top of the distance for them, there're a raft of superstitions about this country. Plus there's just been a change in the head of the Voroshk family. Somebody called the Old One died unexpectedly about the time we climbed onto the plain. His replacement seems to be more action-oriented."

"And you got all that by talking to crows?"

"They're smart birds, Swan. Smarter than a lot of people. They make wonderful scouts."

Doj asked, "What is our strategy now?"

"We sit tight. We wait. We let the Black Hounds play. They like to tease horses."

Everybody looked at me with that exasperated expression I recalled from those days when I was the Captain and played my cards close to my chest. I shuddered, forced myself to open up further.

"They've separated a small light cavalry force in order to make more speed. The Unknown Shadows will start tormenting the horses after nightfall. Subtly, of course. We don't want to lose them. The bigger ones are going to work on the forvalaka by letting her see them as One-Eye's ghost. I'm hoping she'll rush on down here ahead of her friends. So we can kill her and get out before they get here." There. I had shared.

I felt lousy. I felt like something was sure to go wrong now that I had talked about it.

Silence. Which stretched. Until Murgen finally asked, "Will it work?"

"How the fuck should I know? Ask me again this time tomorrow."

Lady asked, "What're we going to do about Goblin?"

"Keep an eye on him. Don't let him get near One-Eye's spear." That all seemed self-evident to me.

Silence stretched again. Then Swan said, "Here's a thought. Why don't we leave Goblin here when we pull out?"

I grumped, "I thought he was your friend."

"Goblin was. But we've already decided that this can't be the Goblin we knew. Right?"

"But there's a chance the Goblin we knew might still be inside him waiting to be let back out. Like the rest of us when we were buried under the plain."

"And us guys who weren't aren't so sure about you."

"Just say I've developed a soft streak. We'll treat the guy like Goblin till he does something that makes us want to hang him. Then we'll string him up." I had to posture some. It was expected of me.

Murgen observed, "The Captain is still solving her personnel problems by exiling the questionables to Khatovar."

"And that's funny?" Because he was smiling.

"Of course it is. In the sense that neither you nor I nor Lady would've considered doing anything like that while we were in charge."

"Everybody's a sarcastic social critic," I told Lady. "Don't you let on that you can't kick Goblin's ass all the way to Hsien when he gets here. I'll try to keep him so busy he doesn't have time to get into trouble. But it'll help if he believes he has to walk a narrow line, too."

"He won't have to be convinced of that. He isn't stupid."

"How much longer you going to need us?" Swan asked. He had begun shuffling a deck of cards. Murgen and Thai Dei seemed eager to join him in a pastime that had made a comeback during our sojourn in the Land of Unknown Shadows.

"Go ahead. There's not much to do now but wait. And watch Uncle Doj sneak around with all those snail shells like he can't even conceive of the idea that anybody would be alert enough to notice." That was how the Unknown Shadows had crossed the plain and gotten here. So who on my team was in cahoots with Tobo and the Captain?

I could not wait forever, though. Nor did I have any intention of facing any Voroshk soldiers. My only quarrel with the Voroshk sprang from their presumption that the Company existed only as an as yet untapped resource.

I deplore that attitude wherever I encounter it.

There was a full moon in Khatovar that night. I went strolling in the moonlight. My ravens came and went. They traveled like lightning as long as I did not try to watch them do it.

The Unknown Shadows are every bit as wicked and dangerous as Hsien folklore indicates. It was almost too easy for them to taunt and lure the forvalaka away from the umbrella of protection offered by the Voroshk sorcerers.

Shadowlands:
Breakout

The Captain slithered up beside Suvrin, lifted her head just enough to be able to see the Shadowgate separating the plain from home. "We're only thirty miles from where you were born, Suvrin." She had tried for years now to think of a better nickname than Suvrin, which meant Junior in Sangel, his native tongue. She had not found anything more exotic that fit.

"Less. I wonder if anybody'll remember me."

Behind them thousands waited anxiously. Hungrily. Way too much time had gotten wasted crossing the plain. Sleepy brushed aside a twinge of guilt.

"How many of them are there?" she asked. A camp lay just below the Shadowgate. Built on the remains of old Company camps, it looked to have been there a long time. Its shelters had a makeshift but permanent appearance. They were part of a squalor which characterized all things military under the Protector's rule.

"There are fifty-six people. Including nine women and twenty-four children."

"That isn't exactly enough to stop a breakout attempt."

"We aren't why they're there. They're armed but they aren't real soldiers. They don't pay any attention to the road or the gate. During the day most of them just work their fields." Several feeble examples of primitive agriculture lay scattered along the banks of the creek at the bottom of the hill. "I thought about jumping them but decided I'd better wait till Tobo could look them over. I think they're really here because of the shadows."

"We'll send commandos down after sunset. Roll them up before they know what hit them." The Captain was not pleased with her protégé's indecision.

Suvrin said, "Better have Tobo check them out first. Really. They're always more active after dark."

"Excuse me?"

"It's almost twilight now. Hang on. You'll see what I mean."

"Don't make me wait all night, Suvrin." Sleepy eased back. Once she could rise without being seen from below she did so, strode to her waiting staff. "There's a garrison in our way. Not a large one. Shouldn't be any trouble because they don't appear to be expecting anything. I want to make sure none of them get away once we move. Runmust. Iqbal. Head back up the road. Have everybody fall out. Maintaining plain discipline. Tell them to eat. To get their weapons ready. No fires permitted, though. We don't want to show any smoke or light. We might not go in till after midnight but I want everyone ready to go when I say it's time to go."

Relays of messengers carried word back along the column.

There. Watch. That's what I mean," Suvrin said, pointing. Tobo and the Captain lay to either side of him. The garrison below had begun an exhaustive examination of the area around the Shadowgate, illuminating the area from several directions using a variety of sources of light. "They're obviously looking for leaks right now. It'll get more interesting in a minute."

Soon afterward a three-man team brought up a thin-necked earthenware jar of about a gallon's capacity mounted in a wooden rack which they crowded right up against the sorcerous boundary that prevented the shadows, the Unforgiven Dead, from leaving the plain.

The lighting was bright but still not good enough for even Tobo's sharp young eyes to discern clearly what was going on but, whatever they were up to, those people were being extremely cautious.

"I've got it!" Tobo said after watching intently for about ten minutes. "They're trying to catch shadows. They've got a tiny little hole bored through the barrier there and they're hoping an overeager shadow will pop through it into their jar."

"They work for Soulcatcher," Sleepy said, maybe just to dampen the boy's enthusiasm. She now understood why Suvrin had been so cautious.

"Of course they do. Who else? We need to think this over. If she has a whole bunch of shadows under her control. . . ."

"It's too late to turn back." As though he had suggested anything of the sort. Sleepy rolled onto her back, rubbed her forehead with her left hand. The stars above were the stars of her childhood. She had not seen them for far too long. "I missed our stars."

Suvrin replied, "I did, too. I've spent a lot of time here just enjoying them."

"You haven't sent even one scout through yet?"

"I really haven't had the chance. I didn't want to commit you to anything by taking everything into my own hands. Anyway, I had to fix the gate before I could do anything else and I've gotten maybe an hour a night when I could get down there to work on that."

"It's ready, now, though. Isn't it? I've got twelve thousand men up here. Don't tell me we have to wait some more."

"You can go through any time."

Tobo grunted. "The Nef."

Sleepy rolled back onto her stomach. Sure enough, the dreamwalkers had appeared down by the locals. They remained transparent. They jumped and gestured. The workers beyond the barrier ignored them.

"They can't see them," Tobo said.

The Nef abandoned their effort to communicate with the shadowcatchers and swept upslope to harangue the watchers on the lip of the plain.

"What're they trying to tell us?" Sleepy asked.

Tobo replied, "I don't know. I can actually hear a whisper sometimes but I still can't understand them. If Dad was here. . . . He was almost a dreamwalker. I think he might understand them a little bit."

"It's probably safe to assume that there's something they don't want us to do. That's what it always has been once somebody does figure it out. But doing what we want hasn't ever led to trouble for us. Has it?"

The wait stretched. Suvrin said, "It's always like this." He rolled over. "Why don't we watch for shooting stars?"

Tobo said, "I'm going down there. I want to hear what they're saying."

"Ignoring the fact that they'll see you, when did you learn to speak Sangel?" Sleepy asked.

"I've picked up a few words from Suvrin. We had to do something during those tedious journeys to the Shadowgates. Although I don't think these guys will be speaking anything but Taglian. They have to be people the Protector trusts. Meaning people whose families are where she can eat them up if she's disappointed with anybody's behavior. They aren't going to see me."

Doj had taught him well. He was all but invisible descending that slope, using no magic at all. The shadowcatchers noticed nothing. But the dreamwalkers did. They became agitated. Then the few shadows in the vicinity, not swarming beside the road with all their kin, hoping some soldier would stupidly break the protective barrier, also began to scoot from hiding place to hiding place erratically. One darted up and through the pinhole into the earthenware jar.

The shadowcatchers congratulated one another. In a moment they had both jar and barrier sealed, the latter with an almost invisible bit of bamboo. Tobo sensed powerful spells in its wood. Soulcatcher did not want the more potent shadows pushing through that valve.

The capture of a single shadow satisfied the shadowcatchers. They packed up for the night.

"That's it?" Sleepy asked.

"That's the first time I've actually seen them catch one," Suvrin replied. "I guess it doesn't happen very often."

Moments after the shadowcatchers left, Tobo stepped through the Shadowgate into the world of his birth. Suvrin had made his repairs correctly.

The boy took a deep breath. He listened to the soft noises made by the commandos already coming down from the plain. There had been no alarm as he had passed through the Shadowgate and there was none when the commandos began to ease through. Plainly, the Protector did not fear the south. Though she had leapt up from the grave a few times herself, she did not anticipate that kind of refractory behavior on the part of her enemies.

"Water sleeps," Tobo told the night, and began to cast a spell that would send the shadowcatcher crew into a deep sleep. He had learned the spell from One-Eye, who had stolen it from Goblin over a hundred years ago.

Always his thoughts found their way back to Goblin.

Kina was the Mother of Deceivers. Suppose she had done nothing whatsoever to the little wizard? Nobody would believe that. And nobody would ever trust him again. Tons of time and resources would be wasted keeping an eye on him.

Was that it? Was Goblin just a diversion? Was there any way to find out?

He was supposed to be on fire with the creative brilliance of youth. He ought to be able to devise something workable.

The prisoners looked on in wide-eyed amazement as battalion after battalion marched down off the plain. An army this size had not been seen since the Kiaulune wars. Soulcatcher had won the laurels in that round because the Company had been hopelessly outclassed in matters of sorcery.

The Radisha Drah and the Prahbrindrah Drah had prominent places in that parade. Clad in imperial finery, accompanied by dozens of Taglian royal banners, their presence was a declaration Sleepy wanted made early and often.

It was a declaration that was wasted here, of course, because none of these witnesses would be allowed to carry the news out ahead of the advance of the invasion force. But Sleepy thought it would be a good idea for the Prince and Princess to begin practicing to reassume their historic roles.

Suvrin was gone already. As were scores more pickets and scouts and recon soldiers. The Soldiers of Darkness were loose. Poor Suvrin was having to run ahead again, now tasked to close the southern end of the pass through the Dandha Presh. A job for which he needed no special training. It was the one he had held at the time when Sleepy had taken him prisoner, while on her way to release us poor old Captured from our durance beneath the plain.

Once Suvrin was sure the pass could not be used by rumor-mongers from the south side he was supposed to go on through and seize the military works at Charandaprash. Which were likely to have no garrison at all, considering Soulcatcher's attitude toward her armed forces.

Suvrin would know that layout well before he got there. Tobo had brought sack after sack of old snail shells off the plain once the way was open. An unseen flood had begun to spread across the region once known as the Shadowlands. Tobo would know everything his creatures knew. Tobo would have those creatures carry the news to anyone else who needed to know it.

Tension ran high and continued to rise. Those who knew Soulcatcher knew she would hear of the invasion eventually. Her response was sure to be violent and showy, swift and unpredictable and nothing anyone wanted to endure.

The Taglian Territories:
The Blind Measures of Despair

Narayan groaned when the girl wakened him. He regained control quickly, however. The Protector was out there somewhere, never closer than she had been these past two days. The Daughter of Night's valiant efforts, using talents she did not understand, had been just enough to prevent their capture. But it was a close thing every day. And the game might not last much longer. He and the girl had nothing left. If the Protector brought in some of the shadows she controlled . . .

"What is it?" he breathed. He fought the pain that was with him always nowadays.

"Something's happened. Something big. I can feel it. It's . . . I don't know. It's like my mother woke up, took a look around, then went back to sleep."

Narayan did not understand. He said so.

"It was her. I know. She touched me." From confusion the girl moved swiftly toward assurance and confidence. "She wanted me to know that she's still there. She wanted me to hang on. She wanted me to know things will be getting better soon."

Narayan, who had known the girl's birth mother well, suspected the child took after her aunt, the Protector, far more. The Protector was changeable. The Daughter of Night's moods could shift with a change in the breeze. He wished she were more stable, like her mother. Although Lady could become obsessively focused. For example, she was determined to even scores with him and the Deceiver cult. She had been Kina's tool but had no love or respect whatsoever for the Goddess.

"Did you hear me, Narayan? She's there! She's not going to lay low much longer."

"I heard. And I really am as excited as you are. But there are wonders and wonders. We still have to get away from the Protector." He indicated the sky to their west. Crows swarmed not half a mile down the long, scrubby slope.

Soulcatcher had her obsessions, too. This chase had gone on forever, successfully for neither party thereto. Did the Protector have no other work to do? Who was managing Taglios and its territories? Deviltry was sure to flourish in her absence.

From the beginning of the chase Narayan had been confident that Soulcatcher would get bored and would turn to something else. She always did.

But not this time. This time she was dogged.

Why?

No telling with the Protector. She might have had a vision of the future. She might be unable to think of a more amusing hobby. She was twisted inside. Her motives might not always make sense even to her.

The crows began to fan out to the north of what must be Soulcatcher's position. They seemed to be interested in a slice of pie arc. They drifted on the breeze, not working hard, slowly moving away. Narayan and the Daughter of Night watched without moving. Crows were sharp of eye. If the two most holy Deceivers could see them, the crows could see the Deceivers in turn—if the girl's erratic talent failed for even a moment.

A single bird glided to the southeast, rather drunkenly, Narayan thought. Soon no black bird could be seen in any direction.

Narayan said, "Let's move on now. While we can. You know, I think that haze down south might be the Dandha Presh. We'll be in the mountains in another week. She won't have a hope of catching us there."

He was whistling in the dark. And they both knew it.

The Daughter of Night led the way. She was far more mobile than Narayan. Frequently she grew impatient with Narayan's inability to keep up. Sometimes she cursed him and hit him. He suspected that she would desert him if she had any other resource. But her horizons never did extend far beyond the boundaries of their cult and she understood that the living saint had far more influence with the Deceivers than did any ill-schooled female messiah whose status as such was accepted only because it bore the living saint's chop of authenticity.

Narayan's lagging actually saved them. The girl was squatting in brush, looking back with ill-concealed irritation. "There's a clearing. It's big. Not much cover. Shall we wait until dark? Or should we work our way around?" It was much too difficult for her to keep them invisible when they were in the open.

Narayan sometimes wondered what she might have become had she grown up with her birth mother. Lady would have turned her into a dark terror by now, he was certain. Not for the first or even the hundredth time he wished Kina had allowed him to sacrifice Lady the day he had claimed the newly born Daughter of Night. His life since would have been much easier had the woman died then. "Let me look."

Narayan crouched. Pain clawed his bad leg as though someone was slashing him with a dull knife. He peered out at a stony waste almost devoid of life—except for a stunted, twisted stump of a tree smack in the middle. It stood just over five feet tall. There was a familiar feeling to it. He had not seen it before but knew he should recognize it. "Don't move," he told the Daughter of Night. "Don't even breathe fast. There's something not quite right out there."

He froze. The girl froze. She never questioned him in these things. He was right every time.

It came to him eventually. He whispered. "That's the Protector, that stump. Wrapped inside an illusion. She's used the trick before. I heard about it when I was a prisoner of the Black Company. It was one of the devices she used when she was stalking them and they kept telling each other to look out for it. Look carefully at the root of that branch that twists around twice and ends in a cluster of little twigs. See the crow hiding there?"

"Yes."

"Back away carefully. Slowly. What? . . . Freeze!"

The girl froze. She remained unmoving for many minutes, until Narayan began to relax. She murmured, "What was it?" Neither the stump nor the crow had done anything alarming.

"There was something. . . ." But he was no longer sure. It had been there in the corner of his eye for an instant but not there when he looked directly. "Over by that big red boulder."

"Hush!" The girl stared in another direction. "I think . . . There. Something . . . I can't see anything but I can feel it. I think it's watching the tree. . . ."

Grrr!

Both felt rather than heard the growl from behind them.

Such was their self-discipline, after years on the run, that neither so much as flinched. Something large and dark and not quite there trotted past. The living saint's mouth opened wide but no scream came forth. The girl drifted closer to him without making any sudden movement.

What seemed like a series of large black cutouts of an unfamiliar animal flickered across the open ground. It looked nothing like a dog. It had too many limbs. But in its brief moment beside the stump it lifted a hind leg and loosed a river.

And then, of course, it was not there anymore. But Soulcatcher was, in her own form. And she was in a towering rage.

"Something has changed," Narayan gasped through his pain.

"Something more than Mother."

Something more than the Mother of Night.

Something that, from that moment onward, left them feeling as though they were being watched every moment—even when they could see nothing around them anywhere.

Khatovar:
The Lords of the Upper Air

My ravens worked hard. Within the same hour I learned that Sleepy had broken out into our homeworld and that the forvalaka had left the Voroshk and was rushing our way. I began issuing orders immediately. Bowalk could not possibly arrive for hours but I wanted to make sure that each of my companions was exactly positioned and that all of my resources could be brought to bear almost instantly.

Willow Swan followed me around reminding me that most of the fussing I was doing was exactly the sort of half-ass officiousness I resented from Sleepy.

"You want to make your future home in Khatovar, Swan?"

"Hey, don't kill the messenger."

I grunted unhappily, went and collected my sweetheart. "It's time we got dressed up. Get ready for the show."

"Ooh!" she said. "I've always had a weakness for men in black with birds on their shoulders."

Our preparations were complete. Our dozen surviving fireball projectors were positioned, I felt, to perfection to bring the forvalaka under saturating fire as she attacked me. If that did not destroy her itself it would drive her to me, directly onto One-Eye's black spear. I looked forward to our confrontation. That was unusual for me. I am not one of those men who enjoys the killing side of this business.

The ravens had the monster just an hour away. People were having a last meal so we could get the fires all put out before it arrived. There was a pig that Doj had killed. It went fast. Not many vegetarians in my crew.

Murgen joined Lady and me where we were playing paper, rock, knife with Willow Swan. "Goblin's here. He just came over the rim of the plain. There's two guys with him. That's a good look for you." He had not yet seen the new Widowmaker armor in action.

"Bless the Captain and her infinite wisdom," I grumbled. "That was quick. Let's keep an eye on the little shit." Like that needed repeating. I asked Lady, "Should I put him to work?"

"Absolutely. Right out front. One-Eye was his best friend, wasn't he?"

"Murgen, when he gets down here, after we talk to him, I want him positioned down there where I put the pair of two-inchers. We don't know if either of those has anything left in them. Then have those guys fall back to cover the approach to the Shadowgate. You and Thai Dei stay with Goblin."

Murgen offered me a carefully blank look.

"If you have to, stick him. Or bop him over the head. If he gives you a reason."

"Which might be?"

"I don't know. You're an intelligent adult. Don't you think you can tell if he needs smacking around?"

"Don't you think that that's what those guys with him are there for?"

I had not thought of that. It did seem probable. "Are they men we know well enough to trust completely?"

"I couldn't make out who they were yet when I came over here."

"Then the instruction stands."

I studied Goblin intently. I had not seen him since before I had gone under-ground. He had aged a lot. "Last I knew of you, you'd deserted."

"I'm sure One-Eye explained all that." The voice was the same but there was an indefinable difference in the man that, probably, had more to do with time and the betrayals of memory than it did with any evil new within him, but I have never gone far wrong by being suspicious.

Goblin's stature approached the extreme low altitude end of normal humanity. And he was wide, despite not having eaten well in recent years. And he had almost no hair at all anymore. Nor did he smile readily. He seemed infinitely tired, as though he labored under a weight of weariness that stretched all the way back into antiquity.

My long nap in the cave of the ancients had not been all that restful, either.

"One-Eye was a notorious liar. The way I heard it—fifteen years after the fact—was that it was all your idea and he just got dragged along."

"The Captain was satisfied." He did not argue and he did not make light. And that was the last clue I needed. There was no humor left in this Goblin. That was the big change.

"Good for her. You've arrived just in time. The forvalaka is only minutes away. We're going to kill it this time. You didn't lose any of your skills while you were trapped, did you?"

Something stirred in the deeps of his eyes. It seemed cold and angry but might have been just his irritation because so many pairs of eyes peered at him so intently, so suddenly.

"Captain?"

That had to be one of the real old hands. Everyone else was out of the habit, though many still called Lady "Lieutenant" because Sleepy never filled that position officially. Sahra did much of the work despite her official status as an outsider.

Why did we set such store by these tiny distinctions?

"What?"

"There's movement out there. Probably the Black Hounds coursing the for-valaka. Which means the monster is getting close."

"Full alert. Murgen, show Goblin his post." I clattered and clanked. The armor was mainly costume but it was real and it was heavy.

"Captain!" From farther away. "Down there!" A man stood out of his conceal-ment, pointing.

I gawked.

"Shit!" Lady exploded. "Why the hell didn't your crows tell us about that?" She dove for cover.

Three flying things were headed toward us from the west, in a V formation. My man had spotted them so far away that, despite their speed, we had time to observe their approach. Eagle-eye there was a guy who deserved a bonus.

The flyers had made the mistake of approaching at an altitude calculated to avoid the notice of the Unknown Shadows. That left them completely vulnerable to detection by the naked eye because it silhouetted them against the clear blue sky on the one day the weather chose to be neither overcast nor rainy.

Lady snapped. "You concentrate on the shape changer, darling. This is a diversion. I'll deal with it." She shouted orders. I boomed a few of my own.

She was wrong, of course. The forvalaka was the diversion for those flying Voroshk—though Bowalk would be convinced that the reverse was true. Once they moved closer the airborne sorcerers appeared to be rippling lumps clinging to long fenceposts. They were wrapped in and trailed acres of something resembling black silk cloth.

They must have had some reason to believe that we would not be able to see them. They made no effort not to be noticed.

When they slowed their approach I suspected immediately they wanted to co-ordinate timing with the forvalaka—and I was right.

A burst of screams and dark fury erupted a scant hundred yards from our most forward post. Unknown Shadows were all over the forvalaka. Exactly as they were supposed to be, suddenly and briefly, at that point.

The moment Bowalk stopped charging to rip at the spooks they faded away.

For that moment she made a wonderful target.

The fireball projectors opened up.

Unfortunately, most that worked sped their blazing, unpredictable missiles toward the Khatovaran sorcerers. Only two light bamboo pieces remained trained on the monster. And one of those gave up the ghost after projecting just one bilous green ball that flew in erratic skips and jerks but did graze the beast along the flank scars she had gained during our previous encounter. She took a solid hit in the shoulder from the other projector.

She could scream.

I did not look away. Lady kept talking, keeping me informed. She told me the flyers had been surprised completely. That made me suspect that there had been little honesty between Lisa Daele Bowalk and the Voroshk sorcerers.

They should have known. All of them.

The Voroshk were not entirely unprepared for trouble. They had surrounded themselves with protective spells which did shunt the lightest fireballs aside—usually from the path of the leader into those of the trailing two. But those spells could not turn everything and they weakened quickly.

I was bracing to receive the charge of the forvalaka when one of the flyers streaked across in front of me, behind Bowalk, tumbling, all that silk aflame. A scream ended abruptly as the sorcerer impacted somewhere to my right.

My strategy was to channel the forvalaka toward me and One-Eye's spear, hurting it as much as possible as it approached. I had mounted the black spear in the end of a twelve foot bamboo pole to give myself a little added reach. Once Bowalk was pinned, the people with the fireballs could finish her off. Assuming One-Eye's spear had not lost its potency with his death.

And assuming the people with the fireballs were not busy with the distraction overhead. I risked a glance. The lead flyer was circling back. Whatever he had intended to do he had not, because he had been forced to concentrate on his defenses instead. The remaining Voroshk had come to a halt several hundred yards east of us, smoldering, drifting on the breeze, evidently still alive but just barely. Before I shifted my attention back to the forvalaka I noted that that flyer was gaining altitude very slowly.

A swarm of javelins and arrows buzzed around the werepanther. The darts were all poisoned. Just in case a few did penetrate her skin.

Wonder of wonders! A lot of arrows were sticking. A sort of black haze seemed to cover the monster, making the boundary between her and the rest of the universe appear poorly defined.

Lady was yelling. A lot. Fire discipline was critical. We would be able to create no new fireball-spitting bamboo poles until we were safely back in our own world. Half of those we started this fight with were out of action already. The guys had not been in a real fight for years but they did remember what was what. The fireballs stopped going up even before my wife started yelling again. Several men did take the opportunity to put fireballs into the forvalaka, though. Poor Lisa had no friends.

She was not as invulnerable as I had expected. She began to stagger drunkenly well before I had hoped she would respond to the poisons. The endurance and stamina of her kind were legendary and in our experience were exceeded only by the ferocious vitality of the sorcerers who had belonged to the circle that had been known as the Ten Who Were Taken. Of whom Soulcatcher and the Howler were the last. Of whom there would be no survivors much longer.

I was determined. I had a whole list of people who were going to blaze the way to hell for me.

Now the monster was up again, evidently shaking off the effects of missiles and fireballs and chemicals. She was gathering herself for the charge that would get her in amongst us and render her safe from our most dangerous weapons just when she could start using her jaws and claws.

I do not know what the Voroshk tried to do. I know the fireballs flew again, there was a shudder in the ground like somebody had hit it a few yards away with a ten-thousand-pound hammer, then the forvalaka launched herself my way in a sort of weak, half-hearted leap, one hind paw dragging in the dust. Smoke came off her at a dozen points. The stench of burnt flesh preceded her.

I glimpsed the last Voroshk streaking across the sky behind the monster. He was tumbling.

Bowalk batted at my makeshift pike as she flew toward me. Her effort was weak and slow. The head of One-Eye's spear entered and passed through the flesh of her right shoulder, which had been injured badly already. I felt it bounce off bone. She screamed. Her weight ripped my weapon out of my hand even though I had the butt of the bamboo pole set firmly against the ground.

Her momentum spun her around. She managed to slap me with a paw and send me ass over appetite before she landed and became preoccupied with the black spear. My armor withstood her claws. I barely knew up from down for a moment but I did keep my head attached to the end of my neck.

I regained possession of my bamboo pole but not of the spear. The forvalaka was writhing around, screaming and snarling and snapping at the spear while my comrades were careful to stay out of her way. The occasional arrow or javelin continued to dart in, when there was no risk of a miss.

The Voroshk remained out of the struggle. One burned on the slope east of us. One rose higher and higher, now yielding streamers of smoke. The last circled cautiously, either looking for an opening or just observing. Each time he started to dart in, a score of bamboo poles pointed his way, offering to welcome him. I suspect most were dead. But he could find out the truth of that only the hard way.

A huge black sword of a design similar to Doj's Ash Wand came with the Widowmaker costume. I drew it as the forvalaka tried to come at me. I felt almost foolish behind the excitement and fear. It had been decades since I had used a sword anywhere but in practice sessions with Doj. I did not know this one at all. It might be little more than a showpiece. It might snap the first time I struck a blow.

The shapeshifter staggered forward a few steps. Someone hit it a glancing shot with a fireball. Javelins and arrows continued to arrive. It snapped at the wound where One-Eye's spear stood forth, again. The arrows and javelins all fell out eventually but not that black spear. It was working its way slowly deeper.

I stepped in, struck. The tip of my blade bit several inches into the big cat's left shoulder. She barely stumbled. The wound bled for seconds only, then closed, healing before my eyes.

I struck again, near the same site. Then again. Not despairing. Her vitality was no surprise. But her wounds were not healing as fast as once they had. And that spear was worming its way deeper. And she seemed to be losing the will to fight.

Shouts!

The healthy Voroshk was boring in on me, coming fast, his protection turning first the fireballs rising to meet him, then the arrows and bolts. I pranced around and braced myself to flail away when he got close enough. He raised one hand as if to throw something. But before he could, my white crow appeared out of nowhere and hit him from behind. In the head. His chin slammed against his chest.

I doubt he suffered any damage but he did forget me for the moment. He flailed at the raven. The ghost bird had secured a perch on his shoulder and was trying to peck his eyes.

Even up close I could see no face. That was hidden by wraps of the same cloth enshrouding everything else.

I swung away but misjudged the Voroshk's speed. My blade chopped into the post he was riding a foot behind his butt and tore itself from my hands. Then he hit ground. Then, howling, he bounced into the air and streaked away in a lazy curve that tended northward, all the while spinning round and round the axis of his flying post. His robes or cape or whatever billowed all over the sky. Tatters tore loose and fluttered down.

The forvalaka continued to weaken. Cautiously, some men left cover and surrounded the beast. Lady and Doj joined me within striking distance. Each carried one of the debilitating fetishes Tobo had created using the tail and bits of skin Bowalk had left behind when she killed One-Eye. Lady had shown him what to do. The fetishes were particularly effective because Lady and Tobo had had Lisa Daele Bowalk's true name to work with.

I said, "Swan, take a squad to check out the one that's burning over there. Be careful. Murgen, keep an eye on the other two." The Voroshk who had streaked off rolling was under control again and headed our way at a crawl, gaining altitude, moving toward the Voroshk who remained airborne and still rising slowly. That one had begun drifting with the breeze and showing some evidence of actual flames.

I asked my darling, "Darling, is there any chance you're keeping an eye on Goblin?" Our mysteriously resurrected brother had remained extremely quiet during the exchange of greetings between the Voroshk family and the Black Company. Unless I had missed something while I was preoccupied.

"There are two guaranteed-good bamboo poles aimed at him right now."

"Excellent. You are going to be able to make more of those things once we get back home, aren't you? They're the best weapons we've ever had."

"I'll make some. If there's time. Once my sister knows we're back we're going to get extremely busy."

Egg-yolk light suddenly drenched the world. It faded before I looked up and saw a thousand-armed starfish of a cloud blossoming where the smoldering Voroshk sorcerer had been drifting.

The other Voroshk was headed north again, this time end over end. And someone was falling directly toward us, vast expanses of black cloth fluttering behind, smoke boiling off that. There was no sign of the log the Voroshk had been riding. Its fall seemed terribly slow.

Meantime, undistracted from his task, Willow Swan was bellowing across the slope. He wanted a stretcher.

Lady observed, "That one is still alive."

"We have a hostage. Somebody poke that thing with a pike. It's probably playing possum." The forvalaka had stopped struggling. It lay on its back, tilted slightly to one side, both hands grasping the shaft of One-Eye's spear.

"Hands," Murgen said as Thai Dei prodded the monster with one of the longer fireball projectors.

"Hands," I said, too. The change was coming over her. The change she had longed for ever since we had murdered her lover-master Shapeshifter, way back during our first assault on Dejagore.

Lady said, "She's dying." She sounded both puzzled and a little disappointed.

Khatovar:
Then Start the Fire

A rising shriek rushed us from above. The falling, flailing Voroshk smashed through the leaf roof of a shelter. The shrieking stopped. Bits of roof flew upward. I said, "Murgen, go check that out."

When I looked back to the forvalaka, I discovered that Goblin had joined us. He pushed through the crowd and stood over the monster, staring down. She was about halfway changed, her arms and legs having become a badly scarred, naked woman. She was aware enough to recognize Goblin.

The frog-faced little man said, "We tried to help you and you wouldn't let us. We could've saved you but you turned on us. So now you pay. You mess with the Company, you pay." He started to reach for One-Eye's spear.

Men jumped every which way. Half a dozen bamboo poles swung toward Goblin. Crossbows came off shoulders.

The little wizard's mouth opened and closed several times. Then his hand slowly withdrew.

I guess news of One-Eye's dying words had gotten around.

Goblin squeaked, "Maybe you shouldn't have rescued me."

Lady told him, "We didn't," but did not expand upon her remark. She drew me away. "He has something to do with Bowalk dying so easily."

I glanced over there. "She isn't dead yet."

"She should have been much tougher."

"Even considering the fetishes and One-Eye's spear?"

She thought about that. "Maybe. When she's done dying you'd better make sure that thing is hard to reach. I don't like the look in Goblin's eye when he stares at it."

That look was there now, though the little wizard showed no inclination to do anything certain to inspire a swift and violent response.

Swan and his gang were approaching, four of the men at the corners of a makeshift litter. Trotting ahead, Swan puffed, "Wait'll you get a look at this, Croaker. You ain't going to believe it."

At the same moment Murgen called for another stretcher. So the other Voroshk had survived, too.

Swan was on the mark. The girl on the stretcher was impossible to believe. Maybe sixteen, blonde, as gorgeous as every boy's fantasy. I asked my wife, "Darling, is this for real?" And to Swan, "Good job, Willow." He had bound and gagged the girl so as to disarm most of a sorcerer's simpler tricks.

Lady said, "You men get back." There was not much left of what the girl had been wearing. And more than a few of the guys were the sort who would count her fair game for having tried to attack us. Some were the sort who would dish out the same treatment to a male captive. They might be my brethren but that did not make them less cruel men.

Lady told Swan, "Take Doj back over there and collect anything you can find that belonged to her. Her clothing and that thing she was riding in particular." And to me she said, "Yes, dear, she's the real thing. Except for just a touch of makeup. I hate her already. Goblin! You come over here and stand where I can see you."

I stared down at the Voroshk girl, not focusing on the lushness and freshness of her but on the blondness and whiteness. I have read all the Annals, all the way back to the first volume—albeit, admittedly, a several-generations-removed-from-original copy—that had been begun before our forebrethren ever left Khatovar. Those men had not been tall and white and blond. Could the Voroshk be another out-world scourge like the Shadowmasters of my own world and Hsien?

At that moment Lady removed her helmet, the better to menace me for staring. And I realized she was quite white herself, even if not blond.

Why expect the peoples of Khatovar to be any more homogeneous than the peoples of my own world?

Murgen and his crew came jogging up, carrying another body on another crude litter. The first had escaped most of the effects of impact and fire. This one had been less fortunate.

"Another girl," I observed. That fact was hard to ignore. She was more obvious than the first.

"Younger than the other one."

"But just as well put together."

"Better, from where I'm standing."

"They're sisters," Lady growled. "You have an idea what this means?"

"Probably that the Voroshk had so little respect for us that they sent out some kids so they could get in some practice. But after what's happened, Daddy and Grandpa will take a closer interest." I beckoned. "Gather round, gentlemen." Once everyone not doing something closed in, I said, "In a short time we're probably going to have a sky full of unfriendly company. I want you to start pulling up stakes and getting the animals and equipment back through the gate. Right now."

Lady asked, "You think that third one will make it back to the Voroshk army?"

"No way will I bet against it. My mother's optimistic children have all been dead for fifty years." I glanced at the forvalaka. It was almost entirely Lisa Bowalk now. Except for the head. "Looks like some mythological beast, don't she?"

She was not dead yet. Her eyes were open. They were no longer cat's eyes. They begged. She did not want to die.

I told Lady, "She doesn't look any older than the last time I saw her." She was still a young and attractive woman—for one whose formative years had been spent surviving the worst slum of a truly ugly city. "Hey, Cratch. Grab Slobo. I want you guys to bring all the firewood over here and pile it on this thing."

Goblin said, "I'll help."

"I'll tell you what, runt. You want a job, you can build me a couple of good litters so we can take our new girlfriends with us."

Lady asked, "Are they fit to travel?"

"The older one could probably get up and limp along on her own if she was conscious. I'll need a closer look here before I can tell how bad this one's hurt, though."

"You watch what you're poking and squeezing, old man."

"You'd think that, at your age, you'd have developed a little better sense of humor, old woman. Don't you understand that every profession has its perks? A surgeon gets to poke and squeeze."

"So does a wife."

"I knew I forgot something when we did that ceremony thing. Shoulda brung a lawyer. Cratch! Nobody touches that spear till we start the fire. And I'll do any touching that gets done. Where are my birds? I've got to get the Black Hounds called in." We could not leave them here. They were going to be critical weapons in the war with Soulcatcher. Sleepy was, probably, missing them desperately already.

Swan and three others approached, straining to carry the post the older girl had ridden. Swan puffed. "This goddamned thing weighs a ton!" The four of them started to drop it.

"No!" Lady barked. "Gently! You recall what happened to the other one? Up there?" She pointed. Smoke or dust or whatever still smeared the sky. There was still an occasional crackle of toy lightning inside the cloud, too. "That's better. Goblin! Doj! Come and take a look at this thing."

"Check this cloth," Swan said, offering me a bit of black rag.

It felt like silk and seemed almost weightless. It stretched when I pulled it without tearing or getting any thinner. Or so it seemed.

"Now watch this." Swan stabbed the cloth with his knife. The knife did not penetrate. It did not cut when he slashed, either.

I said, "Now isn't that a handy little trick? We're lucky we had the bamboo. Honey, check this out. Show her, Swan. You, men. Get the post thing on the other side of the gate. Let's get moving, people! These folks can fly. And the next bunch that shows up aren't likely to be as friendly." No one really needed my encouragement, though. A solid line of men, animals and equipment was moving upslope already. The older Voroshk girl was headed uphill already, too, bound to Goblin's first litter.

When Swan finished showing that cloth to Lady, I told him, "See if you can't find a log or post in one of the huts that might look like that flying thing from a distance."

Lady, Goblin and Swan all stared at me. This time I stood on my command right and did not explain. I had a hunch the Voroshk would not want to lose the post. Which my comrades might understand but if I said so they would just ask for further explanations.

I said, "This one has broken bones, bad burns, punctures, cuts and abrasions and probably internal injuries."

"And?" Lady asked.

"And so I think she won't be much use to us. Probably die on us. So I'm going to do the best I can for her, then leave her for her own people."

"Going soft in your old age?"

"Like I said, she'd be more trouble than she's worth. Plus, the sister ought to be up and around in no time. So if I do right by the one I leave here, the Voroshk might be less inclined to run around behind us trying to get vicious."

"What're they going to do?"

"I don't know. I don't want to find out. I just take into account the fact that they were able to get Bowalk onto the plain and off again, once each way, without wrecking any Shadowgates. I'm hoping they don't have what it takes to move an army the same way."

"They wouldn't need to grab us if they did. Odds are, Bowalk's trip was possible because of what she was and the fact that she'd bulled through it all once before."

I looked at the forvalaka. Even its head was Lisa Daele Bowalk now. The same Lisa Bowalk who ruined Marron Shed a thousand subjective years ago. Her eyes were shut but she was still breathing.

We would have to fix that.

Lady told me, "Cut off her head first. Then start the fire."

Khatovar:
The Opened Gate

The Voroshk were not sneaks. They came out of the northwest in an angry swarm, eager to get at us. There were at least twenty-five in the first wave.

My people were all on the uphill side of the Shadowgate but many of the Unknown Shadows had not made it back. I had left snail shells scattered around the woods so they would have somewhere to hide. I would get them out later, once the excitement was over.

The swarm streaked in, vast flutters of black cloth billowing. Even though they could see that we were beyond the Shadowgate and our main body was already on the plain they dropped down and streaked over our empty camp, shedding a rain of small objects which turned little patches of ground into puddles of lava and caused vegetation to combust almost explosively. None of our shelters or corrals survived. But nothing touched the injured girl or the forvalaka's funeral pyre.

"Glad I don't have to run between those raindrops," I said. A couple of the Voroshk had tried to award me that experience but the barrier between Khatovar and the plain repelled their missiles easily. And ate their magic right up. They did not activate, even when they dribbled to the ground.

Lady said, "They're all kids, too."

The members of the swarm all seemed to do whatever they wanted, going their own ways, yet none of them collided. Once their assault failed to produce results most of them settled to earth around the injured girl.

On my side of the Shadowgate we leaned on bamboo poles and watched.

A trio of latecomers formed the second wave. They appeared several minutes after the first flood. "These will be the leaders," Lady said. "Being a little more cautious than the youngsters." Even more black fabric billowed around these three.

"The highest ranking members of the Family making the journey," I conceded. "There sure are a lot of these people. Considering the size of the army they brought." Not counting the Voroshk themselves, my spies numbered the approaching force at about eight hundred. The light cavalry hurrying ahead numbered fewer than fifty men. There was a good chance we could have beat them up if they had not had all those post riders in the sky looking out for them.

When they grounded, the Voroshk flyers did stand their conveyances on end, like fenceposts that would not tip over without a push from a human hand.

The elders circled a few times before they set down. Then they took time to examine the unconscious child before paying any more attention to us.

I gave a small hand signal as soon as we were on. Men on the slope who had been hanging around gawking resumed moving. The Voroshk chieftains were allowed to see the other girl being led away and what looked like four men lugging a captured flying fencepost. While the heart of my heart and I posed just behind the gate in our best killer costumes. I know there was a huge smirk hanging around inside my helmet.

Out there among the Voroshk, so far ignored but not unnoticed, the headless corpse of our ancient enemy crackled and popped inside a roaring fire. I wished we still had the Lance of Passion to show those guys, too. My ravens had not been able to tell if the Voroshk were aware of who we really were.

I said, "The past always comes back." I waved. Then I told Lady, "I think it might be a real good idea if we got going now. Their good feelings about us having taken care of that kid just aren't going to last."

"You've probably stretched it too long already, showing off." She started up the slope. She did not look at all bad in that armor. She set a brisk pace for such an old gal, too.

Soon all the flying sorcerers were staring uphill, pointing and jabbering at one another. They seemed to be much more excited about us carrying off their flying log than they were about us taking the girl. Maybe she was not anyone important. Or maybe they figured she was old enough to look out for herself.

One of the elders stepped away from that fluttering black crowd. He had a small book in his hand. He turned a couple of pages, found the one he wanted, ran a finger along a few lines as he read. A second elder nodded and apparently repeated what he had to say, with gestured accompaniment. After a moment the third elder took it up, his gestures similar but not in step with those of the other two.

"It's a round," I told Lady. We had overtaken the slowest of our people. "Row row row." I made some gestures myself. "You do anything you're going to be sorry."

The Voroshk all spun, presenting their backs to us.

The flash was so bright it blinded me for a moment. When my sight returned another of those hundred-legged starfish of brownish-grey smoke had materialized. This one was not upstairs. This one was right where the Shadowgate had been. Centered right where I had hidden the captured flying post under some "abandoned" tenting.

"Warned you," I murmured.

"How did you know?" Lady asked.

"I'm not sure. A hunch, I guess. Uninhibited intuition."

"They've just killed themselves." There was almost a hint of compassion in her voice. "They'll never stop the shadows from flooding through that."

Some of the Voroshk already recognized the magnitude of the disaster still unfolding. Black fluttering shapes scattered like roaches suddenly exposed to the light. Flying posts took to the air, streaked northward so violently that bits of black cloth ripped off and fluttered down like dark autumn leaves.

The three elders held their positions. They stared our way. I wondered what was happening inside their heads. Almost certainly not any recognition of the fact that the disaster was a direct result of the magnitude of Voroshk arrogance. I have never met one of their kind who would admit any fallibility whatsoever.

I was sure there would be some grand squabbles over where to fix the blame during the time they had left. Human nature at work.

"What are you thinking?" Lady asked.

I realized that I was no longer moving, that I was just watching the Voroshk watch me. "Just looking around inside me, trying to figure out why this doesn't bother me the way it would have years ago. Why I recognize the pain more easily now but am not touched by it nearly so much."

"You know what One-Eye used to say about you? You think too much. He was right. You don't have any more obligation to him. Let's go back to our own world, see about spanking our little girl and getting my baby sister straightened up." Her voice changed severely as her thoughts turned. "One thing I demand. Still. Narayan Singh. I want him. He's mine."

I winced inside my helmet. Poor Narayan. I said, "I still have one thing to do here."

"What?" she snapped.

"After those three leave. I have to get Tobo's friends back."

She grunted and resumed walking. She had to make sure the road across the plain could be closed behind us, so that we would not become victims of the explosion, too.

The Shadowlands:
The Protector of All the Taglias

Soulcatcher's survival instincts had been honed to a razor's edge by centuries of adventures among peoples who considered her continued good health a liability. She sensed a change in the world long before she had any idea what that change might be, good or ill or indifferent, and ages before she dared hazard a guess as to its cause.

At first it was just that sense. Then, gradually, it became the pressure of a thousand eyes. But she could discover nothing. Her crows could find nothing either, other than the occasional, unpredictable, flickering glimpse of their quarry, the two Deceivers. That was ancient news.

Soulcatcher abandoned the hunt immediately. It would not be difficult to get close to the Deceivers again.

She learned nothing more before nightfall—except that her crows were extremely unsettled, getting more and more nervous, less and less tractable and increasingly inclined to jump at shadows. They could not make clear the nature of their malaise because they did not understand it themselves.

That began to grow clearer as the twilight gathered. Messengers interrupted Soulcatcher's meditations to inform her that several of the murder had fallen prey to a sudden illness. "Show me."

She made no effort to disguise herself as she followed her birds to the nearest feathered corpse. She picked it up, rolled it carefully in her gloved hands.

It was obvious what had killed the crow. Not illness but a killer shadow. No cadaver looked like one did after a shadow finished with it. But that could not be. It was still light out. Her tame shadows were all in hiding and there were no rogue shadows around anymore. Nor would wild shadows have wasted themselves on a crow when there was human game in the vicinity. She should have heard Narayan Singh and that wretched niece of hers screaming long before any crow. . . . There had been no sound from the bird whatsoever. Nor had there been from any of a half dozen others the murder knew to be gone. The survivors had plenty to say. Including stating plainly that they were not about to stray away from her protection.

"How can I fight this if I don't know what it is? If you won't find out for me?"

The crows would not be bullied or cajoled. They were geniuses for birds. Which meant they were just bright enough to have noticed that every one of the dead had been completely alone when evil had befallen them.

Soulcatcher cursed them, then calmed herself and convinced the most valiant birds that they had to, therefore, do their scouting in threes and fours until darkness closed in completely. At that point she would have bats and owls and her own shadows available to take over.

Darkness came. As the Deceivers correctly observe, the darkness always comes.

With nightfall came a silent but horribly vicious warfare with Soulcatcher poised at the eye of the storm.

Initially she had to hold on desperately against unknown assailants until her own shadows could bring in enough swift reinforcements. Then, spending shadows profligately, she took the offensive. And when dawn came, and she was almost without supernatural allies because of the cost of the struggle, she gave way to exhaustion, having gained a knowledge of a portion of the truth.

They were back. The Black Company were, with new formations, new allies, new sorceries, and still without a dram of mercy in their hearts. These were not the Company she had known in younger years but they were the spiritual children of the cold killers of the olden days. No matter what you tried, it seemed, you could kill only men. The ideal lived on.

Ha! An end to the boredom of empire stood at hand.

Bravado and pretense did not lessen the inexplicable fear. They had fled onto the plain. And now they were back. That had to mean much more. She needed to interrogate shadows who had existed on the glittering stone during those silent years. When there was time. Before she did anything else she had to do what she always did so well: survive.

She was out here hundreds of miles from any support. She was besieged by things that would not yield to her will or sorcery and which she could detect, it seemed, only through her own shadows or when one of them attacked her directly. They were as fierce as shadows but strange. They were more otherworldly than her spirit slaves and seemed possessed of a higher order of intelligence.

Each one she extinguished personally infected her with both a vast sorrow and with the certainty that she was battling only the most feeble of their kind. Always there was a powerful presentiment of demons or demigods to come.

What she could not comprehend was why all this frightened her so. There was nothing here more deadly or threatening or bizarre than a thousand perils she had faced before. Nothing here matched the sheer dark menace of the Dominator in his time.

There were infrequent moments when she still longed for those dark and ancient times. The Dominator had taken her and all her sisters, had made one of them his wife and another his lover. . . .

He had been a strong, hard, cruel man, the Dominator. His empire had been one of cruelty and steel. And Soulcatcher had revelled in its pomp and dark glory. And would never forgive her rival, her last surviving sister, for having brought all that to an end. Blame the death of the Dominator on the White Rose if you wanted. Soulcatcher knew the truth. The Dominator never would have gone down if his whining virgin of a wife had not helped his destruction along.

And who had fought and conspired so hard after their resurrection to keep the Dominator in the ground? His loving wife, that was who!

She would be back. She would be out there somewhere, wherever the Black Company had been hiding. She was not here yet but she would be soon. Having been buried alive again would be no impediment to the inevitable, that grim moment when they would settle their differences face-to-face.

Soulcatcher could will herself blind in some quarters, despite centuries of cynical experience. She would not see that fortune could be just as erratic and insane as she was.

Soulcatcher's powers of recuperation were tremendous. After a few hours of rest she rose and started walking northward, her stride long and confident. Tonight she would gather an army of her own shadows around her. Never again would she be as threatened as she had been the night before.

So she told herself.

By late afternoon her confidence was as high as ever it had been and fragments of her mind were already peeping past today's crisis to scout out what might be done to sculpt the future.

Soulcatcher had long been intimate with the knowledge that horrible things could and did happen to her but always she had enjoyed the certainty that she would come through everything alive.

Khatovar:
Leave-taking

Looks clean," Swan said. Murgen and Thai Dei grunted agreement. I nodded to the Nyueng Bao. What he had to say meant something here. His eyes were still as sharp as those of a lad of fifteen. I was damned near blind in one and could not see out the other.

"Doj? What do you think? Did they run away? Or did they sneak back just in case *we* sneaked back?" Element of surprise no longer my ally, I did not want to run into the Voroshk again. Especially not those old men. They would be bitter and in a mood to drag me down to hell with them.

"They went away. They went back to prepare for the onslaught. They know horror and despair are headed their way but they also know they're strong enough to weather it if they remain calm and work hard."

I suspect I gaped. "How do you figure all that?"

"It's just a matter of mental exercise. Take what we know about them, about sorcerers as a whole, and about human beings in general, and the rest follows. They've been through this before, in a smaller way. They'll have worked out what to do if it happened again. All this empty country, from here to the other side of their Dandha Presh, will serve the same function as the cleared ground surrounding a fortress expecting to be besieged."

"You've convinced me. Let's just hope they're not so ready that they figure out how to come looking for us after they wrap up their pest problem." As badly as the Shadowgate and nearby barrier had been damaged I doubted the Voroshk would have much energy to spare for generations.

Swan said, "He had me for a minute, too, but here comes the argument that proves what I always knew: Uncle Doj is full of shit."

A half dozen billowing black forms had emerged from the vegetation down the slope. They were walking very slowly, two by two, hands extended away from their sides, their flying posts tagging along behind at waist height.

I said, "I don't know what the fuck is going on but I want Goblin and Doj ready for anything. Murgen, you and Thai Dei spread out so we can hit them from in front and both sides with fireballs." Me and my pals had three live poles, literally all our band had left. Lady said there were just six usable fireballs between the three. She hoped.

One for each of the Voroshk.

Swan said, "You sure we really need to round up those spooks? Life would be a lot easier. . . ."

"Right here. Right now. But what happens back home when we've got Soul-catcher coming at us and we yell for Tobo to let loose the Black Hounds and there ain't no Black Hounds? And the rest of the Unknown Shadows say, 'Fuck that shit! I ain't getting skragged for these guys who wouldn't even try to bring the Hounds out of Khatovar.' "

Swan growled. Goblin sneered, "A little passion, Captain? I thought you'd lost it all."

"When I want shit out of you, runt, I'll kick it out. What did he just say?" The Voroshk had stopped coming toward us. One had spoken. And, O wonder, his words sounded like something I ought to understand. "Say that again, buddy."

The sorcerer got the idea. He repeated himself, loudly and slowly, the way you do with the hard of hearing, the dim of wit and foreigners.

"What is that noise?" I asked. "I know there were words in there that I should recognize."

"Remember Juniper?" Goblin said. "It sounds like he's trying to speak what they spoke there."

"Makes sense. Bowalk came from Juniper. So listen close." Goblin had served in Juniper, too. A *long* time ago. I have a knack for languages. Could I get enough of this one back fast enough to do us any good? We did not have many hours of daylight left.

Something began to get past the fact that the Voroshk had a horrible accent and his grammer was atrocious. He butchered tenses and inverted his verbs and subjects.

Goblin and I compared notes as we proceeded. The little wizard had never spoken the language well but he had had no trouble understanding it.

"What's going on?" Swan demanded. He was holding one of the bamboo poles. It was getting heavy.

"Sounds like they want us to take them with us. That they think the end of the world is coming and they don't want to participate."

Goblin nodded, agreeing. He added a caveat, "But I wouldn't trust them for a second. I'd always assume they were sent to spy on us."

"Yes," I said. "I'd do that with just about anybody."

Goblin ignored the jibe. "Make them strip. Bone naked. Doj and I can go over their clothes like we're looking for nits."

"All right. Only I'm taking Doj with me to help collect my snail shells." I began telling the Voroshk what they had to do if they really wanted to go with us. They were not pleased. They wanted to argue. I did not argue even though I hoped to get my hands on a flying post or two so Lady and Tobo could study them. Damn, having a few of those sure would be handy.

I told the Voroshk, "If I don't see naked bodies I'd better see the backs of people getting away. Anybody who isn't doing one or the other by a count of fifty will die where he's standing on his dignity." The language came back to me quite well, though I did not really make my statement that clearly. The two Voroshk who were probably the brightest began disrobing almost immediately. They proved to be as pale and blond as the girls we had seen already, though red with embarrassment and shaking with fury. I watched carefully, not with much interest in their flesh. How much determination they put into something humiliating would give me a hint or two about their sincerity.

It was too much for one young woman. She got just far enough for her true sex to become evident before she found that she could not finish.

"Better run, girl," I said. And she did. She hopped aboard her flying log and scooted.

Her desertion had a definite impact on one of the young men. He changed his mind even though he was already naked. I did not hurry him as he dressed.

That left four, three boys and a girl, all in their early to middle-teens.

I waved uphill, confident that by now Lady would be watching and could guess what I needed. She is clever that way. And shortly a couple of guys were headed downhill lugging bundles of odds and ends with which to dress our prisoners.

They did not yet quite understand their new status.

I brought them through the Shadowgate one at a time, watching carefully. I did not expect them to try anything but I am alive at my age because I make a habit of being ready for trouble when it seems most unlikely. I asked, "Anybody got any reason to think whoever goes out the gate is going to get into trouble?" To their further humiliation the Voroshk kids found themselves with their hands bound behind them as soon as they were dressed.

The fellow with the feeble command of Juniper's lingo protested the indignity. "It's only temporary," I assured him. "Just while us few are on the outside." I shifted to Taglian. "Murgen, Swan, Thai Dei, you keep these guys on a short leash."

Bamboo poles lashed the air. Despite age and its attendant cynicism, those guys could put on a show of enthusiasm. Mainly faked. Swan promised me, "Anything happens to you, there won't be anything left of them but grease stains and toenails."

"You're a good man, Swan. Doj, you go through first." The elderly Nyueng Bao drew the sword Ash Wand and stepped through the damaged Shadowgate into Khatovar. He positioned himself. I said, "Your turn, Goblin." By hand sign I told Murgen not to be shy about flinging a fireball at surprise targets outside.

What followed was anticlimactic. I took a sack around to all the places I remembered seeding earlier and collected snail shells. Those in which something had hidden itself had a distinct feel.

My ravens returned while I was involved in the harvest. They reported the Voroshk feverishly preparing for nightfall. They believed our defectors were genuine. Terror and panic were spreading across the world as fast as Voroshk messengers could fly.

The birds made the recovery of our shadow companions much easier. They let me know which shells were a waste of time and where to find the ones I had forgotten. We were all back through the Shadowgate an hour before sunset.

Goblin was still examining the clothing removed from the Voroshk kids. The little wizard piped. "This is some truly amazing material, Croaker. I think it might be sensitive to the thoughts of whoever is wearing it."

"Is it safe?"

"I think it's completely inert as long as it isn't in contact with whoever is keyed to wear it."

"A little something more for Tobo to play with during all the spare time he's going to have in the middle of a war. Bundle it up. Put it on a mule at the front of the column. We need to get going." I shifted languages, told the unhappy youngsters, "I'm releasing you now. I'm going to bring you back out here, one at a time, so you can get your posts. You won't be allowed to ride them. You'll travel at the rear of our column." I went on to tell them about the dangers of the plain while they were following instructions. Their fear of the shadows gave me a good chance to retain their attention. I tried to impress them that a screw-up on the plain would kill not just the fuck-up but the whole crew, so they should not expect my people to be gentle if their behavior was unacceptable.

I was the last of the Company to leave Khatovar's soil. Before I departed I indulged in a little personal ceremony of farewell, or perhaps of exorcism.

The youngster capable of some communication wanted to know, "What is the meaning of what you just did?"

I tried to explain. He did not get it. In time I determined that he had never heard of the Free Companies of Khatovar. That he knew almost nothing of the history of his world before his ancestors had taken power. That, furthermore, he did not care.

He seemed a shallow young man, overall. No doubt his companions were much the same.

The Company was going to be a revelation for them.

L ady and I stayed at the end of the road, waiting to make sure we had sealed it successfully against shadow incursions. The sun set. The sense of presence that comes when a large number of killer shadows are gathering grew powerful as darkness came. A rising excitement informed that presence, as though the Host of the Unforgiven Dead knew that some change had taken place even though they could not come out and scout around in the daytime.

The skies remained clear over Khatovar. The moon rose just before sunset, so there was ample silvery light to reveal the opening stage of the shadow invasion.

A trickle of small explorers gradually slithered through the shattered boundary. The scream of a dying pig reached us. More shadows descended the slope. Though they did not appear to be communicating with one another, somehow more and more and bigger and bigger shadows became aware of the opportunity.

"Look there," Lady said. A line of Voroshk flyers had begun passing near the moon. Before long little balls of light were bubbling into existence within the dense vegetation down the slope. "Maybe something like our fireballs."

The fireballs had been created, originally, to destroy the floods of darkness the Shadowmasters insisted on throwing against us.

"They're going to put up a fight, anyway. Will you look at that?" That being the Nef.

"The dreamwalkers are going out? I wonder why."

"Too bad we couldn't let the shadows all get out, then slam the gate shut behind them."

Even Shivetya would agree, I supposed. He was not pleased with some of the improvements made on his plain during recent millennia.

Lady said, "We should get moving. And you might want to put some thought into what to do with our new children once we get to the other end and they become tempted to run away."

Yes. I should. We did not need any more psychotic sorcerers getting under foot.

The Shadowlands: Tobo's Chores

Tobo finished interviewing the black raven that was not really a bird, sent it racing back to Croaker. He found his mother and Sleepy with Sleepy's usual fellow travelers studying a map of the territories north of the Dandha Presh. They were trying to determine the most favorable route northward, once the force finished crossing the mountains. Little colored patches represented the last known positions of the Protector and of Narayan Singh.

Sleepy asked, "News from Croaker?"

"He's finished it. He's on his way. But it turned stranger than he expected." He relayed the full report.

Sleepy told him, "You'll have to go back. We can't risk the chance of another gang of sorcerers getting loose over here."

"I suppose." Tobo had no enthusiasm for that.

"I don't like it. Why didn't he just kill them after he had their flying things and that remarkable clothing?"

"Because he doesn't do things like that." Not to mention the fact that dead people are not real cooperative when it comes time for them to share their knowledge.

"No. He lets people get away with stuff, then hunts them down thirty years later." She made a growling noise. "How can I keep moving if I don't have you here?"

"If Croaker is on this side all the Unknown Shadows will be on this side, too. The Black Hounds will be running out front in no time. A day or two later we'll be able to see what's going on anywhere we want to look." Sleepy needed that reassurance. She was worried about everything going on out where she had no ability to see. Reminding her that most people, including most captains, went through whole lives far more blind than she had ever been, did nothing to improve her temper.

Sleepy was spoiled. Throughout her association with the Company, one way or another, we had owned some ability to find out what was happening far away from us. You let anybody have something for a little while, they soon consider it their birthright. Sleepy was very much no exception to that rule.

G oblin crabbed, "I understand that you need Tobo here before you can let the prisoners leave the plain. But why shouldn't the rest of us go ahead? We aren't getting anything useful done just sitting here."

"You're getting done what I want you to get done. Now be quiet. Before I gag you."

I became impatient myself before Tobo finally appeared. He was subject to the constraints of normal travel. We had no flying carpets anymore, though there was hope that the Howler might create some once he was reawakened. (Nobody had yet tried.) And now there was the possibility we might gain the secrets of the Voroshk flying posts.

Tobo came in astride the superhorse that had attached itself to Sleepy. Bred originally to serve the Lady of the Tower up north, a number had come south with the Company. This was the last known survivor.

"How long do those things live, hon?" I asked Lady as Tobo approached.

"Maybe forty years. At the extreme. This one is pushing the limit."

"Looks pretty spry." Despite having run forty miles the animal looked almost fresh.

"I did good work in those days."

"And you miss them now?"

"Yes." She would not lie to me. She did not love me any less for missing being what once she had been, either. Near as I can tell, she never regrets anything she does, good or evil. I wish I could be that way.

Tobo dismounted right outside the Shadowgate. I passed him through. He got straight to business, though he smiled and waved to his father and uncle and Doj. "You have five prisoners? All major wizards?"

"I don't know about that. They could be complete no-talents, far as I can tell. But they did go flying around on fenceposts wearing a kind of super-fabric that Goblin says can be manipulated by thoughts. This comes across as a 'You'd better be careful, Croaker' kind of sign."

"We can communicate with them?"

"We have two brothers whose father studied and managed Bowalk while she was in Khatovar. The father could force Bowalk to resume human shape for an hour or two sometimes, but he couldn't keep her there. He thought the problem was a dead-man-loop Shapeshifter built into the shape-changing spells. Shifter didn't trust her. The loop activated when One-Eye killed him.

"Anyway, this Voroshk's kids picked up some of Bowalk's native tongue from being around her, which has been for all of their lives. When the Voroshk blew up the Shadowgate one of them got the bright idea that he could talk us into taking them to safety somewhere else. He rounded up some friends who were just as scared and came to us. He assumed we all spoke the same language as the forvalaka. He had some strange notion that we would recognize the innate superiority of the Voroshk and take his bunch in as honored guests. He couldn't imagine it being any other way because that's the only way it could be in Khatovar. He's vain, stupid and arrogant. They all seem to be. The other brother more so. He won't even talk."

Tobo smiled a little unpleasantly, perhaps recalling similar attitudes amongst Hsien's warlords. "I expect they've all suffered one disappointment after another."

"Absodamnlutely. Life has become an unimaginable hell for these kids. I have to remind them over and over that they're still alive."

"Let's go meet them, shall we?" The kid looked like he was excited by the challenge.

As we approached the refugees I warned Tobo, "They're all gorgeous but I really don't think they have a brain between them. At least they show every sign of being slow learners."

We stopped several yards from Khatovar's forlorn children. They huddled together beside the road as Black Company men and mules began to move out through the Shadowgate. Only one of the girls had ambition enough to look up. The little one. The one we had taken prisoner.

She stared at Tobo for half a minute. Then she murmured something to her companions. They looked up, too. Only the ringleader and his brother betrayed their native arrogance. And it had not been that long or arduous a journey.

They seemed to sense something in Tobo that was not apparent to me. It awakened hope. Several babbled questions in their own language.

"When they stop yammering tell them who I am. Don't feel like you have to be entirely honest, either."

"A little exaggeration couldn't hurt?"

"Hardly ever."

The interview lasted longer than I anticipated. Tobo was remarkably patient for his age. He worked hard to make the Voroshk understand that they were no longer in the land of their fathers, that here it did not matter who they were or who their parents had been. In our world they were going to have to sing for their supper.

We broke for a snack. The Voroshk and their guards were the only people left on the plain side of the Shadowgate. I told Tobo, "I admire your patience."

"Me, too. Already I want to kick some of them. And it's not really all patience, anyway. I'm trying to learn more about them by reading what they don't say and what they do let slip. You're right. They don't seem very bright. Though I'm guessing that's as much because of the way they were educated as it is any natural stupidity. They have no idea whatsoever of their own past. None! Never heard of the Free Companies. Never heard of the Lance of Passion. Didn't know that some really great wizards from Khatovar erected the standing stones that are all over the plain, at great peril to themselves from shadows. Didn't even recognize the name Khatovar, though they do know Khadi as some vague, old-time demon that nobody cares about anymore."

"How do you know that? About the memorial stones."

"Baladitya got it from Shivetya. You did notice that the runes on the flying logs are almost identical to the ones on the standing stones?"

"I didn't notice that, no. Mostly I've kept busy watching Goblin. The little shit speaks a bit of the language. He's been sneaking around talking to them."

Tobo chewed and nodded and looked thoughtful. "You ask him about it?"

"Hardly. I don't trust that guy, Tobo. One-Eye told me not to just before he passed."

"Nobody is going to trust Goblin for a long time, Croaker. And he knows that as well as anybody else does. He'll be the carefulest Goblin you ever saw. You won't even recognize him."

"We're talking about Goblin here. He can't help himself."

"He got into most of what he got into because One-Eye dragged him along. Think about it, Croaker. If he's somehow turned into Kina's tool, his assignment will be a long-term one. 'Bring on the Year of the Skulls' kind of stuff. He won't get himself killed trying something trivial."

I grunted. That made perfect sense on a rational level but I remained unconvinced. Goblin was Goblin. I had known him for a long time. The things he did did not always make sense, even to him. I asked, "What'll we do with the Voroshk?"

"I'm going to educate them."

Damn! I did not like the way he said that.

He replaced my guards with his own cronies, Taglians led by a senior sergeant called Riverwalker. All these guards were fluent in the language of Hsien and possessed a working knowledge of Nyueng Bao, which was a close cousin of the language spoken in the Land of Unknown Shadows.

Tobo instructed the guards, then the prisoners. Through me. Explaining the facts of life. "These men will be your teachers. They will teach you languages and the skills you will need to get along in this world. They will expose you to our religions and laws and the ways we have for getting along with one another."

The boy doing the translating started to protest.

Riverwalker smacked him in the back of the head hard enough to knock him down.

Tobo continued, "You have to understand that you're guests. You bought passage out of Khatovar with your knowledge. Your lives will be as comfortable as we can make them so long as you cooperate. But we are at war with ancient and powerful enemies. We won't be inclined toward patience with anyone who doesn't cooperate. Our patience will be especially short with people we consider dangerous. Do you understand?"

Tobo waited for me to finish translating. I asked an extra time to make sure the kids really grasped the gravity of the situation. Youngsters have a hard time getting it when the cruel and deadly applies to them personally. They also tend to agree to almost anything just to stop hearing about it.

Tobo had me tell them, "The rest of today and tonight you can rest. Tomorrow you'll begin an intensive education in Taglian. While we're hurrying to catch up with the rest of our army. I'll travel with you and will help you as much as I can."

The leader boy wanted to argue again. He had not listened closely enough to what he was translating. Riverwalker knocked him down again. Tobo told me, "That one's going to be trouble."

"There's a good chance they all will be. They couldn't get along at home." They had to be misfits. Shifting languages, I told the kids, "If you make yourselves more trouble than you're worth these people will kill you. Come on. I think I see some chow waiting to make our acquaintance."

One of the girls said something in her own language. The captive, not the one who had come along with the boys.

I responded to the whine. "Tell her she can't go home. It's too late for that."

Meantime, Tobo remarked, "But everybody here is running away from something."

"Some," I stipulated. "How soon do you think we'll get a chance to sit down somewhere? I've got a lot of writing to catch up on."

Tobo laughed. "You'd better stage a coup, you want a chance to sit down. Sleepy won't take time off until the corpses are piled high enough to make fences."

The Voroshk seemed to enjoy their evening meal. They were hungry enough to appreciate anything. We started teaching them Taglian nouns. Tobo studied both them and the wonders they had brought with them. He seemed less impressed by their flying posts than he was by the clothing they were no longer permitted to wear.

He told me, "Those posts look like a variation on the same sorcery Howler uses to operate his flying carpets. I should be able to work it out eventually. If I can get around some spells that're meant to make the posts destroy themselves if they fall into the wrong hands."

I told him about the two I had seen explode.

"Pretty potent self-destruct, then. I'll be careful."

"Be careful of those girls, too. I think the little one's already staked you out."

Come morning the leader kid could not be wakened. He was alive, all right, but no one could rouse him. "What did you do?" I asked Tobo, whispering, having leapt to a conclusion involving Tobo wanting the potential troublemaker out of the way without us losing access to his post and clothing.

"I had nothing to do with it."

Lady examined the boy after I did. She said, "This looks a lot like the coma Smoke went into for so long."

I agreed. But Soulcatcher had been responsible for that, we believed. And there was no way this could be her doing. The Unknown Shadows knew every move she made. And would turn aside any monsters she sent against us. I wondered aloud, "Were any of your invisible friends around here last night? Maybe they saw something."

"I'll check."

By dint of ferocity I got the unconscious kid's brother to admit that he could communicate. I made him understand that they needed to bind his brother onto one of their posts. Otherwise he would get left behind when we moved out.

The kids were terrified.

"Handy disaster," Lady remarked.

"Yeah. But for whom?"

Taglios:
The Message

Mogaba swore softly but virulenty, foully and steadily. Crows had been arriving for over an hour, each bird carrying a fragment of a long message from the Protector. Being birdbrained, no one crow could carry much of the whole. And because they were vulnerable to a thousand misfortunes, every fragment had to be sent again and again.

The Great General hated putting these puzzles together and this one was the worst ever, by an order of magnitude. There should not be this many crows in the whole world.

He had twenty scribes working on the message already.

Some points became clear quickly.

He sent for Aridatha Singh and Ghopal Singh. This message would affect all of them.

By the time the others arrived, enough of the puzzle had come clear for Mogaba to reveal what, for him, was the most critical detail. "They're back."

Aridatha jumped, startled by Mogaba's intensity. "Back? Who's back?"

"The Black Company. The Protector destroyed them. Right? Root and branch. Right? But now she says they're back. They're patching her message together in the next room right now."

Ghopal asked, "What are you talking about?"

"There's a huge message coming in from our employer. She's given up her quest. She's on the run, headed home. The Black Company is pouring through the Shadowgate. Thousands strong. Well-armed, well-clad, well-trained. With the Radisha Drah and Prahbrindrah Drah in their train and blessing them. And we have nothing much in their way for hundreds of miles. She's headed back here. She expects to lose her ability to watch them shortly. They have some unfamiliar kind of supernatural help coming off the plain with them. Evidently something like the shadows but more dangerous because they're smarter."

Aridatha observed, "Sounds like pretty good intelligence gathering for somebody who's on the run from an enemy who knows her capabilities." Singh's handsome face had lost some of its color. His voice had gone husky.

"A thought which did not escape me. She is Soulcatcher, after all. On the other hand, though, she can't learn anything when there isn't anything to see."

Aridatha and Ghopal nodded. In all ways, except in their hearts, they remained dedicated servants of the Protector.

Mogaba said, "The enemy being familiar with the Protector's capabilities means they'll try to take them away from her. We don't know who's in charge but doctrine is doctrine. They'll try to blind her first, then they'll try to take away her capacity to communicate. They couldn't have come at a better time for them. She's a hundred miles from nowhere. She can't spread the word much faster than rumors will spread. And you know the news that the Radisha and her brother are coming back will spread like the plague."

Ghopal said, "I'll seal this part of the Palace off, then. We don't want those people in there running to their temples or whatever and telling too much of the truth to someone who'd use it as a tool against us."

"Do that." That would look good to the Protector's invisible spies. But, on the other hand it might be very useful to have some of the news get out. Taglios might fall into a state of chaos. A state in which there would be opportunities. Chaos could be very useful. Chaos could make wonderful camouflage.

Perhaps when the Protector was nearer Taglios.

Right now it was necessary to prepare for the advent of the Company. That would be expected from all quarters.

Where did they find so many men? Or shadows of their own? What other surprise cards did they have in their hand?

Some, surely. That was their nature.

Mogaba said, "We've got to leak some of the news. Like it or not. We have to get ready for war. We're headed for a fight. Unless we give up without a struggle. I don't plan to do that myself. I couldn't live with the consequences."

The Singhs exchanged glances. The Great General showing a sense of humor? Remarkable.

Ghopal said, "People are afraid of the Black Company."

"Of course they are. But when was the last time they won? We beat them over and over during the Kiaulune wars." Mogaba was proud of his work back then. His thinking and planning had contributed to every Taglian triumph.

"But we didn't wipe them all the way out. The trouble with the Black Company is that if you leave even one of them alive, before long they're coming right back at you again."

"My brother unforgiven." That slogan haunted Mogaba's nightmares. He had his regrets.

"How soon can we expect the Protector?" Ghopal asked. "I'll have preparations to make."

Mogaba said, "She was on foot when she started sending her message. But she'll get to a courier station eventually. Then she'll start making good time. I wouldn't count on having more than another two or three days if she gets in a real hurry."

Ghopal grunted unhappily.

Mogaba nodded. Nothing ever went easily.

Aridatha asked, "Did she catch the Deceivers?"

Once again Mogaba thought the man betrayed a curiously skewed interest. Possibly a personal interest. "No. I told you, she said she was breaking off the chase. Enough. We all pretty much know what we need to do. Aridatha, I want the entire courier battalion here as soon as possible. The garrison commanders will need to be advised. I'll let you know right away if any critical news comes in."

Watching the message continue to approach final form, the Great General reviewed his unit commanders and the readiness and reliability of their commands. He was troubled. At first glance it would seem he could call up the resources of an empire. But the Protector had not concerned herself with the upkeep of her armed forces when she was not directly and immediately threatened. And she was not remotely popular, never had been and never wanted to be. She preferred rule by raw strength.

The Prahbrindrah Drah and his sister returning was particularly troubling. They had been popular in their era and in time's crucible had gone through the first stages of sanctification already. Some would hail them as liberators. Hell, if Croaker was still alive they might give him his old title back.

There would be desertions, both at high levels and among the soldiers. Mogaba was more concerned about the troops. The nobility and senior priests, who owed their positions to the Protector, would play it carefully. Taglios had received several painful lessons regarding the price to be paid for betraying the Protector.

Where would it be best to bring the Company to battle? And how could he force battle upon them if they were reluctant to hazard a major encounter?

He was sure that his best chance lay in forcing an early confrontation, before what forces he did have began to evaporate.

The Nether Taglian Territories:
The Barrens

Soulcatcher hastened along the bank of a creek that was almost as still and deep as a canal, looking for a way to cross. She had miscalculated when she had chosen to cut across these moors and downs to reach the shabby stronghold at Nijha. Clinging to the road would have meant a longer walk but there would have been bridges for times like these.

When she encountered obstacles of this sort she had no choice but to guess which way to turn. She did not know the country. She was blind. There were no bats or owls to send scouting. There were no shadows tonight. She had sent all those to safety, along with her crows. She knew she was capable of dealing with the hobgoblins following her around.

Something rose from the water behind her. It had a shape like a horse. A voice whispered in her ear, telling her to come and ride. She barely glanced at it, and then only in total scorn. These things might be smarter than shadows but they could not be by much. How stupid did they think she was? She did not have to be familiar with the folklore of Hsien to understand that the water horse would drag her under.

She ignored the monster, not knowing it was an afanc, actually of centaur shape rather than equine. A half hour later she ignored one of its cousins, which took the semblance of a giant beaver. Then there was one resembling a crocodile, though this creek was four hundred miles from anywhere warm enough to support those giant reptiles. They all whispered to her. Some of them even knew her true name.

She found a plank footbridge evidently put in place by the seldom-seen, horse-stealing natives of these highlands. As she started across, something whispered to her from underneath. She did not understand its words but their menace was plain enough.

"You don't want me crossing, come up and do something about it." The voice she chose was that of a small child who was severely annoyed, but not frightened.

Something came up. It was huge and dark and ugly. In spots it glowed with a leprous inner light. It had way too many teeth. They stuck out of its mouth at all angles. It would have trouble when it came time to eat.

All those teeth and fangs snapped open as the monster prepared to lunge.

Soulcatcher's gloved right hand drifted forward. A spray of sparkling dust floated onward to meet the evil spirit.

It screamed.

Soulcatcher leapt off the bridge an instant before it shattered to kindling. She backed away, watched the fiend thrash and melt. From behind her mask came a soft wee sound like a little girl's skip-rope song, with a refrain that went, "It was fun to watch you die."

The Taglian Territories:
Somewhere North of Charandaprash

The Daughter of Night actually seemed to be thriving now that the Protector was stalking them no longer. Narayan was worried.

"You're always worried," she chided. She was happy. Her voice was musical. The light of the campfire made her eyes sparkle—when it did not make them glow red. "If someone is after us you worry about getting caught. If we're safe you worry about me not being a perfect replica of this image of the Daughter of Night you've invented inside your head. Narayan, Narayan. . . . Papa Narayan, what I want more than anything is somehow to fix it so you don't have to do this anymore. You've been the one for so long. . . . You deserve to put it all down now and relax."

Narayan knew that was not possible. Never would be. He did not argue, though. "Then let's bring on the Year of the Skulls. Once Kina returns we can loaf for the rest of our lives."

The girl shivered, seemed puzzled. Then she shuddered violently. She grew more pale, leaving Narayan wondering how she managed that when she was always as pale as death to begin. She stared out into the night, obviously troubled.

Narayan started to dump dirt—piled there for that purpose—onto the fire.

The girl said, "It's too late."

A huge shape rose behind her—then faded away as though dispersed by the wind.

"Kid's right, old man," said a voice Singh had not heard for years and was hearing again far sooner than he had hoped.

Iqbal and Runmust Singh—no relation to Narayan—appeared at the edge of the firelight, wavering, as though they were a mist coalescing. Other men appeared behind them, soldiers in a style of armor Narayan had never seen. Amongst the soldiers he saw drooling red-eyed beasts of species he had never seen before, either.

Singh's heart redoubled its wild pounding.

The girl observed, "Now we know why my aunt quit chasing us."

Runmust Singh agreed. "Now you know. The Black Company is back. And we're not happy." Runmust was a great shaggy Shadar whose sheer size was oppressive.

Iqbal Singh smiled, perfect teeth glistening in the middle of his brushy beard. "This time you'll have to deal with your mother and your father." Iqbal was as shaggy and nearly as huge as his brother but somehow less intimidating. The girl remembered him having a wife and several children. But. . . . Did he mean her birth mother? Her natural father? But they were supposed to be dead.

Her knees went watery. She never had seen her natural parents.

The living saint was unable to keep his feet. Kina was going to test him yet again. And he had no energy left to spend in the fight for his faith. He was too old and too feeble and his faith had worn too thin.

Runmust gestured. The soldiers closed in. They were careful men who made certain they did not get between their captives and the crossbows threatening them. They put the girl's hands into wool-stuffed sacks, then bound her wrists behind her. They gagged her gently, then pulled a loose woolen sack over her head. They were aware that she might work some witchery.

Narayan they placed up on an extra horse, then tied him into the saddle. They were doing him no kindness. They were in a hurry. He would be too slow if they made him walk behind them. They were more gentle with the girl but her immediate fate was identical.

Their captors were not gratuitously cruel but the girl was sure that would change when they found themselves with adequate leisure time. The strange young soldiers in the clacking black armor seemed highly intrigued by what they could see of her pale beauty.

This was not the way she had imagined herself becoming a woman. And her imagination had been extremely active for several years.

38

The Taglian Territories: The Dandha Presh

We were high in the pass through the Dandha Presh when the news arrived. The grinding weariness dragging my ancient bones down slipped my mind. I was at the head of the column. I stopped walking, moved aside, watched all the tired mules and men trudge past. Man and animal, we hoped the main force had not stripped Charandaprash of food and fodder.

The Voroshk had sunk deep into exhaustion and despair. Tobo traveled with them, talking all the time, trying to teach them through their pain and apathy. The kids had not had to walk anywhere ever before.

Their flying logs followed right behind.

Lady finally came up. I joined her. I sensed that rumor had reached her already, even though nobody seemed to have any breath to waste on conversation. Rumor is magical, maybe even supernatural.

I told her anyway. "Runmust and Iqbal have captured Narayan and Booboo. They never stopped heading our way after Soulcatcher left off chasing them."

"I heard."

"You as nervous as I am?"

"Probably more." We trudged along for a while. Then she said, "I never got a chance to be a mother. I never got a chance to learn how. After Narayan kidnapped her I just went back to being me."

"I know. I know. We have to keep reminding ourselves not to get emotionally entangled in this. She isn't going to think of us as Mom and Dad."

"I don't want her to hate us. And I know she will. Being the Daughter of Night is her whole life."

I thought about that. Eventually, I told her, "Being the Lady of Charm was your whole life once upon a time. But here you are."

"Here I am." Her lack of enthusiasm would have disheartened a lesser man than I.

She—and I—were of an age now where we spent too much time wondering how things might have gone had we made a few different choices.

I had plenty of regrets. I am sure she had more. She gave up so much more.

Willow Swan went puffing past with some remark about old folks slowing everybody down. I asked, "You guys keeping an eye on Goblin?"

"He don't fart without we don't know about it."

"That goes without saying. The whole countryside knows."

"He's not getting away with anything, Croaker."

I was not confident about that. Goblin was a slick little bastard. If I had the time I would stay right beside him myself, step for step.

Lady said, "Goblin hasn't done anything suspicious."

"I know. But he will."

"And that attitude is beginning to win him some sympathy. I thought you ought to know."

"I know. But I can't help recalling One-Eye's warning, either."

"You noted yourself that One-Eye would try to get his last lick in from beyond the grave."

"Yeah. Yeah. I'll try to take it easier."

"We need to move a little faster." The rear guard was almost up to us.

"We could lag behind and sneak off into the rocks for a while."

"Maybe you're not as worn out as you thought, then. Get a move on." And after a moment, "We'll talk about that tonight."

Some motivation, then.

Taglios:
The Great General

Thus far Mogaba had contained the worst reaction to the seething rumor cauldron that Taglios had become. His most useful tool was the carefully placed half-truth. His representatives did not deny that something big and dangerous was going on down south. They did, however, suggest that it was an uprising by the same sort of Shadowlander troublemakers who had supported the Black Company during the Kiaulune wars. They were milking that connection from the past, trying to intimidate opponents and encourage friends. There was no Black Company anymore.

Rumor had not yet discovered the Prahbrindrah Drah and his sister. Mogaba would offer the suggestion that those people were imposters when stories did begin to circulate.

"This is actually going better than I expected," the Great General told Aridatha Singh. "None of the garrison commanders have refused their marching orders. Only a handful of the senior priests and leading men have tried to pretend neutrality."

"I wonder if that state would persist if we lost the Protector."

Mogaba had been trying to find out for some time. The Prahbrindrah Drah had yet to produce an heir. His only living relative was his sister, who had run Taglios and its dependencies for years in fact, if not in name. At one point she had proclaimed herself her brother's successor. Though the culture militated against a female ruler she might be allowed to take over again if her brother preceded her in death. No one knew what would happen if brother and sister were both gone, as most of the population believed them to be.

The question was entirely an intellectual exercise, these days. Power in Taglios belonged to the Protector almost exclusively.

Mogaba never pressed his questions beyond a purely speculative level. None of his respondents suspected a deeper purpose. Nor did anyone volunteer to participate in an effort to get rid of the Protector, though it was no secret that most Taglians would prefer to do without Soulcatcher's protection.

Communications with Soulcatcher had ceased. The crow population had suffered a dramatic decimation, whether from disease or enemy action remaining unclear. Their numbers had been dwindling for decades, until murders in the wild were almost unknown. Bats could not carry significant messages. Owls would not. And there was no one at the Taglian and trained to manage and communicate with shadows. That was a rare talent indeed and the Black Company had exterminated the brotherhood who had shared it back when they were still running things their way.

Soulcatcher had scoured the Shadowlands, whence those people had sprung, length and breadth. She had turned up just a few old women and very young children who had survived all the wars and purges. They seemed to be a people unrelated to any other in the south, had been unknown there before the advent of the Shadowmasters, and among themselves had a oral tradition of having come from an entirely different world. Those old women and babies had lacked any useful knowledge or talent.

When his duties granted the time, Mogaba walked the main route from the Palace to the city's southern entrance. The walls had been under construction for decades and remained unfinished but the southern gate complex, the most important, had been completed and put into use ages ago. By channeling traffic through its bottleneck the state managed to tax all incoming travelers.

He was looking for the perfect place to put an end to the Protectorate. Four explorations had not revealed it yet. The obvious sites were just that: obvious. Soulcatcher would be alert. She was intimate enough with human nature to realize that rumors fed by the crisis in the south would reawaken opposition to her rule.

There seemed to be no way to manage it in the streets. And the longer it was delayed the more certain she was to become suspicious of her captains. It would be impossible for them to conceal their nervousness.

It would have to be instantly upon her arrival or immediately upon her entering the Palace. Or never.

They could forget the whole thing, go back to being her faithful hounds, and wait with her for the disaster from the south.

When Mogaba thought of the Company he shuddered and was most sorely tempted to abandon the plot against the Protector. Soulcatcher would be a potent weapon in that war.

The gate. The south gate. It had to happen there. The complex had been engineered for exactly that sort of thing, although on a larger scale.

When he returned to the palace he found Aridatha Singh waiting. "There was a messenger, General. The Protector has reached Dejagore. She took time out to review the troops assembling there, though it would seem the enemy isn't that far behind."

Mogaba made a face. "We don't have much time left, then. She won't lag long behind our couriers." Unspoken, but understood, remained the fact that they were running out of time to chose their final commitment.

Then Mogaba grunted. He had realized, suddenly, that the Protector could pluck the whole opportunity right out of their hands. Easy as snapping her fingers.

The Taglian Territories:
Below Lake Tanji

We overtook Sleepy in the hills beyond the north shore of Lake Tanji. Lady hurried ahead. She knew better but could not help herself.

Runmust Singh's rangers were still somewhere out ahead of the main force. They were close enough for their campfires to be seen across the barrier hills but recent hard rains had flooded the ravines and creeks between here and there. Which was the only reason we had caught Sleepy so soon. The flooding had slowed her down.

"It won't be long," she told us. "Unless we get more rain. These washes drain fast."

I knew. I fought the Shadowmasters across these hills, many years ago.

My wife was exasperated. She turned on Tobo, who, with his father, was renewing acquaintances with Sahra. "When are you going to learn enough about those damned posts so we can use them?" A little flooding would slow nobody if we could fly.

Tobo told Lady the truth, which was the last thing she wanted to hear. "It might be months yet. Maybe even years. If we're all so anxious to become more mobile, why don't we wake the Howler up and make a deal for some flying carpets?"

Debate was immediate and brisk with almost everyone feeling a need to offer an opinion. Goblin, Doj, Lady, Tobo, Sahra, Willow Swan, Murgen, Goblin again. Even Thai Dei looked like he had a viewpoint, though he kept it to himself.

I realized that Sleepy had not stated her opinion. In fact, her eyes had glazed over. She was far, far away. Her intensity was disturbing.

One by one, the others fell silent. A foreboding emotional murk began to gather. I looked for Unknown Shadows but saw nothing. What was going on?

Tobo spoke up first. "Captain? What's the matter?" Sleepy had begun to lose color. I got up to go find my medical kit.

Sleepy came out of it. "Tobo." Her voice was so intense silence spread in all directions. "Did you remember to restore the Shadowgate so it won't collapse if Longshadow dies?"

The silence deepened. Suddenly we were holding our breaths. And staring at Tobo. And every one of us knowing the answer even if we had not been there and did not want it to be true.

Sleepy said, "They've had him in Hsien for as long as we've been here. He was a frail old man. He won't last."

Without saying a word Tobo started getting ready to travel. Groaning, I clambered to my feet and began getting my stuff together, too. Tobo began telling his father and Uncle Doj how to manage the Voroshk. "You have to keep them engaged. Keep them trying to learn. Keep them away from Goblin. You'll need to force-feed the sick one. I don't think he's going to last much longer."

I was not sure I overheard that last remark. He spoke very softly.

He was right. The kid was slipping away. I could not stop it.

I looked hard at Lady, who had shown no sign of getting ready to do what had to be done. I told her, "You need to come. Following Tobo you're our best gate mechanic." I offered a hand.

Murgen, I noted, was paying his son's instructions no attention. He was getting ready to travel, too.

Lady's expression hardened. She accepted my hand. Upright, she stared northward. The fires in Runmust's camp were not visible now. Rain was falling between here and there.

Several others, including Willow Swan, quietly began getting ready to travel, too. No names were named, no orders were given. Those who needed to go or thought their presence would be useful began packing. Nobody grumbled. Nobody said much of anything at all. We were all too tired to waste energy doing anything but what had to be done.

No fingers got pointed, either. It took no genius to understand that Tobo had been swallowed up by his own workload, with people wanting something more from him every minute. Sleepy bore the heaviest responsibility. It was her job to see that everything got done. She should have had a checklist. But she had been singleminded in her desire to move faster than resistance could coagulate in front of her.

For that she could not be faulted. The Company had seen no fighting yet, though nearly a quarter of the Taglian empire could be accounted disarmed. It was the most remote and lightly populated quarter but the strategy remained sound.

The wealth Sleepy had brought off the plain would let her exploit the territories we held far more effectively than would Soulcatcher's capacity for generating terror allow her to exploit what she held.

Of course, if the Shadowgate collapsed all that would be moot. Our world would be in greater danger than Khatovar. Unlike the Voroshk, we could not defend ourselves.

Tobo did not bother collecting the few bamboo fireball throwers left. If we became desperate enough to need them that handful would not do any good.

There were eight of us. Tobo and his father, me, Lady, Willow Swan, and Thai Dei because Murgen never got out of rock-throwing range of Tobo's uncle. Then there were two older-than-average hardcases from Hsien, solid veterans of the warlord conflicts. One we knew as Panda Man because his real name sounded like that. The other was Spook. He was Spook because he had green eyes. In Hsien demons and haunts are supposed to have green eyes.

The Unknown Shadows refuse to conform. Every one of those haunts that I have actually seen had the more traditional red or yellow eyes.

Many of the Unknown Shadows traveled with us. At night, under the moon when it made its infrequent, shy appearances, the ground surrounding us seemed to be a sea in motion. Tobo's pets did not mind being seen just now.

Before long my two ravens rejoined me. I had seen nothing of them since shortly after we had left the Shadowgate.

Tobo told me, "I've sent scouts ahead. Now I'm going to ride ahead, too." He was mounted on Sleepy's superhorse. "The rest of you follow me as fast as you can."

He surged ahead. Most of the churning darkness went with him, though we retained enough shadowy outriders that no danger would take us by surprise.

"I'm sorry," I told Lady.

"Not your fault this time." She was not happy, though.

"You gotten anything out of Kina yet?"

"No. Nothing but a few infrequent touches while we were up there with Sleepy. They were pretty faint and probably just because we were close to Booboo."

Damn. "You think we can get back to the gate in time?"

"You think Longshadow will fight for life if he knows that the only thing he can accomplish is to save the people who pulled him down and turned him over to his oldest enemies?"

That was not the answer I wanted to hear.

The Nether Taglian Territories:
Leaves of Misfortune

Runmust and Iqbal rode northward slowly, at a pace their whole band found comfortable. Life would not be too hard until the Captain caught up. She would be put out because the rangers did not meet her as soon as possible. She would get over it.

The prisoners were given no opportunity to enjoy life, but they were not tormented directly. The Singhs would not have allowed that even had they known that Sleepy would not mind.

There was no formal arrangement between the Singhs and the dark spirits out of Hsien but Unknown Shadows paced them always. Communications remained crude. Runmust generally just got a really bad feeling when it was time to watch out. The problem was his. A religious failing. He was allowed no congress with demons. His innate human knack for rationalization had not yet exonerated the Unknown Shadows from being spawn of darkness.

Runmust began to have one of those bad feelings. It grew worse fast. Iqbal's uneasiness said that he had been touched, too. Even some of the soldiers were becoming troubled.

Quick hand gestures. The ranger team halted. Everyone dismounted. Scouts crept forward while the men assigned the duty for the day began moving the prisoners and horses into a gulch off the road.

The warriors of Hsien could be remarkably quiet and patient. Runmust admired their skill in using the available cover in terrain, boasting only tangled, scrubby brush, rocks and lots of gullys. He could not do what they did. Of course, he was twice the size of the biggest and a decade older than the oldest.

Minh Bhu, one of the best, intercepted him in his slow advance, after signing for absolute silence.

Minh brushed leaves aside and smoothed a patch of dirt. He used a forefinger to sketch the ground ahead, indicating the approximate positions of a well-chosen ambush site.

Runmust signaled a general withdrawal. He looked for crows or other creatures traditionally associated with the enemy. He saw nothing. "How could they
know we were coming?" he asked when he was far back enough to whisper. "How
many of them are there?"

Minh shrugged. "We're not going to get a head count. There are a lot more of
them than there are of us. And as for how did they know, from that hilltop you can
see all the country we crossed the last two days. They were probably just sent out to
see if this is the route north the Captain picks." He pointed back south. The dust
and sparkle of the main force were obvious.

"Why an ambush?"

"They can see there aren't many of us. It would look like a chance to take some
prisoners."

"Uhm." Runmust scanned the slope. Could he turn the tables on those people?
He wished he had developed a more intimate relationship with the Unknown
Shadows. "Iqbal. Talk to me."

"We're outnumbered, we should back away. There's no reason to get in a fight.
Or even make contact. We've got important prisoners to protect. So let's stay away
and wait for the Captain."

Iqbal was a married man. He did not favor major risks.

Even so, Iqbal was right. Withdrawal was the only course that was not crazy.
Runmust asked, "What would they do if we did stroll into their trap?" He wished he
could catch a couple of them. A few questions answered would tell a lot about
enemy plans and what the other side thought was happening.

"They see Sleepy coming. They'll pull out pretty soon."

"Why do I keep getting more and more nervous?" Runmust knew the Unknown
Shadows wanted him to know something and he just was not hearing it.

In the hills ahead horses began screaming. Men cursed. Several dozen arrows
rose into the air, fell where the enemy evidently thought the rangers were hidden.
None of the arrows came close.

Muttering curses himself, Runmust waved his men back again. They began
slipping away. Wildly sped arrows fell all across the slope. "Idiots," Runmust muttered. "Recon by fire." The Protector's soldiers would charge any outcry. Or any
other obvious reaction. They were an opportunity to inflict disaster just waiting to
happen.

A Taglian soldier sprang up not ten feet from Runmust, barking in pain as he
swatted his ass. Runmust froze, hoping the Taglian was too preoccupied to notice
him—though now he heard other Taglians pushing through the dry brush and
knew he could not sneak off fast enough to get away untouched.

Iqbal carried a fireball launcher. He was supposed to use it as an emergency signal, not as a weapon. It was believed to contain just one charge. It was ancient.
There was no guarantee it would work at all.

Iqbal, unseen by the man who had now spied Runmust, rotated, the handgrip trigger on that piece of bamboo.

An intense yellow ball slammed right through the Protector's man and rattled around in the brush behind him. In seconds a dozen fires were burning.

Runmust and Iqbal ran. No point doing anything else now.

They had almost reached the gully hiding the animals and prisoners when a random arrow found the unprotected meat of Runmust's right thigh. Singh flung forward in an uncontrolled dive. His beard protected his face as he ploughed through the brush but he left large tufts behind. He squealed with the unexpected pain.

Iqbal stopped to help.

"Get out of here!" Runmust growled. "You have Suruvhija and the children." Which moved Iqbal not at all.

The Taglian troops blundered down the hillside, scattered, in no order, without discipline or thought. Officers, sergeants and men, they had no practical experience and very little training. They had come out of the Nijha fortress because Soulcatcher had told them they might achieve a startling triumph. But once the situation on the ground deviated from their expectations they were lost.

Stumbling, dragging the leg with the arrow still embedded, Runmust clung to and leaned on Iqbal. Both men heard the exultant Taglian soldiers plunging through the brush behind them, swiftly bringing the inevitable.

The rangers were men chosen from those who had seen prior action serving the warlords in Hsien and who both understood Company doctrine and accepted it. They set an ambush of their own. The Taglians came to it as though guided by maleficent demons.

The result was a bloodbath. It was a tactical triumph for the Black Company. It was not unalloyed by bad news. In the end, in the heat of the moment, the rangers did fail to acknowledge doctrine. They did not fade away while the Taglians were confused and panicky. They maintained contact in hopes of making sure Runmust and Iqbal escaped.

The Singh brothers did survive. But when the light cavalry, flung forward by Sleepy right after she recognized the fireball signal, arrived they found most of the rangers wounded or dead after having been overrun. The horsemen pursued the fleeing Taglians. They cut down most of the enemy wounded and stragglers.

Sadly, they failed to recapture the Daughter of Night.

A particularly bright Taglian officer had recognized what he had stumbled across and got the girl moving to the rear immediately. Her grub-colored skin had given her away.

When that day's sun set it was a tossup which side would consider the encounter the greater disaster. The Company had lost a huge treasure and some of its most valuable men, at least for a while. The Taglians had endured a huge massacre with only one sullen, if exotically beautiful, pale, dirty young woman to show for all the deaths.

42

The Nether Taglian Territories:
After Battle

The Captain herself reached the scene of the fighting just an hour after its end. She stomped around. She nagged the survivors with questions. Most of the rangers had survived but only two had managed without suffering serious wounds. Sleepy interrogated prisoners even more emphatically. The cavalrymen had retained sense enough to capture a few Taglians who offered to surrender, presuming they would continue to cooperate to save their skins.

None of the prisoners knew anything about the Daughter of Night. None even knew that name.

The Captain's prowling took her near Narayan Singh. She kicked the old cripple. "Hellspawn." She turned, bellowed, "Why didn't we know about this ambush ahead of time?"

Some bold soul told her the truth. "The Unknown Shadows probably did know. But nobody asked them. Tobo is the only one who knows how to talk to them the way it takes to get them to do the kind of spying you want."

Sleepy growled. She kicked Narayan Singh again. She paced. "What do we know about this fort?"

Blade came forward. He would save the others. Sleepy's wrath fell less heavily upon him. Usually. Some thought she was a little afraid of Blade. In fact, she was just not sure of him, though he had been around longer than she had. Like Swan and Sahra, he was not actually a sworn brother of the Company. But he was always there and always involved.

Blade said, "The old Captain established it. It was a remount station for the first courier post. The wall got added because the natives kept trying to steal the horses. Soulcatcher eventually expanded the fort and garrison during the Kiaulune wars because she wanted a stronger presence here in case her enemies tried to sneak north this way. Assuming she did here the way she did everywhere else, she forgot the place as soon as the fighting was over. The garrison might be a hundred fifty or two hundred. Plus hangers-on."

"Pretty big gang for out here."

"It's a big territory. And half of them are out of business now."

"What're the fortifications like?"

"I've never been there. I hear they're barely good enough to stop horse thieves. Which means not real impressive. Some kind of rock wall, since that's the available material around here. I've heard there's a ditch that was never completed. Didn't you come this way when you ran south? Didn't you see it?"

"We took a trail west of here. The old trade road. We avoided the courier routes."

"You might send some cavalry to surround the place before they can move the girl out."

Sleepy mused, "It's probably too late to stop them yelling for help."

Blade said, "I don't think you need to worry about sneaking. By now Soul-catcher's got the whole Taglian empire alerted."

Sleepy grunted. Then she sent for cavalry officers. And after she sent them off she visited Runmust and Iqbal. Those two had been close friends for two decades. She asked Iqbal's wife, Suruvhija, "What did the surgeon say?"

"They'll recover. They're Shadar. They're strong men. They fought well. God will watch over them."

Sleepy glanced at Sahra, who was helping tend the wounded. Sahra nodded, meaning Suruvhija was not just wishful thinking.

"I'll include them in my prayers as well." Sleepy squeezed Suruvhija's shoulder reassuringly, thinking the woman was too perfect to be real. At least as men saw wives. But she was Shadar, too, and she believed, and the roles of all members of the family were clearly defined by her religion.

Sleepy took time to talk to Iqbal's children, too. They were bearing up bravely. As they would, for they were good Shadar, too, despite the strange lands and societies they had seen.

When she was around Iqbal's children, Sleepy sometimes even vaguely regretted having abandoned the woman's role. But that never lasted more than a few seconds.

"Blade. Pass the word. I want the whole gang up to this fort before sunset. If that's possible. Once they see some numbers I'm sure they'll give up."

Blade told her, "You know you have to stop before long. The animals need time to graze and recover. And we have a tail of stragglers that has to stretch all the way back to Charandaprash."

People got hurt or sick or just could not keep up. It irked Sleepy but it was a fact of life. Her strength was down maybe a thousand men already. That would worsen rapidly if she continued to drive hard.

"When they get here the most worn-out ones can take over as our garrison." That was a tactic as old as soldiering.

She would not admit it but she needed a rest herself. She could not imagine when she would get one, though.

The Taglian Shadowlands:
The Shadowgate

Seem like there's much point dragging my weary ass over there?" I asked Lady. There was just enough dawn-light to show the vague outline of the slope leading up to the Shadowgate. Which was still miles and miles from where we had spent the night. This part of the journey was one of those where you spend the whole day trying not to look ahead because every time you do it seems you have not gotten ten feet closer. Way to our left a smoky haze concealed the New City and the lower half of ruined Overlook. A lot of unpleasant memories connected us with those places.

"What do you mean?" My sweetheart was as tired and morning-cranky as I was. And her bones were a lot older than mine.

"Well, we didn't get killed last night. That means the gate hasn't collapsed yet. Old Longshadow's still holding out."

"Evidently."

"Wouldn't that mean Tobo's got everything under control? So why beat ourselves up getting on over there?"

Lady smirked at me. She did not have to tell me. We would cross the valley because, in the end, I would want to see everything for myself. Because I would want to get it all into the Annals, right. She had chided me fifty times during the ride south because I was trying to work out a way to write on horseback. I could get so much more done if I could do it while we were traveling.

Then she chirped, "You are getting old."

"What?"

"A sign of advancing age. You start obsessing about how much you have to get done in the time that you have left."

I made noises in the back of my throat but did not argue. That kind of thinking was familiar. So was being unable to fall asleep because I was tracking my heartbeat, trying to tell if something was wrong.

You would think a guy in my line of work would make his peace with death at an early age.

We ran into several locals while crossing the valley, the bottom land of which was decent farmland and pasture. We did not receive one friendly greeting. I did not see one welcoming smile. Nobody raised a hand in defiance but I had no trouble feeling the abiding resentment of a tormented nation. There had been no serious fighting in these parts for years but the adult population were all survivors of the terrible times, whether they were natives or immigrants who had come in to settle the depopulated lands and to escape even worse horrors elsewhere. They did not want the evils of the past to return.

This land had suffered grotesquely under the Shadowmaster Longshadow. It had continued to suffer after his defeat. The Kiaulune wars devoured most everything that Longshadow and the Shadowmaster wars had not. And now the Black Company had returned. Out of the place of glittering stone, an abode of devils. The season of despair appeared to be threatening again.

"Can't say I blame them," I told Lady.

"What?"

I explained.

"Oh." Indifferently. Some attitudes never wither. She had been a powerful lord a lot longer than she had been just another tick on the underbelly of the world. Compassion is not one of the qualities that endeared her to me.

We found Tobo impatient with our dawdling. "I see the old gal's still here," I said of the Shadowgate. Lady and I produced our keys and let the crew cross over, Murgen first so he could make sure his boy still had all his arms and legs and fingers and toes.

"It is," the wonder child confessed. "But probably only because Longshadow still hasn't left the plain."

"What?" Lady was irritated. "We made promises. We owe the Children of the Dead."

"We do," Tobo said. "But we won't be allowed to kill ourselves. Shivetya knew we forgot to disarm Longshadow's booby trap so he kept Longshadow from leaving."

"How do you know that?"

"I sent messengers. That was the news they brought back."

Lady's mood had not improved. "The File of Nine will be smoking. We don't need them as enemies. We may have to flee to the Land of Unknown Shadows again."

"Shivetya will release Longshadow the second we finish refurbishing our gate."

My companions were nervous. Willow Swan was pale, sweating, dancing with anxiety and, most of all, un-Swanlike, silent. He had not, in fact, spoken all day.

Thinking about the shadows can do that to you if you have witnessed one of their attacks.

Tobo asked, "You two ready to go to work?"

I shook my head. "Are you kidding?"

Lady said, "No."

Tobo told us, "I can't finish this alone."

I replied, "And you can't finish it with assistants so tired they're guaranteed to make mistakes. I have a premonition. Longshadow will keep till tomorrow."

Tobo admitted that he would. Shivetya would see to it. But he did so with poor grace.

Lady said, "Let's go set up camp." Murgen, Swan and the others probably should have been doing that instead of standing around being anxious.

Once we crossed the barrier Lady wondered, "Why is Tobo in such a hurry?"

I snickered. "I think it might have to do with Booboo. He hasn't seen her for a long time. Sleepy says he was completely smitten."

While I spoke her expression transformed from curious to completely appalled. "I'd hope not."

Murgen suggested, "There were two rather attractive Voroshk girls. One of them might have something to do with it."

44

The Shadowlands:
Gate Repairs

The dreamwalkers came during the night. Their presence was so powerful that even Swan, Panda Man and Spook saw them. I heard them speak clearly although I never understood a word.

Lady and Tobo did get something out of them.

They put their heads together over breakfast. They decided that the Nef wanted to warn us about something.

"You think so?" I sneered. "There's a new interpretation."

"Hey!" Tobo chided me. "It has something to do with Khatovar."

"Like what, for example?"

The youth shrugged. "Your guess is better than mine. I've never been there."

"Last time we saw the dreamwalkers they were headed out into Khatovar in the middle of all the shadows on the plain. You think they saw something they think we ought to know?"

"Absolutely. Any idea what?"

Lady asked, "Have you had your Unknown Shadow friends try to talk to the Nef?"

"I have. It doesn't work. The Nef don't communicate with the plain shadows, either."

"Then what was the Unknown Shadows' problem last night? The Black Hounds kept carrying on so bad they woke me up several times."

"Really?" Tobo was puzzled. "I never noticed."

Nor did I. But I am deaf and blind to most supernatural stuff. Plus, for once, I had not been tossing around listening for my heart to stop.

"Let's get to work."

"Booboo isn't going anywhere, kid."

Tobo frowned. Then got it. He did not become embarrassed or defensive. "Oh? Oh. You don't know? She's already gone. There was a fight with the garrison from Nijha. Runmust's troop got overrun. The Taglians captured the Daughter of Night. Sleepy has cavalry trying to run them down now."

I shook my head and grumped, "It won't do her any good. A million horsemen won't be enough now."

"Aren't you pessimistic."

"He's right," Lady opined. She lapsed into an old northern language I had not heard since I was young and which I never had understood completely. She seemed to be reciting a song as a poem. It had a refrain that went something like, "Thus do the Fates conspire."

We were on the inside of the Shadowgate, hard at it. Tobo was making tiny, elegant adjustments to the strands and layers of magic that made up the mystic portal. The training I had received had elevated me to the level of a semiskilled bricklayer. Compared to me Tobo was the sort of master artisan who created panoramic tapestries by weaving them instead of embroidering them. I was nothing but the lead finger man on the bow-tying team.

Even Lady was little more than a hodcarrier on this job. But hodcarriers are needed, too.

"Thanks for the compliment," Tobo said after I tried out my similes. "But I'm mostly doing embroidery and plain old-fashioned knot tying on broken threads. Parts of this tapestry were plain outright crippled. It'll never be completely right, even if it's stronger than when it started."

"But you can weasel Longshadow's booby trap out of there?"

"It's kind of like lancing a boil and cleaning it out, but yes. He actually made a pretty crude job of it. Obviously, he didn't know much about Shadowgates. He did know that there was no one in our world who knew more. What he didn't understand was that there were more keys."

"Of course he knew," I said. "That's why he sent Ashutosh Yaksha, his apprentice, to infiltrate the Nyueng Bao priests at the temple of Ghanghesha."

Tobo looked puzzled, like he did not recall that story.

"He knew they had a key there and he wanted it. So he could get back to Hsien. If you don't know that story you'd better corner your uncle. Because that's what he told Sleepy."

Tobo smiled weakly. "Well, maybe. I suppose."

"What do you mean, you suppose?"

Lady paused what she was doing. "Don't play Doj's games, Tobo. You won't be fooling anybody. I was there. Inside the white crow. I know what the man said."

"That's probably it. Doj told Sleepy a bunch of stories. Some were probably true but some he probably made up. Stuff he thought might be true because it sounded plausible based on what he did know. Master Santaraksita spent years searching the records at Khang Phi. The history of our world's Nyueng Bao isn't much like what Doj might've wanted you to believe."

"Which was it?" I mused aloud. "Was he lying or making it up?" I have known plenty of people who would not admit ignorance even in the most obvious circumstance.

Tobo said, "Master Santaraksita says our ancestors left Hsien as fugitives, sneaking out like snakes using a secretly manufactured key. They were trying to get away from the Shadowmasters. There was supposed to be a regular, gradual evacuation across the plain. Because they were persecuted followers of Khadi they did favor the organizational structure we've seen in other bands of believers but those people weren't mercenaries and they weren't missionaries. They weren't a Free Company. They weren't a band of Stranglers. They were just running away because the Shadowmasters insisted they had to give up their religion. Master Santaraksita says their priests probably made up a more dramatic history after they'd been settled in the river delta for a while. After several generations spent wandering. Before they arrived the only people in the swamp were Taglian fugitives and criminals and a few remote descendants of the Deceivers Rhaydreynek tried to wipe out. Maybe the Nyueng Bao wanted to impress them."

Tobo's hands never stopped moving while he talked. But their movements had nothing to do with what he was saying. He was mending things that I could not see.

"How much did Doj lie?" I was determined to pin that on him. I never did trust that old man.

"That's the intriguing part. I don't know. I don't think he really knows. He did tell me that a lot of what he told Sleepy originally he said just because it sounded believable and like something she wanted to hear. When you get right down to it, except for his skill with Ash Wand, Uncle Doj is a bigger fraud than most priests. Most priests actually believe what they preach."

Lady said, "Sounds like he's spent time hanging around with Blade."

Tobo continued, "The key my ancestors used to cross the plain was created secretly in Khang Phi. It went back to Hsien so the next group of fugitives could use it. They never got the chance."

"But they had the golden pick." Which was the key that Sleepy eventually found and used to get onto the plain so she could release us Captured from underneath Shivetya's fortress.

"That must have been the key that belonged to the Deceivers who hid the Books of the Dead back in Rhaydreynek's time. They must've hidden the pickax under the temple of Ghanghesha. The temple has a long history. It started out as a Janaka shrine. The Gunni took over and used it as a retreat. Then the survivors of Rhaydreynek's pogrom chased the Gunni out. But they faded away. Nyueng Bao folklore talks about bitter fighting over doctrine in the early days. A century later Gunni holy men from the cult of Ghanghesha began to come back to the swamp. Eventually most Nyueng Bao forgot Khadi and adopted Ghanghesha. A few generations back the pick turned up when the temple was being repaired. Somebody realized that it had to be an important relic. It wasn't till more recent times, when Longshadow, and later Soulcatcher, found out about it, that anyone realized how important it had to be."

"What about the pilgrimages?"

"Originally people from Hsien were supposed to meet our people at the Shadowgate with news from home and more refugees. But the Shadowmasters found out. Plus on this side my ancestors lost touch with the past. Contrary to legend, and unlike the way things are now, there wasn't that much pressure from outside. Hanging on to old ways and old ideas wasn't that important a way to maintain the identity of the Nyueng Bao.

"Whatever Doj says, most Nyueng Bao aren't devoted to tradition and keeping the old ways. Most don't remember anything anymore. You saw that while we were in Hsien. The Nyueng Bao aren't anything like those people over there."

Lady and I exchanged looks. Neither of us assumed Tobo was telling any more of the truth than Doj ever had. Though the boy was not necessarily lying consciously. I glanced at Thai Dei. He gave nothing away.

I said, "I've been wondering why Doj never found any Path of the Sword guys over there."

"That's easy. The Shadowmasters wiped them out. They were the warrior caste. They kept fighting till there weren't any of them left."

I had, for years, wondered why a sword-worshipping cult would be part of a people descended from a band of worshippers of Kina, who, in my world, did not believe in shedding blood. I still did not know. But now I knew that nobody else was likely to know, either.

I told Lady, "I'm surprised Sleepy never picked up on the fact that the supposed priest of this Nyueng Bao band went around carving people into steaks."

"Deceiver people at that," she added. "He slaughtered them by the score at Charandaprash."

Tobo is a clever young man. He understood that we did not find his version of history more convincing than Doj's.

I still was not sure whether he believed what he was saying.

It did not matter.

Lady poked me. She whispered, "Murgen and Willow Swan have drawn my attention to an interesting phenomenon. You'll want to see for yourself. Tobo, drop doing what you're doing and look at this, too."

By then I knew it would be something I did not want to see. Thai Dei, Murgen and the others were debating the best places to take cover already.

I turned. Lady pointed. A trio of Voroshk flyers, appearing only slightly larger than dots, hovered above the rim of the plain. They were way up high and a long way away, motionless.

I asked, "Anybody want to guess how well they can see us?"

Lady said, "They can tell we're here but that's it. Unless they have a farseeing device."

"What're they doing?"

"Scouting around, I imagine. Now that their gate is gone they can get onto the plain whenever they want. During the day they're safe as long as they stay off the ground. And they probably won't have much trouble with shadows even at night if they stay high up. We've never seen shadows go higher than ten or fifteen feet above the surface of the shielding."

"Think they're looking for us? Or are they just looking?"

"Both, probably. They'll want revenge. And maybe even a safe new world."

The Voroshk did not move while we were talking. I pictured similar trios ranging to all points of the plain, perhaps hoping they could open the way without us. "Tobo, can they get off of the plain?"

"I don't know. They won't be able to here. Not without one of my keys. I'll install something that'll kill them if they try."

I admired his confidence. "Suppose they have somebody as slick as you are? What's to keep him from undoing your spells the way you're undoing Longshadow's?"

"Lack of training. Lack of the knowledge we got out of Khang Phi. You have to know a little about these things to redo them."

Lady asked, "Can they break through the gateway into Hsien?" The knowledge was there.

"I don't know. They got the forvalaka through. Maybe they could shove their own people through on a slow, one-at-a-time basis. They never tried before. But they've never been desperate before. And time isn't on their side."

"What about Shivetya? What's his take on this?"

"I'll find out. I'll send a messenger in just a minute."

One of the soldiers from Hsien—Panda Man, I think—asked, "What about the men with Longshadow? If he hasn't left the plain. One is my cousin."

Tobo drew a long, deep breath. "My work is never done."

Lady said, "If you're going to do something you'd better do it fast. They have a key. It's at risk."

"Damn! You're right. Captain, I'm going to borrow your ravens. Lady, lean out the gate and yell for Big Ears and Cat Sith. They'll hear you. Tell them I want them. It's an emergency."

"One damned thing after another," I grumbled. "It never lets up."

"But you're alive," Swan said.

"Don't you be jumping around on the other side of your own argument." We amused ourselves with some good-natured bickering while Tobo sent supernatural messengers off to Shivetya, the guards at the Hsien Shadowgate, Longshadow's keepers, and our folks up north.

Along the way Murgen asked his son, "What's to keep those jokers up there from just flying off the plain? I remember times when crows came and went." And he used to do so himself, all the time

"They could do that because they come from our world. Crows from any other world we wouldn't have seen at all. Even if they were there. Yes. The Voroshk can fly out any time they want. But when they do they'll end up in Khatovar. Every time. If they want to get off the plain into another world they'll have to come onto it through their Shadowgate and leave it through another Shadowgate. Shivetya restructured it that way."

It can be confusing. I guess that happens where realities overlap, with a deathless demigod in the middle who feels compelled to make it hard for the human species to realize its darkest potential.

45

Nijha:
The Stronghold Falls

There were fewer than fifty soldiers to hold Nijha's walls, most of them injured already and all of them thoroughly terrified after having endured a night overrun by the Unknown Shadows.

The defenders were accorded the honors of war and allowed to march out without their weapons, taking their families and what possessions they could carry. They were admonished to clear the road whenever the Black Company passed.

If the Nijha stronghold had surrendered any faster Sleepy would have worried that she was walking into a trap. As it was, she did send Doj in first to make sure Soulcatcher had left her no special little gifts.

She had not.

Put Narayan somewhere where he can't embarrass me," Sleepy ordered after the stronghold had been declared secure. "I'll decide what to do with him in a day or two." She would have preferred handing him over to Lady and Croaker right away. "Battalion, regiment, and brigade commanders and all senior staff are to assemble in the local headquarters building in one hour."

Sahra asked, "You think there'll be room? I really thought this place would be bigger."

"So did I. Even though we knew it was a glorified remount station. Gosh, I wish Tobo was here instead of down there."

"So do I." Sahra hated having her whole family so far away. She had become accustomed to having a real family again during our years in Hsien. "I've been thinking. Wouldn't it be reasonable to keep Tobo and Murgen from going to the same dangerous places?"

"Like the Shadowgate?"

"Like that. Or anywhere else where one bad blow could take them both away."

Sleepy understood Sahra's agony. Sahra had lost two children and one husband to malignant fortune already. The husband did not trouble her much. His removal had improved her life. But rare is the mother who will not ache forever over the loss of her little ones.

All part of the wondrous cruel experience of the siege of Jaicur, or Dejagore, that has twisted so many members of the Company and burdened them with vulnerabilities and obsessions that will shape their minds and souls for as long as they survive.

"That's a good idea," Sleepy said. "Although you can count on getting resistance from the men. Can you imagine Runmust and Iqbal being willing to go anywhere where they're not elbow to elbow with each other?"

Sahra sighed. She shook her head slowly. "If the Gunni are right about the Wheel of Life then I must have been something more wicked than a Shadowmaster in a previous life. This one never stops punishing me."

"Let me tell you, it's harder being Vehdna. You don't have other lives to blame it on. You just go crazy trying to figure out why God is so angry with you in this one."

Sahra nodded. The moment had passed. She was in control again. "You'd think I would've made my peace with this life by now, wouldn't you?"

Sleepy thought that she had, about as well as she could, but did not say so. She did not want to push Sahra back onto the path of self-examination. That could get tiresome fast.

"We have a major staff meeting. I want your help. I want you to think in broader terms. I'm rethinking my strategy. The distances are turning out to be too great for a headlong rush. We're getting weaker fast while our enemies are getting stronger. I want your thoughts on different approaches."

"I'll be all right. I have to have these spells once in a while just to get by."

46

Nijha:
The Darkness Always Comes

Darkness came to Nijha. With it came an almost supernatural silence. Within the crude walls the senior commanders were clustered with Sleepy and Sahra. Outside, the soldiers were cooking, repairing harnesses and equipment, or, mainly, just sleeping the sleep of the exhausted. A night's rest was never enough to recover fully from a hard day's march. Weariness accumulated, and more so when a force covered a lot of miles in a hurry.

For the first time since his liberation Goblin found himself unsupervised, overlooked, forgotten. He did not trust his observations for a while. These were sneaky people. Possibly they were testing him.

Eventually it became evident that he really was running free, unmonitored. This was early in the game and way remote but no better opportunity was ever likely to arise.

Narayan stirred warily, though his despair was such that he could generate little concern about his own continued well-being. Already he had been separated farther, if not longer, from the Daughter of Night than ever before since her birth. If he lost her there would be no reason to go on. It would be time to go home to Kina. There would be nothing more he could do. And there was little chance he would get any opportunity ever again, anyway. He was alive now only because these people were saving him as a plaything for the girl's birth parents. Again.

His days and hours were numbered and once again his faith was being tested sorely.

He heard a faint, breathy sound that seemed vaguely familiar. And it should be, he thought. His heart began to hammer. That was a Deceiver recognition sign meant for use in darkness exactly like this, where the usual hand signals would not work. He murmured countersigns. The effort set off a coughing fit.

The exchange continued until Narayan was satisfied that he had been located by a religious brother. He asked, "Why have you come? It won't be possible to rescue me." He used the secret Deceiver cant, which amounted to the final test. It would, at least, advise him of the status of his visitor. Not many recent converts were yet that advanced in their studies.

"The Goddess herself has sent me to relay her love and her esteem and her appreciation of all your sacrifices. She bid me to assure you that your rewards will be great. She wants you to understand that her resurrection is nearer than any nonbeliever suspects. She wants you to know that your efforts and your trials and your steadfast faith have made the difference. She wants you to know that her enemies soon will be overwhelmed and devoured. She wants you to know that she's watching over you and that you'll stand at her side when we celebrate the Year of the Skulls. She wants you to know that of all those who have ever served her, even of her many saints, you were her most favored."

The Shadowgate:
The Repairmen

The encampment below the Shadowgate became the hub of a flood of Unknown Shadow traffic as Tobo tried to head off the Voroshk threat. He remained especially worried about Longshadow's keepers till Shivetya somehow assured him that they were invisible to Voroshk eyes.

"Do you trust him?" Lady asked. She being the most naturally paranoid of any of us at the Shadowgate. "He might try to make a better deal with the Voroshk."

"What better deal? We're going to give him what he wants. Without trying to control him or even to get much out of him."

"Bet he thinks we're too good to be true, then." She was in a mood.

I asked, "What happened to the golden pickax? The Deceiver key to the Shadowgates."

After a pause to make up his mind about what to admit, Tobo said, "I left it with Shivetya. We may need it again. When it's time to kill Kina. I couldn't think of any other place where it would be safer from her followers." He was troubled as he looked the rest of us over. He was thinking he should have kept that to himself. The golden pickax was an extremely holy Strangler relic that could also be used to help set Kina free.

He was afraid that at least one of us was sure to tell somebody what we had just heard.

I t was a long night followed by what promised to be a longer day.
For the uninvolved members of the band these were trying times. There was nothing for them to do but play cards and wonder if the people of the New City would be crazy enough to attack us.

Panda Man and Spook mostly watched the game. They did not do well when they played. Tonk is one of the simplest games ever invented, rules-wise, but a huge part of it is the table talk that goes along with the actual picking up, discarding and laying down of cards. A group accustomed to one another is an entirely different animal from one where the players barely speak the same language. Wherever the Company stops for fifteen minutes a tonk game soon develops. The tradition began ages before my time. It will persist long after I am gone.

Gone. I tried to imagine what life might have been like had I left the Company sometime in the past. My imagination was not up to the task. I confess. I do not have the strength of personality to abandon everything I know, even when all that is just a meandering, unhappy path that, too often, wanders through the outlying marches of hell.

I was a zombie most of the day, carrying that hod for my young bricklayer while most of me was elsewhere, boldly adventuring across those fields of might-have-been.

Sometime late in the afternoon I told Lady, "I probably should tell you this more often. I love you and I'm glad Fate conspired to bring our lives together."

I stunned her into silence. I know Swan and Murgen gaped and spent some time trying to figure out if I thought I was dying.

T he Voroshk had not overlooked us. They were cautious. They showed themselves briefly several times during the day. Their customary arrogance seemed in abeyance.

Once I left my own preoccupations behind I asked Tobo, "What do you suppose they're up to?" We had talked about it before but I am never entirely comfortable taking a sorcerer's motives at face value.

"Looking for hope. Or anything that will give them an edge. I expect that, right now, their world is more like hell than almost anything any priest ever imagined. Most of the surviving shadows from the plain must be running loose there. One family of sorcerers, however wonderful their weapons, just has no chance to stop what's happening. Not before the devastation reaches the scale of an end of the world catastrophe."

Once upon a time I might have felt bad for the Voroshk and the people of Khatovar. This time when I examined my soul I found not much more than indifference within me.

"How much longer before you've finished making all your modifications?" Lady demanded. She was anxious to head north. From oblique remarks I gathered that she wanted to rejoin the main force before disaster struck it. What she could do to avert a disaster was beyond me. She did not have enough magic currently to start a fire without adding flint and steel to the mix.

"Ten minutes, tops," Tobo replied. "There's this one last braided strand that needs reweaving and we'll have us not just a completely healthy Shadowgate, it'll be the toughest there ever was. Tough enough that what happened to the Khatovar gate can't happen here. In fact, it's already all those things. What this spell rope is going to do is create a little pocket of darkness that's invisible from outside so killer shadows can be turned into invisible sentries. They'll be there ready to jump out at anybody who tries to get through who isn't already approved by us or Shivetya."

"Neat," I said. Lady scowled. She was determined to believe that we were placing too much trust in the golem.

She seemed unable to recognize that trust was not a large part of this equation. She said, "We're going to have company in a minute."

I looked up. Two Voroshk sorcerers were coming down the slope, following the old road, inside what would have been protection if they had not blown up their own Shadowgate. A third post-rider remained a dot above the horizon, a remote witness. I asked, "You think they did more damage getting through the barrier and onto the road?"

After only a glance, Tobo said, "No. I think they came in the far end and flew here, following the roads. The other one paced them from above."

Admirable stupidity, I thought. The two at ground level had no chance of getting back out before dark. Did they think we would protect them from the night? If so they were huge daydreamers.

The Voroshk dismounted a hundred yards away. They walked toward us like walking was a foreign experience. Riding the flying fencepost had to be a huge status symbol back in Khatovar. So huge, walking was never done where your inferiors could see you.

"How long now?" Lady asked Tobo.

"Fifteen seconds. After that I'll fake it for a bit. Then we all step back through the gate. Are Dad and the others alert?"

Alert was not strong enough a word. A variety of missile weapons were ready. So was one fireball projector but it would not see use while the Voroshk remained on the plain side. The barriers could be damaged by fireballs. Arrows and crossbow bolts, however, could pass through and the wounds they made would heal in moments.

Not that arrows were likely to accomplish much against these chunky old men.

They did seem overweight. They projected an aura of fatness behind the constant stirring of their black cloaks.

"There. I think that should do it," Tobo said.

Click. Click. Click. That swiftly we three backed through the Shadowgate into our own world. Tobo sealed the way. We waited. The kid said, "One of these will be the father of our two troublemakers."

Probably. The Voroshk did appear interested in communicating. They knew someone on our side spoke the language of the forvalaka.

Their luck was in. Of all the Black Company people who could have been there with Tobo they got me and Lady.

They would get no happiness out of that, though. Their kind rubbed me the wrong way. I would make nothing easy for them.

The Shadowgate:
The Warlords of the Air

These Voroshk, who actually introduced themselves—as Nashun the Researcher and the First Father—both spoke the language of Juniper. Nashun the Researcher had by far the best command. Neither had social skills of a sort likely to put a smile on the face of many mothers. It was clear that the demonstration of manners toward persons outside the family was an exercise with which they had little familiarity.

After the introductions I stated the obvious. "You people sure got yourselves into big trouble."

You could feel the Voroshk closing their eyes and sighing inside all that black material.

"We will survive," the boss Voroshk declared. He strained to keep anger and arrogance out of his voice. He had less success with confidence, which made me wonder if he did not really mean it.

"No doubt. What I saw of your family's capabilities impressed me. But honestly, you realize that your family's survival will require more than just fending off the shadows."

Nashun made a dismissive gesture with one gloved hand. "We come to you because we want our children back."

He spoke clearly and slowly enough that Lady caught that. She made a surprised little noise that might have been half a laugh.

"You're out of luck. They may prove useful. Nor have we any incentive to give them back."

Their anger seemed a palpable force.

Tobo felt it. He said, "Warn them that any power they use to try to break through will bounce back at them. Tell them that the harder they try the worse they'll get hurt."

I translated. Our visitors were not impressed by anything a boy said. Neither did they experiment. They did recall events at their own Shadowgate. The Researcher said, "We are prepared to make an exchange."

"What do you have to trade?"

"You still have people on this plain."

"Go for it. They're covered. When the dust settles you'll be picking up dead family members." Of that I was confident. Because Tobo trusted Shivetya completely. "You're powerful but ignorant. Like an ox. You don't know the plain. It's alive. It's our ally."

Smoke should have rolled out of their ears. Goblin sometimes did that in the old days. But these men had no sense of humor.

Their desperation overcame their anger.

"Explain," Nashun hissed.

"You know nothing about the plain but you're arrogant enough to believe that your power will be supreme there. In a realm of the gods. Evidently you don't even know your own world's history. The people you're facing, that you believe you can threaten, are spiritual descendants of soldiers sent out from Khatovar five hundred years ago."

"What happened before the Voroshk does not signify. However, you demonstrate ignorance of your own."

"It *is* of consequence. You want something from the last Free Company of Khatovar. And you don't have anything to offer in exchange. Except, possibly, that disdained history and a little contemporary knowledge."

Neither man commented.

Lady told me, "Ask them why they want these kids back so bad. They're safe over here."

I asked.

"They are family," the First Father said.

His voice had a quality which made that seem not only plausible but possibly even true.

I said, "They're a long way away. They've been travelling northward steadily since they arrived. One is deathly ill."

"They have their *rheitgeistiden*. They can get down here in a few hours."

"I think this guy is for real," I told Lady. "He's really got some mad-ass notion that I'd give those kids their toys and turn them loose, just on his say-so. They sure don't have to work to survive in Khatovar."

The Researcher picked up the one word. "I mentioned your ignorance. Listen, Outsider. Khatovar is not our world. Khatovar was one city of darkness, where damned souls worshipped a Goddess of the night. That evil city was expunged from the earth before the Voroshk arose. Its people were hunted down and exterminated. They have been forgotten. And they will remain forgotten. Never will any Soldier of Darkness be permitted to return."

Once upon a time, on a lazy day, ages before he had become the vessel he was now, Goblin had told me that I would never get to Khatovar. Never. It would forever remain just beyond the horizon. I could get closer and closer and closer but I would never arrive. So I had imagined I had set foot in Khatovar. But I had only been to the world where Khatovar had existed once upon a time.

"Time itself has evened the score. That which Khatovar sent out came back. And the world that killed Khatovar will die."

"Did you catch that?" Lady asked.

"Huh? Catch what?"

"He used the world evil. We don't hear that much in this part of the world. People don't believe in it."

"These guys aren't from this part of the world." I returned to the language of Juniper. "Given a complete, working breakdown on the construction and operation of your flying logs, and of the material from which your clothing is made, I'd say we could give you what you want."

Lady did her best to keep the others up-to-date on what was being said. She did not always get it right.

Nashun the Researcher could not grasp the enormity of my demand. He tried speaking three different times, failed, finally turned to the First Father in mute appeal. I was sure his hidden face was taut with despair.

I told my guys, "It might be wise to back away from the Shadowgate. These people are about out of patience."

I felt wonderfully wicked. I always do when I frustrate overly powerful, responsible-to-no-one types who think all existence was created only for their pleasure and exploitation.

I told the Voroshk, "It'll be dark soon. Then the shadows will come out." And, as the Voroshk exchanged glances, I borrowed from Narayan Singh. "When dealing with the Black Company you would do well to remember: Darkness always comes."

Lady's expression was one of less than one hundred percent approval when I turned away. "That could've gone better."

"I let my feelings intrude. I should know better. But talk wasn't going to get us anywhere, anyway. They think too much of themselves and too little of everyone else."

"Then you're giving up the dream of returning to Khatovar."

The Voroshk made their first furious attempt to bust through the Shadowgate. I did warn them.

They did not want to listen.

It was worse than I had imagined it could be.

It was worse than Tobo had predicted.

The countermagical blast hurled both sorcerers all the way up the slope to the edge of the plain, bouncing and tumbling all the way. By some miracle neither broke the barrier protecting the road. Maybe Shivetya was watching over then.

One still had shown no sign of recovering when I gave up watching. I told Tobo, "I reckon it's time to go, now. Those guys might have gotten the message this time."

I did not look back. The trials the Voroshk faced left me confident that they would never become a problem to my world.

As we descended the hill I asked, "Anybody think there might be a connection between the Shadowmasters and the Voroshk? They seem to have gotten their start about the right time. And the Shadowmasters tried to sever all connections with the past in Hsien. It was just too big a job. I wonder what we'd find out if we talked to some ordinary farming stiff over there?"

"I can ask Shivetya," Tobo said. "And the prisoners." But he did not sound particularly motivated.

49

Nijha:
Place of the Dead

Sahra kept calling for more torches. As though bringing in enough light would nullify the disaster. By the time the Captain arrived there were fifty torches, lamps and lanterns illuminating what had been a stable before the Company arrived.

"Strangled?" Sleepy asked.

"Strangled."

"I'm tempted to use the word 'ironic' but I fear there's no irony in it at all. Doj. That white raven of Croaker's was hanging around outside. Find it. There were little people hanging around here, some of them supposedly watching Singh. I want to know what they saw."

Sleepy had a good idea what she would hear from the Unknown Shadows. It would be a variation on reports she had had before. She said, "I'll want to send the news south, too."

Nothing happened around the Black Company without some hobyah there to witness it. The soldiers from Hsien understood that perfectly. They took it for granted. They tended to be well-behaved. But someone without experience of life in Hsien would not take the Unknown Shadows as seriously.

A minute later, Sleepy asked, "I don't suppose anyone's seen Goblin, have they? I don't reckon anyone knows who was supposed to be watching him?"

Riverwalker said, "He was right over there till a minute ago."

Sleepy looked, considered, muttered, "No doubt right up to the second I decided to consult the Unknown Shadows about what they saw." Which would have been the same moment he would have realized that his recent history was no mystery to anyone. The moment when he realized that Sleepy had been paying out the hangman's rope while seeing what she could learn.

Riverwalker asked. "Want him rounded up? In one piece?"

"No." Not now. Not when the best wizard she had was an old, old man whose skills, outside using a sword, were too weak even to put hexes on people and animals. "But I wouldn't mind knowing where he is." Doj could manage that. The

Unknown Shadows communicated with him. Sometimes. When the mood took them. "What you do need to do right now is get extra guards around the Voroshk. Goblin showed a lot of interest in them while we were traveling. I don't want anything happening to them and I don't want them wandering off." It did not occur to her to reinforce the company responsible for the comatose sorcerer Howler. But Fortune stood behind her there.

Goblin, it developed, had grabbed a couple of fast horses and some loose supplies and had gotten himself out of Nijha, headed north, all without attracting any particular notice. Sleepy very nearly indulged in profanity when she received the report. Someone pointed out that the little wizard always had had that knack. Sleepy growled, "Then somebody should have been watching for him to take advantage of it."

Uncle Doj told her, "I can't stop him or control him but I can make life miserable for him."

"How?"

"His horses. The Black Hounds can have a lot of fun with them. And when he tries to lead them to water . . ." He chuckled wickedly.

"Send them." Sleepy beckoned Sahra. "I kept leaning both ways during the meeting. Looking for a sign. I've just had it. We're not going to rush in anymore. We'll move ahead slowly, into more hospitable country, and stop somewhere where we can support ourselves without much trouble. We'll wait till everyone catches up. And issue a call for volunteers willing to support the Prabrindrah Drah and the Radisha." If anyone even remembered them.

"Wait especially for my son. Yes." Sahra was angry and unhappy but too tired to fight much. "Now that Murgen is no longer the major tool."

"Especially for Tobo, yes. Tonight it was clear that without Tobo we're in trouble bad."

Sahra said nothing more. She was tired of fighting a battle in which even the men she wanted to protect refused to honor her concern.

50

The Taglian Territories:
The Palace

The Taglian field army slowly assembled astride the Rock Road in lightly settled country midway between Dejagore and the fortified crossings over the River Main at Ghoja. Another, less powerful force, consisting of troops from the southern provinces, assembled outside Dejagore. And a third gathered outside Taglios itself. There seemed no reason to suspect that the force at Dejagore should have any trouble denying that city to a force such as that the Black Company was bringing up. Mogaba expected his enemies to swing west once they descended from the highlands, possibly marching as far as the Naghir River, which they could follow north, then swing eastward again and try to get over the Main at one of the lesser downriver crossings. He intended to let them march and march and wear themselves down. He intended to let them do whatever they wanted till he slammed the door shut behind them. Once he had them north of the Main he could build a ring around them and slowly squeeze.

The Great General was feeling quite positive. Taglios was restive but not rebellious. Even the most remote garrison commanders were bringing their soldiers to the assembly points with their units at near strength even though some harvesting would commence in the far south before the end of the month.

Harvest season inevitably precipitated higher desertion rates.

Best of all, the Protector was staying away. Her tinkering and interference always made his task more difficult. And, of course, it was always his fault when a bastardized plan fell apart.

The Great General gathered his senior staff and inner circle, which included a dozen generals as well as Ghopal and Aridatha Singh. He told them, "The plan appears to be coming together perfectly. With a couple of nudges and timed withdrawals I think we can lead them to the ford at Vehdna-Bota. I still wish we had better communications with the Protector. But she can't find enough crows anymore. Some plague is wiping them out. I seldom hear from her more than once a day. And then, often as not, she'll waste time on weather news or a flue epidemic in Prehbehlbed."

Nor were there any shadows about, nor any of the Protector's lesser spies. Mogaba did not mention that. Taglians were dedicated conspirators. Let them continue to think that there might be eyes in the corners, watching.

Only his own conspiracy need go forward.

The Great General had more to preoccupy him than how to isolate and destroy his enemy. He suspected there was a definite question about the identity of Taglios' most dangerous foe.

Something about this incarnation of the Black Company had Soulcatcher so concerned that she insisted on focusing all her attention there. Something about this incarnation of the Black Company had touched almost everyone of substance within the Taglian empire, though news of their return had barely had time to spread and there were no eyewitness reports available at all. All customary enmity and internal friction seemed to be dwindling at a time when, normally, factionalism should be exploding as old antagonists tried to use the situation to their advantage.

And Mogaba had found that he was thinking less and less about the practicalities of eliminating the Protector, more and more obsessively about destroying the Black Company. Not just defeating them but obliterating them. To the last man, woman, child, horse, mule, flea and louse.

After decades of unhappy fortune Mogaba was naturally wary of everything—including his own emotional state.

He had begun keeping a personal journal the day he had made the decision to betray Soulcatcher, to track his thoughts and emotions during the subsequent, stressful days. It was a journal he opened only in brilliant sunlight. It was a journal he would destroy before actually taking action against the Protector because there were names in it he did not want betrayed if he failed—and was lucky enough to die before she captured him.

Lately he had noticed an evolution in his thinking about the Company. An accelerating evolution. A frightening evolution.

He had become suspicious of his own reason.

Following a general meeting to consider policy for the empire the Great General met with the men responsible for the capital city.

"Kina is active again," Mogaba murmured. Ghopal and Aridatha listened politely. He was referencing events from before their time, that they knew only by repute. "She's doing that thing where she gradually shapes everyone's prejudices."

They offered him blank looks.

"Not history buffs, eh?" Mogaba explained. "The strangest part was, nobody ever wondered why they were terrified. They just didn't remember that three years earlier they'd never heard of the Black Company."

Ghopal said, "What you're saying is, the Strangler Goddess has a particular fear

of the Black Company. She wants the whole world to climb all over them and destroy them. Even if blood has to be spilled."

"Isn't this an interesting quandary," Aridatha said. "If we can overcome the
Black Company, we'll still have to deal with the Protector. If we knock her down,
too, then we'll still have to handle the Stranglers and Kina, in order to prevent the
Year of the Skulls. Wave after wave. No end to it."

"No end to it," Mogaba agreed. "And I'm getting to be quite an old man." He
had begun to nurture an outrageous notion almost as soon as he had determined
that he was being manipulated. "There are a couple of old records I want to check.
I want you both back here same time tomorrow."

The Great General did not lack courage. The next evening he led Ghopal and
Aridatha into the brightly lit room. He presented a more convincing case for his be-
lief that Kina had awakened, drawing heavily upon excerpts from copies of Black
Company Annals residing in the national library.

Aridatha Singh said, "I believe you. I just wonder what happened to wake her
up again."

"Ghopal?"

"I'm not sure I understand. But I don't think I have to. Aridatha does. I trust his
wisdom."

"Then I'll talk to Aridatha. But you listen." Mogaba chuckled.

Aridatha listened to his idea, the reasoning behind it, frowning all the while.
Ghopal seemed aghast. But he kept his mouth shut. Aridatha went off alone with his
thoughts. After a while he nodded reluctantly and said. "I have a brother in Dejagore.
I'll find a reason to go visit. I know some people who might listen to what you have to
say if it's me doing the talking."

"What?"

Aridatha said, "You recall a few years ago when the Company underground
here started kidnapping people? Willow Swan, the Purohita, and so on? I was one of
the people they snatched."

Ghopal wanted to know why, and Mogaba wondered how he had gotten away.

"I got away because they let me go. They only picked me up because they wanted
to show me off to somebody they were holding already." Aridatha took a long, deep
breath and revealed his great secret. "My father. Narayan Singh. They were showing
him their power."

"Narayan Singh? *The* Narayan Singh? The Strangler?" Ghopal asked.

"That Narayan Singh. I didn't know. Not till then. Our mother told us our father was dead. She believed it, I think. The Shadowmasters conscripted him into
their labor battalions during their first invasion, before the Black Company ever arrived from the north. I was the youngest of four children. I'm pretty sure the older
ones knew the truth. My brother Sugriva moved to Dejagore and changed his

name. My sister Khaditya changed hers, too. Her husband would die of mortification if he knew."

"You've never mentioned this before."

"I think you can understand why."

"Oh. I do. That's a cruel burden to bear." Mogaba already found himself responding to the Deceiver connection. With exactly the sort of paranoid fear everyone did to any Deceiver connection. It was inevitable. Aloud, he said, "I wonder how those people ever trust each other?"

Aridatha replied, "I suspect you'd have to be inside and a part of it all to understand. I think the biggest part of it, though, would be their faith in their Goddess."

The Great General looked at Ghopal Singh. "If the Greys have objections I need to hear them now."

Ghopal shook his head. "Only one Grey is going to know about this. For now. The others wouldn't understand."

"Aridatha. You have someone you trust to take charge while you're gone?" The City Battalions did not know they were part of a conspiracy to free Taglios from its protector. It was necessary to keep firm control there.

"Yes. But no one in the know. If you have unusual requests you'll have to justify them based on what's going on in the city." The soldiers understood that their role was to keep the peace if the population became too restive for the Greys alone.

Mogaba asked, "Are there enough provocations to make any excuses sound good?"

Ghopal showed a large array of teeth. Shadar were proud of their well-kept teeth. "That's almost amusing. Since the news reached the street that the Black Company really is back, there's actually been less related graffiti. As though real Company sympathizers don't want to risk identification and the non-Company vandals responsible for most of it suddenly don't want to be identified with any terror that's for real."

"Terror?"

"You were right, what you said last night. There's a growing fear of the Company out there. Like you said, it was in olden times. I don't understand but it's helping keep the peace just when I expected a lot more trouble."

"If you need provocations and the villains don't provide them, feel free to create your own. Aridatha, you know what needs doing. Do it. As quickly as possible. Before events move so fast they rob us of more chances." Though it could happen almost momentarily, Mogaba had abandoned any real hope of catching the Protector unaware as she returned to the city.

At the moment it seemed she did not plan to return until the Black Company invasion was settled.

51

The Taglian Territories: The Middle Ground

Soulcatcher, in full leather and fuller ire, stalked the perimeter of the encampment midway between Ghoja and Dejagore. A dozen frightened officers followed, each silently appealing for mercy to his choice of god or gods. The Protector in a rage was a disaster no one wanted to experience. Her excesses made no more sense than do those of a tornado.

"They haven't moved. For six days now they've hardly taken a step. After hurtling northward like the storm itself, so fast we were killing ourselves trying to pull something together fast enough to stop them. What're they doing? What changed suddenly?" As always when she was under stress Soulcatcher was a babble of conflicting voices. That added to the uneasiness of the men tagging after her. None had had any experience with her before her arrival in camp. The actuality was more unnerving than the stories predicted. She seemed every bit as cruel and capricious as any god. Several graves beyond the perimeter attested to the violence of her temper.

These sycophants would never find out but those who died had been chosen only after extended supernatural espionage. Not one had been a devoted servant of the Protectorate. Each had said so aloud. Additionally, none had been particularly competent leaders and that had been clear to their soldiers and compatriots. They had attained their positions through nepotism or cronyism, not ability.

Soulcatcher was culling her officer corps. She was disappointed that necessity prevented her from doing more. That corps was terrible. But she would take no responsibility for that. Of course.

How poor would it have been without the efforts of the Great General? Probably an awful, corrupt joke without a punchline. Without Mogaba's dedicated nurturing there would have been little to assemble here.

How to keep it here? The desertion rate was supportable now but showing signs of rising. Was that the enemy strategy? Wait until the Taglian armies melted because of the demands of the approaching harvest? Would they charge north again then? It sounded like a Black Company sort of thing to do. Indications were, they had the wealth to maintain a force in the field a long time.

Mogaba's messages indicated his own suspicions concerning a similar strategy. He was tailoring his own approach toward getting his enemy to take the long way around, into a trap.

Soulcatcher did not believe there would be any chance to trap the Black Company. Their intelligence resources were much too wonderful. While her own continued to fade. All species of crows were becoming endangered. Mice, bats, rats, owls, those sorts of creatures had no range. There seemed to be no modern sources of quality crystal or worthy mercury with which to create a scrying glass or bowl. The shadows she still controlled were few and feeble and frightened and she refused to risk them in enemy territory, often because each time she did a few more would not come back. And for now she was cut off from her only source of replacements.

She glanced skyward, saw vultures circling to the north, over woods which ran from right to left for as far as she could see. The growth followed a shallow stream. Her sister had won a small victory over the Shadowmasters there, ages ago, soon after the Black Company had suffered the disaster that led to the siege of Dejagore.

"I'm going to walk up there and see what those vultures find so interesting."

No one gave in to the urge to protest.

Maybe the vultures would dine on her.

"None of you need to come with me."

Relief was obvious.

52

The Nether Taglian Territories:
Lady Made Grumpy Noises

Lady was in a towering rage. I could not recall ever having seen her so close to losing control. "How the *hell* could they let that happen? Somebody was supposed to stay in that little shit's pocket every second!"

No one bothered to respond. She did not want answers. Not really. She wanted somebody to hurt.

Tobo was quietly busy talking to things that were there only when you looked away. Big things, little things, human-looking things and things that had escaped from madmen's nightmares. Goblin was going to be found. Goblin was going to be tracked and harassed and hurt if at all possible, all the live-long day. Insofar as this fragment of the Company was concerned Goblin was going to be the main mission from this day forward. He was to be hunted down and exorcised—or exterminated—before he could engineer any more disasters on Kina's behalf.

Though long out of practice and definitely out of the habit, Lady hurled a deadly spell at an inoffensive scrub pine. The tree began to wilt almost immediately.

"What the hell was that?" I demanded. "I thought you couldn't . . ."

"Be quiet. Let me think." So astonished was Lady that she forgot to be angry about Goblin.

I was quiet. I gave her all the thinking room a girl could want.

Was there a silver lining inside our latest black cloud?

My at-the-moment not very lucky wife called, "Tobo. Next message you send north, ask if the little shit got away with one of the gate keys. Or anything else un-usual."

Tobo made little gestures to the air, then replied, "I checked on that already. He got away with nothing more than two horses and one saddle. Not even a sausage. He's probably eating bugs. The only unusual thing mentioned is that nobody no-ticed him. An eventuation almost certainly artificial in origin."

"Because?"

"Because he's being damned hard to notice right now. The Black Hounds shouldn't be having trouble finding and following him. But they are. He's as elusive as a ghost. Each time they do make contact it's because he's been following the road, without deviating, and they can just wait for him to show up."

"Following the road where?"

"North. Toward the junction with the Rock Road. Though because he isn't talking his plans are unclear."

Tobo still had a sense of humor about what was going on.

I asked Lady, "How did you manage to murder that tree?"

She mused, "A good question. Without a good answer. I never felt any sharp-ened Kina presence."

"You think it might have to do with Goblin? We know Kina must've put a piece of herself into him or he wouldn't even be alive."

"I would've sensed something before. I think. Tobo. Did you feel anything weird about Goblin?"

"Of course." The boy was curt. He was trying to work. Old folks kept interrupting. "He wasn't Uncle Goblin anymore. But he wasn't any more powerful than he was before, either."

I said, "Maybe it was something that didn't come out until he got the chance to kill Narayan."

Debate on the why increasingly focused on the fact that crippled old Narayan had been in no shape to run or do anything on behalf of his Goddess and, if left in our hands, would have been compelled to reveal whatever he knew eventually. And while most of us would view his murder as a betrayal by his Goddess, what we knew of Deceiver doctrine suggested that he might actually see it as a reward. Having been strangled for the Goddess, Narayan would go directly to Deceiver paradise where, no doubt, his rewards would be commensurate with his service.

I tend toward the cynical view where religion is concerned.

After a silence so extended I decided she was not listening, my beloved responded, "You might just be smarter than you look. She'd expect us to be suspicious enough to watch every breath Goblin took. So she'd want him to seem as normal as possible until he got a solid chance to get away." She began to pace. "Poor Goblin. That would've been mostly him, maybe even really trying to help his old friends as much as he could. And he'll still be partly Goblin, but a prisoner inside his own body." The hollowness of her voice indicated that she might have been through that herself, once upon a time.

"Which tells us nothing of his purpose. Or of Kina's."

"She's in prison. She wants out. That doesn't take any special figuring."

"But there'll be a grand plan. Old Goblin didn't get his soul eaten up just so he could be flung across the pond of the world like a skipping stone. He's going to go somewhere and he's going to do something and if he gets away with it all the rest of us are going to end up really sorry."

Lady grunted. She was still mostly angry.

I said, "He headed north. What's up there that would interest Kina?"

Tobo interrupted his sweet talk with his pets. "Booboo." He sounded as unhappy as I felt. "He's going to take Narayan's place watching over the Daughter of Night."

"Yeah. Only there'll be a big chunk of Goddess in him so he'll be a lot more dangerous than Narayan ever was."

Lady glared around her with an expression that made me think she did not have much trouble seeing Tobo's friends. "Do you think my sister can be made to hear one of those?"

You could have heard a stack of pans drop. Even the animals quieted down.

I asked, "You have something in mind?"

"Yes. We send her a message. Tell her what's going on with Goblin. It's as much in her interest to stop him as it is in ours."

"And she has a personal interest," Tobo reminded us.

I understood immediately but Lady needed it explained. "Goblin is the reason Soulcatcher has a bad leg."

"Oh. Of course. I remember now."

She ought. She was there, spying on everything through the eyes of a white crow, during the kidnapping of the Radisha. That same night Goblin managed to trick Soulcatcher into springing a booby trap. The result had been serious and irreversible damage to her right heel.

Tobo said, "She gets around pretty well now. She wears a special boot and brace and is supported by several specialized spells. She only limps when she's really tired."

"Ah. She'll definitely want to chat with Goblin, then. She's always been a sore loser."

"Just a thought," I offered. "What happens if Soulcatcher turns Goblin into her own version of the Taken? And maybe Booboo, too? Word is, there were times when she showed a few powers of her own."

"Make a slave out of a Goddess?" Lady was incredulous. I raised an eyebrow. She protested, "What I did wasn't the same thing at all. What I did was pure parasitism. I wormed in so she couldn't get me out without hurting herself."

"And now you're getting a little of that back?"

"But it doesn't feel the same. Tobo. Can you send a message to my sister or not?"

"I can try. In fact, I *can* do it. Easily. The real question would be whether or not she'd listen."

"She'll listen or I'll kick her butt."

It took all of us a moment to realize she was joking. She did so so rarely.

Tobo began concentrating on the task of getting an extended message to Soulcatcher.

Again I cautioned, "There's a risk in this."

Lady just made one of her grumpy noises. She was turning into a cranky old witch.

53

The Taglian Territories:
A Haunted Wood

Soulcatcher glanced back before entering the wood. "So where are they all?" And in a firm male voice she demanded, "What happened to all the suck-ups?"

Another voice, "Somebody should've wanted to kiss up."

A puzzled voice asked, "They always do, don't they?"

"Are we losing it here?"

"I don't like it."

"This isn't fun anymore." Petulant, spoiled child voice.

"Most of the time we're just going through the motions. There aren't any challenges here."

"Even when there are it's almost impossible to get impassioned enough to care."

Most of those voices were businesslike but jaded.

"It's hard to keep going on fuel like hunger for revenge alone."

"It's hard to be alone, period."

That remark brought on an extended silence. Soulcatcher did not have a voice for expressing the emotional costs of being who she was. Not out loud. Ferocious mad-killer sorcerers do not whine because nobody likes them.

The growth along the creek had a sharp boundary. In another time the land must have been groomed by human occupation. Soulcatcher listened. The wood, which was a little more than a mile wide, seemed remarkably silent. There should have been a racket from work parties harvesting firewood and timber for use around the camp. But there was nothing. And she did not recall authorizing a holiday. Something had frightened the soldiers away.

Yet she sensed no danger.

After a moment, though, she did detect a supernatural presence.

She glanced upward. Those vultures continued to circle. They were lower now. They seemed to be wheeling above the presence she sensed.

Warily, she probed farther and deeper. She had remarkably well-honed senses when she cared to concentrate.

This presence was like nothing in her experience. Something like a powerful shadow, yet with a strong implication of working intelligence. Not a demon or some such otherworldly entity, though. Something that felt like it was a part of nature but still having about it a hint of not belonging to this world. But how? Not of this world but not otherworldly? . . . Something very powerful but not driven by malice. At the moment. Something timeless, accustomed to patience, mildly impatient right now, again a smart-shadow thing like those stalkers down south had been.

Soulcatcher extended her senses to their maximum. This thing was waiting for her. For her alone. It had repulsed everything but those vultures. She had to be careful. Despite her ennui she did not want to trigger a fatal ambush.

There was nothing.

She stepped forward.

She did so while assembling a quiver of sudden and deadly spells. She squinted behind her mask, looking for this thing that wanted to see her.

It grew stronger but less focused as she moved toward it. For a moment it seemed that it was all around her—even while being in one place somewhere ahead of her. When she did arrive where her senses told her it ought to be, she saw nothing.

That place was a small clearing just off the Rock Road, across the shallow stream. She saw several Vehdna grave markers and a few Gunni memorial posts with time-gnawed prayer wheels on top. This must be where her sister fought the Shadowlander cavalry during her flight from Dejagore. In a time so long ago that she still had believed Narayan Singh to be her friend and champion.

Sunlight tumbled through the leaves overhead. It dappled the clearing. Soulcatcher settled on a rotten log that protruded from what might once must have been an earthwork. "I'm here. I'm waiting."

Something large moved at the edge of her vision. She got the impression of a black feline. But when she turned she saw nothing.

"So that's the way it's going to be, eh?"

"Thus it must be. Ever." The response seemed to come from nowhere in particular and it was not clear whether she heard it with her ears or inside her head.

"What do you want from me?" Soulcatcher used a deep masculine voice heavy with menace.

The presence was amused, not intimidated. "I bring a message from your old friend Croaker."

Croaker was no friend. In fact, she was distinctly piqued with that man. He had not been entirely cooperative when she had tried to seduce him and now he had refused to stay buried after she had tried to kill him. Still, he was the reason she had a head on her shoulders these days. And that tiny edge would be why this communication was arriving in his name.

"Go ahead."

The whatever-it-was did as she bid. As she listened she poked around in an effort to fathom its true nature. While searching for some handle she could grasp to make it over into an agent of her own.

It sensed what she was doing. It was amused. Not troubled. Not frightened. Not inclined to react. Just amused.

Soulcatcher reviewed the story carefully once the spook had finished relating it. It sounded plausible. If incomplete. But why expect those people to be entirely forthcoming in such a situation?

Try as she might she could discover no obvious trap. They sounded worried down there. This news could explain their sudden shift of strategy.

Goblin possessed by Kina. Narayan Singh dead. The Daughter of Night running loose. . . . Not running loose at all! In the hands of her troops, on the Rock Road somewhere south of Dejagore, very probably looking for an opportunity to get loose.

Goblin might arrange that.

She bounced up off the rotten log, ennui gone. "Tell Croaker he can consider communications opened. I'll take steps to deal with the situation. Go! Go!"

A flicker. Like a shadow passing through and deserting at the same time. It left a deeply felt chill and one more uncertain glimpse of an impossibly large, catlike form moving away at an impossible pace.

From the nearby Rock Road came the rattle and clop of a large party headed south. Camels seemed to be involved. That meant civilians. There were no camels in her armies. She hated camels. They were filthy animals with nasty tempers even on their best days.

She leapt across the creek and hurried to the edge of the woods, emerging not a hundred feet from where a caravan was doing the same. Civilian it was, but most of the wagons and camels and mules would discharge their cargo in her camp.

The caravaners spied her. They were startled. And frightened.

Her blood was moving again. She always enjoyed the impact she made when she appeared unexpectedly.

As she turned and raised her gaze to the circling vultures she thought she glimpsed a familiar face among the merchants and teamsters. Aridatha Singh? Here? How? Why? But when she looked more closely she saw no Aridatha. Maybe it was just someone who looked like Singh. Maybe it was her reawakened zest reminding her that it had been a long time since she had enjoyed a man. Aridatha Singh had a definite masculine allure. Few women failed to notice that, though he seemed entirely unaware of the effect he had.

Time enough to think about that after she alerted Dejagore and got troops of cavalry out to round up her niece, that willful, difficult child.

There must be some way to gain control of her and add her talents to the arsenal of the Protectorate. Possibly she might even take Goblin—despite the fact of his possession.

Goblin never had been much of a wizard.

How sweet revenge was when it arrived after a long delay.

Then let that bitch Ardath and all her dogs come on! A lot of ancient debts would get paid off.

As she approached the encampment ditch she glanced back to consider the vultures again.

The carrion birds had broken their circle. Only a few remained in sight, cruising the sky in search of something rank and tasty again.

Soulcatcher found a voice she had not used since she was young. With it she began to sing a song of springtime and young love, in a language recalled from the springtime of life, when love still lived in the world.

The sentries were extremely frightened.

54

The Taglian Territories:
The Thing in the Cesspit

I have a question," Murgen said. The stronghold at Nijha was in sight. "Who's going to tell Sleepy we're in bed with the Protector?"

I replied, "I don't reckon anybody has to. Not putting it that way, anyhow."

"She's a reasonable woman," Lady opined. "She'll understand what we did and why."

Tobo laughed. Murgen just grinned weakly. The boy wizard said, "You must not have been paying attention. Or you must've mistaken the Sleepy I know for somebody else."

I told him, "She'll get over it. How's Soulcatcher doing on cutting Booboo off?"

"She has pickets out in a line south of Dejagore. The line keeps spreading out wider, to either side of the Rock Road. She doesn't entirely trust me to send her solid information. And I'm not giving her everything I know because I don't want her guessing how well I can keep an eye on her. She's not talking about this to her captains, by the way. My guess is she's afraid she'll start losing them if they begin worrying about Kina."

What a bold lot we were. When first the Company arrived in the Taglian Territories a fixed part of Taglian culture was that the Goddess was never named lest her attention be attracted. If a name just *had* to be used people would reference the watered-down avatar from Gunni myth, Khadi.

The fact that the name Kina is now widely used in daily speech is one more indication of the magnitude of the impact the Company has had these past few decades.

Maybe those old-timers had been right to be terrified of us. We have shaken a civilization to its foundations. And its future does not look bright.

They asked for it. All we ever wanted was to pass on through.

"We won't have to deal with Sleepy for a few days yet," Tobo told us. "She's moving out of the highlands onto the plain, following the south bank of the Viliwash right now. She's only moving a few miles a day. The countryside there has enough of a surplus to support her easily. She's started trying to recruit. In the name of the Prahbrindrah Drah. The Prince and his sister are showing themselves off."

I had a feeling they would not sell well in those parts. That was territory that had been conquered by the Black Company in Taglios' name. "What about Booboo?"

"Almost up to the Protector's picket line now. Sticking to the Rock Road. The Black Hounds have instructions to make sure she gets caught."

Lady grumped, "I thought she was caught already. That she was a prisoner."

"That's true. But right now she seems content to have it that way. I understand that her guards aren't nearly as attentive to her security as they ought to be."

Having read Sleepy's Annals I was not surprised. Booboo seemed capable of having a mind-numbing impact on nearby male-type people.

"Then that's something you need to let my sister know. Otherwise she could get a surprise that would leave all of us unhappy."

We were approaching the Nijha wall. I said, "You experts ought to give this place the once-over. See if our bitty old buddy left any evidence behind." That earned me frowns and scowls. Here came a chance to rest and I was talking about more work. Not for me but for them. I changed the subject and asked Lady, "You said Sleepy burned the Books of the Dead? The real ones? You were a direct witness?"

"I was a witness through the white crow. She burned all three of them. Shivetya himself has their ashes. He's been having Baladitya dispose of them a pinch at a time by having them carried away by anyone who's traveling the plain."

Tobo said, "I moved a lot of them back when Suvrin and I were exploring the plain. What's up?"

"An old man natural's curiosity, I guess. Everyone, and the Deceivers seemed to agree, thinks the Daughter of Night—or whoever inherits her job if she fails—will have to have the Books of the Dead to complete the rituals of the Year of the Skulls. No books, no resurrection. Right?"

I did not get an answer. There was no answer anyone could give. In actual fact nobody really knew. Possibly not even my befuddled daughter or poor old Deceiver and now very dead Narayan Singh.

Lady stipulated, "The old witch is still in there trying, isn't she?"

"Isn't she?"

L ady and Tobo found nothing of interest at the Nijha post. Goblin had not shed his skin or left any secret Deceiver hex signs. He had just started running while the getting was good, as soon as somebody realized that he might be responsible for Narayan's murder.

Uncle Doj rejoined us at Nijha. So did some stragglers who had accumulated there. Sleepy would not have much trouble with desertions. These men knew no one outside the Company and spoke not a word of Taglian or any other local language.

With the stragglers added we would number more than a hundred when we resumed traveling. Of the original group we lacked only Spook and Panda Man, who had been awarded the dubious honor of staying behind to watch the Shadowgate.

Once she finished looking for other evidence, Lady cornered Doj. "Where's the body?"

"Huh?" The old swordmaster was baffled.

"Narayan Singh. What did you do with his corpse?"

Tobo and I exchanged looks. That question had not occurred to either of us. It might be a good idea to make doubly certain just who had died. Narayan Singh had been a veritable Prince of Deceivers, beloved of Kina.

One of the injured men left to garrison Nijha volunteered, "They threw him in the old cesspit, then filled it with dirt and rock from the new latrine, ma'am. Which was built according to your specifications, sir."

I have had a reputation as a martinet along those lines ever since I joined the Company. And when health, hygiene and waste disposal are handled my way the Company tends to experience significantly fewer disease problems than do people who do not do things my way. It remains impossible to reason with some men, though, so I just give orders and make sure they are carried out.

"Dig him up," Lady directed. And when nobody rushed to grab up picks and shovels she began to glow darkly and swell up and even to develop fangs.

Then people started looking for tools.

"That was interesting," I told her.

"Been working on it since I ambushed myself and that tree. It doesn't take much effort or power but it ought to be visually impressive."

"It definitely was that."

*   *   *

The exhumation satisfied Lady. There was a body. It resembled Narayan Singh, even including his bad leg. And it was unnaturally well preserved considering where it had been buried.

"Well?" I asked after she had gone so far as to open the body up. I do not know what she expected to find.

"It does seem to be him. Considering who he served, who seemed to love him, I was almost certain there wouldn't be a body. Or it wouldn't be Narayan's if there was."

The truth was, she had not wanted it to be Narayan. She did not want Singh evading her vengeance this easily.

"There's no dramatic unity in real life," I told her. "Save it up and take it out on Goblin."

She offered me a wicked look.

"I mean on the thing that's taken possession of Goblin." The real Goblin would be my oldest surviving friend.

She carved Narayan's corpse into little pieces. She left a trail of those for the bugs and buzzards over the next several days. But the man's head, heart and hands she kept in a jar of pickling brine.

I did not ask why or if she had a plan. Narayan's escape had left her in much too black a mood for small talk.

A couple of times I did overhear her cursing the fact that there were no great necromancers left in the world.

She would call Narayan back from paradise or hell to make him pay for taking our daughter.

The smaller Voroshk girl, the captive, came out to see us. In not bad Taglian she told us, "Sedvod just died." She stared at Tobo the whole time.

I went to check. The sick boy had, indeed, passed on. And I still had no idea why. I figured the Goblin thing probably deserved the blame.

55

The Nether Taglian Territories: Along the Viliwash

Sleepy surprised us all. She was irked about us dealing with Soulcatcher but she made no great fuss. "This situation isn't the one I prepared for. Tobo. I trust you're taking steps to prevent the Protector from observing what we're doing."

"She sees what we want her to see. Which means she doesn't see what we're doing, only what our mutual enemies are doing."

Which was not much on Booboo's part. Despite her best effort to vanish during the night after her captors first encountered Soulcatcher's pickets, she remained a captive. She would be turned over to Soulcatcher herself within a few days.

Goblin, moving faster than the girl's captors were, had been gaining ground fast and Tobo now placed him only about thirty miles behind. I suggested that he would be more trouble to Soulcatcher than Booboo ever could.

Thinking out loud, I said, "I wonder if this is how myths get started."

People looked at me like they were not sure they wanted to know what that was all about.

I explained. "Here we've got a bunch of people visiting strange places most people couldn't get to even if they wanted. We've got close relatives squabbling and even trying to murder each other."

"That's reaching," Murgen said.

"I like it," Tobo said. "A thousand years from now they'll remember me as the god of storms. Or something."

"Or something?" his father asked. "How about the small god who makes littler rocks out of runty stones?"

Earlier Tobo had gotten caught making stones explode. He had been doing it for the sheer joy of watching them shatter and hearing the fragments ricochet. He was embarrassed. But you have got to have fun once in a while. Today's Company is not nearly as much fun as it was when I was young.

I snickered. "We marched forty miles every day. Uphill all the way. In the snow. When we weren't in the swamp."

"What?"

"Thought I'd start practicing for when I get really old. How do you make rocks explode?"

"Oh. That's easy. You just kind of feel what they're like inside. You find the water. You make it hot enough and the rock goes boom."

Find the water. Inside a rock. And the rock goes boom. Right. I had to ask. I changed the subject. "How are those Voroshk kids doing?" Despite everything he had to do, Tobo found time to spend with our captives.

It was amazing how much the kid could handle in a day.

I could recall when life worked that way for me. Back when we were marching up all those hills. With cold, wet feet.

"Uncle Doj has them speaking Taglian like they were born in the delta, in the shadow of the temple of Ghanghesha."

"Excellent." He was poking fun, of course.

"They're picking up the language. Shukrat and Magadan could get by now. Arkana is having trouble but she's catching on. None of them are mourning Sedvod. Gromovol, the brother, is being stubborn. He doesn't like not being the only conduit. He likes to be in control. Of something. But even he is making progress."

"Gromovol is the pain in the ass, then? Which're which with the other names? I haven't heard any names before."

"That's because they hadn't given up hope that their family would rescue them from their own dumb mistake. Even more than the Gunni do, they believe their names can be used against them. There's a connection with their souls."

"Which means that Shukrat and Magadan and whatnot won't actually be real names."

"They're real public names. Work names. Just not true names."

"I've never understood the concept but it's one I've learned to live with. Which one is which?"

"Shukrat is the shorter girl. The one who crashed."

"The one who's working up a crush on you."

Tobo ignored me. The ability to ignore seems to be coupled with a talent for sorcery. "Arkana is the ice queen. Which I definitely would not mind melting. Magadan is the quiet guy."

Magadan, in my estimation, would be the dangerous one. If he so chose. He observed and studied and prepared. He did not bluster or invoke the threat of powers from a world away. "Did you tell them what happened at the Shadowgate?"

"They didn't want to believe me but they did enough to decide to introduce themselves. Enough to conclude that they're likely to be a part of our world for a long time to come."

"You did remind them that that's what they asked for?"

"Sure. Shukrat even managed to joke about it. She has a great sense of humor. For a girl. Who *didn't* ask to be here."

Considering the females in his experience I could see how he might think a feeble sense of humor was a sex-linked characteristic. Only Iqbal Singh's wife ever smiled and joked. And Suruvhija's lot was the poorest of all the women associated with the Company.

"But all you can see is long legs, long blonde hair, big blue eyes and a monumental set of gazoombies." Once we got up into settled country we needed to find the kid a whore. Twenty years old and never been laid.

On the other hand, harnessing all that energy the way we were right now had a lot to recommend it. We were not headed into an era where we could let our most talented wizard be distracted by nature.

Maybe we should find him a traveling companion.

I could just imagine what his mother would say about that.

"The future," I said, raising my hand as though holding a drink. "We have to get Swan and Blade set up in the brewing business."

Murgen said, "That's what I miss most about One-Eye, too."

"Here's a thought. Maybe Goblin will get so thirsty he'll shake Kina off and set up a still."

I had to mention Goblin. That took the pleasure out of the moment.

Everybody who remembered the old Goblin had to deal with those memories each time the man's name came up. Those memories were going to be treacherous if ever we confronted the revenant himself. Even if they caused just a moment's hesitation.

If we had to go after Goblin hard we would be better served to send people from Hsien. They would not be sentimental about him. Their exposure was entirely hearsay.

I did not want to hasten the day.

I asked, "Tobo, now that we've slowed down, what are we going to do about the Howler?" An entire infantry company had been saddled with that sleeping sorcerer from the day he and Longshadow had been brought up out of the earth. That company had no other duties but transporting and protecting the Howler. "Something's got to be. If she don't wake him up and make a deal we'd better kill him. Before Soulcatcher figures out that we've got him and steals him so she can use him herself."

I was worried that Sleepy was not taking the Howler seriously enough. She had no experience of him. Not enough to understand just how dangerous he could be, which was just as dangerous as Soulcatcher. And he was crazier than she was.

The Howler was no dedicated enemy of ours though he had worked against us far more often than otherwise. His nature seemed to make him a follower. He gravitated toward where the strength seemed to be. He was so powerful I would prefer he was with us rather than not. Or, if not with us, dead.

"There's a certain amount of debate. Sleepy would rather just leave him for the jackals. Mom would, too, only she keeps having these premonitions. You know how big premonitions are with the women of the Ky family."

"One got your mom and dad together."

"No use crying over spilled milk," Willow Swan said. "How about somebody tells Sleepy if she's not going anywhere in a hurry why don't we set down in one place? It's a pain to set up and tear down every day if we're not going anywhere."

Our northward drift did allow for a lot of camp time. I used it to work on these Annals. Lady used it to get several wagon loads of large bamboo poles collected so she could begin manufacturing a new generation of fireball projectors. Tobo used it to teach the Voroshk youngsters. I joined him occasionally. The boy Magadan seemed to have a healing touch. We needed to nurture that.

Arkana remained the ice queen. Shukrat grew more relaxed with us. And Gromovol decided he wanted to become my buddy—in support of whatever scheme was shaping up inside of him.

Although he did not spread it around, Tobo figured out the basics of riding the Voroshk flying post. At least, a particular flying post. I suspect Shukrat helped him. It was her post he sneaked out in the middle of the night, indulging all of a young man's joy in adventure.

The Nether Taglian Territories:
The Manor at Gharhawnes

Ten days into the Amble on the Viliwash we had traveled barely forty-five miles. A third of those we covered in a single day when it became apparent, to the amazement of all, that there really were people in the Taglian Territories disinclined to celebrate liberation from the Protector's reign. A coalition of regional nobles and priests tried to resist, then tried to hole up in a stout manor called Gharhawnes. In the field Tobo used his talents to weaken their will to resist, before the soldiers got a real chance to beat up on them.

We surrounded the manor at dusk. Fires sprouted. The outer wall of the manor house seemed to boil with a dark mist as the Unknown Shadows stormed the place.

Results did not become obvious for hours. Tobo's friends preferred to be indirect. And preferred the cover of darkness.

We had the place surrounded. Our bonfires sent harmless shadows scampering over the manor walls. I told Sleepy, "This place looks nice and comfy, Captain. We're in no hurry. We could hang around here for a while. Long enough to learn its name."

She was underwhelmed by the suggestion. "Gharhawnes."

"Bless you."

"Gharhawnes is the name of the place, you idiot."

"And it's the best place we've seen. Maybe we should set up the prince and his sister here. Sort of get them back into the swing of being royalty." The gods knew they got no practice with us savages. We just dragged them hither and yon like so much duffel, in case they became useful someday.

"Don't you have some writing to do? Or a boil to lance?"

"Not at the moment. I'm all yours and full of advice."

Before she could put together a suitable reply without using profanity, a party of several men slipped out of the manor, bringing women and children with them.

I had a feeling our camp looked pretty impressive.

It was supposed to look like a horde was on the move.

Tobo and his parents materialized. The boy said, "The haunts are working faster than I thought they would." He extended an arm, hand palm downward, then whispered in what sounded like the language of Hsien. A moment later a cry of rage came from a high manor window where a pair of archers had been about to snipe at the defectors. One somehow managed to fall through the opening.

The Captain said, "Have those things start whispering that anyone who surrenders before dawn will be allowed to take their possessions with them. They'll even be allowed to go home unharmed if they take an oath to the Prahbrindrah Drah. Captives taken after sunrise tomorrow will be conscripted into our forced labor battalions."

We did not have forced labor battalions. But those were a part of siege warfare and were often the fate of prisoners of war and peasants who were insufficiently fleet of foot. The threat was plausible. And the Black Company had a long reputation for being unimpressed by caste, noble birth, or priestly status, too.

Once it was clear we would provide covering fire to defectors a flow developed. Usually the soldiers set to keep deserters from using the posterns were the first to come over.

The people engineering the resistance were not popular with their conscripted followers.

So some folks wanted to see the Protectorate continue but the people who had to do the work were not interested. The few I got to talk to had no real convictions in the matter. Who ruled made little difference in their lives. But it was getting on toward harvest time.

One of the great truths was getting some exposure to the light here.

Our men entered the manor early next morning. I was still asleep. Tobo's pets spread confusion. Our men cleaned up behind them. None of our people died. There were few wounds of any consequence. Sleepy felt magnanimous. She turned most of the men of standing over to the Radisha and her brother for judgment. Only those Tobo identified as irredeemable creatures of the Protector faced the Company justice.

"Spread that around," Sleepy told Tobo. "Make it sound a lot bigger than it was."

"Tonight little people will be whispering in the ears of sleepers everywhere within two hundred miles."

57

The Nether Taglian Territories:
The Resurrection

That far Taglian province shared religions with the rest of the Taglian Territories, with the majority being Gunni. It's language was closely akin to that spoken around Dejagore. Sleepy could manage the dialect with only a little practice.

What I called a manor house was really more like a village completely enclosed within a single blockish structure. The principal building material was an unbaked brick kept carefully plastered so it would not wash away in the rain. Inside there was an open central square with both cisterns and a good well. Stables and workshops opened on it all around. The rest of the structure was a warren of halls and rooms where people obviously lived and worked and ran shops and lived life as though the place was indeed some sort of city.

"It's a termite mound," Murgen told me.

"The Prince and his sis ought to feel right at home. It's as bad as the Taglian Palace. On a miniature scale."

"I want to know what they ate. The smell is overpowering." The odors of spices clogged every hallway. But that was true in every Taglian city and town. These odors were just an alien mix.

Thai Dei caught up. He had actually allowed Murgen out of his sight for several minutes. Maybe he was slowing down, too. He brought a message. "Tobo says to tell you that Sleepy has decided to take a chance on wakening the Howler."

You could tell Thai Dei was worried because that was one of the longest speeches I ever heard the man make.

Sleepy chose to undertake the awakening with full pomp, ceremony and drama. Following an evening meal we gathered in what had been a temple hall, when everyone was rested, well fed and supposedly relaxed. The place of worship was poorly lit and boasted far too many multiheaded and multiarmed idols in its corners to lead me to consider it strictly benign.

None of the idols represented Khadi but all Gunni deities make me uncomfortable.

I was present in a demigod role myself. I appeared as the creepy armored monster Widowmaker. I do not enjoy the role.

My dearly beloved, on the other hand, just loves any excuse to assume the guise of Lifetaker. For a few hours she can wear the ugly armor and pretend that these are still the good old days when she was something much more wicked than this Lifetaker thing is supposed to be now.

Our role in the proceeding was to sit there in the gloom with colorful worms of sorcery slithering over us. We were supposed to look intimidating while others got the real work done.

Tobo just came as Tobo. Hell, he did not bother putting on a clean shirt and trousers. But he did bring his Voroshk students.

The rest of the audience consisted of senior officers and regional notables who had come in, mainly, to assess the Prahbrindrah Drah and to discover what they would need to do to weather our presence.

Conquerers do come and go.

The hall was crowded. All those bodies produced a lot of heat. And I was inside that armor, sitting motionless on a stool behind the action, One-Eye's black spear held upright in my right hand. That was supposed to be my entire part.

It mostly involved not fainting in front of witnesses.

Sleepy had set the stage pretty well, with the low lighting and enough advance rumormongering to make the audience understand that the Howler was both foaming-mouth mad and yet a sorcerer who was as powerful as the Protector.

Poor Howler. Despite his part in the Shadowmaster wars he was almost forgotten now.

The Voroshk, I noted, eventually settled right up front. Tobo was treating them as good friends, particularly the well-rounded, freckled little blonde. He chattered with her until Sleepy growled and told him to get on with it.

Even I felt a little let down by the awakening. Tobo indulged in no mumbo jumbo and no showmanship. He felt that his part was no more exciting than working in a stable.

But his effort was more impressive to thoughtful minds. A few people, maybe the right people, understood that Tobo was so good he could make something big look routine.

I thought the boy's efforts said a lot about his character, too. His ego did not need a lot of feeding.

I noted that three out of four Voroshk got it right away. Gromovol actually got it, too, but he did have an ego disease.

Tobo freed Howler from his long trance in a matter of minutes.

I do not know the whole story. You never do with their kind of people. But I do know that Howler is ages older even than Lady. He was one of the men who helped her first husband, the Dominator, build the Domination, an empire that collapsed into the northern dust about the time the original Black Company crossed over from Khatovar. Howler's pain and deformity are a legacy of that time. So is the kind of thinking that led Soulcatcher to proclaim herself Protector.

The woman does not have the obsessive focus and drive necessary to create a true replica of that old empire of darkness.

I never have seen Howler outside the layered rags he wears, rags so long unchanged that a whole ecology has developed between the Howler's skin and the surrounding world. It includes numerous invertebrates, molds, mildews and a variety of small green plants.

The Howler is smaller than Goblin or One-Eye ever were but Lady insists that that was not always the case.

When Tobo finished, the almost shapeless little ragbag sucked in a deep breath, then let out one of the shrieks that had given him his name. It seemed an egalitarian mix of agony and despair. I shivered despite the heat. It had been a long time since I had heard one of those cries. I could have waited a lot longer to hear this one.

The little wizard sat up.

Swords made metallic sounds. Spearheads dropped. Several of the half dozen existing, new-production fireball projectors swung to point Howler's way.

But he did nothing more. He was at least as disoriented as the worst of the rest of us when he awakened.

Tobo signalled. A man stepped forward with a pitcher of water. Howler would be fiercely thirsty. He would drink as much as he was allowed for the next couple of days. The first few of us to be awakened four years ago had made ourselves sick drinking too much water.

We learned to ration.

Howler wanted water by the gallon, too.

He did not get it.

He opened his mouth. A terrible howl came out. He could not control that frightful habit.

As rationality returned the little wizard looked around and was not pleased with his situation. He did not recognize anyone immediately. He asked, "How long has it been?" He used a tongue of the north so ancient no one but Lady spoke it. She translated into the language of Hsien, adding, "Right now he thinks he's been resurrected into a whole new age."

I suggested, "Break his heart fast. We don't have time to waste."

Howler asked questions again, in a series of languages, trying to elicit an understandable response.

I watched him wilt as he began to acknowledge the possibility that he had been asleep so long that the nations of his own age had been forgotten. But he was not entirely numb mentally. Though they differed in detail from the originals he soon recognized the armor Lady and I wore. And recalled who was who. He addressed himself to Lifetaker. The language he chose was an old one that they had shared in another age. There had been a time when I could read it, written, but could only guess at the meaning of the spoken words.

Just when everyone started to relax he let rip another bone-chilling shriek.

Lady announced, "Howler sees the general situation. Once he's had a little more explained I think he'll be amenable to an alliance."

I used the language of Hsien to respond. "Howler has been part of my life most of my life. And all that time he's been one of the people trying to kill me. I don't think I can be real comfortable having him on my side."

"Well, that would be stupid, wouldn't it? We don't have to trust him, darling. The Unknown Shadows will keep him trustworthy."

Of course. "And you do remember his true name. Which you could pass along to Tobo."

"If I have to."

I nodded, thinking it might be a damned good idea for her to tell Tobo right away. Because the Howler was not the sort to be shy, reluctant or slow about eliminating a threat.

Howler let rip another terrible cry.

Sleepy had begun to simmer because she did not know what was going on.

Lady talked to the Howler about our situation while I told the Captain what was going on.

The Howler howled. There was some passion in this cry. He did not like the situation at all. But he had been there before and my sweetie was amply blunt in making it clear that there would be only one other choice available.

One reason the Howler had become the Howler was his powerful aversion to death. Nor did he have any reason to love Soulcatcher, who had buried him in a hope that that would last forever. And who had played him cruelly a time or two farther in the past.

The little sorcerer howled again.

In the language of Hsien I wondered aloud, "Tobo, do you think Shivetya has the power to cure this little shit's screaming?" It really got distracting after a while.

Tobo shrugged. "Possibly." He was not paying much attention. "I can find out." He was trying to hear what Riverwalker was whispering to Sleepy. Riverwalker had been called away a few minutes earlier. He was back now with Suvrin and a cavalry officer named Tea Nung. Nung's troop was supposed to have picket duty so I supposed something important had happened out there.

Sleepy nodded, said something affirmative. Riverwalker, Suvrin and Tea Nung withdrew. Sleepy started to snap something at them but whatever the thought was, it had come too late. Sleepy shifted her attention back to the matter at hand. She seemed less than totally focused now. She had developed a case of the fidgets. And she seemed to have brightened up.

She leaned over to confide something to Sahra.

Sahra was startled. Then she became smiley and conspiratorial, possibly even teasing.

The Captain did appear to be embarrassed.

Lady coughed indiscretely to cue me that it was Widowmaker's turn to speak to our leader. So I said, "Captain, the Howler would be honored to throw in his lot with the Black Company. He'll create flying carpets for us and he'll help with our weapons program. I wouldn't trust him a whole hell of a lot, though. And I'd keep him away from the Voroshk." All this stated in the language of Hsien, so the little sorcerer would not follow.

The youngsters remained in their unhappy clump, trying to understand. Almost perky little Shukrat understood enough Taglian already to keep her companions accurately posted as to what got said in that language.

Riverwalker and Suvrin returned. A tall, handsome man accompanied them. He was dusty and obviously exhausted but he was alert. He ran an inquisitive eye over everyone. He seemed to recognize several people. He even bowed slightly to the Radisha.

Sleepy rose to greet him. There was a deference in her manner I had not seen before, though it was so subtle as to lurk on the border of imagination. Obviously this was someone she knew. But not someone she cared to announce. After a tentative clasping of hands she, Sahra, Riverwalker and a few others, including the Radisha, slipped away.

I wondered immediately if they had not done something stupid by bringing the man into a crowded hall when a meeting with him needed to be private. Yet a glance around showed me nobody buzzing. Excepting Sleepy's cronies from her years underground in Taglios.

Might the visitor be some Company brother who had been left behind? Or some past ally?

The glance around also showed me all the Gunni idols apparently stirring. That had begun to divert the attention of the audience. Tobo was grim with concentration. He had his spectral allies hard at work.

That pretty boy had to be somebody special.

A moment later Widowmaker moved for the first time during the festivities. He stood up suddenly. The tip of his spear snapped down, pricked the rags surrounding the Howler, who had managed to stifle his screams and was in the process of beginning to ooze away.

Lifetaker's great black sword fell an instant later, blocking his line of sight.

Gharhawnes:
The Traitor General

It was deep in the night when a limping Runmust Singh dragged me out of bed. Out of a real bed. It had been ages. And this one came with a real woman in it. Runmust insisted that she had to get up, too. The Captain wanted us both.

Lady was grumbling something about restructuring the chain of command when we left our cubicle. We ran into Murgen right away. He was waiting for Thai Dei, who had not gotten a personalized wake up call. Sahra was nowhere in sight.

I asked, "When are you two going to work it out so you can go your own ways?" Thai Dei was one of very few Nyueng Bao still dedicating himself to bodyguarding.

"I don't think that'll happen," Murgen said. "He doesn't have anything else since Narayan died."

"Ah." Thai Dei's son had been slain by Stranglers. Thai Dei was another who had been waiting in line to get some paybacks.

The obligation to protect Murgen had become a convenient fiction for both men. I should have recognized that a long time ago. I who have made such a big deal out of brotherhood for so many years.

Thai Dei bustled up. We set off after Runmust. I said, "Singh, you should let me take a look at that leg. It should've healed faster than it has."

"It'll mend fine once I get some real rest, sir. And I believe we expect to stay here for some time."

What good would that do if the man refused to take the opportunity to rest?

I could have Tobo knock him into a coma.

Runmust led us to a room barely big enough to fit a dozen people. Sleepy and Suvrin, the Prahbrindrah Drah and his sister, Tobo and Sahra were there already. So was the handsome stranger.

"Sit," Sleepy said. Then she got straight to the point. "This is Aridatha Singh." Beside me, Lady winced, recognizing the name and thinking of her trophies. "Aridatha commands the City Battalions in Taglios. He, the Great General and Ghopal Singh, who commands the Greys, form the triumvirate who're running Taglios while the Protector is out of town. Aridatha tells me that he and they—the Protector's top henchmen—have decided they need to get rid of her."

From one side, in back, Willow Swan grumbled, "Ghopal Singh is a general now? He was a damned sergeant when he worked for me."

Aridatha responded, "The Protector prides herself on her ability to recognize outstanding talent."

A joke of sorts had passed between the two. I guess you had to have been part of the situation to follow it.

While we sat around with our mouths hanging open, looking intelligent, Sleepy told the outsider, "These people are here to offer their advice. That's Croaker. He was the Liberator, once upon a time. That's Lady. That's Murgen. They've all led the Company at some time. The others you'll recall from the last time we met." She passed over Thai Dei, which lent him an air of mystery, nor did she introduce the Prahbrindrah Drah.

I asked, "Did Mogaba send you?"

"I volunteered. Because your Captain knew me. And because your Company has no personal grievance with me."

Lady stirred. She was willing to invent one.

Sleepy said, "It would seem that there are limits even Mogaba refuses to exceed. And Soulcatcher has managed to discover them."

Aridatha said, "You have ancient grievances with the Great General."

"I want you to know that he isn't an evil man. He *is* an obsessed man, though his obsession has weathered away with age. He's realized that history won't record his name on the roll of great conquerers. There's no longer time. He hasn't entirely made his peace with that but he does see that it's his own fault. Because of his untimely defection during the siege of Dejagore he has been forced to serve a procession of deranged and incompetent masters. But that's of no moment now.

"Between us, he, Ghopal, and I have concluded that Taglios should be spared any more torment by the Protector. She's like a deadly rot. She's destroying everything slowly. Even our religions and culture. And the only force able to put an end to that is the Black Company."

Murgen suggested, "You guys could whack her yourselves. She's not immortal. And she trusts you. As much as she trusts anybody. That gets you close enough. . . ."

"That plan was in place even before you people resurfaced. But she's stayed away from the city since the beginning of that crisis. Her messages to the Great General all affirm her determination to keep after you until she's accounted for every member of the Black Company personally. She was extremely put out because so many people who were supposed to be dead started turning up alive."

"Believe me, I know how exasperating that is," Lady said. "For twenty years I chased the Deceiver Narayan Singh. The man had more lives than a cat."

Aridatha caught the past tense. "Has the living saint of the Deceivers passed to his reward, then?"

"He got away from me through the only exit he had left." Lady sounded extremely bitter. Like she thought Singh had beaten her by cheating blatantly. Her hatred of Narayan was stronger than I had suspected.

"Then that's one distraction that no longer needs concern us."

"Incorrect," Sleepy said, reclaiming control. "The Daughter of Night is still out there. And Kina still hopes to bring on the Year of the Skulls. Whatever else happens, Kina and her followers still have to be managed. Tell my associates why we should trust anything you tell us, Aridatha."

"I am, of course, damned to walk in the shadow of a man I met only once in my life, after I was a grown man, and then for only a few minutes, several years ago, in your presence. That's the legacy of the Deceivers. The cult destroys trust. My answer is, all men should be judged by one standard: their behavior. By the deeds they do. The gesture of good faith I have to make in this instance is, I think, generous."

Sleepy interrupted. "Aridatha has a brother who lives in Jaicur. Under an assumed name. This brother, real name Sugriva, is going to help us take the city. He'll scout out the best gate for us to get at in the middle of the night. We'll use it to prance in and take over before anyone can put up a fight."

I opened my mouth to argue but stopped before anything stupid came out. Sleepy's mind was made up. All I could do was my best to make sure everything worked out right. "Soulcatcher has an army between here and there. One that outnumbers us, I hear."

"And one that's little better than a rabble, according to Aridatha. Some of the poorer soldiers are armed only with hammers, pitchforks, sickles and such."

"A guy goes away for a few decades, everything turns to shit," I said. "I had everybody tall enough to reach his mother's hand armed up, once upon a time. What happened to all those weapons?"

Riverwalker explained, "When the Protector took over, times got so bad that almost anybody with anything to sell sold it. Weapons were a glut on the market. The steel got forged into other things."

"And the Protector didn't care," Aridatha said. "The Great General finally gave up trying to make her see the point of maintaining arsenals in peacetime. I think it won't be long now until she understands what he was talking about."

Sleepy told us, "It isn't necessary to trust Aridatha or Mogaba to test Jaicur's defenses. We're expected to swing west toward the Naghir River. We'll make a show of doing just that. But Blade, with the light cavalry, will split off the rear of the column and loop back around eastward. The hidden folk will find a route along which the horsemen can approach Jaicur unobserved. In the meantime, the main force will turn again and head for the Rock Road north of Jaicur. That ought to stir up an ant's nest. And make Soulcatcher forget Jaicur completely for a few days."

Why had Sleepy bothered calling the rest of us in? She had it all worked out already. And pretty soundly, I thought.

Tobo said, "We do have a more immediate problem than that, Sleepy. You brought General Singh in during the reanimation ceremony. And he's been seen around camp. It's inevitable that some of our outside visitors will be Soulcatcher's creatures. And it's possible one of them recognized him."

Sleepy admitted, "I didn't think fast enough. I'm open to corrective suggestions."

"I'm already working on it. But I do want to warn you. I don't think I can be a hundred percent successful in identifying them and cutting them off."

"Then you'd better consider what would be the best way to warn the other conspirators in Taglios, hadn't you?"

Aridatha said, "Ghopal and the Great General won't be taken unawares. The Protector possesses no means of traveling faster than the rumor of her coming. When she heads for Taglios they'll know before she gets there. And what she brings with her will betray her intentions."

I nodded. The reasoning seemed sound. And you did have to be really sneaky to outfox Mogaba. Soulcatcher was not sneaky these days. She had developed the habit of just bulling straight ahead because she was the biggest power around.

Sleepy elected to assume a stance which made it look like we were just going to sit and rest. But Tobo scouted the country north of Gharhawnes in ever greater detail, sometimes even going out in person, when he went flying with Shukrat.

The two of them were getting very chummy.

In private I observed, "This is getting distinctly weird. We're allies with Soulcatcher against our daughter and Kina. We're allies with the traitor Mogaba against your sister. We're allies with a demigod whose price for supporting us is that we murder him."

Lady chuckled weakly. "You did say it has a mythic ring."

"You know something? It's got me scared."

She stared at nothing, waiting for me to explain.

"Scared in a generalized way, not scared like when we're in a fight. Scared of the shape the future might take." I had a bad, bad feeling. Because on the surface everything looked just too marvelous for the Black Company.

59

With the Middle Army:
When Guests Arrived

The Goblin creature proved difficult to catch. What should have taken just a few days took two weeks and, in the end, necessitated Soulcatcher's personal intervention—with, to her chagrin, considerable coaching from the shadowy cat thing she could never quite see and never quite ambush and bind to her own service.

In the meantime she amused herself with the girl.

The Daughter of Night was imprisoned in a cage inside Soulcatcher's tent. That was the largest and most ostentatious tent in the midway camp. The girl had been stripped naked, then had been decorated with a variety of chains and charms. She would not be guarded by or even approached by anyone male. Soulcatcher knew only too well how men could be manipulated by the women of her blood.

Though the girl did not seem interested in listening, Soulcatcher said, "To this day I'm not quite sure how you and that old man managed to get away from me. But I have some suspicions. And it won't happen again. You're far too important to your mother to be running around loose." The voice Soulcatcher selected was annoyingly pedantic.

The girl did not respond. She was alone in her own reality. This was not her first time as a prisoner of someone who planned to use her. She could be patient. Her moment would come. Someone would slip up. An impressionable guard would be assigned. Something. Somewhere, sometime, she would have an opportunity to deceive someone into loving her long enough to want to set her free.

The girl's continued indifference pricked Soulcatcher into trying to hurt her with news she had wanted to reserve. "He's dead, you know. Your old man. Narayan Singh. He was strangled. They threw his body in a cesspit."

That blow did strike home. But after an initial flinch and a brief, black look the Daughter of Night lowered her eyes and settled back into her pose of patient indifference.

Soulcatcher laughed. "Your freak Goddess has abandoned you."

To which the girl offered her only spoken response since her capture. "All their days are numbered." Which was like a slap in Soulcatcher's face. It was one of those slogans Black Company–inspired graffitists had used to taunt her for years.

Soulcatcher snatched a whip, flailed away without doing the girl much harm. The cage itself prevented that.

Someone shouted for Soulcatcher's attention from outside the entrance to her tent. In that respect her soldiers were well-trained. They did not bother her with trivia.

Responding, Soulcatcher found a gaggle of soldiers with a dead man on a crude litter. The corpse was twisted. Its features were severely distorted. Raindrops slid off the ruined face like tears. "You," she said, picking a man. "Tell it." A cavalryman covered with mud, he must have been on picket duty.

"This man came up from the south. He gave the proper recognition signs. He told us that he was bringing you important news about traitors but wouldn't say anything else."

"He arrived healthy? How did he get this way?"

"Just before we got to camp he stood up in his stirrups and screamed. His horse reared and threw him. After he hit the ground he shuddered and twitched and made gurgling noises trying to scream. And then he died."

"Traitors?" No doubt there would be many of those to pay off before this played out. These situations brought them out from under every rock and bush.

"That's all he said, ma'am."

"Bring him inside. It's possible I can still get a little something out of him. Be careful where you track your mud." She stepped aside, even held the flap for the soldiers. Reluctantly, a few found courage enough to bring the body forward. Soulcatcher's soldiers shared a common opinion that it was not good to catch the Protector's eye. These stepped carefully, leaving as little mud and moisture as possible.

In a merry young voice Soulcatcher observed, "You must all have mothers."

S oulcatcher had the corpse partially stripped, disassembling its apparel thread by thread, when there was another disturbance outside the tent entrance. Irked, she responded, hoping this would be the news she had been awaiting so long: that Goblin had been captured at last.

As she was about to open up she caught motion from the corner of her eye. She spun. For an instant she thought she glimpsed a tiny man, maybe eight inches tall, ducking down behind the corpse.

The racket outside remained insistent.

It was not the news she wanted. The soldiers there—they always came in groups—pushed one of their number forward. "A courier just came in, ma'am. The enemy is on the move again. Westward."

Mogaba had called it right, then. "When did this start?"

"The courier will be with you in a minute, ma'am. With dispatches. He had some physical needs he couldn't put off before he could see you. But the command staff insisted you get the main news immediately."

In a casual tone, Soulcatcher observed, "The drizzle seems to be letting up."

"Yes, ma'am."

"Get that courier here as fast as possible."

"Yes, ma'am."

The reports from the south did indeed have the rested Black Company forces moving westward but not on the track previously anticipated. Part of their journey would have to be made without the benefits of roads, over rough terrain.

Soulcatcher said, "They must be striking for Balichore by the shortest route. Why? Can anyone tell me what's special about Balichore?" Soulcatcher controlled a sprawling empire she knew only a little about.

After an extended silence someone tentatively suggested, "That's the farthest upriver heavy barge traffic travels. Cargos have to be portaged and loaded on smaller boats or onto wagons."

Someone else recalled, "There's some kind of problem with rocks in the river. A whatchamacallit. Cataract. The Liberator once ordered a canal built around it but the project was abandoned. . . ."

A couple of pokes in the ribs were necessary before the speaker recalled who was responsible for the neglect of public works in recent times.

Soulcatcher did not respond, however. She concentrated on the transport idea.

A large portion of the Company had barged up the Naghir River after fleeing Taglios five years ago. Could this new Captain be in a rut? Or was she thinking she could catch Taglios by surprise, from the river side, where there were no walls and no defensive works and the peoples of those poorer quarters tended toward nostalgic recollections of the Prahbrindrah Drah, the Radisha and even the Liberator.

Soulcatcher asked, "Does anyone happen to know how long it takes to get a barge down the Naghir, through the delta channels, and upriver to Taglios?" She knew barges manned by veteran crews traveled day and night, unlike soldiers afoot or on horseback.

Another disturbance at the entrance arose before anyone produced a reliable answer.

The drizzle had ended, she discovered. Yet the men demanding attention were covered with mud. And they had brought her a present.

"For me? And it's not even my birthday."

Goblin was a present who looked way the worse for use. He was bound and gagged. His head and hands were wrapped in rags as well. His captors had been determined to take no chances.

Soulcatcher gloated. "He stumbled into one of my traps, didn't he?"

"Yes he did, ma'am."

There were hundreds of those out there, taking many forms. Soulcatcher had begun to put them out as soon as it had become evident that the new, improved Goblin could evade the best efforts of her soldiers. "He's still alive, isn't he?" If he was dead her concern that he might have allowed himself to be caught would slide down her list of worries.

"Your instructions were perfectly clear, ma'am."

Soulcatcher memorized that man's face. He was mocking her behind a mask of rectitude. She preferred open defiance. That she could crush without mystifying anyone. "Take the mask and gag off. Set him up over here." The Daughter of Night, Soulcatcher noted, was interested enough to forget to hide her interest.

She could not know the little wizard's significance, could she?

No. Impossible. The girl was just doing what she did whenever anything happened inside the tent. She paid attention because she might learn something useful.

Soulcatcher waited until she judged that Goblin was sufficiently recovered. She told him, "Your former brothers really don't like turncoats, do they?"

Goblin stared at her with eyes colder, deeper and more remote than those of the Daughter of Night. He did not reply.

She stepped closer. Her mask was just a foot from his face. She purred, "They came to me for help settling your account."

Goblin twitched but remained silent. He did try to look around.

He smiled when he glimpsed the Daughter of Night.

Soulcatcher said, "They told me all about it, little man. They told me what you are now. They expect me to just kill you because of what you did to my foot. They really just want you dead." She rubbed her gloved hands together. "But I think I'm going to be a lot cruder." She giggled.

"All their days are numbered," Goblin said in a whisper. The voice borrowing the taunt only vaguely resembled that of the man who had gone down into the earth to challenge the Dark Mother.

"Some more closely than others." Soulcatcher's voice was old and emotionless. Her right hand lashed out, sliced across Goblin's face. Blades a half inch long on the ends of her fingers destroyed his eyes and the bridge of his nose. He shrieked, at first as much in surprise as in pain.

The Protector turned on the men who had brought the prisoner in. "Bring me another cage like the one the brat is in." The cage did in fact exist already. Such had been her certainty that she would capture Goblin.

The blacksmith had orders to create three more, suitable for housing her sister, her sister's husband, and that treacherous Willow Swan.

Later, in Taglios, she meant to work with a glassblower to bottle them all so they could be displayed outside the entrance to her palace. They would be kept alive and fed until they drowned in their own ordure.

Such was the fate that the Dominator often bestowed upon his most important enemies, in his time.

Gharhawnes:
Tobo and the Voroshk

The Howler certainly kept busy. He completed his first functional four-passenger flying carpet two days after the soldiers marched westward. Gharhawnes seemed deserted, though there were enough of us around to bloody a bunch of noses the morning the former tenant took a notion to steal his home back.

Sleepy had a dozen carpets on order, from single-rider scouts to a monster she hoped would carry twenty soldiers. I do not know who she expected to fly them. Only Howler and Tobo—and, possibly, the Voroshk—had the power to manage the things.

I insisted that we have a couple of modest-sized carpets first. Those should not take too long to make and would be the size most useful to us right away. And since I was in charge of the left-behinds and the Dejagore strike I got what I wanted. Well, I got the one carpet.

Tobo had the flying post thing figured out, too. Both Shukrat and Arkana seemed eager to get along now. One or the other would allow Tobo to borrow her post when he wanted to run out to visit Sleepy, which he did by night so he would not be seen from the ground. I never felt comfortable when he did that. We had too many potentially unpleasant and unfriendly people back here in the manor. Including a lot of hostages from the leading families of the region.

Both Magadan and Gromovol were increasingly determined not to be won over, each for his own reasons. I told Magadan, "I'd be tempted to send you two home just so I don't have to worry about what's going on behind my back." I was not worried, really. Tobo's supernatural friends saw everything.

Magadan told me, "I don't want to go home. Home no longer exists. I want to be free."

"Sure. You Voroshk showed what you can do when you're free. I've spent my life killing people like you. That's people who believe it's their destiny to make slaves out of people like me. I'm in a war with another one of them right now. I'm not about to cut you loose and let you start making peoples' lives miserable, too."

None of which was absolutely true but it did sound good. And Magadan bought it. Some. The part that really was true. That I would kill him before I turned him loose on the world.

That was the moment when he decided he might want to go home after all. From then on he brought that possibility up each time we crossed paths. The hidden folk said he was sincere. He was trying to get the other kids to go along with swapping what knowledge they had for an escort back across the place of glittering stone.

Lady did not believe it. She thought we should put him and Gromovol down because of the trouble they could cause.

My sweetie has a very direct approach to problem-solving.

Sometimes I do find what little conscience I retain a damnable handicap.

Howler, though, did successfully work his way out of the top ten on my shit list. Tobo's appeal to Shivetya had resulted in word from the golem saying he did have the ability to intervene in Howler's screaming and shrinking problems. Shivetya did not have much of a reputation as a liar so even Howler took him at his word. After which the smelly little wizard became extremely cooperative.

Though we still had no cause to trust his long run intentions. Nor he any call to trust ours, either.

L ady cornered Tobo. "We have a dangerous situation, here. And like a pet cobra it's going to bite us someday. We have to do something."

The boy sounded puzzled. "What're you talking about? Something about what?"

"Those Voroshk. They aren't as strong or as bright as we first thought but there are four of them and only one of you."

"But they're not going to. . . ."

"Pardon me for being an old cynic," I said. "Magadan keeps telling me, in so many words, that he wants to be anywhere that isn't here with us. And there's at least the implication that he'll do whatever it takes if we don't help him go home.

And Gromovol is going to be trouble eventually because his personality requires it. If you go out to visit Sleepy or just on a flying date the rest of us are stuck here with no better hope than the Howler."

"And speaking of flying," Lady said, "don't you *ever* go out with both of those girls again. Hush! You're only familiar with the women you've grown up around. I'm telling you right now that Arkana is exactly like Magadan. But she has one more weapon than he does and she means to use it to cloud your mind."

"But . . ."

"Shukrat I'm not sure about. There's a chance Shukrat is exactly what she seems."

I agreed. The kid was likable. And according to Tobo the hidden folk agreed. They offered no reason not to trust her.

Tobo was not used to arguing with anybody but his mother, even when he thought he was right. He did not want to think ill of Arkana but would not fight us.

Lady demanded, "So how do we make sure of them? You have to think of something before we move against Dejagore. We'll be scattered, distracted and extremely vulnerable then. And because you spend time with the girls, out amongst the rest of us, all four will know what's going on. They can plan accordingly."

Again Tobo did not get a word in before I said, "I would be."

Lady reminded him, "You've never been a prisoner."

"Now there's a joke. I was born a prisoner. A prisoner of a prophecy by an old woman who died years before I was born. A prisoner of the expectations of all you people. Gods, I wish Hong Tray was wrong and I could've been a normal kid."

"There aren't any normal kids, Tobo," I told him. "Just kids who fake it better than the rest of us do."

"And that name. Tobo. That was my baby name. Why does everybody still call me that? Why didn't we ever have a ceremony to give me a grown-up name?"

Nyueng Bao do that. And Tobo was years past the appropriate birthday.

Lady told him, "You'll have to take that up with Uncle Doj. Meantime, the other thing needs addressing right now. Blade is moving already. In three more days Sleepy will curl back to the northeast and it'll be too late to stop anything. I want to be sure that we won't get stabbed in the back just when things get exciting."

An hour after we nagged him Tobo asked Shukrat to go flying. He borrowed Arkana's log. Arkana was not pleased. When an hour later she told me Magadan had said he did not mind if she used his post to join Shukrat and Tobo I told her, "But I mind. If you need to talk to Tobo do it when he gets back."

Arkana was the brightest of the Voroshk. She recognized that things were tightening up.

When Tobo did return he stayed just long enough to round up Magadan. He took Magadan flying. It was the first time Magadan had been aloft since he had entered our keeping. He did not appear excited, which I would have expected.

They returned within a half hour. Magadan's hand-me-downs, appropriated from Gharhawnes' former occupants, were ragged. He looked like he had been in a fight and the other guy had kicked his butt. A good long way.

Tobo gave instructions for Magadan to be isolated, then found Arkana and took her for a fly.

The ice queen, I noted, had replaced her confiscated robes with native garb that served her to considerable visual advantage.

"Down, boy!" Lady said.

"It's a good thing I didn't run into her before I met you, isn't it?"

That earned me a not entirely playful swat.

Arkana came back looking rougher than Magadan had. And she was not smiling. Tobo had Arkana put in with Magadan. He collected Gromovol.

Gromovol was not interested in going anywhere with Tobo. Tobo insisted. They were not gone long. Once they returned Tobo had the Voroshk returned to their quarters. He gathered their flying posts in the main hall. Lady and I joined him.

I asked, "What was that all about?"

"I took them out and dueled with them. Except for Shukrat."

I stopped Lady before she explained—probably at great length—how unsmart doing that could have proven. Sometimes she could fuss as much as Sahra. I said, "I'm sure there was a reason."

"I wanted to find out just how much we really do have to fear from them."

"And?"

"They're frauds. The only power they really have is what they draw from their post and their clothing. Without those even Shukrat isn't as powerful as One-Eye was at the end. Gromovol is about Uncle Doj's equal. Lady, even as weak as you are right now, you could manage any of them but Shukrat."

I snorted. "I guess that would explain why Gromovol's pop was anxious to get the kids back. Were most of the Voroshk limited talents? Were most of them carried by a few strong members of the clan?"

"I'd guess that's likely. The point, though, is that for right now there's a better chance our Voroshk will attack us with knives than with sorcery." He looked at us, saw no obvious eagerness to embrace his theory. "Don't you think that if they had any real power they would've used it to try to escape?"

I realized that he was upset. He had believed he was making friends with the Voroshk. Our worries had led him to test that and he had learned that his friends were not as close as he had hoped.

"You're telling us we don't have to kill them to be safe," Lady said.

"That, too."

"You have the Unknown Shadows at your command and you didn't figure this out until today?" Lady can find something to suspect in everything. I would suggest we retire and settle down somewhere where we do not have to worry all the time but she would suspect me of ulterior motives.

"I've thought it for a long time," he admitted sullenly. "But the hidden folk can't report things that they don't hear. The Voroshk don't discuss their weaknesses. Or much of anything else, actually. Because of their present situation nobody likes anybody very much anymore."

I said, "I didn't want to kill them, anyway. Maybe I'd like to thump Gromovol a little, now and then, but . . ."

"So that's settled. Heck, turn them loose if you want. Once they've had a dose of the real world they'll come back. Meantime, let me get to work on these things."

Lady asked, "You've finally found their secret? You can make more?"

"I've learned how to change who they recognize as their master. None of the Voroshk know how the posts are made. They're not even sure of the theory behind them. I know more than they do just because I've studied the things. I don't yet know how they pull their magical power. But I don't know how I do that, either. Someday I will know. But it'll be a long, slow, dangerous process, finding out. They're booby-trapped."

I told him, "Life is booby-trapped, kid."

As we left the hallway Lady was speculating on whether the original Voroshk had invented their magics or if they had just stolen them from an ingenious but unwary predecessor. I did not care, so long as no Voroshk made my life more difficult than it already was.

The Taglian Territories: Nightfliers in Dejagore

Three flying posts formed the goose flock formation. Tobo had the point with Willow Swan riding pillion. Swan was in the throes of an apparently severe religious relapse, muttering a continuous polysyllabic one-word prayer. With his attitude toward heights he would be bruising Tobo by hanging on so tight. His eyes would be closed so intently that he would have muscle cramps all the way back to his ankles.

Lady and Shukrat flew the other posts. Lady had Aridatha Singh aboard behind her. Shukrat carried Uncle Doj.

Murgen, Thai Dei and I shared the flying carpet with the Howler, whose shrieks were being contained inside a big glass bowl sort of thing Lady had put over his head. It worked well enough to save trouble with people who did not know we were coming.

Murgen and Thai Dei were along only because Sahra had to be placated. She did not want her baby going into harm's way alone. People everywhere were irked because the boy's father and uncle had had to be flown back to Gharhawnes before the raid could be launched. But Sahra had been stubborn and loud and Sleepy had given in rather than lose a friend.

Sahra's recollections of and fears of Dejagore remained abiding and debilitating.

I hoped Murgen and Thai Dei handled it better, though at takeoff time Murgen had been sweaty, pallid, shaking and appeared to be having trouble breathing. And Thai Dei had seemed more self-engrossed than ever.

I had spoken to each alone and had tried telling each that I was counting on him to keep an eye on the other and carry him if the emotional strain became too much. I have found that assigning major external responsibilities like that can get many of my brothers through times of deep emotional stress.

Howler kept the carpet in the pocket of the formation. We moved northward at a pace that created a cold wind strong enough to pull the tears out of my eyes. Murgen and I occupied the carpet's rear corners. I told him, "I'd forgotten just how much I don't like this. Why didn't I send some of those eager young bucks from Hsien?"

"Because you're just like every other recent Captain of the Company. You've got to have your pointy nose right in the middle of things so you can make sure things get done your way."

Up ahead Tobo lifted the shutter on a red lantern. He winked the light several times. There was an answering signal from the ground, miles off our track and much farther forward than I expected.

Blade and the cavalry had made good time and were already in the ring of hills surrounding Dejagore. The moon would rise in an hour. It would provide the light they needed to filter through the hills and descend the inner slope.

We passed over the rim and discovered the scattered lights of Dejagore. We slowed to a crawl. The flying posts gathered together. Aridatha tried to explain to Tobo where we needed to go.

I told Murgen, "You should've gone with Tobo. You know Dejagore better than anyone else."

"Dejagore twenty-five years ago, maybe. It's a whole new city since my day. Aridatha belongs with him. It's only been weeks since he was there."

Few details could be distinguished by starlight but as we moved closer the walls and main buildings matched my recollections almost exactly.

The logs formed up in line astern with Lady and Aridatha leading. Howler fell in behind. We resumed moving.

Ten minutes later we were on the ground. Five minutes after that Aridatha hustled us into his brother's shop.

Sugriva Singh seemed to be a shorter and older version of Aridatha. He had done well for himself. He had the whole downstairs of a building for his business and everything above for his family—none of whom were ever in evidence.

Sugriva's past good fortune assured his deep displeasure at our invasion. All of a sudden he had ten villains in amongst the vegetables and only his brother and the bountiful little blonde did not look willing to roast him for a prank. He had a great deal to lose here. And maybe more to lose if he did not cooperate. The Strangler cult was hated in the extreme in Dejagore. Just a whisper about his relationship to the living saint of the Deceivers would destroy him and just about anyone who had ever spoken to him.

Aridatha dispensed with introductions. Sugriva did not need to know his visitors. Chances were, he recognized a few of us anyway.

Aridatha told his brother, "Our father is dead. He was murdered a few weeks ago. Strangled."

Sugriva was the elder by a decade. He remembered the Narayan Singh who had sold vegetables and doted on his children before the invasion of the Shadowmasters. He was stricken as Aridatha had not been stricken. "And that should be no surprise, should it? Is that what you mean?" Sugriva said through tears that might have been due as much to rage as to pain.

He needed a few minutes to collect himself.

To his credit Sugriva Singh did not rail against the inevitable. He understood exactly how his arm was being twisted and, though events were not going to proceed quite like Aridatha had led him to expect during his previous visit, he chose to cooperate. He wanted to get it over as fast as he could, then he would pray that the new administration would be as indifferent to him as he was to the one presently in place.

Things were not exactly working out the way Aridatha had hoped they would, either.

Sugriva said, "You haven't chosen the best night to do this. The moon is going to expose anyone moving toward the city from outside."

Tobo chuckled. "You might be surprised. The night is our friend, brother Sugriva."

"I rather expect you'll find that my father believed the same thing, young man."

And his father's son? Sugriva had been unhappy, even angry, when we turned up, but not really surprised. What kind of vegetable dealer was not surprised to be wakened in the night? Inside a city that closed its gates with fanatical devotion when the sun's lower limb touched the western hilltops?

Could Aridatha's big brother be some sort of crook?

Aridatha told his brother, "The reason we're troubling you is that we don't know how the gatekeeping is managed."

"You told me before. I looked into it. There's a company of soldiers assigned to each gate. The west gate is the most closely controlled because it sees more traffic than the other three put together." One of Dejagore's quirks was that most of to-day's roads to the city joined outside it, to the west, so there was not much traffic elsewhere. The north and south gates were used only by people involved in agricul-ture and its produce.

"The east gate looks like it should be the easiest to seize and control," Sugriva said. A true road did connect with the east gate but there was little out that way but a few distant villages. "The guards are slackers, at all levels. None of them are na-tives. None of them are old enough to remember the last time Jaicur was attacked." Sugriva had adopted the local accent and the local name for the city when he had assumed a Dejagoran name.

The trouble with the east gate was that Blade was west of Dejagore. But he was well ahead of schedule. There was time, before sunrise, if he hustled.

Tobo suggested, "Lady, why don't you go tell Blade that it has to be the east gate?"

"Because I'm going to be getting dressed."

Widowmaker and Lifetaker were coming to the party. They had been away for far too long.

Half a minute later Shukrat said, "I guess it's time to find out if you can really trust me, Tobo."

I jumped in before the boy could speak. "I suppose so. Tell Blade not to waste time. We need as much of the night as we can get. And we won't stay unnoticed long once we start. Tell him we'll be waiting when he gets to the gate."

A smile tickled Shukrat's freckled, almost pudgy face. She bounced up onto her toes and gave Tobo a peck on the cheek. Bold, bold behavior by any standard in this part of the world. They must do things differently among the Voroshk.

She bounced away. Tobo was completely flustered. I grinned till Lady poked me in the ribs. Evidently I was enjoying the bouncing part a little too much.

Murgen said, "I suggest we get to work here, folks. I don't want to be inside these walls a minute longer than I have to." He was holding it together but the strain was obvious.

Thai Dei was frazzled, too, and with even better reason. A lot of people very close to him had died here during the siege. No matter how tough a man pretends to be, such losses gnaw at his soul. Unless he is not human at all.

"The man has a point," I said. "Start getting ready."

Lady and I had the most to do. We had a big show to put on. We retreated into a small separate room, colder than the main shop. As we strove to turn ourselves into walking nightmares I asked, "Hon, have you really got that post-riding stuff figured out?"

"It isn't that hard. Except for staying on. Any idiot could do it. There are some little black rods and slidy things you move around. You go up or down, or faster or slower, or whatever, when you do. Why?"

"It occurs to me that it might be better for us and him both if we got Aridatha back to Taglios. He's been gone a long time. Mogaba needs to have him back where he can show him off before news of tonight's business gets around."

She did not stop donning the Lifetaker armor but did look at me in a way that I do not see often. It was like she was looking right through me, at all the secret places inside. It was frightening sometimes.

"All right. We'll have to move fast if I'm going to be aloft before daylight."

"Will the log make it that far?" Not knowing how those things worked I did not know what you might have to feed it, like a horse. The posts did seem to work on a different principle than Howler's flying carpets, which required a strong-willed, powerful sorcerer to drive them. They demanded his undivided attention every moment they were aloft.

"I'm sure it will. What do you want me to tell Mogaba?"

The long-time taunt, "My brother unforgiven," came to mind, along with, "All their days are numbered." But this was not the time.

62

Dejagore:
The Occupation

My original intention had been to make a huge show of our invasion. I do like a big ration of drama. Lightning. Thunder. Fireworks. But I waited until we had the gate open to let it start.

Early on there were alarms from the south wall as a tide of darkness and whispers passed by. But no sentry saw a single horsemen. They spied only vague shapes that stirred secret fears of things far darker and crueler than any conquering soldier.

The city was restless and troubled but remained unaware of our presence. It did sense approaching change.

The thunder and lightning came after Blade's men started coming through the gate, six hundred men in Hsien's strange armor, under strict orders not to betray their humanity until the city was captured. Most Dejagorans were Gunni. The Gunni believed in demons who could take human shape to make war on men. And most of the people of the outlying Taglian Territories had by now heard that the Company was allied with ghosts and devils.

Each soldier had a bamboo wand carrying a banner affixed to his back. The color of the banner declared the man's unit affiliation while characters painted on the banner stated that unit's martial slogan. Widowmaker and Lifetaker rode at the head of the invading column. She carried a burning sword. Widowmaker carried One-Eye's spear, which was crawling with maggots of light. His shoulders bore a salt-and-pepper set of oversized ravens.

And, even so, much of the city slept on.

Ugly worms of fire crawled over our hideous armor. Bannermen marched ahead flailing big flags supposed to be our personal ensigns.

Witnesses brought out by the flash and boom and the rattle of horseshoes remembered old stories and ran away weeping.

Yet most of the city slept on.

Doj, Murgen, Thai Dei and Swan remained at the gate, holding the hostages we had taken there. Aridatha stayed out of sight at his brother's place. Howler, Tobo and Shukrat circled high above. Howler's glass bowl continued to contain his shrieks. We hoped he would remain a secret for a while.

The real fireworks began when we reached the citadel, where the Protector's still-sleepy governor deluded himself into thinking he could refuse to surrender and make it stick.

Fireballs flew. The citadel gate exploded. Holes appeared in its walls. People inside began to scream.

Every dark place in the streets had something moving inside it. Hundreds of somethings, many of them vaguely familiar in those instants when anything could be clearly discerned.

Those flooded in through the broken gate of the citadel. They weaseled through the holes in its walls.

Lifetaker and Widowmaker followed moments later.

The terrified inhabitants of the tower put up no fight at all. Our sole injury was a broken arm suffered by a dimwit who tripped over his own big feet and rolled down a stair.

Lady and I stood atop the citadel. The city below still was not fully aware that it had been conquered. I said, "It hurt a lot less getting here tonight than it did last time."

"That was the night we made Booboo."

"Which was a real booboo."

"Not funny."

"That was the night One-Eye made the enemy that stalked us for twenty years, too."

"We'll make new enemies this time. I have to go if I want to have any hope of getting Aridatha into Taglios unnoticed."

"I don't think you can, tonight. Not without flying so damned fast the wind rips the skin off your face."

"I'll see if Tobo can't help."

It was difficult to kiss her good-bye. We still wore all the costume armor.

The Taglian Territories:
The Middle Army

The Protector's reconnaissance troops had warned her that something unusual was taking shape. The warning confirmed her suspicions. Her nonhuman spies had been having almost no success keeping track of the enemy. Which meant the enemy was taking pains to be less visible.

Soulcatcher raised the state of alert and stepped up training. She redoubled her own, personal preparations.

When word of the disaster at Dejagore reached her—one lone rider managing to get through with the news—she had known for fourteen hours already that the Company main force had left its westward track and had begun hustling up a line that would slice between her Middle Army and the newly orphaned force outside Dejagore.

That would evaporate within days, she presumed. Many of those soldiers came out of the city itself—a disproportionate percentage of them officers—while the rest would now hear the call of the harvest much more loudly.

What the hell had happened down there? The messenger had brought very few details, just word that the city had awakened to find itself occupied. The invaders had been swift and thorough. They seemed to have had outstanding intelligence. Heavy sorcery might have been involved.

"The next fight won't be so one-sided," she promised her officers. "Next fight they'll have to deal with me. Me like they haven't seen me in a long, long time." She was angry and awake and no longer handicapped by any shred of boredom. She was feeling more alive and filled with hatred and bitterness than she had for a generation.

Within hours her new mood had electrified those around her.

Officers who failed to become equally electrified quickly suffered permanent replacement.

64

Dejagore:
The Orphaned Army

After losing their base at Dejagore the generals of the fading, confused army nearby ineptly tried to invest the city in a way that would not result in economic disaster. Then, six days after the fall, news came that the enemy main force was rushing straight toward them.

There had been skirmishes with the cavalry occupying Dejagore. Those had not gone well for the locals. And now ten times as many well-disciplined, perfectly-armed, trained killers were about to fall on them.

A third of the army went home under cover of darkness the night after the news arrived. Those who stayed endured almost continuous psychological torments by things they could never see.

The murderous army from the south never materialized. That was never necessary. The Dejagoran soldiers in the Taglian force all deserted. The cavalrymen occupying Dejagore scattered the army's steadfast core without outside help.

Taglios:
The Palace

Mogaba's level of discomfort—he would not think the word "fear"—had risen substantially since Aridatha's return. The stakes kept rising. The risks kept expanding. Lady had been seen by Palace servants. So far those believed they had seen the Protector, whose comings and goings were secretive and unpredictable. But someday Soulcatcher might overhear some mention and know she could not have been two places at once. Nor would she believe the manifestation to have been one of the haunts now regularly seen in the maze of passageways for which the Palace was famed.

Mogaba told Ghopal and Aridatha, "I'm tempted to drop everything and run."

Ghopal asked, "Yeah? Where would you go?" It might not be as personal but his doom was every bit as certain as Mogaba's was if the Black Company reconquered Taglios and restored the ruling family. Life would turn cruel for any Shadar who had belonged to the Greys.

"Exactly." Mogaba ran his palm over the top of his head. Keeping it shaved required less and less work. "So I remind myself what honor demands."

Aridatha said little. He had not talked much since his return. Mogaba understood. Singh had seen things he did not want to believe were true. He had learned things about the stakes that left him paralyzed with indecision. There appeared to be no road leading toward the light. Wherever he turned he beheld another face of the darkness.

It was important to Aridatha that he do what he perceived to be the right thing.

Singh's visit with his brother had fueled him with a determination to offset some of the evil his father had done.

Aridatha was Gunni by faith but his character was much more suited to the Vehdna religion. He thought *this* was the life where wrongs had to be made right.

Mogaba said, "The news from the south is uniformly disasterous. The Black Company is meeting very little resistance. They have superior sorcery, superior weaponry, superior troops, equipment and leadership. Not to mention intelligence so good we're wasting our time trying to keep anything secret. So it seems our fates actually depend on how fast those people can get here. The Protector won't stop them. They'll pluck the strings of her ego, tickle her pride, and just when she thinks she's ready to make her kill they'll hit her in the back of the head with a sledge-hammer she'll never see coming. You have to be more than just powerful to deal with those people. You have to be more than clever and treacherous. You need to be psychic."

Ghopal asked, "Then why don't we ride down there and take charge?" He smirked.

"Not funny. Two reasons. First, she doesn't want me to. She still thinks we can get them into a pocket between us. I don't know how. And, more importantly, if I got anywhere near her there'd be no way I could hide my thoughts and no oppor-tunity to put them into effect before she could protect herself. You two, you might be a little luckier."

Ghopal observed, "The city is remarkably calm in spite of the news."

Tidings of the fall of Dejagore were making the rounds but hardly anyone seemed to feel that the Protector was in any peril herself. There had been no disor-ders. Graffiti was becoming more common, though. Mostly the same old taunts, though rajadharma was becoming more common. Then there was a new one: You shall lie in the ashes ten thousand years eating only wind. And one not seen for years had reappeared: Thi Kim is coming.

No one knew quite what that meant. Maybe not even its framers. Some people thought "Thi Kim" might be a Nyueng Bao phrase. In which case the name could mean something like Walking Murder.

If it was not Nyueng Bao it made even less sense. Or no sense at all.

Aridatha asked, "If we do nothing to support her and she gets beaten, how do we defend ourselves?"

Mogaba said, "I'm going to tell you right now, *you* don't have a problem unless the Protector wins. The Company and the royals have no quarrel with you. You've done a good job running the City Battalions. If you just sit on your hands you'll probably end up inheriting my job."

Aridatha shrugged. "You must have talked about these things when *she* was here."

"Oh, yes. She said nobody would chase me very hard if I had sense enough to take off before they occupied the city."

Ghopal asked, "They're that confident? That they can discount your help? What about me?"

"She's that confident. Which is probably too confident. She didn't say anything about you. She didn't know who you were. She suggested that if you think you have reasons to fear the return of the royals you should join me in looting as much treas-ure as you can before you run away."

"Shadar don't abandon their oaths of service."

Aridatha, with little to fear from defeat, suggested, "Let's just do our jobs. Like we've always done. And see what opportunities Fortune places in our hands."

Sarcastically, Ghopal responded, "Of course. The Black Company and the Protector could end up destroying each other. Like a couple of rams getting their horns locked."

A consideration which left all three men thoughtful, with Mogaba in particular reflecting on how fate might write the joke that would end with that unexpected punchline.

66

The Taglian Territories: Midway Between

Oh, we looked good, ten thousand strong, all lined up as if for a parade. Every man wore his armor. Every man had his personal banner whipping in the breeze. Every battalion wore its own color of armor. Every weapon was perfectly honed and polished. Every horse was groomed and caparisoned as though for review. Every standard was in place and gloriously new. We were a general's wet dream, pretty and dangerous, too.

The gang opposite us, though they outnumbered us three to one, looked like they would be no challenge. Men over there were still trying to find their assigned places in ranks.

Good as it all looked I had my doubts about the wisdom of offering battle, however confident our guys were and however much confidence the men opposite us lacked. But Sleepy wanted to crush them fast and harry Soulcatcher back to Taglios where, because she would be hard-pressed, she might not be wary enough to elude ambush by Mogaba and his henchmen.

She was assuming too much would go our way. When things are going good is when you really have to watch your back.

But I was not the Captain. I could only advise, then do my part in the show once a decision had been made.

Tobo was more confident than Sleepy was. He believed the enemy only needed a nudge to crack. One vicious shock and they would collapse. He guaranteed it.

Trumpets sounded the ready. Drums began to talk, counting the cadence for the advance. A thousand men would remain in reserve. Well behind them were the recruits we had acquired. Those surrounded the Radisha and her brother, nominally forming the royal lifeguard. They would be used only in desperation.

The trumpets sounded the advance. The ranks stepped out, lines dressed, cadence perfect, weapons exactly on line. Positioned in front of the wings, Lifetaker and Widowmaker lit off in blinding flashes and began to advance themselves. But they halted before they entered missile range.

From that closer vantage I could see that Soulcatcher had formed her troops up in three successive forces with a hundred yards of separation each between them. The frontline unit was the most numerous but looked like the lowest quality. The second formation appeared much more solid.

That was a device I understood, having used a variant myself. But you have to be confident that your real fighters will not catch the panic of the scrubs when they run away.

There were things going on behind Soulcatcher's third line but they were too far away to be made out clearly.

Then the advancing soldiers made seeing much more difficult. Then the next stage of enchantments surrounded me, concealing me from enemy eyes, making it impossible for me to see anything either.

67

The Taglian Territories:
Inside the Middle Army

This is going to be tricky," Soulcatcher reminded staff officers compelled to take her genius on trust. Her previous demonstration, during the Kiaulune wars, had come before their time.

The enemy trumpets sounded the ready. His drums began to rumble.

Soulcatcher said, "Once they sound the advance they'll be too busy to spy on us."
The advance sounded.

"I want the word spread on the second line that the collapse of the first line is
part of my plan. Tell them it's a deliberate ruse. I don't want anybody running because the first line does. Tell them that anybody who does run is guaranteed worm
food. Then tell the third line the same thing about the first and second lines. I want
them to believe I'm luring the enemy in where I can use sorcery to destroy them.
And I want the reserves backed off to the edge of the wood. Right away."

"But that means . . ."

"Forget the camp. If we don't win this fight the camp won't matter. I want the
reserves spread out along the edge of the woods so they can collect up men who run
away and get them organized. But before they do that I want them in here to move
my guests back to the north bank of the creek."

Blank looks stared her way.

Anger began to creep into her voice. Anger they knew to be the sort that soon
saw corpses arriving on the cemetery ground outside camp. When Soulcatcher was
angry enough she would not let the Gunni burn, and thus purify, the bodies of
those she had slain. "Form them at the edge of the woods! Ready to kill any cowards!" Then in a calm, almost beatific voice she added, "If the soldiers fail to rally
and throw back the enemy their generals won't long survive defeat." Soulcatcher
had very strong feelings about how this engagement should proceed. "In fact, the
wise general will make plans not to outlive his standard bearer. His passing will be
much less painful that way."

She had been preparing for days. But she was compelled to fight with flawed
weapons. The most rigid control had to be exercised.

"Get busy!" She stepped past the officers, left the tent, climbed up a reviewing
stand that would let her see the action. As she took her place there the enemy, with
the precision of a drill team, collided with her forward deployment.

The slaughter was slighter than she had anticipated. The enemy seemed content to
shatter opposing formations. They did not pursue. They halted, removed wounded,
dressed their ranks and repaired their equipment. And took their time doing it. Which
pleased the Protector. That meant more time for the beaten companies to collect
themselves at the edge of the wood.

Soulcatcher glanced back as men carried her prisoners' cages out of her tent. Goblin, his eyes regenerated already, offered her a little mocking salute. The girl looked
straight at her and smiled.

One more time and she would throw the brat to the soldiers for a few hours.
That would take the sass out of her.

The soldiers managing the removal seemed calm enough, despite the terrified
fugitives beginning to enter the camp.

Soulcatcher was irritated at herself for having overlooked the chance that the fugitives might not flee all the way to the woods. She should have had the palisade demolished.

No matter. Only a few would take refuge here.

She gave orders to seal the gates.

The enemy resumed his advance.

The second line gave a better account of itself but the outcome was identical. The troops broke without doing much real damage to the foe.

This time none of the fleeing soldiers got into the camp.

Once again the enemy stopped to handle his wounded and dress his lines and repair his armor. The cavalry screening the enemy flanks were having trouble holding back. Soulcatcher guessed that discipline would crack once the third Taglian line fell apart.

Those idiots had better be ready back at the wood.

Soulcatcher left her vantage as the enemy sounded the advance again. "Very businesslike, this new Captain. But how well does she think on her feet?"

Very businesslike, Soulcatcher's personal removal to the wood, where she growled new orders at her officers before she retired to the big tent she had had prepared, as a pretended forest getaway and as a place where she could meet messengers from the allies who were trying to butcher her now. Goblin and the Daughter of Night had been deposited there.

Both prisoners seemed amused by her arrival. As though they had shared some particularly hysterical joke, entirely at her expense, just a moment before she appeared.

Soulcatcher paid them no attention. She was much more concerned about how troubled her sister would have grown because of the absence of sorcery on the battlefield. If no one became too suspicious for another fifteen minutes . . .

The Taglian Territories:
Fire on the Middle Ground

Behind the brilliant fog of light masking Widowmaker I climbed down off my horse, then clambered onto the Voroshk flying post I would share with my former understudy, Murgen. The post had Magadan's name painted on it in his native script. Over on the left, Lifetaker, too, was preparing to soar with that noted devotee of high flying, Willow Swan. All of the flying logs were ready to go up, each surrounded by an absurd wicker and bamboo framework carrying numerous makeshift attachments.

Somewhere back where I could not see them, Tobo and Howler were getting ready to take up a flying carpet creaking under the weight of warlike unpleasantries. The screaming wizard was still muttering under his breath because he had been forced to reveal his flying secrets to Tobo.

A huge volume of raw nastiness would be taken aloft, to be launched either when Soulcatcher betrayed her location or our attack began to bog down.

The latter did not happen. The evaporation of the Taglian front line was a daydream come true. The second line lasted only a little while longer. The third line, evidently comprised of the best and most motivated of the Protector's troops, was more stubborn. Having spent too much time too close to Soulcatcher myself, I could imagine why the third force might have had a little extra motivation. Soulcatcher was not a thoughtful, forgiving commander.

Give her her due, though. She would not expect love or forgiveness from anyone superior to her, either. In the world where she had come of age that had been the norm. That world, of the Domination, had demanded ruthlessness and cruelty. It had forgiven neither kindness nor compassion.

The third line's stubbornness failed to withstand the precision and confidence of our men. Fainthearts began to slip away and run toward that distant treeline, where somebody appeared to be rallying survivors.

The rout had only just begun when a dome of cardinal light popped into existence in an instant, straight ahead. It faded in seconds. I was making a clumsy effort to gain altitude when a second dome of light, this time carmine, appeared and faded to my left.

There were a half dozen more flashes, each in the family of reds, before I felt confident that I was high enough and dared to divert attention from the post's controls long enough to see what Murgen had been babbling about throughout our climb.

The sorcery in progress appeared to have turned the earth a uniform black. Upon that surface something kept painting red flowers that spread from a pinpoint in an eyes' blink, almost black at the center but fading to flame yellow as the circle ended its expansion at perhaps twelve yards in diameter. From on high nothing but the sudden red chrysanthemums, blooming randomly, were readily visible. The earth looked like some bleak gameboard upon which a garden of deathflowers continue to blossom and gradually fade.

Whatever was happening, it was passive. Not coming to us. The sorcery had been in place already and was being tripped by our advancing soldiers. Who were not getting off lightly.

Soulcatcher did not make herself evident anywhere.

Way off to my left Lady and Willow vanished behind smoke as all the bamboo fireball launchers attached to their post sprayed the Taglian camp. Dozens of fires broke out down there but the red circles kept blooming amongst our soldiers.

I pushed my post forward half a mile. I told Murgen, "Saturate the wood. She's in there somewhere. Where the hell are my crows? They're never around when I need them." They had disappeared during my climb to altitude. Maybe they did not like getting too far from the surface of the earth.

There was no sign of the Unknown Shadows anywhere. But I did not expect to see signs. Tobo had sent most of the hidden folk away last night, for their own safety.

You notice strange things in times of stress. I remarked the absence of crows around the battlefield. A rather bizarre lacking which I had not witnessed before, ever. But vultures had begun to circle above the wood.

Murgen shouted something about the enemy taking heart from our misfortune. I said, "Put the fireballs along the treeline, then." Which was really my task since I had to point the Voroshk post where I wanted the fireballs to go.

Child Shukrat, better schooled in the use of the post, swept in from the east, low, laying her fire down upon the Taglian line. She wasted hardly a fireball.

Our ground advance halted. Sleepy did not withdraw but neither was she willing to face any more killing sorcery.

I would not see how bad that had been until I was back on the ground. Which was soon enough because once we exhausted our fireball supply there was nothing more Murgen and I could do from above.

I had no trouble imagining Soulcatcher over there in those woods laughing her leathers off at how she had hurt us.

The Taglians launched one uncoordinated, inept counterattack which turned disastrous when they began to run away again. Soulcatcher's sorceries did not distinguish between friend and foe, only between directions of travel.

We grounded well to the rear. I remounted my horse and went forward. Soulcatcher's sorcery had been terrible. The site where each flower of light had bloomed remained defined as a red so dark it verged on black. The black itself was fading from around the circles, trampled grass gradually becoming visible like winter wheat sprouting. But weirder crops appeared within the circles.

Men, sunken into the earth, some only ankle deep, some up to their hips and more. Frozen in the advance, still in their lines. All suits of armor no longer tenanted by even a ghost of life.

Somebody had tried opening several suits. Inside there was nothing but charred flesh and bone. A quick calculation suggested we might have lost four or five hundred men to this horror, which had taken place almost faster than it can be told.

"There's something wrong here," I said. "Soulcatcher has stopped."

"What?" Murgen asked. He was probing a deadly circle. He discovered that it was cool now and the visible surface was no thicker than a fingernail. "What's that?" Later, when we collected the dead, we learned that they had not sunk into the earth. The apparently sunken portion was not there when we dug out around them. Possibly they had melted.

"Soulcatcher stopped playing with us. She had to be controlling those circles somehow. Otherwise they would've killed her own soldiers the first time they retreated. But that isn't working anymore. What's changed? What's happened?"

Suddenly, the vultures above the wood all spiralled down rapidly, as though planning to attack something.

I said, "Let's see what Sleepy is up to."

Sleepy was sending scouts to explore the limits of the danger. So far no death flower had bloomed on our far flanks.

The vultures stopped their descent just above the treetops but continued to look more like raptors than carrion birds. One suffered an impulse to descend a little farther.

A golden-brown urine-colored strand darted up like a gigantic toad's tongue. A splatter of light surrounded the bird. It seemed to become a black cutout of a vulture. The cutout shattered into a hundred fragments. Those fluttered down like falling leaves.

The remaining vultures chose to take their business elsewhere.

Nobody but me seemed to notice what was happening.

Where were my damned ravens? I could send them to see what was happening while keeping my own sweet ass high and dry. What was the point of taking on a mythic character if I did not get to do mythic kinds of things?

Moments later Tobo and Howler were above the woods, dropping prosaic firebombs on the Taglian forces.

Lady joined us before Sleepy's scouts had found out if we could safely slide around the ends of the killing zone. She had a map she presented to the Captain. One glimpse told me my sweetie had not wasted her time aloft. She had charted the deadly circles. And a pattern was apparent. The positions of those not yet tripped were evident. Unless Soulcatcher had been aware of our airborne capacity. Then the death circles would be there solely to herd us into something far more gruesome and cruel.

Sleepy summoned her battalion commanders immediately.

Midway Between:
The Unanticipated

Soulcatcher's soldiers fought stubbornly for a while, along the edge of the wood, but had been too badly mauled already to last long under determined attack by our professional bloodletters.

Most of the Taglians had no desire to see their wives and children lose their husbands and fathers. Sleepy gave orders to let anyone who abandoned his weapons go.

Any Taglian economy inherited by the Prahbrindrah Drah would be better off if it was not crippled by a great slaughter of the empire's young men. It was only now recovering from the horrible losses suffered during the Shadowmaster and Kiaulune wars.

"It wasn't anywhere nearly as eloquent a victory as I'd hoped. But I'll take it," Sleepy said. "Despite our casualties. This war may have been won today."

That earned her a lot of bewildered or disbelieving looks. Soulcatcher was still out there, in a really foul temper now. More unpleasant surprises could be expected.

"But if we keep after her she'll be distracted when she reaches Taglios."

Mogaba's plans were a longshot. I said so. "And whatever sweet nothings his conscience whispered to him a couple months back, he'll be a whole lot more worried about saving Mogaba's skin once he has old enemies pounding on his door for real."

Sleepy started to say something about Aridatha Singh but thought better of it.

A carmine flash appeared on the killing ground. Using Lady's chart Tobo had triggered a booby trap by bombarding it from the Howler's flying carpet.

Sleepy told Runmust Singh, "After Tobo's done I want you to march some prisoners back and forth through there. I don't want any of those things left active. Some kid might wander in there and get himself killed." Like the countryside was swarming with stupid children.

I said, "I'd be more pleased if we could grab a few of those things for our own use. If Mogaba had something like that he might stand a chance of killing Soulcatcher."

Lady ruined the fun. "She'd smell it out. She created those things. There'll be safeguards so they can't be thrown back at her."

A whole lot of shouting started in the woods. Tobo and Shukrat darted that way, in case the soldiers needed help. Moments later Howler's carpet streaked back our way.

Tobo did not bother to dismount. He just announced, "They've found the Daughter of Night. She's in a cage. Soulcatcher ran off and left her."

Lady and I exchanged looks. That seemed completely unlikely. Unless the girl was bait in a truly deadly trap. Which might be. Soulcatcher had sown the field of death that had consumed our soldiers without the Unknown Shadows noticing her doing it.

Midway Between:
The Capture

The cage was inside a halfway collapsed tent. Several fireballs had ripped through the fabric but had failed to set it afire. I told everyone, "Be extremely careful here. If there was ever a time when Soulcatcher would try to spring something on us this would be it."

Sleepy had her henchmen push curious soldiers back. We were already closer to the tent than Lady liked—though that had as much to do with who we expected to meet here as it had to do with concern about sorcerous deadfalls.

Nobody had yet been able to sense anything active in that line.

Lady told Tobo, "Go over everything three more times. Then check it again.

Howler, you go over it, too." Of no one in particular she asked, "Where's Goblin?"
When she got no answer she turned on the men who had found the tent, all of whom
were in perfect health despite having taken time to scrounge souvenirs before they
reported their find. "Where's the little man? The one who got away at Nijha."

Shrugs. They might not know what she was talking about. But one brave soul
did say, "There's another cage under there. It's tipped over and broken. Maybe he
got away."

Lady and I exchanged glances. Why would Goblin leave without the girl?

He would not.

Tobo called out, "There's no danger here."

Howler tried to concur but his voice gurgled off into a scream.

I said, "Something definitely ain't right. Tobo, send your unseen pals out to
scout around. We especially need to know where Goblin and Soulcatcher are. As
soon as we can. We have to keep after them."

Sleepy nodded irritated agreement.

Lady and I approached the tent warily.

Booby traps come in many forms.

As we had been warned, one broken cage was empty. The other lay on its side,
door downward. One fine-looking woman lay sort of splattered all over inside,
wearing not a stitch.

Lady stunned me by starting to rush forward saying something about her poor
baby. I caught her arm. "Easy." The body looked, to me, like it had been posed. It
would excite Soulcatcher's sense of humor for decades if she could get us to jump
to our deaths over a child who had no more feeling for us than she did for the
horses, cattle, and whatnot that passed through her life.

Lady paused but would not remain patient long. "What?"

"That isn't Booboo. I don't think." But that naked flesh could not be an illusion,
could it? Goblin used to do that sort of thing. . . . But Tobo said nothing magical
was going on.

I squatted, groaning as my knees creaked, reached through the bars and pulled
dark hair away from the woman's neck, which it had concealed.

I pulled Lady down beside me. Her knees popped as badly as mine had. "Look
there. I do pretty good work, don't I? You can hardly see the scars." I exaggerated.
The scarring was ugly. But not all that ugly for somebody who had had her head
sewn back on.

"Check the foot. Which foot got hurt? The right one, wasn't it?"

I uncovered the woman's right foot. The injury done by Goblin's booby trap,
and Soulcatcher's own crude self-repairs, were immediately obvious.

"I hate her even more than I used to," Lady said. "Except for that heel and her
scars she's still looking just as sleek as she did on her nineteenth birthday. What's
wrong with her?"

I said, "I can't tell from here. But I'm not getting any closer till I know it's safe. Where'd Tobo and Howler go? Get them back here." This remained a potentially explosive situation, even if no sorcery was active. Soulcatcher would be in a foul temper when she regained consciousness.

Lady mused, "The child must have a low opinion of our intelligence if she thought this would fool us."

I wondered. Maybe we just showed up before the trap could be fully prepared.

When Tobo returned he told us, "Cat Sith just spotted Soulcatcher at the north edge of the woods. She has Goblin on a leash. She's rallied some soldiers and has them building earthworks." He became increasingly distracted as he stared at my sister-in-law.

Now was that not an interesting set of developments?

Sleepy blurted, "The Daughter of Night is pretending that she's the Protector?"

Tobo almost reeled back when he realized that he was lusting after a woman five hundred years his senior.

Lady, always an advocate for swift and decisive action when she had been in command, insisted, "We need to press her. Whoever's in charge. Every second she gets to pull things together will mean more casualties and difficulties for us later."

Sleepy did not disagree. It was hard to argue with the truth. She went off to restore order and resume the advance. It was weird that the Taglians, already broken twice and neither well-trained nor motivated, would be rallying. But Tobo insisted that they were doing so and he was not subject to fantasies. Of that sort.

It seemed unlikely that the Taglians would be well-armed. Most of the Taglian soldiers had thrown down their weapons the first time they fled.

Lady gripped my hand for a moment. "Think we'll ever really get to see her?"

"You begin to wonder if she's any closer, or any more real, than Khatovar, don't you?"

Willow Swan came bounding up. "Is it true? Have we caught Soulcatcher again?"

"News spreads fast," I said. "Yes. That's her. I'm pretty sure. You're welcome to join me while I examine her. To make sure." He had gotten closer to her than I ever had as her one-time physician and surgeon. He would have a better chance of spotting physical evidence that this was one of Soulcatcher's elaborate tricks. If he remembered anything at all after five years away.

I did not believe this was a trick. There was something badly wrong with my honey's little sister. I felt that before I got my close-up look.

Swan examined and grumbled. He had no happy recollections of the way Soulcatcher had used him way back when. But he was not driven by any particular hatred of her, either.

Sleepy said, "You keep what this woman did to you firmly in mind, Willow Swan. I don't want to see it happen again. And if I do get a whiff, you can count on getting kneecapped before you score."

Swan wanted to rage and protest that there was no damned way that witch was going to get inside his head again. But he did not. He was only flesh and he recognized that that flesh was incapable of rational thought around any female who shared Soulcatcher's family blood.

His record spoke for itself.

"Then why don't we just kill her?" he asked. Wounded pride burned through his cool. "Right here. Right now. While we've got the best chance we'll ever get. End it all forever."

"We won't because we don't know what Goblin and Booboo did to her," I snapped when Lady seemed strangely reluctant to disappoint a fellow whose passion had fixed upon her originally. She would not be developing a sense of compassion at this late date, would she? Or of family? She and her sister were one another's oldest surviving enemies. "Soulcatcher won't help us more than she absolutely has to but she will help. For a while."

Lady nodded. Her sister was insane but her insanity was pragmatic.

Sister Soulcatcher showed no signs of recovering.

I did not say so but my outburst was part whistling past the graveyard. I was increasingly certain that there was something gravely wrong with Soulcatcher. I feared she might be dying. This was the thing that had claimed Sedvod. And nobody else saw it.

The others were all too excited by the prospect of having her at our mercy.

Midway Between:
Unpleasant Truth

Getting Soulcatcher awake and aware enough to understand and begin suffering because of her circumstances preoccupied Lady and Swan for some time. Murgen and Thai Dei, Sahra and Uncle Doj joined them. In time they meant to strong-arm Soulcatcher into assisting us but first they wanted to fatten up on a feast of gloating.

Soulcatcher did not cooperate. She remained steadfastly unaware, exactly the way Sedvod had done.

The racket of skirmishing rose and fell in the distance, never becoming intense. Our guys did not sound much more ambitious than were our enemies. I did not blame them for a disinclination to get killed when the battle's outcome had been determined already.

Riverwalker jogged into sight. "The Captain's compliments and could you all come up and help her? She has a situation. She'd like some advice."

"I'll be damned," I said. "Just when you think you've seen everything."

"What kind of situation?" Murgen asked. He was not distracted by Soulcatcher. He understood that when the word "situation" was used this way it meant that his son was about to be asked to jump into something particularly hot.

"We're having trouble coming to grips with what's left of the enemy."

I suggested, "Why not just leave them the hell alone now? They're on the run." Riverwalker ignored me.

"At about a hundred yards the soldiers start losing interest. The few who do manage to go on and get within fifty yards say they find themselves thinking how awful they are for interfering with Her and that they really ought to be helping Her fulfill Her holy destiny. 'Her' not being defined but they assume they're thinking about the Protector because the Protector is the devil they know and the devil they thought they were supposed to be chasing."

Lady waved me closer. She murmured, "I'll handle this end. Take the carpet and posts up and bombard the Taglian command from outside spell range."

"We're almost out of fireballs again."

"So drop rocks. Or burning brush. Or anything else that will make her concentrate on staying out of the way. Every time she moves a few more of her troops will drift outside the spell. Whereupon they'll suddenly get smart and run away."

Her confident prescription suggested that this was an effect she knew of old.

I told everyone, "First thing we do is load up on arrows. We'll just drop them from higher than she can reach. From five hundred feet up they ought to be good and deadly." My gut knotted. I was talking about bombarding my own flesh and blood.

But part of me was certain that the girl would avoid personal damage. And part believed that a confrontation had been inherent in the situation from the moment Narayan Singh had snatched our baby from Lady's arms.

It did work. The girl, wearing her aunt's costume, darted around, followed by Goblin. The last few fireballs and firebombs got spent. Their infallible lack of accuracy refreshed my cynical view of our chances of catching a break.

The pair tried to fight back. Whenever a flier descended below a certain level a string of urine-colored lights flung upward. But I kept them too busy skipping out of harm's way to concentrate on their marksmanship. I could not tell which was the source of the deadly light.

I noted that the girl seemed unaware that the guy overhead in the ugly suit was her doting papa.

Our soldiers grasped the situation quickly and seized those opportunities offered by the shifting perimeter around the Taglian forces.

The Daughter of Night was no soldier but she was quick and decisive and did have a source of advice in a man who had spent more than a century soldiering.

Goblin told her to attack, to get what use she could out of the troops she held in thrall. She did attack. Straight toward Sleepy, ignoring the missiles falling around her. Our people had no choice but to run from her while trying to weaken her from extreme rage. Anybody who got too close underwent a sudden change of heart and took up arms on behalf of the Deceiver messiah, without understanding what was happening.

Because she was indifferent to how many of her helpers perished, Booboo was able to chase around everywhere, breaking up everything before it got organized, gaining a recruit for each two or three men she lost, making it emotionally ever more difficult for our archers to hurl missiles at soldiers who had been comrades not that long before. The girl even came near recapturing Soulcatcher.

Then Tobo screwed up.

He assumed that his strength, combined with that of the Howler, would be enough to overpower an untrained girl if they came at her suddenly, from an unexpected direction. And maybe he was right. But he forget that her companion was not the Goblin he had grown up around. This Goblin was infected with wicked godhood.

That urine-colored light caught the flying carpet a glancing blow just before the Howler and Tobo cut loose with the best they had. A chunk of carpet turned into fluttering black scraps. Howler and Tobo and the rest of the carpet hurtled ahead, safe from spells but not from a brutal beating by the branches of the trees into which they plunged. The Howler got off a couple of heartfelt shrieks.

The urine-colored bar of light did the magical equivalent of jostling the mystical elbows of the young sorcerer and the ancient one alike. Their spells did a lot of damage to Booboo's defenders. They even managed to stun their intended targets. But because the spellcasters were bouncing around in the branches in the woods, instead of reporting in, the rest of us never got a chance to take advantage.

Midway Between:
The Rescuers

We had a standoff of sorts. We could not get at Goblin and the Daughter of Night when they were most vulnerable. Their thugs did not know that we had lost our most potent weapons, at least for a time. My ravens, who had returned conveniently only when it was time for them to become Tobo's mouthpieces, informed me that Howler and Tobo had survived but were hurt. They were hidden in the woods a few dozen yards from where the Daughter of Night and Goblin, barely recovered enough to keep breathing, were hunkered down.

I tried to let Sleepy know quietly but Sahra was too alert. In moments she worked herself into a state that even Murgen could not soften. "You've got to do something!" she shrieked.

"The Daughter of Night will hear you," Murgen growled.

"You've got to get him out of there!"

"Be quiet!"

I agreed. Somebody had to do something. That somebody might be me. But the only useful help I had was my two raven assistants. They alternately reported Tobo unconscious or quietly delirious. They could not get reliable orders from him. They refused to let me use them to transmit orders to the other Unknown Shadows. Those were gathering in numbers such that it was impossible not to catch glimpses of them when you turned or moved suddenly.

"We can't get close to him," Murgen told Sahra. He shook her. She was not listening. If she listened she would have to hear uncomfortable truths.

Shukrat stepped forward. She told us, "I can bring him out."

Sahra shut up. Even Sleepy stopped pulling the remains of our army back together and offered her attention for a moment.

"I'll need my own clothing back," Shukrat told us. Her accent was slight. "The enchantment won't touch me if I'm protected by my own clothing." Her use of Taglian had become conversational.

Sahra's hysteria faded immediately. I will never understand that woman. I would have bet on it getting worse.

The rest of us exchanged glances. We could not survive without Tobo. Not in this world. Not with our enemies. We had to get him out of there before the Daughter of Night discovered the opportunity that fortune had thrown down at her feet.

Shukrat said, "You've got to trust me sometime. This might be a good time to take a chance."

Maybe she was not as dumb as she put on.

Tobo trusted her.

I looked over her head to where Sleepy had resumed expostulating angrily with Iqbal Singh and an officer in badly dented Hsien style armor. She had heard. She waved a hand and nodded to indicate that the decision was up to me. I knew the Voroshk kids better than she did.

"All right," I told Shukrat. "But I go with you."

"How?"

"I'll put on Gromovol's . . ."

She was more amused than alarmed, though she *was* troubled. She was very worried about Tobo.

Because I have this obsessional thing about loyalties and brotherhood and keeping faith with the past I sometimes have trouble believing that other people respond as flexibly to their situation as they do. I could not have made my peace with such a dramatic shift in circumstances as easily as Shukrat had.

I said, "That won't work, eh?"

"No. The clothing is created specially for each of us. Individually." She had only that slight accent, no greater than my own, but she did not yet possess a large vocabulary. Her speech was simpler than it might have been. "Though it can be adjusted by a tailor of sufficient skill. The skill takes twenty years to learn, though."

"All right. Where's that stuff stashed? In Tobo's wagon?" The kid had so much junk he needed his own wagon and teamsters to haul it around. The wagon contained things as diverse as marbles and miracles. He had been indulged all his life and would not leave anything behind. "Let's go."

I hoped he had not left any protective spells where they would keep us from getting at the tools we needed to save his scruffy young butt.

73

Midway Between:
The Rescue

Fully attired in her family uniform Shukrat seemed a lot more formidable than the cute little freckle face who hung around with Tobo. Her apparel seemed to be alive, seemed excited to have rejoined her. The black cloth kept stirring around her, restlessly. She resembled an Unknown Shadow who had chosen to let itself be seen. Her blue eyes sparkled. I suspected she might be having fun.

I told her, "Tobo's dad and I will come along as far as we can," although she did not seem to need reassurance. She did understand that having Murgen along meant Thai Dei would be there, too. And Thai Dei did not trust her at all.

Our sometimes odd personal entanglements did not interest Shukrat. Not that she would ever *talk* about them with an old fart like me.

Shukrat forgot that she was wearing that same outfit the day she fell into our hands. When she was not alone. She forgot that she was not invincible.

Sorcerers never lack for self-confidence. Especially young sorcerers.

Those whose self-confidence is justified live to become old sorcerers.

A platoon of elite fighters would creep along behind us, far enough back not to irritate Shukrat's pride but close enough to salvage her cute little behind if her confidence was not completely justified.

For Tobo's sake I would try to make sure she became an older sorceress, by at least one more day.

Murgen scrounged up fireball projectors for himself and Thai Dei. Uncle Doj scrounged up himself and Ash Wand and invited himself into the game. He might be older than dirt but he was still spryer than me. He and his disciples stole through the battered wood in silence so total I wondered if my hearing was going. My old bones were less cooperative so I ended up as rearguard. Today my whole body insisted on reminding me that I had been critically wounded not all that long ago. Although it did that almost every day.

I wore my Widowmaker armor. Though the Hsien reproduction was quieter than the metal original that Soulcatcher made I still seemed to be all clang and clatter.

I took One-Eye's spear along, against Lady's advice.

Shukrat's flying post trailed behind her. My ravens rode it, one offering directions, the other poised to carry news or unexpected holiday greetings to the rear.

It would be a holiday somewhere in the world. And fate offered me a glimpse of Goblin in the distance, evidently passed out, much as he had done after proferring the holiday excuse for being drunk, half a lifetime ago. I hefted the black spear.

I glimpsed the girl, too. She was moving but doing it like a drunk on the brink of passing out. I recalled another time, long ago, when a brother named Raven and I had ambushed a sorceress called Whisper on Soulcatcher's behalf. Circles of fortune. The madwoman had been our employer at the time. Now she worked for us. Or would be given the opportunity to work for us if I could keep her alive. That might be a tough assignment.

Seeing the girl and my old friend hurt. I wished I had a weapon I could use to end this here, now.

One-Eye's spear seemed to turn in my hand.

I pointed out the view to Murgen and Thai Dei. I breathed, "On the way out. After we have Tobo and Howler." I indicated their bamboo poles.

Murgen worked to keep a blank face. Thai Dei did not have to work. Thai Dei did not come equipped with facial expressions, so far as I could tell. Uncle Doj nodded. Uncle Doj was old friends with unpleasant necessity.

I told Murgen, "I'll do it if you can't." Sometimes you have to build a wall around your heart.

A few steps onward we encountered the emotional phenomenon the soldiers had reported. But with the girl stunned it did not overcome reason. I just had to concentrate on not giving myself up to love for the Daughter of Night.

I did wonder how much worse it had been when she was in control of all her faculties.

We reached Tobo without incident. Howler lay not ten feet away, miraculously silent. The gods do play amazing games.

I examined Tobo before I let anyone move him. His pulse was strong and regular but he was covered with cuts and abrasions and had suffered a lot of broken bones. He was not going to be much use to anybody for a long time.

Shukrat whispered. "He would have been fine if he had been wearing this." She indicated her apparel. That seemed spellproof, too. As promised, she was suffering none of the effects of the Daughter of Night's emanations.

It was a struggle for the rest of us, and getting more difficult as Booboo regained her senses.

We got Tobo aboard a crude litter that we slung underneath the flying post. Howler we hoisted onto the log itself. We tied him into place. He was not badly hurt, just persistently unconscious. His rags had served him better than any armor.

He needed to find himself an alley and do some ragpicking. He needed a new outfit desperately. What he was wearing no longer came up to the standard of rags.

I told Thai Dei and Murgen to collect as many scraps of flying carpet as they could without alerting the Taglians to our presence. No telling what could be learned from them. We did not need Goblin and Booboo getting any brilliant notions about improving their mobility.

Howler chose that moment to wake up, stretch and greet the world with a good scream. I clamped an armored hand over the little bastard's mouth but I moved a beat too late.

Booboo's men started scrambling around. Goblin woke up and glared around, but in apparent confusion. Somebody eager to hurl himself into the gap between peril and the Daughter of Night smashed into the girl violently enough to knock her off her feet and leave her groggier than she was already.

The "love me" spell weakened significantly.

Half a dozen Taglian soldiers materialized. The first two stopped instantly when they got a look at me and Shukrat. Those behind them piled into them.

Doj leaped forward like a man a third his age. Ash Wand glittered in a dance of death.

More soldiers appeared. Lots more. Murgen and Thai Dei emptied the bamboo fireball projectors they carried, then drew swords and joined Doj in weaving a tapestry of steel.

Shukrat told me, "Go. Now. Just push the rheitgeistide. It will go ahead of you." In a straight line only, I discovered instantly, unless a couple of people pushed and pulled it real hard to get it going in a straight line in some other direction.

I did not have anyone to help me right away. Tobo's male relatives were busy turning the Taglian army into bite-sized bits of crow food. Shukrat was playing hard to hit with a band of Taglian archers.

When their arrows reached her she seemed to lose definition momentarily. Her cloak swirled around her, almost cloudlike. Nothing touched her.

A cloud of a thousand glittering little obsidian flakes boiled off Shukrat. Despite a breeze blowing into our faces, the cloud headed for the Taglians. In moments enemy soldiers were swearing, slapping themselves, forgetting to be bellicose toward me.

Most excellent.

I had seen One-Eye and Goblin pull similar stunts frequently over the years, usually with bees or hornets. One time one of them stirred up an army of ants to attack the other. Much of their creativity for much of their lives had gone into inventing new ways to harass one another.

I missed the little shits, aggravation and all.

It was not a good time to be a Taglian devotee of the Deceiver messiah, willing or otherwise. Tobo's family was making the blood fly.

That damned Goblin exploded like a starving vampire popping up out of his grave. He landed amongst his own soldiers. Three or four went down. Doj, Thai Dei and Murgen all got thrown around like they weighed nothing. Their swords seemed incapable of doing any harm. The fiercest blows sounded like they were slamming into a waterlogged tree trunk. And did about as much damage as they would have done to a huge old watersoaked log.

I recalled One-Eye's last hours. And was in motion already when I did, the black spear extended way out in my right hand, head starting to glow.

The Goblin thing whipped to one side fast enough to avoid getting skewered. It did suffer a cut that would have been enough to require stitches if it had been the true Goblin.

Its flesh felt tougher than an old smoke-cured ham.

The Goblin face betrayed complete astonishment, then horrible pain. The spear flashed and smoked in my hand. Goblin shrieked. For an instant I saw the real Goblin looking out of tormented eyes.

I fought for my balance and tried to get him with a truer thrust.

I did not get him at all. He flung out of there in complete terror of my weapon. His wound looked like it had gone gangrenous already.

All this took only moments. The troops I had asked to tag along behind wasted no time rushing up to help. Still down, Booboo was not radiating enough "love me" to disrupt their ability to fight. They started grabbing the rest of us and dragging us out of there.

"I can walk!" I snarled. Though I had almost no strength left. I got hold of the flying post and started walking it.

The soldiers carried Doj and Thai Dei. Murgen looped an arm over the shoulder of another fighter who had managed to get himself injured already.

This did not look good for the Ky family.

More of our men rushed up.

I leaned into the log. I tried not to worry. Behind me the skirmish got rowdy. More men came up on both sides. Fortunes shifted as the girl found strength or weakened. Evidently using the "love me" enchantment sucked the strength out of her flesh.

I hate this kind of fight," I told Sleepy when she came over to see how the survivors were doing. She kept her back to the ranks of the dead.

Howler was up and around already. I had a whole team working on Tobo. Murgen was going to make it. He just needed time. But time had run out for Doj and Thai Dei. Soldiers live.

I kept doing what I could for Soulcatcher, too, mostly when my wife was not watching. "You can lose a lot of men without accomplishing a thing." I meant that as a subtle suggestion.

"They've realized they can't win. They've started moving north. Before we can finish surrounding them." I heard nothing in her voice expressing disappointment. "How bad is Tobo?"

"Not as bad as his uncle and Doj."

"Croaker."

"Sorry. We're out of business. Maybe for a long time. If Tobo has a bone that isn't broken I can't find it." I exaggerated only a little. The kid had a broken leg, a broken toe, a broken arm (two places), a concussion and a whole rack of crushed or broken ribs. "Unless you're willing to face Mogaba without him."

"Outnumbered by the best troops we'll face, commanded by the only intelligent commander we're likely to meet?" Meaning a general she had fought during the Kiaulune wars but never had beaten. She eyed Soulcatcher. "Counting on Howler to give us his best? I think not."

"Then we'd better fall back to Dejagore and get comfortable. Or move up to Ghoja."

"Ghoja," she decided instantly. "We want control of that river crossing. And that barrier."

"Mogaba isn't likely to come out right away. He'll want to know exactly what's going on before he commits himself to any course. Hell, he might not come out at all if we update him on what's going on with the Daughter of Night."

She agreed. "If we let him know, he might find a chance to do something beneficial to all of us. See that he gets the appropriate information."

How was I supposed to do that?

I did not ask.

I knelt beside Soulcatcher. Her breathing was ragged. She seemed to be getting weaker. I did ask, "How's Sahra?"

"She'll be all right. She's lived with this idea for a lot of years. She knows nobody gets out of here alive. Even if they don't have one of those silver badges. I'll let you know what she decides about funeral arrangements."

I grunted.

She left me with a final caution. "Just don't let her boy die. Things would get unpleasant."

74

Midway Between:
Escape Artists

Sometime during the excitement the Voroshk kids decided to run away. But before they ran they had to argue about how to manage it and who should be in charge after they succeeded and then they kept bickering until they wasted most of the time when the rest of us were diverted first by Soulcatcher and then by Booboo.

Nothing got decided completely. After sundown they surprised their guards using feeble disorientation spells. Gromovol killed several soldiers, mostly because Magadan cautioned him not to. As soon as they were loose Gromovol started looking for his flying post. Arkana and Magadan believed it was more important to find their clothing. Without that they were almost powerless. They wrote Gromovol off. They knew the Black Company well enough already to want to distance themselves from the doom taking shape in his future.

Arkana told Magadan, "We'll have to take one of those keys to their Shadowgate, too. Otherwise we'll never get out of this world."

"If we get the chance, yes. But the main thing we need to do is to get away from these madmen." Even after several months Magadan still did not understand what was happening in this world. It was too alien. Nothing made any sense.

His own world had known no real war since his forbears had come to power.

Two hundred yards away Gromovol did something stupid and betrayed himself as he tried to steal a flying post. An alarm sounded. In minutes rage flooded the camp. The murdered guards had been found.

Arkana swore. "That idiot! We'd better surrender to somebody important right now. If we keep on running the soldiers who catch us won't listen to any explanations."

"Shukrat . . ."

"Shukrat's gone native. Shukrat's decided there's no way she'll ever get home so she might as well do the best she can for herself over here. It's probably because of her mother."

"What?"

"Her mother. Shukrat's been totally weird ever since the First Father put her mother aside for that woman Saltireva. Besides, she's infatuated with Tobo."

"He is gorgeous, isn't he?"

"Magadan! Well, yes. Exotic, anyway."

"I hear his mother was one of the great beauties of this world when she was younger. But his father grew up eating nothing but ugly soup." All the while they talked Magadan kept drifting away from the excitement. He had no destination in mind but no intention of giving himself up. There would be no chance like this ever again.

Arkana said, "Shukrat could be right."

"What?"

"Suppose she hasn't really gone native? Suppose she's just winning their trust? Maybe someday she'll just stroll off with one of their keys and leave this world."

"Damn."

"Shukrat won't do it. But we could adopt that strategy." It had not taken Shukrat long to get her post and clothing back. She was becoming an important part of the Black Company. Already.

"Why didn't we think of that?" Magadan grumbled.

Arkana said, "Because we're almost as stupid as Gromovol is. As blind to anything that isn't the way it was at home. Shukrat isn't bright. But she does see that this isn't home and never will be. I'm turning back. You do what you want. When the shouting stops I want them to find me right where they left me. I refused to run away. It was all that idiot Gromovol's fault."

But, darling ice princess, don't you know you never do anything alone?

The Voroshk never fully grasped the fact that the Unknown Shadows are with all of us always. If Tobo wanted he could catalog every breath they took. The hidden folk tap emotion. They learn to understand what is being said far faster than even language naturals like myself. The Voroshk could no longer speak secrets.

Sometimes misfortune likes to get into the game.

Magadan told Arkana, "You go ahead. Be friendly. Flirt. Do what Shukrat did. When you get your key come find me. I'll walk you home."

"Come back with me."

"I can't. They'll blame me for what Gromovol did."

The devil named appeared suddenly, running straight toward them, the light of campfires exaggerating the terror distorting his face. Gromovol had expected to fling open the door to freedom but had found it to be the door to hell and no one on the other side cared who he was.

Before it could all be sorted out and the troops calmed down Magadan had been killed, Gromovol had been wounded badly, and Arkana had been raped several times. She brought a broken leg and several cracked ribs into my care as well.

In time I heard all the true details from my ravens, who seemed more inclined to be communicative while Tobo was out of action.

Soldiers whose friends have been murdered are not kindly people. In a Company without Lady and a female Captain no discipline would have been assessed at all. As it was, the discipline was light and directed mainly at those who had assaulted Arkana sexually. That could not be overlooked.

Taglios:
The Palace

Mogaba was not yet aware of the disaster that had befallen the Army of the Middle when he found the two women in his quarters. Lady he recognized. The young blonde he did not. She would, he presumed, be a sorceress, too. Fear cramped his stomach. His heartbeat doubled. But he betrayed nothing outwardly.

He had had to mask his emotions in the presence of madmen and a madwoman for decades. The madmen were gone. With luck the madwoman would follow. And he would persist.

He bowed slightly. "Lady. To what do I owe the unexpected honor?"

"To disasters. Of course."

The Great General glanced at the younger woman. She was completely exotic, like no woman he had ever seen. Though white and blonde she did not resemble Willow Swan otherwise. There was an alien feel to her.

She must be from wherever the Black Company had hidden the last several years. He said, "I'm sure you didn't come this far just to stand around looking cryptic."

"The Daughter of Night and the thing inside what used to be Goblin somehow overwhelmed the Protector. The girl put on Soulcatcher's leathers. She's pretending to be her. She's squandered ninety-five percent of your Middle Army. She's headed this way. We aren't in any condition to chase her. My husband thought you should know. He wants me to remind you that the Daughter of Night exists only to bring on the Year of the Skulls. I want you to know that Kina is real. Doubt any of the other gods you want but not this one. She's out there. We've seen her. And if she gets loose none of our other squabbles will mean a thing."

Mogaba did not need to be reminded that the Year of the Skulls would be an atrocity far huger than any of Soulcatcher's random cruelties. Catcher was mere Chaos. Kina was Destruction.

"We have a plan for handling the Protector. It should work as well against someone pretending to be the Protector. Possibly better." He did not ask what had become of Soulcatcher. He was content to hope that phase of his life was complete.

"The girl doesn't have Soulcatcher's finely honed powers but she does have plenty of raw talent. She's somehow surrounded herself with an aura that makes anyone within a hundred feet want to love her and do anything to please her. This has manifested itself before, in smaller ways, so I fear we can expect it to grow as she comes to understand it and exercise it."

"That isn't good. That's not good at all. That'll make sniping difficult. Any way around it?"

From the blonde's slight start, Mogaba judged Lady's, "Not that we know of yet," to be less than honest. But in her place he would have reserved something, too. And what they had obviously was not reliable. Otherwise they would have used it themselves.

The Great General said, "Thank you for the warning. We'll make use of it. Was there anything more?" Down deep he nurtured the tiniest hope that there could be a reconciliation. A hope he knew was unrealistic. But everyone nurtured impossible dreams. Even the gods were pursuing the impossible.

Mogaba stated the facts as they had been reported to him. He made that point clear. "We aren't their friends. They just want someone else to assume part of the cost of eliminating the enemies they have to go through in order to get at us."

Ghopal Singh asked, "What about the truth of the report? Are they just trying to trick us into attacking the Protector? If they could get us to make the attempt and we were to fall at a time when they were close behind the Protector they'd reach the gates just when Taglios was falling into chaos."

Aridatha groaned. "*We* went to *them*, Ghopal. Remember me chasing halfway to the other end of the world to tell them we were going to try to get rid of the Protector? Remember me helping them take over Dejagore as a sign of good faith?"

"Circumstances have changed."

Mogaba interjected, "Ghopal, I've given this a lot of thought. I think it's true. The Protector is out of the game. Possibly only momentarily. Hell, probably. She's made unlikely comebacks before. What hurts my feelings, of course, is that those people don't consider us much worth worrying about in terms of the greater struggle."

Aridatha grumbled, "Which might not be that unreasonable when you think about it dispassionately."

Ghopal asked, "And you're equally sure that the Middle Army has been destroyed?" Even military insiders had not yet fully digested the news about the losses of Dejagore and the Southern Army that had clung to it's skirts. A lot of people were still waiting to hear how Dejagore responded to it's change of masters.

The nature of that response would have repercussions throughout the Taglian empire.

Would the return of the royals be celebrated? Or resented? The Dejagoran response was likely to set the fashion for all the cities and towns that came under the Company sway.

"I'm sure of it," Mogaba told Ghopal. "But I'm less sure of the condition of the invaders afterward. I got the distinct impression that their defeat of the Middle Army was neither cheap nor easy."

Aridatha said, "We've got to have better intelligence."

Mogaba took a moment to stifle his sarcasm before confessing, "I'm open to ideas. Any ideas."

No inspirations sprouted immediately.

Aridatha said, "We could always do something mythic. Like damning ourselves by bringing in an ally worse than our enemies. One that will devour us after it finishes doing what we brought it in to do."

Mogaba and Ghopal recognized the effort but did not get Aridatha's joke.

"It's an allusion. Or a parable. Or something," Aridatha explained. "Like all stories about Kina. The Lords of Light created her or brought her in for the demon plain war. And probably would have been better off if the rakshasas had won, ultimately."

Mogaba did have a sense of humor. He just had not brought it along tonight. "I guess you had to be there. Anyway, there's nobody we could bring in. We're on our own. So suggestions are in demand. Practical suggestions will be particularly welcome." That was something in the nature of a jest so, perhaps, he had brought part of his sense of humor.

Ghopal said, "All we can do is send out more spies and set up more remount stations so the spies can get their observations to us faster."

"And we have only one courier battalion." Mogaba sat quietly for half a minute. Then he asked, "How is our support among the priests and bourgeoisie? They've had time to think about the royals coming back. They plan to desert us?"

"We're the devil as far as they know," Ghopal replied. "The Protector has been their benefactor. And only a few of the slickest talkers can hope to benefit if we get thrown out. We worked hard to eliminate the Radisha's friends once we could no longer hide the fact that the princess was gone, not just hiding out feeling sorry for herself."

The Great General proposed, "Let's try the same strategy. Make believe we haven't lost the Protector. Aridatha. You seem to be distracted."

"I keep thinking about the girl. The Daughter of Night."

"And?"

"I saw her once. Five years ago. There's something about her. . . . Makes you want to throw her down on her back. And makes you want to worship her at the same time. Makes you feel like you should do anything you can to please her. It's scary when you step back far enough to realize what happened."

"She's all grown-up that way." Mogaba explained what Lady had told of events to the south. "That girl got hundreds of men killed. We'll have to assassinate her remotely somehow. See if some mechanical engine can be contrived."

"I have a question," Ghopal said.

"Go."

"What's that thing you're fiddling with? You've been playing with it ever since you got here."

"Oh. Some kind of snail shell. They're all over the Palace. Nobody knows where they come from. Nobody's ever actually seen one crawling around. They're sort of relaxing when you roll them around in your fingers."

Both Singhs eyed the Great General as though thinking his behavior was distinctly odd.

Ghopal said, "Regarding the Daughter of Night. We might consider poison. There're some talented poisoners in Chor Bagan, the thieves' market."

The years had changed Mogaba. He did not immediately reject the suggestion as unworthy of men of honor.

The Taglian Territories: Another Origin Story

I suggested, "How about a standoff weapon we can launch from outside her influence? Hell, if we take the logs and carpets up high enough we can just keep dropping rocks till we get her." There was some optimism. We did not have even one carpet since Booboo knocked Howler and Tobo down. What we did have was bits and pieces of half a dozen carpets that Howler had been working on when nothing else took up his time.

Lady glared at me so intensely I began to wonder how soon I would start melting.

Killing Booboo was not yet on her list of options. Her emotions were engaged much more deeply than mine, though the problem of the girl was a torment to me, too.

My entanglement was more with the idea of the child than with the specific daughter.

Lady *wanted* to fool herself into believing there might be some way that Booboo could be redeemed.

"You're wasting time," the Prahbrindrah Drah said. The collapse of Soulcatcher's Middle Army had brought him to life. Suddenly, he believed his restoration was just a matter of marching to Taglios and yelling, "I'm back!" He had leaped into the embrace of self-delusion.

There was a lot of that going around.

Murgen joined the conference as the Prince began to bicker with Sleepy about her plans, a situation guaranteed not to persist for long. Sleepy would let him know who was running the show. Murgen announced, "I just finished reading a really long message from Baladitya. Who is well and loving every minute of his new life, thank you very much, Sleepy. Which he did not fail to point out several times."

I asked, "What're you doing getting mail from that old goofball?"

"He wasn't writing to me. He doesn't know me. The message was intended for Tobo."

Sleepy, who was thoroughly cranky because nothing was going the way she wanted, grumped, "I'm sure you're going to share every exciting detail with us, too, even though what we all need is some sleep."

"Since you insist." Murgen grinned. He had no particular job assignment while he was recuperating so he could do just about anything he pleased. "His letter mostly concerned the prisoners Shivetya is holding up there. The First Father and Gromovol's dad. Who Shivetya took in originally just to protect them from the shadows. Of which there are hardly any left anymore. Them and the Voroshk have almost wiped each other out. Sorry." He patted Shukrat's shoulder. Nobody missed that gesture. Murgen approved of Tobo's girlfriend—if that was what she was.

I wondered what he was doing bringing Shukrat to a staff meeting.

Sahra, of course, bristled like a hedge hog. There were no eligible Nyueng Bao girls anywhere within two hundred miles and she had married a foreigner, Murgen, for love herself, against the will of most of her family, but what did that have to do with today?

Sahra could restrain herself most of the time, these days. In public. If Murgen was around to calm her and remind her that Tobo was not a four-year-old anymore. But she was under tremendous additional strain now, with all her family dead or wounded. She had not yet pulled herself together well enough to make decisions about funeral arrangements for her brother and Uncle Doj.

He restrained her now, with just a gentle touch.

"You got a point to make?" Sleepy said. "Or can I get back to work figuring out how to get us through this on terms that suit our needs?"

Swan muttered something about the little bit needing a good dose of man to relax her. Sleepy snarled. Swan grumbled, "Did I volunteer? I don't think so. Not recently. So don't fuck with me."

Hurriedly, Murgen told us, "Guys, Shivetya came up with another Kina origin cycle. He got this one from the Voroshk. Evidently they don't mind talking history if they're bored. In this version Kina's husband put her to sleep. When she kept acting up after she won the demon plain war for the gods by sucking the blood out of all the demons. This version of the Goddess has ten arms instead of four. Her husband, known as Chevil in the world of the Voroshk, has four arms and is a lot like the Kina we know. Sometimes he's called the Destroyer, too. But sometimes he can be cajoled or seduced into going easy. Kina can't."

His audience rustled. In some stories Khadi, one of the gentler Gunni forms of Kina, had had a husband, Bhima, who also counted the Destroyer among his many names.

All Gunni Gods have bunches of names. They get a little hard for an outsider to keep straight because when they change their names they also change their attributes. It gets particularly confusing when you have two aspects of the same god getting into an ass-kicking contest with each other.

"And this Chevi has what to do with Kina's origins?" Sleepy demanded.

"Oh, he's the one who did all the mean things to her, like chopping her up and scattering the pieces all over. But she also kills him. And brings him back to life."

"Murgen. I'm considering sending you back to the Taglians for some more rework."

"All right. Chevi has more than one wife. But there used to be only one. That was Camundamari, who has several other names, naturally. Camundamari was very dark-skinned. The other gods mocked her and called her Blackie."

Interesting. Both Khadi and Kina can mean black in some Taglian usages, though "syam" is the common and conventional word.

Murgen continued, "When Chevi himself started taunting her she flew into a huge rage, tore her skin off, and turned into Ghowrhi, the Milky One. The shed skin became Kalikausiki, which filled itself up on blood sucked from demons, then became Khat-hi, the Black One."

"Kina is a skinwalker!" Suvrin cried, startling everyone. Skinwalkers were a demonic terror little known outside Suvrin's homeland. Skinwalkers killed a man, sucked out his flesh and bones, put on his skin and stole his life. The details are pretty gruesome. Skinwalker folklore strikes me as a way for ignorant people to explain radical and bizarre changes in personality. Shifts I believe are due to poorly understood diseases. Or maybe just due to getting old.

Murgen was startled by Suvrin's outburst. Which seemed excessive to me, too. "Not a skinwalker in the way you mean," Murgen said.

Was there something in Suvrin's background?

The concept of a monster able to steal someone else's identity that way is particularly grotesque. I have seen a lot of strange and ugly things. Tobo's hidden folk are only the latest on a long list. But skinwalkers are one horror that just seems too terrible to be true.

Like the gods themselves of late there have been no manifestations before reliable witnesses. We were talking ancient legends tonight. Suvrin had referenced one of the most obscure.

I said, "Believe me, Suvrin, if there were any real skinwalkers down your way you can bet the Shadowmasters would've rooted them out and used them up. What a weapon, eh?"

"I guess," Suvrin admitted. Reluctantly.

"That's wonderful," Sleepy grumped. "Ghost-story time is over, boys. Now we let Murgen finish. He is going to finish, isn't he? Because I want to get back to what this meeting is supposed to be all about." She swung a deadly finger. "Don't you even think about puking up another wisecrack, Willow."

Swan grimaced. He had live ammunition and no ready target. Then he grinned. A time would come.

I said, "Murgen?"

"There isn't much more. Baladitya says most of the high points of the mythology agree. There's more of a death goddess to her nature over there. She's always referenced as living in a cemetery."

"She does that here, doesn't she?" I asked. "When Sleepy and Lady and you, especially, talk about your nightmares, that place you go with all the bones? That could be a Gunni style cemetery."

The Gunni burn their dead to purify them before their souls line up for reassignment in the next life. But the fires are never hot enough to consume the major bones. If a burning ground is near a major river the leftovers are generally deposited there. But a lot of places are not near a major river. And some are not near a source of firewood. And some families never save up enough to buy wood that is available.

Bones pile up.

These places are not often seen by anyone but the priests who attend them, the men in yellow who revere Majayama but watch over their shoulders because Kina and her pack of pet demons supposedly lived beneath the bone piles. Even though Kina is known to be chained up under the glittering plain until the Year of the Skulls.

I said, "I've got a lot of time to think these days. One of the things I've been pondering is why there are so many different stories about Kina. And I think I've figured it out."

My ego got a boost. Even Sleepy seemed interested, despite herself. My wife, perhaps less enthralled, suggested, "Do go on," in a tone implying that she knew there would be no stopping me anyway.

"In those days the Company . . ."

"Croaker!"

"Sorry. Just seeing if you were listening. What clued me was the fact that there isn't any uniform Gunni doctrine. There isn't much of an hierarchy amongst Gunni priests, either, except locally. There's no central arbiter of what constitutes acceptable or unacceptable dogma. Kina isn't alone in being the subject of a hundred conflicting myths. The whole pantheon is. Pick any god you want. When you travel from village to village you'll find him wearing different names, different myths, getting mixed up with other gods, and on and on and on. We see the confusion *because* we're travelers. But up until the Shadowmaster wars almost nobody in these parts ever went anywhere. Generation after generation, century after century, people were born, lived and died in the same few square miles. You only had a few gem traders and the Strangler bands moving around. Ideas didn't travel with them. So every myth gradually mutates according to local experience and prejudice. Now first the Shadowmasters and then we land in the middle of all this. . . ."

We? A glance around showed me just three other people who had not grown up in this end of the world. For a moment I felt ancient and out of place and found myself recalling an old piece of poetry that said something to the effect: "Soldiers live. And wonder why." Meaning, why am I the one, of all those who marched with the Company when I was young, who is still alive and kicking? I do not deserve it any more than any of those men. Maybe less than some.

You always feel a little guilty when you think about it. And a little glad it was somebody else, not you.

"That's it. We're travelers. That's why it all seems alien and contradictory. Wherever we are, most of us are outsiders. Even when we do belong to the majority religion." A glance around showed me that hardly any of my audience were Gunni, either. "Well, that's my piece."

"All right, then," Sleepy said. "Back to practical problems. How do we deal with the Daughter of Night and the Goblin thing?"

"That's practically the same thing as a skinwalker," Suvrin said. "Kina put him on like a suit of clothes." Suvrin had skinwalkers on the brain tonight.

"The Daughter of Night!" Sleepy snapped. "I want to hear about the Daughter of Night. Not about Kina. Not about skinwalkers. Not about old Voroshk sorcerers, not about old librarians and not about anything else. And, Lady, if you really don't want the girl killed, then come up with an idea for disarming her that's better than any idea for taking her out. Because you're the only one here letting emotion get in the way."

Above Ghoja:
Seeking the One Safe Place

Goblin and the girl both rode, though their mounts remained skittish and frightened and Goblin's had to be kept in blinders so that it could not see its rider. Neither animal was allowed to look back. Goblin himself wore a rag to protect his damaged but nearly healing eyes.

The handful of soldiers who joined their flight from the middle ground fell away rapidly. Driven by the "love me" spell they gave it everything they had but eventually every man drifted outside the spell's influence, then vanished immediately.

Only the two touched by Kina crossed the bridge at Ghoja. They reached the north bank as dawn began to paint the eastern sky. It was still only the morning after the destruction of the Taglian Middle Army. They had killed several post horses but even so had not arrived ahead of rumors of the disaster to Taglian arms.

"Our enemies have been here before us," the Goblin-thing said. He wanted to be called Khadidas, Slave of Khadi. The girl simply refused to address him by that appellation. "These people have been warned and threatened but they will raise no hand against you because of who they think you are." *Not* because of who she *was*.

The Daughter of Night played Protector with a blend of arrogance and small-mindedness nothing like her aunt's but the garrison commanders found her sufficiently convincing. And she ached every second because it was clear that these unbelievers would never yield themselves to the service of the Dark Mother. She knew that they would have tried to destroy her had they known she was not her aunt. This world deserved the Year of Skulls.

The aura the girl radiated got her through her brief confrontations.

"I'm exhausted," she whined to Goblin. "I'm not used to riding."

"We can't stop here."

"I can't go on."

"You will go on. Until you are safe." The Khadidas's voice left no doubt who it believed to be in charge. "There is a holy place not many leagues further. We'll go there."

"The Grove of Doom." There was no enthusiasm in the girl's response. "I don't want to go there. I don't like that place."

"We will be stronger there."

"It'll be the first place they'll look for us. If they don't already have soldiers there waiting." She knew that was unlikely. Those people were not yet prepared to tell their soldiers that the woman inside the black leather was not the Protector anymore, but they did have the capacity to move their game pieces from afar. They seemed able to thwart the Goddess whenever they liked.

She said, "They already know what we're going to do. Because we just talked about it."

"We're going to the Grove. I will be much stronger there." No argument would be allowed.

The Daughter of Night was no less devoted to her spiritual mother today but she did not like this creature who bore a fragment of Kina inside him. She found it difficult to articulate even to herself, but she missed Narayan. She missed him because he had loved her. And she, in her self-centered way, had loved him enough in return that now her life was one ongoing trail of loneliness and desolation . . . leading where? This new hand of the Goddess seemed incapable of any emotion but anger. And he refused flatly to indulge her in any way, or even to acknowledge her humanity.

She was a tool. That she was a living thing with wants and emotions all her own was just an annoyance, a nuisance, an inconvenience. There was an ever stronger implication that she should learn to abandon her distractive qualities. Or else.

Goblin said, "We need a place where we can be safe and our power is strong because there is much we need to do before we commence the actual rite of resurrection." By which the Daughter of Night understood him to mean bringing on the Year of the Skulls.

She became attentive despite her inclination to be rebellious. It sounded like the Khadidas was going to impart some real information at last. Hitherto, the possessed little man had done nothing more than present his bonafides, then tell her what to do. They had been together for only a few days but throughout them he had been completely unforthcoming.

She asked, "How can we possibly bring on the Year of the Skulls? Our cult has been exterminated. I doubt that there are a hundred devout believers left in the entire world."

"There will be hands enough to undertake the holy task. Narayan Singh did well in his last years. But before we bring them together we must recover the Books of the Dead."

The Daughter of Night had to pass on the cruel truth that had been used to torment her all the while she had been a captive of the Black Company. "The Books of the Dead no longer exist. The woman who commands our cruelest enemies burned them personally. Not even a scrap survived. The monster that dwells in the place of glittering stone, that prevents my mother from rising, had the ashes scattered throughout all the realms that touch upon the demon plain."

"That's true." The Khadidas grinned evilly. "But books are knowledge. The knowledge contained within the Books of the Dead is not lost. The knowledge also resides within the Goddess herself. And whatsoever there was within her that needed to be brought forth into this world she placed within me before she sent me forth."

"You know the Books of the Dead by heart?"

"I do. Which is why we must find our one safe place. The scriptures are no good locked up inside me. They must be out, in written form, to assume their full power. They must be there so that the cantor priests can sing from them continuously during the time of resurrection. Come. We must travel faster."

The Daughter of Night hurried her pace, her exhaustion pushed back briefly by the stunning implications of what she had just heard.

The holy books were not lost!

She was ashamed that she had suffered even a slight wavering of faith.

Midway Between:
Bad News

People began to scurry as though in near panic. I knew the signs. News had come in and it was not good. I suspected the cavalry force sent to probe the defenses at Ghoja had suffered some major misfortune.

I headed for Sleepy's tent without being summoned. By the time I ducked inside I had overheard a half dozen rumors already, not a one of them reassuring.

Generating rumors is one thing even the most inept armed force does exceedingly well.

Sleepy was heads-together with Suvrin and Runmust, Riverwalker and several brigade commanders from Hsien. Tobo was there but was goofy with painkillers.

Howler and Shukrat were not present. Tobo looked a little peeved. My guess was that he had brought the bad news but could not keep himself together well enough to contribute anything beyond his report.

I had given up on him. If he wanted to cruise around on a post trying to do things while he was all busted up and in casts I was not going to nag him anymore. He had a half-crazy mom to handle that.

Sleepy glanced my way, for a second revealed extreme irritation. That turned to resignation as other former Captains let themselves in behind me. Even Willow Swan invited himself to sit in.

Sleepy did face a unique challenge. No other Captain in the Company's history has had such a cabal of ex-Captains looking over his shoulder. Even though none of us intrude, or even offer much unsolicited advice, Sleepy's particular insecurities leave her feeling like she is being judged whenever she had to Captain in front of us. And, of course, she is, though like proper old ladies we do it only behind her back.

"Since everybody but the cooks and grooms is here, I suppose I should get on. . . . No. Tobo is here. He can tell it better than I." She deferred to the kid as soon as her gaze fell upon him. I glared at her. She had no business putting him through . . .

Tobo's eyes focused. He shut them, took a cleansing breath, started talking. "The hidden folk have been tracking Goblin and Booboo the best they can, though it's hard even when we know what route they have to take." He was something less than intimidating, strapped into position aboard a Voroshk flying log, so covered with casts and splints that he was able to use only one hand. "They travel inside a fog of, for want of a better description, divine darkness and confusion. By knowing their route, though, I was able to have the Black Hounds seed the way with snail shells. . . . I got lucky. One of the hidden folk eavesdropped on an argument between Goblin and the girl." His words came in a soft, swift gush that forced his audience to stay quiet and lean forward.

Tobo paused. For effect, I would have suspected in normal circumstances. The kid liked his drama.

The boy made the grim announcement, "The thing inside Goblin knows the Books of the Dead by heart. Once the Daughter of Night transcribes them they plan to start the rites associated with initiating the Year of the Skulls."

Fox in the henhouse, oh, my, oh!

It took Sleepy several minutes to get everyone settled down. In the interim Tobo grabbed the opportunity to relax. When a measure of calm returned he said, "That's not as bad as it sounds. Remember, there're only two people involved. Should we kill either one, the resurrection fails. For the rest of our century and beyond. And, as anyone who ever worked on the Annals will tell you at great length, it takes a long time to write a book. Even if you're just copying. I saw the Books of the Dead before Sleepy destroyed them. They were huge. And the Daughter of Night will have to transcribe them error-free. So we don't exactly face an immediate crisis even though this is trouble that we never anticipated."

I jumped in. "If you got one of your critters close enough to find out all that then you probably know right where they are. We can set up some kind of ambush." Lady and Howler were supposed to have been ransacking the cobwebby cellars of their minds in an effort to recall some ancient device whereby Goblin and the girl might be distracted, disoriented, distressed and destroyed. Or just disarmed, in the case of my missus. Realist and pragmatist though she was, she nevertheless nurtured a blind bit of self-delusion wherein she would turn Booboo around. Though she would never admit that, of course.

Tobo said, "All right, Master Strategist, Architect of the Destruction of the Shadowmaster Evil, tell me how you ambush somebody you fall in love with before they get inside crossbow range."

"Kid has a point," Lady said, eyeing me expectantly.

"Your snail-shell lurker didn't fall in love with her, did it? It just hunkered down there and eavesdropped till it decided to come running to you with its gossip."

"And?"

"So the Unknown Shadows aren't affected by the Daughter of Night. Is the opposite true?"

"They couldn't do her much physical harm."

"Skryker? Black Shuck? That big old jumping duck thing? You're shitting me."

"No, really."

"Well, they really wouldn't have to, anyway, would they? They'd just need to haunt her. Keep interfering with her sleep. Driving her crazy. Jogging her elbow whenever she tries to write. Really be guilty of all the annoyances they're blamed for back in Hsien. They could piss in her inkwell. They could hide her pens. They could spill stuff on whatever she's trying to write. They could make food go bad and milk turn sour."

"They could keep her husband from performing on her wedding night," Sleepy snapped. "You're roaming a little far into the future, Croaker. And possibly targeting the wrong victim. The Goblin thing is the one who has the Books of the Dead locked up inside his gourd. He might be able to manage without the Daughter of Night. I'm pretty sure she can't manage without him."

Points worth considering.

"Both are just ephemeral tools," Sahra announced in a hollow, oracular voice. "Both can be replaced. In time. So long as Kina herself persists the threat from the glittering plain lives on."

That took all the cheer right out of the gathering.

Everybody stared at Tobo's mother, the injured boy himself included. There was a creepy feeling to her, like something had taken control of her, to speak using her mouth.

Murgen later said Sahra had looked and sounded exactly like her grandmother, Hong Tray, when she issued her prophecies, decades ago.

She scared the shit out of Murgen and Tobo both. They used all the energy they could muster to insist that Sleepy's concern about Goblin and the Daughter of Night was not yet critical.

The Taglian Territories:
In Motion

Sleepy reaffirmed her determination to move north. We limped along, accommodating the injured. We encountered no direct resistance at Ghoja, though forces loyal to the Protector had damaged the main span of the great bridge over the Main. It took our engineers more than a week to restore the bridge. Throughout that week the Prahbrindrah Drah and his sister preached to the people and soldiers of Ghoja. They managed to win the hearts and allegiance of the majority.

The Prince was quite good with people when we let him run around loose. He preached his own restoration with an evangelical passion. He won particular favor amongst old folks nostalgic for the quiet changelessness that had characterized the world of their youth—before the coming of the Shadowmasters and the Black Company.

Except for a small memorial pasture where the fighting had been bloodiest, the battlefield on the north bank, where the Company had won a signal victory in what seemed like another lifetime, was completely built over. Back then there had been a hamlet and watchtower on the south bank, beside a ford that could be crossed only half the year. Now Ghoja threatened to become a city. The bridge, begun at my suggestion ages ago, was a strategic gem both militarily and commercially. There were strong forts and big markets on both banks now.

The girl and the Goblin thing should have done more to keep us from crossing over.

We made camp twelve miles north of the bridge, in rough, bare country still not claimed by peasants. I doubt that it was good for much but pasture. Which meant it was a wasteland amongst vegetarians. But had the ground been better I doubt many farmers would have immigrated. It was too near the high holy place of the Deceivers, the Grove of Doom.

We left the Prince and his sister at Ghoja, along with many native recruits. Sleepy thought it was time the royals got a taste of independence. She was confident that they would not conspire against the Company again. They had been included in our councils often enough to know that Tobo's hidden folk would always be close by.

Ten hours after we set camp, in the middle of the night, Sleepy changed her mind. She wanted to move a little closer to Taglios, to get between the City and the Grove of Doom.

I was awake when Riverwalker brought the news, writing by lamplight and keeping an eye on our injured. Some of them had not weathered the journey well. I was concerned about Soulcatcher in particular.

The change in plan did not irritate me as deeply as it did Lady. She had to be dragged out of a deep sleep. The way she snarled and threatened great evils left me wondering if she had not begun having nightmares again.

Riverwalker murmured, whispered. "I'm getting me a head start."

"Run, River, run. You'll need every yard you can get."

Lady gave me a look that made me wonder if I should not yell at him to wait up.

W e established the new camp near a dense stand of trees which, I learned, surrounded and masked a sprawling Shadowlander cemetery that hailed from the first Shadowmaster invasion of the Taglian Territories. From before the Company's arrival. Almost no one knew about that. I had not, though I had campaigned in the region. Of the entire host only Suvrin showed any interest. He thought he might have a relative or two tucked away there.

He would have plenty of opportunity to visit tombs and graves. Sleepy planned to stay put, recruiting and training and harrying the edge of the Grove of Doom while Tobo and our other casualties recuperated. The trouble with the cemetery was, time had vandalized most of the Shadowlanders' slapdash grave markers.

The Goblin-thing and the Daughter of Night settled down, too, and they really did nothing but sit. They did not begin transcribing the Books of the Dead because they had no supplies. They did not consult with Deceivers making pilgrimages into the holy grove. Those men we left alone, every future step to be dogged by Unknown Shadows so we could follow their routines once they returned to their home environments. There were not many Stranglers left alive. This way we could find out who those few were.

Handy as it is, being able to see whatever you want takes a lot of getting used to.

The Grove of Doom was always a cruel and wicked place, filled with ancient darkness. The hidden folk hated it but they endured going in for Tobo's sake.

Their devotion to the boy gets scary when I think about it too much.

Gromovol and Arkana were mending at a pace equaling Tobo's, which was amazing but not magical. Gromovol's arrogance remained undiminished by misfortune. Arkana was understandably withdrawn.

Soulcatcher worried me increasingly. Not only did she show no improvement, she seemed to be growing weaker. She was headed right down the grim trail Sedvod had blazed.

There was a lot of sentiment favoring letting her slide, and for possibly easing Gromovol along the same dark path while he was sleeping. The jury remained out on Arkana even though the hidden folk had exculpated her in all ways but calculation and manipulation. There were random moments, widely separated, when I felt sorry for the girl.

I remembered the loneliness.

I was the only one who would talk to her, excepting Gromovol. She turned her back on him every time he tried to do so. During our reluctant chats I tried to learn more about her homeworld and, especially, Khatovar. But she did not have much to say. She knew nothing. She had a full measure of youth's indifference to the past.

Shukrat shunned Arkana completely.

Shukrat was almost pathetically eager to fit in. Shukrat really wanted to belong. I have a strong feeling she did not belong before she joined us. And maybe Arkana had, which might illuminate Shukrat's spite toward her now.

80

The Taglian Territories: In Camp

Life is never like a canal, flowing gently through a straightforward and predictable channel. It is more like a mountain brook, zigging and zagging, tearing things up, sometimes going almost dormant before taking an unexpected and turbulent turn.

I was setting out some similar proposition to Lady and Shukrat while examining Tobo to see if he dared put any weight on the broken leg. He thought he was feeling better and was getting extremely restless, which is usually a sign that the patient is, indeed, getting better but is not nearly as far advanced as he wants to believe. We were in my VIP hospital. Soulcatcher and Arkana were present as well. Shukrat was putting on a show, fussing over Tobo while making it clear that Arkana no longer existed. Lady was on her knees beside her sister's pallet, hands flat on her thighs, motionless. She had stayed that way for almost an hour. For a while I thought she was meditating. Or she had gone into some sort of trance. Now I was starting to worry.

The women looked more like mother and daughter than sisters. Poor Lady. Against the years all men campaign in vain. And of late, time has been particularly unkind to my love.

Now that we were settled and had little to do but wait for people to mend, Lady spent time with Soulcatcher every day. She could not explain it herself.

She finally came around, looked back, asked the question that tormented her. "She's dying, isn't she?"

"I think so." I admitted. "And I don't know why. It looks like the same thing that got the Voroshk kid. So I don't know how to turn it around. Howler doesn't know how, either." Though the screaming sorcerer never had been renowned for his skills as a healer.

"Goblin must've done something to her but it isn't sorcery." I added, "Not that anybody recognizes. And it isn't any of the diseases I see in the field." In most armies more soldiers die of dysentery than fall to enemy arms. I am proud that that has never been true in my army.

Lady nodded. She resumed staring at her sister. "I wonder what it is. Something Goblin did. We'd have to wake her up to find out, wouldn't we?" After a heartbeat, "The little bastard was right there when Sedvod took sick, too. Wasn't he?"

"I'm afraid so." I passed Tobo to Shukrat. "Take it easy on him, girl. Or we'll need to get you two a separate tent."

Tobo blushed. Shukrat grinned. I turned to Arkana. "You think you're ready to take up your dancing career again?"

"Is nothing ever serious with you?"

She caught me by surprise. Frivolity was not a crime often attached to my name. "Absolutely. None of us are going to get out of this alive so we might as well grab a laugh while we can." So One-Eye used to claim. "Cranky this morning?" I leaned forward and whispered, "I would be, too. Broken bones are no fun. I know. I've had a few. But try to smile. You're through the worst of it."

She put on her best scowl. The worst of it was still inside her head. She might never recover emotionally. She had not been brought up in a place and station where it was even conceivable that such horrors could overtake her.

"Look at it this way, child. No matter how bad you think it is right now, it can always get worse. I've been in the soldier racket a long time and I promise you, that's a natural law."

"How could my life be worse than this?"

"Think about it. You could be back home. Where you'd be dead. And you would've gone through hell getting that way. Or you could be a prisoner instead of my guest. Which means that every day could be like your one bad day. There're plenty of guys out there who think we let you off too easy. Which reminds me of another natural law. Once you're outside the circle of people who agree that you're special, you're just another human body. And that's hardly ever a good situation for a woman. You're actually better off here, where we have women running stuff, than you would be almost anywhere else."

Arkana retreated inside herself, evidently thinking that I was threatening her. I was not. I was just thinking out loud. Maundering. Old men do that.

I told her, "You need to take it out on somebody, put Gromovol's name at the head of your list."

Lady said, "She's the only connection I have left with ninety percent of my life. The only connection with my family."

The stream takes its wild turns.

"You do anything that saves her, the first thing she'll do when she gets on her feet is try to cut you off at the knees and make you dance on the stumps."

Tobo started to say something. I poked him. We had discussed this several times. His opinion was bloody-minded.

"I know. I know. But every time I turn around it seems like someone else is gone and we're getting to be more and more alien. . . ."

"I understand. I've felt completely dislocated in time since One-Eye died. There's almost nothing left of my past." The nearest thing was come-lately Murgen. Lady and I had chosen the way—and now we were refugees from our own place and time. Though why should I be surprised at this late date? That was what the Company always was: the gathering of the landless, the hopeless, the fugitive and the outcast.

I sighed. Was I about to start creating another past as an emotional crutch?

I knelt beside Lady. "I don't think she'll last more than another week. I'm having trouble getting food down her. And more keeping it there. But I've thought of something we can do to stall death. And maybe even get a sound diagnosis."

Lady turned a gaze on me so intense I shuddered, recalling ancient times, when I was a captive in the Lady's Tower at Charm and about to face the Eye of Truth. "I'm listening."

I noted that, even now, she would not touch her sister. There was a strong selfish underpinning to her emotions. She wanted to save this mad devil sister entirely for her own sake.

"We can take her to Shivetya. We know he can cure Howler. . . ."

"He says he can. Telling us what we want to hear."

What Howler wanted to hear. I had no emotion invested in the runt's well-being. I thought the world would be improved by his extermination.

Lady's tone did not support her words. A spark of hope had been struck.

I said, "Let's have Howler get another carpet put together, then we'll slip away to the glittering plain, get him fixed up and find out what Shivetya can do for Soul-catcher. Even if he can't do anything we can stash her in the ice cavern till we have time to research what's wrong with her. That ought to be a real challenge for Tobo."

That was the course I preferred. I figured that once we installed Soulcatcher in the cave of the ancients Lady would lose interest eventually. The effect on the world at large would be the same as if we had killed her right away while Lady could sustain her tether to her roots via the pretense that she would jump in and resurrect her sister one day soon.

Lady said, "I like that idea. I'll see how soon Howler can get a carpet put together."

"All right." I peeled back one of Soulcatcher's eyelids. I saw nothing promising. I got the feeling that her essence might be absent, out wandering, lost. Paybacks, Murgen might say, if that was true.

As soon as she left, Tobo said, "You're up to something besides what you told her, aren't you?"

"Me?" I shrugged. "I have some ideas. Some of them I might have to clear with the Captain."

Shukrat then said something that ruined her dumb blonde image for me. "You know the reason that Soulcatcher followed you all down here from the north is the same reason that Lady wants to save her now? I'll bet that if she really wanted to badly enough she could've killed you all just about any time she wanted."

I stared. I looked at Tobo. I stared some more.

Shukrat reddened. She murmured, "Neither one of them ever learned how to say, 'I love you.'"

I understood. It was the same thing Goblin and One-Eye had had going for all those years, at a somewhat less lethal level. When they were sober. It was the sort of thing I see all the time amongst my brethren, who cannot, or believe that they dare not, express their real feelings. I added, "Only those two don't even know they need to say it."

The Shadowlander Military Cemetery: Laying To Rest

Willow Swan stuck his head into the tent. "Croaker. Murgen. Anybody who's interested. Sahra's ready to do her thing with Thai Dei and Uncle Doj."

About damned time, I thought but did not say. There were moments, lately, when I wanted to have the whole damned Nyueng Bao Community lined up and spanked. They had dragged the two corpses a hundred fifty miles while they argued bitterly about what to do with them. I did manage to keep my mouth shut but kept wanting to scream, "They don't care anymore! Do *something*! They smell. Bad!"

Not the sort of thing you do with grieving relatives, of course. Not unless you feel like you have developed a shortage of enemies.

The Nyueng Bao had prepared a pair of ghats in a prominent place near the center of the Shadowlander military cemetery. Though only a few swamp folk remained with us those survivors were gathered in cliques, according to the funeral option they believed best honored the dead.

Who would believe a funeral could become savagely political? But people can find reasons to squabble about almost anything.

Thai Dei's send-off was less controversial, of course. He had not believed in much of anything but his own honor, himself. A ritualistic passage through the purifying flame for a warrior who would not bend, troubled only a couple of conservative old-timers who thought the ceremonies too foreign. Uncle Doj was the great bone of contention.

With Doj the burning group were in dispute with the exposure group, who wanted to lay the corpse out on a high platform and leave it till its bones were clean.

This was supposed to be the proper send-off for a high priest of the Path of the Sword—though no one could say how, why or when that idea had arisen. None of the men from Hsien, some of whom had grown up in Hsien's martial arts monasteries, had heard of any such practice there. The people of Hsien buried their dead.

Doj's cronies insisted that his predecessors had been exposed exactly the way they wanted to do him now.

As we filed past the ghats, each tossing on an herb packet and a folded piece of paper carrying a prayer the fire would send along with the dead, Suvrin suggested, "They might have acquired the custom when they first passed through my country. Some of the peoples back home, back then, did expose corpses that they were especially afraid would be seized by skinwalkers."

Skinwalkers again. One of those monsters no one has ever seen, like vampires and werewolves. With all the real monsters loose in the world, seen and suffered often enough, why did so many people trouble themselves about things no reliable witness ever saw? "Wouldn't fire work just as well?"

"Burning wasn't acceptable. It isn't even in modern times, even though so many northerners have come across the Dandha Presh."

I grunted. It must have to do with religion and religion seldom makes sense to me.

"The common people, the poor, anyone that wouldn't attract a skinwalker, gets a normal burial. Just like here." He indicated the graves around us. "People who might attract a skinwalker will be exposed. So there won't be a good suit of skin to steal." He gestured. "The above-ground tombs. They must contain priests and captains who were being stored temporarily, until they could be properly exposed. Their army must have been hard-pressed. They never got back to deal with it."

Actually, I could see several fallen collections of poles with bits of rag and bone beneath that might have been exposure platforms a long time ago. "Looks like your skinwalkers never got here to take advantage, either."

That earned me a scowl.

I was not quite sure why Suvrin was Sleepy's favorite and probable designated successor. But I never understood why Murgen picked Sleepy, either. Yet he had chosen well. She had brought the Company through the Kiaulune wars and the era of the Captivity. And there had been a lot of raised eyebrows when I had chosen Murgen to become Annalist. And Murgen had managed despite never having been quite certain of his sanity.

Sleepy saw something.

Suvrin did not agree. Suvrin insisted that he was going to leave us. But I noted that he had passed up several wonderful opportunities to do so already.

As was her right, being Thai Dei's closest surviving relative, Sahra asked Murgen to join her and Tobo in placing the torches into Thai Dei's pyre. Fitting, I thought, although the old men grumbled. Murgen and Thai Dei had been as close as brothers for a long, long time.

Sahra asked no one but Tobo to help bring the fire to Doj.

Even I saluted the dead swordmaster, though in life I never trusted him.

Lady leaned against me from my left. "I suppose you'll have to admit that he was trustworthy now." Mind reading.

"I don't have to admit any such thing. He just kicked off before he could screw us over."

"No fool like an old fool."

I stopped arguing. She would win every debate by dint of outliving me. I changed the subject. "You still feel like you're getting stronger?" For an age now she had been able to steal almost no supernatural power from Kina. But long ago she had been able to parasitize enough to come close to being Soulcatcher's equal. She believed Goblin's attack on the Goddess was why there was so little power left to steal.

It seemed reasonable to me that Goblin returning as Kina's tool would mean fresh power available but it had not worked that way. Not until Goblin and the girl had entered the Grove of Doom.

"It's coming. Little by little." She sounded like she did not want to wait. "I can do a few parlor tricks now." The way she thought, that might mean she was limited to destroying small villages with a single wink. "I need to get closer to see what helps."

I did not follow up. I could feel her excitement. She hid it well but if I got her going she would drive me nuts talking about stuff that was entirely beyond me.

I could do that, too, either going on with my theories about diseases or about the Company's history.

Definitely a match made in heaven.

I told her, "Soon as we're done paying our respects, how about you see Howler? Find out if my idea gets him moving on the carpets any faster."

"If you give him what he wants now he won't have any incentive to stay with us."

"Where's he gonna run to?"

"He'll find somewhere. He always has."

And, somehow, that always ended up in our way. "Then I expect we'll push him hard to get us a couple, three carpets. And you can hang around playing apprentice while he does, sister Shukrat."

"Yech! No way! He's creepy. He stinks. And he has more hands than some of those four-armed Gunni gods."

"He's little," Tobo called from the chair we had brought along so he could rest between ceremonial stints. "Spank him."

"That's probably what he wants."

"Get somebody to carry me around and I'll go with you," Tobo told Shukrat. "I make the Howler nervous. Croaker. What'll we call him if Shivetya cures his screaming?"

"Stinky might work. Or the Stinker for formal."

The flames of the funeral pyres leapt higher. Tobo ignored me now. I let it drop, too. Time to say good-bye, old man. They never took the oath but Thai Dei and Doj were brothers in their hearts. Their stories were warp and woof of the Company tapestry.

With the Company:
Going South

Sleepy always saw idleness as a vacuum in need of filling. No way was she going to put up with ten thousand men sitting around, maybe spending an hour or two each day training. When they were feeling particularly ambitious.

Just miles away stood a perfectly ugly wood desperately in need of clear-cutting.

You put a whole lot of people to work on a place like that, starting from the outside and working inward, making sure you get even the tiniest twigs and shoots, you can get some great bonfires burning. The evening of the second day the soldiers had one entire horizon hidden behind ramparts of smoke.

Sleepy was *daring* Goblin and the girl to come show us what they had.

I had doubts about the wisdom of that. Sleepy was not impressed enough with the fact that Goblin had a slice of Kina stuffed inside him. And Kina's bad-ass reputation was well-deserved.

But I was not the boss. I could advise but I could not make anyone listen. My worries just earned me one of Sleepy's enigmatic smiles.

"You ready to go for a fly?" Lady asked. "Howler's got a carpet ready."

"You in a hurry?"

"You told me Sileth's only got a week. That was three days ago."

"I did, didn't I? How big is that carpet?"

"Big enough."

"I mean it, hon. It's got to have room for six people."

She stared. After several seconds she said, "I don't think I'm even going to ask. Except maybe who."

"You and Soulcatcher. Howler. Gromovol. Arkana if she wants to go."

"Still playing games, Love?"

"No game. Progress. We lost the most promising one of those kids when Magadan got killed. That was a bad career move on his part. Gromovol is as useless as teats on a bull. I'd just as soon kill him. But if we give him back to those two old Voroshk demons Shivetya's got tied up down there we might score a point or two."

She frowned.

"Thought you were the master manipulator of the greatest empire. . . ." She pointed a finger. An invisible darning needle began to sew my lips together. She *was* getting the power back. "I'll just explain then, shall I?"

"There's the man I married."

Bullshit. But I was not going to argue. "We got the top two Voroshk locked up out there on the plain. They've got no home anymore, far as we know. As far as Shivetya is letting anybody know. They have no future, nowhere to go. An apparent act of kindness might add a couple of heavyweights to our ranks just when it would be handy to have them."

"You're evil."

"I try. Let me go blow in Arkana's ear."

"You do and you'll wake up in the morning wondering how long before you get your first hot flash."

Well, well. Maybe that explained some recent crankiness. Hers. Mine was caused by the iron-strapped, rock-headed obtuseness of the people who insisted on tangling my feet. That was a whole different hunk of monkey meat.

I went to blow in Arkana's ear. Verbally.

I'm not going to give Gromovol a choice," I told Arkana. "This is a chance for me to maybe make peace with his old man. Which is the only good that can ever come of the idiot. If I keep him here he'll eventually do something stupider than anything he's done already. I've told you before, I've been in this racket a long time. When you come up with a liability as big as Gromovol you look for a way to use him. Or you kill him. I've been getting soft in my twilight years."

Her skeptical expression told me how well I had sold that fairy tale.

"You, you're special. You get choices. You can go back if you want. You can tag along for the visit and stay with us when we're done. Or you can hang around here and not go at all."

"Oh, I'll go. I can't not. I'll decide what else I need to do after we get there."

We went aloft by night, under the light of a full moon, with Lady, Soulcatcher, Gromovol and Arkana aboard Howler's new carpet. Tobo, Shukrat, Murgen and I witched along on flying posts. Despite Sleepy's objections, and Tobo's aches and pains, Tobo insisted on coming along because Shukrat was coming. So Murgen rode with me because Sahra refused to fly. The youngsters larked about us fearlessly, engaged in some dragonfly mating ritual.

Murgen and I dropped out briefly at Dejagore. Sleepy insisted we check up on Blade and his occupation force.

Drifting down toward Dejagore's citadel, I asked, "You think Sahra's been having visions or something?"

"Huh?" Murgen's thoughts had been wandering.

"This frantic mother stuff. I swear she keeps getting worse. I thought you might have noticed her having psychic seizures. Or something."

"She don't talk about it. If she does."

"What do you think?"

"I think that if she hasn't she's definitely afraid that she might start."

"Yeah?"

"When we were young she worried about turning into her mother."

"Sometimes she's damned crabby."

"She's no Gota the Troll, though. Her body doesn't hurt her enough. So now she's terrified she's going to turn into Hong Tray. Her grandmother."

"And?"

"And maybe she will. She's started to look like the old woman did. Whenever she starts cranking about it I remind her how calm and accepting Hong Tray always was. Like a solid rock in a wild river."

"Doesn't work, does it?"

"Not for a second. Well. Somebody must've smelled us coming."

We had not yet settled to the top of the citadel tower but Blade and his chief lieutenants were there to meet us. Blade called up, "We were expecting Tobo, the way the shadows were all spooked up."

"You got lucky. The kid's hurt so you get the old farts instead. Captain wants us to check up on you. So you give us a couple of good drinks, we'll tell her you're doing a kickass job, no need to even think about you guys."

"I think we can handle that."

83

Taglios:
Decision

The sharpest-eyed spy can be misdirected or deluded if you know he is watching. Having been of the Company once and having been victimized by the Company more than once, the Great General understood its policy of deception. His understanding had served him well during the Kiaulune wars, where the trickery had gotten the best of him rarely.

He and Aridatha Singh were observing large-scale close order drills from the wall of a fortress that bestrode a hill just south of Taglios. The soldiers had begun to show some interest in improving their skills lately. The approach of a powerful enemy was a mighty motivator.

The Great General asked, "They all went?"

"I've had the report from two independent sources within the last hour. They went out right after moonrise. A flying carpet and three flying poles. They headed south. They passed close enough to Haband's tree for him to identify the Howler, Lady, Croaker, Murgen, the boy wizard and three of those white wizard children I saw when I visited. They aren't worried about us."

"There'd be more of those."

"I'm sure the rumor is true. I've had it confirmed too many times. They're dead."

The Great General refused to take anything at face value where those people were concerned. "Where would they go?"

"Maybe something's happened at Dejagore. Or farther south."

Farther south would have to be beyond the Dandha Presh. Support for the Protector had evaporated outside those territories still directly under the Great General's control, near as his agents could determine, though there had been no outbreaks of enthusiasm for the return of the royals. The mood of the empire was indifferent, excepting amongst those who could profit, one way or another.

Same as it always was, Mogaba reflected.

Mogaba played with a snail shell as he talked. Doing so seemed almost a tick anymore. But he startled Aridatha by popping his arm back suddenly, snapping the shell out as hard as he could throw. "Time for a full-scale field exercise. Let's find out how good their intelligence is with wonder boy away."

Aridatha asked a few brisk questions. These days he commanded the division that would form the left wing of Mogaba's army. It was backboned by his own City Battalions.

The Great General said, "Make all your preparations exactly as you would if we were going down there to fight. Issue appropriate rations. But prepare in a relaxed manner. We just want to see how ready we are. So we know where we need to do more work. Don't encourage questions. And from now on I want to see our spies personally when they bring in news."

Aridatha went away wondering what Mogaba really had in mind.

The Great General sent for the rest of his staff and commanders. He spent a particularly long time, in bright midday sun, conferring with his cavalry captains.

Beside the Cemetery:
Confusion

Willow Swan stuck his head into Sleepy's cabin, which had been built for her from the better logs harvested from the Grove of Doom. "Another contact with Mogaba's cavalry. Three miles west of the Rock Road."

This happened periodically. It was one way the Great General kept track of his enemies. The probes became more numerous when Mogaba wanted to provoke a response. Sleepy grunted, untroubled.

"I'm a little concerned," Swan told her. "This time they're pushing harder. Since we don't have any good way to get anything out of the hidden folk who didn't run off after Tobo, we don't have any idea what Mogaba is doing. We're as blind as he is."

"Is his main force maneuvering behind his cavalry screen?"

"I get that impression."

"Then he's trying to harass us into another panic." Twice already Taglian forces had come south and demonstrated until Sleepy responded, whereupon they had retreated rapidly. Mogaba was trying to get his virgins some confidence-building experience under the stress of near-battle. No doubt he would push them a little closer this time. "Run one brigade up behind the pickets and have them make a lot of noise. Keep another brigade in camp. Everyone else can see to their normal business. I think we're due for a reaction from the Daughter of Night pretty soon."

Her campaign against the Deceiver messiah and the Goblin-thing was much like the Great General's against her.

Swan reminded her, "We have official Deceiver titles for those two now." A fact one of the hidden folk had discovered in far Asharan, of all places, just before Tobo's departure. Asharan was a small city to the southwest unlikely to have any impact on any events unless through its band of Deceivers. "Khadidas. Khadidasa."

Slave of Khadi. Or Kina. "Is that one or both of them?"

"Those are the male and female forms. One for each."

"Willow, that girl won't be called a slave by anybody. She has the same blood as her mother and aunt. Daughter of Night suits her just fine."

Swan shrugged, departed. Tobo had said that there was no love lost between the girl and the Khadidas. That, in fact, they tended to bicker. That, further, the girl had begun to appear almost disillusioned.

The Great General's cavalry continued to harass Sleepy's scouts and pickets. Skirmishes popped up everywhere. Commercial traffic dwindled on the Rock Road. Sizable troops of horse probed the brigade deployed to screen the Company force. They were mostly Vehdna. Vehdna had a tradition of being excellent horsemen. These horsemen showed well against Hsien's professional infantry. Sleepy brought the other brigade out of camp and handed the backup role off to the native recruits.

"I'm getting worried," Swan told Sleepy.

"It must be escalating. You were just concerned before."

"Exactly my point. Why is Mogaba working so hard to make us think he's working up to a straightforward attack? Why is he trying to force a response?"

"Because he wants to see what we'll do. Unless he's trying to distract us from something else. Any chance he could've made a deal with the Deceivers?"

"Narayan Singh's son is one of his cronies."

That struck a spark. "Aridatha Singh is no Deceiver! Nor is he a Deceiver stooge."

"All right. Don't get excited."

Moments later, though, it became clear that it was time for everybody to get excited about something, fast. The unexpected and deadly happened.

Mogaba's cavalry faded away. They were replaced by the infantry of Mogaba's Second Territorial division, as numerous as Sleepy's whole army. The Taglians drove straight into the defending force, hurling them back, while the cavalry began to leak around the ends of the friendly line.

Sleepy had messengers flying around and horns blaring before it became entirely clear that this time Mogaba was not just teasing. She snapped at Swan, "We have to keep them from getting inside the camp. Whatever that costs."

"I'll handle that," Swan replied, though he was no official member of the heirarchy. "I'll use the recruits. You grab anyone else you can find." He sprinted away. If Mogaba captured the camp he would gain control of the treasure that had come down off the glittering plain. That might win his war for him right here, right now.

Swan began sorting the confusion in the camp as soon as he located the Hsien sergeants in charge of training. He announced that the enemy had launched a reconnaissance in force. Some elements might try to reach the camp.

Once he had the recruits assembled facing toward the enemy, Swan sent trusted men to move the treasure into hiding inside the old Shadowlander military cemetery. And well he did, too. Mogaba's attack was much more vigorous than expected. When it reached the camp the recruits did not long withstand it. They allowed elements of Mogaba's force to get into the camp itself.

All did not go well for the Great General, though. Soon after his own division caught the attention of his enemies, a second was supposed to rush forward east of the Rock Road, to catch the disorganized troops rushing back from the Grove of Doom to help Sleepy. The commander of that force, not sure if he was being led into a clever trap himself, vacillated until his attack had no chance of attaining success. Shortly he would find himself free to pursue new career opportunities. Many lesser officers would join him.

On the extreme left Aridatha Singh launched his attack exactly on schedule. Its initial goal was to occupy the Grove of Doom. Then it was supposed to carry on southward and westward and cut the enemy's line of withdrawal. But before Aridatha's force was well into the maneuver he received a dispatch from Mogaba directing him to pull back. The enemy had collected himself. A counterattack was expected shortly. Mogaba feared that if Sleepy discovered Aridatha she would cut him off and exterminate his division. Aridatha was a novice on the battlefield.

The Grove of Doom:
A Big Surprise

The Daughter of Night was ready to scream with the boredom and psychic op-
pression of life in the Grove of Doom. Life with Narayan had not been perfect
but she had understood it. Life with the Khadidas was intolerable. The possessed
little man was insufferable. Every day, all day, there were lessons. Almost always
about things she already knew. Unless it was philosophical stuff about how she
ought to give herself up completely to the will of Kina. About how she should strive
to rid herself of even the most stubborn tatters of personality and become nothing
but a vessel for Kina, not the Daughter of Night anymore but the Khadidasa.

The Khadidas droned his arguments at her while she sat with arms around
shins, chin on her knees, on the steps of the Deceiver temple. Visiting Deceiver pilgrims came and went, cleaning the temple. She paid no attention. She was recalling
more than one other time when she had been right here with Papa Narayan. Looking back, those days seemed almost a normal family life, now.

She began to replay thoughts from times past, immediately became restless,
and wondered why. She had not thought of men in that way since she had heard
about Narayan's death.

Someone came down from the temple, passed by her. He set himself to fling a
pail of dirty water. There was a solid thump. The bucket man made a startled little
squeak and toppled backward. He fell on the steps beside the girl, looking up at his
messiah from amazed eyes. She watched the light fade from them.

An arrow stood out of his chest. It had struck him through the heart. The girl
did not notice the colorful markings on the shaft, which identified not only the
archer's unit but the bowman as well. She started to look around. Thumps and cries
surrounded her. Arrows hissed close and thumped behind her as they found her
new companion. She started to dig inside, to release the "love me" effect. A blunt arrow struck her squarely in the breastbone. A second struck her lower. She pitched
forward, trying to puke up her anklebones.

The first few arrows seemed not to inconvenience the Khadidas at all. But they kept coming. And coming. And then there were Taglian soldiers all over. A high officer shouted, "Cut off the heads. We'll take them with us. Leave the bodies in the boneyard. For the ravens."

Another officer strode toward the Daughter of Night. The other Taglians all deferred to him. The girl's first response was to notice that he was incredibly handsome. Then she recalled having seen him before, years ago, when she had been a captive of the Black Company. He had been brought to see Narayan. "My brother Aridatha," she gasped out. "It seems my fate is to spend life as a prisoner." She continued to clutch her stomach. A huge Shadar soldier stood over her, ready to club her at the first hint of anything untoward.

The Taglian officer was startled but only for a moment. He grasped the part about being her brother. "You're the Daughter of Night. It's my job to make sure you don't fulfill your destiny." He eyed the thing lying beside her, motionless now but not dead. In the conventional sense. He had met Goblin that night, too.

"That is the Khadidas now," she said. "Not the wizard. It's not dead. And you can't kill it. It has the Goddess in it."

The Taglian made swift gestures. Soldiers bound the Goblin thing, then stuffed it into a hemp sack—after yanking the arrows out of its flesh. "I wouldn't count on that."

"Kina is in him."

"Suppose I chop him into little pieces, Booboo? Then have my men burn the pieces at places separated by a hundred miles. I didn't know my father and I certainly don't honor what he was. But, even so, that creature murdered him."

"What did you call me?"

"Eh? You mean Booboo?"

"Yes. That. Why did you do that?" She forced herself to look away from what was happening to the martyred Deceivers as she forced her mind away from the accusation leveled against the Khadidas.

"Your mother and father and everyone in the Black Company who cares about you calls you Booboo. Because it isn't as unwieldy as 'the Daughter of Night.' Come on. Get up. I have to keep these men moving. No tricks, either. If you misbehave you'll get hurt. These men are very scared of you."

A twinge of surprise ran through the girl. They were concerned enough about her to have a pet name for her? Narayan had not dared go that far, though she knew that he had been devoted to her.

Despite Aridatha's warning she tried to turn on the "love me" effect. It would not come. She could not tell if that was because she was so rattled or because of the Khadidas. The Goblin thing had shown the ability to interfere with her before, usually when she was not conforming to the standards it set.

For an instant she hoped her captors *would* shred the Khadidas and roast the scraps in a hundred scattered trash pits. Then she forced her personal feelings aside.

This was no time. This was the time to concentrate on making sure she and the Khadidas survived until they found their opportunity to begin their great work.

That that chance would come she did not doubt. Kina would find a way. Kina always did. Kina was the darkness. And the darkness always came.

The girl remained completely docile and cooperative. She could not help noticing how restless she became each time the handsome general came near her. But he was too busy to notice her. He had received orders changing his mission.

86

Beside the Cemetery: More Confusion

There's another division out there, east of the Rock Road somewhere," Swan told Sleepy and her staff. "My impression is that it was supposed to push past and get behind us. But it suddenly turned back north. Without us taking prisoners or getting help from the hidden folk we'll never know why."

The Unknown Shadows became a hot topic. There were a few still around but they would not be bullied into helping. Tobo had not told them to help.

Tempers did not improve during the discussion. Everyone was tired, cranky and impatient. Sleepy in particular. With no solid evidence whatsoever she was beginning to believe that Mogaba had gotten the best of her yet again. And the thing was not over yet.

The Great General had not yet broken contact entirely. He seemed willing to continue skirmishing indefinitely.

Swan told everyone, "I think we did well. The casualty ratio ran in our favor, certainly."

Sleepy snapped, "But, strategically, Mogaba must be celebrating. He's pleased with what he accomplished." She had no way of knowing any such thing, of course. She knew only that she was not pleased. Mogaba had surprised her again.

She overlooked the fact that she had managed to drive off a much superior force once the fighting started, that Mogaba might have been too subtle and clever for his own good.

Willow Swan did not overlook that. He said, "Mogaba may be back. Once he understands that he did surprise us and could've rolled over us if he'd just charged in without all the maneuvering."

Heads bobbed. One brigadier noted that were he in charge on the other side he would attack again even if he thought his enemies expected him. He would do it just to see what would happen. And to build in the minds of the attacked a belief that they had to stay alert. Keeping ready to repel an attack would grind a force down after several days.

Sahra wandered in. Late and uninterested in the discussion. To no one in particular she said, "It's started to rain."

Because that was important news that might have a serious impact on operations, Swan stepped out for a look.

The sky was overcast. The smell of rain was in the air. But it was not raining now and did not look likely to start until well after nightfall, which was only a short while away. Swan went back inside shaking his head.

That Sahra might have been speaking figuratively or metaphorically became evident a short while later, when a patrol brought in news that the Grove of Doom had been cleansed of Deceivers.

"Even of the Daughter of Night and the Goblin thing?" Sleepy demanded.

"We didn't find their bodies, Captain. And there were plenty of bodies there. All with their heads missing. Maybe those two managed to escape."

"Maybe. I wish Tobo would get the hell back here. I really hate this being blind."

"You're totally spoiled," Swan told her.

"And loving every minute of it. Tso Lien. More work for your recon people. Find out what happened. And find out if we can run anybody down. Keeping in mind that it would please Mogaba no end to lead us into a lethal trap."

"It shall be done, my Captain."

Swan sneered at Tso Lien's flowery response. The man hailed from a province where styles of speech were as important as what was being said. He was another of those fiercely competent professional officers who had wanted to shed the feudal chains of Hsien in hopes of making his fortune.

Swan wondered if the men from the Land of Unknown Shadows might not begin concentrating more on staying alive than on winning a war. Their future fortunes were in Company hands already, hidden in that cemetery.

Glittering Stone:
Fortress with No Name

O h, so alert the observing eyes when Lady and I opened the Shadowgate. I tossed in several unnecessary steps just for drama and confusion. Then we were moving again, flickering southward along the shielded road toward Shivetya's great wintry fastness.

The entire plain seemed a chill, grey, wintry place, lacking all glitter. The standing stones seemed old and tired and not much interested in making any effort to proclaim the glories of the past. I did not spot any new ones. Not once did the wind grow warmer than the heart of a loan shark. We saw patches of ice and snow.

Tobo suggested the plain was getting its weather from somewhere where the season was less comfortable than our own.

"You think?" I said. "With the Khatovar gate busted completely?" There was no sense of menace to the plain today. Could the shadows have become that few?

Shukrat said, "Only, it would be the heart of summertime at home, now."

I grunted. I adjusted my flying log to make more speed. The kids had no trouble keeping up. I heard Lady curse in the distance as Howler's carpet fell behind. Howler could not hurry because his conveyance nearly filled the protected area. He had to be cautious.

A s we neared Shivetya's fortress, Tobo shouted, "It's safe to go up now!" He and Shukrat shot toward the sun. Or where the sun would have stood had the weather not been vile.

"Don't you dare!" Murgen barked.

"Too late, buddy. Hang on." I was rising already, though not with the derring-do of some immortal teenager. When Murgen squawked I said, "You don't like the ride, get off and walk."

In moments we had a god's-eye view of the glittering plain.

It was not a view I had seen before, nor was it one I had heard described. From a half mile up the plain resembled the floor inside the main chamber of the fortress. That did not surprise me. But the plain's boundaries did.

Each of the sixteen sectors centered on a Shadowgate. Each had its own weather, season and time of day, which became obscured and confused approaching the midway points between Shadowgates.

"It's like looking at the rest of the universe from inside a crystal ball," Murgen said.

"How come you never mentioned that it looks like this?"

"Because I never saw it like this. Maybe from the ghost realm you can't see this."

From up there color came to the plain. Never before had I seen so much color in the place of glittering stone.

Tobo and Shukrat shot past us, headed down, whooping with glee. I said, "Fun time is over." Howler's carpet had come into view, creeping along the line of the road down from our own world's Shadowgate.

We entered the fortress through a hole in its roof. That seemed the only damage that never repaired itself. Maybe the guardian demon found a hole more useful than a dry floor. Certainly he had no cares about weather.

Although it was daytime outside, our agent on the scene, ancient Baladitya, was napping. These days he probably spent more time snoozing then he spent awake.

By the time Murgen and I set down, Shukrat was involved in a bitter argument with Nashun the Researcher and the First Father. She and the Voroshk sorcerers used their native tongue, of course, but exact words were of no consequence. At heart the squabble was as old as humanity itself, fug-headed antiques locking horns with omniscient youth.

"Smells in here," Murgen observed.

It flat-out stank. Evidently the Voroshk were waiting for the serving staff to clean up after them. "Guess Shivetya doesn't have a sense of smell. If I was him I'd stop feeding them till they learned to take care of their chores." Baladitya, I noted, kept up his share of the housework despite tendencies toward absentmindedness and single-mindedness.

The racket raised by Shukrat and her relatives finally disrupted the copyist's snores.

Baladitya was a hairy old scarecrow desperately in need of a change of clothing. His ragged apparel was all that he had ever worn in my experience. He was almost as bad as the Howler, although less densely wrapped.

A close encounter with scissors, comb and a tub of warm water would not have been amiss, either. Tangled wisps of fine white hair floated all around his head and face. I thought bits might begin floating away, like seeds from a dandelion.

The inside of the fortress was completely creepy. I never relaxed there. It rubbed me the same way Uncle Doj always had. Wrong. Suspiciously wrong. In a quiet, unobtrusive way. A way that left me incapable of relaxing. Baladitya zeroed in on Murgen, wanting to know all about how Sleepy was doing, about how his old friend Master Santaraksita was doing, about how Tobo was. He had the Annalist bug. Also, though he had chosen his life out here for the intellectual adventure, he did miss people.

I suspect the Voroshk were not excellent company. They probably whined constantly in a language he did not understand, making no effort to communicate other than by yelling louder and slower.

I glanced upward, wondering when the others would get around to showing up. Then I strolled away a few steps, to the outer fringe of the dome of sourceless light that illuminated Baladitya's work area. I stared at the vast, indistinct bulk of the demon Shivetya.

The darkness around the devil was deeper than I recalled it, deeper than others had recorded it. The great wooden throne was equally ill-defined. The humanoid bulk nailed to the throne by means of silver daggers seemed less substantial than I remembered. I wondered if the golem became more ethereal as he gave of himself to sustain his guests.

Visitors have to eat. Shivetya sustains his guests and allies by exuding large, mushroomlike growths of manna. I recall the taste as slightly sweet and mildly spicy in that way that leaves you trying to figure out exactly what the spice might be. Just a few bites provide immense energy and boost your confidence dramatically. But nobody gets fat eating the stuff. In fact, it is a little repulsive and you do not touch it until you are hungry or hurting.

Obviously, Shivetya himself was not going to remain chubby forever, either.

I realized that big red eyes had opened. Shivetya was regarding me with more interest than I was regarding him.

The golem did not speak aloud. We believed that it could not. When it chose to communicate it did so by speaking directly inside your brain. Some found the experience no problem. I had not endured it myself, to my recollection, so cannot describe it. If Shivetya invaded my dreams during the half generation I lay enchanted in the caverns below I had no recollection of that, either. I have no memories whatsoever of that time.

Murgen and Lady do remember. Some. They will not discuss it. They prefer to let what made it into the Annals speak for itself.

It must not have been pleasant.

The shadows left Shivetya looking like he had a dog or jackal's head, which sparked a momentary recollection of childhood idols. I guess he *was* a sort of lord of the underworld. He just did not do much recruiting.

One huge eye closed, then reopened. The demon of glittering stone showing off his sense of humor. Knowing that wink would obsess me for days.

Hands took hold of my arm. I glanced down. My sweetheart had arrived. And in this dim light she looked much younger and happier. I whispered, "You guys finally made it."

"Howler is turning into a timid little old man. He's got the idea that he might have a future."

"Let's stroll off that direction about half a mile and get lost for half an hour."

"Well. I'm certainly tempted. But I'm wondering what's gotten into you."

I pinched her behind. She squeaked and swatted my arm. I said, "Whoops!" Both of Shivetya's eyes were turned our way now.

Lady said, "That sort of takes the edge off the moment, doesn't it?"

It did. So did several pairs of eyes watching from where the rest of the crowd were gathered. The youngsters in particular were appalled.

"Oh, well. Life's a bitch."

Fortress with No Name:
Recruiting Excitement

The squabbling amongst the Voroshk went on and on, seldom subsiding for long. I suspect there were several occasions when those two old men wanted to punish the rest of us but were held in check by Shivetya. Tobo paid them no mind. He remained busy communing with Baladitya or the golem. The latter seemed to be contributing to the boy's already excessive arsenal of power.

Whenever it became too much for them, Arkana or Shukrat would retreat to wherever I happened to be, usually ending up seated on the floor, facing away from the family. "They're afraid of you," Arkana explained. "They think you're the real terror and Tobo is all for show. They think you destroyed our world."

"I didn't destroy anything." Curious. Her accent was not nearly as pronounced out here, when she wanted some protection.

"I know that. You know it. Even they probably know. But they don't want it to be their fault. Inside, they're almost as bad as Gromovol and Sedvod. For a couple of hundred years now to be Voroshk has meant to be perfect in every way. Without fault."

"So how come all the arguing?"

"Because Shukrat wants to stay with you. Because Sedvod died without proper rites. Because they don't want to believe that Gromovol did so many really stupid things, including getting Magadan killed. That'll really cause terrible Family political trouble when the news gets back home. Magadan's father is the First Father's brother and they really hate each other."

Evidently the surviving Voroshk preferred to pretend that their Family still ruled in a land not wasted by murderous shadows.

"And why are they yelling at you?"

Arkana sighed. She tucked her head down in between her knees, where I could not get a good look at her expression. "I guess because I really kind of said I don't think I want to go home, either."

Arkana really used the word "really" a real lot. "Despite what happened?"

"They don't know that part yet. They don't need to know about it."

"They won't hear about it from me. But Gromovol might . . ."

"Even Gromovol isn't stupid enough to talk about it. There's no way he can talk his way out of that being his fault. By the rules of our own people. If that came out even his own father would desert him."

Wearing a somewhat dazed expression Shukrat retreated our way. Arkana moved over a few feet but otherwise did not acknowledge her existence. Neither did Shukrat deign to see Arkana. Shukrat settled on the stone floor, arms around her legs and chin upon her knees. There were tearstreaks on her cheeks.

"Well?" I said. "Do I need to go over there and spank somebody for being rude to my little girls?"

Shukrat laughed weakly. "You'd have to hit the other end. About ten thousand times. With a blacksmith's hammer."

"Just to get their attention," Arkana said. Posed as they were now the family resemblance was clear. Only when they were up and moving under the direction of their divergent characters did they seem so different.

The girls had a point. Even the destruction of their world had not been enough to shake those two old boulders loose from their dry riverbed of fixed thought.

I asked, "Arkana, are you pulled together now? Want to come translate for me?" I could use the tongue of Juniper, of course, but this would give her a chance to feel like she was useful.

She thought about that for a moment. She exchanged glances with Shukrat. Both girls looked at me.

I promised, "I'll only bully them a little."

The older Voroshk were keeping their fangs sharp by gnawing on Gromovol. If the kid had not fucked up so badly I might have felt sorry for him. He did not have the option of returning to our world. He would have to take whatever those two chose to hand out.

"You've been a little hard on my girls," I told the First Father. "Time to knock it off. Either one of you bothered to go back and see how things turned out at home?"

No response. Other than ugly looks.

"So you don't really know how things stand. . . ." An epiphany. "Arkana, sweetie. They ran away. Coming after you kids was their excuse. And when they used it up they couldn't go back. I'll bet you Shivetya hasn't been forcing them to stay here at all." I recalled that once there had been three of them. Somebody must have gone. And maybe did not live to bring back news.

Those old men were cowards? It fit.

For the first time in generations the Voroshk faced something the Family could not overwhelm as easily as stamping a mouse. And the only way some of them could deal with that was to run away.

These two would not want to go back now in case there *were* survivors.

I said, "I'll be right back." I trotted over to Tobo, interrupted, gave him the short version. "How long are you going to be? Do I have time to take a run through the Khatovar gate with those old men so we can find out what the shadows really did do over there?"

The boy's eyes went blank.

When I was about ready to slap him to get his attention back he refocused, told me, "Shivetya says that would be a huge health risk. Shivetya says you're right about the Voroshk. They did run away. Shivetya says more courageous members of the clan are still active back there. A lot of shadows are active there, too. Shivetya says the gate is growing closed. With almost every surviving shadow on that side of it. Shivetya says leave it alone. Shivetya says go ahead with your scheme. Shivetya says not to worry about Khatovar. You can't reach it. Trying will only get you killed. And it will still be there when everything else is done."

Was that Tobo speaking or was the demon using his lips? "Shivetya, I fear, contains an awful lot of stinky brown stuff. For a guy who never eats."

"You think it's unreasonable, him being a little selfish about the order things get done? Considering the scale of his contributions?"

"Humbug." I stamped back to Arkana. I wondered how anybody was supposed to murder a goddess—and survive it so the Goddess's jailer could be hustled down the dark path right behind her. "Sweetheart, tell those old farts that I want them to fly out to your homeworld with me. That I want to see what's happened there. And that I really do want to see what's left of Khatovar."

Arkana took several little sideways steps that moved her around in front of me, putting her back to Nashun and the First Father. "You really mean that?"

Softly, because that half-wit Gromovol seemed to have become interested in what was being said, I responded, "As far as they need to know, I do."

The old men did not do much faking of any reason for avoiding a trip home for a fact-finding tour. They did make it clear that they would not go.

"What do you plan to do with your lives?" I asked. "Shivetya won't let you loaf around here forever."

They suspected they were about to be sucked into something. And they were right, of course. I added, "The Company always has room for a few good men." Or bad men, as the case might be. I was not so sure about chickenshit and mediocre men—though having a couple extra sorcerers sounded worthwhile enough to make the try.

Trouble was, if I did seduce these two, how would I keep them under control?

That sounded like something Lady ought to ponder. It was the sort of question she had dealt with regularly before I stumbled into her life.

I could hear the clockwork kerchunking inside Voroshk craniums. Their thoughts were obvious. Tell Croaker anything. Tell Croaker what he wanted to hear. Get off this cruel and frightful plain. Run away. Find a place where they have not heard of the Voroshk, where they have no major wizards of their own. Set up shop there and slap together a whole new empire.

Just as the Shadowmasters had done before them.

"Tell them I'll come back after they've had a day or two to think it over."

As she retreated with me Arkana told me, "If they agree to join you they'll give you more trouble than Gromovol did."

"Really?" I chose a tone that was supposed to let her know I might not be as dumb as I looked. "How do you suppose we could keep them from doing that?"

She did have some ideas. "Do what you did to us. Make them strip naked. Take their rheitgeistiden and their *shefsepoken*. Make them stay on the ground where they're vulnerable. But promise them they'll get everything back after they show you that you can trust them. Then you stretch it out."

"I'm going to adopt you. You'd make a wonderful daughter. Hey, evil-minded future daughter number two. You heard Arkana. What do you think?"

Grudgingly, Shukrat admitted, "I think she's right."

"Excellent! Let's go ask your wicked future mother's opinion."

We found Lady reading what Baladitya was spending his final years recording, which was, more or less, Shivetya's biography. "Darling, I've decided we need to adopt these two marvellous children. They're turning out every bit as blackhearted as we ever wanted our Booboo to be."

Lady awarded me a suspicious look, decided I was fooling around but meant what I said. More or less. "Tell me about it."

I said, "Go to it, girls."

89

Beside the Cemetery:
More Confusion

Expecting the Great General to remain offensive-minded was not enough, Sleepy knew. She had to outguess him. This one time she could not let Mogaba slide around her.

She took a twinned approach to planning, setting up two distinct staffs. The first consisted of Iqbal and Runmust Singh, Riverwalker, Sahra, Willow Swan and others who had been with her since the Kiaulune wars. She even summoned Blade up from Jaicur because Blade actually knew Mogaba personally and, at one time, had been fairly close to him.

The second general staff consisted entirely of officers from Hsien. These men knew Mogaba only as a bugaboo. And they had no knowledge of the surrounding territory beyond what they could learn from maps and scouting on their own.

Sleepy hoped to find something useful in the gap between diverging visions.

She kept her cavalry busy, scouting, chasing Mogaba's scouts, skirmishing with enemy patrols, trying to locate the bulk of the Great General's forces.

Mogaba was doing the same. Both sides relied heavily on questioning civilians passing through. Traffic on the Rock Road had slackened but had not stopped entirely.

Each staff proposed several likely enemy campaigns. Sleepy had their opposite numbers play out a counter campaign. And in the end, after two almost sleepless days, she felt no more illuminated than she had at the beginning.

So she chose to go with intuition. That had served her best during previous dances with the Great General, anyway.

By the Cemetery:
Still More Confusion

The Great General told his commanders, "I'm growing concerned that all this maneuvering helps them more than it does us. It's obvious that they're without mystical support. But every hour we maneuver is an hour nearer the time when they get those advantages back."

Aridatha Singh asked, "Aren't we still at a disadvantage in a direct confrontation?"

"Soldier for soldier, possibly. But we have three times as many soldiers. And they're still trying to cover a line running all the way from the Grove of Doom to this stand near their camp. That's too much to hold with ten thousand men."

No questions came. No suggestions arose. The Great General seldom solicited advice. When Mogaba gathered his captains he planned to issue instructions. Their job would be to see that those were executed.

"I'm returning to the original plan. I'll drive straight forward, in the middle, with the Second Territorial. I'll engage and hold. Singh, you advance along your previous route with your same mission. Once you're behind them form your division in battle array and advance up the Rock Road. If the rest of us have done our jobs you'll only have to sweep up fugitives."

Mogaba rested a hand upon the shoulder of a young officer named Narenda Nath Saraswati, scion of an old aristocratic family, of the third generation of that family to serve under arms since the opening skirmishes of the Shadowmaster wars. Two days earlier Saraswati had been a regimental chief of staff with an aggressive attitude. The Great General having been disappointed by the timid performance of his remaining division, Saraswati's aggressive nature was about to earn him a chance to shine.

Mogaba said, "Narenda, as soon as I have the enemy engaged, I want you to take your whole force forward on a narrow front, along the edge of this wood." That division having been shifted to the right since the previous engagement. "Overrun their camp. That shouldn't be difficult. They appear to be holding it with raw recruits. Once you clear the camp, reform and advance so as to strike the enemy left wing, rear, and reserve. *Don't* begin your initial attack until I do have the enemy solidly engaged.

"One more thing. I want you both to leave your main standards with me. If the enemy sees those maybe they'll think I'm concentrating everything in one place."

He paused. There were no questions. All this had been planned out before. The necessity now was renewed vigor.

"I'll go in at midmorning. Behind scouts and skirmishers. Make sure your men are well-provisioned. I'll personally strangle any officer who fails to see to the welfare of his soldiers."

The Great General's attitude was well-known, if not universally applauded by his officers. Corruption was so deeply ingrained in Taglian culture that even after more than a generation of cultural collision and occasional bloody change there were still those who failed to understand that theft from the men you commanded was not an acceptable way to supplement your income.

Whatever their differences, the Black Company, the Protector, the Great General, all the northerners who gained power, strained to increase the efficiency of their regime by rooting out graft and corruption. More than anything else, that made the outsiders incredibly alien.

"Aridatha. Wait. I've had a thought. If things go well it's likely Saraswati will break the enemy before you can get into position behind them."

"I was thinking of leaving during the night and going into hiding inside the Grove of Doom."

"Good idea. What I'm thinking, then, is, you should come out in a long line so you can catch most of the fugitives running southward. I'm especially interested in catching the kind of people who go underground and five years later turn up with a whole damned new army."

"I'll do my best."

Mogaba growled. That was a promise he hated. It sounded like an excuse being put into place beforehand. Though Aridatha was never the sort to excuse his own shortcomings. He was more the sort who found good reasons why others failed.

91

By the Cemetery:
Even More Confusion

Today's the day," Sleepy told her Captains. "I can feel it." She went on to excoriate Croaker, Tobo and that bunch for taking so long. Then she began telling people what she wanted done. She started getting arguments right away. She snapped, "Mogaba is going to split his force again. For that he's going to pay. If you want to argue with me I'll accept your resignations now. There're officers who'll do what they're told and keep their mouths shut."

A few hours later the Great General appeared almost exactly where she expected him. He was spread out over a lot of ground and had a lot of banners flying. For a time she feared she might have guessed wrong and Mogaba was just going to come straight ahead and roll right over her. But he did not attack as vigorously as he should have if that was the case.

Sleepy did not press in her turn. Not right away. She did not want to make it obvious that she had not concentrated her forces, either. She engaged in skirmishing and harassing tactics but stepped back whenever Mogaba responded in any strength. He came forward both because he had to stay in contact and because Sleepy was pulling back toward the second jaw of his trap. He seemed willing to be led that way.

When the division on the far right rushed from concealment behind a low ridge, it lost all cohesion. The troops had to cover most of a mile. Their commander was more interested in striking before his foes could respond than he was in presenting a pretty picture advancing.

The men in colored armor who came out of the hidden cemetery marched in perfect order. Some carried recently manufactured fireball projects. They began slaughtering the rabble before most of the Taglians were aware that Fortune had dealt them one from the bottom of the deck. They lasted as long as they did only because there were so many of them.

92

By the Cemetery:
Confusion Piled Higher

They've begun to stiffen on their right," one of Mogaba's companions announced. "But they're falling back on the other wing."

"There's something wrong," Mogaba declared. "There should be more of them."

"Why don't we rush them?"

"Do sound a general advance. But at the slow cadence."

The first confused message arrived just minutes later. Narenda Nath Saraswati's division was on the run. Saraswati himself was dead. Most of the division officers had been captured or killed.

Before he could make sense of it, Mogaba heard the horns on his right and saw the different colored blocks, every soldier with his own banner on his back, advancing. A flurry of cavalrymen swept stragglers, and fugitives, and foolish resistance out of the infantry's path.

The Great General needed only a moment to understand that Sleepy was about to kidney-punch the Second Territorial with her best. "Full attack!" he ordered. "Fastest cadence!" If he got the soldiers moving forward before they recognized their peril he could use his numbers to overcome. "The little witch finally caught me." But there was still Aridatha, moving in behind. It remained to be seen who would have whom in the end.

Mogaba drove straight toward the enemy camp. If he could get inside its palisade. . . .

Beyond the Grove of Doom:
Confusion Grows

Aridatha learned of the developing disaster from Vehdna horsemen who had been forced to flee in his direction, around the eastern end of the battlefield, because enemy skirmishers had blocked the way north already. Aridatha was able to intuit the truth from the complete confusion of the reports.

He ordered his division to form for battle.

Backboned by his own City Battalions the force was well-drilled, if not veteran. Within two hours Singh had the enemy in sight. The invaders and their traitor native allies were involved in a huge, bloody melee with all of the Taglian troops Mogaba had been able to hold together or who had not been able to run away. Evidently the invaders had not remained sufficiently concerned about Singh's division.

Aridatha's advent was close to a complete surprise. As for its effectiveness. . . . His soldiers had no experience dealing with the terror. And they all knew that their brothers in the other divisions had lost their battle already and were busily doing their dying.

The exhausted armies disentangled as the day waned. The soldiers on both sides had endured so much horror that, gradually, they just stopped trying to interfere with an enemy who seemed willing to go away without causing trouble.

But who won?

On that day arguments could have been made both ways. Final determination would be in the hands of those historians who examined the effect the battle had on Taglian society and culture. It could be a watershed or it could be nothing important, depending on what followed and how the population responded.

94

Beside the Cemetery:
Sorrows Gathering

Not even Sleepy had the physical or mental energy left to do anything useful. She slumped against the saddle of a dead horse, let the twilight and exhaustion wash over her. She felt no exhilaration even though she had broken the backbone of the last Taglian army and had, for the first time, been the one who held the field when the fighting ended. Mogaba, if he lived, was the one slinking away this time.

A big contributor to her mood was the fact that this accomplishment, such as it was, was as much Suvrin's responsibility as her own. Suvrin, alone, had not abandoned all thought of the third Taglian division. He had been able to move his brigade in response, feebly, when the rest of the enemy appeared. But for Suvrin's cool head, the Great General would be here, holding the field, yet again. Though the numbers of dead and dying, likely, would be much the same.

Suvrin settled beside her. He said nothing for a long time. Neither did she. For the first time in decades she wanted to hold someone, wanted to be held by someone. But she did not act upon that want.

Finally, Suvrin spoke. "Willow Swan is dead. I saw his body a while ago."

Sleepy grunted. "I have a feeling there'll be a lot of old friends to mourn once we collect the dead. I saw Iqbal and Riverwalker go down."

"No. Not Iqbal. Who'll take care of Suruvhija?" Singh's wife was not all that bright.

"The Company, Suvrin. Until she chooses to leave." And Runmust, if he had survived. It was his obligation under Shadar religious law. "She's one of our own. We take care of our own. Do we have anyone capable of handling picket duty?"

Suvrin responded with an interrogatory grunt.

"That's the Great General over there. Iron Man Mogaba. If he's still even a little bit healthy and can pull together some kind of night attack he'll be back. Maybe even if he has to do it all by himself."

Suvrin took several deep, thoughtful breaths. "We have quite a few recruits who didn't do much but hide in the cemetery. I've already shamed some of them into picking up the battlefield."

"It won't matter if they run away as long as they run toward us."

"Uhm."

"Willow? He never did. . . . Never found his dream."

"I always pictured him as your basic everyman. Just drifting wherever the tides of life took him. Showing a flash sometimes but never really getting up and grabbing the reins. He might have been a hopeless romantic, too. According to the Annals. He had a case on Lady once. And a case on the Protector, where he was much more lucky but lived to regret it. He even had it for you for a while, I think."

"We were friends. Just good friends."

Suvrin did not argue. But there was a quaver in Sleepy's voice that made him wonder if, possibly only once or twice, there had not been something to lend substance to rumor.

It was none of his business.

"I should've avoided this mess until Tobo and the others got back."

Suvrin observed, "Mogaba wouldn't have let you. So don't beat yourself up. He would've chased you hard, trying to take advantage of the fact that they were gone."

Sleepy knew that was true but truth did not alter her emotional state. A lot of people were dead. Many of them had been comrades of long standing. It was her mission to preserve them, not to waste them. She had failed.

And the full, grim scope of the tragedy remained to be revealed.

95

Fortress with No Name:
Down Below

She looks so peaceful," Lady intoned. We stood over her sister, in the cavern of the ancients. Soulcatcher now filled the identical spot that Lady had occupied during the Captivity.

I needed a moment to realize that she was being sarcastic, repeating the inanities you hear at funerals. She was sure Soulcatcher was partially aware of what was happening. And she could not interact with her sister in any more intimate way.

I said, "We've done what we came to do. We need to think about getting back to the Company." Though I remained tempted to hazard a recon run through the Khatovar gate before it healed completely.

And I had a notion to take a gander at the dark thing that had been toying with our lives and destinies since before we ever heard any of her names.

"Yes," Lady said. "There's no telling what mischief Booboo and the Khadidas and Mogaba have gotten into without Tobo and Howler there to baby-sit."

I said, "If Mogaba realizes that Sleepy's got no wizards, he'll be all over her like a snake on shit."

"That was colorful, if nonsensical." I noted that she did not include herself with Tobo and Howler. Yet I suspected strongly that she was capable of sucking Kina's power like a queen vampire nowadays. Sometimes I wondered what that augured for the day it came time to pay up to Shivetya. She *really* hated turning into something old and dumpy and grey that looked way too much like the mother she barely remembered.

"I just remembered a Company sergeant from before your time. A man named Elmo. He had an unusual turn of phrase."

"You are getting old."

"I spend my whole life living in the past, darling. Let's saddle up." We had come down the long stair to the cavern aboard Voroshk flying posts. What a marvellous way to deal with stairways when you are no longer twenty years old.

Lady started to pat her sister on the shoulder, an ordinary little action. "Don't!" I barked, with enough urgency to cause a couple of small ice stalactites to fall somewhere back in the depths of the cave.

"Oh. I wasn't thinking."

There were frost-encrusted old men all along the sides of the cave. No one knew who they were. Except, possibly, Baladitya. Most of them were still alive. They were, like Soulcatcher, exiles from some unsympathetic power. But a few, including way too many Company brothers from the time of the Captivity, were dead meat. And all it had taken to kill them was a thoughtless, gentle or friendly touch.

Lady pushed past me. I surveyed the local population. As ever, it seemed the open eyes all stared right at me. I met Soulcatcher's dull gaze. For no reason I understood, I winked. We were old conspirators. We went way back. I knew her before I knew her sister, in olden times of terror.

It may have been a trick of the light or of my imagination but it seemed there was a flicker of response.

W hen we returned up top we found the others involved in the initial stages of getting ready to leave. Howler was exulting, loudly, to all and sundry, in his new ability to remain silent. He seemed almost grateful. Being an old cynic myself I have strong notions about the true value of human gratitude. It is a currency whose worth plunges by the hour.

Though thoroughly confused, the two old Voroshk sorcerers were collecting themselves for the journey, too. Which meant that they had surrendered to Tobo's blandishments while Lady and I were down below. They had surrendered their flying posts and special clothing rather than be forced to return to their own world.

They must have gotten some really unpleasant news.

"You understand what this means?" I asked Tobo.

"Uh?" The kid was relaxing by flirting with Shukrat. I got the impression that those two might have started sneaking off into dark corners. They had developed that goofy way of looking at each other. And they could not stay away from one another.

That would not instill Sahra with great joy.

"It means we have to stash Gromovol downstairs, too. Or kill him. Which wouldn't be politic. Because there's no way I'm going to give him the opportunity to give us any more grief by letting him come back with us."

"I'll talk to Nashun and the First Father." He turned to Shukrat. "Come on, honey."

Hah. Honey.

A procession of flying posts went down to the cave of the ancients. Oh, that was so much easier than clambering down and up. The elderly Voroshk, in borrowed rags, rode behind Tobo and Shukrat. Gromovol rode behind Arkana. I figured she owed him one. Her cast did not cause her any problems flying. She would be out of that soon.

Gromovol whined and begged until he became an embarrassment to everyone.

I could claim I had no mercy but that would not be true. Had I been appropriately merciless, pieces of Gromovol would have gotten distributed over half a world after I made a few cutting remarks about his character and bad behavior.

I felt like one of the Voroshk now. I *looked* like one of the Voroshk. So did my beloved. The deal with the old men compelled them to refit their wondrous black costumes for us.

Those would make marvellous complements to our Widowmaker and Lifetaker armor.

Tobo and Shukrat, too, boasted the black and undefined look, Tobo having helped himself to Gromovol's outfit.

It took only minutes to inter Gromovol, not far from the frozen corpses of several men who had been my friends. His final pleas still echoed when I told Lady, "I'm going down to the bottom of this hole. I want a look at that old bitch who's been fucking up our lives for the last fifty years."

"Are you crazy?" Tobo yelled. "I wouldn't go down there. I'm nervous just being this close."

"Then go back upstairs. Shukrat. Answer a couple of technical questions for me before you leave. Please?"

The black barrier that had frustrated Blade so was back in place. It put a terrible pressure on my mind. But the flying post did not notice it at all. The post kept moving. The Voroshk costume I wore stirred slightly, enclosing me more securely within its protection.

Although I know the names now I refuse to call post and costume by their proper, clunkily cumbersome Voroshk titles.

I passed through the barrier. Lady made a funny little sound as she came through behind me, like she did when we made love.

The scene was pretty much the way it had been described by others. What seemed to be a vast, open cavern without evident bounds, illuminated by no evident light source, and that extremely feeble. All that could be seen was a huge, ugly sprawl of flesh the color of polished eggplant. It did not move, even to breathe.

Kina looked like Shivetya's homely big sister. Kina *looked* like the embodiment of all the dark attributes I had heard assigned her, under all her many names, since first I became aware of her existence. Kina looked like many dark things.

My memories of the next few minutes are completely unreliable.

Almost immediately the great hairless head turned our way. Kina's mouth was open, exposing ugly dark fangs. She seemed to have a snake or lizard tongue. I did not recall that having been reported before in any of the conflicting myths, though her tongue was supposed to be long, the better to lap up demon blood.

The eyes of the Goddess began to open.

The immensity of her will smashed at me like a tidal wave breaking. The lights went out. For me.

Looks like you were lucky this time," Tobo told me. "Your post got you out of there."

I wanted to tell him luck had nothing to do with it. I planned it that way. I set it up with the help of his girlfriend. But I barely had energy enough to keep breathing.

I did manage to gasp, "Lady?" Had to check on my honey.

"Better off than you are. Sleeping right now. Said to tell you to just rest. Here's some Shivetya manna. It'll give you a kick in the ass. If you can keep it down."

I managed to roll my head until I could see the demon.

Shivetya was looking back at me. A white crow was strutting around on his shoulder. Not my white raven. The demon revealed a few teeth in what he might have thought was a smile. Bizarre. I did not recall him ever having moved before.

He must have seen the inside of my head. Must know I thought I had a notion about how to get to Kina.

I hoped the Goddess could not look inside my head, too.

Someday. Down the road. If I could get all the pieces to fall into place.

The white crow sneered. I believe they can do that, those birds.

Tobo understood that something was happening but did not catch on. I think my new daughters understood better than he did.

The Shadowgate:
Bad News, Bad News

I was outside the Shadowgate gossiping with Panda Man and Spook, who were telling me that keeping an eye on the gate was the best duty they had ever endured. The work was easy and the locals were friendly. If the damned ugly spooks from the plain did not keep nagging you. . . .

Tobo and Shukrat came through.

Almost immediately Tobo let out a cry of despair. He shouted, "There's been a battle!" A moment later he shot into the air, headed north, black cloth streaming behind him. An instant later still Shukrat shot off in his wake, gaining slowly.

Panting, Lady asked, "Does that mean we should be worried?"

"That would be my guess. The little shit must've gotten something from the hidden folk."

"And it was bad enough to set him off like that." She looked as troubled as I felt.

No good could come of any battle fought while we were away.

She asked, "Aren't you going to rush off and see what happened, too?"

"Don't see the point." I jerked a thumb in the direction of the carpet, which was creaking and sagging under the weight of people we dared not trust. "There isn't anything I could do, anyway. Look at that." A ripple, a distortion in the fabric of reality, seemed to be running over the face of the earth, chasing after Tobo and Shukrat. "The hidden folk following their hero."

"Why were they here?"

"Waiting around for Tobo."

"But they should've been with Sleepy. They don't do us any good hanging around the Shadowgate when . . . oh. They don't care if they do us any good."

"Exactly. What they care about is Tobo. Anything they do that benefits the rest of us they do just to please him. Which is why two-thirds of the time I don't have the two ravens that're supposed to be my permanent shoulder-ornaments and messengers and far-seeing eyes. They keep forgetting to stick with me. They wander off to find the kid. Bet you they turn up before we catch up with Sleepy, though."

"Sounds like a sucker bet to me."

After crossing the Dandha Presh I steered a course mimicking that Sleepy had followed heading north. When Lady asked why I was not heading straight north as fast as we dared push the carpet, I told her, "Because I thought I saw something I shouldn't have on the way down. I have to check on it. I'm hoping it was my imagination." But my brief conversation with the guards at the Shadowgate suggested that the nightmare might be real.

She was curious but did not ask. At the speeds we could make airborne a bit of circuitous flight would not delay us much.

I found what I was seeking on the path Sleepy had taken from Gharhawnes, at almost exactly the point where she had doubled back to get behind Dejagore. By then my confederates were extremely crabby.

"There!" I told Lady, catching just a glimpse of something moving fast inside a stand of scrubby oaks.

"There what?" She had not seen.

"The Nef."

"The Nef? The Nef are in the Voroshk world. Trapped there."

"Not according to Spook and Panda Man. They say the Nef come around every night."

"All right. But how would they get through the Shadowgate?"

"I don't know." I was flying in a circle now, giving up altitude. Once down to treetop level I cruised back and forth. I spotted nothing. Nor did I find a sign when I descended lower still and began to glide between the tree trunks.

I never found a thing. Not even a hint of a thing.

People began to yell down at me.

All right. They had a point. There were things we needed to do way north of where we were now.

Beside the Cemetery:
Among the Dead

It had been over for more than a day but the surgeons remained hard at work.
Men still lay in long rows awaiting attention, moaning, screaming, some delirious. And some dead. A burial detail walked the rows, picking up those who had
gone. Too many of those had died alone amidst the hundreds, without comfort.

The glory of war.

The ultimate fear. Mine, anyway.

I checked quickly to make sure that everyone was conforming to my decrees concerning cleanliness and sepsis. A few of the wounded would stand a better chance if
the surgeons and their helpers cleaved to the rules. Even when they were exhausted, as
they were now, and the temptation to cut corners became overwhelming.

Beyond our wounded lay those from Mogaba's army. They were likely to get no
treatment at all, except what they could manage for themselves. I was sure that our
medical supplies were as strained as our medical staff was. It looked like this was a
much bigger fight than I had expected. Or, at least, a more desperate encounter
with more casualties than expected in a short time.

Runmust Singh on crutches took me in to see Sleepy.

She appeared disoriented. I knew that look of old, having been there myself.
She was on the edge of collapse. She had not done more than catnap since the fighting started. "You can't do it all yourself, Captain. You'll be a lot more effective if you
just trust the rest of us to get things done and get yourself some rest. If Mogaba comes
back now you won't be able to think fast enough or straight enough to do anybody
any good."

She eyed me irritably but was too exhausted to squabble. "I take it you didn't
come here past the dead."

"I came through the hospital area." She knew that I would have to do that. After
we talked I would, probably, go back to offer what little help an old man with a
bum hand and a bad eye could.

"Then you don't yet know that there isn't anybody left for me to trust while I take a nap. Swan is dead, Croaker. Blade is dead. Iqbal Singh is dead. Riverwalker is dead. Add Pham Huu Clee, Li Wan, both the Chun brothers and your old engineers, Cletus and Loftus. There's going to be a lot of opportunity for advancement. Name a name. Almost everybody is dead or injured. Hell, even Sahra may be dead. We haven't been able to find her."

"We're back," I said. That ought to take a load off her shoulders. "Successfully, I might add. What about Suvrin?"

"Suvrin made it through. Suvrin saved the day. Suvrin and I have agreed to take turns resting as soon as we're sure Mogaba isn't coming back. Right now we're taking turns holding everything together."

Based on what I had seen and heard already the Great General would not return any time soon—unless he came on his own. His soldiers had had enough.

Mogaba would have been back already had he had any troops he could use. Caution and procrastination were not sins you could pin on the Great General.

I heard Tobo's voice outside, overhead. He was addressing the folk of the hidden realm. Before long we would know all we wanted to know about Mogaba's current situation. In moments thousands of wraithlike things would be involved in the search for Sahra—and everyone else still missing.

The kid was taking charge.

Sleepy mumbled, "I shouldn't have engaged him till Tobo came back."

Unwittingly, I repeated comments she had heard from Suvrin already. "Mogaba wouldn't have given you a choice. He doesn't have our intelligence resources but he does make use of the tools he has. That was our failing. Not remembering that. We should've given at least the appearance of having left a sorcerer in camp."

Sleepy nodded. "Water down the creek. Which I'll thank you to remind me whenever I begin to feel sorry for myself and start picking the thing's bones to indict myself for doing things differently."

"You're a strange bird, little girl."

"What?"

"Sorry. One-Eye's been on my mind lately." I did not explain. As long as I kept my genius sealed up inside my head there was a fair chance Kina would not find out anything she would make me regret. I asked. "What about Goblin and the girl? If there was fighting in the grove . . ."

"We don't know yet. I assume Tobo will inform us. I assume everything is going to be just peachy now that Tobo is back." She was striving for sarcasm but it was not working. She did not have strength enough to speak in anything but a monotone.

"Lady and Murgen will be here in a few minutes. Let them manage the little shit while you get your rest."

*   *   *

I went for an excursion amongst the unburied dead, to make good-byes. They were laid out in rows, awaiting disposal. The weather was cold and damp so putrefaction was not far advanced but there was stench enough of blood and open bowels. Flies were rare, it being the wrong season. And crows of any sort were a rarity these days. Buzzards circled but dared not come down because the welcome they received from the living tended to be discouraging.

Once someone identified one of the fallen, Taglian prisoners moved the body to the appropriate funeral procedure group. Recruits and additional prisoners were busy building ghats, burning corpses, digging graves and filling them, or erecting exposure platforms for the few whose fate it was to leave the earth that way.

A lot of corpses had been dealt with already but I could see that, despite the season, we were going to have to dig mass graves for the Taglian fallen. There would not be time to get each man a decent funeral. Although civilians who had had men serving with Mogaba had begun to show up already, hoping to reclaim their dead.

I wondered if, in some mystical fashion, new standing stones were materializing on the glittering plain, their faces crawling with golden memorial characters.

A subaltern from the Land of Unknown Shadows approached me. It was obvious he was not pleased about having been assigned to the funeral detail. He must have embarrassed himself during the fighting. The unpleasant duty would be his reward. "Sir," he said, with a salute so crisp it should have gotten his sentence commuted, "it would be a great help if you could offer me the funerary preferences of your old comrades." There was a mildly repulsive fawning edge to his otherwise businesslike demeanor.

He led me to a spot where he had isolated non-Taglians who did not hail from Hsien. My former henchmen and a couple of Nyueng Bao occupied that little square.

"Soldiers live," I murmured. Now there was only Murgen and Lady left from the farther shore of the Sea of Torments. "Bury Swan and the engineer brothers. Inside that cemetery over there. Make sure that their graves are clearly marked. I'll want to find them later in order to put up a proper memorial. They deserve more than a parting mention in the Annals." I wondered what Swan would think of lying to rest beside all those Shadowlanders. He and Blade and Cordy Mather had helped put most of them there.

I had no idea what funeral customs obtained amongst Blade's people. Neither I nor anyone else ever learned who those people actually were. "Lay the black man down in a grave near Swan. Maybe they can be buddies in the next world, too. Maybe they'll finally get to start that brewery they always wanted."

The subaltern was puzzled by that but did not comment. The soldiers of the Land of Unknown Shadows were growing accustomed to the religious absurdities of the new world. I walked on, across ground covered by the corpses of men Sleepy had recruited during the time of Captivity. Their number was disturbing. Before long she would be as isolated from her own generation as I was isolated from mine.

A great many excellent soldiers from the Land of Unknown Shadows lay upon that cold, hard ground, too. And, unsurprisingly, so did many men who had joined us recently, locally. Poorest trained, they had stood the least chance during the fighting.

I surveyed all that death and hoped Sleepy had reached a watershed here, that henceforth she would seek solutions that did not require headbutting until somebody staggered away and collapsed from concussion. Not that all this could be blamed on her. Based on information available I could fault none of her decisions. And she was a better tactician than I had been.

Above the Cemetery: Mogaba Accedes

Twenty-six hours after his order to break contact Mogaba abandoned all hope of pulling together an attack that would take advantage of the enemy's despair and disarray. His own men had been too badly mauled to set aside their own despair and disarray. Only Aridatha Singh's division retained its cohesion. Its reward was the task of screening the retreating army.

Which consisted mainly of survivors of the Second Territorial. Of Saraswati's former right wing force not one man in ten could be accounted for anymore.

Enemy cavalry remained very active. The Captain seemed disinclined to let him get near her again.

A pair of billowing black shapes passed low overhead. They radiated a chilling psychic scream. Suddenly, instinctually, Mogaba knew that he was being watched by something he could not turn fast enough to catch staring. He knew that his best opportunity had ended. He summoned his latest aide-de-camp, who had been in place only a few hours. The man's several predecessors were still down there on the field. "Bring me the Deceiver prisoners."

"Sir?"

"The prisoners General Singh captured in the Grove of Doom. I want to see them." He thought he could offer them a deal. The girl could pretend to be the Protector for a while. Taglios would be less restive if the Protector appeared publicly sometime soon.

"Those prisoners were sent north, sir. Under special constraint because of the danger General Singh told us they present."

"And he was right. That was the best thing to do. We don't want them to fall into unfriendly hands." Publicly, Mogaba insisted on treating the recent encounter as a triumph. He expected his officers to do the same.

Mogaba spent a moment considering what options he might have. It took only a minute to conclude that withdrawal toward Taglios was the best course.

Oh, but he hated that. No matter the true facts, rumor would call it a defeat and a retreat. That would cost.

The Great General considered his aide. He did not know the man well enough to be aware of his family status. "Tonjon, is it?"

"Than Jahn, sir. A remote male ancestor is reputed to have been Nyueng Bao. My family is Vehdna."

"Excellent. Perhaps you can share religious anecdotes with the enemy Captain."

"Sir?" Sounding both baffled and irked.

"I'm sending you south under a flag of truce. To arrange for an armistice. So we can collect our dead." If anything the Great General ever did won him favor with the Taglian people, it was his effort to bring back the fallen sons so their families could honor them with all the appropriate last rites.

This time would be a bitch. There was no way he was going to recover all the Taglian dead. "Find me some priests. Every kind we have." He needed advice about what to do with so many bodies, this close to home.

The Company, Mogaba was sure, would just fling their share of Taglian corpses into one big ugly hole, cover them over and forget about them.

99

By the Military Cemetery: Missing Persons

Tobo was distraught. Murgen was distracted. He walked around bumping into things, trapped inside his own interior world. I had not seen him so lost since his Annalist days.

No trace of Sahra had surfaced, even with the Unknown Shadows hunting. So far Tobo had determined only that she had not fallen into enemy hands. The Taglians were not looking. They were unaware, even, that they ought to bear the woman a grudge.

Sahra always had had a knack for going unnoticed.

"She's dead," Lady told me. "She was hurt, she crawled in somewhere to hide, and she died there." Which was plausible enough. Several bodies had been discovered in circumstances that fit the scenario. And Sahra was not alone in being missing. Every company in the force was unable to account for someone. Most, probably, had run away or were prisoners of war. But the hidden folk kept finding others dead in places where no one had yet thought to look.

I hoped Lady's simple explanation was the correct one. I dreaded the chance that Sahra had been captured by somebody who would use her to manipulate Tobo.

The upside was that there was a paucity of villains who might be interested. Mogaba was exonerated. Soulcatcher was buried. Booboo and the Khadidas were entombed in the big fortress guarding the southern approaches to Taglios, behind a door that could not be opened by any key still within the stronghold. Others who might have tried something sly—say the Howler or the Voroshk—had perfect alibis.

So it came down to Sahra being dead and lost or lost and wandering around in a shock so profound that she could not recall who she was or where she belonged.

Sleepy posted a huge reward for "the capture of an older Nyueng Bao woman wanted for questioning in regard to espionage against agents of the Prahbrindrah Drah." Murgen provided a description that included the shapes and locations of moles and a birthmark unfamiliar to anyone else.

"It doesn't make much sense, does it?" my darling whispered to me. "People go at the oddest times and from the oddest causes."

"Soldiers live," I murmured.

"You're turning that into a mantra."

"You feel guilty. You wonder why him and not me, then you're glad it was him and not you, then you feel guilty. Soldiers live. And wonder why."

"One soldier lives because the gods know that I still haven't gotten my fair share of loving. Put that pen away and come on over here."

"You've sure turned into a pushy broad in your old age."

"Yeah? You should've seen me four hundred years ago."

Tobo announced, "Mogaba's had the Khadidas and the Daughter of Night moved to the palace. In a remarkable coincidence the Protector was seen publicly for the first time in months only a few hours later. She was extremely angry with the Taglians and brought one of her punishments down on their heads." He grinned. "Most likely that had something to do with all the graffiti that's begun appearing. All the good old stuff. 'Water sleeps.' 'My brother unforgiven.' And even some that aren't my doing. 'You shall lie in the ashes ten thousand years, eating only wind.' I love that one."

That one caught my attention. I had heard it before, somewhere. But I had heard them all before.

"'*Rajadharma*' is everywhere. Anyone who can write seems to put that one up. Then there's '*Madhuprlya*' which means 'A Friend of the Wine' and is a popular nickname for Ghopal Singh. Seems the lord of the Greys has a taste for the grape. The one I don't get, and which seems to trouble the Greys more than '*Madhuprlya*,' is, 'Thi Kim is coming.' It doesn't make sense. Everybody assumes Nyueng Bao are involved because Thi Kim is translatable only from Nyueng Bao. As 'death walk.' Except that here it's written as a proper name."

I said, "If it's used as a name or title it would more properly come through as 'Deathwalker' or 'Death Walking.' Not so? In olden times a Deathwalker was a suspected plague carrier."

"Goblin," Lady said. "It's Deceivers announcing the coming of the Khadidas. A dead man still walking around. By the grace or curse of Kina. And a plague carrier, too, if you count the religious side."

"Maybe." Tobo did not seem convinced. I did not blame him. I had a feeling it was something more sinister myself. Based on nothing whatsoever, because Lady's suggestion *ought* to be true.

I nodded in the general direction of where Sleepy should be. "She said anything about what she's planning?"

"Not unless you count her complaining about the headbutting she's been doing with our friends from the Land of Unknown Shadows. Every brigade commander is whining about needing replacements. But none of them want local recruits—because of the language problem more than because of their lack of equipment and training—but none of them wants to see their own brigade disbanded so its soldiers can fill open slots elsewhere."

But there was no choice and everyone recognized that fact. The best answer was simple enough. And Sleepy found it without consulting me.

Instead of disbanding the hardest hit units she took the one least distressed and distributed its people amongst the others, keeping whole groups together. Being with people you know and trust is critical to a soldier. She made sure the officers got better jobs whenever possible. The displaced brigade commander became her chief of staff, with the assurance that he would be given command of all the native troops we raised, however numerous they might become.

Maximum result with least distress to oversized egos. Only a few men ended up completely disappointed.

Life has turned into a preoccupation with administrative detail.

Is that what happens when you get old? You worry more about people and their interaction than you do about drama and the violence and the wicked deeds those people do?

That is us. The Black Company. Wicked deeds done dirt cheap. But by damn! You had better pony up when payment is due. Otherwise, if we must, we will come back from the grave itself to make sure our accounts are properly balanced.

I said some of that aloud one afternoon. Tobo told me, "You're mad, old man."

"As a hatter." A reflection. "Speaking of which. You know whatever happened to One-Eye's old hat?" I was going to need that disgusting flea farm one day soon. Desperately. One-Eye had told me I would but I had not listened closely enough. I *had* listened and understood that One-Eye's wondrous spear would have to be employed in ways that the little wizard had defined well back into his healthier days. But that hat had been such a commonplace, and so foul, that it had not clung to its place in my mind.

"It may be in my junk wagon," Tobo told me. "If it's not there it'll be with mom's stuff." He winced. Sahra remained missing. "We took everything of his and Nana Gota's when we left Hsien."

"I need to find it. Fairly soon."

Tobo wondered why but did not ask. What a good boy. He did say, "If I was you I'd think about getting my stuff together, ready to move." For this Annalist all the junk and paper and pens and ink and notes and whatnot can build into piles that threaten to swamp. "Sleepy would rather stay here and spend some treasure refitting and recruiting and training and getting stronger but I convinced her that won't work. Things aren't going to slow down anywhere else. Right now we have more sorcery available than ever before in the Company's history."

"I've said so myself." More than once, in jeremiads about counting too much on powers and skills not part of the traditional Company arsenal.

"Yes, you did. But you didn't say anything about it fading away."

"Sure I did."

"You *want* it to go away. And it will. Because these aren't the kind of people who're likely to be content to do what we've got them doing. So we ought to use them up while we can."

"Meaning?"

"We need to go after Taglios while we have the power to hit it hard."

Was he starting to sound just the slightest bit bigheaded? Like he might know better than the Captain what we ought to do? Was it going to be squabble on with Sleepy now that his mother was no longer around?

Might better keep an eye on our baby boy. He was overdue to outgrow all that.

I said, "You could be right."

100

Taglios:
The Palace

Ghopal Singh's report was not reassuring. "The graffiti is everywhere but we just can't catch anybody doing it. It's much worse than it was five years ago. Nowadays, with a lot of people on our side, you'd think we'd be able to come up with a clue. All we get is nonsense about ghosts and demons and things you can see only if you're not looking for them."

Mogaba steepled long fingers under his chin. "The thing is, Ghopal, I've seen both demons and ghosts with my own eyes. When I had just become part of the Black Company one of the Company wizards had a pet demon. It later turned out to be our enemy, but that doesn't matter. It was a demon. And during the siege of Dejagore ghosts often came and went. We all saw them, though hardly anyone ever talked about them.

"Most people blamed Nyueng Bao conjurers."

Aridatha Singh observed, "The reality of demons and ghosts doesn't affect the situation. Whether spooks or clever agitators are writing these messages, the messages are there. And enough people can read that the whole population knows what's being written."

"What would you do about it?" Mogaba asked.

"Keep watching for vandals but ignore it otherwise. If the people believe we're indifferent to the criticism they won't take it seriously either."

"A notion I hoped to put forward myself," Ghopal said. "Because people in the street have no more idea than we do who's putting that stuff up. Which makes them just as nervous as it makes us."

Mogaba grimaced, "Approved, then. With this caveat. Some of those slogans don't fit the traditional mold. 'Thi Kim is coming.' We still don't know what that means."

"The Walking Death is coming," Ghopal said. "You have to think that means the Daughter of Night's companion."

"You think it's Deceiver work, then?"

"That's my guess."

"But Thi Kim is Nyueng Bao. I've never heard of any Nyueng Bao Deceivers."

Ghopal grunted. That had gotten past him.

Aridatha made a joke of it. "We'll know him when he gets here. People will start dying."

"Ha, and one more out of charity, ha," Mogaba replied. "In the meantime, we need to make a decision about our guests. We'll have a lot of trouble keeping them under control. Especially the wizard. Goblin. Who insists on being addressed as the Khadidas. He did help cow the mob when we had the girl pretend she was the Protector. But he has no interest in our cause. He'll devour us the instant he stops seeing us as valuable to *his* cause. Which is bringing on the end of the world."

Neither of the Singhs responded. Each understood that there was more to the Great General's words than he was actually saying. That something particularly delicate would come up had been evident from the moment it had become clear that no one else would participate in the meeting.

"I'm thinking we should get rid of him. Right now. Before he gets too comfortable and sure of himself."

"And the Daughter of Night?" Aridatha asked.

"She's not much threat on her own." Meaning the Daughter of Night could be spared. If that was what Aridatha wanted. "Though my guess is, she's too set in her ways to be redeemed."

Aridatha's coloring was pale enough to betray his embarrassment. "*That* isn't what I had in mind."

Ghopal came to his rescue. Inadvertently, having failed to catch the unspoken. "How do we get close enough to do anything? She'll make us love her so much we'll want to chop off our own toes."

"There must be ways around that."

"I'd be happy to hear suggestions."

"Well, it's obvious she can't do it all the time, whenever she wants, or Aridatha couldn't have caught her."

"Unless she wanted to be caught."

Mogaba feared there might be something to that suggestion. "And that power doesn't work on weapons. Or poisons."

"Sorcery might be a possibility," Ghopal suggested. "You think anyone knows either of their true names?"

Mogaba shook his head. "I don't think even our enemies could do much there. The girl hasn't had any name but the Daughter of Night. The Goblin thing is two creatures in one, with the Kina side ruling. The man who knew the Goblin side's secrets is dead. So we can focus on treachery and poison right away."

"I don't want to harp," Aridatha said, "but I do have to remind everybody that the girl's parents aren't that far away. And right now our prospects don't look that great."

Mogaba suspected that to be a subtle invitation to discuss his plans. He did not accept.

He did not accept because these days he no longer had any grand plan. He believed his days were numbered, as some of the graffiti insisted. ALL THEIR DAYS ARE NUMBERED. But the things that made him Mogaba, positive and negative, compelled him to struggle on.

Beside the Cemetery:
Plans

Lady had been preoccupied since our visit to Shivetya's fortress. More than usual. A couple of times I walked in on her while she was practicing her sorcery. I did not ask. The answer was plain. Her ability to steal Kina's power had returned full strength just when the Khadidas had come forward to take control of Goblin.

Lady had herself locked down, under rigid control. Being someone who has crawled all over her for years, I knew she was battling hope.

She was addicted to the power.

She had given it up, not entirely of her own volition, to prevent that old horror, her first husband, the Dominator, from resurrecting himself. Then she had gone away with me, knowing there was no way she could survive, powerless, in the world she had created. But she remembered being the Lady. And as years fled by she missed that more and more. And, I think, she missed that most when misfortune led her to a close encounter with a mirror.

A personable Dejagoran youngster we knew as Mihlos Sedona made the rounds, summoning the insiders to join Tobo and the Captain. The kid was only about sixteen but had charmed himself into a job as Sleepy's personal gopher. A smile and a winning personality is worth more than genius and sour most any day.

I thought well of Sedona myself. He had remembered to invite me to the party.

The camp was in turmoil. Sleepy had ordered preparations for movement toward Taglios. Those with the necessary expertise were producing parts for artillery pieces or siege engines to be assembled once we reached the fighting zone. Those without expertise were doing the donkey work. I wondered why Sleepy was having the work done when we did not yet know if we would need the equipment. I expect she just wanted everyone kept busy.

Can a bird sneer or smirk? The white crow observed from the arm of an incomplete, mobile stone-thrower. In my eye it seemed to do both. "Long flight for you, eh? You·just get in?"

The bird jumped but did not fly away.

"Be good," I told it. "I know who you are and I know where you live."

Crow laughter, a little strained. Soldiers who remembered when crows were plentiful and dangerous paused to stare.

The crow winged it toward the cemetery.

I grumbled, "I do believe our old pal Shivetya is hedging his bets."

The day was chilly but the sky was clear. The Captain seemed to think a meeting out in the fresh air would be good for everybody. I slipped around behind her headquarters tent.

Tobo spoke first. "The Great General and his henchmen plan to keep fighting, despite our advantages. Both Generals Singh think it would be better to recognize the Prahbrindrah Drah and save Taglios the damage from heavy fighting. But loyalty is a matter of pride and honor for them, too. And the Great General isn't the Protector. They consider him their friend. As long as he's still standing I'm afraid they're going to stick with him."

No surprise there. Not to mention that Ghopal Singh did not have much choice. As director of the Greys he had no friends outside the present establishment. He had committed himself to the Protectorate, not to Taglios.

Aridatha, on the other hand, and despite his participation in the recent fighting, could be considered apolitical and committed to Taglios. The job he had done was the same job that would have been demanded of him by anyone who happened to be in power.

That was the consensus. Maybe we were just making excuses. Everybody who met Aridatha liked the guy and wished him good fortune.

"Enough of that," Sleepy snapped. "The man's a paragon. The sort we all want our daughters to marry. Fine. Tobo, get on with it."

"Last night the generals decided to destroy the Khadidas. He and the Daughter of Night can't read minds but they did sense trouble. They broke out of their cells. Which means one of them has more power than they've been showing. They're hiding somewhere in the abandoned part of the Palace. The Greys and the Palace Guard haven't found them yet. The Khadidas did something that distorted reality around them. Even the hidden folk lost them. They haven't been able to find them again. Not long after their disappearance somebody raided the kitchen. They stole a lot of food. Then somebody broke into the offices of the Inspector General of the Records and stole a shitload of paper and ink."

Murgen blurted, "They're going to reconstruct the Books of the Dead!" This was the first real emotion he had shown since Sahra's disappearance.

"Evidently," Sleepy said. "Not something they can accomplish quickly but something they'll manage eventually. If we don't interfere. And we are going to interfere. Tonight the whole bunch of you are going to fly to Taglios. You're going to pull the same stunt you did in Jaicur. Using all the power you have available. I want you to capture Ghopal Singh and the Great General. Capture the girl and Goblin. Put Aridatha Singh in charge. Then hunker down. I'll start the army moving tomorrow. As soon as we're past the city gate I'll send for the Prahbrindrah Drah."

I tried to exchange glances with everyone, anyone around me. Nobody seemed interested. They all seemed embarrassed. Or something. Like maybe they thought Sleepy had turned simpleminded but it was up to somebody else to point that out to her.

I would bet you saw a lot of that around Mogaba. And a whole lot more around Soulcatcher before her forced retirement.

"It shall be done," Sleepy's proud new chief of staff intoned. Though he spoke Taglian that formula hailed from the Land of Unknown Shadows.

I miss One-Eye. One-Eye—or Goblin in his time—would have given that officious little asshole a mystic hotfoot. On the spot. Or maybe a case of fleas. The size of tumblebugs.

Those were the days. Except that those guys had not always gotten it right. They had screwed up and gotten me a few times, too.

There was a brief debate about whether or not to include the older Voroshk in the raid. The implication being that Tobo might not have what it took to keep an eye on so many people of dubious loyalty. Arkana appeared to have become one of us, but we did not yet *know* that. Arkana was the one who had advised Magadan to do whatever it took. . . . Our hold on the Howler was weaker now, too. The little sorcerer had become almost invisible since he no longer announced himself every few minutes. The senior Voroshk, of course, were trustworthy only until they figured out a way to mess us over. If that long. They did not seem much smarter than Gromovol had been.

I said only, "Don't get overconfident because everything's gone our way so far." Not only Sleepy but most of the others turned studiedly blank faces my way. "There're plenty of chances to stumble still ahead of us."

No doubt I would get an argument but I thought our path had run fairly straight and smooth lately. We might be just hours from our final accounting with the traitor Mogaba and only minutes longer from collecting Booboo and extinguishing the hope of the Deceivers. Events had had a ponderous inevitability almost since our first scares in the Land of Unknown Shadows.

"What?" But the question had been directed at Tobo, not me, by a startled Sleepy.

"We can't leave till after midnight. Lady is going to walk me through a raising of the dead. So we can find out what happened to Mom."

Sleepy wanted to argue but instantly understood that this was a battle she could not win. Tobo would do this thing Tobo's way, with Murgen's blessing. And it was not good to squabble in front of the troops.

"Don't take all night."

The Palace:
Better Housekeeping

The Great General picked up a snail shell, considered it. "More of these things around here all the time. But nobody ever sees a live one."

Ghopal said, "I'd bear down on my household staff if this was my place."

A distant crash echoed through the hallways. Greys and Guards had begun demolishing walls at random, to make it more difficult for the Deceivers to hide. And in areas they felt confident were clear they had masons sealing doorways and walling off entire hallways. Additionally, several self-anointed psychics and ghost hunters had joined the hunt.

Mogaba said, "You're probably right." He gestured to one of several young men who had been trailing them. That fellow snapped a slight bow and disappeared. Before long every domestic in the palace was involved in a massive housekeeping campaign. Mogaba observed, "We can't have this place looking a mess when our enemies get here."

A messenger huffed and puffed into the presence. The search had stumbled onto some corpses. From long ago. Three men wearing nothing but loincloths. They appeared to have gotten lost in the maze of the Palace, but had perished of wounds suffered earlier. The searchers were troubled because the corpses had not suffered much from vermin or normal putrefaction.

"Don't do anything with them," Mogaba said. "Don't even touch them. Just seal them up where they are." He told Ghopal, "Those would be some of the Deceivers who tried to assassinate the Liberator and the Radisha when you were still wearing diapers." He sighed. "No matter what we do to hurry this it's going to take an age."

"They do have to eat."

"Eventually, yes. We'll guard the kitchens at all times." And, he said aloud to no one, because these days it was more secure to communicate by passing notes, any food easily reached during quiet hours would be poisoned.

"Keep at it here, Ghopal. Day and night. Use as many people as we can spare." The Great General expected his enemies to come for him and he was making preparations to welcome them.

Mogaba withdrew to his own quarters. There he invested an hour in one of his hobbies before he moved on to the Protector's quarters to nap. He used her apartment now because no one ever went there. No one but the Great General dared. No one but the Great General could pass through the warding spells the Protector had left in place.

It had become his sanctuary.

Mogaba's scouts and spies had reported that Croaker and all his mob had rejoined the Company, back from wherever they had gone, with even more tools of deviltry.

The crisis could come any time now.

Beside the Cemetery:
Search for a Lost Soul

I had been in the neighborhood of necromantic activities before, and other high-order divining, but never any closer than I got that night. I do not plan to get that close again. If my honey wants somebody handy to save her sweet butt when she gets in trouble, I will tie a long rope to her ankle and attach the other end to a horse. If something goes sour I will swat the horse's butt.

This séance did not go well. And before it was over I got a much uglier vision of that place of bones that had claimed so many of the dreams of Murgen and my beloved.

The smell was bad but the cold was worse. I have never felt such cold. I roasted myself beside a bonfire for hours after the summoning was over but mortal flames did little to defeat that bitter chill. It was so bad we did not undertake the Captain's raid that night or even the next and when we did we went only because Her Highness began wondering publicly if us slackers were waiting for summer weather.

Murgen, Sleepy and I were present at the summoning. No one else was invited, not even Shukrat or Suvrin or any of Sahra's friends. And it started going bad right away. Right after starting Lady raised a hand to massage her right temple. Soon afterward I began to catch fleeting, random impressions of things that were not there. The cold came first, then the smell. Before I saw anything there were several moments when my balance became very iffy.

Lady grew more and more excited as things continued to refuse to go the way she wanted. She started over twice. And when she finally did storm ahead she did not get where she wanted to go. Eventually she gave up. But not before the rest of us had gotten a good strong whiff of Kina's charnel dreams.

"I'm sorry," Lady told Tobo. "Kina keeps trying to get at me through our connection. The more power I siphon from her the more easily she can touch me."

Not good. We could have Lady turn kickass powerful—and be in thrall to the Goddess when she did.

She seemed to read my mind. She gave me a dirty look. "The bitch isn't going to get a hold on *me*."

I considered reminding her of whom we were speaking. The Mother of Deceit. Kina did not need control where she could manipulate. And she could manipulate whole populations. In her sleep. Instead, I asked, "Did we find out anything about Sahra?"

Lady's temper was not improving. "Certainly not what we would've if that old devil-sow hadn't decided to wreck our game." Her mind had been affected somehow. She seemed almost drunk. "We couldn't raise Sahra. Couldn't even touch her. Which leaves the matter's resolution ambiguous." Her speech continued slurred, she was aware of it, yet she persisted in trying to use difficult words. "I think she's dead. If she was alive Tobo and the hidden folk would've found her. Nothing hides from the Black Hounds for long."

"Soldiers live," I whispered. "It ain't right, something like that happening." But Fortune does not care. Unless Fortune gets a laugh out of human pain. "There has to be more meaning. . . ."

"You going mystical on us at this late date, Croaker?" Sleepy snapped. "You're the one who always says nothing has any meaning we don't put into it ourselves."

"Sure as shit sounds like me, don't it? Let's go work out our frustrations by kicking Mogaba's antique ass."

Sleepy gave us the once-over, unwilling to send us out while we were in so bleak a mood. We might be dangerous to ourselves.

She was no happier with us later. We did not improve, any of us. Finally, she swallowed her reservations and told us to go.

H owler had completed a large carpet capable of moving twenty passengers. Tonight it carried sixteen of those, plus freight. Amongst the sixteen were both elder Voroshk, a number of commando-trained soldiers from Hsien and Murgen. Murgen had been zombielike since Lady's failed ritual. He had overheard her saying she thought Sahra was dead.

I had urged him to stay behind but he insisted on joining us.

I should have stood fast. He could not help but be a liability.

Tobo was less distracted. He was too involved with Shukrat to be obsessed about his mother being missing. Still, he would bear watching.

Lady and I dressed up in full costume, with Voroshk apparel over the black Widowmaker and Lifetaker armor. My two ravens tagged along. Arkana flew with us, being tested. Which she understood fully.

Down below, dark things were on the move. They had been since nightfall.

Taglios never sleeps. Tonight those with reasons to be out after dark would have cause to worry about what might be lurking in the shadows. Hey, Mogaba. Look out. Darkness always comes.

We were still climbing away from camp when I eased over next to Lady. We flew knee to knee, our Voroshk apparel whipping in the breeze for twenty yards behind us. First we discussed which of our companions needed watching the closest, then we revisited the failed attempt to contact Sahra's spirit. For the twentieth time. Lady insisted, "I do believe she's out there, just as desperate to make contact with us as we were to make contact with her. But the ugly Goddess wants to keep us apart."

"Is Kina awake?"

"More than she has been for a long, long time. At least since Goblin went down there. Maybe since the days when she sensed her doom afoot and commenced her war on us ere ever we entered this country."

Ere ever? Wow. "I have a question on another subject. It's been bothering me for a long time but I've never quite been able to put the words together right."

"Artist."

"Power junkie."

"What's your question, Old Style?"

"What happened to Soulcatcher's shadows?"

Lady looked at me blankly.

"Come on. The old brain can't have slowed down that much. She was an accomplished Shadowmaster. She didn't have a lot of shadows left because Tobo's pets kept picking them off. She stopped trying to use them against us. But she still had some hidden away somewhere. Saved for a rainy day."

Lady growled, "It couldn't have gotten any stormier than it did." But she was not arguing. She had her mind wrapped around the question. "My bet is that the Unknown Shadows finished them all off. There aren't any killer shadows left. If there were we'd still be hearing reports of unexplained deaths."

"Maybe." Probably. If they were out there anywhere the excitement the shadows would cause would be much greater than the numbers justified. The peoples of the Taglian territories had a long history of suffering from killer shadows.

Even so, I moved up until I was flying hip to hip with Tobo, an eventuality Shukrat found distasteful. She drifted away. Rather haughtily adolescent, I thought.

"I don't plan to take over your life." I told the boy about my concerns.

He seemed to agree that they were valid. "I'll find out if there's any reason to worry."

I fell back until I rejoined Lady.

She asked, "What did he say?"

"He'll check it out."

"You don't sound real happy about that."

"He said it the way you do when you agree with somebody just so you don't have to spend time with them fussing over something that doesn't bother you."

104

Taglios:
View from the Protector's Window

Mogaba's eyelids kept getting heavier. Twice he drifted off completely, to start awake violently, disturbed once by some clamor in the city, once by shouting down below that suggested the guards might have glimpsed the Khadidas. It was the wee hours of the morning, when even the heartbeat of the world had trouble thumping on.

They were not going to come tonight. They had not come last night, nor the night before. Maybe they were waiting for a larger moon.

Something dark blurred the glass in the window whence the Great General watched his own quarters and the best part of the Palace's northern face. Including all the significant entrances. He did not even breathe.

The Unknown Shadows could not find a way past the glass and the Protector's permanent wards. Mogaba resumed breathing. Slowly, invisible in the deep darkness of the room, he rose and glided nearer the glass, so that he would have a broader view.

They had come. Not when he had expected but exactly where. The same place their messengers had come every time. That same turret top.

He felt no particular elation. What he felt, in fact, was sorrow. All their lives, his and theirs, had come to no more than this. For a moment there was even the temptation to shout a warning. To cry out that that prideful fool who had made such a stupid choice in Dejagore so long ago had not meant any of them to come to this. But, no. It was too late. Fortune's die was cast. The cruel game had to be played to its end, no matter what anyone wanted.

105

The Palace: The Great General's Place

Lady led the way, grim as ever when she donned the Lifetaker persona. I was not pleased. Someone with more power ought to have been first down the stair. But Tobo was sure he needed to go last. Otherwise the Howler and the Voroshk might not feel motivated enough to participate. And Howler would not go first because he had to manage his carpet until everybody was off.

The stair was crowded. No one wanted to be there in that darkness, though only Lady, Murgen and I were old enough to remember when darkness was our determined foe. I tried to stay close to Lady, my foolish mind somehow afflicted with the notion that I had to protect her.

There went a joke of cosmic proportion.

We made it down the stairwell without mishap. And, despite a horrendous racket, without causing any alarm. Lady murmured, "Mogaba must be sleeping the sleep of the innocent. All that noise should've raised the dead."

"Uhn?"

"His quarters are straight ahead."

I knew that. We had rehearsed this raid before we left. In a half-ass sort of way. Which means not thoroughly enough to satisfy me.

"He's a heavy sleeper," I said. That was one of the few knocks against him before his defection. That and an intensity even his brother Nar had found oppressive. But I was speaking to the night. She was pulling ahead.

Someone generated a light, a feeble glowball that drifted above our heads. It had an alien feel so I assume one of the Voroshk was responsible. As the light grew so did a sense of relaxation, of confidence.

Maybe one of those cranky old men was not as dim as he let on.

"The light is my familiar," someone murmured in one of the dialects of Hsien. The phrase possessed the rhythm of ritual. Later I would learn that it was part of an incantation meant to repel the Unknown Shadows, those being disliked by everyone but Tobo.

The hidden realm was there, too, all around us. And so troubled that even I could feel it.

Tobo whispered, "There's something strange here. I had hundreds of the hidden folk put into the Palace. But none of them are reporting. As far as I can tell they aren't here anymore." He whispered to the creepy darkness. Things unseen moved around us, jostling us from directions we were not looking. Some of the stress oppressing me went away.

Lady beckoned soldiers forward. It was time to break into Mogaba's quarters. Though that implies more force than was needed. His door was not locked. Nor had it ever been before, according to Lady.

She and Shukrat took point. They knew their ways around. Unless clever Mogaba had rearranged his furniture.

Soldiers followed. The Voroshk and Howler crept inside. Murgen followed them. Lady and Shukrat began to argue sharply, in whispers, about who should find a lamp. Somebody stumbled into somebody else. Somebody fell down. Another somebody crashed into something. Then somebody else stated categorically, "Oh, shit!"

Arkana was just sliding into the room, a step ahead of me, when Tobo echoed those sentiments from behind me. He started to push. "Out of the way, damnit!"

A huge crash of breaking pottery. I had not known that Mogaba was a collector, though there were some marvellous craftsmen in this part of the world. . . .

A man screamed.

Before his lungs were empty other screams joined his. And fireballs leapt from small projectors. And I knew why so many men were screaming and why they were so panicky they were blowing holes through one another.

Shadows.

The old evil. Killer shadows.

Deadly shadows off the glittering plain. Shadows, the exploitation of which had given the Shadowmasters their name. Shadows of the sort Soulcatcher had used to prop up her Protectorate until the coming of Tobo's allies from the Land of Unknown Shadows.

I had the answer to the question I had addressed to Lady and Tobo.

People panicked completely. Fireballs flew everywhere, caused far more carnage than mere starving mad shadows. One of those ripped through my Voroshk cloak. The cloak seemed to whine but pulled itself together around me. A shadow hit me. My apparel repelled it, a fact I did not fail to note despite the rising chaos. It also shed the next fireball that found me.

I saw Lady hit several times, rapidly. I saw one of the Voroshk succumb to shadows.

I tried to bellow into the madness, to calm them down, but the panic had them all. Even Howler and Lady caught it.

But Shukrat did keep her wits about her. She crouched in a corner and let her cloak form a barrier impervious to fireballs and shadows alike.

Men fought to get out the door. Howler loosed a spell that flashed so brightly it blinded everyone not in Voroshk protective clothing, including the little sorcerer himself. His effort did not avail. A moment later he screamed with more enthusiasm than ever he had before his cure.

"Get out of my way!" Tobo bellowed. He hurled me aside. His father was inside that room.

Before I regained my feet the tower was creaking under the psychic mass of Tobo's unseen friends. Their battle with the invisible killers was brief but belated. And, probably, needless, because the fireballs ate shadows alive. Unknown Shadows as well as the traditional lurkers in darkness.

I did not know if I wanted to get off the floor. It was very still in that other room now, except for Arkana crying. But I had to get up. We had to get moving. The rest of the palace was not silent anymore. An alarm had been sounded. People with sharp instruments would be coming to get us.

I t was impossible to tell who was dead, who was dying, and who was only mildly injured. For a while it was too dark.

I got Tobo to provide another light. Then I started getting the fallen moved back to the tower top. Arkana and Shukrat and Tobo's hidden allies kept the Palace Guard at bay. I kept my emotions turned off while I lugged bodies. At the moment I could not afford to indulge.

"How are we going to get these posts and the carpet out of here?" I demanded. Lady, both of the elder Voroshk, Howler, Murgen were all out of action. So were most of the commandos.

"Shukrat and I can handle the carpet. You and Arkana will have to tow the posts."

"You hear that, new daughter?" Minutes earlier I had been about to slap the girl around to crack her shock. But she had solid stuff inside her. She was dragging the dead and injured now, calmer than most of the others.

"I know. I'll need something to use for tethers."

"Find it fast. I'll lug bodies."

A crossbow bolt buzzed past without doing any harm. An instant later the section of wall whence it had come was shattered rock and boiling flame.

Tobo was not in a kindly mood.

I told Arkana, "You get those posts out of here right now. All but mine." She had gotten some rope from aboard the carpet.

Good girl, Arkana. She got busy. Like Shukrat, she focused on the task at hand.

Funny, I thought, how the Company seemed to attract good women.

The Palace Guards and a surprising number of Greys responded to the alarm.

And they refused to be intimidated by Tobo's violence and by Tobo's half-seen friends. Brave men, they. There are always brave and honorable men amongst one's enemies. Missiles filled the air. A few found targets.

I began to wonder if this would not be a good time to reconsider my lifelong determination never to leave Company people behind.

But I was incapable of leaving without my wife. And I needed the old Voroshk. Even if they were dead.

The Palace:
View from a High Place

Mogaba felt no elation as he watched the disaster unfold. In fact, he became more troubled. He could see that there would be survivors. Those people were still strong enough to hold off the Guards and Greys while they evacuated their casualites. That meant that, unless he enjoyed a gargantuan turn of luck and they were all killed by missiles before they could get away, he still faced a final battle.

He had no tricks left in his bag.

The shadows had not been completely effective. Which proved what he had suspected for some time. The enemy had a similar force at his disposal. And that force had responded in time to save some of the raiders.

He watched crossbow bolts, arrows and even javelins bounce off the creatures in the great seething black cloaks. Only one of those people got hurt.

A fireball's flare, as the big carpet backed away from the parapet, gave just enough light for Mogaba to distinguish the Lifetaker armor.

"Lady," he murmured. Awed.

That same flash must have reflected off his eyeballs or teeth, betraying him somehow. Because when he glanced at the post riders he found the one in the Widowmaker armor hurling straight at him, black cape expanding to shut out the sky.

107

Taglios:
Soldiers Live

I saw Mogaba behind the window. Rage devoured me. I drove straight at him, accelerating. And even as I did some tiny remnant of rationality wondered if what
I had glimpsed was real, not my mind seeing what it wanted because I needed
somebody else to hurt as much as I had begun to do.

If the Mogaba I saw was my own creation it vanished before I smashed into the
window glazing.

The glass did not break. It did not yield at all. My post stopped dead. I did not.
The post rebounded. I smacked into the glass. Then I bounced back. And fell. I had
time for one very enthusiastic howl before I reached the end of my tether, then I was
flailing around ten feet below my post.

The post kept driving forward, kept rebounding. I tried to climb back up but
could get nowhere with only one reliable hand. The motion of the post got me
swinging like the weight on a pendulum. One end of each swing brought me into intimate contact with the Palace wall.

The Voroshk cloak protected me well, but unconsciousness eventually came.

I was still dangling when I recovered. The ground was only a few yards below and
moving slowly. I seemed to be flying along above the Rock Road, barely clearing
the heads of travelers. I tried twisting so I could look up but could not manage. The
tether was attached to me in the back, just above my waist. I did not have strength
enough to twist around.

I did have a bit of pain when I struggled.

I lost consciousness again.

I was back in mankind's natural state, on the ground, when I wakened again. A
pointy hunk of chert was trying to gouge a hole through my back. Somebody said
something in one of the dialects of Hsien, then repeated himself in bad Taglian.
Arkana materialized overhead, face somber. "You going to live, Pop?"

"All the aches and pain I've got, it's a sure thing. What happened?"

"You did something stupid."

"What else is new?" a second voice demanded. Sleepy's face materialized opposite Arkana. "How soon you going to get off your back, part-time? I need some help. This disaster show you guys engineered is about to put us out of business."

"Be right with you, Boss. Soon as I get my leg bones unbraided and my feet hooked back onto my ankles."

The effort of trying to get up, because I wanted to find my wife, pushed me over into the darkness again.

Rain in my face wakened me the next time. My physical pains had turned to dull aches. They had gotten something into me. Cataloging, I decided I had a lot of bruises but nothing was broken or permanently damaged.

Just when I started to make an effort to get up I floated upward. After a momentary panic I realized that I was on a litter, being moved in out of the rain. Being lifted onto the litter was what had interrupted my sleep, not those first few misty raindrops.

I got a better grip this time. I remained rational when Sleepy turned up. "How's my wife?" I asked, with only a small squeak in my voice.

"She's still alive. But her situation isn't good. Though it's better than it would've been if she hadn't been wearing the Voroshk outfit. I'd guess she might recover. If we can get Tobo to stay focused long enough to help."

I heard the unspecified offer of a job assignment in there somewhere. "What's the kid's problem?"

"His father got killed. Where were you?"

I grunted. "I was afraid of that." Maybe I had tried to shut it out. It was going to hurt.

Sleepy seemed to think we did not have time for pain.

I had begun to trust her instincts.

"You had it right, Croaker. Soldiers live. Only three people got out of that scrape unhurt. Tobo, Arkana and a very lucky soldier named Tam Do Linh. Howler, the First Father, Nashun the Researcher, Murgen and all the other soldiers, didn't. The rest of you are hurt. Tobo feels guilty. He thinks he should've done more. He thinks he should've realized it was a trap."

"I understand. What about Shukrat?"

"Bruises and abrasions and emotional distress. The Voroshk clothing took good care of her. It knew her so well it adapted faster than Lady's could. As I understand it."

"Murgen could've worn Voroshk protection." But he had refused. Damn him. There had not been much fight in him since Sahra's disappearance.

"I want you to straighten Tobo out. We need him back. We need the Unknown

Shadows. If I was in Mogaba's boots I'd have another attack force headed our way already."

"I don't think so."

"The man doesn't wait around, Croaker. His gospel is, seize the initiative."

I could only make an ass of myself arguing with a woman who had fought the Great General more years than I had known him. Who had lived in Taglios for as many years as I had, much more recently. Evidently I was just another cranky old man raising a fuss for the attention. Except when she needed something. "Then we'd better arrange for it to get really dangerous for him personally if anything happens to any of us."

I felt stupid before I finished saying that. For Mogaba there was little chance life would ever be more dangerous than it was already.

I had forgotten an early lesson. Try to reason like the enemy. Study him until you can think just like him. Until you can *become* him.

Sleepy told me, "You need to find yourself an apprentice, too. If you're going to keep getting involved in lethal stuff." *At your age* was implied—until the Captain actually said, "You're too long in the tooth to be out there right where it's happening. It's time you eased up and started passing your secrets along."

Sleepy went away, leaving me wondering. Who was I supposed to tap? I was inclined to pick her buttboy, Mihlos Sedona, except that the kid had one huge shortcoming. He was totally illiterate. And I did not have any inclination to put in all the hours needed to alter that condition.

Then the man I maybe should have been thinking of turned up on his own, voluntarily.

"Suvrin? What the hell's gotten into you? You're going to leave us most any day now."

"So perhaps I've had an epiphany. Maybe I need to learn the Annals because I've decided to face my destiny."

"Is that the fragrance of bullshit wafting on the breeze?" Being an old cynic I thought it was more likely that he thought this would somehow get him laid. But I did not suggest anything. I just accepted him, then groaned upon discovering that Sleepy's wonderfully educated young man neither wrote nor read a single word of Taglian, which has been the language of these Annals for the last twenty-five years.

Lady's book was the last written in another language. And Murgen had translated and updated that, along with a couple of my own that had not really needed any polish.

"Think you can learn to read and write Taglian?" I asked. "You might never *need* to do either. . . ."

"Unless I want to read the Annals. The holy scriptures of the Black Company."

"Yeah. If I go, you'll be on your own unless Sleepy makes time or Lady recovers."

I had had time enough now to put together an act of indifference. But I was not convincing anybody.

Suvrin stared, waiting for the punchline.

There was none, really, except that he ought to make an effort to see that I stayed healthy long enough for him to develop the needed skills.

Two days after Suvrin became my understudy Sleepy stage-managed a ceremony that formalized his appointment as Lieutenant of the Black Company and her heir-apparent.

We were outside that big, nameless hilltop stronghold which broods over the Rock Road approach to Taglios. A large plain had been leveled and prepared as a place where troops could camp or could practice the close-order skills necessary for success in battle. Or as a place where forces defending the city could engage an advancing enemy.

No one bothered us there, other than small Vehdna cavalry bands made up of youths who wanted to show off their courage. But I advised both Sleepy and Suvrin against leaving the stronghold unvanquished behind us.

Sleepy was no more interested in advice than ever before but these days she did pretend to listen. Her own approach to conquest had been a disaster mitigated only by the fact that a few of us had survived.

108

Taglios:
Someone at the Door

Upon reflection, after we beat back a relief sortie by troops from Taglios, the commander of the fortress offered to surrender on terms. He wanted paroles for himself and damned near everyone who ever bore arms in the three nearest counties. Which was not all that unreasonable, I thought, considering we were going

to turn all this over to the Prahbrindrah Drah as soon as the deal closed and the
Prince could get his ass up here from Ghoja.

Even after all her years in the real world Sleepy retained some Vehdna notions
about right and wrong that had nothing to do with the practicalities of the moment.

"Even if this Lal Mindrat is the worst human monster since the Shadowmasters
themselves, you have to consider what your moral rigidity can cost the rest of us," I
told Sleepy. Evidently Lal Mindrat had betrayed some of our allies during the Kiaulune wars. I had not heard of him before Sleepy started getting uppity so it could
not have been a major betrayal.

A good many friends of the Company had been turned by the Protector in
those days. Soulcatcher had had the power and wealth.

"Be flexible," I advised. "But treacherous when *absolutely* necessary."

She understood. With some half-ass help from Tobo and his friends, and the
appropriate promises of parole and safe passage, Sleepy got our enemies to evacuate the stronghold with no more violence than occurred when Lal Mindrat came
out with his lifeguard.

Thus the Captain finished her business with a minor traitor from her own era.
For the time being.

M ogaba made our approach hell, at least for those of us who pulled the recon,
picket and vanguard duties. Horsemen never stopped harassing our forward
elements. The Voroshk girls and I went out whenever the enemy's behavior became
overly obnoxious.

Eventually we reached the great South Gate of Taglios, something that had not
existed in my time. These days a truly substantial wall stretched into the distance at
either hand. The soldiers on the ramparts seemed much too small. The wall reared
up like a vast cliff of limestone.

"Wow!" I told Sleepy. "There's been some changes made." The entrance to the
city was a fortress in itself, outside the wall but attached to it. I could not tell from
the ground for sure but it looked like an equally formidable structure guarded the
pass-through from within.

Sleepy grunted. "Been a few since I was here. Methinks the Great General must
have inveigled some appropriations out of the Protector somehow. They've added
several feet to the height of the wall. And that barbican complex . . ." She shrugged.

As I remembered city politics, public works were particularly vulnerable to graft
and corrupt practices. "Somebody in the treasury offices must have been blowing in
the Protector's ear."

Sleepy grunted again, uninterested in my opinion. She was watching Suvrin
spread the troops out facing the city, offering battle. No response was expected. No
response was what he got.

I said, "They don't have to be careful of anybody's property, at least." More than the immensity of the wall itself, I was awed by the existence of a thousand-foot-wide band of empty ground lapping the wall's foot. What had it taken to get people moved off that ground? How did the state keep them off?

"In a few months there'll be grainfields and vegetable patches as far as you can see. That grid of pathways marks the boundaries of the patches. They started that back right after Sahra and I first came to the city."

"Tobo's going to be a busy boy."

Sleepy examined our forces, left and right. They did not appear threatening against the backdrop of the wall. Nor did anyone atop that wall appear concerned.

"He will. I expect him and the girls to hit hard, with everything they have, right from the start, so people in there will be stunned by the fury of it. Is he going to be able to do it?"

"I can't guarantee you his heart'll be in it."

"What about you? Is your heart going to be in it?"

I heaved a huge sigh.

Sleepy asked, "How is she doing?"

Another major sigh. "Honestly? I'm worried. She just lays there, midway between life and death. She gets no better; she gets no worse. I'm starting to wonder how much the Kina connection has to do with all that."

It took a major effort to let that out. Because of what the Captain might consider if she grasped all the implications. And she began to see some right away.

I said, "If I can pull Tobo through his grief he may be able to find out if Kina's gained any control." I dreaded the possibility that the Dark Mother was setting my wife up as an alternate route of escape from her ancient prison. I could imagine a scenario wherein I struck the sleeping Goddess and freed Shivetya only to see the darkness return through the woman I love.

Not that it would take the Mother of Night to accomplish that. She was entirely willing to welcome in her own breed of darkness.

Aren't we all.

The Captain said, "I haven't heard a direct answer. Can I count on you to actually pay attention when the arrows start to fly?"

An old, old formula came to mind, from back when I was very young indeed. "I am a soldier." I said it first in the language I had spoken then, then repeated myself in Sleepy's own Dejagoran dialect. "I've been distracted before. I'm still alive."

"Yeah, soldiers live. You only get one mistake, Croaker."

"Go teach your granny to suck eggs." Which was a waste of colorful language. The expression had no meaning amongst these peoples.

"What's that?" Sleepy asked, pointing at something rising above the city.

"Looks like a big-ass kite."

109

Taglios:
No Excuses Accepted

Damn it! No matter how much I wanted it Mogaba refused to be stupid. Facing
potential problems with an infestation of airborne wizards? Take advantage
of the season's almost constant winds. Put up about ten thousand giant box kites with
poisoned sharp things hanging on tails made of braided fibers almost too tough
to cut.

There would be no zooming about with youthful exuberance over Taglios. Especially not after dark. Those kites would not be able to hurt us in our Voroshk clothing but they could entangle us and knock us off our posts. Whereupon whoever lost
their seat would need someone else to come along and bring them out. Unless . . .

Shukrat once fixed me up with a post that would travel on its own when its
master could not manage it.

I issued an order.

Just hours later Shukrat's post brought the girl herself back virtually mummified in cord and deadly sharps that took hours to overcome. But she had cleaned
away scores of kites.

I made Tobo untangle her. I was having a real problem getting him engaged
with life. But Shukrat was supposed to be important to him.

She certainly thought so. Once he finished freeing her, too slowly to suit her, she
popped him in the middle of the forehead with the heel of her right hand. "How
about you at least pretend to be interested, Tobe?" And, moments later, "You're
making me wonder just how bright I am."

Tobo was a real young man. He started to protest. I tried to warn him by shaking my head. No way was he going to break even here. Shukrat cut him off, unwilling to grant him the validity of any excuse. After that I tried not to hear what they
were saying.

I mused on Shukrat's swift, nearly effortless grasp of Taglian. She had almost no
accent at all, now. And she appeared equally adaptable regarding strange customs.

Arkana was having more difficulty but she was coming along marvelously, too.

Having allowed the girlfriend time to make her point, I approached Tobo. "Tobo, we need to know about what's going on behind those walls."

He did not look like he cared much.

Shukrat punched him.

I told him, "You have to let go."

He gave me one ugly look.

"You have to let go of the guilt. It wasn't your fault."

I doubted that telling him would do any good. These things never are rational. Your mind goes on chasing the irrational even when it *knows* the truth. If Tobo wanted to feel guilty about his father and mother he would find ways to do that in the face of every argument, of any bit of evidence, and of all the common sense in the universe. I know. I have suffered through that bleak season a few times myself.

I had a little of it going right then, featuring my wife.

Shukrat said, "The Great General did it, Tobe. The Taglian supreme commander. And he's inside those same walls."

There you go, girl. Appeal to the darkness within, to the stores of rage and hatred. We really needed to get those emotions cooking inside the most powerful sorcerer left in this part of the world.

Taglios:
Misfortunes

The Unknown Shadows told Tobo that Mogaba and his cronies were hunkered down, waiting us out. They thought we might begin to fade away before long, despite our wealth.

They could be right. Though Sleepy had plenty of treasure left, many of the soldiers from Hsien had signed on for only one year in the field. I did not doubt that many would stay as long as their pay was on time but I did not doubt, either, that homesickness would begin to bleed us, too.

We cleared away kites faster than Mogaba could put new ones up. We made a few high altitude raids each night. We dropped firepots on the properties of known allies of the Protector, the Great General, and the Greys. But fire is a cruel and unruly ally. Some that we started spread way beyond their targets. Even more smoke than usual clung to the city.

A second midnight approach to the occupied portion of the palace provided us with some distinctly unwelcome news. We learned that Mogaba's efforts to seize our encampment beside the Shadowlander cemetery, while tactically disastrous for his loyalists, had not been entirely unprofitable.

Sleepy's chief of staff decided he needed a firsthand look at the Palace. For planning purposes. He was a thorough man. At Sleepy's urging he and other selected folk had been getting training using the Voroshk flying posts. We had seven available with only five regularly assigned. And Lady was not using hers these days. Sleepy hated seeing resources going to waste. Sleepy being Sleepy.

The chief of staff had Mihlos Sedona join us. Mihlos was the most competent of the part-time flyers though his only excuse for getting the opportunity was that the Captain liked him. And wanted his observations. No way was she going aloft herself.

I went along to make sure those two had somebody to bail them out if they got in trouble. I made them wear Voroshk apparel, too. If we were seen we could expect missile fire. Mogaba's people never gave up trying.

You just need one lucky break.

Mihlos Sedona had not yet realized that he was not immortal. He ventured too close to the enemy. Then we all learned how Mogaba had profited from disaster.

A fireball ripped through the darkness. The boy escaped the worst of it by hurling himself to one side. The fireball struck him a glancing blow, which, however, was enough to knock him off his post.

General Chu ignored my shout and went after Sedona. And actually managed to get close enough to get a hold on his post. As fireballs streaked in from half a dozen sources.

One struck Chu's post dead solid.

The explosion of that post was violent enough to set off the other. And the two in concert were violent enough to smash in an acre of Palace like an invisible giant's foot stomping on eggshells.

More Palace continued to cave in around the initial collapse.

A wicked wind flung me around like a rogue dandelion seed. Once again I lost my grip and fell off my steed. While dangling I caught rolling glimpses of flames beginning to peek through cracks in the rubble, of panic beginning to prowl amongst the soldiers atop the palace.

Taglios:
Sleepy Flew

We're going to start strapping you down, Pop," Arkana told me as she towed me into camp. She had been on a routine patrol kite-clearing when the explosion happened. In rushing to see the results she almost got knocked out of the sky by a daredevil swinging from a flying fence post.

"Just get me down. Fast. Preferably right in front of the Captain's tent." Sleepy had to know. Now. And somebody needed to go watch the Palace. If the whole damned thing caved in. . . . If Mogaba and his henchmen died in the disaster. . . . If the Khadidas and the Daughter of Night escaped in the resulting chaos. . . .

Some hearty fires were burning over there now. A strong glow silhouetted the city wall now.

I kept having to explain as more notables reached the Captain's tent. And I kept urging Sleepy to make whatever move she was considering making right away. Never again would the other side be as confused and disordered as they must be now. She agreed but pointed out that our bunch were not terribly well organized right now, either.

The Captain dealt with the problem of interruptions in the most amazing fashion I could imagine. After delegating Suvrin to begin preparing an attack, she told me, "Take me up there. Show me what's happened."

"You?"

"Me. I'll keep my eyes closed until there's something to see. Before we leave I'll throw an old blanket over my seat so I won't get your post all wet."

I shook my head, disconsolate. "I wish Swan was still around. A straight line like that shouldn't go to waste. Let's do it."

"Wait. Suvrin." She issued more instructions. So he would have something to do in his spare time.

Her absence would slow nothing down.

"Tie yourself on good," I told Sleepy. "I might decide to do a few loops while we're up there."

She growled like a whole pack of angry rats. Made it clear that if she fell off I might as well just keep on going.

"All right. But coming home hanging underneath like a carp on a stringer is a lot better than the alternative."

"If you don't mind a little embarrassment."

"I don't mind at all if I'm alive to get red in the face." Something you learn as you get older. Or, at least, you should.

We were passing over the gateway complex when I realized that I had gone right back up without having paused to check on my wife.

Was I not a little old to feel guilty about everything? She would not be going anywhere any time soon.

It was not possible to get dangerously close to the Palace. The fires were huge now. The heat was intense, even through the Voroshk clothing. And the higher you flew the more turbulent the air became. There were no kites anywhere nearby anymore.

I figured Mogaba would give up on the kites soon. They were not doing us any harm.

Sleepy clung to the post with white knuckles. I wondered if we would need a chisel to break her grip once we got back on the ground. But she did manage to keep her voice sounding normal. "What in the world is burning? That place isn't anything but a big old stone pile."

The flames were not limited to the Palace now. Several fires were burning nearby. The entire area was crawling with people, most being gawkers who just got in the way of the soldiers, officials and volunteers actually trying to accomplish something.

"Somebody's still thinking," I told Sleepy. "They've put troops around the place." I dropped lower and moved close enough to spot Aridatha Singh out working two thin lines of soldiers, one facing outward, holding the mobs back, the other, stronger, facing inward. The latter were more heavily armed. Anyone leaving the palace was going to get a good hard look. "I hope they got those guys in place before the Khadidas and the girl got away."

"Back to the gate. If we're ever going to invade this city, now is the time."

"You found enough boats yet?"

She tensed up. She did not answer for a moment. "You figured it out."

"Logic suggests that it makes no sense to storm those walls with no more men than we have. Particularly when Taglios has almost no defenses on the river side." A point which would have occurred to the Great General, too.

"There is no easy way in," Sleepy told me. "The defenses on the river side just aren't as obvious." She proceeded to explain about log booms and chains that controlled traffic, forcing it into narrow channels well-ranged by massed artillery ashore. A barge loaded with attackers could be pounded into driftwood and fish food in minutes.

I said, "I see where this is going."

"Do you really? Will I attack by day or by night?"

"It's dark now but by the time you can get anybody to the point of attack the sun will be up."

"Take me back. I have to get things moving faster."

Taglios:
Under Siege

Ghopal Singh looked terrible. He had been close enough to the fire to have had his beard singed. He had blisters on both face and hands. His turban was gone. The rest of him was rags and smoke smell.

"You'll never pass inspection," Mogaba told him.

Singh's sense of humor was moribund. "We've got it controlled inside. It'll burn itself out. Out there in the city. . . . Pray for unseasonable rain."

"Good luck doesn't always work out, does it?"

Grudgingly, Singh said, "No way we could know what would happen if a fireball hit one of those flying things."

"No. Of course not. Here comes Aridatha. Like a crow. There'll be more bad news." Mogaba glanced eastward. Not even close to dawn yet. Why was this night stretching out so long? "You've got a spot of ash on your right trouser leg, Aridatha."

The commander of the City Battalions actually paused to deal with the matter before he realized that the Great General was teasing him. More or less. Aridatha said, "They're trying to take advantage of the confusion. I'm getting reports about ghosts and terrors at work around the South Gate and the river forts."

"They're really coming?" Ghopal Singh could not believe the enemy would assault Taglios with so few soldiers. He had expected them to just sit tight in hopes they could forge alliances with disaffected elements inside the wall. "Where?"

"The river," Mogaba predicted. "They've had time to scout. That's where we're the weakest."

"Maybe they just want us to think . . ."

"They can't get a strong force into place for a while yet. When they attack from the air we'll know they're on their way and where they think they can get through."

Minutes later word came that enemy commandos were atop the wall half a mile west of the South Gate, ferried there by flying carpet. They were being reinforced rapidly. Neither the City Battalions nor the Greys had much strength in that area. The bulk of the Second Territorial was on the waterfront. The garrison of the barbican was responding to the threat as best it could.

Mogaba looked to the east. Once the light came the enemy would lose the advantage of his unseen allies. Then the city's defenders could exploit their big advantage in numbers.

Ten minutes later news came that swimmers armed with small fireball projectors had cut the chains and broken the booms at the upstream end of the city. Firebombs were falling amongst the artillery engines.

"You were right," Ghopal said. "It'll be the river."

"Possibly. Where are their wizards?" Mogaba wanted to know. He understood that the post riders need not be sorcerers. "If we don't see wizards we have to remain skeptical about their commitment to any particular attack. All I see now are diversions."

"Shall we go out there?" Aridatha asked.

"Out where? Would you care to bet that other attacks won't break out sometime soon? This is the best place for us to be. We're central." It had occurred to him that he was being watched. That the Captain's plans might hinge on his own behavior. Whatever he did might direct enemy efforts where he was not. It was what he would have done, given their resources. "We'll stay central. Let's get a tighter cordon around the parts of the Palace where the girl might be. That'll let us free up some more of these men."

Hundreds had been freed up already, because the gawkers had begun to melt away when fires elsewhere proved too fierce to contain. As soon as there was a specific defense to mount Mogaba would send reinforcements.

News came of fierce aerial attacks on the South Gate complex itself. Massive volleys of fireballs were riddling the stonework with thousands of holes. The sheer profligate expenditure of fireballs awed everyone.

"That's the point, you know," Mogaba said. "This Captain is more willing to fight than her predecessors were but when she does she rachets the level of violence as high as she can. She wants to stun her enemies so they'll be too numb to react while she overwhelms them." A glance around told Mogaba that the Captain's technique was enjoying some success right here, right now. And neither General Singh was eager for a lecture on the subject of combat psychology.

So Mogaba just noted, "And we'll be at a disadvantage until we know which probe will become the real attack."

And that, he suspected, had not yet been determined on the other side, either. She could just be trying to find out where she could get the best return for her investment. They never liked wasting their men, the Company Captains.

"At this point we'll let the district commanders respond to their own crises. We'll reinforce them only to stop a disaster. What I need from you two is regular gauges of the mood of the mob. So far they don't seem to care but we wouldn't want any unwelcome surprises."

Ghopal offered, "I'd say the masses favor us. It wasn't us who started all those fires."

Mogaba glanced eastward. There was a little color over there but he felt no elation. Ghopal had reminded him of the oppressive amount of work ahead once he suppressed the enemy's attacks. Fires would leave tens of thousands homeless and destitute in a city where a third of the population already enjoyed that distinction.

Maybe he should just walk away and leave all the problems to Sleepy.

Taglios:
Attack

It became clear to me that Sleepy wanted control of the South Gate itself. She was flinging people and material around everywhere and using up those of us able to fly, but when you did the numbers over half of our efforts were taking place within a half mile of the barbican. And the barbican itself had suffered immensely from above. Parts looked like slag pierced by ten thousand holes.

I had better information than Mogaba did. But I knew that the Great General would catch on soon enough. He possessed a well-honed instinct for things warlike.

How flexible was the Captain's planning? Could she shift her point of attack fast once Mogaba did catch on? I did not know. Whatever level of planning had gone into this, I had not been invited to participate. Only Suvrin had a real grasp of the whole picture. And I was not that sure about him. This Sleepy was as close as I used to be when it came to sharing her thoughts.

That seemed to go with the job. My predecessors had been the same way. Someday it would hurt us.

I t was just past noon. Striking suddenly from all directions and enjoying maximum support from above and from Tobo, our troops pushed into the barbican complex. The defense seemed doomed once the assault teams got inside and got the outer gates open.

Mogaba did not respond. The streets near the gate complex did empty as civilians decided this seemed like a good time not to be visible. Bands of Taglian wounded retreated deeper into the city. Still no one came forward to reinforce or relieve the defenders of the barbican. Soldiers from Mogaba's own Second Territorial began saying unkind things about their boss.

Something was not right here. Mogaba was way too passive. The man had to know that he had to do something before the night returned and the Company waxed far more powerful by grace of the Unknown Shadows.

Somehow, we had to be doing what Mogaba wanted us to do if he was doing nothing to prevent us from doing it.

Yeah. You can drive yourself crazy trying to work your way around all the angles of that kind of stuff.

S leepy sent everybody but Tobo off to intensify the attack on the upriver waterfront defenses. Evidently we had gained a good foothold there, cheaply, so the Captain wanted to expand it.

I had begun to suspect that Sleepy really did have no fixed plan. Other than to seize whatever Mogaba was willing to let go.

An hour later, when loyalist troops did respond to the threat on the waterfront, the South Gate again became the focus of our attack.

I hoped she decided soon. I was worn out. And we still had hours of daylight left.

I was right in the first place. She chose the gate.

Back when the men on the walls finally broke into the gate houses a signal had gone up, to alert the Captain and Lieutenant. There were two gate houses and both had to be cleared. One had proven much more stubborn than the other. In the interim every man not engaged elsewhere gathered outside, ready to attack.

Now Sleepy signalled the advance. The officers all had orders to push through the barbican and drive straight on to the heart of the city. They had guides to show them the way. The Captain wanted the Palace captured swiftly. She believed we would face little resistance in the rest of Taglios once its symbolic heart had fallen.

Word was out already that the Prahbrindrah Drah was on his way, to reclaim his family's dominion.

Me, I would have had the Prince in my hip pocket first, ready to flash in front of the mob right now. I would have him lead the charge. But nobody asked me how I would handle things anymore.

Taglios:
Bad News, White Crow

Mogaba received the news about the South Gate in grim, expressionless silence. He asked no questions, just looked to the west to see how much daylight he had left. He turned to Aridatha and Ghopal. The latter nodded slightly.

Once a messenger had departed, the Great General asked, "Are they continuing their attack on the waterfront?"

Aridatha responded. "At last report they were stepping it up."

"Send another company. Their main force will head straight here. With all their sorcery supporting it. A counterattack down there should have an excellent chance of succeeding."

"And what should I do about the invaders?" Aridatha asked.

"We've had that set for months. Just follow the plan. Let it unfold."

Aridatha nodded, plainly wishing there was some way to reduce the bloodshed. He was less pessimistic about the outcome of this conflict than was the Great General. But he feared the price would be so crippling that victory would be the greater evil for the city as a whole.

Mogaba told him, "I want you to return to your own headquarters now. Continue to direct your troops from there."

"But . . ."

"If this goes badly and you're here with me when they come you'll have to pay a crueler price than necessary. Do as I say. Ghopal, you take over here. No one goes into the Palace. No one comes out. If the enemy gets this far make sure they know about the Khadidas and the Daughter of Night. I expect you to stay out of the way yourself. The best people to get the information to are the two wearing the fiery armor. Widowmaker and Lifetaker. They'll listen to you. They're the girl's natural parents. Aridatha, why are you still standing there? You have your instructions."

Ghopal asked, "What'll you be doing?"

"Readying a pair of counterattacks that'll make these strange foreign soldiers wish that they'd never left the land where they were born." The Great General projected immense confidence.

He did not feel a bit of it inside.

Nevertheless, his stride was that of an arrogant conquerer as he walked away from the Palace, a gaggle of messengers and functionaries scurrying behind him. He spun off orders as he went.

Mogaba spotted the white crow watching from a cornice stone. He beckoned. "Come down here." He patted his shoulder.

The bird did as it was bid, startling Mogaba's entourage.

The Great General asked, "Are you who I think you are?"

115

Taglios:
The Special Team

There were some tasks too important to entrust to anyone but family. The responsible captains at the South Gate were always related to Ghopal Singh, though they were officers in the City Battalions. They were all men who dared not be disloyal because their pasts were all tangled up with the Greys, the Great General, and the Protectorate.

Also, they were men who were mentally disciplined enough to retreat without running away. They were men who had prepared themselves and their followers for this day. Though, originally, they had expected the Protector herself to be entering their killing zone.

116

Taglios:
Outrageous Fortune

The passage through the barbican seemed a maze from inside, though there were only a half dozen turns. From above it did not look that bad. Until huge blocks of stone fell out of the walls, blocking the way ahead of and behind the Captain, trapping her, her staff and another dozen men.

The falling blocks initiated a train of mechanical events, the first of which was the launching of a storm of poisoned darts. Horses screamed and men cursed. And, as I sent my flying post downward to try to get the Captain out of there, burning oil sprayed from ports in the walls.

So this was how they had planned to get rid of Soulcatcher.

The heat drove me back. The black Voroshk clothing could not stand up to much of that.

Sleepy had chosen to place herself at the middle of the invading column. Which meant our forces had just been split in two.

A massive counterattack was sure to develop.

I pushed myself up beside Arkana, who was numb with the horror. "Get ahold of yourself! I want you to find Suvrin. Tell him I'll take charge on the city side. He can build steps to get the rest of the men past that mess. He can use the lumber meant for siege engines. Go on! Get going!"

Once again I did not have to whack her to bring her out of her stupor.

Once again Mogaba had dealt us one off the bottom of his deck. This time our chances of surviving did not look good.

We should have been prepared for it. He had *told* us that there were arrangements in place.

Sometimes you just do not hear what is being said.

I checked the sun before I reached the ground.

We would have to hang on for a bit longer than what inspired me with optimism.

*　*　*

It won't be long," I insisted to the commanders on the ground. "We need to put ourselves into a position to hang on until nightfall. Once darkness comes . . ."

"The Unknown Shadows."

"The Hidden Realm."

Shouts. A scatter of arrows fell.

"Push a company along the wall that direction," I directed. "I want those steps under our control when the others start joining us." I had to show an optimism I did not feel. I *hoped* Suvrin would press his half of the attack.

No man could question the courage of the soldiers from Hsien. They mauled the City Battalions badly. They mauled reinforcements from the Second Territorial. Unfortunately, the City Battalions and Mogaba's Second Territorial elite mauled them right back. It did not take long to see that Sleepy might have taken too big a bite. The Great General seemed to have plenty of reserves, though he was parsimonious when it came to investing them.

Vigorous support from Arkana, Shukrat and Tobo kept us from being overwhelmed.

Once Tobo woke up enough to begin thinking more than mechanically the tide began to turn. Once he recalled that he was good for something more than dropping rocks and firepots. Once he added his sorcerous skills to the girls' weaker ones we got stinging insects, painful worms of fire, lemon and lime snowflakes that pitted armor and flesh.

Nevertheless, the enemy kept us confined until darkness came.

Darkness always comes.

Taglios:
Night and the City

The Great General took charge of the riverfront defenses personally. He found morale abysmal when he arrived, accompanied by reserves from the Second Territorial. The long succession of military disasters had the soldiers suspecting that defeat was inevitable and that they were being wasted in a hope-less cause.

The Great General himself led his own lifeguard in a counterattack of such fury and finesse that the enemy soon lost everything that it had taken them all day to capture.

The invaders got no support from above. The Great General interpreted that to mean that they were in desperate straits at the South Gate.

There was not a lot of communication between forces. Nobody knew what any-body else was doing, really. The best anyone could do was cling to the plans and hope the enemy did not get too much enjoyment from his advantages.

Mogaba's opponents tried reinforcing themselves with recent recruits. That did them little good. Those men entered the fighting in groups too small to make any difference.

The last attackers fled in the barges they had used to make their initial landings, drifting downriver because they did not have enough men healthy enough to row against the current. All the barges were overburdened, one so much so that it shipped water at the slightest rocking. It did not remain afloat long.

Mogaba treated himself to a long breather. He turned his mind off completely, closed his eyes, let the cold winter air chill him.

When he was calm and breathing normally again he allowed himself to return to the moment.

He could get the best of this thing yet. If he could get these men to the South Gate and get in a hard blow he might damage the enemy enough to earn his own people a fair chance of making it through the night. If he succeeded, victory would be his. *They* would not be able to survive everything he would throw at them to-morrow.

He opened his eyes.

The white crow stared at him from a perch on a broken cartwheel scarcely a foot from his face.

The crow started talking.

That bird was a much better messenger and spy than the crows he had known in earlier days.

The Great General listened for a long time. And wondered if the mind behind the bird was aware of his disloyalty.

He would not bring it up first.

The Great General dragged himself upright, ignoring the complaints of aching muscles. "Sergeant Mugwarth. Spread the word. All officers. Round up every man who can walk. We're moving up to relieve the South Gate."

*　　*　　*

The enemy's aerial advantage betrayed the trap before it could close. Mogaba left the soldiers to their work and hastened toward the Palace. He arrived as dusk began to deepen shadows. The view from that eminence included half a dozen fires still burning. Smoke and trickles of fire still attended the fallen parts of the Palace, too.

Awaiting him was the news that the enemy had reduced most of the defenses at the downriver end of the city. Their forces there had been augmented by the survivors from upriver. These outsiders were stubborn fighters.

"Send reinforcements?" Ghopal asked.

Mogaba thought a moment. Those foreigners ought to be near their limits. "Yes, actually. These are all your men here, around the Palace, aren't they?"

"I thought that would be best. Makes them all men I can trust."

"Let Aridatha's soldiers take their place. Send yours to the waterfront. And gather up any of your brothers and cousins who're still alive, I want them here."

"What? . . ."

"Do it. Quickly. Quickly. And round up all those captured fireball throwers."

"I think we used most of them up."

"That means they're some of them left. I want them all."

Darkness came. And soon after it did messages reached the Great General informing him that his enemies, inside both their footholds, were hunkering down for the night rather than pressing forward when their shadowy allies could come out to play.

The Great General refused to let the night intimidate him. By his example he inspired those around him. And it did seem that the enemy's spooks meant to do little more than yell "Boo!"

The Great General reorganized the city's defenses, shifting almost all responsibility into Aridatha Singh's hands. Then he led Ghopal Singh and the man's kinsmen, armed with fireball throwers, toward the waterfront conflict.

Ghopal asked, "What're we doing?"

"This is a false peace," Mogaba replied. "They lost their Captain this afternoon. The trap in the gate worked to perfection. They lost most of their command staff, too." He did not explain how he knew that. "They'll need to work out who's in charge and what they're going to do now. They might even decide to go away." He shivered, told himself it was the winter air.

But he knew that Croaker had survived the day. He knew the Company would not be going away. He knew the succession there had been assured and the new Captain would attempt to complete the work of the old.

118

Taglios:
A New Administration

I'm not ready to take over," Suvrin argued.

"And I'm too old to come back," I countered. "And the only other qualified person is in a coma." Lady was not, literally, in a coma, but, practically speaking, the effect was the same. She had nothing to contribute.

Suvrin grumbled under his breath.

"Sleepy picked you. She thought you could handle it. She's been giving you opportunities to get a feel for the job."

Sleepy was a big part of the problem. Her death, so sudden and cruel, had stricken everyone. Most of us were still in a daze.

I said, "We take too much time here; we'll give the Children of the Dead too much time to think. We don't want them looking at how bad the numbers thing has gone since they've been on our side of the glittering plain."

A moment of self-loathing followed. That was exactly the sort of thinking I found repugnant in the Company's employers.

Suvrin reflected briefly. "We can't spend time grieving, can we? We have to go ahead. Or call it off."

"No decision there. Go ahead. I've tried to get messages to Aridatha Singh. He seems like a good man, willing to put Taglios first. He might be willing to spare the city some pain."

"If you can convince him that the Great General isn't going to eat us alive. The way Tobo tells it, Mogaba isn't particularly worried."

"He will be. Once we get settled in here I just might take the girls general hunting."

Suvrin still showed some of that pudgy, baby-fat look he had always had. He needed to get busy and develop the hardened, piratical look of a Captain.

He yielded to his hidden desires. "All right. I'll be the Captain. But I reserve the right to quit."

"Excellent. I'll spread the word, then I'll go smack Mogaba around." My hatred for the Great General was no longer virulent, though. It was more like a bad habit these days.

"I'm the Captain now, right? Completely in charge?"

"Yeah." Spoken with a twinge of suspicion.

"My first directive as Captain, then, is that you should stop putting yourself at risk."

"Huh? What? But . . ."

"Croaker, you're the only one left who can keep the Annals. You're the only one left who can read most of them. You didn't finish teaching me and you haven't trained anyone else. I don't intend to lose our connection with our heritage. Not at this last stage. Therefore, henceforth, you're not going anywhere that'll put you at risk."

"You sonofabitch. You jobbed me. You can't do that."

"I'm the Captain. Sure I can. I just did. I'll have you restrained if that's what it takes."

"You won't have to." Because I buy into the whole Company mystique, like a religion. Because I cannot defy orders just because I do not like them. Ha-ha. How long would it take to find a way to weasel around this if I felt a genuine need? "But I wanted Mogaba."

"We'll catch him for you. Then you can skin him or whatever you want."

I went out and spread the word that we had a new Captain and that the officers should attend him. Then I looked for Arkana, who was off somewhere wasting a valuable part of her life sleeping.

As I stumbled around, shivering because things unseen were everywhere in the night, I realized that Suvrin, unwittingly, had given me orders of critical importance. If I kept running around, getting into the middle of everything, and I got myself killed for my trouble, more than the Annals would die with me. So would the little plan I had worked out for fulfilling our commitment to Shivetya.

I had not shared that with anyone, and would not unless I was convinced I was dying.

Words never spoken cannot be overheard by sleeping Goddesses.

119

Taglios:
Messenger

Guided and masked by the folk of the hidden realm, Arkana penetrated Aridatha Singh's headquarters undetected, flying post and all. The general was alone. He had collapsed of exhaustion an hour earlier. Solicitous subordinates had put him to bed. They had left sentries outside his door to keep him from being disturbed.

Arkana got in through an open window, lying flat upon her post. She was not especially nervous. She was confident that she could manage any trouble that came her way, at least for the moments it would take her to escape.

She had been instructed to flee at the first sign of trouble. She believed in those instructions with the fervor of a new convert.

Once inside she dismounted and turned her post so she could get away without any delay. She kept herself tethered to the post so it could drag her out even if she was not in the saddle. Even if she was unconscious. Maybe even if three guys were hanging onto her, trying to keep her from going.

She found a lamp and lit it. Then she awakened Aridatha Singh.

The general did not waken quickly. But he did so quietly and cautiously, understanding that he was in a dangerous situation. Maybe it was the Unknown Shadows. The sense of their presence was strong. Because they were all around.

Singh rose into a cross-legged sitting position. He moved slowly, keeping his hands in sight. He asked his question by expression alone.

Arkana strained to ignore his looks. She had been warned. . . . She was not an idiot like Gromovol. "The Captain wants to know if you received the Annalist's messages. The Captain wants to know if you're ready to spare Taglios the agonies of further conflict." She enunciated carefully, having no desire to be misunderstood.

"Of course I do. But how do I get you people to go away?" He could not tell much about his visitor because of the Voroshk clothing.

"Here's an idea. You can have your soldiers lay down their arms." As one of the

Voroshk that sort of statement directed at an outsider would not have troubled Arkana at all. But here, tonight, she was just another refugee and freelance. And a very young one at that, with limited confidence in herself. Maybe Croaker's confidence was misplaced.

That clever old man. He had set her up so she would risk her freedom rather than let him down.

That was a characteristic of old men. All old men in her experience, anyway.

Aridatha said, "There's little I'd like more than to end this fighting before even one more person gets hurt. But I have no control when it comes to making the choice between war and peace. I've undertaken obligations. I've given my word. Right now Taglios is in the keeping of the Great General. If *he* gives the order to stop fighting I'll do so instantly."

And he said no more. That was as clearly as he could speak. Even that much clarity troubled his conscience.

"That's your firm response, then?" Arkana's confidence had begun to swell.

"There is no other position open to me. Your Captain will understand."

"Your honor could get you killed. And there'd be no one to sing your praises." Arkana departed before Singh could figure out what that meant. He thought it sounded like something foreign that did not translate well.

Aridatha was a little less exhausted than he had been before he collapsed. But he did not fall asleep again for a long while, and not because of the potent sense of alien presence still filling his bedroom. He kept hearing the visitor's last words and remembering his father. Narayan Singh. A man of high honor, within his own world. Now without a soul to sing his praises. Unless maybe his beloved Goddess sang him lullabies within her terrible dreams.

And Narayan's murderer was still hiding somewhere inside the remains of the Palace.

120

Taglios:
Thi Kim Was Always Here

Mogaba did not participate much in the fighting. He told Ghopal, "The spirit is willing but this body is just too damned old and tired. I'll just sit here and tell you what to do." But mostly he visited with the white crow, which had begun scouting for him despite the presence of unfriendly ghosts. The bird could see those ghosts quite clearly, for it warned him regularly when it was time to keep his mouth shut.

When Mogaba suggested that the unseen things did not seem to be helping the invaders much the crow told him that the folk of the hidden realm were completely devoted to making their master happy. What little they did contribute they did in response to the will of their messiah, Tobo, whom they worshiped almost as a god. As Thi Kim. Which, in the canonical language of the priests who had created the Unknown Shadows, meant One Who Walks with the Dead.

Startled, the Great General demanded, "You mean to tell me that Thi Kim isn't Nyueng Bao?"

The title came from a language closely akin to the Nyueng Bao of four centuries ago.

"So Deathwalker is the half-breed kid?"

Not Deathwalker. One Who Walks with the Dead.

Mogaba was too tired to wonder much about the difference. "Go find Aridatha Singh," Mogaba said. "I want to know what he's doing."

The bird was not pleased about being given orders. But it went.

Mogaba called for Ghopal immediately. He asked, "What're your feelings toward this city?" He knew but wanted to hear it from the man's own mouth.

Ghopal shrugged. "I'm not sure I understand. Like everyone who lives here I love it and I hate it."

"Our enemies have reorganized their chain of command. Right now they're resting. But they'll resume their attack while there's yet darkness enough to conceal their hidden allies. I'm sure now that our forces will survive the night with more than enough strength left to be able to counterattack tomorrow. I think we'll be able to hurt them badly when we do attack but their damned sorcerers will save them and when night comes again their allies will finish us." The Great General said all this without having seen any proof that the Unknown Shadows were capable of doing anything lethal. "And I think Taglios will suffer a great deal more destruction during that time. I believe that, eventually, both sides will be so weakened that, no matter who wins, neither will be able to restrain the religious factions, nor be able to contain the ambitions of the gang lords, priests or anyone else likely to take advantage of a state of disorder. We might even see rioting between the followers of the different major religions."

Ghopal nodded in the darkness, unseen. As chief Grey managing unofficial ambition had been his task. He had been particularly hard on criminal gangs. Mogaba had not dug for details but knew that something in Ghopal's past drove him to shatter criminal enterprises.

"What're you trying to say?" Ghopal asked.

"I'm saying that if we continue this war the way we are now, we can win—probably—but we'll destroy Taglios in the process. And, even if we do lose, the results will be anarchy and destruction."

"And?"

"And our enemies don't care. They didn't come here for the city's benefit. They came to get you and me. And the Khadidas and the girl. Especially the Daughter of Night."

Mogaba felt Ghopal's growing suspicion.

The white crow would be back soon, too.

"I think we should walk away, Ghopal. And save Taglios the agony. The garrisons in the eastern provinces are loyal. We can continue the struggle from there."

Ghopal was not fooled. Neither did he raise the objection that they had little hope of success against an enemy seated in the capital, armed with a crew of wizards and well-supplied with funds.

Ghopal had known his commander a long time. The Great General was a stubborn warlord, imbued with no weakness whatsoever. Unless that was his secret love for his adopted city, that he had revealed several times lately. Ghopal found he had no trouble believing that the Great General could walk away rather than let Taglios be destroyed as a monument to his ego. This Mogaba was not the arrogant youngster who had held Dejagore against the worst the Shadowmasters had been able to deliver. "Where would we go?"

"Agra. Or possibly Mukhra in Ajitsthan."

"Vehdna strongholds, both. A band of heretic Shadar aren't likely to be welcomed. Particularly if the strife puts any more strain on religious tolerance."

"That could happen," Mogaba admitted. "Or it might not."

"Nor have we mentioned families." Family was extremely important to the Shadar. "I have only my brothers and cousins. But most of my brothers and cousins have wives and children."

Mogaba said, "I suppose they could stay here, cut off their beards and pretend to be people who haven't been getting much sun. Ghopal, I'm being completely unfair. I'm putting this all squarely on your shoulders. Stay and fight? Or go away and spare the city?"

As if to punctuate his remarks a mushroom of fire rose above the heart of the city. For an instant it resembled a gigantic, glowing brain. Flying shapes hurtled across its face.

Mogaba said, "That respite is over."

121

Taglios:
Sleeping Beauty

It was driving me crazy, having to hang back over friendly territory, observing an aerial assault on a cluster of buildings anchoring a defense stubbornly blocking our advance toward the Palace. We had brought the knowledge of war to this end of the world and we had taught our students too well. These Taglians refused to yield even in the face of sorcery and the Unknown Shadows.

Someone had pointed out that the troops of the City Battalions were mainly Vehdna and Shadar. Both religions assure swift access to rivers of wine and acres of eager virgins for the man who falls in battle. Though originally that only meant warriors who perished in the name of God.

I wondered what the Vehdna paradise was like for Sleepy.

We had not yet been able to identify her body. The corpses in that passage had been burned that badly.

"Why don't we go around these guys?" I wondered. And the answer was, they would not let us. They had an interlocking defense nicely laid out. The only way past was through. Or over.

Over we could do.

Over we did go, twenty insanely courageous Children of the Dead at a time, with a Tobo so tired he was cross-eyed doing the lifting.

The Unknown Shadows supported their pal from every possible direction, sometimes so blatantly that I could see them clearly from where I hovered, doing nothing whatsoever that was useful to the cause.

I had a wife in the camp outside the city. It had been a while since I had gone to see how she was doing. That might be considered doing something useful.

So I did leave my brethren to go visit my wife. While a fight was going on. A fight that would, no doubt, be completely unique amongst all the fights ever fought, so that somebody really should be right there to record every nuance of its unique ebb and flow.

Lady remained unchanged. She lurked halfway between life and death. She kept talking to herself in her sleep. What I saw did not inspire me with hope. What I heard only confused me. Mostly it was incoherent. Such individual words as were recognizable did not fall together at all sensibly.

A few minutes of that reminded me why I always resisted visiting till I had forgotten the despair a visit inspired.

Taglios:
Unknown Shadows

Only two unmarried second-cousins of Ghopal chose to leave the city with the Great General and the commander of the Greys. Because they had families the rest all chose to take their chances with the invaders.

Mogaba understood. In the coming confusion scores of his allies would be finding new looks, new races to be, while the conquerers scoured the city for enemies. Many would somehow fail ever to have heard of the Greys, let alone have contributed to that organization's criminal oppressions.

"Here," Mogaba said, leading the way out onto an ancient, rickety dock. "This one will do." He indicated an eighteen-foot boat that, from its aroma, had been bringing in fish since sometime early in the last century.

Mogaba invited himself aboard. Ghopal and the others followed warily. Shadar and large bodies of water had a relationship somewhat like that between cats and bathtubs. Mogaba said, "Untie those ropes. You really *do* know how to row, don't you?" Ghopal had made the claim.

Singh grunted. "But not competitively."

To Mogaba's astonishment they stole the boat without a challenge. He was amazed that a vessel so large had been untenanted. There should have been at least one family aboard. But tonight the entire waterfront was silent and unpopulated, as though the riverside nights were too terrible to endure.

Mogaba's internal struggle waxed and waned. He reminded himself that it was fast becoming too late to change his mind, to give in to his prideful, arrogant side. That weakness had brought about these terrible end days. How different his life and the world would have been had he been able to control his interior demons during the siege of Dejagore.

He would hardly be a hated and lonely old man whose memories were all of serving faithfully and well a parade of despicable masters.

The white crow found them while they were trying to work out the mechanics of raising the boat's lateen sail. There was a good breeze blowing, capable of carrying them up the river far more swiftly than could their incompetent rowing.

The bird settled in the rigging. "What are you doing? I did not give you permission to flee. Why are you running away? No battle has been lost."

The Shadar gawked. Mogaba thumped himself on the chest. "No. A great war has been won. Here. At last. Now I go somewhere where I will do no more harm anymore forever."

Ghopal looked from him to the crow and back, gradually gaining understanding of both. He grew increasingly agitated and afraid as he did so.

The bird was capable of a range of voices, though it was only a haunted crow. "Turn this vessel shoreward. Now. I will tolerate no disobedience."

"You hold no terror for me anymore, old whore," Mogaba replied. "You hold no power over me. I won't be your toy or cats-paw tonight or ever again."

"You have no idea how much you will regret this. I won't be imprisoned forever. You will be the first chore on my list when I return. Ghopal Singh. Turn this disgusting tub around . . . awk!"

Ghopal had whacked the bird with the flat of his oar. Flailing, losing feathers, shrieking, it flung from the rigging into the fetid, muddy river. The retiring commander of the Greys observed, "That bird has an amazingly fowl vocabulary." He grinned. Then he began digging through the bag he had carried aboard. He really needed a sip of wine. His kinsmen scowled. "Glower all you want, you magpies! I'm my own man now!"

The tenor of the bird's incessant natter changed suddenly, becoming pure corvine terror. It flapped in panic as the surface of the river lifted it up.

The rising water tilted the boat precariously. Ghopal lost his grasp on his bottle.

One of his cousins took a wild swing with his oar, swatting a gallon of water out of the thing taking form. His effort had no enduring effect.

"Holy shit!" Ghopal said from flat on his back. "What the hell is that?" He was staring over Mogaba's shoulder.

A *thing* loomed against the light of fires burning in the city. A thing resembling a huge duck capable of a grin filled with wicked, glistening teeth. And the thing was not alone.

"Oh, man," one of Ghopal's cousins sighed. "They're all around us. What are they?"

Mogaba sighed himself. He did not say that the monsters were not the sort of things people saw and lived to describe.

Taglios:
Crow Talk

Aridatha Singh had just gotten back to sleep when fiery pain pierced the back of his right hand. He leapt up and flung his arm out. He thought his lamp had somehow spilled burning oil and feared his cot would be on fire. But the lamp was not burning.

Not fire. Something had bitten him, then. Or maybe clawed him. And he had thrown it across the room, where it was struggling feebly and making incoherent chicken noises. Those people were attacking him directly now? He shouted for the sentries.

Once light filled the room he discovered that his visitor was an albino crow. One of the men threw a blanket over the bird and wrapped it up. Another examined Aridatha's hand. "That's one ragged looking critter, General. You might want to see a physician. It might be diseased."

"Send for soap and hot water. . . . It doesn't look like the skin is broken much. . . . What is that?"

The blanket with the bird inside had begun talking.

"It's talking," the soldier said, so utterly amazed that he could do nothing but state the obvious.

"Seal the window. Close the door. Get yourselves ready to hit it with something when we turn it loose." He recalled that one of the Company chieftains sometimes carried ravens on his shoulders. And one of those was white.

Escape was no longer an option for the bird. Aridatha directed, "Turn it loose now."

The crow looked like someone had tried to drown it, then had decided to pluck it featherless instead. It was in terrible shape.

The bedraggled beast cocked its head right, left, surveying the chamber. It made an obvious effort to put aside its anger, to collect its pride and dignity.

Aridatha did not think this was the raven he had seen with that man Croaker. This one seemed smaller, yet more substantial.

The bird studied Singh first with one eye, then with the other. Then it eyed the sentries. It seemed to be awaiting something.

"You have something to say, say it," Aridatha suggested.

"Send them out."

"I don't think so." He motioned two soldiers into positions where they would be better able to swat the crow.

"I am not accustomed to . . ."

"Nor am I in the habit of taking back chat from birds. I assume you bring a message. Deliver it. Or I'll wring your neck and go on about my business."

"I fear you will live to regret this, Aridatha Singh."

In that moment, with the bird's voice changing, Singh understood that he was in touch with the Protector. But her enemies had buried her beneath the glittering plain. Had they not? "I await your message. If it's just a threat I'll have Vasudha step on your head."

"Very well. Until the day, Aridatha Singh. Aridatha Singh, you are now my viceroy in Taglios. Mogaba and Ghopal are no more. I will instruct you as to what steps to take. . . ."

"Excuse me. The Great General and General Singh have been killed?"

"They tried to do something foolish. For their trouble the enemy's shadow creatures destroyed them. Which elevates you to . . ."

Aridatha turned his back on the crow. "Jitendra. Get that word out. I want every company to disengage. The only exception is to be where the enemy won't let them. And get the word across the lines that I'm prepared to discuss terms."

The white crow flew into a cursing rage.

"Throw the blanket on that thing again, Vasudha. We may have some use for it later but I don't want to listen to its nagging now."

"You could get you a wife if you needed that, General."

Taglios:
The Sandbar

Already there were stories on the street about how the Great General had sacrificed himself in order to void the strictures of all the oaths and vows binding him and his allies. Because he had wanted to spare the city further devastation by the invading rebels and outlanders. Amazing. We had just started taking charge and already people were nostalgic for the good old days of the Protectorate.

Hard to blame them, I suppose. It was a generation ago that the Prahbrindrah Drah last saw the inside of his capital city.

Let them feel however they wanted. As long as they stayed out of my way.

Tobo and I drifted above the Palace, studying the ruin. Smoke still found its way out of the rock pile. Every few hours a little more caved in. A third had collapsed already. That third included almost all of the occupied modern sector. Maybe the abandoned parts had been constructed from sterner stuff. They had survived generations of neglect.

Even during the worst fighting Aridatha had used volunteers from the City Battalions to keep sifting the ruins for survivors to rescue and bodies to deliver to distraught relatives. He continued in that role, now reinforced by units formerly committed to the fighting. Elsewhere, whole battalions now engaged the more stubborn fires instead of invaders.

I asked Tobo, "You really think they're still in there somewhere?" I meant Booboo and Goblin.

"I know they are. The hidden folk have seen them. They just can't remember how to get to them."

"Strange as it may seem, I need them out of there alive. Without them I can't keep my promise to Shivetya."

Tobo grunted. I had not included him in my planning. In fact, the inner circle still consisted of a council of one. Me. And I intended to keep it that way. Nothing spoken, nothing betrayed.

"I think Arkana's in love." Below, the Voroshk girl had come up with another excuse to consult Aridatha Singh.

Tobo grunted again. He was better than he had been but victory had given him no satisfaction. He would be a long time getting over the loss of his mom and dad.

I asked, "Have you found any trace of Mogaba or Ghopal Singh?" Aridatha said they were dead. He claimed to have been told so by the white crow—not an entirely reliable witness.

The boy studied me before responding. "They drowned. While trying to escape upriver. By boat. Evidently the boat capsized."

"I see."

My tone made him stare at me intently. I could not see his expression, of course. The Voroshk apparel concealed that. And mine masked my features. We continued to dress up because some people did not approve of our conquest. Incidents abounded.

Mostly, though, Taglios had heaved a huge collective sigh and began getting on with the business of life. Thus far there had been almost no retribution against those who had served the displaced regime. Most people seemed of the opinion that the Greys had done more good than harm, since they had repressed criminal behavior with a ferocity greater than they had shown to enemies of the Great General and the Protector.

In general, the masses of people were entirely indifferent to who ruled Taglios and its dependencies. The who seldom touched their lives deeply, one way or another.

The human species never ceases to amaze me. I would have bet more people would have cared a lot more. But from the inside nothing is ever what it looks like from without.

RAJADHARMA graffiti continued to appear. Some folks are never satisfied. THI KIM IS HERE was turning up now, too. I had not pressed the kid on that. He did not want to talk about it.

I would let it ride even though that mystery was not yet solved to my satisfaction. There had to be more to his relationship with the Unknown Shadows than had become obvious so far.

I left the boy and circled the Palace. Our men had replaced the City Battalions on that perimeter. They made a colorful line. City troops were clearing rubble, particularly in areas where Tobo's friends believed people were trapped. A number remained alive, caught inside interior rooms that had not collapsed. Now thirst was their implacable enemy.

All was going as it should. It seemed. But I was not comfortable. I had a sense of there being a wrongness somewhere. Intuition. Based upon subconscious cues.

I drifted away from the Palace, waving in passing to Shukrat, who just had to see Tobo after having completed a courier run to the approaching Prahbrindrah Drah and Radisha. Once out of sight I put on speed and headed for the river.

I started at the downstream end of the waterfront. I drifted upstream. The boats were out. As they would have been had the fighting still been under way. I asked a few questions of terrified fishermen, not at all sure what I might find. The current had had ample time to carry bodies and wreckage down to the delta swamps.

Or perhaps not.

There is a miles-long sandbar just off the curve of the north bank. It has been there so long that it is an island now, with grass on its flanks, brush above that and trees along its highest parts. The channel on its north side is narrow, shallow and choked with mud. An overturned boat lay in the mouth of that channel. One dead man sprawled in the mud. A dozen Taglians clad only in loincloths were trying to right the boat preparatory to dragging it off the bar. None of those men showed the least interest in the corpse. But it was obviously Shadar and they were all Gunni.

The scavengers had a definite interest in not being anywhere around when people came swooping out of the sky in a billowing black cloud. A couple jumped into the channel and swam for the north bank. Others ran into the growth on the island's spine. A few tried to make it back to the boat that had brought them. It had beached a hundred yards down the bar.

The dead Shadar appeared to have been an officer of the Greys. I discovered a second corpse underneath the boat, also Shadar. There were disturbed crows in and above the nearby trees, which was interesting because we saw so few of those birds anymore.

I made a couple of lazy passes overhead, to finish scaring the birds away, before dropping carefully through the branches.

Mogaba was recognizable only because of the unique color of the bits of skin left to him. Ghopal Singh I identified only by deduction. They had been tortured. Terribly, and for a long time. Mogaba maybe for days. His corpse was not that old.

I slid downstream behind the island and eventually rejoined my own people. I searched out Arkana. "We need to talk, adopted daughter." I jerked a thumb. Somewhere up high, in the brilliant noonday sun.

She picked up on my concern. She drove upward a thousand feet, tending south, as though we were going to check on the Prahbrindrah Drah's progress. In fact, a sizable dust cloud could be seen to the south.

"What is it?" she asked.

"I think Tobo may be out of control. Or so close to it as makes no difference. If we're not careful we might all be sorry his mother isn't here to scold him. And that Sleepy and Murgen are gone. He may be a grown man but he still needs direction." I told her what I had found on the sandbar.

"Why tell me? You don't let anybody in on anything, Pop."

"Because I've seen you making moon eyes at General Singh. And he was a partner with the Great General and Ghopal Singh. If Tobo's really unhinged he might go after Aridatha next."

"Why do you blame Tobo?"

I led her through my reasoning, which relied heavily on my assessment of the character of the Great General. "Mogaba knew Aridatha wanted to spare Taglios from the fighting. He wanted that himself. He couldn't surrender, though. And Aridatha's sense of honor wouldn't let him desert Mogaba. So Mogaba decided to arrange it so Aridatha wouldn't be encumbered. And Tobo got him."

"You didn't say why you blame Tobo."

"Because only Tobo could've known what Mogaba was doing and where he would be doing it. There was something badly wrong on the river that night. All the waterfront people felt it and ran off to hide in the city."

"All right. Suppose it's true. What're you going to do?"

"I just did it. I told you to be careful. And now I'm going to see if my wife's gotten any better since this morning."

I knew Lady would not have done so. I had begun to lose hope for her.

Taglios:
An Afternoon Off

I took Lady out for a picnic. With a little help from my adopted daughters. In the vain hope that some sunlight and fresh air would make a difference when even Tobo's best effort could not shake the enchantment holding her. According to the boy wizard I was supposed to consider myself lucky. If she had not been Lady, had been some ordinary person, she would have been long dead. He assured me this was not the spell that had claimed Sedvod and still gripped Soulcatcher. I could not see any obvious difference—except that Lady was getting no worse.

His best advice was to take my questions to the perpetrator once we found him.

The girls left me alone with my honey. I held her hand and rambled on about a thousand things: recollections, current affairs, hopes. I shared my suspicions and concerns about Tobo, too, which might have been dangerous since I had no idea what might be listening.

Nothing I did helped her even a little, nor did it seem to do me any good. I fought the good fight against despair.

A squeaky clean, thoroughly polished corporal from Hsien trotted up. "Captain's compliments, sir, and could you come to the Palace? They think they may have located the Khadidas and the Daughter of Night."

"Damn! Yes. I'll be there as soon as I can. Tell them not to mess with anything. Tell them to be *very* careful. Those two are extremely dangerous."

They knew that, of course. And Tobo would be right there to remind them. But repetition never hurts. Not when it helps get you through the deadly times.

Shukrat and Arkana came running. "What's up?" Shukrat asked.

As I explained I reflected on how much better the girls were getting along. They seemed to have shed the conflicts they had brought into Captivity.

As we three got Lady ready to go back to my tent I asked Arkana, "Will you want to go home someday?"

"What?"

"Home. Where you were born. The world I used to call Khatovar. Do you want to go back? I think I could make it happen."

"But it's all destroyed."

"Not really. The First Father and Nashun the Researcher said so, but that was just to excuse their cowardice."

"I'm not sure I want to believe that."

"Good. Excellent. That's the way I want my kids to be. Skeptical. That's the truth according to Shivetya. And I'm not a hundred percent sure of our demonic friend myself."

"Why didn't you ask me if I want to go?" Shukrat demanded.

"Because you don't want to go. You just want to be where Tobo is."

"That isn't exactly a secret. It isn't a crime, either. But I'm not bereft of my senses. You'll sure never see me do some die-for-love kind of thing. If you guys do go, tell me. I'll decide what I want to do then."

126

Taglios:
Royal Return

I did not make it to the Palace. Shukrat beat me there and came right back with instructions to head for the South Gate. The Prahbrindrah Drah was about to arrive and Suvrin wanted *somebody* there to greet the man we had been touting as the city's legitimate ruler.

Per instructions I rounded up a few men from the City Battalions, along with a handful of their officers, and off I went, grumbling all the way. I expected the Prince's homecoming would be a huge disappointment for him and his sister.

Taglios did not care.

I told several people to spread the word, to try to get something going.

That did very little good. The route inward from the gate was never more than sparsely populated with spectators and the rare feeble cheer we did hear came from really old people.

I hate to waste pomp and pageantry. Not that we did put much on. Aridatha got to bring out his marching band, a little late. Never would have been better. They were terrible. And not just because what passes for music here is so alien. I have spent half my life in this end of the world. I asked Singh, "Those guys practice much?"

"They've been too busy being soldiers."

Aridatha had an attitude I appreciated. Each one of his men was expected to be a soldier first, and whatever else secondarily.

Singh said, "I do have to tell you, this Prince doesn't look very impressive. I hope he's a better ruler than he is a showman."

I was no longer sure bringing the Prince back would be good for Taglios, myself. There had been big changes in the city and bigger changes in the man. They might have nothing in common anymore.

I shrugged. "He's old. If he hasn't got what Taglios needs Taglios won't have to put up with him for long."

In the old days the Prince and I had gotten along well. Until he had turned on us. As an officer in my command he had shown a hunger for learning and a lust for doing the best thing. So I told him straightaway, when we met inside the South Gate, that his first order of business, now that he was back in business, had to be the establishment of a generally acceptable line of succession. Otherwise chaos would follow his demise.

"*Rajadharma*, old buddy. Let's get the job done."

My remarks earned me a tired growl and not much more. The Prince seemed used up and worn out. His sister showed more spark but had a lot more years on her because she had not shared the stasis of the Captivity with her brother. Chances were, nowadays, that she would go first, despite being the younger.

She could not be titular ruler, anyway. When she did exercise the power, during all those years, there had been a pretense of a regency, in place until the legitimate ruler could resume control. Because the Prahbrindrah Drah was still alive somewhere. Neither custom nor law allowed a woman to rule in her own right.

Arkana came to meet me with the news. "They've definitely found the Khadidas and the Daughter of Night, Pop." She was a willing participant in that charade now and, more and more, helping herself to a job as my personal assistant. Now, if I could just teach her written Taglian. . . . I suspect the frequency with which I crossed the path of Aridatha Singh had something to do with all that. Singh, I noted, had not failed to recognize what a tasty morsel my little girl was, either, though Voroshk protective apparel seldom flattered.

Tobo remained patient enough to wait until I reached the Palace. Barely. And only out of impatient courtesy, because that was my real daughter and my former friend in there.

My real daughter. A grown woman, whom I had never seen. Arkana, known less than a year, was more daughter to me in life. And Narayan Singh was more a father to Booboo.

Aridatha was there and interested. I wondered why. Then I recalled that he had seen Booboo a few times before and those women have a way of getting under your skin without ever trying.

It did not occur to me that he might be thinking more about the Khadidas.

At first the Prince was put out by everyone's sudden loss of interest in him . . . then he got a good look at what had happened to the Palace.

He moaned aloud, a textbook cry of anguish. He managed some respectable gnashing of teeth.

Suvrin stepped in. The little pudgeball could be weasel-slick handling people when he wanted. Which might be the ideal leadership skill for the times. I turned to Arkana, gave her special instructions. She flew off to my rooms in the building we had taken for our headquarters. Once upon a time it had been a Greys barracks.

Most of the Greys have vanished. We all pretended not to notice that there are a disproportionate number of Shadar in the City Battalions, say compared to when we were duking it out with them in the streets.

Aridatha was sharing his own good fortune. Though there was less popular in-clination toward vengeance than I had expected. And that little focused entirely on individuals.

The Radisha Drah also let out a disconsolate wail on discovering the state of the Palace. She and her brother remained still and silent for minutes. Then she slew the silence with another cry of pain.

I told Suvrin, "I hope they don't decide that this is all our fault and they just have to get even." I did not think they would be that stupid, after having survived what they had suffered for having turned on us before, but with royalty you never know. They think differently than real people. The real world never quite seems to reach them.

Smoke still trickled out of the ruins, here and there. While we watched a small avalanche of weakened masonry cascaded down.

The Prince observed, "The stonework must have suffered more than we thought during the earthquake."

"Hunh?" That had happened so long ago that I had forgotten it. "You're proba-bly right. Plus the Protector never wasted a copper on maintenance while she was in charge." I approached Tobo, who continued to prance about impatiently. "Where are my treasures?"

As I asked, Arkana swooped down, black cloth popping and crackling in the wind. She carried One-Eye's spear and his ugly old hat. The hat still smelled of the ugly old man who had worn it.

"Right there where the red flag is."

Poles with colored streamers indicated points where the Unknown Shadows had detected something human under the rubble. There were just two red ribbons. The rest were black. There would be no rush to dig there. The red streamer not in-dicated by Tobo was the focus of frenzied activity.

I asked, "What's over there?"

"Ten to twelve people trapped in one of the treasury strong rooms. We're send-ing water and soup down through bamboo pipes. They'll be all right."

"Uhm." I could imagine the nightmares they would suffer for the rest of their lives. "Just hang onto that stuff," I told Arkana. I studied the stone around the base of the red-streamer pole. "Tobo, are they conscious down there?"

"I don't think so."

"I'd hate to think they're just waiting to do something obnoxious when we dig them out."

He said, "We can just leave them there. Without water they'll die."

"It's a solution." But not one that interested me. Only Booboo would really suf-fer. "Suvrin, may I?" When he nodded I beckoned some men who were standing around awaiting instructions. If the girl was aware I was sure we would get a dose of "love me" real quick. Which meant only people in Voroshk clothing should do the final digging.

The Khadidas and Daughter of Night had crawled into a corner of their hiding place when the collapse came. The walls had held up just enough. But they had not had time to collect food and water.

Sadly, my baby did have a lamp and supplies and did make a valiant attempt to keep right on enscribing the Books of the Dead, perhaps in hope of lending Kina enough strength to save her. She could not have had much hope otherwise.

I thought a lot about what Booboo had been through in her near quarter century. About what had been done to her and what she believed she was. The loving part of me thought it might be a priceless mercy if she was saved the cruelty of reawakening.

It never got beyond being a notion. No argument I could present would ever convince Lady that that was appropriate. She wanted a little Lady so badly.

I discovered the Radisha beside me. It was amazing how much she had aged. She even carried a cane. "It's true, you know," she said in a weary voice.

"What's that?" Though I knew what she was going to say.

"The coming of the Black Company did mean the end of Taglios. Just not the way we imagined."

"All we ever wanted was to pass on through."

She nodded, keeping her bitterness contained.

"You think we were hard on Taglios? Consider how happy the Shadowmasters must be."

"But you haven't finished with Taglios," the Prahbrindrah Drah observed, joining us. "I've just heard what happened to Lady. How is she?"

"Stable." He was another of those men who had been infatuated with my wife at one time. "And you're right. In a way. As long as people try to push us around people get hurt. But that shouldn't last much longer. We're close to where we have to go." I stepped forward, spoke to the men digging, first in the language of the Children of the Dead, then in Taglian. "We're getting close. Hold up till those of us who are protected can help. Tobo! Girls. They're almost through over here."

Not far off more interior brickwork surrendered to the seduction of gravity.

127

Taglios:
And My Baby

The soldiers created a precarious opening through which someone might wriggle. I asked for a lantern, meaning to be first inside, but Tobo seized it when it arrived. I did not argue. He was better equipped than I.

Seconds after the boy began to duckwalk a blast of urine-colored light ripped through the opening. It glanced off Tobo, hit a block of stone, scattered. It was a potent blast. Stone melted. And one stray ricochet found the Prahbrindrah Drah.

The results were ugly. And instantly fatal.

"That was it," Tobo called back, unaware of the disaster. "That's all he had. He's out of it now. Croaker, help me drag them out."

The Radisha began to wail.

The boy recognized the scope of the disaster immediately. The Taglian empire was, as of this moment, without an acceptable helmsman. Was without legitimate direction. "It'll have to wait a minute," I said. "The Prince is hurt. I want to get him to medical care right now." Maybe, just one more time, we could pretend the supreme authority was fine but staying out of sight. Soulcatcher got away with it. The Great General got away with it. Why not my own band of opportunists?

I feared there had been too many witnesses, though Suvrin and Aridatha took up the pretense immediately and the Radisha herself joined me after only a few heartbeats. She put on a creditable show of threatening me with serious unpleasantness if her brother happened to die.

Now aware that political disaster threatened, Tobo launched some glitzy distraction. To which I paid little attention because I was desperate to get the Prince out of the public eye. There was a lot of flash behind me, and changing colors playing through the ruins. A big bunch of masonry went down. And Shukrat began helping Tobo pull the Khadidas out of the ground.

Aridatha's men hauled the Prince's litter away.

The Prince seen to, Arkana and I began to ease through the rubble toward the hole. I beckoned more stretcher-bearers. The thing being dragged into the light did not look dangerous. It looked like an old, worn-out version of a Goblin who was already dead.

"You want these now?" Arkana asked.

"Hang on just another minute. Get him over here, guys. On the stretcher. Easy. Easy! Tobo. Can you wake him up? Just for a second? Long enough for him to recognize me and what I'm doing?"

"Probably. If you want to risk it." There was a choke in the boy's voice. He looked at the spear and the ugly hat and wanted to believe that I had a way to reach the Goblin trapped inside the Khadidas. The Goblin who was always like an uncle to him.

"Oh, shit!" I said. "Wait! Wait!"

"What?"

"I just had an ugly thought. About how Kina might react through Lady if we drive the devil out of Goblin."

Tobo sucked in a bucket of air, released it. "I don't see how she could work that. But why take a chance? She is the Mother of Deception. Shuke, honey, do me a favor. Get the small carpet from my room. Just fold it up and bring it back. We'll use that to haul them away."

Shukrat jumped onto her post and zipped away. While he waited Tobo had an awning erected to keep potential rain off Goblin, then snaked back into the hole. He did not ask for help so I stood back with Aridatha and Arkana, insides turning over, awaiting my first glimpse of Booboo.

I asked Singh, "The fires under the rubble never go out. What the hell keeps burning?"

"Five hundred years worth of archives. Everything that belonged to the Inspector General of the Records. It'll make for interesting times when we try to put things back together."

Shukrat, the little darling, obviously knew her way around Tobo's quarters. She was back with a small, folded flying carpet before the kid himself poked his head back out of the hole. With Arkana's help she snapped the frame into position, stretched the fabric taut.

Arkana finally found nerve enough to speak to Aridatha directly, in a nonbusiness capacity. "You think it's going to rain?"

You could see she wanted to melt like a slug freshly sprinkled with salt. All that work to find the nerve to speak and something that feeble was all she could get out. When fat raindrops had begun plunking down at random intervals nearly a minute before.

She was just a kid.

They had the Khadidas on the flying carpet now. And a couple of soldiers, one Taglian and one from Hsien, had hold of a pair of ankles.

"You all right, Pop?" Arkana asked, holding onto my left arm.

"She looks just like Lady did the first time we met." In a time of terror. There was terror here, now, but of an entirely different sort.

"Then your wife must have had some filthy hygiene habits in her younger days."

"Ah, but she was eager to learn. Tobo, can you make sure Booboo doesn't wake up until I want her to?" I did not want to have to cope with her witchery. "And let's keep these two away from each other from now on. We don't need them getting their heads together."

"We don't need them, period," someone muttered. Shukrat, I realized. Shukrat did not like the way Tobo kept eyeballing the Daughter of Night.

Nor did my other adopted offspring particularly approve of the contemplative stares of Aridatha Singh.

Tobo called, "Croaker, you want to wake up yourself? Just for a minute? So you can take a look at her? See if anything's missing or broken?"

One of the city soldiers told another that everything looked just fine to him. A little soap and some clean clothes . . .

I never thought I would be a father and have to pretend not to hear such remarks.

The man was right. She was a beautiful child. Exactly like her mother. And like Lady's, most of her beauty lay right on the surface. I had to remind myself not to be taken in by what I saw or by what I wanted to feel. My emotions would not be trust-worthy. They might not be my own. The Mother of Deceit had not left the game.

I knelt beside my daughter. My emotions were engaged indeed. I felt a thousand years old and utterly powerless. It took a major application of will to touch her.

Her skin felt cold.

In moments I reported, "She's got lots of bruises and scrapes but there isn't any serious damage. Nothing permanent. She is dehydrated." She shook each time I touched her, as though I was massaging her with pieces of ice. "She'll recover, if we take care of her. Put her in with Lady."

Tobo said, "You'll need somebody to stay with her. Somebody who can control her."

"I will."

"I will."

Shukrat and Arkana both volunteered.

Well. Were they *that* concerned about competition from a beat-up, unconscious woman who knew absolutely nothing about men?

I would bet Tobo was grinning when he said, "All right, ladies. Work yourselves out a schedule. Croaker, what do you plan to do about Goblin?"

Suvrin seemed a little irked. Events were going forward without consulting the new Captain of the Black Company. But in matters concerning Booboo and the Khadidas he was no expert.

"Stash him. I'll wait till I'm well-rested to deal with him. Meantime, we need somebody to crawl into that hole and collect up all of Booboo's scribblings. Somebody from Hsien, preferably. Somebody illiterate. We'll take no chance anybody will read that stuff. I'll take care of it. But right now I'm going to go take a nap. I'm totally exhausted."

Taglios:
Another Great General

I was worried. I pranced from foot to foot like a little boy at a wedding who really needed to pee. It was another day and I still had not gotten started with Booboo and the Khadidas. Giving them and their Goddess any time at all was bound to lead to mischief.

But I had more immediate responsibilities. The fighting was over. Our obligation to the dead had to be handled now. And a huge city, with many dead of its own, had to be kept on a tight rein. Recent disasters would encourage plotters and conspirators.

The Children of the Dead knew how to put on a memorial for fallen comrades. Deep-voiced drums muttered and grumbled. Horns conjured forth the mood and gloom of a chilly, rainy morning despite a bright, cloudless winter sky. The soldiers paraded in all their brilliant colors, with all their thousands of banners. The locals were suitably impressed. We sent Sleepy off in more style than she could have hoped for while she lived. We said our good-byes to a great many people.

Then we stood back and rendered appropriate honors as Aridatha Singh directed equally large, if not nearly so dramatic, ceremonies honoring those who had fallen on behalf of the Protectorate. And when that was done we joined the local soldiers and the most important men of the city in honoring the Prahbrindrah Drah.

His funeral was the grandest I ever attended. I developed the distinct impression that all those leading men had gathered, however, to eyeball one another suspiciously rather than to mourn the passing of a ruler none had seen since they were young.

Aridatha Singh was popular with these men. Because Aridatha Singh had gathered to himself the loyalties of the survivors of the Second Territorial Division, the Greys, and the commanders of the rural garrisons nearest the city. Aridatha Singh had become the most powerful man in the Taglian Territories, despite having done little to acquire that power—except to be competent and a nice guy.

They say that when the hour comes, so will the man. Sometimes fate will even conspire to put a competent, honest man in the right place at the right time. Almost overnight the graffiti began giving Aridatha Mogaba's old title, Great General.

Now, if he could just manage to get by without antagonizing the occupiers.

I tried to keep an eye on Tobo but that was difficult with a kid so talented.

129

Taglios:
Open Tomb, Open Eyes

The hours of ceremony ground me down. I wanted to put myself away for another long nap. But I refused to give the Queen of Darkness any further respite.

"These are them," Arkana told me in perfectly colloquial bad Taglian, indicating eight bitty wooden kegs. "Eight different men took turns crawling in there and stuffing papers—and everything else they could find—into a keg. Which I had sealed up as soon as the man came out. By an illiterate cooper."

"You are a treasure indeed, daughter dear. Gentlemen, let's build us a bonfire." I had brought a couple of carts loaded with wood purchased from a wood seller whose usual customers were people who needed firewood for funeral ghats. I had been surprised to find he had any stock left, considering recent events.

The gentlemen I spoke to all hailed from Hsien. They knew only that the eight kegs contained the hopes of life of a monster more blackhearted than the legendary Shadowmasters who had tortured the Land of Unknown Shadows. And that was all they needed to know.

The pyre went up quickly, the kegs scattered throughout it. A fraction of me bemoaned the fate of the latest incarnation of the Books of the Dead. I hate seeing any book destroyed. But I did not interfere when the oil splashed and the fireballs zipped in.

My reluctance might be Kina trying to manipulate me.

I stayed there until I was confident that my natural daughter's life's work had been consumed completely by the flames.

In some myths Hagna, god of fire, is Kina's mortal enemy. In others, when she is in her Destroyer avatar, he is her ally.

The more I am exposed to the Gunni pantheon the more confused I become.

"What task now?" I wondered aloud.

Everyone but Arkana and a few curious street kids, the near-feral ones called jengali, had moved along. A ragged, bemused white crow had been hanging around, too, but it had nothing to say. It had been doing a lot of sticking close and keeping its beak shut lately.

"Time to wake somebody up, Pop. Your wife, your daughter or the Khadidas."

I surveyed the workmen clearing rubble. Most were civilians now, supervised by soldiers there just to keep them from stealing any treasures they unearthed.

The masonry had stopped collapsing. The fires had burned out. The popular consensus was that an all-new palace should be erected, once the old structures had been cleared away.

I could not imagine what treasures and surprises might surface if they did demolish and remove the whole rambling monster. No one ever knew the palace in its entirety. No one but a long-dead wizard named Smoke.

The death pyre of the Books of the Dead attracted more jengali, who wanted to take advantage of the warmth.

S hukrat glowered at Arkana. Seemed Arkana was not doing her share of Booboo watching. And Arkana did not care if Shukrat was pissed off.

I noticed a change in Lady. She did not seem to be in a sort of coma anymore. She seemed to be in a normal but deep sleep. I threw open a window. I am a firm believer in the health benefits of fresh air. The scruffy white crow appeared almost immediately. I asked, "How long has this been going on?" I had my back to Booboo. Cleaned and groomed and dressed in decent clothing she was quite the sleeping beauty. I tried not to look at her long. Seeing her still ripped at my heart.

"What?" Shukrat asked. She stuck her tongue out at Arkana.

"The snoring. Lady didn't snore before." I meant since she had fallen under the spell. Before, she had snored for as long as I had been sleeping with her. Though she refused to believe it.

Shukrat said, "She started right after we brought the Daughter of Night in. I didn't think anything about it."

"No reason you should."

Arkana nodded. "I never noticed her not snoring."

The white crow chuckled from the window sill. I asked, "Did she snore when she was a kid?"

The crow made a noise. The girls looked at me, then at the bird. No dummies, they realized right away that it was not just an albino with bad personal habits. Being sorceresses they soon understood that it was a genuine crow, too, rather than some creature whose usual form was no form, and out of sight.

"Assuming she is sleeping, she's been there a long time. You'd think she would've wakened on her own." I touched my wife gently. She did not respond. I shook her, much less tenderly. She groaned, muttered, rolled onto her side, pulled her knees up. I said, "Don't give me that stuff. It's time to get up."

The girls smiled. They felt my relief.

She *was* just sleeping now, even if that had been going on for a long time and might go on for a while more.

"Come on, woman! We've got work to do. You've had enough sleep for ten people."

"She's sure been getting my share."

Lady cracked an eyelid. At the same time she muttered something incoherent that sounded suspiciously like one of her traditional early morning threats.

I said, "All that rest hasn't improved her disposition any. I'll remember this next time she claims lack of sleep is why she's cranky."

"You want me to dump a bucket of cold water on her?" Arkana asked. She could be a presumptuous little witch.

"She does need a bath."

Lady growled again, but this time in a lame attempt to be cheerful.

I told her, "Don't even try to be nice." The way the human body works, returning from a coma in a good humor is flat impossible.

Her throat was dry and tight. After we dealt with that, she asked, "Where are we? How long was I down this time?"

I had lost track.

"Fifteen days? At least. Probably more," Shukrat said. "You were sleeping for all of us. We were all too busy."

Lady examined her surroundings. She knew she had not been here before. She could not see Booboo from where she sat.

I told her, "The war is over. We won. Sort of. Aridatha Singh surrendered. We offered them good terms."

Lady grunted, mind not working swiftly. "Mogaba let him do that?"

"The Great General isn't with us anymore."

"I need to talk to you about that, Pop," Shukrat said. "I went out to that sandbar."

I signed her to silence. Something from the hidden realm would be around somewhere. I continued talking to Lady. "A lot of people aren't with us anymore. Including almost everybody who went to town with us the night you got hit. Sleepy, too, later on. In an ambush. Suvrin took over. He'll be all right. He'll grow into it. As long as we help him."

Arkana added, "Don't forget the Prince and General Chu. And Mihlos. I miss him."

"Because he panted around behind you like a horny hound dog," Shukrat sneered. "And you just led him on."

"And who went out of her way to make sure she wiggled and jiggled whenever he was around?"

"Girls?"

"What?"

"I'm just jealous. Where were you when I was Mihlos's age?"

Lady interrupted. "What else do I need to know?"

"The Palace fell down. We've occupied the city. Aridatha Singh is in charge now and gets Arkana wiggling and jiggling whenever he comes around. We don't know how the succession will work out. We captured Booboo and the Khadidas. We destroyed the Books of the Dead. Again. Booboo is right over there. If you want to see her." I extended a hand to help her rise. If she wanted. "She's pretty."

"I want. But I won't be able to stand up by myself. I don't think I'll even be able to sit up for long without help."

The crow snickered.

Lady gave the bird a long, hard look. Then she offered me its twin.

I asked, "How's your connection with Kina?"

"What do you mean, how is my connection?"

"Did I stutter? Is it still there? Is it stronger? Is it weaker?"

"Why?"

"Because I want to know. Why not answer me?"

The girls were startled. They looked like they wished they were anywhere else. But they spread out.

"She didn't take me over while I was sleeping, if that's what you're after. I did have some awful nightmares, though. It was like I was trapped inside her imagination for an age. But she ignored me. She had something on her mind." She came close to grinding her teeth with each word. She did not want to open up. "The nightmare went away a while ago."

I could understand. The only place I want to reveal myself, even a little, is here, where hardly anyone will ever notice.

"Did you have any sense of time? I'm thinking maybe something happening here changed what you were going through there."

"Sense of time? It was forever. And no time at all. Kina doesn't experience time the way we do. I don't think. She sure doesn't let it oppress her. Come on. Show me my baby. Before I collapse." She strained to get up.

Shukrat and Arkana got hold of her arms and helped her up. Arkana asked, "She always this cranky when she wakes up, Pop?"

"You're going to become part of the family, get used to it. You will if you don't take it personal." I chuckled when Lady asked me how I would like it if she stopped getting personal. "She's not bad today."

The crow hissed. Clearly, it did not care if Lady figured it out. In fact, what it said sounded like, "Sister, sister." Which was the taunt Lady had employed a few years ago, when she was looking out from behind the eyes of another crow.

Curious, the white crows. There has been one around, off and on, since the siege of Dejagore. Back then Murgen had been the mind behind the bird's eyes. Most of the time. Apparently. But was Shivetya the mind behind the crow-riding minds? Could he have had that much power to affect events outside the glittering plain?

That would explain a good deal. Maybe even Murgen's former difficulties with his place in time. But that would mean that Soulcatcher was not responsible for much of what we believed were her crimes. I was not sure I wanted it to be that way.

The bird snickered. Like it could read my mind.

Soulcatcher always had had a knack for reading me.

"We lost Murgen, too," I said as we moved into position facing one another over the unconscious girl.

"I understood that. From your having told me how many we lost. That would be everyone not wearing Voroshk clothing. Correct?"

"Except for one damned lucky soldier from Hsien who managed to be behind the right person at the right time. Lucky is now Tam Do's official nickname."

"Must be in the blood," Lady muttered, forcing herself to look at the girl. "The women of my blood are fated to spend most of their existence trapped and asleep." She rested her weight more fully on the girls, extended a hand to touch Booboo's cheek. She lapsed into the language of the Jewel Cities. "Asleep like this was the only way I ever saw my mother. She was the one they told the first Sleeping Beauty stories about. Her Prince Charming never came. My father did. And he was content with her the way she was."

Now there was a slice of horror to lug around in the back of your brain: knowing that your mother was not even aware that you had been born.

And we like to whine about how cruel the world is today.

They were giants in the olden days.

We will be giants ourselves five hundred years from now.

"So this is our baby." She stared. "Conceived on a battlefield." Her emotions were plain upon her face. Never had I seen her looking more vulnerable.

"This is our baby."

"Shall we wake her up?"

"I don't think so. Not now, anyway. Life is insane enough right now without asking for more trouble."

That did not set well. Not at all. Lady wanted to establish some kind of emotional dialog with this flesh of her flesh. For my part, I found that now I had been exposed directly, the emotional distress was fading away. I do not believe my thoughts were skewed by might-have-beens and wish-that-weres.

Lady did concede that it might not be a good plan to waken Booboo without Tobo there for backup.

She did not do anything untoward but she did have the girls breathing nervously for a while.

Taglios:
Khadidas

Tobo was there to help when I wakened my old friend Goblin, who had become the unwilling vessel of the Khadidas.

It was not that difficult once Tobo's controlling spells had been cancelled. Tobo shook Goblin while I stood by. And once the little shit began to stir Tobo stood by while I nagged.

The little man's eyelids snapped open. The eyes behind them were not the eyes of the hedge wizard Goblin. I was looking straight into large chips of the darkness. Those eyes seemed to want to suck me in.

The mouth of the Khadidas opened, preparing to vent some infamy or blasphemy. I interposed One-Eye's ragged old hat between Kina's slave and myself. The effect was electric. The Goblin body convulsed as though I had whacked it with a hot poker. I slapped the hat down on its head.

"Lift," I told Tobo, who had placed himself at the head of Goblin's cot, out of the Khadidas's field of vision. I held the hat in place while Tobo raised Goblin into a sitting position. "It works. Better than I hoped."

"Better than I thought it would, for sure."

"One-Eye always did underplay it when he did something right." The wicked light had left Goblin's eyes. Now he just looked empty. Not even a thousand-yard stare, there. More like nobody at home at all.

"Do the spear."

I did the spear. But, man, was I reluctant to trust the wisdom of a dead man when it came to putting that potent a tool into the hands of a devil.

I stood it up in front of Goblin, its butt between his heels. I wrapped his hands around the black shaft. Then I shoved One-Eye's filthy felt relic down onto his head even more solidly. *Then* I gripped his hands hard, squeezing them onto the silver-and-black wood.

Life began to enter his eyes.

I told Tobo, "Not as dramatic as watching a baby being born but dramatic enough." Even a dummy like me did not need a map to see that we were conjuring up the real Goblin.

A Goblin in pain so deep I was aware immediately that only Lady could begin to understand.

I settled myself on a stool. Tobo eased Goblin onto a chair with an upright back, then planted himself on the edge of the cot. Goblin kept turning from one of us to the other, tears streaming but unable to speak, however hard he tried. He reached out to Tobo in a silent plea for contact.

"Careful of that hat," I said. "I'm already thinking about nailing it to his head." And thinking about how wonderful a friend One-Eye had been, too. Because he had foreseen some possibility like this and had invested his final years in making a rescue feasible.

I choked up for a moment, thinking I never had a friend who would go that far for me. Then I recalled that Sleepy had spent fifteen years working to exhume the Captured. And now, barely five years later, all those people but Lady and I were gone. Belly up. Up in smoke. Finished.

Soldiers live.

Not once had Sleepy ever behaved like she believed that she had wasted her life. But I am sure she had thought it sometimes. Regarding some individuals.

I said, "You ought to keep at least one hand on the spear, Goblin." We had done nothing to rid him of the Khadidas. The monster had been pushed back into the pit where it had lain till it had sprung forward to seize control, but now behind feeble barriers. The monster was much stronger than Goblin. We would have to work hard to keep it suppressed.

"What're we going to do with you?" I asked. And felt a twinge of guilt. Because I had plans for him already. Plans that might change the world.

"What do you think, Goblin? You going to help us help you hang on?"

Goblin was getting some muscle control back. He managed a weak, "Yeah," as he nodded his head, too.

I'm going to leave everything in the hands of you two gentlemen," Suvrin said. He nodded politely to Goblin. "I scarcely knew this man. And then mainly from the perspective of being the butt of practical jokes he and One-Eye played. Meaning I might not be disinterested even if I tried. What is that stuff around the bottom of that thing on his head?"

"Glue. That *thing* is a hat. You must've seen One-Eye wearing it. The old fart rigged it up with some spells, planning for something like what did happen."

"You told me."

"All right. The glue is because we don't want the hat to come off. Ever. If we could come up with a way that would leave him free to feed himself and scratch his butt we'd glue his hands to One-Eye's spear, too."

There is something about becoming Captain that takes the humor out of a man. It had gotten to Suvrin already. He never cracked a smile. He asked, "You gotten any useful information out of him? Not yet? When?"

"I don't know. He's coming around. Really. Remember, in practical terms he's been dead for six years. He's having trouble figuring out how to use his body again. Especially his tongue. Meanwhile, the Khadidas is still inside of him trying to take over again."

"And Lady?"

I was more concerned about my wife than I was about Goblin. She was acting strange. It did not seem like I knew her anymore. I had resurrected all my earlier worries about her connection with Kina. Kina was the master manipulator and planner. Kina schemed schemes ages long and many layers deep.

But Kina was slow. Very slow. Which was why she favored plots that required years to ripen. She could not handle swiftly changing fortunes.

"Lady is a puzzle right now," I confessed. "But a benign one."

Goblin made a gurgling sound. The Khadidas was working hard to keep him from talking.

Suvrin asked, "Do you know anything about the leading men of Taglios?"

"Not the current crop. Except for types. My advice would just be, don't ever turn your back on any of them. You could talk to Runmust Singh. If he survived the latest fighting." I had a feeling he might have been with Sleepy in that ambush. "Or you could just ask Aridatha to loan you a couple of advisors."

Suvrin seemed unusually amenable to consulting for a Captain of the Company. He told me, "We need to resume our lessons. So I can study the Annals."

I responded, "We need some peace for that. Maybe a few years. We could build a new Company while we're at it."

Goblin gurgled again and nodded.

The little creature was like a puppy in some ways.

I told Suvrin, "I need to talk to Goblin a while." Once our hesitant new commander stepped out, I said, "We need to work out ways around the Khadidas's interference."

Nod.

"And that's how we'll do it, I guess. Unless it can control more than your speech." I peered at the little man. He did not respond. I realized that I had not posed a yes or no question. "Can it do that?"

No.

"All right, then. The most critical question of all. Is the Khadidas in direct contact with Kina?"

No. And yes. And a shrug. So we proceeded to play a game of a thousand questions during which I seemed to go the wrong direction, no matter where I went, making him gurgle in frustration. His best efforts to speak seldom produced more than one recognizable syllable.

Eventually, despite my density, I got it. The Khadidas could communicate with the Goddess only when it was in control of the Goblin flesh. It could not do so when it was not in control.

That made sense. Some. Though I had been cautioned to remember that the Goblin I was interviewing was actually a ghost that had not been able to leave when its body died and had been reanimated by the breath of the Goddess.

"That is exciting news, Goblin. Look, I have a plan." Difficult as it was, I dredged a form of it up from its hidden place deep down inside me, hoping the Goddess had no way of listening in. My plan depended entirely on my understanding of the Goblin I had known for so long, hoping he had not altered drastically during the past two decades. A man might change a lot in that much time—if he had to spend part of it dead and enslaved by the Mother of Deceivers.

On the surface Goblin seemed to like my plan, as I presented it. Seemed willing to participate. Even seemed enthusiastic about plunging One-Eye's spear into the blackest of hearts.

I told him, "I don't want to waste one minute I don't have to. You understand?"

Nod. Even a gurgled, "Yes!" With enthusiasm. With outright eagerness.

"I'll be back soon." I felt almost bad, not telling a dead man all of the truth.

Around Taglios:
Aerial Recon

I found Arkana and asked if she wanted to go flying, nodding to indicate that she really did want to make a tour of the upper air. For the benefit of the curious I mentioned wanting to check rumors that troops loyal to the Protectorate were headed toward the city. One force had crossed the Main at Vehdna-Bota. Another was gathering out east, near Mukhra in Ajitsthan, where Mogaba had enjoyed considerable popularity among the tribes. Since those rumors were beginning to make a lot of people nervous nobody would be surprised that I would want to take a look.

And that is what we did while we were aloft, because it was work that had to be done. Doing the work, though, gave me time to talk to Arkana.

She replied, "I can see one big problem with your plan. Maybe. What happens to the plain and the Shadowgates? You asked me if I wanted to go home. The answer is yes. I don't think to stay, though. Just to see what happened there. To bury my dead, I guess you could say. But I don't see how that could keep from complicating everything else if I had to do it first because there wouldn't be any way later."

"You're right. And I need to do what I've got to do as soon as I can. Before Kina catches on." If she had not foreseen the possibilities already. Or learned of them from Goblin. Or Shivetya. Or from Lady, who was smart enough to guess what I was thinking. Sometimes. "Particularly before my wife catches on. Or starts thinking I'm chasing around."

We were approaching the River Main, heading for Vehdna-Bota. There were pillars of smoke north of the ford, away from the small settlement. But not many.

Arkana told me, "That's not much of an army."

"Not in any hurry to get into harm's way, either, looks like. There's plenty of daylight left they could use for traveling."

Not in any hurry. When we went down for a closer look we found men scattering like startled roaches.

"Somebody covering his ass," I said. "Making a show of honoring his obligations. That bunch will never actually get to Taglios."

We went back up. We talked, not just about what had to be accomplished. Arkana seemed able to relax, now. Seemed to have made peace with the bad times. Some manage that with comparative ease. Others remain crippled for life. Those are not the sort who remain soldiers. They become ex-soldiers and get intimate with wine or poppies.

I asked about her leg.

She laughed. "I can be one of the old folks now. I can use it to predict the weather."

"It's all right otherwise?"

"Yes."

"I do good work."

"Lots of practice."

"You get that in this racket."

We flew back toward Taglios, chatting in a relaxed way, me thinking that this was what it would have been like had Booboo grown up with her parents. Me fooling myself. Lying to myself. No child would grow up even as normal as Arkana if they had Lady for a mother and me for a father.

Maybe I had found the way. Adopt them after they have gotten through their formative years.

We were passing south of Taglios, going to scout the forces gathering in Ajitsthan, when Arkana spotted a billowing figure climbing toward us. "That's Shukrat."

"Have you two made peace? Real peace?"

"Sort of. Mainly because we've only got each other. From back home. If it wasn't for that we wouldn't even be talking. Partly it's because of family stuff. Things our parents did to each other. And partly it's us. She's too cute and too sweet and dumb as a bucket of rocks. But all she's ever had to do is make big eyes or bounce a little and look helpless."

"And you were the smart one. Always expected to figure it out for yourself."

"Yes."

"Well, you're growing up to be the prettier one, too. Shukrat's going to be all freckles and frump before long."

We slowed so Shukrat could catch up. She came up on my other side. I asked, "What's up, other daughter?"

"Croaker, I wanted to talk about what happened to those men on that island. That scares me. Really bad. I really like Tobo. A lot." I was sure she was bright red behind her facial wraps. She did blush easily. "But I don't think I want to be involved with anyone capable of doing that."

"We're all capable of that, Shukrat. Put in the right place at the right time and given a motive. It's the people around us that keep us from doing it."

"What do you mean?"

"I mean, Tobo cares about you. Probably a lot more than he's willing to admit. He's a passionate kid.

"Because he's what he is he's always had the capacity for huge evil, Shukrat. You know, nobody starts out to be a villain. Not the Shadowmasters. Not my wife or her sister. Not even the Voroshk. But being powerful can turn you villainous. Because there's nothing to stop you from doing whatever you want to do. Except for something inside you. For Tobo, for a long time, that something was his love and respect for his parents. He fought with Sahra every day but there was no way he was ever going to do something that would disappoint her. While she was alive. After she disappeared the brake on his dark side became his father. But now Murgen is gone, too. So there's only one more person whose good opinion is important enough to him to keep him from letting himself go."

Shukrat had to think about that for a while. She was nowhere as dim as Arkana claimed but there were times when it took her a while to get her mind wrapped all the way around complex issues.

"You're saying me caring about him is what will keep him from doing that stuff again?"

"Yes. I think that. But I also think you have to confront him with your knowledge and make him understand that you won't accept *any* excuses for behavior like that. Don't nag. Don't carp. State your case firmly and clearly, then shut up. Don't negotiate. You have to mark out an absolute limit he'll always know is there. And stick with it. You always have to know it's there, too."

Shukrat nodded.

While I waited to see if she got it I told Arkana, "I might turn out to be pretty good at this fatherly advice stuff."

"You're definitely long-winded enough."

"Thanks a lot."

"For the record, I think you're right. What you said to her."

"You know what she's talking about?"

"She warned me. In case I wanted to watch out for General Singh. Not long after you warned me about it. I had to go see what you were excited about, didn't I?"

The girl rose in my estimation every damned day.

T he force gathering at Mukhra was much more of a threat than that at Vehdna-Bota. It would mean major new trouble if Aridatha, as the new Great General, was unable to sell the concept of peace to Mogaba's old allies.

132

Taglios:
Wife and Child

Lady was sitting beside Booboo again. Or still. I pulled up a stool opposite her. "Want me to take over for a while? Give you a chance to get out and about and stretch your legs? The Green Dragon Banner Company have a wicked lamb stew going. Don't ask me where they found sheep in this madhouse."

She lifted her face. There were tear tracks on her cheeks. "Help me, Croaker. I can't stop thinking about how much was taken away from me when Narayan Singh stole her. How much that one event changed my life."

It changed all our lives. It affected everyone in this end of this world and hundreds of thousands in at least two others. But she was completely self-involved right now.

"Get up and get out of here," I told her. "Go get something to eat. Go flying. It's a beautiful, cool day. There're signs that things are going to start greening up soon. Go take it in. I want you to get hold of yourself before I go. I don't want to leave you here if you don't think you're all right."

"Go? Where are you going?"

"It's almost time to release the first contingent of the Children of the Dead. Some of us are going to scout the way south and across the plain. And get the guys at the Shadowgate busy collecting supplies. Why don't you come along? It'll get your mind off things."

"No. I couldn't. There isn't anyone here who can take care of her."

Damn! Now I saw where she was vulnerable. I saw the door the darkness would use to get in. If it had not done so already.

Clever me, though. I knew how to close that door. Forever. And I had just set myself up to take care of it without interference.

"Go get some stew. Strut around. Make the soldiers hate me for being lucky enough to have you." There was a time when every man did. When every man responded to Lady the way women did to Aridatha Singh. But those days were gone. And so were all those men but me.

I glanced down at Booboo, then up at the silent white crow standing in the open window. It certainly seemed to run in the blood.

The white crow was around a lot now, but was quiet about it. So far I had not forgotten to look around before I said anything I did not want overheard. I needed to keep my fingers crossed for the future, though.

Lady dithered.

I said, "If you don't get going I'll call some guys in here and have them hold you down while I paddle you."

For a moment the Lady I love peeked out of the dark place. She flashed a smile, said, "Promise? That might be fun."

Once she left I collected Booboo's hand and indulged in a little of the same despair. The girl's fingers were cold as death. But she was breathing.

The white crow found it all amusing. "You've become sickeningly domestic, lover."

I growled something.

"Ah, I know. You were so stubborn when I had you. But it might be fun to see what happened if somebody said you weren't, after all these years."

I grumbled.

"Well, maybe not fun for you." And, after a moment, in a different, sorrowful, almost little girl voice, "It could have been something amazing."

No doubt. And fatal besides, probably.

Glittering Stone:
A Dangerous Game

Only four of us flew south. Five if you counted that ragged-ass lazy crow riding the tip of Goblin's flying post. The little man was flying independently but his movements were limited by a tow rope and a safety harness, each of which connected him to a different companion. We told him it was for his safety while he was learning to manage the post but even dead he was smart enough to see through that. We did not want him haring off if the Khadidas regained control.

Goblin was much stronger now. He could manage most self care without assistance and many other uncomplicated tasks as well. He had a vocabulary of maybe thirty words. He could lay One-Eye's spear down for minutes at a time without risk of wakening the demon within.

We were blazing along through blue skies, cloaks streaming thirty yards behind, at an altitude low enough to panic livestock and send children running to tell skeptical parents. The girls whooped and shrieked, having a wonderful time. Whomever's turn it was not to mind Goblin soared and dove.

Spring was going to spring soon. With these kids that might become an adventurous season.

With spring would come the rainy season, too. Lots of wet and lots of ferocious weather.

I made a couple of brief side trips. The main one was a brief look at Dejagore, where life had settled into a semblance of normalcy and nobody was mourning the passing of one of the city's most famous daughters. Probably not one in a thousand people outside the garrison knew that Sleepy called Dejagore home.

The other side trips involved looking for evidence of the Nef in places where I thought I might have seen them before. I found nothing.

Since there had been no sign of those ghosts of the glittering stone, outside my own glimpses, I was pretty sure what I had seen had not been the genuine articles.

Tobo had expressed a suspicion that, had I not been imagining things, what I had seen were some of his hidden folk trying out disguises.

He believed some would do that just for the hell of it. The folklore of the Land of Unknown Shadows supported his contention. In fact, that sort of prank was a huge favorite.

So, probably, the Nef were less of a problem than I had feared. But a problem even so. Unless they *were* trapped in the Voroshk world.

Panda Man, at the Shadowgate, robbed me of that foolish hope. "They're out there begging and whining every night, Captain."

"Looks like you guys have made yourselves right at home." They had built themselves a tiny hamlet, complete with women and livestock, most of both showing signs of gravidity.

"Best duty we ever had, Captain."

"Well, now is when it starts getting tough." I spun out a gaggle of orders. Then me and my daughters, my pal the white crow and my dead friend, passed through the Shadowgate. Though I could see nothing I thought I could sense the pressure of the Nef inside.

The plain boasted a thousand patches of dirty snow. Old snow lay drifted against the standing stones on their west sides. The air was bitterly cold. The place was getting its weather from somewhere other than my native world. And it had an air of neglect. As though the residents had given up housekeeping and maintenance.

The neglect was less evident inside the nameless stronghold. The stench of human waste was gone. Evidently Baladitya had cleaned up after Shivetya's Voroshk guests. But there was a taint of wasted human.

"We need some light," I told the girls. Still competing with one another in some ways, both hastened to create those little will-o'-the-wisp glowing balls that seem to be the first trick any sorcerer learns.

The source of the odor was obvious instantly. Baladitya had fallen asleep at his worktable and had not yet awakened. The chill, dry air had done a lot to preserve him.

I was unhappy but not surprised. Baladitya must have been an antique when I was born.

Arkana and Shukrat made appropriate noises expressing sorrow.

"This isn't good," I muttered, staring at the copyist's remains. "I was counting on him to help me talk to Shivetya."

From somewhere in the darkness the white crow said, "Hi, there, soldier. Looking for a good time?"

Fumbling around after oil with which to refill Baladitya's empty lamps, I said, "Ah, yes. You. All is not lost. But neither is it found."

"What?" That voice was a high-pitched squeak. I wondered how she managed to produce so many of those, even when using a bird to do her talking.

"Trust." I recalled a time when anything she said scared the shit out of me. I guess familiarity does breed . . . something. I was almost comfortable with her. "Why on earth would you expect me to trust anything you say?"

It helped my courage, knowing she was buried and in a sort of undying coma.

"Shivetya won't let me lie."

Right. Call me a cynic. But I had a notion that the golem might have been with us more than Kina had, over the years. A notion that it would be impossible to untangle his manipulations from hers. A suspicion that he might be just as much a deceiver as she was when it came to maneuvering toward the end of the world.

"Right, then. Got your word, do we? I'm comfortable with that. Let's get started. Does the Goddess know we're here? Does she know what's in my mind?"

"Her attention is elsewhere."

The girls took over filling and lighting the lamps. They were good girls. They had learned to do for themselves. And they watched their daddy at work with respect and awe. Or, at least, they wondered what I was doing, talking to a crow that looked diseased. And having the crow talk back, like it was intelligent.

I told Arkana, "If you could read and write Taglian you'd understand all about this because you'd be able to keep up with the Annals."

"No thanks, Pop. Not even a good try. I said no yesterday, I'm telling you no to-day, and all you're going to hear is no again tomorrow. I'm not going to get pulled any deeper into your mob than I already am."

Which is what Suvrin used to say. Suvrin, who started out as a prisoner of war.

Shukrat said, "Don't even bother to look over here."

I had not considered Shukrat. I would not. But I did think Arkana might work out. If she would give it a chance. She had a personality suitable to be one of the gang.

"Recruiting season over?" the crow demanded.

"For now." I peered into the darkness, trying to make out more details of the golem. There was not enough light. But the demon seemed to be asleep.

Or at least uninterested. Which puzzled me, since I was there to set him free.

I shrugged. His indifference would not slow me down.

I collected Goblin. I led him well out onto the floor of Shivetya's vast hall, away from other ears. Had I brought a lamp along I would have been able to see how lovingly the floor detailed the features of the plain outside.

I reviewed for the little man. "Kina is a very slow thinker. We need to get this done before she understands that we're already here, that we intend to strike, and that we do have a weapon puissant enough to do the job." One-Eye's spear shimmered all the time here. Filaments of fire slithered over it in unpredictable patterns, excitedly. The edges of its head groaned as they sliced the air itself. It seemed to sense that it had come home.

No one could argue that the spear was not a masterpiece of a peculiar sort of art. No one could deny that in creating his masterwork One-Eye had reached a level of inspiration seen nowhere else in his long but rather pathetic life.

Many an artistic masterpiece has fallen into that same category: the sole triumph of the genius of its creator.

"Once we reach the black veil across the stairwell she'll start to realize her danger. You'll have to move fast. Get up as much speed as you can so you can drive the spear as deep as you can. The Lance of Passion wasn't potent enough. But it wasn't made for godslaying. One-Eye's spear is. You could name it Godslayer. You know. You were there during most of the years he worked on it. When we were in Hsien it became his whole career."

Goblin had been there. But that Goblin had been alive, not a ghost still trapped in the flesh it had worn in life. At least part of the time this Goblin was an agent of the very monster this Goblin was going to kill. Or maim. Or just irritate.

As the doubts began to circle round me like Tobo's hidden realm friends I kept right on talking, explaining yet again why he was the only one of us who could make the strike. And he really did find my arguments compelling. Or else his mind was made up and the hopes and wishes of others no longer mattered.

The Goblin thing climbed back aboard his flying post.

I pushed my own forward, so I could see the tip of his and make doubly sure I knew which one he was riding. "Let's go downstairs, then," I said. "I'll be right behind you. Your post is spelled to come back on its own if you're unconscious." He knew. He had been there when Shukrat fixed it to do that. "If that doesn't work I'll swoop in and grab you, drag your ass away. If you want, I even brought an extra hundred yards of line to hook onto your safety harness. We can tie it to your belt."

The little man looked at me like he thought I was trying too hard. He had been working himself up for a suicide mission, convinced that the destruction of his flesh was the only way he could rid himself of his parasite and find rest himself.

I played the whole scam by ear. I had no real idea what Goblin really wanted or what he hoped to achieve with the false life he had been given. I had not been able to guess much about him when he was alive. The only thing I knew for sure was that he was working crippled. Doing without One-Eye was, for him, like doing without one of his limbs.

And he did want to hurt Kina. That was never in doubt.

A long, difficult discussion ended up with me chagrined a bit as I finally got the message that Goblin was not deeply interested in backup that would pull him out if things went sour. He wanted backup that would make sure the job got done even if he failed.

I do not know why I had so much trouble recognizing and understanding Goblin's program. Possibly because I was concentrating on getting things to go forward exactly the way I wanted. Goblin had told me almost everything before, one time or another, when I had been focused enough to ask.

Personally uninclined toward mortal self-sacrifice, I had trouble overriding my cynical nature—particularly as regarded someone as self-indulgent as Goblin had been for so long.

Goblin brandished One-Eye's spear and told me what I had already told him but had not done. "Time to go downstairs, Croaker." He got it all out in a single, bell-tone clear sentence.

I patted myself down. Final check. Still not sure I was ready for this.

Taglios:
Best Served Cold

The only check on Tobo was Lady, who could not maintain her level of interest. The only check on Lady was the wonder boy. And he had other things on his mind. And altogether too much of that touched by the darkness.

No Shukrat, no Croaker, no Lady paying attention. Nights in the city lost their traditional noisome urban charm. Some people began to compare the new age to a time when the Protector had loosed her murderous shadows upon the city, for no more obvious reason than existed behind the unleashing of the horrors out there now.

The fact that there were few actual deaths went unremarked.

The Unknown Shadows enjoyed themselves greatly, tormenting the living. As did Tobo, who found himself free to do anything he wanted.

Except in his dreams.

A woman had begun to haunt those. A beautiful Nyueng Bao woman who seemed to be the embodiment of sorrow. He understood in his heart that this was his mother as she had appeared when she was young, before she had met his father. Usually she was not alone. Sometimes she was accompanied by a young, unbent Nana Gota. And sometimes by another woman, always gentle, always with a smile, forged of steel tougher than that of Uncle Doj's sword Ash Wand. This woman, who had to be his great grandmother, Hong Tray, never spoke. She communicated more with a disapproving eye than Sahra could say in a hundred words.

His vengeances were unacceptable to all these women who had created and formed him.

Tobo could not determine if he was being touched by the ghosts of his ancestors—a possibility entirely in keeping with Nyueng Bao beliefs—or if the women were the product of some conscience-stricken cellar of his mind. The darkness within him was strong enough to make him want to defy them.

None of them wanted to be avenged.

Sahra's ghost warned, "You won't just hurt yourself, darling. If you go on you'll be running into a trap. Put aside your pain. Embrace your true destiny and let it lift you up."

Hong Tray studied him with eyes like cold steel marbles, agreeing that he had come to a crossroads. That he was about to make a choice that would shape the rest of his life.

He knew, of course, that the words the ghost women spoke, and the ghosts themselves, had to be metaphors.

He had no trouble with his conscience when he was awake. So he tried to avoid sleep.

Sleep deprivation clouded his judgment even further.

The hidden folk always reported the same thing: Aridatha Singh would not leave his offices. He worked day and night, seldom doing more than catnap, as he tried to hold the Taglian world together by the weight of his own will. The struggle to maintain control ought to have beaten him down and have shredded his spirit in days. Most men would have started cutting throats to more swiftly facilitate reconstruction and assuage frustration. Aridatha just beat people down with reason and public opinion. He treated with no one in secret. He made sure the world knew when someone refused to handle the city's business publicly.

Obstructionists were becoming known. The mood of people displaced by strife and fire was not forgiving of traditional factionalism.

The unthinkable happened. Several men of high caste were beaten savagely. Shadar were seen in the crowds, encouraging the violence. No one wondered, though, and Aridatha Singh did not appear to be aware of that personally.

It was deep night but a light traffic continued to and from the City Battalions barracks containing Aridatha Singh's headquarters. A dark fog slowly gathered around the place. People grew sleepy. Shadows scampered among the shadows. For an instant, here and there, little people or little animals were visible briefly—had anyone been awake to see them.

Tobo came walking through it all, so tired his eyes were crossing, so sure of himself that he had not brought his flying post nor had he armored himself in Voroshk black. So sure of himself that he did not double-check reports from his Unknown Shadows.

He expected to walk in, complete his revenge, and be gone with no one the wiser. Aridatha Singh's fate would become a great and terrible mystery.

The hidden folk could tell him nothing about Singh's office. They could not get inside it. It was kept sealed airtight. But the sentries outside were snoring.

Tobo shoved the door. It gave way only grudgingly, swinging inward. He stepped inside, panting. Across the room three men had fallen forward onto a worktable or lay sprawled in their chairs. "Not good," Tobo muttered, unexcited by the presence of the potential witnesses.

"Not good at all," Aridatha said, lifting his face off the desktop.

Tobo just had time to catch the swish of air behind him before something hit the back of his head with force enough to crack bone. He went down into the darkness knowing he had been betrayed, that he had walked into a trap. The Unknown Shadows scattered in every direction, going mad, making Taglios a city of nightmares.

Sahra, Gota and Hong Tray all awaited Tobo on the other shore of consciousness. All three told him that this was a disaster entirely of his own devising. He could have avoided it simply by doing the right thing.

He had been warned beforehand. He had not listened.

Sahra's sorrow was deeper than ever Tobo had known it before.

Taglios:
The Mad Season

Lady dealt with the temptation easily for several days after Croaker departed. She kept reminding herself that all she had to do was hang on till he got back. By then the Daughter of Night would not be the Deceiver messiah anymore. She would be just plain Booboo.

Sense told Lady to be patient. But emotion knew no patience. And emotion threatened to devour her. Despite her long history, emotion had stolen control.

She broke after only four days.

Lady took a quick look into the hallway to make certain no one was likely to intervene, then settled on a stool beside her daughter's bed. She plucked the ends of strands of spells keeping the girl asleep and constrained. She worked quickly and deftly. She had been studying Booboo's bonds all those four days.

Those spells unravelled almost as if they had a will of their own.

Lady proceeded with an uncharacteristically naive haste. That part of her that had grown hard and bitter in the real world mocked her for her childishness. This was the world. Her world. The real world. There was no reason to expect any good to come her way.

Booboo's eyes snapped open with mechanical suddenness. The color was right but still they were not the family eyes. Nor were they Croaker's eyes. They were eyes colder than Lady's own in her cruelest hour. They were the eyes of a serpent, a naga, or a deity. For an instant Lady froze like a mouse caught in a snake's stare. Then she said, "I'm an incurable romantic. The essence of romance is an unshakable conviction that next time will be different." She tried to assert control while the girl was physically too weak to act.

The girl's "love me" aura had touched Lady already, so subtly that she remained unaware of it until it was too late.

Lady had not worn her Voroshk costume. There was no shelter from the storm.

A vibration developed down deep inside her, at glacial speeds. As it built she watched the power of the Goddess slowly fill the Daughter of Night. The buzz within Lady included a trace of mirth. She understood that her unpracticed maternal emotions had been discovered and manipulated, ever so subtly, for a very long time. So subtly that she had not suspected. Worse, so subtly that she was not adequately prepared to respond to any disaster.

Nevertheless, she was a woman of incredible will, having had ages to practice employing it.

There was a countermove left.

In an instant Lady made the cruelest decision of her life. She would regret it forever but knew the choice she made would leave her with the least painful longterm wounds.

The Lady of Charm had centuries of practice making terrible decisions quickly, and just as many years of practice living with the consequences.

From her belt Lady drew a memento of her brief passage as Captain of the Black Company. The dagger's pommel was a silver skull with one ruby eye. The ruby always seemed to be alive. Lady lifted the blade slowly, her gaze locked with that of the Daughter of Night. The sense of the presence of Kina grew ever stronger between them.

"I love you," Lady said, responding to a question never asked, existing only within the girl's heart. "I will love you forever. I will always love you. But I won't let you do this thing to my world."

Lady could do it, in spite of all. She had slain as dear before, when she was not yet as old as the child lying beneath her knife. And for less reason.

She felt a madness creep through her. She tried to concentrate.

She could kill because she was filled with a conviction that there was no better thing she could do.

Kina and the Daughter of Night both strove to crack Lady's terrible will. But the dagger descended toward the girl's breast, its progress inexorable. The Daughter of Night quickly became the hypnotized prey, unable to believe that Lady's blade kept falling.

The tip of the knife touched cloth. It passed through, found flesh, then a rib. Lady shifted her weight so she could drive the blade between bones.

She never sensed it coming. The blow, seemingly struck to the right side of her head, was powerful enough to hurl her sideways a half dozen feet, into a wall. Darkness closed in. For an instant there was a living dream in which she saw herself trying to strangle her child instead of stabbing her.

The Daughter of Night felt fire rip across her chest as her would-be killer flung toward the wall. She screamed. But the agony that moved her was not that of her wound. It was a black explosion inside her mind, a sudden tidal wave of knife-like shards of a thousand dark dreams, of a scream harsher than ten thousand whetstones sharpening swords, of a rage so vast and red it could be called the Eater of Worlds.

That blow was violent enough to fling her upward and to one side. She came down sprawled across the still form of her birth mother. But she did not know. She was unconscious long before gravity placed and posed her.

A whiff of old death, of graveyard mold, hung in the air of the room.

Fortress with No Name: Godstalking

Goblin was too eager. Twice I felt compelled to yell at him to slow down. He plunged down the dark stairwell at a pace I could not match. Even wearing the Voroshk apparel the bruising impacts with the walls became too much for my nerve.

We had not yet gone as deep as the ice cavern where Soulcatcher lay when I bellowed an order to stop. Wonder of wonders, this time Goblin heard me. And listened. And responded when I told him we had to go back up.

"What?" He turned the word into a two syllable whisper from an old tomb.

"We can't do this in the dark. We'll beat ourselves unconscious before we get down there. Or at least get there too beaten up to think."

He made a sound that signified reluctant agreement. He had had a few unpleasant collisions of his own.

"We have to go get lights." Why had I overlooked something so obvious? Because I was too damned busy looking for the subtle and the sneaky, I suppose.

The stairwell was much too tight to turn the flying posts. We had to back them up. That was a slow, humbling, sometimes painful task. And things did not get much less humiliating when we did reach the top.

The girls and the white crow awaited us. In attitudes so smug they could be read even though the ladies were clad for action. Arkana swung a lantern back and forth.

For an instant I suffered an entirely irrelevant worry because I had not brought my Widowmaker costume. It seemed appropriate to the situation. But definitely not necessary.

All that armor ever was was a costume.

Now Shukrat waved a lantern back and forth. And laughed.

"Not a word," I grumped.

"Did I say anything?"

"You're thinking it, darling daughter."

She raised her lantern higher, the better to see what I was wearing. My apparel was in slow, creeping motion all around me, repairing extensive damage. "Not a word from me, old-timer. You know your Shukrat. Honors her elders to a fault. But I'm going to laugh, now. Please don't jump to conclusions and think that it's at you."

Arkana laughed harder.

Goblin made a series of noises, depleting his vocabulary fast.

"He's right. Give us those lanterns. We need to get this done." I hoped my dimwit failure to consider the need for light would not be the one little thing that got us destroyed. And that that was the last little thing I had been dumb enough to forget.

Goblin took the lantern from Shukrat. He headed down into the earth again. He was not nearly so hurried this time. Possibly his lust for revenge had begun to cool.

I took Arkana's lantern. The white crow flapped over to the tip of my post. Before I finished telling it that traveling with me might not be a good idea Shukrat had another lantern going and was helping Arkana get herself another lit.

The girls had been ready for us.

I bickered with them all the way down to the ice cavern. They had fun with me all the way. They refused to listen to my warnings.

The white crow decided the cave of the ancients would be a fine place to detour.

I bellowed, "Don't touch anything in there! Especially don't touch yourself." I continued, mumbling, "When will I learn to keep my big damned mouth shut?" It would be a great and wonderful irony if the bird's touch was Soulcatcher's undoing, after all her lucky years.

Goblin got the hurries again. When I tried to slow him down he told me, "There's something going on with Kina! She's starting to stir."

"Shit!"

Keeping up was impossible, until we reached the black barrier. There Goblin's nerve failed him. There he froze, recalling the horror of the years he had spent on the other side.

"Goblin. We're almost there. We've got to do this. We've got to do it now." Numb as I was to things supernatural even I could sense Kina's proximity and her heightened awareness. Which must not be our fault. Her attention was focused elsewhere. "Now!" I said with more force.

Behind us the girls had begun whispering, troubled. They sensed much more than I ever could.

I told them, "You two go back upstairs now. I guarantee you that you'll be glad you did. Especially if things don't work out for us. Goblin."

He reclaimed his courage. Or maybe just found his hatred again. His face hardened. He started forward.

"Don't rush," I stage-whispered as he passed through the black barrier. "Girls, I mean it. Start running now. There *have* to be some survivors." I pushed through the terrible barrier behind Goblin, nearly messing myself with the fear. Despite what I had told the little man this was no time to be slow or tentative. Once we breached the barrier Kina knew that we had come. Her slowness would be our only ally.

Once I breached that barrier I flung myself into the anteroom area outside the entrance to Kina's prison. Goblin lined himself up to charge. I had to do several things at once: encourage him, prepare myself to weather what was about to happen and do my thankless bit to make this deicide work.

Got to keep the whole picture in mind. Got to do each thing on time, in the right order, just the way you worked it out over the last few months.

As Goblin surged forward I placed my flying post into the angle where the floor met the left-hand wall, then plastered myself against the wall above it and willed my Voroshk clothing to form a protective scab over it and me. Then, in light almost too dim for use, I found the right page in the First Father's notebook. I kept my protection open just enough to let me watch Goblin hurtle straight at Kina and, to my surprise, drive One-Eye's spear into her temple. I had expected him to go for the heart.

I completed the cantrip that would destroy Goblin's post, finished shutting me and my post in. Then I allowed myself to feel lower than snake shit because of what I was doing.

I had been hard at work justifying myself to myself for months. And had carried on. But now it was happening. And when it was over I would have to live with my deceits forever.

The entire universe shook. The cavern where Kina lay was big but it was confined. The stairwell was the only escape the products of that violence could find. The energy wave pounded at my protection.

I clung to the stone wall, beneath layers and layers of Voroshk material, while the universe howled and shuddered. I swore that if Kina was powerful enough to get through this I would enlist in her service myself because the only thing tougher than her would be the guys who tied her up. And they had not been seen for several millenia.

The noise began to fade. But I had trouble hearing it go. The roar had deafened me temporarily.

I hoped the girls did head back up the way I told them.

I hoped the violence did no damage elsewhere. I doubted that it would. A major earthquake had split the plain open without destroying the ice caves or doing any harm down here.

I willed the Voroshk clothing to open a crack through which I could see. If need be, if Kina *had* survived but was injured, I would push my post in there and blow it, too. And if I survived a second blast I would start hoping that I did not suffer a heart attack or starve to death while trying to climb those miles of steps.

The material protecting me had been so traumatized that it took ten minutes to respond. It twitched and shivered and crawled, moving in small surges, as it tried to heal itself.

Once I had an eyehole I discovered that there was nothing to see. Intense bright light still burned inside Kina's cell. It might have been fading but it was going slowly if it was.

It was half an hour before I could look for details without having my eyeballs hurt. Just as well. It took that long for my protective outfit to heal and relax sufficiently to allow me off the wall.

Those outfits are made smart. They take just long enough recovering to keep you from doing something stupid.

I mounted my post and moved forward, knowing, as I went, that my protection would not survive another blast soon.

At first I could find nothing. Later, after the light faded some more, I began to discover bits of what might once have been tooth or bone embedded in various surfaces. Of flesh, be it Goblin's or the Goddess's, there was no sign.

In fact, I doubted that any of the tooth and bone fragments could have belonged to any mere mortal. The explosion had been that violent. More violent, even, than those that had destroyed the Voroshk Shadowgate, that had initiated the collapse of the Palace.

Kina's destruction had somehow added vast energy to the explosion.

My post was not behaving quite right. It stuttered and was slow to respond. It must have gotten rattled around some even though I had done my best to protect it.

Once the light faded round where the Goddess had lain I saw what looked like a long black snake lying in the rubble of Kina's rock bed. It was the only nonwhite thing in the place, other than me.

I approached carefully. For all I knew that was the bone of darkness that had snuggled next to Kina's heart. And I was prepared to believe that anything I saw or experienced in this place would be illusion.

Kina was the Mother of Deceit.

One of the great powers of the Deceivers was their ability to leave you doubting everything and trusting no one.

The black thing was no snake. It was the deformed remains of One-Eye's spear. It had come through the violence with surprisingly little damage. It was just twisted and bent a little, and lightly charred on its surface. The metal inlays had been only slightly distorted by intense heat.

Man, he must have put some artful protective spells onto that thing.

I gathered the spear, went and made sure that I was securely attached to my post, then gave it the command to take me back to base point.

Taglios:
The Melancholy Wife

We wobbled down out of the sky like a family of mangy buzzards. My Voroshk clothing still had not healed completely. The girls were more tattered than I. The blast had caught them climbing the stairwell. They had bruises over most of their bodies.

The real miracle was how well all the posts had come through, though none remained unscathed.

The Grove of Doom rose to meet us, welcoming us like a mother greeting lost children.

Bizarre thoughts and images kept worming into my mind now. They worried me. They made me doubt that Kina was actually gone, not just in hiding.

Jokingly, Shukrat told me what I ought to be worried about was Kina's father and husband wanting to get even. I did not laugh. To me it seemed like a worthy concern.

The Grove of Doom was empty. Of humanity. But some birds had moved in already and there were a few small animals in the underbrush now.

There was no sense of grim foreboding about the place anymore.

"We did it," I sighed. "Finally. For real. No more Kina to torment the worlds."

Not having spent their lives under the threat of the Year of the Skulls, the girls were less excited.

The white crow settled on a nearby branch, divested itself of a dirty feather. "Are you sure?" The beast was having lots of fun tickling my fears. She and I seemed to be headed for a long and unpleasant relationship—unless I kept my promise to Shivetya.

I said, "If there was any place in this world where Kina's survival would manifest itself, that would be here. This place has been almost a part of her since her cult began. And that might have been here. I don't think she could disengage herself from the Grove even if she wanted to."

"Then let's get going," Shukrat said.

Arkana sneered, "She can't wait to get her hands on Tobo again." She was not being mean-spirited. And Shukrat's counterfire included a mention of Aridatha Singh and Arkana's terminal timidity. Which did turn Arkana serious.

"Hey, Pop. What do you think Kina being gone will mean to the Daughter of Night?" Walking on eggshells. But worried by the glances she had seen Singh lay upon the girl, not entirely believing that every man reacted like that. "Is she going to turn normal?"

Shukrat showed a sudden interest, too.

"I don't know, baby doll. I worry, though. She's been connected to Kina from the second she was conceived. Seems like to her it would be about like you or me having our liver ripped out."

I was more worried about my wife. Her losing her connection to Kina would devastate her. Everything she was, in her own heart, was tied up in her being the terrible sorceress. Without Kina to leech from she would be just another middle-aged woman gone dumpy and grey.

The weather had been problematic all the way up from the Shadowgate. We had had to skirt rain storms and thunderheads again and again. That had cost us more than a day.

Now, only twenty miles out, there was no evading the weather. Except by going up way high, where it was icy cold and almost impossible to breathe, then zigging back and forth between seething mountains of cloud while being tossed and taunted by turbulence. Shukrat and Arkana were dead set against getting caught aloft in a thunderstorm. Arkana told me, "Think what might happen if you got hit by lightning."

I did not think long. There was no one I wanted to see badly enough to have my post blow up between my legs. I headed for the ground. We holed up in a Gunni farming village where the locals treated us with the same cautious respect they would have shown a trio of nagas, the evil serpent people Gunni myth has living deep underground but surfacing to plague humanity on numerous occasions, always a couple, three villages away.

We did not steal any of their babies or maidens, nor their sacred cattle, nor even their sheep. I found it interesting that they were sufficiently flexible religiously to raise sheep for sale to folks like the Vehdna, who were going to gobble them right down.

The lightning quit stomping around soon after midnight. We left our hosts with coin enough to have them blessing our names. Which we never mentioned.

There was no lightning now but there was a steady, light rain. The Voroshk apparel helped, but only some. I was cold and miserable and my pet crow, now riding right in front of me in order to get under a fold of my cloak, was so far gone in the miseries that it no longer bothered to complain.

The Company barracks seemed both unnaturally quiet and abnormally alert. Armed sentries appeared everywhere. "Looks like Suvrin's worried about an attack."

"Something must have happened."

I hovered. "You girls sense anything?"

"Something definitely isn't right," Arkana said. "I don't know what."

"We'd better find out." Gone less than two weeks and everything had gone to hell?

Survin explained. I controlled myself and did not run off to see Lady before I got the whole story. Suvrin told me, "General Singh has Tobo in a cell that's isolated so the Unknown Shadows can't reach him for instructions. Singh won't let anyone visit Tobo. We do know the kid is hurt, though."

"Obviously. Or he wouldn't put up with this. He tried something stupid?"

"Oh, yes. And I don't have the horses to get him out of it."

"Now you do. If you want to bother. What about Lady?"

"We don't know what happened. Nobody was there. And I've had no reports recently. Last I heard, she was conscious but sullen and unresponsive. And the girl is worse. Your effort was successful?"

"Pretty much. Which probably explains Lady and Booboo." I did not expand. "It feels creepy around here."

"Gets more that way every night. Tobo's friends aren't happy. And they get unhappier by the hour. But Aridatha isn't intimidated."

"We'll see if we can't change that. After I see my wife." Or the person who used to be my wife.

I took Arkana with me. Just in case. "Don't say anything. Just stay in the background and cover me," I told her.

There was a guard outside my quarters but he was not there to keep anyone in. Probably not to keep anyone out, either. He was an early-warning marker for Suvrin. He and I exchanged nods. He broke Arkana's heart by failing to notice that she was an attractive young woman. I guess that was supposed to be obvious despite the Voroshk outfit.

Lady sat at a small table. She stared into nothingness. At some time she had been playing a solitaire-type card game but had lost interest long ago. The lamp beside her was almost drained of oil. Black smoke boiled off it because its wick needed trimming.

Wherever she was looking, it was plain she saw nothing but despair.

She had lost all interest in maintaining her appearance.

I laid my good hand on her right shoulder. "Darling. I'm back."

She did not respond right away. Once she did recognize my voice she pulled away. "*You* did it," she said, more thinking out loud than actually speaking to me. "*You* did something to Kina." Only in the "you" was there any human emotion.

I glanced back at Arkana, to see if she was paying attention. This would be a critical moment. "I killed her. Just the way we contracted to do." If there was any fragment of the Goddess in her now, that ought to provoke a reaction.

It did but not the physical attempt at revenge I would have preferred. Almost.

She just started crying.

I did not remind her that she had known this day was coming. Instead, I asked, "How is Booboo? How is she taking it?"

"I don't know. I haven't seen her."

"What? Before I left we couldn't get you away from her long enough to eat."

The dam broke. The tears started. She became a woman I had not seen before, busted open like an overly ripe fruit. "I tried to kill her."

"What?" She had spoken very softly.

"I tried to kill her, Croaker! I tried to murder my own daughter! I tried, with all my will and strength, to put a dagger in her heart! And I would've done it if something hadn't knocked me out."

"I know you. So I know there was a reason other than you just thought it might be fun. What was it?"

She babbled. Years of holding everything together gave way. The floods swept all before them.

The timing matched my assault on Kina. Lady's violent reaction to Booboo could have been caused by fear leaking through from the Goddess. Booboo's own behavior would have been shaped the same way.

Lady sobbed for a long time. I held her. I feared for her. She had fallen so far. And I had been ballast almost every foot of the way down.

All my fault? Or just the spark and romance of youth's summer turning to the bleak seasons of despair of old age?

Arkana was a good daughter. She stood by patiently throughout the emotional storm. She remained there for me without intruding on my wife's black hours. After we left I thanked her profoundly.

"You think she'll be able to pull herself back together?" Arkana asked.

"I don't know. I don't know how to make her want to. If she did, I wouldn't have any worries. She's got an iron will when she wants to direct it. Right now I'm just going to try to keep on loving her and hoping something happens to sting her with a spark of hope."

"I don't know if I could stand being completely powerless, either. I might kill myself."

"Nine hundred ninety-nine people out of a thousand live their whole lives without having a millionth of your power. And they get by."

"Only because they're completely ignorant of what they're missing. Nobody mourns losing what they never had in the first place."

She had me there.

The full meaning of Lady's melancholy would be denied me forever because I was never able to experience life as she had at the opposite extreme. Whereas she knew my way of life very well indeed.

And that might be contributing to her despair as well.

138

Taglios:
The Lost Child

Booboo was worse than Lady. She was lost inside herself. She had real guards watching her. They told me she had not done anything but stare into infinity since she recovered consciousness. Not once had they felt any urge to serve her or ravish her.

One guard was a Shadar who had followed Sleepy since the Kiaulune wars. He told me, "Suruvhija Singh and her children are taking care of her."

I felt a slight twinge. Iqbal Singh's widow. Favored by Sleepy. But I had been unaware that the family had survived the fighting south of Taglios. I had been too centered on my own preoccupations to look after the welfare of Company dependents.

The Daughter of Night was clean and well-groomed and had been dressed carefully. She sat in a rocking chair, which was an unusual piece of furniture in these parts. She was aware of nothing outside the boundaries of her mind. She drooled on her pretty white sari, which was only a shade paler than her near-albino skin. Someone had placed a rag where it would catch the drool.

Speaking of albinos. The white crow had managed to arrive before me. But it was being very careful not to piss me off these days.

It had overheard enough, here and there, to suspect that I might have a great deal of influence on its future.

Shivetya had given us an unbelievable amount of help in return for our promise to end his stewardship of the glittering plain. I meant to keep that promise. I try to keep all of the Company's promises. Keeping our promises is what separates us from people like the Radisha, who try to screw us rather than keep their word when that seems inconvenient.

I circled Booboo twice. She gave no sign she was aware of me. I knelt in front of her. Her eyes were open. Her pupils were tiny. Her eyes did not track when I moved a finger back and forth in front of them.

I backed off and considered options. Finally, I led Arkana into the hallway, told her what I wanted to try and how she could help.

We rejoined Booboo and the bird. Neither appeared to have moved a muscle.

Arkana and I separated, each moving slowly, as though hoping to drift around behind Booboo without being noticed. Once there we just waited. And waited.

It is hard to be patient when you are Arkana's age. Eventually she began to fidget. Which caused the occasional faint whisper of motion, after which she would even stop breathing for a while.

After a time so long even I began to get restless I signalled Arkana forward. Doing her absolute best to remain totally silent she dropped to her knees beside Booboo's right rocker, out of sight behind the girl's right ear but with her face so close Booboo might be able to feel the warmth of her presence. I did the same on the left. Neither of us moved till my knees were about to kill me. We tried to avoid breathing on the girl.

I nodded.

Arkana whispered, "Sosa, sosa," so softly that I could not hear her. So softly that even someone who did hear the words whispered directly into her ear would not be able to make them out.

I have no idea why she chose to say that. I leaned closer so the warmth of my presence would be a hint more obvious. I nodded.

"Sosa, sosa." No louder than before.

The skin on Booboo's neck twitched.

I smiled at Arkana, winked.

Treachery will out.

"Sosa, sosa."

Slowly, the girl began to turn her head toward Arkana, the child within unable to restrain her curiosity.

It was not that she had been faking. Just that nothing obvious was going to sneak past her palisade of despair.

I got up and drifted so she would not discover me without making a special effort.

Arkana gave me a look which asked how I had known that Booboo could be reached. I shrugged. Just intuition, I guessed. A conviction that her curiosity could be wakened if it was teased with sufficient subtlety.

But what now? How to hold her attention forcefully enough to keep her from running away again?

Soon the girl was seeing and hearing us perfectly well. But still she did not respond. Still she would not answer questions.

She had no will to live. And I could see why. At no time had there ever been anything in her life but Kina and the struggle to release the Goddess. Never had there been anything but the quest to bring on the Year of the Skulls.

Suruvhija appeared. I had not known her in the days when she and her husband joined the Company. She might have been a beauty, then, but I doubted it. She was not now. And none of her children made you want to jump in and hug them. But they were good people, if sad.

"You got her to wake up!" Suruvhija said. "That's great."

"Now we need to keep her that way. Any ideas?"

"Why?"

We all turned to the girl.

I asked, "What?"

"Why do you trouble me? Release me. I have no reason to live. There is no future. There will be no salvation and no resurrection now. There will be no age of wondrous rebirth."

She was wide awake now, but bleak, depressed. I dropped to my knees in front of her, took her hands in an effort to keep her engaged with the world outside her head.

"What does that mean? What you just said."

She seemed puzzled by the question. I spent a few minutes demonstrating my ignorance of her faith. I hoped a chance to explain might animate her.

I have not yet encountered a true believer who could resist an opportunity to expostulate upon his particular truth. Booboo was no exception, though she was a slow starter.

I did not interrupt until near the end. Until that point she did not mention anything I had not heard before, somewhere, in some version. "Excuse me," I said. "I think I missed something. The Year of the Skulls isn't the end of the world?"

Suruvhija's oldest boy, Bhijar, arrived with food and drink. I made sure Booboo got served first. She sucked down a pint of water before telling me, "Yes, it *is* the end of the world. Of *this* world, the way it is *now*. It's a *cleansing*. A time when all *evil* and *corruption* get swept away and only those souls with a *genuine* chance of redemption get left on the Wheel of Life."

I felt confused. I felt lost. I did not understand. I knew the Deceivers wanted to hasten the coming of the Year of the Skulls. That was pretty much what their cult was all about. I knew most Gunni wanted the opposite, but believed that the coming of the Year of the Skulls was inevitable. Someday. It was one of the Ages of Creation, the Fourth Age, ordained at the dawn of time. But this was the first I ever heard that there was supposed to be something on the other side. Particularly something apparently positive.

I murmured to myself, "All evil dies there an endless death." Then I asked, "You're telling me Kina's ultimate task was to clear away all the human dross so that good and righteous men can pass on to paradise?"

Exasperated by my density, she shook her head violently, then went to work trying to explain.

I whispered to Arkana, "Have them bring my wife."

I am not as dim as I pretended with my daughter that evening but I admit I never did get what she was trying to explain. However, I did realize that she truly believed that by destroying Kina I had deprived the world of any opportunity to get past its current age of sin and corruption into an age of enlightenment.

I guess Kina had been meant to devour all the demons again, only this time those would have been the devils of human kind who make life and history over into torture chambers.

The Lords of Light were going to have to take it from the top, hatching themselves a whole new scheme for worldly redemption. Assuming they were still around somewhere themselves.

Lady arrived, accompanied by Bhijar. She melted the moment she saw that Booboo was awake.

I watched, numb, as she took my place on her knees in front of the Daughter of Night. This was my wife? This clump of raw sentimentality was the woman who used to be the Lady, once able to inspire an entire empire with the terror of her name?

I did not listen. I have to admit that I was embarrassed by her behavior. Because I had not realized that there was so much sloppy emotion bottled up inside her. Around me Lady always clung to shreds of her old image . . . whenever she was not lost in her own realm of self-pity.

The whole scene seemed to amaze the Daughter of Night. She did not know what to make of it.

Suruvhija became embarrassed, too. She hustled her brood out of the room. The boys went quickly, unable to stand so much sentiment. Suruvhija herself offered me a look of commiseration before she shut the door.

I tried to tell Suruvhija I was thirsty. My throat was too dry. I went after her. I stumbled as I crossed the room. Not that that made any difference. Mental clumsiness was my real downfall.

I stepped into the corridor and called after Suruvhija, "Please bring some more drinking water. We're all still dry."

She nodded her understanding. She was embarrassed again, this time because she was alone with a man who was not her husband. I was about to say something to spare her when Arkana yelled at me.

It took me a moment to get back through the doorway.

Booboo had a rumel, a Deceiver strangling scarf, wrapped around her mother's throat. Her eyes were dark with the last ghost of Kina. Her strength was, obviously, supernatural. Arkana was having no luck breaking her hold. And that little blonde was no weakling.

I needed not die to get sent to hell. I had an instant to pick which torture I wanted to suffer for the rest of my existence.

I slapped Booboo with my bad hand. She did not let up. I punched her. She rocked. Blood gushed from her nose. She did not ease up on the yellow silk cloth. I drew the dagger that is with me all the time, that normally gets used only when I am eating. I reached out and pricked the skin right under her left eye.

And still she did not stop.

The white crow said, "This is Kina's revenge, Croaker."

Which hell?

Lady was almost gone.

I stabbed the girl in the arm.

She hardly even bled.

I stabbed again, trying for the elbow joint.

No good.

I tried to cut the tendons in her wrists.

All the while Arkana was still trying to pull her off from behind or to break her grip on the silk cloth or to cut that cloth.

I launched as violent a blow as I could manage. When that did nothing but rock the girl's head back again I lost control. As the saying goes, I saw red.

When Arkana finally stopped me I had stabbed my own daughter more than twenty times. I had not killed her, though. Yet. But she had given up her hold on the strangling cloth.

Possibly too late. Lady was hacking and gasping, still choking. I got down and started trying to clear her windpipe. There seemed to be some damage to her larynx.

Arkana remained calm. She summoned help.

"Where did Booboo get the strangling scarf?" I asked. "She didn't have it before we went south." She had been stripped naked, scrubbed down, and dressed in new clothing. Then she had been placed in this room. So someone had brought her the rumel. A secret Deceiver. "We need to find out exactly who visited her." I did not want it to be Suruvhija, though she was instantly the logical suspect. Except for the fact that she was a woman. Hitherto, my wife and daughter had been the only women we knew to have been admitted to the secret brotherhood.

Still, this was a time of great changes. Suruvhija's sorrow and slowness of wit could be an act.

They do not call them Deceivers for nothing.

139

Taglios:
The Great General

The villain was not a Deceiver after all. He did not understand what a Deceiver was. He being Suruvhija's son Bhijar, whom Booboo had pulled in with her "love me" effect, working him only when no one else was around. She had sent him to a secret member of the Strangler brotherhood. He had gotten the killing scarf there. That had happened while we were in the air, coming home from the glittering plain.

The boy received only what punishment his mother thought was appropriate. The Deceiver who supplied the rumel, though, soon went the way of his Goddess. Along with a number of friends. There would be no mercy for Stranglers until the last was dead.

While others rooted out the truth I stayed busy with Lady and Booboo. I soon realized that I did not have the skills to save either. I summoned the best physicans from the Land of Unknown Shadows. To a man they told me what I did not want to hear.

Sorcery was the only hope for either woman. And Tobo was the only one with a command of the appropriate sorcery. Arkana and Shukrat could not help much. They knew little about the healing arts.

I told Suvrin, "Regardless of my personal motives, the boy is one of us. We can't leave him in a Taglian cell."

Suvrin had a little too much of the politician in him. Too much of the kind of mind willing to let an individual go so the rest will not be inconvenienced. He wanted to avoid a confrontation with Aridatha Singh.

I continued, "You *do* need to get into the Annals, Captain. You need to understand completely what it means to be a brother of the Black Company."

"Maybe I do. Until I do I'll run things the way I am now."

I did not argue. I had not expected any other answer. I met Shukrat outside, shook my head. She tested her sleep spell on the men Suvrin sent after me to make sure I behaved. That spell worked perfectly.

Shukrat and I went looking for the Great General.

Arkana kindly flew high cover.

We were going to bust Tobo out.

The flaw in that plan was, we did not know where Tobo was being held.

So we had to go ask Aridatha. Being more careful than Tobo had been when it came to invading the Great General's quarters. Shukrat prepared the way with her sleep spell. It all started out so well I was hard pressed not to look on the dark side and expect a trap.

Singh was not easy to handle unconscious. At least not easy for a gimp old man and a mite of a teenage girl. Nevertheless, we got him aboard my post before he was missed, then took him way up high into the clouds, and through, into the moonlight.

I had Shukrat wake him up.

"We need to talk, Aridatha. And you need to stay calm while we do. Because it's almost a mile down to the ground."

Singh was a cool one. He collected himself. "What do you want?"

"Tobo. Where is he? I'm asking, counting on you to continue being concerned about Taglios. About what new fighting would do to the city."

Singh did not say anything.

I told him, "You're doing a good job of riding the tiger. But that tiger is going to get a chance to run wild if I end up having to drop your ass from a mile up in the sky."

He considered that, suspecting that I might not be bluffing. "You could start a new war."

"*You* could."

"The man tried to assassinate me."

"He won't do that again," Shukrat told him. "We're going to have a talk, Tobo and me. When we're done he'll stop doing stupid things forever." She did not sound like she had any doubts. She did make it sound like Tobo had a surprise coming.

I said, "To lay your mind at rest, it won't trouble me a bit if we get into a new fight with you people. I don't have much left to live for. I can burn Taglios to the ground without compunction. Unlike some, I don't love the place. It's done nothing to win my heart."

Arkana said, "If he kills you there won't be anyone to look out for the Radisha." The Radisha had become regent despite tradition because Aridatha Singh insisted. Strongly. And nobody wanted to argue with the Great General. Even out in the provinces resistance to the new order seemed to be weakening, almost as if it was just too much trouble to fight over all of this when things were going so well otherwise.

Arkana did not give a rat's ass about the Radisha's welfare. She just wanted Aridatha to survive this incident.

"Just tell us where Tobo is," I said. "Shukrat and I will bring him out." Slowly, slowly, I tilted my post forward. Timing its arrival well, a gap in the clouds appeared below, allowing the moonlight to get through and reflect off the surface of the river. We discovered that, when he could actually see how high he was, Aridatha Singh had a fear of heights. It proved to be one of those fears which evades reason's control.

We set him down on the north bank of the river. Arkana stayed with him. I wondered if she would find the nerve to betray her interest.

Taglios:
Brain Surgery

Before Tobo could help me with my women, I, with the help of the best physicians and surgeons among the Children of the Dead, had to bring him back from his head wound. His Taglian captors had done nothing for him. He was two-thirds of the way down the path to a lonely grave.

There were no other Nyueng Bao with the Company anymore. The handful who had reached Taglios with us had stolen away to their native swamps soon afterward.

Tobo required delicate surgery to clear a dozen dangerous bone chips off the surface of his brain. I did most of the work myself, using my fellow surgeons as my other hand. The job took twelve hours. Shukrat was there every second. Sometimes I thought the ghost of the boy's mother was looking over my shoulder.

I collapsed moments after we finished, my physical and emotional reserves utterly spent. Some kind souls saw to it that I got into a bed.

Taglios:
Family Matters

I t had to be afternoon. Storm season thunder rocked the old Greys barracks. The roaring hiss of the deluge ate up almost all other sound. The air was cool to the point of feeling nippy. I told myself to enjoy the cool while I could. Once the rain stopped the heat would return. And the air would be damp enough to steam vegetables.

A whole different, pounding roar developed as wild winds began to slam and kick the barracks. Hail had begun to fall. Heavily. The streets would be filling with Taglian children determined to harvest the ice. Some surely would be injured by large hailstones. It happened frequently.

Shukrat came in. She did not look cheerful. Suruvhija followed her, bringing food and drink.

I asked, "How bad is it? Is it infection?"

Shukrat was puzzled for a moment. "Oh. No. Tobo is all right. He was even awake for a minute a little while ago."

So. The way she did not go on told me where the real problem lay.

When I jumped up, nearly injuring myself in my haste, she barked, "Take it easy! Getting in a dangerous hurry won't help." And, when I failed to calm myself enough to suit her, "You won't be fit to help anybody if you show up emotionally too ragged to cope."

She was right. An old man like me, in my professions, got plenty of exposure to that truth. Not only fear, but most emotion, is the mind killer. We do stupid things when we let emotion take over. Then we are forced to endure the consequences for the rest of our days.

I took deep breaths and drank cold water. I told myself I could handle even the worst news because I have been dealing with bad news all my life. "Lead on," I told Shukrat.

Soldiers live. Bad news is part of the life.

Arkana and the white crow were with Lady and Booboo when I arrived. Suruvhija had gotten there ahead of me. She slipped out right away, with a murmur of gratitude for excusing her son from the worst consequences of his actions.

It was not a good day for me physically either. I was having to use my cane.

Both of my women were lying on their backs, making no noise. I saw no immediate cue as to what the crisis might be. The crow paced back and forth on a shelf above Lady's cot. Arkana perched on a chair beside my daughter.

I went to my wife first.

Lady was breathing. Barely. And having to work extremely hard at it, gasping and fighting for every breath. I groaned. "I may have to cut her throat open below the obstruction." The operation might save her life but her vanity would be sorely tested. The results are never pretty.

I felt relieved as I turned to the girl. And guilty, because I felt so much relief. Soldiers live.

Booboo was gone. But it had only just happened.

That ripped my guts out.

Arkana told me, "There was someone with her every minute, Pop. It was like she just didn't want to make it." She made me take the chair.

"Oh, I understand that part. She didn't have any reason to go on. We took everything that meant anything away from her. But knowing she wanted out, in here," and I tapped my temple, "doesn't do anything to stop the bleeding in here," tapping my chest. I drew a deep breath, let it go in a long sigh. "Tell Suruvhija to come back in."

Once the little Shadar woman returned, I told her, "Buy as much ice as you can get. I want to pack my daughter in ice." I touched Booboo. She was still warmer than the surrounding air.

Shukrat asked, "What's up? What're you going to do?"

"I'm going to take her down to the ice cave." We had to go back to get the Children of the Dead back across the plain and to keep our word to Shivetya. Maybe sooner was better than later.

The white crow made a little sound, simply a device for getting my attention.

I said, "She's first in my heart. If that's what it takes to save her, then I'll put her down there with you, too."

Suruvhija was gone. I hoped she got no grief trying to buy ice. If anyone tried to keep her from getting the money I would be tempted to break some bones.

I did not reflect on what my response, as Captain, would have been toward an underling with my present attitude. The Words Immortal are: That Was Different.

The first ice arrived not much later. Booboo had chosen the perfect time and season to die. We bundled her in a quarter ton of hailstones, inside heavy blankets, which we sewed shut. Lady's flying post, slaved to Arkana's, was just able to hoist the weight.

The fly of indecision bit me. I wanted to get the girl into the safety of the cavern before nature had its way. But I did not want to be away from Tobo and my wife and run the risk of disaster here.

Shukrat assured me, "I'll damned well make sure Tobo is all right. And as soon as he's able I'll have him help Lady. If you're not back. Now go. Do what you have to do."

"Come on, Pop," Arkana told me. "Once we put on some altitude that ice isn't going to melt nearly so fast."

"Yeah. Shukrat. If anything happens . . . get more ice. Come on down. Maybe Shivetya can help."

Before we left I did have to visit Suvrin, to let him know what was going on and arrange it so he would know what to do if the fates ordained that this was the time when Croaker would not be coming back.

Even when you fly with the wind it takes a long time to get from Taglios to the fortress with no name. It seems to take forever when worry is your most intimate traveling companion. The white crow was not good for much of anything but an emergency source of provender. Arkana was a dutiful daughter, more helpful than she needed to be, but she was just too young. Most of her earnest conversation seemed so naive, or even foolish, that it became hard to recall a time when I was that age, still idealistic and hurling myself at life headlong, believing that truth and right must inevitably triumph.

I kept my opinions to myself. After everything she had suffered already Arkana did not deserve to have her surviving optimism skewered by my bitter cynicisms.

Perhaps her youthful shallowness was useful as a shield. It might help her shake off those early traumas. I have known people like that, who live only in the present moment.

142

Glittering Stone: Bitter Desserts

Soon after we placed Booboo in the cave of the ancients, a scant few yards from her aunt, I was stricken by a series of horrible thoughts.

What got me nervous in the first place was the way the imprisoned Soulcatcher's gaze seemed to follow me everywhere as we brought the girl in and settled her, while Arkana set the stasis spells on her—as relayed to her by the white crow.

Paranoia struck deep.

Soulcatcher had control of the bird. And she knew all the ins and outs of the sorcery necessary to lock someone into the ice caverns—or to release a prisoner. She could let herself go.

The bird was not right there when that thought hit me. Else she would have known that I had realized the possibility. I covered up before it noticed.

I stood in the weak, sourceless, pale cold light and stared for a long time, without really seeing. My baby. Hard to believe.

"I never knew you, darling." A tear rolled down. I thought of all the cold, hard men I had known and wondered what they would think if they could see me now, having turned into a maudlin old man.

They might be envious of the fact that I had hung around long enough to become an old man.

The white crow came flapping in from wherever it had been, landed on my right shoulder. Wings slapped my face, stinging. "Goddamnit!" It had not taken the liberty before.

I do not know how long I wallowed in self-pity before the bird stirred me. Far longer than I realized at the time. The crow brought me back to this world of real trials and deep pain. "Arkana. We'd better head back now." My separation from Lady would be more than a week long before we reached Taglios.

It was going to be longer than that.

Arkana did not respond.

"Arkana?"

Arkana was not there.

The flying posts were not there.

Emotion is the mind killer.

In my worry about my women I had forgotten that my adopted daughter was the one Voroshk with a brain. The one who had said she was going to bide her time and pick her moment.

That moment had come and gone, it seemed. There was nobody down in that cavern but me and the scruffy white bird.

She had not been completely cruel. She took the key to the Shadowgates so the gimp old man had no way to get away but she did not make him climb all the way up out of that hole. Only part of the way. She left my flying post just far enough up to give herself a few hours' head start. Just long enough that I had no chance to catch her.

Shivetya manna makes a tiresome diet, however good you feel for the first few hours after you eat. Self-pity and self-accusation make bitter desserts. And a crow haunted by your oldest and dearest enemy makes for a somewhat less than ideal partner in exile.

After the anger faded and the despair subsided I helped myself to Baladitya's writing materials and went to work on bringing the Annals up to date.

There was no time in that place so I do not know how long that took. It seemed longer than it probably was. I began to worry because nobody came to see why we had failed to return. I feared that meant there was no one who could come. The most likely someones who might not be able to come being Tobo or Lady.

But Shukrat was healthy. How come she did not show up?

With no one else there I found myself talking to the crow more and more. And more as time went by, in an effort to defeat the gathering despair.

Shivetya watched from his huge wooden throne, evidently amused by my predicament. While I was amused by Soulcatcher's.

She did have the knowledge to get herself out of the ice cavern. She just did not have the hands. And I thought that was delicious.

I was five or six sleeps into my exile when the Nef returned, first appearing inside my dreams.

143

Fortress with No Name:
Sleeping with the Demon

Soulcatcher kept reminding me that she was in touch with the demon. That, in fact, as long as she remained attached to the white crow she would be little more than Shivetya's tool. This information did not seem newsworthy or particularly important until I suffered the visit from the Washene, the Washane and the Washone.

I had not been especially sensitive to them in the past. I knew them better from description than encounter. This time around made clear why that was.

Their ugliness invaded my dreams but only as a sense of presence little more concrete than that of the Unknown Shadows. Golden glimmers of hideous beast-mask faces in the corner of dream's eye, and scattered single syllable fragments of attempted communication, were all that I recalled after I awakened, sweating and shaking and filled with undirected terror.

Shivetya's gaze, directed my way, seemed more amused than ever.

I soon learned that his amusement had limits.

I had made him a promise. He could look inside me and see that I intended to keep it. But he could also see that I meant to stall for as long as it took me to arrange my own life to my satisfaction.

He had been patient for ten thousand years. Now, suddenly, his patience began to wilt.

I became aware of it first while I was sleeping. On a night when the Nef were almost getting through, my dreams filled unexpectedly with a presence that pushed in like a whale driving through a pod of dolphins. A big, unseen thing that approached like the darkness itself but without containing a thread of evil. Just a vast, slow thing that was.

I knew what it was and understood that it was trying to make a mind-to-mind contact the way it had with others before me. But my mind had a hard shell around it. It was difficult for ideas to get through.

Good thing Goblin and One-Eye were no longer around. They could have gotten hours of joy out of a straight line like that.

A couple sleeps more, though, and my mind had become a sieve. Me and Shivetya were yukking it up like a couple of old tonk buddies. The white crow was put out because she did not have a job translating anymore. I guess the demon had the sheer mental brute force to make contact with anyone.

I learned from the golem in the way that Baladitya had learned before me. I learned by being taken inside the demon's living dream, where past was almost indistinguishable from present. Where the wondrous pageant of the plain's history, and the history of the worlds it connected, were all remembered, in as much detail as Shivetya had cared to witness at the time. There was a great deal about the Black Company. He had chosen the Company as the instrument of his escape a very long time ago, long before Kina chose Lady to become her instrument inside the enemy force and the vessel that would birth the Daughter of Night, who was the intended instrument of her own liberation. Long before any of us were the least aware of all the pitfalls we were going to encounter on our road to Khatovar. But Shivetya chose better than did Kina. The Goddess failed to look closely enough at Lady's character. Lady was too damned stubborn and selfish to be anyone's tool for long.

There were just seven of us when some inexplicable urge made me decide to retrace the Company's olden journeys. And of those seven, now there is just me.

Soldiers live.

The Black Company is in Suvrin's hands now. Such as it is. It is headed south now, according to Shivetya's dreams, satisfactorily avenged, planning to cross the glittering plain back to the Land of Unknown Shadows. There are only a handful of Taglians and Dejagorans and Sangelis left to miss our world. The Company will become a new thing in a new world. And pudgy little Suvrin will be its creator.

Never before had there been anyone of the Black Company who had survived so long that he could see how vast are the changes time will sculpt even upon a band determined to stay one with its past.

When my thoughts ranged those bleak marches Shivetya always filled my head with ripples of amusement. Because those were almost invisible changes when compared with those that *he* had witnessed in *his* time. He had seen empires, civilizations, entire races, come and go. He remembered the gods themselves, the ugly builders of the plain, and all the powers that had come into and changed his estate and then had faded away again. He even recalled a time when he was not alone in the fortress with no name, a time when his devotion to duty caused his mates to nail him to his throne so they could desert without him interfering.

At long last I began to understand what had happened to Murgen in those long ago days when he had had so much trouble clinging to his place in time. Murgen was crazy, some, and Soulcatcher was involved, some—those were the days when Soulcatcher had found her way onto the plain—and Murgen never had a clue himself what was happening but behind everything else was Shivetya, carefully setting up his path into retirement. And, of course, Shivetya does not see time like the rest of us. Unless we demand his attention right here at the vanguard he floats everywhere, everywhen, reexperiencing rather than remembering.

Gods, how I envied him! The entire histories of sixteen worlds were his to *know*. Not just to study and interpret but pretty much to *live* whenever the mood took him.

I did have a question. *The* question of supreme importance if I was going to set the demon free. He had to answer it to my satisfaction if he wanted me to fulfill our agreement.

What would happen to the glittering plain if he was no longer here to manage it?

Fortress with No Name:
Arkana's Tale

Shivetya was never as powerful as Kina but he was a whole hell of a lot faster on his mental feet. It had taken the sleeping Goddess years to impact the world outside and create a vast paranoia concerning the Black Company. Shivetya it took just weeks. It would not have taken that long had he not reached out for a specific someone with a mind shell thicker than mine: Shukrat.

The demon was disinclined to connect with Tobo. Tobo had been his good buddy before but Tobo's behavior recently hinted at potentially troublesome character flaws.

Shukrat finally began to get the idea that there might be a problem causing the prolonged absence of Arkana and her beloved adopted daddy. Even when she did start to worry, though, she did not want to leave Tobo. Tobo was less popular with the Children of the Dead than he was with the Unknown Shadows. The men from Hsien might not give their utmost to pull him through.

The boy's health kept suffering one setback after another complication. The fact that the army was moving would not help his recovery.

Shivetya could show me the Company's southward progress. And did regularly. But I would not look in on Lady. My wife's condition was more grim than Tobo's. There was nothing I could do about it but it upset me so I just did not go where the pain was going to get me. Sometimes the blind eye is the least terrible way of suffering what we cannot make right.

Then there was Arkana.

The little blonde had run off in accordance with her own stated doctrine. Home to the world of the Voroshk. She used the key we had brought to enter the plain to make her exit. Because Shivetya was interested the once shattered Voroshk Shadowgate was almost completely whole again.

In Arkana's homeworld the war with the shadows continued, but sporadically. The shadows had been reduced to a tenth of their original number. The Voroshk had suffered as badly. Their world had been all but destroyed. Not one in a hundred peasants had survived an invasion so enthusiastic it is almost impossible to find a shadow on the plain these days.

Shadows kill. They prefer people but will prey on anything they run into. Even things you find under rocks. People are smart enough to figure out ways to get through the night. Not much else can.

The few survivors in the Voroshk world were starving. They had lost so many draft animals they could not plant. Their livestock had all been taken, if not by the shadows then by the Voroshk themselves. The Voroshk had no intention of sharing the common suffering.

Arkana had gone, had seen, had changed her uncertain mind. This was not what she wanted. But she had waited too long to turn back.

She was seen. Family closed in fast. And deprived her of her post and clothing. She became a prisoner of her relatives, who began formulating big breeding plans immediately.

The Shadowgate disaster had left the Voroshk with few women of childbearing age.

Arkana got elected to become queen ant for a whole new mob.

She would do what she had to do to survive. She would bide her time once again. Her uncles had confiscated her key to the Shadowgates but were unaware what it was. And she was not talking. They were the sort of men who would abandon the disaster they had created and go coursing off in search of new worlds to conquer. So much easier than rebuilding.

It was a good thing Shivetya had power enough to will the shattered gate to heal itself, though that might imply that the nonfunctional gates had failed because of benign neglect. In fact, recalling what Tobo and Suvrin had reported concerning their explorations, all the Shadowgates were crippled somehow.

Shivetya did not like anyone very much these days.

I let him know, "I have a couple of things left to do." Since my mind was no longer a mystery, he knew what already. And he did have a little patience left.

A pretty indulgent partner in crime, that old devil.

145

Glittering Stone:
Then Shukrat Came

Shukrat arrived while I was sleeping, dropping in through the hole in the roof. So entangled with Shivetya was I now that I knew she was there without noticing or paying much mind. My friend the white crow came and did the wake-up dirty deed. I sat up, rewarding the bird with some rude remark or other.

"Just trying to be helpful. You aren't leaving me much to do these days."

"Funny how being a prisoner reduces your options, isn't it? What goes around comes around and all that? But we can still be friends, can't we? Hi, cuter daughter. You finally got here."

Shukrat was exhausted but game. "So what's going on, Pop? Where's Arkana?"

"Well. Arkana got a wild hair, ran off home and now is knee-deep in shit." I explained.

Shukrat's reaction was, "Yuch!"

"Hey, you could be the most popular girl in town yourself if you give them the chance."

"They might try. They'll be sorry if they do. I didn't waste all my time with Tobo playing games. How come you know all that if she took your key and you can't go out poking around?"

"Shivetya and I have been getting to know one another. There isn't much else to do around here when you're waiting for your slower child to start wondering if you haven't maybe gotten yourself into some trouble."

"I see you did some writing, too."

"I'm running short on time, daughter," I said, revealing a secret never even shared with my wife. "I've had so much luck, for so long, that the law of averages is overdue to catch up. Any day. There's only one risk left that I'm willing to take. So I want to have all my shit in order before something happens. I want to check out knowing I did everything the Company could ask, and then some." My expectation that I do not have much time left has become an ever more powerful influence on my thinking since our return from the Land of Unknown Shadows. It has approached the level of obsession since I have been back here in the fortress with no name.

Shukrat proceeded with normal, journey-ending business while we talked, unloading her flying post. She swung down a large hemp sack that rattled as she said, "Let me get some rest, first, then we'll go rescue Scruffy Butt. Not because I give a damn what they do to her, you understand. Just as a favor to my Pop."

"I understand. I appreciate it. Maybe she can do the same for you, someday."

"Oh, yeah, that would be good."

"What's in the sack?"

She thought about being evasive, realized that there was no point. "Snail shells. Tobo didn't want me to travel unprotected. He worries about me."

"How is he?"

"He has good days and he has bad days. More bad than good. In his health and in his mind. It scares me. Nobody can tell me if he's going to make it. Or if he'll be sane if he does. I'm afraid it might all depend on his mother."

"What? Sahra turned up?"

"No. She's definitely dead. I think. But her ghost, and her mother's ghost and her grandmother's ghost, keep following him wherever he goes. Whenever his fever gets to him he sees them. And they talk to him. They nag him, he says. He doesn't like it. But my opinion is, he damned well ought to start listening to them. Because he gets these brain fevers every time he starts to do something that his mother wouldn't have liked while she was alive. Even if it's only something like forgetting to clean his teeth."

"You really believe he's being haunted by his female ancestors?"

"Doesn't matter if I do, Pop. *He* believes it. Even when he's fever-free and completely sane he'll say his mother intends to stay around until he no longer needs her guidance. Then she'll be free to join Murgen. Tobo really resents the implication that he isn't mature and his behavior is keeping her from her rest. And Sahra, apparently, is just as resentful of his immaturity, because she'd rather be somewhere besides here baby-sitting a grown man."

"Why do I get the feeling there's something more?"

"Because you're right. There is more. He thinks those women might run out of patience. He's afraid they'll just drag him along with them."

"You mean kill him?"

"No! His mother, Pop. Not kill him. Take him along. Out of his body. The way they say his father used to do. Only they wouldn't let him come back. If that happened his body would die eventually. And before you tell me Sahra wouldn't let her baby die, you need to remember this ghost isn't the Sahra you knew. This Sahra has been on the other side for a while, running with ghosts who have been there a lot longer than she has. And at least one of those was able to see Tobo's various potential futures way back before Murgen and Sahra ever got together."

Sounded to me like Shukrat was just as much a believer as Tobo was.

"All right. Rest, little girl. I'll come up with a plan while you do."

Look at me. Manly man. Older than dirt, limping, one bad eye, short one hand, reads and writes, but a manly man for all that.

The Voroshk World:
Stronghold Rhuknavr

The Voroshk Shadowgate was being watched from the other side. Shukrat's uncles hoped she would find her way home, too, and they were eager to obtain another breeder.

We did not work hard to avoid being discovered by the watchers. But we did come by night and Shukrat did leak some of her most unusual companions through to distract the sentries.

Tobo did not stint when he gave her Unknown Shadows to help her out in her adventures down this way. Unlike when he gave me those two wanna-be ravens that were never around and had not been seen now in months. He assigned her some of the biggest, the darkest, the smartest, that would stand by her and do what she said.

The Black Hounds darted around and over the two watchers, keeping them from flying just long enough for us to get through the Shadowgate and add ourselves to the equation. Shukrat was able to put them both to sleep despite the state of high excitement the Unknown Shadows had aroused.

In moments we understood why.

"They're just kids!" I said, while undressing one. "This one can't be more than eleven or twelve."

The one Shukrat stripped was even younger. "These two are the youngest Tologev brothers. Somebody really is desperate if he's sending kids this young out alone when there're still shadows roaming around."

I thought that was just fine. The thinner the Voroshk were spread, the better.

The two boys we left behind, up in trees for their own safety. We confiscated their posts and clothing.

It was a long flight. We did not show ourselves during the day. Along the way Shukrat showed me the ruins of Khatovar. I did not feel inclined to explore. I did not have time. There were changes going on inside me. I had to hold them off until I got Arkana free.

The white crow mocked me and accused me of cheating on Lady. She refused to believe I was not. I no longer argued. She was still bitter because she had not been able to take me away from her sister.

Arkana was being held in a minor Voroshk fortress called Rhuknavr. We flew in low, to within a mile, then awaited midnight while floating high up in the tops of trees that were old when Khatovar fell. We put out a dozen shadowtraps Shukrat had crafted according to Shivetya's instructions. Once she released the Unknown Shadows, though, the traps were not necessary.

At my insistence Shukrat made doubly sure that the Unknown Shadows clearly understood we were about to butt heads with people who had considerable experience dealing with creatures of darkness. Their advantage over the killer shadows was that they were not just driven clumps of hunger and hatred. They were cunning and wicked and able to reason, although unfortunately weak on the concept of cooperation.

I asked Shukrat, "You think we might have better luck in the daytime, after everybody inside there relaxes?"

"They're not that alert. They haven't had an incident here for a long time."

"How do you know that?"

"I just do. Now that I'm close enough to feel them." Meaning, probably, that she was hiding the whispers of the Unknown Shadows already.

"Uhm? Are you close enough for them to feel you?"

"No. Because I'm alone. And because I'm dressed. And because they aren't trying to feel for me."

"I see." If it was not our unseen associates it must be something like the way I had begun to sense Shivetya. "Bird. Pay attention." It was not my intent to waste any resource. The white crow was a valuable resource. "So where is my other baby, Shukrat? Be as exact as you can because my feathered friend needs to know how to get there to tell her that we're coming and she should be ready to go."

The crow squawked like it had just found a snake raiding its nest. It protested so vigorously that the surrounding night fell into an uneasy silence.

"Good for you nobody in these parts would recognize Taglian. What's the big squawk? You infiltrated how many places at other times?"

The crow continued to mutter something to the effect of, that was different. The difference mainly being whose idea the infiltration was. She understood that I was getting real thick with Shivetya, though, and the golem might have a great deal to say about whether or not she ever got out of the cave of the ancients. Once she got the frustration worked out she was ready to go.

I had Shukrat describe the interior of Rhuknavr the best she could. Which was not that well. She had not been there in ten years. The crow would have to locate Arkana on her own. Shukrat could not pin her down.

I said, "You just tell her we're coming and she should be ready. And, if she can manage it, she might put a sleep spell on anybody near enough to touch."

The crow left. We waited. I stared at the sky. I found this one far stranger than that of the Land of Unknown Shadows. There was no large moon here, apparently. At least none tonight nor during the nights I spent here before. But there were scores of little ones, the biggest maybe a fifth the size of my own. All the moons seemed terribly busy, scampering hither and yon. When I mentioned them to Shukrat she began telling me about her world's unique breed of astrology, which relied upon the motions of all those moons. Even after ages of study those moons still presented the occasional surprise.

"Once, when I was little, two of them banged off of each other. None of the others have moved quite the same way since. And it rained down pieces for years. Only about a hundred miles from here there's a place where a really big piece hit. I was at Junkledesag, which is over that way another eighty miles, and it was still awful. There were earthquakes and noise like the end of the world. There was a fire in the sky that took all night to fade away. It was like when one of the *rheitgeistiden* explodes, only a million times worse. It knocked a huge hole in the ground. Now the hole is kind of a lake."

The white crow dropped out of the night. "Ready."

"Easier than you expected, eh?"

The bird grunted sullenly.

"Show us the way, Fearless Feathered Explorer."

The next stage was anticlimactic. Only three or four actual Voroshk occupied Rhuknavr. In behavior so human I do not know why I did not foresee it, a small faction of survivors were concealing Arkana's return from the rest. For what little advantage controlling a viable breeder gave.

We left our posts nuzzling the fortress beside an unglazed hall-end window. The interior was too tight for flight. The crow showed the way to Arkana's chamber. There were no bars anywhere but there was a sleeping, non-Voroshk sentry slumped on a stool in the hallway. There had been a pretense that Arkana was a guest.

The girl jumped on me the moment we entered. "I knew you'd come."

"Did you?"

"I hoped you would. All right? I'm sorry. I was stupid. I just wanted . . . I had to . . . Thank you. Thank you. Thank you."

"Why not save your talking until we're out of here? The point of sending the bird ahead was so you'd be ready." The critter named flapped out the room's one small window.

She grabbed odds and ends. Not much. "I don't know where my *rheitgeistide* and *shefsepoke* are."

"We brought something for you. Let's go."

All went well until we were sliding out the window. Then a child, rubbing sleep from her eyes, wandered into the hallway, presumably disturbed by some sound. She stared for a moment, then folded, touched by a sleep spell from one of the girls.

Nothing happened immediately. But in time the child would tell somebody. Unless she had a habit of sleepwalking.

Comfortably aloft and heading south, I asked Arkana, "Are you pregnant?"

She took no offense. "No. They hadn't worked out who got to be first. Though every time I turned around somebody was trying to sneak in. Like they thought I couldn't possibly resist them. I passed out enough bruises that even Gromovol would've figured out that that kind of shit could get somebody hurt—but these guys were real optimists."

She had been hanging out with the right people to learn how to sucker a guy who thought girls ought to be easy prey. I said, "I guess we can thank some god for that small favor."

"You can thank Arkana for not putting up with their shit."

"That's my delicate flower."

S oon after sunrise Shukrat spotted seven or eight protean black dots bobbing in the air far behind us. "They're chasing us, Pop."

I checked. "We climb up a little higher, we'll be able to stay far enough ahead."

The girls agreed. But Arkana added, "There weren't that many of the Family at Rhuknavr. They must've sent for help from Junkledesag or Drasivrad. There aren't but fifteen or sixteen of the Family left alive."

I said, "Just in case they do start pressing us, do either of you have an objection to more of them getting hurt?"

Arkana gave me an unhappy look. Despite our hours aloft she was not yet fully clad in apparel taken from one of the boy sentries at the gate. Getting dressed is hard to do when you are riding one of those posts and staying out of sight by skimming the treetops. Not to mention that before she started changing she had to convince the clothing that it now belonged to her, not the boy from the Shadowgate. "How do you expect to manage that, Pop?" She sounded suspicious. And rightly so.

"Same way I got Kina. But you'll have to name me names." I had the First Father's book with me. I had taught myself enough of the Voroshk language to use the codes to blow those guys out of the sky. If I knew who I was turning into a cloud of dust.

"Don't do that. Not if you don't have to."

I gave it a moment. Then, "If you can forgive them, then I can."

"They never really did anything to me."

They would have but I did not belabor the point. Both of these kids were too forgiving and too understanding for their own good. Those guys back there would have done a whole lot of ugly to both of them, given the chance. I know those kind of guys. I have been those kind of guys.

Just for my own pleasure, privately, when the girls were not paying attention, I tripped the codes that would kill Arkana's post. We were too far from Rhuknavr for me to tell if it worked. I hoped not, now. Because after I did it I remembered the sleepy little girl in the hallway.

She would haunt me for a while.

It was closer than it really needed to be, us getting through the Shadowgate ahead of trouble. The key gave me some grief, probably because I was in too much of a hurry.

"Now what?" Shukrat asked once we were safe from the men and naked boys cursing us from the other side of the barrier.

I said, "I guess you two can go back to the army. I'm going to stay here. On the plain. With Shivetya. There's a job I've got to do. A promise I have to keep."

Nobody spoke again until we were close to the fortress with no name. Then Shukrat asked, "What about Lady?"

"If she's in good enough health you can bring her down here to me and I'll do what I can to help her. If she's not, leave her the fuck alone. Her main problem is she's got to heal herself."

Both girls looked at me like I was some really stinky monster that had just popped up in the middle of a bunny farm ripping the fur out of cute and tender throats.

"Look, I love my wife just one whole hell of a lot. There isn't any way I can explain it to you. But the fact is, love her is about all I can do. She's insane. By any standard but her own. And there's nothing I can do to change that. If you were familiar with the Annals you would know that."

Arkana sneered. "You don't ever give up, do you?"

She caught me off balance that time. "Actually, no. I wasn't thinking about finding somebody to keep the Annals. I was trying to clarify my relationship with my wife."

But did I know what that was myself? Even after all these years? Possibly more important, did *she* have any idea?

All that seemed to matter less and less as we drew closer to the fortress with no name.

Fortress with No Name:
Putting the Pen Down

I stood before the golem Shivetya, basking in his mild impatience. I was impatient myself. But the distractions of the world still had their hold on me.

That part of Gunni philosophy is solidly founded. Before you can achieve more than the lowest possible order of spiritual focus you have to learn to put all worldly distractions aside. *All* of them. Right now. Never mind what. Otherwise there will always be that one more critical thing that just absolutely has to be handled before you can move forward.

My one more thing was Lady. My wife. Who continued to wobble on the brink of the abyss without ever quite slipping over. To me it was evident that the missing medicine now was any will to battle on. And the white crow agreed with me.

"Let me work on her," the bird told me. "Ten minutes and I'll have her so pissed off she'll melt mountains trying to get close enough to spank me."

"No doubt. But I like things the way they are. Except for how long it's taking."

Suvrin seemed to be taking forever making any headway coming south. Though he was covering ground much faster than we had headed north. Nobody was trying to slow him down.

I whiled my time exploring the expansive wonders of Shivetya's memories—but avoiding those including Khatovar. Khatovar was a dessert I meant to save until there were no distractions at all. Khatovar was a special treat for a time when every flavor could be savored.

Eventually, I yielded to the inevitable and sent the girls to bring Lady to me. Maybe my big pal on the wooden throne could give me a hint or two how to goose her into getting going again.

The Nef appeared almost as soon as the girls popped out of the hole in the roof. They were in a black humor, eager for a fight, and because I could not communicate with them my mood soon turned just as dark. I hunted up One-Eye's spear. If it could handle a Goddess it ought to be able to polish off three obnoxious, nagging spooks.

Shivetya stopped me. He could communicate with the Nef. He indicated that he would calm them down with an explanation of what we were doing here. His liberation would not sentence them to extinction. In fact, they were about to enter a new phase of existence. They were going to get work maintaining the glittering plain. There were scores of odd jobs and cleanups that needed special attention.

Shivetya and I were now so connected I could see the plain in my mind almost at will and the rest of the world, through his eyes, with only a little more effort. For a while I watched the girls race northward, each occasionally finding a moment to have fun flying.

I slept for a few hours. Or a week. When I awakened I picked up a lamp and walked over to the throne. I carried One-Eye's spear under my other arm, on the bad hand side. Shivetya and I stared at each other for a while.

"Is it time?" I asked. And, "You think we're ready to manage without the daggers, now? Yeah? Just one more little thing, then. I need to leave a note for my girls."

That turned into a letter. Trust the Annalist to go on and on.

A very clear thought. *Have you finished now? Are you certain you are done?*
    "It's time."

My bridesmaids, the Nef, drifted in out of the darkness. They seemed more substantial than ever before. They like me just fine, now.

I am putting the pen down.

Glittering Stone:
And the Daughters of Time

We saw lights from way out. What was that? There are no lights on the glittering plain. We climbed a thousand feet. By then the lights were gone except for what came out of the hole in the dome over the top of the demon's throne room. Before we got there that went away, too.

Then we were too busy getting Lady and Tobo through the hole to worry about anything else. *Rheitgeistiden* are trouble when their riders are not helping.

When we got to the floor we found only one oil lamp burning on that old man's—that scholar from Taglios's—worktable. Croaker left a note. And, that clever old fart, he wrote it in our language. Not very good, but good enough to understand.

I guess he did have the gift for tongues like he always said.

Arkana took the lamp and used it to fire up a couple of lanterns. We went off to look for Croaker. She said, "You know, he was always teasing us but after a while I did start feeling almost like he was my dad." We never ever talk about our real fathers. We would never get along.

"Yeah. He looked out for you. Maybe more than you know."

"You, too."

We found Croaker sitting beside the wooden throne. "Hey. He's still breathing."

"I don't think . . . Shit. Look. Those knives are all gone from the demon." Actually, they were laying all over the floor.

So just then the demon's eyes open and so do Croaker's and both of them look pretty confused and it is only then that I really understand what Croaker was trying to tell us in his letter. It was not some confused religious good-bye, he just did not have enough of the right words to tell us that he and the demon had it worked out to trade places. So Shivetya got to become a mortal for as long as Croaker's body would last and Croaker got to be a big, old, wise sea dragon swimming all around in the ocean of history. So both of them got to go to heaven. And the Nef were happy. And the plain went on. And the white crow kept bitching, riding around on the Croaker body's shoulder. And Arkana and I got in a running fight about who was going to go on keeping the Annals, because both of us hate to write.

So we take turns. When the little tramp will get away from Tobo long enough to pick up a pen and do her part.

A point she missed, probably because she is too dim to notice, is that Lady is recovering. A while ago I saw her spinning tiny fireballs. I think if there was some way she could make love to that big monster over there she would do it three times a day. Because it is from him that the power flows. It is, probably, the best and most meaningful gift he has ever given her and with it she can become anything she wants to be. Maybe even the young and beautiful and romantically sorrowful and remote Lady of Charm again.

But then he would have to turn Soulcatcher loose just to give balance to the world.

I wonder if he was right when he said a thousand years from now we might be the gods everyone remembers.

And I wonder what he might do about his daughter. His flesh daughter. I think there is no hope for her because she has no hope of her own, but I also think that if there is a hope, Pop will find it.

Suvrin is looking impatient. He wants to hitch a ride down to the Hsien Shadowgate. He is not Aridatha Singh but he may have to do. .

I guess it is time to go see our new world. The Abode of Ravens. The Land of Unknown Shadows. Shukrat says the names have a ring. That it sounds like home to her.

I think home is what I carry around inside me. I am a snail with the meat on the outside.

And it is Shukrat's damned turn to write. The sneaking, slacking little bimbo.

Incessant wind sweeps the plain. It murmurs on across grey stone, carrying dust from far climes to nibble eternally at the memorial pillars. There are a few shadows out there still but they are the weak and the timid and the hopelessly lost.

It is immortality of a sort.

Memory is immortality of a sort.

In the night, when the wind dies and silence rules the place of glittering stone, I remember. And they all live again.

Soldiers live. And wonder why.